ALIEN BLOOD

ALIEN BLOOD

PSION
CATSPAW

Joan D. Vinge

Nelson Doubleday, Inc.
Garden City, New York

Quality Printing and Binding by:
Berryville Graphics
P.O. Box 272
Berryville, VA 22611 U.S.A.

CONTENTS

CONTENTS

PSION

*To Carol Pugner,
who always believed in Cat.*

*And to Andre Norton,
who is Cat's spiritual godmother.*

PART I
CAT

THE GEM-COLORED dream shattered, and left the kid gaping on the street. Jarred by passers-by and stunned by ugliness, he gulped humid night air. The dreamtime he had paid his last marker for was over, and somewhere in the street voices sang, "Reality is no one's dream. . . ."

A richly robed customer of the Last Chance suicide gaming house knocked him against a pitted wall, not even seeing him. He cursed wearily and fumbled his way to the end of the building. Pressure-sensitive lighting flickered beneath the heavy translucent pavement squares, trailing him as he stepped into the funnel of an alleyway. Aching with more than one kind of hunger, he crept into the darkness to sleep it off.

And one of the three Contract Labor recruiters who had been watching nodded, and said, "Now."

The kid settled into a crevice between piles of cast-off boxes, where the unsleeping gleam of the pavement was buried under layers of back-alley filth. He didn't mind dirt; he didn't even notice it. Dirt grayed his worn clothes, the pale curls of his hair, the warm brown of his skin. Dirt was a part of his life: like the smell, like the constant drip of sewage somewhere in the darkness, leaking down through the roof of his world from Quarro, the new city that had buried Oldcity alive.

Water striking a metal walkway rang like endless bells through the fibers of his abused nerves. He raised unsteady hands to cover his ears, trying to stop the sound of the water torture and the sounds of the furious argument in a room up over his head. He felt the throbbing of distant music . . . the beat of heavy footsteps coming down the alley toward him.

He froze, sitting as still as death, caught in a sudden premonition. His eyes came open slowly, intensely green eyes with long slitted pupils like a cat's. The pupils widened, his eyes became pools of blackness absorbing every particle of available light—showing him with unhuman clarity three heavy bodies wearing shadow-black uniforms: the carrion crows of Contract Labor, a press gang searching the night for "volunteers." Searching for him.

"Jeezu!" His drug-heavy boay jerked with panic. He dropped forward onto his knees, hands groping in the trash around him. His fingers closed over the plass-smooth coolness of a bottle neck. He pulled it to him as the alley filled with dazzling, confused motion and he was surrounded by men in black. Their hands caught his clothing, dragging him up, off-balance; he was slapped, shoved. Trying to find words, breath, time to protest . . . he found his arm instead, his hand, the bottle clutched in it. He brought it up in one hard sudden rush.

The heavy shatterproof plass struck the side of a man's head with a dull *sponk*; the impact jarred the kid against the greasy building wall, and the recruiter fell. Two were still coming, their faces dark with vengeance, ready to make him pay. He dodged left, right, making them counter; suddenly he kicked out and up with ruthless urgency. A second man went to his knees with a bellow of agony.

The third one was on him as he tried to break away, dragging him back and down. The kid clawed at the pile of crates beside him, twisting like a snake in the recruiter's grip. The load shifted and swayed; he felt it begin to fall—

He sprawled free as the crates came down. He was on his feet and running before the crashes and cursing ended, before any of them were even up off their knees to follow him.

"Kid!"

He had almost reached the alley mouth when the shout caught up with him. He kept running, knowing the recruiters were not armed. Something struck him in the back of the head; he cried out as painstars burst inside his eyes. Warm wetness showered over his hair, sluiced down his neck, drenched his jerkin. He lifted a hand, brought it down from his forehead wet with luminous orange dye, not blood. "Shit." He swore again, half in relief, half in fresh panic: they had marked him for a police pickup. He stripped off his jerkin as he ran, running harder out into the midnight crowds of Godshouse Circle. But the dye had already soaked through to his skin, and even the crowds could not hide him. Night was when the upsiders came slumming, came to wallow in Oldcity sin; and the Corporate Security Police came with them, to protect the rich from the poor. He elbowed aside thieves and beggars, musicians, pimps, and jugglers, along with the silken customers who fed and bled them all.

He had been a thief for most of his life; on another night he would have welcomed this crowd. But tonight startled heads were turning, angry voices were rising, arms waving, pointing, clutching. Somewhere an arm in gray would lift a stungun—

He broke through into the Street of Dreams; its throat of golden light swallowed him up in incense and honey and loud, rhythmic music. He had never run down this street before. He had stood gawking in it a thousand times, seduced by the promise that all his wildest dreams would be fulfilled if only he would step through this door . . . *this* door . . . *my* door . . . *no, mine.* But none of those doors had ever let him past, given him refuge, welcomed or even pitied him. Tonight would be no different. He pushed on through the yielding chaos of real and holo-flesh, feeling the crowd drain the bright energy of his panic. A *mistake, this was a mistake*— Orange sweat ran into his eyes; the street's glaring assault on his tortured senses was making him sick.

Someone shouted, and this time he saw uniform gray. He began to run again, trying to keep the crowd between them; running through nightmare. But he still knew the streets better than he knew his own face. Instinct saved him, and he dodged into a narrow crack below a shadowed archway. He ran down steps, up steps, clattering through sudden light and blackness along a metal catwalk—out into another alley, between rows of silent pillars; navigating by constellations of distant streetlights.

Footsteps and shouting still trailed him, but they were falling behind now, out of sight. He let himself slow, almost missing the break between abandoned buildings—the crumbling wall that left him room enough to squeeze through, just below the hanging entrails of Quarro. He clambered up a fallen girder, his breath coming in sobs. He crouched and leaped, straining to bridge the gap. But his legs gave way; his body had no strength left to give him. His fingers caught, clung, slipped from the lip of broken stone. He dropped back into the rubble four meters below. An ankle cracked as he came down; as his body, abused for too long, betrayed him at last.

He huddled over, cursing the white-hot pain softly, until they came for him. Again he crouched in a yellow wash of light until rough hands dragged him up and held him against the wall. This time there were guns, and this time he didn't try to struggle. He whimpered as they prodded his leg; they made him stand on the other one, hands locked behind him, until the pickup unit arrived. They knew who had marked him. They worked for the Federation Transport Authority, and the FTA took care of its own, they said. They knew his kind, they said; they knew his record, too. He couldn't do what he'd just done and think he wouldn't pay. "Get used to it, kid. This is the end of everything for you."

But they were wrong. It was only the beginning.

1

IT STARTED WHERE it ended, in Quarro. Quarro is the main city on Ardattee, the garden spot of the galaxy, the Hub, the Heart, the Crown of the Federation. Somehow it always looked more like the garbage dump to me; but that was because I lived in Quarro's Oldcity.

My name is Cat. Cat's not my real name, but it fits, and I like it. I don't know my real name. They always called me Cat on the streets because of my eyes: green eyes that see in the dark, that don't look human. I have a face that makes people uneasy. If you want the story of my life, it goes like this: I was standing in an Oldcity alley when I was maybe three or four. I was crying, because the hunger in my belly hadn't gone away, because it was so cold that my fingers were blue— because I wanted somebody to do something about it. Somebody came out of a doorway and told me to shut up, and beat me until I did. I never cried again. But I was hungry most of the time, and cold. And doing dreamtime, when I had any money for drugs—dreaming the kind of dreams they sold on the street. No excuses. To have dreams of your own is the only way to survive, but Oldcity had killed all mine. Reality was nobody's dream.

I didn't have any reason to think it would ever be any different, either. Not at the start—or at least that piece of time where the past and the future come together and catch you in the middle, to make it seem like the start of something.

At the start I was being hauled out of an Oldcity Corporate Security detention center. I didn't really know where I was going, just what I wanted to get away from. I'd been at the station a couple of days, under arrest for beating up three Contract Labor recruiters who'd been trying to do the same to me. The Corpses had done everything they could to make me miserable; then out of nowhere they'd offered me a chance to volunteer for a "psi research project." With no sleep and nothing to do but think up worse things they could do to me, I guess by then I would have said yes to anything. So I did.

And so the Corporate Security officer took me outside into the hot, stinking afternoon and pushed me into the back of a mod with winged FTA insignias on its sides. I'd never been in a mod before; the only ones I'd even seen were the aircabs the upsiders used to get into Oldcity and get out again. Without a data bracelet all you could do was look. Without a deebee proving you were alive you weren't just poor—you didn't even exist. And without a deebee you stayed in Oldcity until you rotted. I didn't have one. The Corpse sat up front and said a few words; the mod floated up from the ground and out of the courtyard. I held my breath as it carried us over the crowds, through the streets half as old as time. I'd spent my whole life on those streets, but everyone I saw, looking down, was a stranger. They tried not to look up; I tried not to think about why they didn't.

The mod reached Godshouse Circle and began to rise even higher: Godshouse Circle was the only place left in the Oldcity where you could move between worlds, between the old and the new. We were going upside, into Quarro. I hunched down in my seat as we spiraled higher into the light, feeling a little sick, trying to remember why I'd always wanted to see Quarro. . . .

Quarro was the largest city on Ardattee, but it hadn't always been. A handful of interstellar combines had split up the planet when it was first discovered. Then after the Crab Nebula sector opened up to colonization, Ardattee became the jump-off point for the colonies.

Every corporate holding on the planet had grown fat off the trade. Finally the Federation Transport Authority moved in to get its cut. It had moved its information storage here, and claimed Quarro to set it down in. Quarro had become a Federal District, a neutral zone where no combine government had official power, but all of them had hundreds of spies and spooks trying to get one up on everybody else's. Not all the dirty deals that were made in Oldcity were made by criminals. Quarro had become the largest cityport on the planet by a hundred times. Earth lost its place as the crossroads of the Human Federation, and Ardattee became the Federation's trade center, economic center, and cultural center. And somewhere along the way somebody had decided that Quarro's old, tired Colonial town was historic and ought to be preserved.

But Quarro had been built on a thumb of peninsula between a deep harbor and the sea. There was only so much land, and the new city went on growing, feeding on open space, always needing more—until it began to eat up the space above the old city, burying it alive in a tomb of progress. The grumbling, dripping guts of someone else's palaces in the air shut Oldcity off from the sky, and no one who had any choice lived there anymore. All of that I knew from things I'd seen on the threedy, even though I didn't understand most of it; even though it didn't make me feel any better.

We were rising through color now, soft, formless, mostly greens. Plants—more plants than I'd ever seen, or even imagined. The Hanging Gardens, somebody had told me once. The Hanging Gardens were Up There. . . .

And then we were up above the gardens, tier after tier of them; moving through the honest-to-God light of day. Towers, shining and flowing, speared the bright blue air on every side, reflecting the sky until it seemed to flow into them and through them. . . . I shut my eyes, giddy and tingling. I looked out again after a minute, at the endless height of the sky and Quarro shining down below me *like . . . like* . . . . Knowing there had to be words somewhere for what I saw, but not how to find them.

The Corpse sat silently with his back against the barrier between us. The city lay like a long slender hand between the bay and the sea, jeweled fingers shining into the haze. *Mother Earth—I really live here?* I felt the binders cutting into my wrists.

But then we were dropping down through the air. We settled on a ledge where a couple of aircabs already sat, halfway down the side of a silvered building wall. There was an entrance waiting for us, one that didn't look like it got much use.

It was some kind of a hospital, I knew it as soon as we stepped inside. A hospital was a hospital, no matter how much they spent to make it look like something else. I stopped dead. "What is this? What do they want with me?"

"It's Sakaffe Research Institute," the Corpse said. "I don't know, and I don't give a damn. C'mon, you asked for it." He was between me and the door, there was no way I could leave, so I went on in.

He asked a passing tech for directions. She was carrying a plastic bag with what looked like someone's liver inside it, floating in purple sauce. It didn't make me feel better. She nodded over her shoulder, and we walked on down the silent hallway to a waiting room. The far wall was a sheet of tinted glass; light poured through it in a blinding flood that made me squint.

"Over there." The Corpse pointed, and then I saw the others, sitting along a cushioned seat below the wall of glass. He reached out and demagnetized the binders on my wrists; they dropped into his hands. He gave me a shove toward the window and told me, "Siddown, shuddup, and don't pull any stunts." Then he went back out into the hall. I knew he'd be waiting for me there in case I did.

There were half a dozen people sitting under the window already. I felt them giving me the eye as I limped toward them across the thick, sunlit carpet. I knew I was something to stare at—smeared with blood and dirt and dye; wearing a paper coat the Corpses had given me to cover most of the bruises, and over my ankle brace, pants so old they were ready for a museum. I wondered why we were all here, and what I'd really got myself into. I wished I had a camph to chew on to steady my nerves.

I stopped in front of the bench and looked for a place to sit down. The group of them had spread out on it like they were staking territory, until there was no room left. There were two women and four men. All the men looked poor, a couple of them looked tough. One of the tough ones had a stretched earlobe with no combine's tag in it—a busted spacer. One of the women looked rich, the other one just looked afraid. Nobody moved. They just stared, at me and through me, or at their feet. Finally the spacer said, "Up there."

So I looked where he was looking. Past the end of the bench, in the wall on my right, there was a closed door with a blue-hazed window. "The front of the line?"

"Pretty smart, Cityboy." He thought he was smarter. "One look at you, they won't be so choosy about the rest of us." He laughed and then they all did; strained, nervous laughter.

I wasn't laughing. "You want to eat that?" I moved toward him.

"Listen, you, don't make trouble," one of the women—the rich one—said. She was dressed like all the ones who came to Oldcity for laughs. Her round face was patterned with tiny red and gold jewels, matching the color of her hair.

"Butt out. This ain't your affair." I glared at her.

But her eyes said that it was. And then I saw that so did everyone else's; they were all looking at me now. Nobody moved.

"Any time, gutter rat." The spacer grinned. "That Corpse out in the hall would just love to see you try it."

I let my hands drop and went to the head of the line. The frightened woman moved in from the end of the bench, either to let me sit down or because she was afraid I'd touch her. I stuck my leg out into the warm sunlight and smoothed the ankle brace, pulled my paper coat tighter to my chest. Then I twisted to look out the window, letting my eyes follow the flow of clouds and towers, pretending I was alone. I looked down, and down, and thought about falling.

The door to the next room opened and someone came out. His face was grim and disappointed; he looked like a gambler who'd lost his Last Chance. And everyone was looking at me; and so was the man standing in the doorway. "All right, who's next?"

Me. I was next. I looked down at the rip in the knee of my pants, and couldn't make myself move.

But then the woman sitting next to me stood up. "I'll go," she said. She looked at me for a minute as if she knew, before she looked at the man in the doorway. "I'm next." I stared at her. She was holding something and she dropped it into my hands. It was a piece of soft cloth, a scarf.

I wanted to say, "What's it to you?" but she was already gone. I looked back at the rest of them, half heard the rich bitch say something snide. I frowned at her, and she said, "What are you staring at?"

I looked back out the window, with the face of the frightened woman still caught inside my eyes. I tried to stop seeing it, wanting to forget about her; but I couldn't. She was older than I'd figured, somewhere in her twenties in standard years. Her hair fell almost to her hips, as black as midnight in an Oldcity alley. Her clothes were dark and peculiar, layers of shirt and shawl wrapping her in mourning shrouds. She was tall, and too thin, and tired. But her eyes: cloud-gray, up-slanting . . . and when she'd looked at me, empty. She'd gone ahead of me to help me, but it hadn't been personal. It was only a kind of reflex action, like pulling away from a flame; something you did to stop your own pain. I felt strange when I realized that; invisible. I didn't know what to think.

So I didn't think about it for long. I didn't need favors from some burned-out fem anyhow. I looked down at the scarf, as green and gentle as moss bunched between my hands. I let it slide between my fingers, feeling the clean softness of it, breathing in a spicy fragrance like incense. Then I spat on it, and began to wipe off my face.

She was in the other room for a long time. I wondered whether she read minds, if that was why we were here. If that was how she'd known. And I wondered whether knowing what everyone thought was what had made her eyes so empty. The thought of having to live like her, like a freak that everybody hated, made my skin crawl. Then I wondered why the Corpses even thought that I could do it. Because I couldn't; I wasn't some kind of freak. Someone had come and tested me at the detention center, and afterward the Corpses told me I was a psion, I could read minds. I told them they were full of it. They just looked at each other, disgusted, and said, "You're a lucky freak, Cityboy." After that they put me on a truthtester and asked me a lot of questions I couldn't answer. And the next thing I knew they were asking me if I wanted to get out of there.

But they were still crazy—I'd never read a mind in my life. That meant I didn't have a chance, if mind reading was what they wanted from me here. . . . I was almost glad, thinking about that woman with her dead eyes, every day of her life spent knowing how much everyone hated her because she *knew*. . . . But then I remembered I sure as hell wasn't glad about how I was going to end up if they didn't choose me.

"Next."

The door was open but the mind reader didn't come back, and the red-haired woman nodded as if she'd known. I got up, stuffing the scarf into my pocket. My legs still felt like they were paralyzed, but somehow I made it to the doorway.

The man who'd been standing there before was already sitting down, behind a desk terminal. Daylight poured over it from the window wall. The desk, the chairs, the tables in the room, were made of real wood. I wanted to touch something, but I didn't. I wished again that I had a pack of camphs on me. There was a genuine sculpture painting on the wall behind him, not a cheap holostill; I'd been around enough stolen goods to know quality when I saw it. I stared at the thick raised wood grain on the curve of his desk and took a deep breath, before I looked up at him.

He was about thirty-five, maybe a little older. His face had a pinched look, like the face of someone who'd been sick a long time; but something about his expression told me he was no easy mark. His hair was cut short and it was already graying. He hadn't tried to hide that. The yellow collarless summer shirt he was wearing was good stuff, imported from offworld—that must have docked him plenty. But he didn't have on a drape or even jewelry, except two plain rings on his left hand, third and fourth fingers: a widower? He wasn't smiling. I tried my best hand-out smile on him. His eyes were hazel—green and brown. They were staring at my face and down at my clothes, back at my face again. I figured this must be the one the Corpses in Oldcity had told me was "Dr. Siebeling," the one they were sending me to see. My leg hurt. I wanted to sit down too, but the way he looked at my clothes kept me on my feet.

"Rather young, aren't you?" That wasn't all he thought was wrong with me. His hands cupped a glass ball with a hazy image inside it. He stroked it with a kind of absentminded need, like it was helping him stay calm.

I shook my head. My own hands tightened. Everyone thought I was younger than I was—softer, stupider, easier to use or push around. It was like I'd been born a victim, somehow; like they could smell it. I had a lot of scars on me from proving they were wrong.

He said, "Prisoner nine-double-oh-five-seven." I nodded, even though it didn't mean anything. He had what must have been the report from Corporate Security on the terminal, and he stared at it for a while before he looked up again. "This says you've got a record of petty thievery, and that now you're charged with assault and battery against three recruiters for Contract Labor. That you attacked one man with a knife—"

"Is that what he said? That croach. I didn't need a knife." He looked up at me with eyes like stones. "It was a bottle."

"Attacked one man with a knife, struck another, and kicked a pile of boxes down on a third. You ran away, and were arrested by Corporate Security after you broke your ankle in a fall. You were out on drugs at the time?" He sounded like he didn't believe it.

I didn't say anything.

"Why did you do it?"

"Because I didn't want to be shipped off to some sewer world where they can't get nobody sane to go, and rot there for half my lousy life. Why the hell do you think? The stinking Crows . . ."

He looked bored. "There was kadge in your bloodstream when you were picked up. That was two days ago, and you're not climbing the walls—you're not addicted?"

I shook my head. "I can't afford it."

"None of them can afford it, but most of them aren't that lucky. In fact, I've never heard of anyone who could take it or leave it."

Neither had I, when I thought about it, but I only said, "You have now."

He glanced down at the report again. "This says you're also no mind reader. You tested wide-spectrum on telepathy but entirely dysfunctional. I've never heard of that before, either. You must have given the techs a real challenge: you show a ten-plus resistance to probe. I show an eight; that's high. You have control like that and you've never used it?"

I was remembering the test: the veil of tingling mesh they'd fastened over my face back at the Corporate Security station, how I'd felt when my mind began to unravel. . . .

"Well? I asked you a question, Cityboy. I expect you to answer it."

"I got a name, sucker! It's Cat." I was starting to believe in hate at first sight.

His hands tightened on the desk edge; I knew I'd put my foot in my mouth. "Don't you get smart with me. I'm sick and tired of you and all the rest. Why the hell can't they send me something besides criminals and addicts?"

"Okay, okay. I didn't mean nothin' by it." I raised my hands. I hoped I looked as sorry as I felt—sorry for me. The last thing I wanted was to give him a reason to send me back out that door, back to the Corpse with the binders waiting in the hall. I tried to make my answer come out smooth and soft. "No. I didn't know I was a mind reader till the Corpses told me so. I never felt—never even f-f—" Black lightning flickering at the core of my mind, someone screaming . . .

Siebeling stared at me with a peculiar expression on his face. All his anger was gone. "What is it?"

I shook my head, rubbed my eyes, feeling cold and confused. "Nothing. . . . No. I don't want to be a mind reader; who would?" The words spilled out before I could stop them. "All the psions I ever seen were crazy. They don't call 'em freaks for nothin'." I grimaced.

"How much do you know about psionics?" His face was empty again. He pushed the glass ball away from him on the desk top.

"Nothing. What do I care about a bunch of freaks?"

"Psionics research"—he let it sink in—"is what you volunteered to participate in."

"Oh." My ears burned.

"That's all. Thank you." He stood up. The door was open. I knew then that the interview was over. And that I'd failed it.

I went out the same way I'd gone in, wishing more than anything that I could make myself invisible. But I couldn't. I walked past the rest of the freaks like I'd lost my Last Chance, and I saw their faces. I felt mine get hot again.

"Wait a minute."

I stopped, and heard Siebeling asking if anyone there was a telepath. One by one, they shook their heads and said, "No."

I looked at him again, even though I was afraid of what showed on my face. He frowned, and then he gestured me back. Suddenly I wanted to walk out on him. I nearly stepped on him instead, getting through that door before he changed his mind.

The first thing he said was: "Don't think this makes anything different. You're here because of your resistance level, but that's the only reason. I'll still drop you the minute you fall short anywhere. Contract Labor has requested you be turned back to them, if that means anything to you."

I laughed, but it wasn't funny.

He stood there like he was waiting for something. "Don't you even want to know what you'll be doing?"

I shook my head, as much because he wanted me to nod as because I really didn't care. "Why? Nobody's gonna miss me." Everything was lousy; at least this was a choice.

But he said, "The experiments we'll be doing involve psionics—'mind over matter.' Mainly it will be a group of people with undeveloped mental abilities working together to learn how to control those abilities. We'll teach you how to be a mind reader without going crazy. That's all you need to know for now." I shrugged. He pushed something on the desk and a door stood open in a wall again. A different door; I uncrossed my fingers. "How long have you known the woman who came in here ahead of you?"

"Why?" I frowned.

"Curiosity. She suggested that I give you a chance. I wondered why."

"I never seen her before today." I couldn't think of anything else to say, so I just stood and waited until he pointed toward the door.

"Through there. They'll tell you what to do."

2

I FOLLOWED ANOTHER hallway, one that didn't try so hard to look like it wasn't in a hospital. The tightness in my chest eased as I walked, and I took deep breaths. At the end of the hall a couple of people in pastel coats were sitting on the edge of an examining table, tossing out game pieces. I stopped. They looked at each other, then put the pieces back into a bowl. "Siebeling sent you?" the old man with side-whiskers asked, like he thought maybe I'd taken a wrong turn somewhere.

I nodded.

"What are you?"

I glanced down my body and up again. I put my hands on my hips. "Tired and hungry and sick of taking a lot of crap."

His face changed, first confused and then annoyed. "What's your *talent*—are you a teek, or a 'path, or what?"

"What?" I said, feeling like an echo.

"Well, he's not a mind reader, Goba." The woman pushed at her hair.

"Wrong," I said.

They traded looks again. The man leaned over and put a readout onto the screen in the tabletop beside him. He stared at it, a frown growing between his thick brows. "Take a look at that."

The woman peered past him. "Total dysfunction? We're supposed to unravel that in reasonable time? God's teeth, where do you start? What strands do you pull? How do you get through that wall?" She touched something on the screen with her finger.

"Like the Gordian knot," the man said, "I think it requires the direct approach." He chopped the air with his hand.

The woman laughed. "Well, this one's all yours, lucky son. If you can find a real telepath in that you can retire." She looked up at me. "If you can even find a human being inside this pile of rags you're doing better than I could."

He pulled at his mouth, starting to look too interested. I began to get uneasy again.

I have good instincts.

The first thing he did when she was gone was call in reinforcements. Together they stripped me and threw my clothes down the trash chute. Then they scrubbed me and disinfected me and gave me a medical that didn't leave anything to their imaginations—all the time telling me they'd tape my mouth shut if I didn't quit howling about it. After it was all over, they finally let me eat, in the hospital cafeteria. I ate until I got a bellyache, and fell asleep while they were telling me they'd told me so.

The tech named Goba and a shifting handful of others took over my life after that. They told me when to eat, sleep, and wash; they gave me the food I ate and the clothes I wore and even the bed I slept in. My life was jammed into a coffin, a soft suffocating prison where every waking hour they were beating on the doors of my mind, trying to get me to answer, to come out or let them in. Nothing like it had ever happened to me before: no one had ever had that kind of control over me. No one had ever told me when to breathe, or had even cared if I kept breathing at all. The techs didn't really care, either. I was a psion, and they weren't; they didn't even like psions—nobody normal liked a freak. They didn't like this job or anyone who made them work at it. But it was their job, and they weren't going to fail because of me. Goba told me they were going to make me into a telepath if they had to crack open my skull to get what they wanted; after a couple of days I started to believe him.

A telepath was what I was supposed to be: a mind reader. Goba told me that the first day. He'd explained it all to me very slowly, like he was talking to a burnout, while I stuffed myself full of cafeteria food. There were other psionic "talents," too: teleportation meant that you could move your own body from one place to another instantly, just by thinking about it; telekinesis meant that you could move objects the same way; precognition, the wild-card power, showed you flashes of the future—or several futures—and left you to sort out the clues that led to the true one. Some psions could do more than one of those things. I only had one talent, telepathy. One too many.

They spents days hypnotizing me, putting my mental guards to sleep while they probed around in my brain with machines I never wanted to know about: finding areas of resistance in my mind and walling them up, drowning the fears, finding my telepathic sense and dragging it out into the open. I woke up after every session thinking everything was fine, because that was how they'd programmed me to wake up . . . but always I woke up soaked with sweat, raw-throated or red-eyed or with a headache the size of a sun. And then they'd throw me into a hundred different exercises that were supposed to loosen the tension that still held my mind shut, to force me to follow and control the strands of my thoughts, to feel the power move and reach out with it. I had to tell them things like what picture they were looking at when I couldn't see it, or what they'd eaten for breakfast, or whether they were telling me a lie.

They always told me whether I was right or wrong, but I didn't need it. I knew when something happened in my head that had never happened before; I felt the alien energy making static behind my eyes, a formless force stirring in buried rooms of my mind. But I couldn't control it. I couldn't shape it into anything like a thought message to project into someone else's mind. I couldn't even focus it clearly on somebody's sendings, no matter how much feedback they gave me.

Because from the first time I felt the psi power wake and stretch inside me, I hated the feel of it; and no matter how often they put me to sleep and made me swear I didn't, that never changed. It was like being forced to do something I was ashamed of in public, over and over, with all of them watching; being smeared with their disgust every time I brushed against their minds: *psions were scum, psions were a threat to every decent human being, because they had the power to invade another person's life. Psions were freaks and they all knew I was one. . . .*

Whenever I got anything right, I figured they ought to be grateful, under the circumstances. But usually they only got sarcastic, telling me I could do that well by guessing, and that I wasn't really trying. I told them I *was* trying, they didn't give me any choice. "What the hell's going wrong that I can't just *be* a stinking telepath? Maybe you're wrong about *me.*" Wanting them to be wrong, wanting to hear Goba tell me it was all a mistake, that I was as normal as he was; even while I was afraid he might really say it, and send me back to Contract Labor.

But Goba caught my jaw with his hand, turning my face until I was looking at my reflection in the side of a metal storage cabinet. He said, "You look at that face, psion, and ask me again if I could be wrong about your mind."

I only shook my head, not understanding.

He looked disgusted, which wasn't unusual. "You are a psion; don't try to kid yourself. You've got a lot of scar tissue in there," pointing at my head, "figuratively speaking. That's what's gone wrong. Something fed you a tremendous telepathic shock once, so intense it burned out the circuits. Your mind could have repaired them itself, but whatever happened was so painful that it never did. So we're trying to do it for you. But you're still resisting. . . ." He sounded like he took it personally.

"What kind of a shock?" I wondered how something that bad could have happened and left me without even a memory of it.

He shrugged. "That doesn't matter. It's not our business to find out. We just repair the circuitry."

"I ain't a machine; you can't reprogram me. It ain't that easy." *Bastard,* wishing he could hear me think it.

"Get back to your exercises." He started to turn away.

I stayed where I was and folded my arms. "I got a headache. I don't think I want to work anymore."

He looked back at me. "Our job is to work around your problems, not to solve them. If you want to know *why,* see a psiopsychologist. Now get back to work."

And so I moved through the days like a robot, answering when Goba told me to, talking to myself if I wanted a real human conversation. The rest of the techs might as well have been robots too, for all they ever said to me. I never even knew the names of most of them. I was just one more experimental animal to them, and every night they locked me in my room. And night after night I had dreams so ugly that I started sleeping with the light on; nightmares I could never remember, that faded into the morning and left my head filled with the echoes of screaming. I never told Goba about it, or any of the others. They could all go to hell, I'd be glad to give them references, but I was damned if I'd ask them for help.

Then one day I got my visit with a psiopsychologist, without even having to ask. Nobody bothered to tell me that was what I was getting. All I knew was that I was going to see Siebeling.

He was more surprised than I was when the tech showed me into his office. He raised his eyebrows when she said, "Here's Cat," and actually looked past her out the doorway before he looked back at me. I felt the sharp stab of his surprise puncture my mind as he finally recognized me. I stopped dead, shaking the surprise loose from my thoughts, fighting my own disgust. I wasn't used to picking up strays; for some reason his mind focused much more clearly than any of the techs' did. There was an afterimage of confusion that cut off suddenly, leaving me alone again and off-balance inside my thoughts.

"Sit down," he said.

I dropped down into the sling of the nearest chair; the metal frame creaked like old bones. Siebeling grimaced. I leaned back, swaying a little, glancing past him. This wasn't the same room I'd seen him in before; this one was higher up and there was a slanting skylight instead of a glass wall. I tried to imagine what shape this building really was. The room was about like the other one except for the skylight, and Siebeling sat behind the desk like he was just visiting in this one, too. I wondered if people treated him the way they treated me around here. I stared at his clothes: probably not. He had the glass ball in front of him again; the picture inside it looked different from what I remembered.

"I almost didn't know you."

I think that was supposed to be a compliment, but somehow it didn't feel like one. I shrugged.

"How's your ankle?"

"They fixed it up all right. . . . What's the matter, did they tell you I'm no good?" My hands tightened over the metal chair frame.

"Who?" He looked blank.

"Them—the techs. They keep telling me you're gonna throw me out of here if I don't work harder. I'm doin' the best I can!" I leaned forward, the seat shifting under me.

"I'm sure you are." He sounded like he meant it; I sat back, easing a little. "They've told me that you aren't making progress as fast as they'd hoped. They say you seem to have blocks they can't effectively break down. That's what I want to talk to you about."

"Why?" I felt my neck getting stiff.

"It's part of the research. All the volunteers here are trying to come to grips with the problems their psionic ability has caused them. You're not alone in having problems. I'm sorry I haven't been able to talk with you about yours before this; but there are a lot of volunteers, and we're only getting started."

"Well, what do you care about my problems? The techs already told me they don't matter. You just like to get personal?"

He looked at me like I'd just spit in his face. "You mean you still don't understand what you've been doing here?"

I looked down at the floor between my sandals. "How am I supposed to know anything? All I ever see are those damn techs. They're all alike and they don't tell me nothing, they don't even speak to me. Jeezu! What am I supposed to know—that this is a prison? Where the hell are all these other psions they keep talking about? I never see any of 'em, and I've been here forever!"

"You've barely been here two weeks. You'll see them when you're ready to work with them. And you are a prisoner—not ours, but Corporate Security's. Until I'm sure you'll work out for our research, you'll go on being their prisoner, and go on being carefully watched." He took a deep breath. "I am Dr. Ardan Siebeling. I am a medical researcher; I am also a psiopsychologist—I specialize in the treatment of emotional and behavioral problems relating to psionics. As a part of this research I'm trying to give all my volunteers—even you—what counseling I can. The whole point of this is to help you control your talents and learn to live with them. Does that answer your questions?"

I nodded, keeping my head down—wishing I could leave, and wondering why everything I said just made me sound stupider, and made him angrier.

"Then let's talk about what's bothering you. Goba said you'd experienced some shock early in life that was so painful you totally rejected your ability to read minds."

"I know. But he wouldn't tell me what it was."

"Apparently he can't. Even under hypnoprobing you never say anything about it. The human mind is full of unknowns; you can take a memory and throw it down a pit somewhere and never see it in your conscious mind again. But it's still there, somewhere, festering. The mind never really forgets anything—it only forgets how to reach that thing, sometimes." He looked down at the glass ball. He covered it with his hands, and closed his eyes for a second. When he took his hands away again, the picture had changed. I stopped listening and just stared; wonder caught in my chest. "You don't remember anything at all about what might have happened? Can you even remember a time when you knew what people were thinking?"

I blinked, and looked back at him. I shook my head.

"Has anything strange begun happening since you've been involved here? Have any peculiar memories surfaced—anything at all? Dreams?"

I nodded. "Dreams. I have a lot of bad dreams. . . ."

"What are they about?" He leaned forward across the desk.

"I don't remember."

He sat back again. "Something. There must be something—a setting, a feeling?"

"Oldcity. They're always in Oldcity." He raised his eyebrows. I shrugged. "Where else would they be?"

"Anything else, then? Close your eyes, remember how you feel just as you're waking."

I shut my eyes, trying to bring it back. . . . "Afraid," I whispered. I wiped my hands on the knees of my pants. "Somebody's s-screaming. . . ."

"What?"

"S-screams!" I opened my eyes, glaring at him.

"Whose? Your own?"

"Yes. N-no!" I pushed up out of my chair. "I d-don't want to do this."

"Sit down," he said, almost gently. I sat down again. "Do you stutter much?"

"I don't stutter!" I remembered what I'd just heard come out of my mouth.

"All right." He nodded, looking up through the skylight. "Let's try something else. How old are you?"

I took a deep breath. "Your guess is as good as mine."

"You must have some idea—sixteen, seventeen?"

"I guess so."

"Have you ever lived anywhere besides Oldcity?"

"No."

"Are you sure? You could have come to Ardattee when you were too young to remember. Did your family—"

"What family?" My mouth twisted.

"You're an orphan, then." He looked like he was apologizing for it, but there was something almost eager in the words that made me uneasy.

"I guess so." I made a sound that wasn't really a laugh. "And I remember living in Oldcity way back. I wish I could forget it, but I remember."

"Before you were, say . . . four years old?" The question wasn't quite casual. His hands closed over the picture ball; the picture changed again. He looked up, watching me watch it.

"Yeah," I said, remembering to answer him. "I got a good memory."

"How did you survive, if you were that young, and alone?"

"I lived off other people's garbage and junk." I felt him pushing me, a pressure I could almost see growing in my head. I twisted the hem of my smock between my hands, not understanding why it was happening. "I been a slip, and a beggar, and sometimes I was even—" I broke off. "What do you want from me!"

His face caught somewhere between disgust and pain. "Just—the answers to a few questions." It was a lie. He kept his voice even, but one question was burning inside him, stronger and deeper than any professional curiosity. I couldn't read him, but I couldn't stop feeling it, either. "What happened to your parents?" That wasn't the one.

"They're dead." I hoped they were; because if they weren't I wished they were, for what they'd done to me.

"Do you know which one was Hydran?"

"What?" I frowned. "What do you mean?"

"Your eyes and the bone structure of your face look Hydran. Your psionic ability makes it even more likely. . . . Do you know about the Hydrans?" he asked finally, when I just kept staring at him.

"They're the aliens." The word was hard to get out. "They come from Beta Hydrae system. I know some jokes. . . . Are you trying to make a joke outa me? It's bad enough bein' a freak. I'm human, I ain't some kind of monster!" I stood up again.

He stood up too, and leaned across the desk top, upsetting the picture ball. It rolled toward me. "You don't understand. My wife was Hydran. I had a son—"

"I don't care if your whole lousy family was alien, you devel I ain't, I ain't Hydran! And I ain't answering any more questions."

He pulled back, straightening away from me. I saw his face harden over with anger, felt his anger sink into my bones. He turned his back on me, as if even the sight of me was more than he could stand.

I looked down from the back of his head at the picture ball lying on the desk in front of me. I picked it up with shaky hands, and put it into my pocket. And then I got out of that room fast.

He didn't try to question me again. That was the last time he interviewed me, and Goba complained louder than ever when they got me back.

But then a couple of days later Goba came into the lab with a stranger: someone who looked like he'd probably come sealed in plastic —everything about him was so neat, so plain, so mass-produced. The stranger looked me over and said, "So you're the shadow walker who beat up three Contract Labor recruiters?" I stood and glared at him. He smiled at me; it made his face look human. (Think you can take me too, telepath?) I heard it, but this time he hadn't opened his mouth: the words formed inside my head—his thought, not mine, and I wasn't even trying to read his mind. He was a telepath.

"God's teeth!" I held my head, looking back at Goba. Goba just smiled like a sadist and left us alone.

I put a table between the stranger and me, and wove my thoughts

into a shield. No human had ever been inside my mind like this before
—it was like a tumor of thought growing in my brain. The feeling made
my stomach turn over. "You keep out of my mind, freak, or I'll show
you what I can do." I held up a fist.

"Take it easy." He spoke it normally, this time. He looked nervous,
which made me feel better. "Pull in your claws, Cat. I'm not here to—"

"I ain't an animal, you piece of meat!" I brought my fist down on the
table. "I'm a human, even if they don't treat me like it around here."

His face changed. "My apologies." He nodded, glancing down. He
looked soft, like somebody who didn't get any exercise. His dark hair
was pulled back and fastened at the base of his neck, the way half a
million other people wore it. It was like he'd done everything he could
to make himself ordinary. His eyebrows were dark and smooth, like
feathers; his eyes were a gold-flecked green when he looked up again. "I
didn't mean to patronize you, and I guess I did. I'm sure they've made
your life more unpleasant than you had any right to expect when you
came here. Just between us, it was meant to be that way. It's all a part
of the . . . uh, research. It helps to know those things; it puts it all in
perspective. Doesn't it?"

I stared at him, trying to figure out what he'd just told me, and what
the hell he was doing here. "Who are you?"

"My name is Derezady Cortelyou. I work for Seleusid Interstellar as
a corporate telepath. I'm also a volunteer in psionic research, like you.
I'm here to help you work on your own telepathy."

I sat down at the table and rested my head in my hands. It hurt, as
usual. "Jeezu. That's all I need."

He sat down across from me, picked up the stack of cards with
symbols on them that I was always having to "see," and shuffled
through them. But he didn't start playing head games; he didn't even
talk about telepathy. He talked about the weather—about everything
but psi. I didn't say anything. Finally, as if he'd run out of ideas, he
pulled out a pack of camphs and put one of them into his mouth. I felt
my own mouth start to water. My fingers twitched.

He glanced at me, but he didn't offer me one. He just sighed, and I
could *feel* how good it felt. . . .

"Gimme one of those?" I tried to make it sound casual.

He smiled and flipped one across the table.

I stuck it into my mouth and bit down on the end of it. The bitterness
numbed my tongue. I swallowed, letting it deaden my throat, knowing

that soon enough it would ease the tension all through my body. I
sighed, like he had.

"Been a while since you've had one?" His voice prodded me, but only
a little.

I didn't care. I nodded. "Seems like forever." Knowing there was no
way I could get out of it, I finally began to relax and let the conversation happen. He held his mind loose and unprotected all the while—I
could have walked right into it and read everything he was thinking if
I'd wanted to. I didn't want to. I kept my own mind as tight as a fist,
but he didn't try to reach me that way again. It was a laying down of
weapons, and even I could understand that much. Which maybe was
why I let myself answer his questions, and after a while even talked
about psionics.

He knew more than I ever wanted to know about telepathy, and
when he found out that I didn't know anything, he made me sit through
it all. The only thing that kept me listening was the camph slowly
dissolving in my mouth, and more where that one came from. But by
the time the lights of Quarro were a net of stars in nebula outside the
window, I knew all about the different degrees of telepathic ability. I
had what should be the greatest, the most flexible: "wide spectrum," the
ability to read everything from conscious thoughts lying on the surface
of another person's mind to buried memory fragments and even pure
emotion.

I'd learned that the mind was a net of electric fire—nerve fibers reacting to every sensation and image, every thought and feeling that let
human beings interact with life. In most humans the input and reactions were woven into a snarl that even biofeedback training could
barely begin to unravel. Psions were born with something more—a set
of self-controls that let them weave the snarl into patterns and, more
than that, to tap and use a kind of energy normal humans were blind to.
Psions had a sixth sense—and their minds were both more open to it
and more protected against it.

Some of them had two or more talents at the same time, different
ways of manipulating an energy as universal as life-force, and as much
of a mystery. Not all psions had the same level of control over their
talents, the way not all artists had the same amount of skill. There were
psions who were born with multiple talents like a crown of semiprecious
stones, and ones born with a single talent like a perfect diamond. . . .

"A 'diamond in the rough.' " I repeated the words, finally understanding them. "That's what Goba called me." A flawed, ugly stone

that needed cutting, he'd said, but that resisted every tool except the hardest. . . .

"He's right," Cortelyou said. "You have a level of control that would make anyone who wanted to be a psion green-eyed with envy." He laughed like that was a joke, but I didn't get it. "Except you've twisted it back on itself. You've used it to weave the fibers of your mind into a barrier, a wall of defense. They've been doing their best to fracture it—"

" 'And they don't much care if I break clean or shatter.' " I finished Goba's speech for him.

His mouth quirked. "I can imagine. I know the type." He sounded tired, suddenly.

I wondered again about what he was, and did. This time I asked, "What's a corporate telepath do, anyhow?"

"I screen clients for Seleusid executives, and sometimes do security checks at their headquarters."

"You mean you're a croach."

"A what?"

"A backstabber. A paid snitch." I shrugged.

His mouth thinned, but if he was angry or insulted, he didn't let it show. "Some people have said that, yes." The words sounded used, like he'd said them too often before. But then he told me that he was also a precog—that he made predictions about the economic and political future of the combine's holdings. I asked if he'd do it for me, but he only said that you couldn't predict when you'd get a prediction, and that they weren't always accurate, anyway. "Besides, we're here to work on telepathy, not precognition."

That was only the first time he came to work with me, and it wasn't long before a part of me looked forward to seeing him. He was a new face, and he didn't treat me like I was a pain in the ass—another change from Goba and the rest. But besides that he was more interesting than he looked. He told me that he had total recall, he remembered anything he saw or heard perfectly; that it was a skill any psion could develop, even me, if I wanted to work at it. I told him I had enough problems. But he must have read nearly everything ever written, and almost anything I asked about he'd explain: stardrives or computer memories or just what my pants were made of. . . .

". . . and telhassium is the thing that ties them all together. It makes the data processing detailed enough and the transportation economical enough so that it's worth someone's while to make cheap denim clothing on Earth and ship it all the way to Ardattee."

"Yeah?" I rubbed the knee of my jeans. "These really came all the way from Earth? Hell, they've seen more of the galaxy than I have." I laughed.

"They have a longer history, too. The original denim cloth . . ." And he was off again. Half the time what he told me was so technical I didn't know what he was talking about, but I tried not to let it show. Sometimes I wondered whether he really understood what he said himself.

But he seemed to enjoy having an audience. Not the way a performer did, or not exactly—it wasn't just that he like to show off. But sometimes I caught flashes of a need that ran strong and deep inside him, felt him aching for acceptance. I was a challenge to him, and from the minute I'd taken that first camph and started answering him, I'd been feeding a little bit of that need. Knowing that, I used his need, because that was what life was all about—using and being used. I knew how to fake interest; and sometimes I didn't even have to fake it when I was listening to him. That just made it easier. "What's—telhassium, that makes things go?"

He smiled, blissed on the pure pleasure of knowledge. His eyes looked toward something beyond the pastel green laboratory walls. "Telhassium is element one-seventy. Its pure form is a blue-silver crystal used for information storage in computers. They lock data into the electron shells, and they can run a whole planet's information system on a crystal as big as your thumb. Telhassium makes starship travel easy, giving navigators the number-crunching computers that can set up a long jump in hours instead of weeks.

"Before they had telhassium, starships cost a fortune, and they couldn't even . . ." He went on into a wilderness of words, all of them longer than my arm. "And now even a fast ship like a patrol cruiser carries less than a cubic meter of telhassium crystals on board for its computations. The big cargo ships only carry a little more telhassium than an entire planet uses; and only in case of emergency, because they use the computers of mainline ports like Quarro to do their navigation. A major spaceport can compute a jump to any important system in the Federation, except in the Crab Colonies, in less than an hour."

"Whew." I rubbed my forehead. My mind was still stumbling in the undergrowth of words somewhere back along the trail. "I feel like I swallowed my brain."

"Then maybe we'd better get down to work." He glanced at his data bracelet, looking at the time.

"Hey, not yet. I got more questions. . . ." I never had enough questions, because once he'd answered all I could come up with, we had to work on my telepathy.

"You must lie awake nights thinking them up." His voice began to show an edge.

"I always work best after midnight." But it wasn't by choice any more. My eyes burned from the lack of sleep. I leaned back in my seat, waiting for him to start talking again. "Gimme another camph, will you?" I put a hand out on the cool white tabletop, palm up.

He didn't move, sitting across from me. (You'll have to work for it this time.)

I jerked and swore, unbalancing my chair. "Don't do that to me!"

(Why not? That's why we're here.)

"No!" I flinched as I heard it come out. "I mean, I know that. But I need more time. I just ain't—ready." I was pulling my thoughts in tighter and tighter, weaving defenses to keep him from getting at me again.

"When are you planning to be 'ready'? Tomorrow? Next week? A month from now, a year? You don't have that long, Cat!" Suddenly he was angry. "If you want to stay in this research program, you've got to show results. You have to be able to control your talent, not just 'feel' it —control it under pressure, in ways you never expected to. You have to learn when not to use it, and how to keep other psions from using it against you—" He broke off.

"Why?" I frowned, matching his own.

"Because those are the rules; and if you want to get along, you learn to obey the rules."

"Not where I come from." I pushed up out of my chair and moved away from him.

"You're not in Oldcity now. But you'll be back there in a hurry, Cityboy, if you can't learn to cooperate."

"What's eating you?" I turned to stare at him. He sounded like a Corpse. He'd never called me that before, or threatened me.

"Maybe that you don't even bother to hide how little you care about all this, about what you're doing here, or what I'm trying to do to help you." He got up, following me but keeping out of my reach.

"What do you mean?" Knowing what he meant, that he'd seen it in my thoughts. "I didn't—"

(The hell you didn't!) His anger and frustration caught me from an unguarded angle, and hit me behind the eyes. (All right, shadow walker, you've been using my patience like a wall to hide behind; but you've finally used it up. No more camphs, no more questions, no more games until you show me some return.)

"Lemme alone, you vermy bastard!"

(No more being left alone! You'll never be alone again unless you *make* me leave your mind—)

"Get out, get out!" I pressed my hands against my ears, like that would do any good. He was through my defenses and on the inside, and I didn't know what to do about it to get him out again.

(Make me.) His words echoed through the circuits of my brain.

"Damn you, damn you—" I was half crazy with the fear that he really meant it, that he'd never get out of my head again. I groped for a weapon—not on the counter beside me, because my body couldn't get at him; but somewhere in my mind, where I could. *(Damn you! damn you!)* Feeling the thought leap like a spark across the gap between my mind and his. Suddenly making the connection, holding onto it, I completed the link of thought, (You slad, you son of a bitch, get out of my mind before I burn you out!), with a jolt of white-hot rage. (Break, break!)

He broke contact: in the same second my mind was suddenly all my own again, my eyes saw him sway and clutch at a chair for support.

I swayed too, reaching out for the counter edge behind me. I swore softly.

"Congratulations." His own voice was barely more than a whisper. "Psion."

"God." I gulped, and wiped my hand across my mouth. A few more words slipped out, more curses, as I stumbled back to the table and sat down.

Cortelyou sat down across from me again. This time he tossed me the whole pack of camphs. "Here."

I pushed one between my lips with shaking hands. Disconnected filaments pulsed behind my eyes—signposts, beacons, patterns that had lain waiting for me to turn my own eyes inward and see them. . . . We sat there for a long time, not saying anything; while I tried to make myself believe what had happened, while the camph calmed me down.

"How do you feel?" he said, finally. He was all solicitude, now.

"You should know." I glared at him.

He shook his head. "I'm not reading you now; you know that."

"Then how do you think I feel?" I looked away, wishing, this room had a window.

"Proud . . . excited . . . like you've made a breakthrough?"

"No. Dirty, lousy—like a freak! That's how you're supposed to feel, ain't it?"

"Did Goba tell you that?" His smile disappeared.

"He didn't have to. Every time I get close to his mind, or any of them, I can smell it." My hands tightened into fists on my knees.

Cortelyou grimaced. "Damn them, why can't they—"

"Why shouldn't they hate me? Who wants to have somebody else know everything you're thinking? I seen people get killed for less than that!"

"And that's why you're fighting this every step of the way." Half question, half answer.

I shrugged, letting him think he understood everything, when he only understood half of it.

"I'm sorry I was so hard on you." He bent his head. "I should have known . . ."

"Why should you be any different?" I wished he didn't apologize so much; it got on my nerves.

"Because we *are* different. We have to be—not just because of what we can do, but because of the responsibility it puts on us. We do things with our minds that most humans could never do, and that makes them afraid of us. 'In the country of the blind, the one-eyed man is stoned to death.' We have to live by a stricter code than the rest of humanity, to prove to them that they have nothing to fear from us. . . ." He leaned forward. "Do you want to know how I feel about my telepathy?"

No. But I didn't say it. I shifted in my seat, hung onto its hard, curving edges to keep from bolting as I felt him reach into my thoughts again. I held my mind loose, let the sparking strands link with his in the invisible space where our senses met. I was shaking with the effort, and I felt his mind cringe with the fear I couldn't damp out.

But he didn't push me away. Instead the weave of his thoughts only loosened, like the first time, as he dropped all his defenses and drew me in. The impressions he wanted me to find shimmered on the surface of his awareness where I couldn't help seeing them: he was proud, glad, grateful for the Gift that he'd been born with. . . . Psionics could lead to a new future for humanity, filled with understanding and free of the fear that fed blind hatred. . . . He would never abuse his Gift, never do anything to make the blind ones think of his talent as a threat. . . . He would do *anything* to gain their trust, to make them understand.

But behind the images he held like banners for me to see, I felt the

brand of a fresh wound laid on him by some psi-hating corporate lackey
—heard the murmur of a thousand other ghosts and shadows. Fury
raged in some deep part of his mind, held prisoner by his will. And I
realized what it cost him to be a corporate telepath, a missionary in a
world of hate-filled deadheads who didn't want to be saved. . . .

I broke contact. "How can you live with that?"

"What?" He looked totally confused.

"They spit on you, they don't give a damn about what you're trying
to prove. It's eating your guts out; why don't you quit whoring for those
bastards?"

His mouth fell open. "Where did you . . . ?" His face straightened
out again. "I've lived with it for years. I'm barely aware of it anymore."
It sounded like something he used to put himself to sleep at night. "I
believe in what I'm trying to do. It isn't an easy thing, but it isn't
impossible." One hand clung to the other. "Haven't you ever endured
something unpleasant for something you believed in?" It was almost a
challenge.

"Yeah. Staying alive—so I could stay alive." The words slid out, just
another smart remark. But then my own mind showed me things I'd
done, and let be done to me, that would probably make him say everything I'd just said to him. "I guess you get used to anything, if you have
to." I looked down. "So long as you don't think about it too much." I
thought about all his facts and figures, filling up his mind until there
was no room for anything else to get in the way of his belief. And I
understood suddenly why this research was important to him, why I
was too, why he'd *had* to make that breakthrough today and force me
to prove he was right. I thought about my being a telepath in spite of
everything—seeing the lines of psi energy shining with life force. I
thought about being born to use them: the Third Eye, the Sixth Sense,
the Extra Ear . . . about a screaming thing locked in a cell somewhere
in the pit of my mind . . . about thinking too much. I took out another camph.

"Do you know what a 'joining' is?"

I shook my head.

"It's a meeting of minds, between a telepath and another psion, so
complete and unguarded that their minds become one—each open to
the other totally, with nothing held back. Their psi powers are heightened, each one's by the other's; they do things they could never do
alone. It's the ultimate form of giving, of belonging. It's like nothing

else you can experience, and it can change the ones who join forever.
. . ." His eyes were alive with longing.

"You ever do that?" I asked, because he expected something.

"Once." His clenched fists opened; I heard more joy and loss than I'd ever heard filling one word before. "A pure joining is very rare. It's almost impossible for more than two human psions. It's a combination of the highest ability and the deepest need. . . ." He looked up at me again, and his look told me I'd never experience it, unless somehow I could make my brain stop chasing its own tail.

"I can't imagine ever wanting to get that close to nobody." I leaned back, away from him.

He leaned back too, and sighed. "Well, a journey of a thousand miles starts with the first step."

After that the steps got longer. Now that I could actually make contact with him, he began trying to teach me all the things he'd said I had to learn about controlling my talent. I didn't see what was so important about most of what we did. But then, I didn't understand most of what was happening to me here, anyway. I hardly even knew when I was confused, half the time.

He told me I'd had it easy working with technicians who weren't psions themselves; their concentration and control was so poor that any telepath could keep them at bay. Working against another psion was going to be something else. He explained to me how trained telepaths could sort out the strands of image that patterned someone else's thoughts; how they could locate one particular pattern, follow it along all its branching ways to their scattered ends and back again. He also told me how another telepath could protect that pattern by weaving a shield—burying it behind and between tangles of other images and information—or by sensing the probe and sidetracking it, braiding the intruder's mind into a false strand, a lie. Most psions were better at protecting themselves from a mindread than normal humans, even if they weren't telepaths, just because they were more in control of their own minds.

I was supposed to be a stronger telepath than he was. It should have been easy to keep him out of my mind. But I hadn't been feeling my mind, exercising my talent—and he had. He told me that if one telepath knew the tricks of thought-tracking and the other one didn't, the greenhorn couldn't hide his deepest secret, no matter how much raw confusion he put up to save himself. Then to prove it, he'd make me nervous or angry. I'd forget what I was doing, and he'd walk right into my mind. He didn't usually go very deep, but he didn't need to. Using my telepathy never got any easier, and feeling him pry into me like that still drove me crazy. And then he'd jump on me anyway for letting him do it. For someone who looked so soft, he was as tough as steel when he was doing his job.

And no matter how hard I tried, I couldn't trick *him*, and that just made it worse.

But in spite of everything, working with Cortelyou I finally began to act like a real telepath. Or I thought I did, even if nobody else did. But Goba didn't have any time left to be fussy, he said, when he finally sent me to meet the rest of Siebeling's psions.

3

THE PSIONS WERE sitting in a circle of chairs, maybe a dozen of them, in a pearly-walled room with a floor of patterned tile. One wall looked out on the sky here, too; farther up in the building, and higher in the air, than I'd ever been before. Siebeling was at the head of the circle when I stopped in the doorway. He frowned at me like I was late and said, "This is Cat. He's a telepath."

They stopped talking. I spotted the red-haired woman from the day I'd first come here, staring at me. I didn't want to go into that room, and know what they were thinking, and be laughed at. What the hell were they staring at, anyhow—? But then I saw the woman with empty eyes who'd given me the scarf. She was watching me too, but her eyes weren't empty this time; and suddenly I saw myself from the outside, clean and neat in a fresh smock and pants, looking like anyone else. I wasn't dirty and dye-smeared now; they were all strangers here, too. A calmness came over me somehow, and suddenly everything was all right. She half smiled at me, and her eyes dropped. I went and sat down, at the end of the circle where all the seats were empty. I pulled a pack of camphs out of my pocket and stuck one into my mouth. Then I finally noticed Cortelyou sitting with the rest of them. He nodded at me.

Siebeling began to talk about how most psions felt afraid or ashamed because they didn't understand their abilities, and society didn't understand psions. Once they learned to control their minds the way they controlled their bodies, they'd see that they weren't freaks; that being a psion could be a good, valuable thing. He called psionic talent the Gift, and he said that it didn't have to hurt them, it was something to be proud of. Learning how to control the Gift was what we were doing here at the Institute. He was smiling all the while he spoke; pride and encouragement filled the words. I'd never seen him like that—it made him look like a different man. I watched other faces around the circle while he spoke, and some of them looked like they'd never smiled much at all, but they smiled now with him.

Afterward we started in on new exercises. Siebeling put a candle on the table behind him and said we were going to use our Gift to help us light it. He held a lighter up in the air and let it go; but it didn't drop. He was controlling it with his mind, by telekinesis. It drifted, past him through the air, and lit the candle. He blew the candle out again and tossed the lighter to the woman who'd smiled at me. "Jule?" I don't know why it surprised me to learn Siebeling was a psion too. A lot of things suddenly made more sense about him. I tried not to stare.

Jule stood up, and then she was standing next to the candle, and then she was back in her seat, before I'd even blinked—she could teleport. The candle was burning, the lighter was on the table. Siebeling nodded; she looked down.

Someone else made the lighter float again, telekinesis, a little shaky; and then Siebeling was throwing it to me.

"What am I supposed to do with it? I ain't a teek." But he didn't say anything. I sat there feeling stupid and angry, and then suddenly words filled my mind. (Fellow telepath. Ask me to light it.) I looked around the circle until I saw somebody grin at me. It was Cortelyou. I asked with my face but he shook his head.

(Ask me.)

His mind was open to mine. I thought, (Will-you-light-the-candle?) gritting my teeth.

He blinked. (Don't shout. I'll be glad to.)

I threw him the lighter. He reached over and lit the candle. Siebeling nodded, and tossed the lighter out again. It went on around the circle, and I started to feel like maybe this wouldn't be so bad after all.

And when the lighter came to the red-haired woman, she just got up and walked over to the candle to light it, as if she couldn't find any other way to do it. That made me smile, but she didn't look embarrassed. Siebeling saw me grinning. He said, to everyone, "Darra's talent is precognition—predicting the future. Psionic skills vary, just as artistic skills do. Sometimes your skill will be the only one that can solve a problem; sometimes it's the only one that won't. Don't feel self-conscious if you have to do something the hard way—like the rest of humanity." Everyone else laughed. Later, when I couldn't move a chair, and neither could Cortelyou, Cortelyou shrugged and thought. (There's always the cards. We're the only ones who can cheat.) I laughed out loud then, so that everyone looked at me, and the woman named Jule smiled again. And I guess I'd learned more than a couple of psi tricks that afternoon.

But then Siebeling said something while I was thinking about that, and everyone got up to leave. I looked across at Cortelyou and thought, (What?)

(It's time for What to Do until Corporate Security Comes.)

I wondered what the hell that was supposed to mean, but I got up and followed everyone else.

It turned out to be another laboratory I'd never seen before. I sat down in a chair in front of a terminal and touchboard like everyone else, and someone at the end of the room began to talk to us about communications. He might as well have been talking backward for all the good it did me. I couldn't understand anything: I sat and felt bored, rolling a camph between my fingers, until he began saying, "Touch the segment labeled ON. Now, spread your fingers across the area marked with . . ."

I stared down at the board in front of me, and put out my hand, and pulled it back. My skin started to itch. I can't . . . Cortelyou wasn't anywhere near me; I couldn't ask him for help. But Jule was sitting next to me, she looked like she knew what she was doing. I tried to reach into her mind. She gasped and her hand went up to her face; her mind drove me out with a bright flash of terror. Then her gray eyes were full of shadow and surprise, staring back at me. She was as afraid of intruders as I was.

I turned away, back to the terminal, my hands clenching. But it was already too late; Siebeling had seen it. He came up behind me, and I felt him look past me at Jule, and then down at the dark screen, before he said, "What's the matter?" I didn't say anything.

"Touch ON." Like he was trying to be patient.

I just sat there, feeling him get angry. "I can't."

"What?"

"He probably can't read, Ardan," the red-haired precog said, loud enough so that everyone in the room could hear it.

"Oh? Is that true?"

I nodded, barely moving my head, feeling like my neck would snap.

"Then I'm afraid you're not qualified to—"

I stood up. "Why do I have to do this? This's nothin' to do with being a telepath! The hell with—" I felt a touch, like a soft hand somewhere in mind, and then all of a sudden I shut up and sat down in my seat again, wondering. A voice said, "It isn't a crime. I'll help him, Ardan. Come on, Cat, it's easy, watch me. . . ."

And I watched Jule touch a corner of the grid, because I was too ashamed to look anywhere else. The screen brightened. She turned it off, and then I tried it. After a minute Siebeling said, "If you can learn to do it, I'll tell you why you have to," and he left us alone.

"You can do it," she said, not looking at me.

"What do you care if I can? Why should you help me?"

Her face changed; she looked up at me with those empty eyes and said, "I don't know." She shrugged. And she didn't know.

I felt stupid and confused again, I was going to tell her to mind her own, but I just said, "I'm sorry, about . . ." and I touched my head. She nodded. I didn't say anything more to her, but I let her help me.

Siebeling came back to watch me work after the others had gone for the day. He almost seemed disappointed to find me doing things right. "If you're going to have this much trouble with everything, I can't ask Jule . . ."

"But I don't mind, Ardan. He wants to stay; I'll help him." She got up. "I have nothing else but time."

"We could use another telepath," somebody said. "He did all right today."

I looked past Siebeling. I'd thought everyone else was gone, but Cortelyou was still standing across the room.

Siebeling frowned. "I just don't think he—"

"I want to stay here. I'll work."

He glanced back at me, hesitated. "All right, then. I suppose I . . . Jule? If you can wait, I'll . . . see you out." For just a second he looked like an embarrassed kid.

Jule had started fading away toward the door; she stopped and came back. I saw Cortelyou grin at nothing behind her, and then he followed her back to where I was sitting.

Siebeling looked annoyed, but he only said, "When I told you what you were getting into, I didn't tell you everything; because I didn't know how you'd work out. Everyone else here already knows the full truth about what they're getting into. You should understand all of it too, before you make your final decision.

"We are psions working with our abilities; the FTA is 'sponsoring' it. Everything I told you about that part is true. But they hope it will be more than simply a research project. They're investigating a matter of Federation security that involves psionics; they think we may attract the

attention of the criminal behind it—someone they call Quicksilver."
The word seemed to burn his mouth. I saw Cortelyou's mouth turn
down; lines of tension formed on Jule's face.

"Nice name," I said, raising my eyebrows. "You all got somethin'
against it?"

"Quicksilver gives all psions a bad name," Cortelyou said, and Siebeling nodded.

"He's a renegade, he uses his psionic talents to commit crimes all
over the galaxy."

"What kind of crimes?"

Siebeling started to frown again. Cortelyou answered the question:
"Expensive ones. Impossible ones."

"Ugly ones," Jule said softly, and all of a sudden I didn't want to
hear the details.

Cortelyou nodded. "He's rumored to have multiple psi talents, all of
them perfectly controlled. Just take one, telekinesis, and let your mind
play with the possibilities. . . . Combines hire him and use him against
rival governments. He'll work for anyone who pays him enough. And
he uses his psi to slip through Corporate Security nets like water. So far
they haven't been able to touch him. They don't know his real identity
—they don't even know what he looks like. But they want him stopped.
That's why we're here."

"We're bait, in other words," Siebeling said, "and if Quicksilver takes
the bait, we'll be expected to act as undercover agents. Nothing at all
may happen; but if we do become involved with this Quicksilver, we'll
be in considerable danger. Because of that I've arranged for everyone to
be credited a substantial—"

"Everybody?" I said. He nodded, and told me how much; my arm
slipped off the back of the chair. "Jeezu you mean . . . I'd have a
rating, a data bracelet, the whole thing? Like a real human being?"

"I suppose so." He glanced at the clock in the lower corner of my
terminal screen. "Is that acceptable to you?"

"Are you kidding?"

"Jule . . ." He turned to go.

"Hey, you gonna tell me any more about it?" Suddenly the strange
questions the Corpses had asked me before I came here, and all the
things Cortelyou had been showing me without telling me why, began
to fit together in my mind.

"I thought you weren't interested in anything but avoiding Contract
Labor."

The others looked at Siebeling, surprised, and then at me.

"Well . . . maybe I changed my mind."

"Do you know anything about the Crab Colonies?" That was Cortelyou, naturally.

"I heard the Crab Nebula is an exploded star. It's . . . out there, someplace." I waved at the window.

"It's forty-five hundred light-years from here," Cortelyou said. "But you're on the right track."

"What's a light-year?"

Siebeling sighed and dropped the folder he was carrying. "If you really want to know about this, you'll have to have more background than you do. I suppose we can give it to you. . . ." So the three of them told me about the Crab Colonies and the FTA and Earth, and what all that had to do with us being here at the Institute.

The Crab Nebula, Cortelyou said, was a cloud of gas and debris—what was left of a supernova, a star that blew itself up before humans ever left home. To astronomers on Ardattee it looked like a smoke ring; and like a smoke ring it was expanding through space. A light-year was the distance light could travel in a year—moving at around three hundred thousand kilometers a second. But even at speeds like that it took thousands of years for the light to reach us here; the real Nebula was even larger than the nearly five-thousand-year-old image they saw from observatories. Several star systems with inhabited planets were located near the Nebula in space; those were the Crab Colonies.

The Federation Transport Authority controlled the Colonies directly, and the rest of the Federation indirectly, because it regulated shipping. The FTA had grown out of something that had been set up long ago back on Earth, before the days of stardrives and space exploration. Its original purpose had been to oversee trade for the confederation of multinational corporations that finally took over Earth's old national governments. As the solar system was settled, making shipping and trade a thousand times more complicated, the FTA became more important. And it grew even more by taking over the distribution of resources during a handful of intrasystem wars. Finally it began to build its own ships and even weapons and hired more security forces than a lot of corporations did.

Then faster-than-light stardrive was invented, and suddenly humans could reach the nearest stars in weeks instead of years. Suddenly Earth's multinational corporate empires had the chance to become multiworld empires, and they started sharpening their knives to carve up the stars. The old toothless Worldgov mutated and survived; it set up guidelines for interstellar law, even though it didn't have the power to back them up. And the new Human Federation began expanding like a bubble outward from Earth. Finally the FTA set up an expedition to prospect in the Crab Nebula for telhassium. Cortelyou had told me about telhassium—an element so rare that it was almost impossible to find outside the heart of a star. The Federation needed it in large amounts to make its new faster-than-light stardrive cheap and simple.

The Transport Authority expedition found a piece of the exploded sun's corpse there, still orbiting the tiny neutron star that was all that was left of its mass after the supernova explosion. They called the thing Cinder, and it was the nearest anyone had ever seen to a solid piece of telhassium ore. Once they began mining it, the citizens of the Human Federation were free to travel between its settled worlds as easily as they'd traveled between continents on just one world.

But they hadn't counted on one thing: The FTA took the telhassium for itself. Controlling the telhassium supply meant that the FTA no longer just oversaw the Federation's transportation, it controlled it. No matter how big any combine was—and especially if it wanted to get any bigger—it had to toe the FTA's line or it didn't get the telhassium it needed to move its ships and process its data. The original shipping empires suffered the most, because the FTA took just about all their independent control away and made them its tools. The FTA wasn't all that unreasonable in what it wanted—power and money—but it cut into the power and profits of everybody else. It also built up a big enough Special Forces arm to actually start enforcing some of the Federation's laws. It kept the combines from the kind of throat-cutting competition they were used to, and they didn't much like that. But they lived with it.

So an isolated Colony of the Federation grew up out around the Crab, controlled by the FTA and independent from everything else. And the rest of the Federation, even though it was still only a few hundred light-years across, wasn't a bubble shape expanding evenly into space anymore. It started to stretch out toward the Colonies. Earth lost its economic influence, and Quarro became an independent Federal District, the new center of power and money and everything worth having.

All of that was why Quarro's District Corporate Security, the FTA's own soldiercops, had gotten involved in something going on way out in the Crab Colonies. The FTA had learned through its spies and informers that some sort of dirty business was taking shape out there, and they figured some combine or alliance of combines was backing it. But they couldn't get any closer to the heart of it; all their leads just kept slipping through their fingers. They were sure Quicksilver was behind the plot, whatever it was. That made them real nervous, because the telhassium supply was out there in the Colonies. But eventually they learned that Quicksilver had contacts here in Quarro—and that he was looking for recruits.

So we were here to work undercover, to find the real source of the trouble and make sure it was stopped before it knocked the Federation on its ass. Siebeling made it sound like making history, like poor psions saving the galaxy. I thought about that, and about me as a big hero. . . .

Siebeling said, "Keep that smirk off your face. This isn't a joke. If you can't take it seriously, I'll send you back—you aren't being given the chance to slide out of anything here."

I sighed. "I'm glad you ain't a mind reader."

Cortelyou laughed and shook his head. Siebeling just turned away, looking toward Jule.

I watched them leave together, all of them going home when I couldn't. My head was crammed so full of information that I felt as if moving it would make everything overflow. I thought about psions plotting out in the Colonies, about going out there and stopping them, about being a hero and a part of history. I looked down at my hands, at my bare wrist that would be wearing a data bracelet in a few more weeks . . . at the broken thumb that had healed crooked after I'd picked the wrong pocket once. And I realized suddenly that I was glad I wasn't going home.

The next day Goba and his techs used hypnosis on me again, giving me a screen of half-true memories that would protect the real truths I knew now from anything but a direct telepathic probe. And beginning the next day Dere Cortelyou worked me harder than ever, forcing me to learn the mind tricks I needed to handle a direct attack. It wasn't any easier; but at least now I knew why I was doing it, so it was easier to keep trying.

And then I really was a part of the research program, playing psi games with the rest of the psions and waiting for something to happen. Before long I began to wish we'd be waiting there forever. Sometimes I think that was the happiest time of my life.

It surprised me how fast I'd gotten used to the Sakaffe Institute,

because it was so different from—everything, from before. I had decent
clothes that fit me. I could eat as much as I wanted to, any time I felt
like it. I even had my private room. They'd stopped locking me in at
night, but by now it didn't matter: the bed was soft, clean, and mine,
and that was all I wanted. There were a dozen different projects going
on at the Institute besides ours, too; and once they'd gotten used to
seeing me, the lab workers let me hang around and watch. Or just sit
and stare at the threedy in one of the lounges, if I felt like it. Nobody
cared. I was never bored. I didn't even miss the drugs; just looking out
any window was like some kind of an alindith dream. I had to pinch
myself sometimes to be sure it was all real.

I even liked to think about what I was supposed to be doing here: I'd
seen a show on the threedy, *Nebula Pioneers,* about Colonists and miners out in the Crab Colonies making a home in the alien wilderness. Life
was hard out on the frontier worlds, but it was exciting, and no one
cared what you'd been before, only what you were trying to be now. It
was a place where you were free to start again, and maybe make it all
come out right this time. I thought maybe I'd like to try that; thought
about using some of my money to go there when this was over. I was
glad we were supposed to be helping them out.

But more than anything else I liked working with the rest of the
psions—even if it meant being one myself. It was hard work, and Siebeling always seemed to make it harder; but I never wanted to quit. I was
getting to be pretty good, too. I think I'd have been good even if I
hadn't been trying to keep Siebeling off my back. I wanted to be good; I
guess I wanted to prove something to somebody. Maybe to myself.

But even so, I wouldn't have been much good without Jule taMing.
After that first day, whenever we had to work with any equipment she
stayed around afterward, and went over everything we did with me
until I knew it from memory. I'd half expected Cortelyou would take
over teaching me, but he only laughed and said he knew where my
attention was now—meaning on Jule—and I might as well follow it. I
swore at him, blushing, and did.

Jule taught me how to use one machine after another: she taught me
letters and symbols that stood for the same thing on different boards;
she worked with me until soon I could pick things up almost as fast as
anyone else. . . .

". . . then that, and that—" I touched the wrong square and the
comm panel lit up with red. "Damn!" I pulled back from the
touchboard, shaking out my hands.

Jule leaned past me and cleared the panel for the tenth time, her dark hair brushing my shoulder. "Those two letters are almost the same; anyone could make that mistake. Try again," she said, still as patient and calm as she'd been an hour before. Somehow she never made me feel stupid.

But that doesn't mean I didn't feel stupid anyway. "Mother Earth, I ain't never gonna get them straight! They don't *mean* nothin'!"

She looked down at me directly for once. "You're tired. . . . Your body is screaming for sleep. Why do you stay awake all night, when you know you have to get up and work?" It wasn't critical, just curious.

I tensed; it still made me jumpy when she knew exactly what I was feeling. She was an empath besides being a 'port: she knew what everybody felt, whether she wanted to or not. I frowned at my hands. "I'm used to it." Back in Oldcity I'd stayed awake all night because that was when the crowds were out, and I lived off the crowds. Now I stayed awake because I was afraid to sleep.

Her face told me that she knew there was more, but she looked away and didn't push it. She had her own fears. She shut off the comm's touchboard, murmuring. "They don't mean anything. . . ."

I followed her across the lab. Outside twilight was staining Quarro a deep violet-blue; lights were coming on. There was a roof garden a few stories down below us; trees moved in the cool air of dusk. Jule lit up another terminal and began to work with it. I stood beside her, looking out; close enough so that my hip brushed hers. And suddenly I couldn't help thinking about how close she was, touching me, the way her hair moved. . . . I felt a rush of heat rise through me, and wondered what she'd—

The thought that she knew everything I felt hit me like a bucket of cold water. I tied my mind into a knot, trapping the thought inside, and moved away from her.

She looked up, startled—either because she'd felt what I felt, or just because her awareness of me had been stopped dead. I looked out the window, taking out a camph, rocking on my heels.

"Cat?" She called me back. I couldn't tell what she was thinking, but for just a second the corners of her mouth turned up a little. She wasn't looking at me as I stopped beside her, but she said, "You move like a dancer. You're very quick and graceful."

"Me?" I laughed, embarrassed. "Comes from walkin' on eggs all the time." I pushed my hands into my pockets. It was the first time I could ever remember anybody noticing something good about me. "What's that?" I nodded at the terminal. It was just a plain bright screen with a couple of control buttons below it. There were three letters printed on the screen.

"That's your name."

I touched it with my hand. "My name?"

She nodded, tracing the symbols with a stylus, naming them, C-A-T spells *Cat.*

I said the sounds after her. "I seen all those letters before."

She nodded again.

But now they really mean something. I reached out, pulled back a little, finally took the stylus she was holding out to me. I touched its tip to the screen, leaving a bright smear.

Someone came into the room. I felt it before I saw them . . . Siebeling, and a Corpse with him. I jerked around, dropping the stylus, looking for another way out—

Jule's hand caught my sleeve. "It's all right. He's not here for you. It's me he wants to see."

"You?" But already I saw that he wasn't a Citicorpse, that he was wearing the insignia of some combine government. "Jule, you got a record?"

She didn't answer. Siebeling came over to us, leaving the Corpse waiting in the doorway. Jule usually started to glow all over whenever she saw Siebeling, but this time her face was set and pale, and her mind was full of darkness.

"Jule, there's someone here to see you," Siebeling said.

She nodded, keeping her head down. "I know. I don't want to talk to him, Ardan. Make him go away, please. . . ." She began to bite a fingernail.

"I think you should talk to him." Siebeling's voice was quiet, but it was almost an order. "Jule, you didn't tell me that you—"

She picked the stylus up and put it into my hand. "Here," she whispered. "Practice." Then she moved away from us, toward the Corpse, her arms folded in front of her and her hands clutching her elbows. She was trying to hold in her tension, but I could feel it like electricity in the air.

"What's he want? She ain't bein' arrested, is she?"

Siebeling glared at me like I'd insulted her. "Of course not. He brought a message from her family."

"Her family?" There was something so solitary about Jule that I'd always thought she must be as alone as I was. Siebeling was the only other person she ever really talked to besides me. The two of them had had a thing going almost from the start; everybody knew it even though they pretended not to. It wasn't easy to keep a secret from a bunch of psions, and Jule was only just learning how to keep her feelings hidden at all. She might as well have shouted it. If she wanted to get involved with Siebeling that was her business . . . even though I couldn't see what she saw in him, myself. "They sent a Corpse to tell her? Whose colors is he wearing?"

"Centauri Transport. It's a shipping combine; the biggest and one of the oldest." And the taMing family controlled its holdings. *Her* family . . . the thought was lying on the surface of his mind, bright with his own surprise.

"You mean she's rich?"

"Does she look rich?" He bit off the words.

I shrugged. "Not from here." She was talking to the Corpse, still hugging herself, still broadcasting resentment. "Don't worry. I ain't planning to mug her." I turned back to the screen, annoyed, and started trying to copy my name.

"What are you doing?" Siebeling said it like he'd caught me defacing property.

"Doin' what she told me to do." C . . . A . . . T. My hand shook; I was holding the stylus like it would jump out of my fist, and the letters looked like pieces of string. I made myself relax. C-A-T. C-A-T. CAT. CAT. CAT. The picture of my name. It got easier and easier. A feeling I'd never known before took hold of me. Maybe it was pride.

"A waste." Siebeling let the words slip out and squash it. His mind showed me an ignorant criminal, a green-eyed Oldcity hoodlum who was wasting everybody's time.

I looked up, smarting with anger, ready to do something we were both going to regret. But a burst of fresh feeling from Jule cut between us—a kind of startled triumph, and then echoes of the same feeling that had started inside me. She was walking toward us again; the Corpse was gone from the doorway. She didn't seem to notice our tension, for once. Her own mind was clenched around the irony that her family only interfered in her life when it was going right. But her gray eyes were shining and alive as she said, "I'm staying."

Siebeling's tight face relaxed into a sudden smile, his relief was almost as loud as hers was. But he said, "Are you sure that—?"

"Yes." She nodded, ending it. She started to look back at me.

Siebeling caught her hand, trying to pull her away; but she broke free. "Wait." Siebeling shot me a dark glance past her. I didn't say anything. Jule looked at what I'd done on the screen. She grinned at me for a second like we'd both had a triumph, and pride filled me again. Siebeling put an arm around her then, the first time he'd ever done that in front of me, and this time she went with him.

I went back to the comm console and switched it on, and went through the sequence she'd been trying to teach me. I did it a few more times, perfectly, and then I went back and wrote my name some more. I thought about asking Jule to show me some other words tomorrow: *maybe I could get an instruction tape, or something. . . .*

But after that there wasn't any more equipment I had to learn, and somehow Siebeling always seemed to have something better for Jule to do than waste her time on me. Without her pulling me, I went back to watching the threedy like the ignorant hood I was, and just forgot about learning anything else.

But that didn't change how I felt about being at the Institute. Being a psion, working with the other psions, was still like nothing I'd ever known. Even if some of them called me "the mental pickpocket" in the back of their minds, when we worked together there was still a bond between us. Because then we were all the same, and nothing else counted. If the psi talent made me angry, I knew that most of them knew how it felt. Only they'd lived with it, and maybe hated it, a lot longer than I had. I knew I'd been lucky in burying it all my life, and that made living with it now easier for me.

I guess it was making it easier for all of us, sharing the changes. I thought some of them even began to like me a little—Dere Cortelyou, for one. And Jule. Back in Oldcity the closest I'd ever come to having a friend was sleeping in the same room with somebody. I'd never even run with a gang. This was the first time I'd ever belonged to anything; I never figured it would feel so right. I finally had something to lose. Sometimes I was afraid I'd pinch myself once too often, and wake up for good.

4

"HERE!"

(Behind you—)

"Got it!" (Thanks.)

"Keep it moving. Again!"

"All right, all right. . . ."

"Here!"

"No, *there!*" Laughter.

We were working together, caught up in what Siebeling called "juggling." Each of us used our psi talents any way we could, to take the others by surprise or warn each other, in a free-flowing, shapeless game. We tossed things and moved things and moved ourselves, reached out with our bodies and minds; making our control surer and more fluid, training ourselves to respond without losing focus or dropping guard—

"Damn!" Or dropping a block, or a bowl.

(Gotcha!) "Gotcha!" More laughter.

"Twenty-three! Time?"

"Catch!"

"Over and under—"

(Cat, *warning.*)

Jule's sending lit my mind a second too late, as the stool that had been sitting clear across the room materialized right behind me. I stepped back into it before I could stop myself; my feet tangled and I landed on the hard ripple-rings of the tile floor. Siebeling had done it to me again. He was good, real good. Too good. I lay on the floor and thought things at him that I didn't have the breath to say out loud, but his mind was woven solid and he didn't feel a thing. *Didn't feel anything, the stinking—* Jule did; I saw her wincing, at my anger or at my pain. Guilt pinched me, and I tried to get control of my feelings, for her sake.

The others stood shifting from foot to foot. I shut my own mind against their muttering thoughts.

"Come on," Siebeling said, and you couldn't tell from his voice how much he must be enjoying it. "Get up, you're breaking the rhythm."

"You're breaking my neck! Why is it always me?"

"Because you're the least experienced," he said quietly.

"No—because you're always on my back, that's why!" I started to pick myself up, piece by piece.

"If I give you more attention, it's because you need it. You obviously need it or you wouldn't have fallen. Stop making excuses."

I got up, rubbing my bruises, and kicked the stool toward him. He watched me with that look I'd gotten to know too well, one dark with something I couldn't ever reach; as if maybe even he didn't know why he hated the sight of me. Then suddenly he looked away from me toward Jule, and the thread of tension snapped. He looked down. He shrugged and said, "That's enough for today. We'll work on this again tomorrow." He gestured toward the doorway at the far end of the hall, making a point of not looking at me now. As he turned, I heard Cortelyou mutter to him, "Quit picking on the kid, Ardan. It's not what he needs from you. You just make him expect to fail. . . ." I moved away from them, straight for the door; wondering if seeing me fail wasn't just what Siebeling wanted.

When I was almost to the doorway, I had a sudden dizzy flash, my mind's eye saw me, like a mirror picking up the image from some other psion's mind. But the image came from outside the room, not through the eyes of anyone here . . . not from the mind of anyone I knew. I stopped, touching my head. We were being watched; someone was waiting in the hall. But when I got outside, no stranger whose mind burned with cold fire was waiting for me. The hall was empty. I went on to the lifts; I got into the first one that came and sent it up before anyone else could follow me.

When it couldn't go any higher, it let me out into the quiet lounge at the top of one of the Institute's peaks. There were a handful of lounges spread through the building's ice-sculpture sprawl; this lounge was one not many people bothered with, because you couldn't see the ocean. Today the sky was weeping, lidded with clouds, wrapping the towers of Quarro in dirty gauze; no one else at all was up here. That suited me fine. I settled down into the formless pile of seat in the center of the room, letting it ease my stiffness as I took out another camph. I leaned back, watching the billowing rain slide down the transparent ripples of

the dome. I'd never seen rain before I came here, except once, in Godshouse Circle. It was warm and brown. I'd felt like Quarro was pissing
on me, and I didn't like it. I remembered how for a long time I hadn't
even known what the sky was.

I'd thought I'd come up here to be angry, but somehow now I didn't
have the strength for it. I just felt tired. My mind lay open, gray and
empty like the sky. I closed my eyes, listening to the patter and drip of
water; but the space behind my eyes filled up with images of Oldcity,
like tears, and I blinked them open again. "Damn!" pinching myself one
more time, just to be sure.

"Cat. Come in out of the rain."

It was Jule: I knew her voice; I knew the quick, shy whisper of her
mind. I hadn't heard the lift come up; but she didn't need the lift. I
turned on the couch and she was standing there half smiling in her
dark, shroud-soft clothes, with her black hair in a heavy braid hanging
to her waist. The room seemed warmer and lighter suddenly, now that I
was sharing it with her. "You still here?"

She shrugged, glancing down at herself. "The world's a prison, and
we are all our own jailers. . . . I was still here the last time I looked."
Jule was a poet—poetry was like psi, she said, like thought, a thing that
compressed images to essence. Sometimes she talked like a poet; she
made a little joke of it, so that you wouldn't mind. I didn't mind,
anyway. She came over and sat down beside me, not too close. She was
like a shadow, somehow too insubstantial to be an intruder. She always
seemed to know what was happening inside me—sometimes better than
I did myself—and whether she should stay or go away again.

I'd asked her once, early on, what it was like to be able to teleport.
She said, "It's good when you want to get away from it all," not looking
at me. The image that slipped out of her mind then was such a surprise
that I didn't believe it. But I knew it had to be true, so after a while I'd
asked the only question I could: "Jule, what made you come here?"
And knowing she'd already shown me half the answer, she said, "One
night I tried to drown myself." She told me about it like she was telling
a story about someone else; how a Corpse who was a telepath had
pulled her out of the lake in the park. He'd spent hours talking to her
about why she hated her life, and in the end he'd told her about this
research program, how they were looking for psions who needed help.
He'd made her promise to look into it, so that she'd have something to
hold onto again. She kept the promise.

I'd told her then why I was here—my side of it. Everyone already knew Corporate Security's side. And it was being able to tell that mattered, letting it out; what we were telling didn't make any difference, as if there was an understanding that no judgments would be made. But she never told me why she'd wanted to drown. She only said, "It happens when you've forgotten all your excuses for not doing it. I've remembered some of them again, now."

Now she sat beside me looking out at the rain. I looked at the smooth profile of her face; I wondered again about questions without answers. But I didn't go after the answers in her mind. Not because I was afraid she'd catch me, but because I knew how she felt about intruders. I knew how I'd feel. Even now she was so shy that she barely spoke to any of the others, except for Siebeling. I didn't know why she still liked to share space with me, but somehow I was glad she did. I didn't want to do anything to make it end.

"Your mind was all gray," she said. "Where was it taking you?" She still watched the rain. It was hard for her to look at anyone for long, she'd said: the eyes were a window to our minds.

"Oldcity." I shrugged, working my twisted thumb, watching the rain.

"Oldcity . . ." She murmured the word, closing her eyes. "Here in Quarro they call it the Tank. Why is that; do you know?"

"No." I glanced back. "Maybe because once you're tossed down there, you can't ever get out."

"Fish tank," she sighed. "Feeder tank." She looked at her own hands; her nails were bitten down to nothing. "When I was a little girl, my father took me to a pet shop. There were hundreds of creatures there, all crying, yearning at me with their hearts; I couldn't choose. Then I saw the fish—two walls full of them, beautiful living jewels, and another tank, half hidden away. The sides of that one were green with slime, and the fish were gasping on the surface for air, or lying stunned and still in the water, waiting for death. I asked why, and they told me that was the feeder tank, it didn't matter how they lived. I could feel them suffering, and no one cared! I started to cry and hold my head. 'Let me have them, Daddy, they're sad, they hurt. . . .' All the animals and all the people in the store began to moan and cry, because I projected it. My father was mortified." Her voice roughened. She folded her fingers under; one hand hugged the other. "His changeling daughter had humiliated the family in public again. He took me away without buying me anything, and never let me have another pet." She looked back at me, finally. "That's what I know about tanks. . . . I've always thought, If they could only feel what I felt, if they could only *know*, they'd never—" She broke off, and her eyes were looking somewhere else, desperately.

I sank further into the couch, hunching my shoulders, and didn't say anything. The spicy end of the camph smarted on my tongue.

We both jerked upright at the chime of the lift arriving, and turned to watch as the door slid open. A man stepped out—tall, middle-aged, rich. He had a neat dark beard, an expensive hairstyle to go with the expensive hand-cast gold at his throat. He wore a summer suit draped with watercolor silk; his clothes were so simple, and fit so perfectly, that they had to have been made for him alone. He was almost as thin as I was, but his face was handsome, in a way that looked like it would last all his life.

And he was dead. I heard Jule suck in her breath beside me, feeling the same thing with her mind: nothing. *No . . . not dead. He was Death.*

"I hope I'm not intruding." He spoke, and even smiled as he came toward us. "My name is Rubiy." He bowed to Jule and made a series of gestures with his hands—something that would've fitted two people meeting in a palace. He didn't even glance at me; I was glad.

"You're a psion," Jule said faintly, more to herself than to him. Her own hands were motionless in her lap.

He nodded. "Yes, I am. Something we have in common." Suddenly the deadness in my mind made perfect sense. He didn't let anything out. But what he had wasn't like my own blind defense; his was the kind of talent that Siebeling had told us about, the kind that none of us could ever hope to reach.

"Are you joining the research?" Jule asked, with a kind of awe.

"No." He smiled politely, but it was just something he did with his mouth. He controlled his body as perfectly as he controlled his mind. I'd seen men with that kind of arrogance in Oldcity. I knew enough to keep out of their way.

"What do you want from us?" I said, finally, because someone like him didn't do things like this for no reason.

"Direct and to the point." He was still smiling. He settled smoothly on the cushioned window ledge, keeping his distance. "I heard about what Dr. Siebeling was doing here, and came to see it for myself. And to offer you a job. I've been more fortunate than most psions, obviously. . . ." He gestured with a ring-covered hand. There was something strange about the way he spoke: not an accent, but just the opposite. The words were all too perfectly shaped, like he was afraid of making a mistake. "My psionic ability has given me everything I could want. But I've never forgotten the suffering that psions endure in this society. And so I've come to offer you the chance to work for me—with me—in a project that could give you all the wealth, all the independence, all the power you ever dreamed of."

I swallowed a laugh. "You're not too sure of yourself, are you? What do you do with your psi, rob vaults long-distance? Heart attacks for hire?" I thought about the rumors and horror stories I'd heard, all the reasons why people should hate psions.

"Telekinesis has its uses." His ice-green eyes narrowed. Suddenly I was afraid—afraid I might be right, afraid of him. "But neither of those possibilities falls particularly close to the mark. My venture is on an entirely different scale."

I glanced at Jule, my skin prickling. Her look said that she was there way ahead of me. I drowned the realization in mind-static before it could form into conscious thought: that this was what we'd been waiting for. The messenger from Quicksilver, the psion who could make the whole Federation afraid of his shadow. I tried to make all my sudden jangling excitement feel like it belonged to what Rubiy had just said; not sure if he was trying to read us, or even whether we'd know it if he did.

"Isn't this happening too fast?" Jule sat forward, surprising me. "You don't even know us."

"On the contrary." He shook his head. "I've been observing you all, privately, for days—studying your talents and your resources, making inquiries . . . deciding who would fit in, and who would simply be a liability. I've already narrowed my list."

I wondered how much more he would have narrowed it if he'd dropped in on us a few weeks earlier, and overheard one of the "special sessions" we'd been put through. . . . I pushed it out of my thoughts again as fast as I could. I was realizing suddenly what it would mean to try to spy on a whole gang of psions. The thought made me sweat. But if Rubiy hadn't seen the truth in my mind or somebody's by now, it couldn't be that simple, even for someone like him. The false images that we'd had put into our memories must be working; and besides, it wasn't that easy to walk into another psion's mind. I ought to know that, if anybody did. I began to relax, just a little.

"You have both telepathy and telekinesis?" Jule was saying.

Rubiy nodded. "As well as teleportation. I am something of a genetic freak, even among 'freaks.' . . ."

I'd thought no human could do all that. Rubiy went on asking Jule questions, answering her own. Her voice was so small that it was hard to hear. I wondered why he'd choose somebody like her, someone so nervous that he could hardly count on her under pressure. . . .

". . . And you are, of course, one of the illustrious taMings," he was saying. It wasn't a question. "Your family controls Centauri Transport. It's rare to find a psion of such distinguished lineage."

Jule frowned. "Most of them are strangled at birth." The bitter sarcasm of it startled a laugh out of Rubiy. I looked at Jule, not really believing those words had come out of her mouth. Her hands twisted the worn black cloth of her shirt. "I'm only a country cousin." But doors shut in her mind; even I knew she was lying. Rubiy had to know it, too; just like he had to know that whatever she'd been once, she was nothing and nobody now.

But he said, "Nonetheless, for what we'll be doing, it's an excellent qualification."

She didn't ask why. I did.

Rubiy only smiled at me, gently.

"Okay, then." I pulled my feet up under me. "Why me? If you've really been watching what we do, you know I ain't worth spitting on as a 'path. I might as well be dead for all the good I'd be to you." I wasn't sure if I was just asking, or trying to talk him out of something.

"You may want to think you're the psionic idiot of this group, but believe me, your potential is greater than anything you'll ever see here." Suddenly his eyes were like spotlights, and my own were like window glass.

No. I looked down and away, shaking my head. "That ain't—that ain't what Siebeling thinks."

"What Dr. Siebeling thinks, and what he really understands, are two different things."

Jule stiffened beside me; a tiny line formed between her brows. I said, "You ought to tell him that."

"I intend to. Because he is a doctor—and for other skills—he is also one of my 'chosen.' " Rubiy nodded, dark humor twisting his face. His foot tapped a silent tattoo on the carpet.

"What makes you sure I'm so good?"

"The obvious: Your shield ability. Your eyes. That clumsy traumabarrier you've built can be broken down. These incompetents have hardly breached it. And then your mind will shine like a star."

My eyes. . . . I rubbed the scar above my left eye, feeling my body tense again.

His face changed, and so did the subject. "You're currently on probation of sorts, from Corporate Security: you didn't welcome the attention of Contract Labor's recruiters. Would it really have been so bad, compared to Oldcity? They say 'Contract Labor builds worlds.' That it teaches you skills, and gives you a stake. That it's a chance to escape from a place like Oldcity, a choice—"

"They say you're better off dead than living in Oldcity, too. But that don't mean I want to find out the hard way. At least in Oldcity I knew what to expect."

"I see." He—understood, somehow I knew it. I could feel it. "And what did you do there?"

"Steal things, mostly; I was a slip. But now I'm just the mental pickpocket around here." My mouth twitched.

And then for the first time I felt his mind make contact—not to intrude on me, not to take anything, but only to give: pictures slipped loose somewhere in his memory and he showed me why he understood. . . . I caught images of a ragged, hungry kid with psi burning inside his head like fire, cursed by the Gift, like too many other psions in too many slums, in too many cities on too many worlds. But not like all the rest—not a loser, not a weakling; selling what he could do with his psi to anyone who'd pay, for anything they wanted. Anything. And they always paid, plenty, or they were sorry they didn't. Until before long he was out of the slum and rich, he didn't need to sell his talent anymore. But he still hired out, on his own terms, if the offer was right; because he was the best and he enjoyed proving it.

And he was sitting there across from me, with his arrogance licking at us like a colorless flame, the sky weeping behind his back: *Quicksilver.* This was Quicksilver himself—suddenly I knew it couldn't be anyone else. He'd come here to choose us personally, not even hiding his face or name, making fools of Corporate Security without even realizing it. He was that sure of himself.

His cold green eyes held me, and I wondered what he could see in my face; but I didn't feel him touch my mind again. "Are you interested in what I have to offer?"

"Yeah." My voice hardly carried to my own ears, but I let him read it in my thoughts. Jule nodded too, but she was only answering the question he'd spoken out loud.

"Good." Rubiy stood up. The audience was over, and somehow it was more like he was dismissing us than leaving. "I'll be in touch with you again." And then he disappeared. A sigh of air rushed in to fill the space where he'd been.

We sat looking at the emptiness and at each other for a long time before either of us said anything. Finally I said, "Quicksilver. That was him, Jule. Right here."

"Quicksilver himself? You mean he—" Jule broke off, glancing from side to side, groping with her mind.

"You might as well finish it, even if he's listening. If he's gonna find out what we're really doing here, it's better if he finds out now," almost wishing that he would. "Before it's too late—for us." I pulled a finger across my throat.

She grimaced. "He . . . he could kill without a thought, couldn't he?"

I nodded. *Or with one.* But the memory of what I'd seen in his mind made the words stick in my throat. He was an iceman; he could do anything to anybody and never feel a twinge. Maybe he'd had feelings once—too many feelings: I'd seen his kind snap under Oldcity's weight and turn into something that wasn't even human. *Alike . . .* were we really so alike?

"I think I've met a truly inhuman being for the first time." Jule wrapped her arms around her like she felt cold.

"Then you've been real lucky," I muttered. *Inhuman, nonhuman, alien. My eyes . . . what about my eyes?*

"We should find Ardan." Jule started to get up. "Tell him. . . ."

I shrugged. "Rubiy's probably doing it for you, right now."

"We'd never be able to hold him here, anyway." She shook her head. "But he won't tell Ardan he's Quicksilver; Ardan won't know who he's really dealing with. He doesn't have the talent for reading—"

"He'll be all right. Rubiy won't try anything here, either. Besides, Siebeling's got a good nose for scum." I folded my own arms, looking away. "At least that's what he's always telling me."

She settled back onto the seat again. "Don't." The tiny frown line came back between her eyes as she read my feelings. "Not now. If we can't hold together now—"

I didn't try to shield it. (*It ain't my fault!*) "Siebeling's the one who's always making it hard. You know it ain't me"—I realized suddenly what I was saying—"you *know* it, Jule. Don't you . . . ?" I leaned toward her.

She nodded, pressing her mouth together. "Yes, I know." Her voice almost disappeared again. "But try . . . try not to hate him, Cat. He's

bleeding inside, there's something so sad, so terribly deep. . . ." She
reached up like she could pull it out of the air. "I don't know what it is
yet, it's too broken, too buried. But something about you . . ." She
shook her head, not meeting my eyes. "He doesn't mean to."

"That's supposed to make a difference? That's supposed to give him
the right to make me bleed?" *Something about me. Something about my
eyes, Rubiy said.* Siebeling had said it too, trying to tell me what I didn't
want to hear. . . . "Jule." I took a deep breath. "What did he mean
about my eyes?"

"Who?" She reached mentally, trying to follow the change of my
thoughts.

"Rubiy. And Siebeling. Both of them said it, about my eyes. My eyes
are green. But 'all psions have green eyes,' " remembering Rubiy's, like
sea ice. "Don't they?"

She looked up at me, and hers were gray, with round, normal pupils;
but I wouldn't let my gaze break. She said, "Oh." Her fingers wove
through the fringe on her shawl. "I know, there's that saying. . . . But
most of them don't anymore. Not green as grass, not like yours. It's
been a long time; most of them are hazel, green diluted with other
colors."

"What about you?"

She smiled; the flash of metal was in it again, gone again. "A curiosity. No one in the family dreamed . . . my parents were certain there
was no tainting of their bloodline. They wanted to forget the early days,
when Centauri Transport . . . But psions don't always have green
eyes," changing the subject almost angrily. "Not anymore. It's been a
long time."

"Since what?"

"Since we met the Hydrans."

My hands tightened on the cushions.

"You know the history—?" she asked, like Siebeling had, when I
didn't answer.

"Not much." My voice was barely louder than hers. "What's to
know?"

"Well . . . that when humanity got a stardrive and began to expand
outward from our home system, they found a humanoid people on Beta
Hydrae III, and on several other inhabitable worlds in the same general
region of space. They were colony worlds of a stellar union that had
begun to pass its peak long before the coming of the humans. At first we
were overjoyed to discover another intelligent species, proof that we

weren't alone in the universe—and to find they were a gentle, nonaggressive people; no possible threat to the Human Federation. But they happened to be psions, too. At first that was just another marvel—their societies functioned on totally different dynamics and sources of energy from our own. We learned a lot about them . . . and in the process we destroyed them. But in the beginning there was a period of peaceful contact, intermarriage, and sometimes even children born of it. The children tended to inherit the Hydran psi, and also eyes that were as green as grass."

"How could they have kids? That's . . . I mean, Hydrans ain't even human. No human marries an alien now. Ain't it illegal or something?" I frowned.

She didn't see it; she was still looking out at the rain. "Some people still do. Ardan did. It's not illegal; it's just not easy. Things have changed over the centuries—attitudes. And the Hydrans have suffered because of it. But the aliens must be 'human,' Cat, or there wouldn't be any saying about green-eyed psions. . . . Or else humans are 'alien.' There have been some people who say that humans are a world of defective Hydrans, mutant—mute. That our psionic blindness has made us lose our true humanity."

"Crap," I said, flexing my hands.

She shrugged a little. "But there are still a lot of hazel-eyed human psions; even if green-eyed ones like you are very rare."

"Because nobody in their right mind would want a half-breed freak for a son."

I felt her look at me. *She always knows, she can't help it—why didn't she understand?* I looked back at her, with my green stranger's eyes. And her mind flooded with shame and grief, reflected pain, confusion, apology. (Sorry, sorry, *sorry!*) . . . Tears were starting. "Please don't *feel* like that!"

I tightened my mind, wove it together—to keep from feeling her, to stop her from feeling me.

She drew a long, shaky breath, pressing her mouth with her hand. "You didn't know that you had Hydran blood? I thought. . . . How could you not know?" The words wavered. "Didn't anyone ever—?"

I shook my head and said bitterly, "Just lucky, I guess." But the bits and pieces were fitting together in my memory: the joke, the insult, the senseless beating—the truth that I wouldn't let myself understand. I'd never figured it out. Maybe because I didn't dare, because I couldn't carry one more weight, one more stone dragging me down. Maybe that was the real thing I'd spent my life hiding from, in dark corners, endless days alone, drug dreams . . . the thing that all the hunters sensed, that marked me as a victim.

Jule's eyes held the nowhere look they got when her mind was on things meant only for her. So I sat staring out at the rain, and thought about being a— *No. It only figures, with your luck.* And maybe it explained my luck, all the way back. Always bad. Maybe it even explained Siebeling—a man who'd had a Hydran wife, who had a half-breed son somewhere in the galaxy. A man who had to be ashamed of his perversion, who hated that secret locked in the closet of his past. Because who wouldn't hate a thing like that? Or somebody who reminded him of it? He'd even told me so. And I'd tried to ignore it, again. But this time there was no escape.

The lift chimed again, and I turned, looking toward it. Jule stirred and turned too, her face stiff. The doors opened and Siebeling was standing there. I didn't have to be anybody's mind reader to know he was upset about something. He came toward us without a word. Jule's face brightened and came alive; I caught a pang of bittersweet from her mind that had nothing to do with anything but the sight of him.

But Siebeling was looking at me, and suddenly I knew we had unfinished business.

"Ardan," Jule said, "he came. Rubiy, the one we've been waiting for. He came here; he told us about his—offer. And Cat thinks he's—"

"Both of you?"

She nodded. "Both of us. I—he was—"

"It has to wait, then." He shook his head. "Until we discuss something more personal." He had something in his hand, and he put it down on the low table between us. It was a clear ball that looked like crystal but wasn't, with a gold and green insect caught in flight inside it. "This is a nice little toy. Where did you get it?"

And then I knew what I'd done wrong. I'd forgotten about that ball. "It . . . ain't mine."

"I believe that." His voice was sour.

I shook my head. "I mean, I never seen it before." I couldn't keep my eyes off of it. I never could.

"Then I suppose it was just in your jacket by accident."

"Look, if you want to call me a thief, then do it. That's what you're thinking." I wondered why I'd bothered to get up this morning.

"That's what I'm saying, then."

"I didn't steal it! I—I borrowed it. I just wanted to . . . see how it worked." I wondered why the truth always sounded more like a lie than a lie did. Probably because it was only half the truth. I'd taken it, all right, off the desk the second time he interviewed me. I'd picked it up for spite, almost without thinking, never meaning to keep it. But I never gave it back. . . . I couldn't. When you held it in your hands, it made pictures, things like I'd never seen—images of some other world. When you were tired of one it made another, and if you wanted one again it came back. I'd never seen anything like it. I just couldn't give it up. So I kept it. I knew I'd be in trouble if anyone found out, so I'd just blocked it out of my mind. The perfect crime. I felt my face getting red.

He put his hand on the ball, gently, and there was a new image inside it. "Why?" His voice strained.

"What?"

"Why did you take it?" That wasn't what he'd meant. His mind was a tangle of burning thoughts I couldn't read, most of them not about me. . . . And suddenly I understood: that it was an alien thing, a Hydran thing. A thing that had belonged to his half-breed son. And I'd taken it. *You gork, you stupid damn fool!* I grimaced.

"Why did you take it?"

"I . . . I . . ." How could I tell him how warm it felt in my hands; how could I tell him about the pictures? How was I supposed to tell him something I didn't understand myself? "It . . . was pretty; I liked it."

"You liked it."

"Yeah, you—" I bit my tongue, trying to keep from saying the rest of it. "All right. I took it, and I kept it. I knew it was wrong. I'm sorry. I won't take nothing again, I swear. All right?" It had to be all right. I was even admitting I was wrong. What else could he want?

He whispered a name—an alien's name. His wife's name. And his wife was dead. Pain filled the memory. He was looking down at the ball, and I don't think he knew he'd said anything out loud. I was sure he hadn't meant for me to hear it. He glanced up at me again. "It shouldn't respond for you, you couldn't even understand. . . ." Like he was blaming me for something.

But he was going to take the ball. I reached out, my fingers touched it. The picture changed.

He grabbed my wrist. "Keep your hands off that, you cheap gutter thief! Maybe you think a fast apology is all you need to save you every time you 'like' something. Well, not with me. If that's the best behavior you can manage, then maybe you're not good enough to go on working here." *(And you won't ever be—)*

"You got no right to think that." I jerked free. "I'm as good as you are. And I'm sick of getting treated like I ain't!"

He picked up the ball. "Then consider yourself dismissed. Get out, I don't want to see you again."

I blinked. "What?"

"You heard me."

"But . . ." Somehow I stood up, numb all over. "I guess we both know why you're doin' this, don't we?" He didn't answer. I looked back at Jule. Her face was pale and her eyes were wet; she was staring down at her hands with the bitten-off nails, and they were twitching. "Jule." I said it quietly; she didn't look up. "It's gonna be all right. You'll see." I put my hand out over hers, the only time I'd ever really touched her. Her fingers curled around mine in a kind of spasm; she clung to my hand for a second. I knew her tears weren't about anything going on between any of us here. "Look, I'm going now. I'll . . . see you later, huh?" She didn't answer me. I didn't figure she would.

When I straightened up again, Siebeling moved between us, forcing me to back off. He leaned over, murmuring something to her. I went to the waiting lift and took it down.

5

THE LIFT STOPPED at the usual floor, because I'd said the number without thinking. I almost stepped out, almost went back to my room; thinking there was nothing else I could do except go there and wait.

But I stood looking down the empty hallway, looking at another world: one I didn't belong to anymore. Siebeling had cut me loose, and soon enough Corporate Security would come for me and make it official. . . . I'd known all along this was too good to last, like any other dream. My fists tightened, the numbness that had me by the throat suddenly let me go. It was over, and I'd been screwed. I owed nothing to nobody. And I was damned if I was going to stay here like a loser and make it easy for them to take me back. The doors slipped shut again, and I went on down.

I got out at the main reception lobby. Its three-story vault was draped with wall hangings that turned every sound into a whisper. I tried to walk like I had a right to be there; but even if I didn't, no one seemed to care. I moved through the changing dance of bodies, trying to believe I looked as normal as everyone else seemed to think I did, until I reached the building entrance. There were no guards waiting, not even a solid door to fill the arching space. A soft tingling, a breath of forced air, and I was through—standing free in the open in the wide fountain square that I'd seen from high above.

It was all so easy. I stood where I was, just letting myself breathe, wondering why I'd never done this before. I could have walked out of here any time I'd wanted to these past weeks, if I'd only tried. I turned back, glancing in through the open entrance. I looked up and up along the smooth mirroring face of the Sakaffe Research Institute, and wondered where my room was inside it. I looked down again, suddenly feeling dizzy, empty, and alone. Knowing why I'd never tried to leave, now that it was too late.

I turned away and started out into the square. The rain had stopped, but the air was still dim and heavy. The fountain was doing things I'd never seen water do before; as I passed it, a drift of spray blew into my path. I moved through it, blinking. The wet heat was suffocating after the coolness of the Institute. I'd forgotten how summer felt, and how much I hated it—almost as much as I hated winter. At least there wasn't the summertime stench that made Oldcity smell like a dead body.

I entered a canyon between two towers. The street was brighter than any street I'd ever known—and quieter, smoother, cleaner. There were only a handful of other people around me, most of them taking the moving walkways or drifting in and out of building entrances. Far up above my head were aircab balconies and passageways threading the building faces together like chunks of jewel; single mods and multimods jostled in the space between them. Looking up as I walked, I couldn't see the tops of the towers, couldn't even guess how high they had to be. . . . I began to think about falling upward into the fog. I looked down, and didn't look up again.

I went on walking for a long time, with my thoughts wandering as aimlessly as my feet. I was caught in a silence that wasn't all in my mind—everything seemed to be happening far up in the air. As the hours passed, the fog melted away and the sky began to clear. Sunlight winked and sparkled between mirroring walls, off them, through them; falling on me in bright showers. Display floaters advertising upside goods caught my eyes and ears, pulled me everywhere, left me standing in my tracks staring at things I didn't believe even when I saw them. Sometimes somebody else would put a hand through the shimmering, transparent security screen and touch something. I wasn't the only one who couldn't believe what I saw.

But when I reached out, my hand felt the screen, soft and yielding—it wouldn't let me past to touch what was inside. I jerked back, afraid that somehow it knew me for what I was. I stood still again for a long minute, with my heart beating too hard. But nothing more happened, and finally I realized that nothing was going to. I started to believe that there was only one thing different about me that it could have known: I didn't have a data bracelet. Not guilt, just *Insufficient Credit*. I noticed that somebody had scrawled something with a marker on the base below the display; a single, simple word. I knew all the letters. I sounded them out, and when I heard what it said, I laughed. I thought about the walls in Oldcity, covered with words like that. I'd put some of them there myself, but I'd never known what I was copying; I never even cared. I just wanted to make my mark somehow, some way, on a world that didn't know I was alive. It was strange to realize there were really people up here who felt the same way. For a second I thought about Jule.

I moved on, with my hands in my pockets, searching for a credit marker or a camph, for anything; knowing in that same sick moment just how empty they were. Then my fingers closed on something solid. I pulled it out into my hand: candy. I'd stuffed my pockets full of the damned things whenever I could, in the cafeteria at the Institute. One piece left. I closed my fingers over it, opened them again. I put it into my mouth, felt it dissolve and the dark, oily sweetness cover my tongue.

It didn't last long. After it was gone, I began to taste the smells in the air around me. There were places to eat here, just like in Oldcity. Even the gods had to eat. Most of it smelled better than anything I remembered—maybe because there wasn't Oldcity's stink mixed into it, or maybe just because it was here and I was hungry. *Hungry.* My throat ached with the thought. It was too easy to forget how it felt to be. . . . *No.* It was too easy to remember. But without a data bracelet I was scared even to try a lift or a doorway and feel it turn me back again.

The day was closing in on evening; there were more people on foot now, children as well as adults. I wondered where they went all day. Maybe just someplace cool. It was getting loud and confusing and hard to move; my mind started to buzz with the feedback of too many other minds. I wove a defense and held it so hard that I couldn't feel a thing, until I could forget that I'd ever even been a psion.

Lights were beginning to show, and I tried to feel like I was back in Oldcity night. But there was no music. Music was the only thing I'd really missed about Oldcity. Sometimes there'd been songs coming out of the walls at the Institute, but they were thin and gutless; listening to them was like drinking water when you wanted hard brew. . . . I wondered whether I was walking on solid ground now, or whether Oldcity, with its noise and smells and darkness, was somewhere just below my feet.

And I wondered if maybe I couldn't pick a data bracelet off someone in this crowd. . . . But I wasn't in Oldcity, I didn't know which way to run; and even if I did, there was no freedrop waiting to take it off me for a handful of markers. And I'd never be able to break the code on someone else's bracelet before they missed it and had it killed. I was lost in this world, I was a ghost—I didn't belong here, I belonged in Oldcity. And if I wanted to go on walking free I'd better start thinking again, about how to get back there before it was too late.

There were signs everywhere, but I couldn't read them. Trying to act like just another tourist, I went up to the closest stranger in the street and said, " 'Scuse me. Can . . . uh, how do I get to Oldcity?"

He looked at me, squinting a little, and I felt the prickle of his surprise, but no suspicion. "Why, just take an aircab. . . ." He waved a pudgy hand at a nearby call stand.

I shook my head. "I don't—I mean, I want to walk there."

"Walk there?" The squint turned wide-eyed. "But you can't. That's impossible." He shrugged.

I opened my mouth, shut it again, and pushed on past, frowning.

"Take a cab!" He yelled it after me.

I went on down the street, asking other people, always getting the same damn answer; until I believed that they all believed it, and started to hate them: *Lousy, selfish bloodsuckers*— But I had to keep trying. I had to believe that if I could just make it to the Hanging Gardens, then . . . " 'Scuse me," bumping into an old woman, putting out a hand to steady her. She murmured something, fumbling and flustered. "What?" I said.

"Are you all right, dear?" She patted my arm.

"Me?" I almost laughed. "Sure. I—I'm looking for the Hanging Gardens."

"The Hanging Gardens?" She smoothed the silken drape across her shoulders with ringed fingers. She glittered with jewels, but most of them were fake, and the cloth looked worn. "Oh. Why, they're very far away." She stretched out a hand, pointing to my left. "Why don't you take a cab?"

I held the frown back, and said, "I want to walk. I mean . . ." Suddenly I was reading into the look she gave me, seeing the suspicious sympathy lying open behind her eyes, "Yeah, I—I'm a little short on credit. If you got some spare markers . . . ?" I held out a hand, forced it to stay steady.

The sympathy didn't disappear the way it always did in Oldcity; it only furrowed deeper into her face. "Oh, you poor thing. No, I never carry markers. But here, open your account,"—she reached for my wrist—"and I'll transfer you a little sum."

"No." I pulled away. "Forget it. . . . It's all right, I'll walk." I pretended to lean down and pick something up. "Here. I think you dropped this." I gave her back the jeweled pin I'd stolen when I bumped into her, the only thing she was wearing that looked like it was worth anything.

"Oh. Thank you. Thank you! I. . . . But, wait!"

I went on, almost running to get out of reach of her gratitude.

I tried to follow the snaking streets in the direction she'd pointed, asking people again and again for the Hanging Gardens. I got farther away almost as often as I got closer, and it was the middle of the night by the time I finally found them. By then my feet were blistered on the blisters, and I felt like I'd walked halfway to the nearest star. The Gardens flowed uphill and down on every side of me, tier on tier of eerie, rustling life from a hundred different worlds, gathered here at the heart of the Federation. But there wasn't much to see that wasn't hung with night shadows even for my eyes, along the dim-lit walkways that I followed up and down through the air between tiers. Not that I cared, by then. By then all I wanted was to be back where I belonged and forget I'd ever even seen Quarro. Finally I reached the lowest tier, the one that ringed the lip of the well above Godshouse Circle. I walked it around and around, looking for a hidden stairway, for a ladder, footholds—anything that would let me down past the sheer supporting rim wall and the impossible stretch of air below it. But there was nothing. There was no way down; no way back.

Hanging out over the fragile fence and looking down, I could see the spire of the Godshouse gleaming dimly far down below, and people moving through the open space around it. A lone aircab and then another rose like bubbles while I watched, rising past me where I stood and drifting on into the night. I could hear the sound of a thousand voices crying and music playing; I could even smell the stench rising on the heated air to make my empty stomach turn. I leaned out farther, going a little crazy, shouting, "Help! Help! Up here—!" like I thought somebody could hear me. Like I thought somebody would care. But my voice was lost in the space between. I was a ghost to all of them down there as much as I was up here, one more shadow among the garden shadows.

The fence swayed and gave under me. I pushed back onto solid ground; not ready yet to go home the hard way. I turned my back on the Tank . . . *fish tank, feeder tank* . . . a fish out of water, drowning in the open air. I threw myself down on the soft, matted grass of the hillside and lay staring up into the black height of the sky; at the stars, the stars, the stars. . . .

It was almost a relief when the patrolling Corpse woke me up just before dawn, and arrested me for vagrancy.

It didn't take long for the Corporate Security data-files to spit up my whole life story. And it didn't take much longer for them to get confirmation that Siebeling didn't want me back again . . . and Contract Labor did. But it was late in the day before the black-suited Labor Crows came to take me away: one more flight above Quarro, looking down at the crest of the city on fire with the colors of the setting sun. Then the mod flashed across the green waters of the bay to the spaceport complex, and buried us alive in the dark sprawl of Contract Labor's holding pens.

Then it was more corridors, worse than the Corporate Security station, with walls the color of grease and cement. I wondered why all government buildings looked like prisons. Maybe because they were. The guards threw me into a cell, and took turns working me over a little. As they left, one of them said, "We got a special treat for you, Cityboy, for all the trouble you gave us. We're going to let you see what you're in for. Enjoy the show." They went off grinning.

"You know what you can do with it, Crows!" I yelled. "I don't care. It's only ten years!" My voice shook a little. Ten years was more than half my life. . . .

"It'll seem like forever." They laughed; the laughter echoed after they were gone.

I wiped my bloody nose, shaking myself out. They hadn't broken anything; lucky for me they didn't want damaged goods. I looked around. The cell was about the size of a closet, and empty except for a foam sleep mat, a toilet, and a sink. At least I was alone. I stumbled to the sink and drank water from my cupped hands. Then I sat down against the wall and thought about when they were going to feed me, to keep from thinking about Jule and Cortelyou and everything I'd lost. . . .

But then the room went dark, and the wall across from me lit up like a threedy screen. A bored voice was droning: ". . . planet number five of a blue-white sun, spectral type B-three-V, listed Survey One-three-nine-six S-One-three-nine-six-dash–five hasn't got a name, because they couldn't think of one that fit. Climate in habitable zone fluctuates . . ."

The voice kept on but I was only half listening. Suddenly the room was steaming hot, and it stank of rotting plants. I felt bugs crawling on me, biting me, and I leaped up—

In front of me a string of dirty, sweating images of men struggled up an oozing path cut through jungle brush, going ankle-deep in steaming mud with every step. Most of them had some kind of heavy mesh baskets slung on their backs, weighing them down; a couple had stun rifles instead. Then one of the laborers stumbled. A guard moved in on him, and something that looked like a load of yellow slime dropped out of a dead tree and landed on the guard's head. There was a shower of sparks, the thing slid off his back. I shouted as it landed on the one on his knees in the mud. He didn't have any protection. I pressed my hands against my ears, but I could still hear him scream.

The scene changed. Someone else was being dragged under in a mud-colored river by something with suckers. A red stain spread on the brown water. Another laborer tried to go after him; one of the guards clubbed him with a rifle. He fell, more red running down his face, over his hands . . . splattering on me. I started yelling for someone to shut it off, but it went on and on, until I thought it would never end; horror after horror happening in front of me and around me and even through me, until I was crouched in the corner, hitting my head against the wall, trying to go deaf and blind. . . .

After a long time I realized that it was light and quiet and cool again in the room. But I stayed where I was. It didn't matter that what I'd seen wasn't real—because it had all been real where it happened, and that was where I was going. *Damn Siebeling! Damn all of them!* Yesterday I was sharing with them and laughing with them, and today I was going to hell and it didn't even matter to them.

The lights went out again and then I was at the door, beating my hands on it, yelling, "Let me out! You bastards, lemme out of here—"

But there was no one to hear it. And there was nothing else, this time, only the darkness—maybe it was night already. I rested against the cool surface of the wall, and then I went back to my corner and sat down, and said, "I wish I was dead." But there was no one to hear that, either.

By the next morning I was more than ready to get out of that room. The guard who came for me grinned and said, "You don't look like you slept too much." I didn't answer, and he thought that was funny, too. He kept trying to get a reaction out of me as he led me down one hall and then another, and finally into a big room full of data storage.

"The kid here's ready for a little vacation. S-One-three-nine-six." The guard flipped a tape bobbin onto the counter. "Lucky boy."

"Go to hell, scumsucker," I said, finally, just to shut him up. He grinned again and twisted my arm.

The narrow-faced woman behind the counter put a readout on her screen and said, "Are you sure? It's not on any direct line from here—it's hardly cost-efficient." She looked down her nose at him.

The guard glared. I figured it was my turn to grin.

"But, if you want to press your point—"

I changed my mind.

"—you could send him through, say, Tillit Sector. You can bond him here and they'll handle the transfers."

"Tillit Sector?" The guard looked surprised. But he nodded. "Do it."

The clerk smiled a strange smile, and I wondered. But then she lit the counter top with an image showing a lot of tiny print. "Sign here." She pointed to a line at the bottom of it. "This is your formal contract, stating your agreement to work. At the end of ten years indenture you get five thousand credits. If you want to buy out your contract before that time, you owe that much to us."

"Like hell! I ain't signing that piece of—"

The guard picked a writing stylus up off the counter and stuck it into my fist. "Sign it or I'll break your hand."

I signed it. But only with an X.

The clerk nodded, but then she caught my thumb and pressed it down on the readout. I looked, and saw my thumbprint there in blue. "Just for insurance." Then she fed the assignment tape to a stamper on the counter. She caught my arm and stuck that in, too. I tried to pull back but her grip was like iron. I felt a hot slash of pain, and thought I'd lost my hand for sure, but all I'd lost was my freedom. What I got for it was a bright red bracelet about two fingers wide. I touched it, wiggling my fingers. It was hard and still a little warm; and bonded to the smarting flesh of my wrist. I thought about how this wasn't the kind of bracelet I'd been expecting to get, up until yesterday. . . . "Thanks for the jewelry."

"He's ready. Take him to Processing."

I got processed. They took away my good clothes and handed me a worn-out jumpsuit. I wondered if somebody else had died in it. Then they asked me whether I was blind or deaf or dead. . . . I said I was, but the examiner said the question was purely rhetorical anyway, whatever that meant. He sent me on again, to more insults, vaccinations, humiliations, until finally I was back in a cell again and this time I didn't have any trouble sleeping. The next day, or maybe the one after, I was taken out and sent onto the spaceport field, jammed into a carrier with a load of other dazed human cargo.

I'd never seen the spaceport before, and I didn't get much chance to see it now. But still a strange kind of excitement tightened inside me at the flashing glimpses I got of energized grids and silhouetted pylons, outbuildings, gantries . . . *ships.* I tried to shake off the choking mind-cloud of everyone else's despair and let myself feel the sight: these were ships that went to the stars, that weren't tied to one place or even one world, that had the freedom to cross hundreds and thousands of light-years from sun to sun. . . . Ships like the gleaming disk with the Centauri Transport insignia on its side, that lay waiting up ahead to take me away from the prison of Oldcity and Quarro and Ardattee—to something a whole lot worse than any of them.

On board I was sedated and strapped into an acceleration sling so I couldn't move. For hours I lay waiting, not knowing what would happen next. Then at last the ship came alive around me and began to lift. I didn't know what to expect when it finally happened. Maybe I was lucky, because they didn't bother to make our free ride easy or soft. I felt my body tense and fight and scream as the ship tore itself out of gravity's fist, pushing upward and outward into clear vacuum with a will that was stronger than universal law.

I never even saw what it looked like to go up from Ardattee, leaving my life behind, or what my homeworld looked like from out in space. But by then it hardly mattered, to me or anyone else, because it was too late anyway, for all of us.

And then there was nothing to do but go on waiting.

I never knew where Tillit Sector was, or even what it stood for. The FTA used Contract Labor to fill its needs for nontech workers, and it used them all over the Federation. There wasn't even a planetside Colony in the system where the ship came out of its final hyperlight jump: only an orbiting way station chained by gravity to a lifeless, lonely world. Not that that mattered, either. All that really mattered was what happpened when I got there.

For days I waited in a gray stale room, with a bunch of others who lay staring at the ceiling, mainly, because there wasn't anything else—hope, or even sorrow. One end of the room looked out on the scarred, angry face of the nameless world staring up at us from below. I sat on the floor in front of the port for hours, staring back. My mind was as bleak and empty as the view, and all I could think about was the red bond tag on my wrist; how there was no way to hide it, no hope for me either, now.

Until finally a guard came into the room and picked me out, glanced at my bond ring and said, "Okay, bondie, you're it. Up." He pointed with his thumb.

"N-now?" My voice shook.

He laughed. "What do you think?" He took me out into the hall.

There was another Crow waiting there; but this one looked like an official, and he said, "Your name is Cat?"

I nodded. *They know about it* here? I wondered if they went to this much trouble to make everyone suffer who'd ever slugged a recruiter.

"All right. We've got a special request on you, bondie."

I touched the bond tag, feeling insects crawl across my mind; seeing something yellow and slimy drop out of a tree. . . .

He cleared his throat. "I understand you can drive a snow vehicle?"

"What?" I stared at him.

"We have a priority request for a snow vehicle driver, from one of our agents. Our records show that you're qualified—?" *(Somebody had paid him to ask me this. He expected me to answer yes.)*

I didn't disappoint him. "Been driving them all my life. Sure." Sure that he could feel the lie seeping out around the edges of my thoughts, like water through a sieve. But why should he care?

"You're already assigned, though." He looked at the bond ring, surprised or confused; that wasn't in the plan. I held my breath. "I'll put through a transfer."

I started to breathe again. We were walking. *Orders on me:* Who had the contacts to bribe the FTA and fix its records . . . and knew about me? *Siebeling*—maybe he'd changed his mind? But Siebeling wouldn't go to that kind of trouble; he wouldn't need to. I tried to pick the official's thoughts, but he didn't know anything about why he'd been sent here to collect me—only that somebody up the line had made it worth his while.

And the one who was waiting for us was nobody I'd ever seen before. His name was Kielhosa, he was an agent for Federation Mining—which meant nothing to me. I looked him in the eye but there was no sign, no sort of recognition—and none lying secretly on the surface of his mind, either. He was as real as the tag on my wrist. I wondered if it could be some sort of crazy mistake after all. I wondered where the other bondie was whose name was Cat. And I hoped they didn't send the poor slad to S1396 instead of me.

Kielhosa had a jaw like a steel trap and hair as gray as an Oldcity morning. And he thought I looked like a street rat; he didn't believe I could drive a snowtrack. He threw a couple of questions at me about how they worked; the Crow started to look uneasy. But I read the answers that lay waiting in his mind and gave them back to him perfectly. For once, I was glad to be a telepath. I tried to find out where I was going, then—but his mind was choked with schedules and delays, deadlines to meet, and the scum of Earth that he was stuck with picking over.

Finally he nodded and signaled to the guard. "I guess this one will have to do. Get him ready."

The guard led me away. I wished I'd had time to find a clear answer; but in Oldcity they always said, "Asking questions is asking for trouble." Wherever I was going, it couldn't be any worse than S1396. So I kept my mouth shut and let it happen.

PART II
CRAB

6

THERE WERE STARS everywhere. I'd been lost in the stars as long as I could remember, beautiful stars and night. I moved in the cold darkness —and cracked my fingers on something slick. The ceiling, about half a meter above my face. My eyes blurred, and when they cleared again, I could see that the stars were only a projection on the wall across the room. And I remembered that I was on a ship again, and where we were going. I felt in the dark for the restamped bond tag; and tried to smile but my face was numb.

They'd given me some kind of drug that had knocked me out back at the way station; getting me ready for a long trip this time, turning me into freight. I didn't remember coming onto this ship and I didn't figure I was supposed to be awake now; none of the others were, lying below me in tiers of bunks like bodies in a morgue. But I'd been awake before. I remembered watching the stars for hours, unchanging, while the ship sat in space and the crew computed the next hyperlight jump. Somewhere back in another life, Dere Cortelyou had told me how the length of a jump depended on knowing the shape of space—and if you got the wrong solution, it was anyone's guess where you'd come out on the other side. One time I saw us take the jump, saw the stars go blank and come back changed before you could hold your breath. I wondered if we'd made the right one; and then I remembered that any jump we made only meant that I was more light-years away from home and everything I knew.

I wondered how far we were going, and how long it had been. One of my arms was strapped down, and something was dripping into a vein. I never felt hungry, or even thirsty; I didn't feel much of anything. I just lay in a bunk in a long dark room and looked at the stars—or their image on the ship's hull: my mind was never clear enough to wonder why they were there. I could hear the crew sometimes, and once one of them came through to check up on us. As he passed my bunk, I let my free arm slip off and hit him in the face. He nearly leaped through the wall. But most of the time I lay alone in the quiet night counting stars, until I lost track of my fingers.

I was starting to count again, when all at once the stars blinked out and changed. And this time I was looking at a world; a new world. But I stared at the image on the wall for a long time before I understood what I was seeing. Inhabitable worlds were always in blues, like Earth on the Federation Seal. I'd seen Ardattee in pictures—soft-edged, smooth, blue and white—and the way station world's sterile reds and browns from orbit. But this was different from either one, and somehow I knew it was all wrong. There was no blue at all. And it was . . . lumpy. Between swirls of pale cloud the mountains rose up too far, like the skin of a shriveled piece of fruit. We were far enough out to see the planet's curve, but over the mountains I looked down into deep valleys of twisting golden green. The atmosphere shivered and glowed with light, and between the mountains the plains were silver, catching fire on the day side, as if the whole world was a piece of gem; until I wondered whether I was really seeing any of this. And I wondered what they needed me for. . . .

When it was over, they couldn't wake me up. I didn't remember a thing about the landing, or how I got to the bed I woke up in, in what turned out to be the tiny port hospital. It was an improvement over the ship's floating morgue, but I wasn't awake enough of the time to appreciate it. The hospital med techs claimed that my internal organs were peculiar, that the drug didn't react predictably but that it would probably wear off in time.

They were right. There comes a time when you can't even sleep any more, and when I woke up for good, Kielhosa was still waiting. I opened my eyes, and the first thing I saw was his face: I remembered then why I'd wanted to sleep forever. I'd come to the end of my journey and my choices, and now I was stuck with the consequences.

I was the only one of Kielhosa's new recruits who hadn't made it to the mines right after we landed; it didn't make him real happy. But when he led me out of the starport at last, I got enough of a shock to make me forget all my problems. The port town was cheap duraplast on one muddy street, but the world around it was . . . beautiful. The mountains rose up on every side in wild fingers with the town lying in their palm, like something out of *Nebula Pioneers* on the threedy. But this was real; I was real, standing with the planet pressing against my feet, breathing in the fresh, sweet air. I felt weak and clumsy, I was shivering, and my eyesight seemed dim somehow. But none of that mattered. I turned around and around, and started to laugh because I couldn't believe it. The sound startled me; I hadn't laughed for a long time.

"What's so funny?"

"It's beautiful!"

"Hunh. This poisonous hole? That is funny. You didn't come here for the scenery, bondie. You're a working boy, remember? It was an inconvenience, letting you sleep it off in that hospital. You'd better be worth it." He started on again. I followed him, hardly listening. "Watch your step, you're moving in one and a half gravities. It makes you awkward until you get used to it."

"Uh, why do you need somebody to drive a snowtrack here?" Maybe it was only for the winter; it was cold here, but I didn't see any snow. It was crazy to hope my luck had changed, but . . .

"You'll see."

I didn't say anything more.

We walked out past the edge of town. A whitish, sandy track ran through a field of rust-colored grass spotted with yellow flowers—and craters, spitting steam, and pale blots of mud. The biggest of them wasn't more than a meter across, and some of them were only dried mud pits; but up ahead the track swerved around a fresh break in the earth, where white mud crusted the dying grass. The scent of flowers and the stink of sulphur mixed in the sharp wind.

On the far side of the field was a blue stone building. Out beyond it the land dropped off like the end of the world. The view as we reached it made me ache. *All of it real:* green hills folding into long, green-golden valleys, bright water spilling over slate-blue rocks all the way down to . . . I shut my eyes and looked again. "What the—" The hills ended, and beyond them the land lay flat clear to the horizon. Endlessly flat and silver, and the sun's reflected light burned your eyes, like sunlight on metal. "Is that—?"

"Snow," Kielhosa said, behind me.

Disappointment caught in my chest. I swore under my breath. Kielhosa frowned and rubbed his head; I'd projected it without meaning to. I shut my mind tight, looking back at the mountains again. They were still green. "But . . . how?" Even I knew that what I saw just didn't make sense.

"Steam heat, in a manner of speaking—lot of volcanic activity in those mountains." He pointed past me, and following his hand I saw plumes of smoke hanging in the sky over a couple of the highest peaks. "Cinder is a piece of star, it was the companion to that sun up there until it blew itself up. The fragment's still hot enough to melt rock at its core. Where the heat leaks up to the surface it keeps the ground warm, makes hot springs and geysers, that sort of thing. That stream down there would scald you. Water freezes solid out past the foothills, though. Temperature never gets up to freezing."

I ignored everything he'd said past: " 'A piece of star' . . . you mean, *Cinder?* Is this the Crab Nebula?"

"Where did you think you were, kid? What do you think all that garbage is up in the sky?"

I glanced up, into a sky the color of sapphires. Shining across it like cobweb was the end of the star that was Cinder. The sun made me squint, but I couldn't see its circle, just a starpoint of light that flickered, cold and pale, like a strobe. It was only six miles wide—that was why everything seemed dim—and they called it a pulsar. I heard Cortelyou's voice in my mind: *Forty-five hundred light-years from home.*

So I'd made it to the Crab Colonies, after all. I looked down again, at the bond ring on my wrist, and down the green-gold valley at the snow.

"Nice view," Kielhosa said. He was laughing at me.

I spat.

We went back to the stone house. It was covered on the outside with the slate-blue rock I'd seen pushing out of the hillside; someone's strange idea of decoration, I supposed. I couldn't see why they were showing off a pile of stones. The inside of the building was wooden; it looked even stranger, with the computer console set into the board walls. We put on thermal clothes from a locker, and then went on through to an outside loading area. "What's that?"

Kielhosa walked over to the transparent room-size bubble hanging from a steel wire. "A cable car. It's the cheapest thing here for moving ore up the hill." He nodded at me. "Get in."

I came up beside him and caught hold of the waiting entrance. The whole bubble moved under my hand, as fragile as a crystal glass. I jerked my hand away and looked back. "Oh, no. I ain't getting into that —" Kielhosa's face said I'd better not give him any more trouble. I caught the doorway again and stepped inside. My feet didn't go through the floor, but the bubble rocked like a hammock and threw me forward; I staggered and fell onto a platform at one end. Kielhosa stepped in just like it was home, and we barely shifted. He sat down on a seat at the other end, balancing our weight. There was a clear square with lights on it; he pushed a button and the lights went green, from red.

The bubble bounced once, and then swung out away from the building . . . into the air. The ground dropped out from under us; I could see it far down below our feet. We were suspended up there between spidery towers in nothing, not even a mod; just a bubble, drifting down. . . .

"Where's your faith in modern plastics, bondie?" Kielhosa thought it was funny.

I stuck my hands into my pockets and tried not to weigh anything.

It was almost a relief to stand in the trampled slush at the bottom of the hill. Someone was waiting with a snow vehicle, though; and out beyond him the snow was waiting for us all.

The other man said, "Get what you came for?"

"I got him, Joraleman." Kielhosa nodded. He treated Joraleman like an equal, not like a bondie. I wondered who he was. "Supplies loaded?"

"Right. Check the list if you want." Joraleman looked over at me. "The new driver taking us back? I've had it up to here with double duty."

I shook my head but Kielhosa said, "That's what he's here for. You're lucky I got you a replacement so fast. Not many 'track drivers end up in the labor pens."

I looked for a way to change the subject. "Uh, why don't you use some kind of mod for moving your stuff? Wouldn't it be faster—"

"The air currents are too erratic, and the gravity's too high. It would take a magician with psi to keep anything flying out there." Joraleman shrugged. He was a big man, tall and heavyset, still young. He had a beard, and his hair was nearly as blond as mine; but his skin was pale and freckled. I couldn't see his eyes behind his opaqued goggles, but when he smiled it wasn't like he thought I was the joke. "We tried it."

"Oh," I said, knowing I couldn't fly a mod either, even with psi. Right then I didn't feel like anybody's magician. "Well, I . . ."

"Let's go." Kielhosa nodded.

"I still feel a little sick. You mind if I don't drive?"

"You've had a week already," he said. "A person might get the idea you were stalling for time."

I started toward the snowtrack. It looked like an orange egg lying on its side on balloons. That didn't help much. It was a lot bigger than I'd thought by the time I reached it. I climbed up into the cab and looked at the instrument panel. Kielhosa sat beside me, and Joraleman slid into the narrow seat behind us. I tried to pick their minds for something to help me; but my own tension got in the way and I couldn't pull out a clear thought to save my life. There was a touchboard with letters on it, but I couldn't tell what most of them stood for. I made a half guess on one and got the power started. It made me feel braver and I touched another. It didn't work. The snowtrack gave a god-awful screech and leaped about a meter. Kielhosa pushed me out of the seat and got it stopped. Then he kicked me out into the snow and called me some things I'd never been called before, and a lot more things I had been called.

When he ran out of ideas, he told me to get up, and Joraleman asked me if I'd ever driven a snow vehicle before. There wasn't any reason to lie now, so I didn't. Kielhosa looked at me funny and I knew he'd finally figured things out. By now it wouldn't take any brains.

"Take them off." He meant my mittens.

I took them off. The cold made my hands smart.

He looked at my bond tag. "It's been stamped over."

Joraleman frowned. He pushed back his goggles and looked at the bond tag, too; then up at me. He said, "Did you decide to gamble?"

I just shrugged.

Kielhosa caught me by the front of my jacket and brought up his fist. "You little whoreson, you're going to be sorry you were ever—"

"Let him be, Kielhosa." Joraleman pulled Kielhosa's arm down. He looked tired, and disgusted. "He'll have plenty of time to regret it when he gets to the mines."

Kielhosa let go of me, grimacing. "If it's one thing I don't need, it's a goddamn godlover standing on my conscience when I have to deal with these animals!" But he only shook his head, and Joraleman smiled just a little.

I backed away from them, looking at Joraleman. "I could learn to drive a snowtrack! Just show me how. I learn fast."

Kielhosa unlocked the doors at the back of the van.

"Sorry, bondie. You didn't learn fast enough." Joraleman gave me a shove. "Get in."

I climbed into the back. All I could tell was that it was dark and full of crates, until my eyes adjusted. Then I saw two other bondies sprawled on the crates. I figured they must be there to do the loading. One of them was asleep; he didn't wake up even when the doors slammed behind me. The other one stared at me with flat black eyes. Both of them had blue skin. I'd never seen anybody with blue skin before. The first thing I said, before I even thought, was, "Where you from?"

He said, "Hell," softly, and shut his eyes. I wondered if that was an answer.

The snowtrack started up with a jerk, dumping me back against the door. I slid down to the floor and stayed there, folding my legs up, since there wasn't anyplace more comfortable. It was a long ride. But not long enough.

I knew from things Cortelyou had told me that Cinder was only a hundred twenty kilometers in diameter; its surface area was hardly equal to a good-size island back on Ardattee. But the gravity was one and a half times heavier than standard, because Cinder was made up of impossible things: compounds with inert elements, superdense rocks with incredible crystalline structures, super-heavy elements that were never supposed to occur outside a lab. Things that would only form naturally in the heart of a supernova—like telhassium. They could mine the rest, but it would barely be worth the trouble by the time they'd shipped them back to the heart of the Federation. The telhassium made everything worth it.

Telhassium ore was the blue stone I'd seen on the building side; maybe half the planet was made of it, and perfectly formed crystals lay all through the matrix of the rock. Federation Mining could go on picking them out forever. Or the bondies could do it for them. Till hell froze over . . . the bondies said it already had. They cursed the day the FTA ever set down on this godforsaken star corpse, and it didn't take me very long to learn why.

I was already wondering, riding stiff and cramped in the freezing hold of the snowtrack; thinking about the faces of the two bondies lying a couple of meters away from me. It was night by then; night and day didn't last long on a world the size of Cinder. The domed mines compound blazed against the darkness like a sun half-buried in the snowfields as we closed the final distance. . . .

I jerked out of dark daydreaming, wondering where I'd gotten that image, when the sealed blackness around me was total now. Then I realized it had come out of Joraleman's mind, falling into my own drifting thoughts like a warm spark. He wasn't a psion, but something about his mind was both looser and more focused than Kielhosa's.

I breathed on the image spark, let it grow and warm my thoughts for a while, until the snowtrack stopped again. The doors banged open; guards shouted us out into the spotlit compound yard. The bondie who'd been asleep from the start didn't get up. A couple of the guards dragged him away. I tried to reach into his mind as they took him past me, hating myself for trying. . . . He wasn't dead, but his mind wasn't anywhere I could reach, either. I shivered.

And then I was in his place, following the other blueskin, unloading crates of supplies. The guard who stayed with us had an electrified prod —a soft, glowing switch with a bite like acid. He liked using it. Joraleman stood watching us work for a couple of minutes, before he turned suddenly and walked away across the yard. Kielhosa stayed, smirking, until we were finished.

I could hardly pick up my own feet by then. My arms twitched and my knees trembled from working in gravity half again as heavy as what I was used to; the backs of my legs smarted with small burns where the guard had used the tip of the prod on them. When he started us away finally to whatever came next, I did my best to stay ahead of him. On every side of us were towers winking with lights, endless black bulks of refinery buildings, cranes and gantries; a grim, dark city grown out of the frozen desert . . . my new home. Finally I began to see low white-lit buildings up ahead—anonymous, silent, expensive-looking. We were heading toward one of them, but the sight of it didn't feel right to me, not with my legs smarting and my breath coming in heavy gulps. Those buildings were only a mask. This wasn't what came next; not for us. . . .

Burial alive was what came next. We went inside one of the buildings that stood away from the rest, and the guard herded us into a freight elevator. It dropped down a vertical shaft that could have gone straight to Cinder's core before it finally stopped and we got off again, some-where deep in the heart of the stone. The controls were print-idented; no one could operate the lift who wasn't meant to. It was the only way down, the only way out.

The guard left us in a long room lit up nearly as bright as day, full of mats, most with bodies lying on them. I just stood and stared, not understanding, until the bondie who'd worked with me went to the nearest empty mat and collapsed onto it. A couple of the others raised their heads, let them drop back again; all of the faces had blue skin. I began to understand.

This was where we slept, or tried to. The small red points of light at the corners of the ceiling were monitor cameras. There was no privacy, no peace, nowhere to hide here, except in sleep. . . . I found a mat and lay down, feeling the light prying through my eyelids. *Ten years.* . . . I flopped onto my stomach and buried my face in my arms, waiting for oblivion. It didn't keep me waiting long. I dreamed about the Sakaffe Institute, about soft beds and good food and laughter, and about touching Jule taMing.

A kick woke me up again, after what seemed like only a couple of hours. I staggered out to the mess hall with a hundred others, and gulped down the plate of slop that was breakfast. And then we went on down the black hole, and I started to learn how long a day in hell could be.

At the bottom of the shaft was a huge vault cut from the stone, fogged with dust, the fog glowing yellow under banks of lights. Someone handed me a helmet with a lamp on it and something heavy that turned out to be a cutter. I followed the rest of the shift through the sulphur-colored haze like a blind man, up ladders on the far wall of the vault into a shadowy gallery half-eaten into the blue-gray rock.

They started in to work, nobody saying a word to me or each other while the guards were watching. The sound of their cutters was almost too high and too low to hear, drilling into my head, echoing and re-echoing against the sound of half a thousand other cutters all through the underground. I stood where I was, watching, trying to figure out how to start. A guard came toward me; the light on my helmet filled in his silhouette as I looked up at him. He didn't look human—until I realized he was wearing a mask against the dust. We didn't have masks. "Get to work." The words were only a mumble, but I didn't have to guess what he was telling me.

I shook my head. "I don't know—" His prod jabbed me in the ribs and I finished it with a yelp, backing into the wall and dropping my cutter. "Wait, listen, will you"—starting to panic as his arm came up again—"just tell me what to do!"

The bondie working next to me reached out for my shoulder and jerked me around. "Shut up and take this." He pushed a clear, silvery tube into my hands. I held it while he dropped a blue crystal the size of his fist into it and sealed the lid. "Stick it into my shoulder bag." I did. The guard watched us, the prod glowing in his fist; and then he moved on.

"Thanks," I said, feeling weak.

The bondie shrugged, pushing stringy blue-black hair back from his blue-stained face. "For what? I need a new partner, you're it. Do everything I tell you, do it fast and right, or I'll beat the crap out of you myself." He broke off, coughing deep in his chest, and spat. "Understand?" He was bigger than I was, and older, and he might still be stronger. His fingers tangled in my hair.

I nodded, too tired to fight or even to resent it. "Anything you say." He let me go. When he didn't say anything more, I asked, "What're you called?"

He almost looked surprised. "Mikah."

He didn't ask back. Finally I said, "Cat. I'm Cat."

"Shut up. Pick up that cutter and do what I tell you with it."

I picked up the cutter and did what he told me.

And every day after that was the same; until I didn't know day from night, buried alive in a blue stone tomb. Day after day we peeled off layers of ore and dumped it, looking for blue lumps of crystal, and everything weighed too much, even your feet felt like lead. Break the stone. Find the crystal and drop it into a tube, before its structure shattered and the matrix fell apart around it. . . . They used human beings because it was a delicate, dirty job; machinery broke down too easily, and was too hard to replace out here in the middle of nowhere. Warm bodies were cheaper than cold machines—when a pair of hands couldn't hold a cutter or pry out a crystal anymore there was always another pair to replace it, or ten, or a hundred: it didn't matter to Federation Mining whether you lived or died. After a while it hardly even mattered to me. Everything that had ever had any meaning shrank down to the simple effort of living through a few more hours of breaking stone.

Then, you tried to get the same plate full of slop into your mouth while your hands shook. You stumbled back to your dormitory and fell onto a mat still hungry, to sleep like the dead under the endless daylight of the spotlights. You tried to do it all over again, at the new shift; a few more hours, one more day. . . . The blue dust from the mines got into your eyes and nose and mouth, into every pore; it made you cough, it stained your skin blue, but nobody cared if you were too tired to scrub it off.

I kept thinking I'd get used to it, the work would get easier after a while. But it never did. I just got more and more tired; too tired to think straight about anything, or even to remember. . . . But over and over I dreamed about the Sakaffe Institute, about the psions and belonging to something good. And always the dream changed, and I was a slave, crawling through mud, digging my own grave out of blue stone, while Dr. Ardan Siebeling stood over me with a whip. I'd wake up coughing and full of hate, and wonder why I'd ever thought I was saving myself from anything by coming to this place.

But I didn't want to be a slave, I wanted out—there had to be a way out. I knew that to get away you had to get back to the spaceport; there was nothing else on Cinder. On a clear day you could see the Green Mountains from the mines compound, if you were lucky enough to be on the surface. Sticking up at a freaky angle, like the ragged edge of spring calling me out of winter—across fifty kilometers of wasteland, where the temperature never got up to freezing and the snow turned to acid when it touched your skin.

I'd heard strange stories about things happening outside, too, that no one could explain away by "snow accidents." The bondies claimed that there were "others" here who hated the mines, but no one would admit it. But they also claimed that Cinder was haunted, that it could drive you crazy, that it tried to get you lost outside so you'd freeze . . . until I didn't know whether to believe anything I heard.

And a blue-stained face wouldn't get me out of that hellhole anyway, so what was the use?

But there was a way—an easy way. Whenever they shipped the telhassium to the spaceport and brought back supplies, they used a couple of the bondies to do the heavy work, the way they'd done on my trip out. It was a free ride all the way to town, and they picked newer men because they were in better shape.

I'd figured Kielhosa would stop any chance I had of getting a break; I guess it was stupid to think he cared that much. But I couldn't believe my luck when one day they called me out for the trip.

Mikah and I loaded crates of crystals and bars of half-refined ores, our bloodshot eyes half-blind in the glaring daylight of the yard, while a guard leaned against the snowtrack and yawned. Mikah was coughing all the time—he was spitting red, something I'd never noticed down in the darkness. I did my own work and half of his, to keep the guard off our backs. Even so, I felt stronger than I had since I'd gotten here; almost human again.

We were nearly finished when the driver came up—the official named Joraleman. He stared at me for a minute, before he grinned and said, "Sainted Sarro, it is you! You've made me a lot of extra work, bondie. We haven't been able to find anyone else that handles a snowtrack like you do." He laughed; I stood blinking at him for a minute before I realized he was making a joke. "Kielhosa's sharp, kid. Nobody's outmaneuvered him like that in a long time." He stopped smiling. "Sorry it didn't do you more good."

I just shrugged, moving my tongue inside my dust-dry mouth, wondering if he expected me to answer. Afraid to try, but afraid to guess wrong, I did something I hadn't even thought of for months: I probed his mind. Lying on its surface I saw his relief at finding me still alive. And below it was something I almost thought was guilt. He was the one who'd gotten me this ride. He'd asked them specifically to find me. I wondered why the hell he should care what happened to me. But I squinted past him at the mountains, wiping my face, and I almost smiled.

The guard gave Mikah and me thermal jackets, shoved us in on top of the crates, and locked the doors. I felt the snowtrack start up, and felt us go through the dome airlock.

After a while I found a check window and got it open. It wasn't big enough to squeeze through, but at least there was light, and something to do. The cold air stung my nose and numbed my face; but once I began to watch, I couldn't look away. The endless blue-and-whiteness burned away the exhaustion that fogged my mind.

I swallowed and swallowed again; my mouth was always dry, no matter how much I drank. "Look"—trying again—"look out there, Mikah. All that snow and sky. The real world—" My voice broke. I coughed up blue phlegm and wiped my mouth. "It makes you remember you're still alive." He didn't say anything. "You want to look?"

"Nah. Somebody could go blind staring at all that snow. What makes you such a poet?" He frowned, scratching inside his jacket.

I flexed my hands, feeling the calluses on my palms. "I ain't digging ore."

"Crap. You think you're going to take off when we reach the port."

"What makes you figure that?" I stared out the window, feeling the snowtrack's hold close around us again.

"They all think it at first. Even me, once."

"How long you been here, anyhow?" trying to change the subject.

"I don't know. What year is it?"

I looked back at him. "Twenty-two seventeen, I guess."

"God," he mumbled. "Is that all? Five stinking years?" I wondered why I hadn't seen anybody down in the mines who was even close to the end of his ten years. Mikah's voice hardened. "Listen to me. Don't try to make a break. Joraleman doesn't come on as strong as some of the others, but he'll stun you as quick as the next if you do. And when you get back to the mines . . . ever see what they do to runaways?"

"What if I did make it?" I remembered how Joraleman had asked for me.

"You wouldn't. But even if you did, you'd never get offworld. They check for the bond tags. It just ain't no use. Look, anything you do this trip reflects on me, too. So don't try anything stupid." He broke off, coughing again. "Damn . . . damn it! Shut that thing, for God's sake. We could freeze in here." He stretched out on the bars of ore and shut his eyes. "I'm going to sleep. . . ." He was asleep almost before he finished saying it.

I reached over to pull the window shut. And then suddenly the world tilted and fell out from under us.

7

COLD . . . SO COLD. My hands were stiff with the cold, stretched above my head; my whole body was numb. All except my head—somebody must have kicked me in the head, but I couldn't remember the fight, couldn't even remember. . . . But then I remembered that I hadn't been in Oldcity, or even on Ardattee, for a long time. I opened my eyes.

I was lying head down in a pile of crates, and far up above me was sky, a deep twilight purple. I watched aurora move silently in the gap of the snowtrack's sprung doors, watched the fog of my own breath blur and combine with it. I sighed, enjoying the peace of the sky.

Somebody moaned. I raised my head, remembering Mikah and then finally everything else up to the end of the world. "Mikah . . . ?" I struggled, kicking broken boxes away, feeling a kind of sweet pain at the sound of muffled shattering as crystals decomposed inside them. I pulled myself up, buried to my knees in the jumble of crates and ore bars. Mikah lay on his back close to me, mostly clear of the ore. I moved what I had to to get him free, glad after all that we'd had to load the snowtrack as full as we did. The front wall was the closest thing it had to a floor, now; if there'd been less of a load, we would have been buried under the ore.

Mikah was out cold, but he was breathing easy, and when I reached into his mind he wasn't far below the surface. I left him alone and stood still for a minute. There was nothing to hear except the sound of his breathing and mine. Nothing. I wondered what had happened to Joraleman . . . what had happened to us all. It looked like we'd fallen into a ditch.

I put a hand up to the knot on the back of my head. My eyes weren't working just right, and I couldn't seem to think about more than one thing at a time. I decided to think about getting up front to Joraleman. Getting help. He must have a radio, or something. . . . The doors were sprung, and I knew I ought to feel happier about that than I did. I started to climb up and out.

As I reached the doorway, the whole snowtrack shifted and dropped a few centimeters under me. I froze, swallowing my heart again as the 'track didn't slide any farther, and pulled myself through into the snow. The snow lay in a wide fan around me, against a long concave wall of ice; snow that had given way and dumped us into this. . . .

I looked past the doors and down. And down. And then I sat back slowly in the snow, pulling my knees up to my chest, and hugged myself against a fit of shuddering. The snowtrack was resting on a ledge, barely. And below it translucent walls of green fluted ice fell away for a hundred meters or more into caverns of shadow. One slip, one shifting, even the tiniest wrong move . . .

After a while my body began to let itself go, too cold and beaten to sit there huddled in a knot forever. My mind eased out of its blind terror the same way. I started to inch forward finally, crawling, trembling, to look down again into the crevasse. Holding my breath, I saw the cab of the 'track hanging over the edge, resting on air. There was no way I could reach it, or Joraleman, or the radio without killing us all. I backed up again, wondering about Mikah. As long as he stayed unconscious, he'd be better off where he was than he'd be if I tried to move him. If he woke up . . .

But I couldn't make myself climb back into the snowtrack's hold, couldn't even make myself touch it. And I couldn't stay where I was, either, waiting for all of us to fall or freeze. So I started to climb, floundering up the face of the broken snow.

I made it to the surface, panting, covered by a clinging white powder. Before I brushed it off, I wadded a handful in the palm of my glove and looked at it. I'd never seen more than a few flakes of snow at once before. Frozen water. . . . I put the handful into my mouth. I spat it out again as my mouth started to burn, remembering too late that this snow had some kind of acid in it.

I got to my feet. Up ahead I could see the Green Mountains, but they were on the other side of the crevasse from where I stood. They might as well have been on another planet. My throat tightened as I thought about how close. . . . I turned and looked back the way we'd come, shielding my eyes against the bloody glare of sunset. The snowtrack's trail disappeared in the distance. There was no sign of the mines compound at all. The wind moaned and cried, sucking up whorls of dry snow, letting them sift down again as its voice fell away into sighs. The snowfields glittered like broken glass. I'd never seen so much open space before. I'd never been lost all alone in so much space; cold, bleak, and empty . . . *so empty.* I stumbled back and covered my eyes.

But I couldn't panic; *I couldn't.* I brought my hands down. Because the shaking that had hold of me now wasn't just fear. I didn't know how cold it was, but it was colder than anything I'd ever known; and with the sun setting it wasn't going to get any better. I had to keep sane and keep moving or I'd freeze right here. I made myself start to walk back along the snowtrack's trail, the only thing I could think of to do. The crust held my weight, as long as I was careful. This was a small world, no matter how it looked to me. It couldn't be that far back to the dome, and warmth, and help. . . . I kept walking, shivering harder.

Something caught my eye as I reached the first long curve of the trail, coming out of blue shadow below the foot of a buckled sheet of ice. I stopped, glancing up the sunlit slope; stood still, with the freezing air catching in my throat. The wind stirred. Sweet chiming music broke the silence, and a shower of rainbow sparks danced on the snow. *Not real.* I shook my head. My eyes weren't seeing this: not a garden of glass fracturing the sunset, a fantasy forest spun out of ice crystal, thorn and teardrop and gossamer. . . . "Not real." I whispered it, remembering the stories the bondies told, wondering if this world was haunted after all.

I picked up a chunk of fractured snow crust, ready to throw it—and then I dropped it again. I stepped out of the rut and started up the open hillside, breaking through the snow crust, staggering and sinking, but always getting closer. I reached the trees at last, plunged into rainbow as I fell down on my knees below their glistening fingers. They laughed and chimed and sang to me. I got up slowly, reaching out to the final proof of my sanity. . . .

And as I reached out, I saw the other, standing like my own reflection beyond the fragile garden of crystal spines. My hand jerked, hitting the branch. It burst open with a sound like shattering windowpanes. Splinters of burning ice flew into my eyes. I cried out, losing the stranger and everything else in a haze of fire. I dug at my eyes. Suddenly a hand was on my arm, solid and real, turning me, pulling my hands away from my face. I looked up but I couldn't see anything, only a fiery blur.

An alien thought probed deep into the core of my mind. Suddenly all my senses burst open—and then I was wrenched into blackness.

I was sitting on my knees on a floor of rough stone; my mind was still trying to settle back into my skull. I wiped at my oozing eyes, swearing. Mikah was lying on his side staring at me, when my eyes finally cleared. I hoped I didn't look as scared as he did. "You"—he gulped— "you alive?"

"I am if you are." My voice didn't sound very sure of it. I felt the lump on the back of my head again, glancing past him. Joraleman was lying beside him. We were in a blue stone room with no windows. "How . . . how long've I . . . we been like this?" *Trees—where were the trees?*

"I just woke up. Where the hell are we? I can't see anything." There wasn't anything to see, but I didn't bother to mention it. He pushed himself up and started to run his hands over his body, wincing and cursing at the bruises.

"Not the mines." For one sick minute after my eyes cleared I'd thought we were back where we'd started. Now I was sure it was somewhere else. But where? "How's Joraleman?"

"I don't know. He's bleeding. Maybe he's dead."

"Well, hell, why didn't you check?"

"Because I was out cold, jerk."

I crawled over to where Joraleman lay. His pale hair was covered with blood from a cut across his forehead, but it looked like the cold had stopped the bleeding. He groaned when I shook him. "He's alive." I noticed that his stungun was gone.

"Tough luck." Mikah rubbed his hands together.

"Shut up," I said, feeling guilty somehow. "He's the only one who might know what happened to us. You better hope he stays alive till he tells us that much." Mikah shrugged. I shook Joraleman and he groaned again. There was a first-aid kit on his belt. I got it open, but I didn't know what to do with the things I found inside it. There was a wet cloth sealed in plastic; I pulled that out and wiped off his face.

Mikah leaned past my shoulder. "Sure is a lot of blood."

"Too bad it ain't yours," I said, disgusted.

He pulled back, starting to cough again. When it was over, he said, "You know, at first I thought we were all dead, and the real hell was a lousy snowball just like Cinder. Damn, I don't ever want to die, if . . ." He didn't finish it. "Did you see anything? About what happened to us? I don't remember a thing till I woke up here."

I sat back on my heels while everything I'd seen played through my senses again.

"Well?" He gave my arm a poke.

I pulled away from him. "Yeah. We—" I pressed my lips together. "We fell into a big hole. Somebody must've got us out. I don't know how." *Or who.* Who else was there? Who had I seen, in that last second before . . .

Joraleman's blue eyes opened, and for a second there was pure terror in them. He'd been conscious before, for long enough: the view through the windshield of the snowtrack was burned into his memory like a brand. "It's okay," I whispered, touching him. "You're safe." He stared at me, and at Mikah, for a long minute before he tried to push himself up. He fell back again, running his hand over his face. "Hell and devils. . . ."

"Yeah, maybe so," I said. "You hurt bad?"

He didn't answer me at first. "My—ribs. I think something's broken. Feel dizzy." His voice slurred.

"There's a cut on your head."

"Aid kit. Get out the large white pills—two of them."

I handed them to him. He chewed them up and swallowed with an effort. He started to breathe more easily then, and he sat up, staring at the walls just like we had.

I leaned back on my hands. "Where are we? What's happening to us?"

"I don't know." He looked back at me, annoyed. "How would I know if you don't?"

I shrugged, and got up. He stuck out his hand, so I helped him stand. He peered around like it was too dark to see clearly. I suppose it was, for them. My cat eyes didn't have any trouble. He went over and ran his hand along a wall. The room was long and high, but rough around the edges, like a hole, and nothing but blue rock. I saw a telhassium crystal glitter as I glanced past. There were no windows, and now I realized there were no doorways, either. There were no openings at all. . . . I let my mind skid on past that without stopping; trying not to think about suffocating, trying to believe that if we'd gotten in, there was a way out, somewhere. Nobody else said anything about doors, either. A couple of lamps that burned with a shimmering blue glow were set into holes in the wall; otherwise the room was empty. "All the comforts of home," I said.

Mikah grimaced. "Where did you grow up?"

"Spooks. It has to be," Joraleman muttered.

"What?" I looked back at him; so did Mikah. "You feeling all right? Maybe you ought to sit down."

He shook his head. "I'll hold for now." Then he frowned at us; his hand went looking for his stungun, and tightened when he didn't find it.

"You—uh, figured out where we are?" I wondered if that crack he'd taken on the head had made him a little gorked.

"I think so." He leaned against the wall and sighed. "We're 'guests' of the Spooks. The snowtrack didn't just drop into a crevasse by accident. Something happened to the instruments. . . ."

"You think ghosts did all this to us?" Mikah said sourly.

Joraleman laughed once. "The sort of 'Spook' I had in mind would be one of Cinder's natives."

"I never heard of any natives," I said.

"I know you haven't." He shrugged. "We don't exactly advertise it while we're mining here. Squatter's rights aren't legally supposed to apply when there's a native culture. But the Federation needs telhassium—and the Spooks weren't about to leave. The FTA did its best to get rid of them. The problem is that they're psionic—they read minds, they can teleport. And they live underground. It makes them hard to back into a corner." He was staring at the solid walls, and he smiled; but he didn't think it was funny. "By the Seven Saints, I don't know why I'm telling all this to you. The point is that the Spooks won't even deal with us on a normal level. In the beginning they pulled some ineffectual sabotage, but it was barely even an inconvenience; I guess they didn't have much to work with. After that they dropped out of sight, literally. And now . . ."

"Why shouldn't they fight?" I said. "It's their snowball." I wondered why that even mattered to me.

"I know that! But why now? That's why we needed a new driver, kid: the last one didn't come back from a trip to town. Neither did the snowtrack. . . ." His voice faded. For a second the terror was back in his eyes.

I rubbed my arms. Green ice, falling away into the shadows. . . . "Why do they call them Spooks?" I remembered the figure I'd half seen waiting for me—and the sense-twisting wrench that had pulled me from the crystal garden to this freezing hole with no exits.

"I suppose 'Spook' was the first thing that came into somebody's head. Nobody has seen one in years; I've only seen a holograph, but you could say there's a resemblance: dead white and spindly-looking. They appear and disappear. And they don't speak—apparently they communicate only by telepathy, although as far as we know they can't or won't link minds with a human."

"Look, what good is all this talk doing!" Mikah wiped his face on his sleeve. "We're just wasting time—we have to get out of here before those things come and kill us!" His voice wavered.

Joraleman pointed a hand at the walls, his face set and gray. I felt his tension rising. "If you've got suggestions on how to get out, bondie, I'd like to hear them. Otherwise, you might as well just shut up and wait." He didn't know how bad he was hurt, and he was keeping his own voice calm with nothing but willpower. He folded his arms against his ribs and slid down carefully to the floor.

I sat down too and rubbed my cold-aching hands, wishing I had a camph. *Psions . . . telepaths.* I wondered. I shut the room out of my mind and stretched my thoughts. It seemed like forever since I'd even tried to use my psi. It was hard to concentrate; it hurt to search, hunting a doorway in the dark and falling over things I couldn't see. I didn't want to do it, I'd never wanted to, I hated it. But somewhere . . . somewhere . . . *there.*

"Hey, you, what're you doing?"

Something snapped and I was looking at Mikah. "Jeezu! You stupid—"

"You look dead, sitting there with your eyes unfocused."

"What do you want me to do about it? I'm thinking." I looked over at Joraleman. His eyes were shut. He wasn't asleep; he was praying. He wanted to be out of this so much that it was almost a physical pain, merging into the pain of his broken body.

"Then think of how to get us out of here, smartass." Mikah got up and started to cough. His own fear crackled like static.

I blocked them out of my mind. I'd done it; for a second I'd found someone, something. I loosened my mind, let it reach out again; this time knowing where to start, spinning out an invisible thread, casting into the dark waters . . . and then suddenly *contact,* feeling, sound, vision, everything: blinding, alien sensory feedback, twisting and warping my mind's sight like crazy mirrors, roaring and ringing, shocking every nerve ending in my body.

I broke contact. I sat with my eyes shut tight, more grateful right then for the emptiness in my mind than I'd ever been for anything; not even wanting to face the real world. But I'd done it. And knowing that I had, that I could, I had to go back again. . . .

This time it was almost easy; I knew the way through the dark. But I took it slowly, keeping control, making the sudden explosion of images and impressions filter through blocks and byways to reach my mind's eye. And I understood this time that I hadn't contacted just one of the aliens. Somehow I'd contacted them all, more minds than I could ever comprehend, all at once. I was looking through hundreds of eyes at once, breaking in on a hundred different lives, plugged into the circuits of enough energy to burn out all my senses if I lost control again. I could barely touch the wild electricity of living a hundred lives at once. My own thoughts began to tangle helplessly. I started to struggle, to pull my mind free. . . . And then suddenly I knew that they knew about me.

I broke contact and tried to disappear. But they followed me back across the broken connections, and my defenses fell apart until nothing lay in their way. I was drowning in image—

I was back in the stone-walled room; Mikah and Joraleman were standing over me. My face hurt, and after a minute I knew someone had slapped me.

"He just went crazy. Dumb twist sits there staring like he's seeing things and says he's 'thinking,' then he starts—"

Joraleman said, "What's the matter with you, kid? Can you hear me?"

I nodded. "Yeah. I made contact—with the Spooks."

"What did I tell you? He's crazy," Mikah said.

"I ain't crazy! I'm a telepath. I got into their minds, and they found out."

"Is that the truth, bondie? You can read minds? Did you find out anything?"

"Yeah, it's the truth. But there was too much, it all ran together." I shook my head. "I'm still trying to get it. . . ." I looked up and away from him.

Two of them were standing there in the room with us. Spooks: a woman with hair like a cloud, whose moon-white skin was netted with age lines; and a man who looked almost human, I thought—I wanted to laugh but I didn't. They wore heavy clothes, like our own but rougher-looking. I felt them searching us with their mind. I tried to deaden my own mind, not even thinking. . . .

"It's him. He's the one you want!" Mikah pointed at me.

8

THE ALIENS WERE startled; I could feel their surprise. They moved toward us. I got up and backed away from Joraleman and Mikah, toward the far end of the room. The old woman stayed where she was, watching them; the man followed me. I looked back at the others and said, "Do something," but they just stood gaping like none of it was real.

The man stopped in front of me, and I couldn't look away from his eyes. They were green, all green like a cat's. And when they met mine, the world stopped. Suddenly I couldn't move. I couldn't even think; my mind was paralyzed like my body. There was only the wall, behind me, holding me up—the wall, the only thing that wasn't a part of an anger that didn't belong to me, a thousand bright fluttering rags of image choking my mind . . . a sudden knife of focused thought sinking home behind my eyes, searching for my soul—

(Wait, stop, what do you *want?*) I felt my memories separating and coming loose, my mind being torn open. He was searching for the answers to a question I didn't even know; and I couldn't stop him, I couldn't reach him—I couldn't even remember how. I couldn't remember my own name . . . I was disappearing, disintegrating, feeling my mind flowing out of me layer after layer. . . .

Until he tore away the last of my defenses, so deep in my mind that I hadn't even known it was there. And the secret walled up behind it burst out: a nightmare of blood and screaming and agony. His own mind reeled back from it. Just for a second he lost control, giving me time to fuse the defenses he'd torn loose and choke off the horror before my mind had to put a name to it. And then I held him away; I let my own rage against what he was doing feed, and focused a thought from somewhere, (C-A-T spells *Cat.*) I built on it, strand on strand, to thicken a shield and force him out: *He didn't have the right, nobody had the right to do this to me.* . . . I felt surprise, but it wasn't my surprise.

He shook my mind and I slipped, but (I'm Cat . . . Cat . . . and I won't . . .)

And then he twisted my mind back on itself and made me see what I was facing: see that all their strength held me—not just his mind, but his mind multiplied a hundred times over. I'd trespassed against them all. They were all there inside his mind, reaching through his eyes, holding me . . . his eyes burning my mind like emeralds burning, green fire, green ice, green as grass—green as mine. (No! Don't hurt me, I'm like you! Look at my eyes, look at my eyes, they're green!)

I stopped disappearing. One frozen moment went on and on, and then the scattered puzzle pieces of my memory came spinning back together, making me gasp, and I was whole again. But before I could do anything else, he—they—reached back through my eyes. I became a link forged into a chain, while they opened up my thoughts again, all of them together reaching into my head, shattering the walls that I'd built for my fears to hide behind—my shields, my armor, my safety, my sanity. Making me stand naked in the circle of their minds with no protection; making me feel every instant of their own lives. My mind was burning out, but I couldn't make a sound, even inside my head; couldn't do anything but help them. . . .

And then, just when I thought I couldn't stand it any longer, all of it was gone. I was alone again: the deep and total bond was broken, and instead there were quiet messages forming on the surface of my mind— the only kind of contact I'd ever known before. But this time it wasn't in a way I'd ever known it. One voice was made up of all voices, impressions formed instead of words. (And it was true . . . they knew my eyes, they had seen through them now; it was true,) with feeling shifts inside it I didn't understand. (They found a mirror in my mind, saw their own eyes trapped in an alien face. I was the one who had been twice-promised, whose coming would begin the righting of all wrongs. . . .)

But I didn't understand it, I didn't want to; I only wanted them out of my mind. All I could think was, (God damn you, for what you did to me!), and I threw it at them. (Everybody thinks they can use me like a garbage can. But I'm human, for God's sake; I got a right to keep some part of me to myself!)

Their mind touched me again, gently, weaving its hundred voices into harmony with mine—healing, fusing, comforting. Showing me that my shame was meaningless, that with them I had no need for shame. My shame melted away; my anger went with it, even though I didn't want it to. And then I realized that all the clumsy barriers were gone that anger and fear had thrown in the way of the Gift I'd been born with. My mind's vision was as clear as open sky. . . .

(Through ignorance they had trespassed in my—self. Now they tried to make amends. . . . But none of the other desecrators, and none of their blue-skinned slaves, had the gift of true sharing. I was the one who had been promised, but they had not realized that I would walk between worlds; not human, not one of them. They wanted to know why I was different. How had I been made this way?)

I shook my head, because it was all I could do. I thought, (I—I don't understand. I don't know. It just happened, I guess. But, we're not different, really; we're all the same) remembering what Jule had told me. (Your people and mine. That's why I'm the way I am.) It came so easily, I didn't know what was happening to me.

I felt the strange surprise fill my mind again, and a flicker of disgust, a wave of disbelief. (All the same, a unity? Not the mindless ones, the destroyers, the slavekeepers, the savages. They were less than animals. It was the will of the One that those who mined the sacred stone be stopped . . . made to do no further harm. . . .) The image blurred behind my eyes; not death, but a nothingness, like everything I knew disappearing. (I was the one they had been told about. It had been promised long ago that one day their own would return from the stars and end their suffering exile. The outsiders would be swallowed up, would disappear, and all wrongs would be righted. It had been promised, and promised again. I was proof that the promise had been kept, and the time had come at last.) The aliens broke contact then, setting my mind free—and leaving it filled.

I stood staring at the alien's human/inhuman face in front of me, into it, through it. Because I'd been half blind all my life, and now I could see. I was in control again, but my mind still absorbed sights and thoughts and feelings that weren't my own, without even trying. Alien, human, everywhere—I sank into them. My mind dissolved like sea foam, until I could hardly breathe. And then the aliens disappeared, both of them winking out as if they'd never been there. After they were gone, my knees buckled and I slid down the wall.

When I finally felt like getting up again, Joraleman and Mikah were still standing where they'd stood all along. I hit Mikah and knocked him down, even though I knew it hadn't made any difference that he'd told the aliens who I was. "Croach."

"I'm sorry, kid," Joraleman said. He looked dazed. "There—wasn't anything we could do."

"Don't make much difference if you're sorry now." I shook out my hand.

Mikah got up and started to come after me, but Joraleman stopped him. "What did they do to you? What happened?"

I tried to tell him what they'd done to me, but it was too personal. I looked away, and only told him what they'd said. When I finished, Mikah said, "You hear that? They're gonna kill us! And not him." He glared at me. "Why should you get off? You vermy rat, you're not special. These aren't civilized aliens, you're not kin to them. You're just a half-breed freak and a lying son of a bitch." He started toward me again.

I looked at Joraleman. He didn't say a thing, trying not to feel the same way Mikah did. I started to back away from them.

Joraleman said, "Stop it!" suddenly. Mikah shut up then, but I kept on backing away. I went to a corner and sat down, watching them. Joraleman put an arm across his ribs and sat down, too. He swallowed more pills from the aid kit. Mikah just stood staring at me, his breath wheezing in his chest.

My mind was still lit up like I was doing dreamtime, although it was fading some since the aliens had gone away. I could still feel everything Joraleman and Mikah were thinking, their fear and anger—more of it than I wanted to. I kept trying to believe it didn't matter; I didn't care what happened to them. But . . . "Look, I'll try to find out what they're planning for us. Maybe it'll help."

Joraleman glanced up, startled, from across the room. He almost smiled.

I closed my eyes and let my mind slide back into alien water, easily now, trying to find the things I had to know, and trying not to drown. These were Hydrans; they had to be, even if I didn't know what they were doing out here so far from the rest of their kind. They were my own kind—my mind fought it—they knew me, had *expected* me. A feeling of cold wonder burst inside me. *Why? How? And the answer came:* (Because they existed to protect the blue stone of this world.) *Telhassium ore.* (They/their ancestors/their god, was/were the One, and the ore was sacred to them, giving life and light to them on this frozen piece of star. The Ancestors, the wellspring of their spirit, had gone from here long ago, but would return; it had been promised. And meanwhile they kept a sacred trust, and preserved the sacred stone.)

They remembered their ancestors' going; they remembered everything. Their memories pooled age on age—every mind among them was bound to every other, present and past, through hundreds of years; totally, freely, holding nothing back . . . in a joining, the ultimate sharing of mind and soul. They were a whole people who joined and were never separate; each individual was no individual but an outlet for the whole. Every image that any of them, living or dead, had ever shared was woven into the cloth of their group mind. But the wearing of years, hardship, and change had faded and torn the oldest images, until they no longer knew the true meanings, but laid new meanings over the old.

And so I saw the truth, although I didn't understand all of it then. That the Hydrans had come to the Crab long before the supernova's shining dust ever showed in Ardattee's sky. That they'd come here from a stellar empire that had passed its peak and was slipping down; looking for telhassium on a cooling piece of star. They'd set up a Colony of their own here, and then the civilization slipped down even more and the Hydrans on Cinder had lost contact with the rest of their people—with the Ancestors. Cinder grew colder and colder, the humans came; time and hardship shrank the lost Colony until the people no longer understood who they really were, or even why they'd come. But they still understood some things. And so they called the telhassium sacred, and the humans desecrators, and they waited, and waited. . . .

And they were a whole people who joined. Because once, at its height, a whole civilization had been able to join. The thing that for even two human psions was a wonder had been the soul of every Hydran, had been their strength, their world, their One. . . . And when I touched the truth in their mind, I felt fear in a way I'd never known, of things I would never understand. Because it was something that had almost destroyed me; and yet some part of me *wanted* it. . . . My mind broke away, but I forced it back again.

(Now the time had come at last; their waiting, their exile, were coming to an end. The key to the place of evil and its destruction had been sent to them, as they had known he would be.) *Me, they meant me.* (Now he would be taken to the holy place, to touch the spirit of the One, who would give them a sign.) And inside the matrix of the thought I saw flame. . . .

I fell back into the real world, and the others were still watching me.

"What is it—?"

"They're gonna burn me!"

Mikah laughed. "That's a switch!"

"Shut up, we don't have time—" Joraleman turned on him, his voice sharp. "Tell me what you found out," he said, looking back at me.

I told him all that I understood of what I'd seen. "And there's a place filled with fire, I saw it, blue fire; it's a holy place. They think I'm sent by their ancestors, they want me to go there and give them a sign. The hell I will. I'm not gonna be burned alive!"

"What's going to happen to you if you won't? What's going to happen to us?"

I looked down. "I didn't stop to find out. But it ain't no happy ending, I guess. Humans are 'desecrators.' "

Joraleman sighed. "Damn. . . . You said the flames were 'blue'? You saw them? Give me some details."

"They were coming right out of the walls, out of the floor. . . . Wait. I saw crystals, like telhassium crystals, everywhere—hundreds of them."

"Like the lamp over there?" He pointed. I remembered thinking that it looked peculiar. Now I finally saw why. The lamp was a bowl shielding a piece of crystal, and it was the crystal that burned.

He went over and brought it down; he moved slowly, like moving was getting to be an effort. "That's a telhassium crystal they're 'burning.' Their 'sacred stone' . . . wouldn't you know they're religious fanatics. Putting a concentration of the crystals together causes a spontaneous deterioration. That's why you put them in shielded containers when you dig them out. If that's what makes this holy place shine, then maybe you've got a chance. What do you think? Is this it?"

"Yeah, it looks the same. But what difference does it make? It's still fire."

He held out the lamp. "Put your hand into it."

"What do you think I am?" I jerked back.

He passed his own hand through the shimmering light. "Ever heard of 'cold fire'? Most of its radiation isn't released as heat. It won't burn you. Here." He held it out again.

I held my breath, pulled off a mitten, and stuck out my hand. I jerked it back again; but I hadn't felt it beginning to burn, so I reached out one more time. After about half a minute my fingers started to go numb. I pulled my hand out of the fire and shook it hard.

Joraleman said, "What's wrong?"

"My hand, it feels like it's dead." I put my mitten back on to warm my hand.

"How long have you been at the mines?" He was thinking, *(Too long; my skin was blue, he didn't know if I could take that much poison . . .)* "What do you mean, 'poison'?" I said. "What's going to happen to me?"

He looked at me, startled. "Oh. All right, then; since you already know. . . ." He looked away. "Telhassium ore is radioactive. The level of radiation is extremely low; but it builds up in the human body, like any cumulative poison, like mercury or arsenic. Exposure to dust poisons you slowly. But contact with this 'cold fire' poisons you fast, the radiation level is much higher. So what happens to you depends on how long you have to make the exposure. If you can cut it short, you should be all right. If you take too long it could kill you." Joraleman wiped his face; he was sweating now in spite of the cold. I turned away from him, from the pressure of his tension and his pain, from the blue crystal shimmering in his hands.

"Hey." Mikah caught at Joraleman's jacket.

Joraleman winced and dropped the lamp. The crystal imploded, throwing blue embers across the floor. He put a hand over his ribs. "What is it?"

"What good is all this doing for us? You've been figuring out how the freak's gonna save his neck, but he didn't say anything about how it's going to help us. How about it?"

Joraleman looked at me. "He's got a point."

"Yeah." I turned back to them, feeling the windowless walls closing in on me. I pulled my mittens off and started to rub my fingers. They'd been frostbitten a couple of times back in Oldcity, and they ached when they got cold. "Well, they think I'm gonna work miracles. If they're right, I'll work one for all of us." I pushed the corners of my mouth up.

Joraleman was getting one of the white pills out of the first-aid kit, and suddenly he reached in and pulled out something else. He caught my hand and slapped the thing down on it.

It stung. "Ow. . . . What was it?"

"A stimulant. If anything will help you, that should."

I hadn't even said I could save him. "Thanks."

"What about us, freak?" Mikah grabbed my wrist and one of my mittens dropped.

But I only looked away, feeling *something*—

The Hydrans were back.

"Never mind," Joraleman said, staring at them. "Do what you can."

I nodded. I turned again toward the door, and the two aliens were waiting for me. They put their hands on my arms. My mind started to flow into the sea of image, and I dropped the other mitten. My hands were cold. I felt a smile start to form on my mouth.

I heard Mikah say, "He wants to go with them," but I didn't, I didn't. . . . I did.

All I could see was flame, blue into blue, burning. But I saw the Hydrans too, dozens of them. . . . Or maybe I only felt them, drifting, whispering against my mind; like dust against a wall, or sand, or snow, or wind. Or flame. . . .

And then I knew where I was, and why, and my mind was my own again. I stood inside the place that I'd seen in my mind, a shelter inside a greater cave of darkness. Its space was lined with blue crystals, piled with them, alive with their shivering light. I knew what it was I had to remember: that this wasn't a place of ancestor spirits, that their god-self was superstitious garbage. That all I had to do was talk to nothing, make it good, and get it over with.

But maybe I'd been wrong. Because now the things I'd seen in the mind of the Hydrans came back to me, and somewhere in my own mind there was a . . . presence stirring. The thing that had hungered for the wholeness of their shared lives, that knew their loss for its own; that said they were right to welcome me, to have waited for me to come home. Because I was Hydran, this was my real heritage, and I should give thanks for my returning at last. . . . I went down on my knees and bowed my head, answering the stranger awake in my mind; and under my knees in the floor was the silver metal of a thing that had been placed there longer ago than anything I knew of. . . .

But as I kneeled there I felt the deadness creeping up my arms and legs, and I knew that if I stayed much longer I wouldn't get up again. I pushed myself to my feet and took a step, and another. It felt like someone else was doing it. But I left the holy place, and my people were waiting for me. Only two of them were physically there with me, the man and the woman; the rest were watching me through their eyes. This time my mind didn't lose its shape. (I did what you asked—) I thought, not knowing where to begin. My stomach knotted in a sudden cramp; I put my hands over it.

(A sign. The cold fire. . . .) It formed in my mind with a kind of awful joy.

I thought they meant the pain, but then something caught my eyes. I looked down, and my hands were glowing blue. So was my face. I rubbed my hands on my pants; but then I remembered the dust from the mines and how it stained your skin. They'd been answered. I let my hands drop and wondered how long it would last. Maybe too long. (What happens now?), wondering what their answer would mean for me.

The answer came: (You are the promised. You are the key, you will begin to unlock the future.)

I licked my lips. My tongue felt thick inside my mouth. I thought, carefully, (What about the others?), picturing, *(Joraleman and Mikah.)*

(It was my wish that the outsiders be returned to their settlement?)

(Yes! Don't hurt them. Let them go.) I was surprised that they actually cared about what I wanted.

(It would be as I asked.)

(And me?) Feeling a giddy rush of power, wondering how much I could ask of them. (I—)

They broke into my thought, (My guardians were waiting for me. I would be taken to them.)

I swallowed hard. (My guardians? Who? What—?)

But there was no answer. I let them lead me away from the shrine. There was a wide stair worn into the rock, as if they humbled themselves by coming to this place on foot. Behind us the blue glow leaped up the walls and was swallowed by the darkness. The stair spread out and down, to a ledge along the cavern wall, and the walls from there dropped away forever. There were things etched into the stone of the wall, strange symbols. I wondered what they said. The blue-silver glow behind and above us lit a path along the cliff face, along night's edge. The thought of walking it made me feel sick. There was nothing below us but darkness, and a few sparks of blue light, far away, like stars. I was shivering with cold, and I wondered if even the Hydrans knew what was out there in the night. And then I felt myself sucked down again into the whirlpool of their mind. . . .

". . . come on, kid, can you hear me? Try to concentrate."

I was shaking; somebody was shaking me. Joraleman. Mikah. "Damn, d-don't shake me!" And I was sitting against the wall of the blue stone room. The shock of being human, and with humans again, left me numb.

"He's glowing," Mikah said.

I looked at my hands. "They think it's a sign. . . . You're free. They said they'll take you back to town. It's all right."

"You mean that? We're really free?"

I nodded.

The lines of fear and strain eased on Joraleman's pale face. "Thank God." He thought his prayers had been answered.

Let him think it if he wanted to. A wave of cramps hit me again, and I held my breath. "They'll . . . be coming back for us."

"How do you feel?" He was worried. He figured I was in bad shape; but I didn't care. Right then nothing mattered, I felt too lousy.

"Hey, freak." Mikah pulled at my arm; I turned my face away. "God, you look like hell." Something about his voice sounded almost ashamed.

"I'm all right; I'm just tired. Don't call me that."

The Hydrans were back again; I didn't have to look up to know it. I got up slowly and moved away from the others until I stood between them and the Hydrans. (Is—it time?)

I thought the woman nodded; but she hadn't moved. She was expecting me to come with them, promising me (the others would be returned to their settlement as I had asked.)

I glanced at Mikah and Joraleman. "They'll take you back now."

Joraleman said, "Wait a minute. Where are you going?"

I didn't turn around. "With them."

"You can't do that! . . . You need medical treatment."

"I said I'm all right."

"Are they getting you free from the mines? Let me go with you, please. I . . . I can't take it there much longer. I don't want to die in that hole!" Mikah's face was tense and blue; he was remembering what Joraleman had said about the ore.

"They're not getting me free." I shook my head. "They just said I've got to go with them. I got no choice. They said somebody wants me. I don't know who, or—or what. Or even why." I was afraid even to guess.

Mikah looked at my face and then he shut his eyes; his hands balled up into fists.

"If I knew I was going free, I'd let you come." I raised my hands and made the truth-swearing oath.

"Sure." He nodded. "What the hell, it was worth a try." He glanced at Joraleman.

Joraleman didn't look angry, like I'd thought he would. He said quietly, "What's your name, bondie?"

"Cat."

He put out his hand, and at first I didn't understand. Then I wiped mine on my pants, but it was still glowing. He shook it anyway.

"Thanks. Good luck, Cat."

I nodded. I could feel the Hydrans waiting restlessly, their mind pulling at me. I started toward them, just wanting to get it over with.

"Hey."

I looked back one last time. Mikah made a funny motion. "Good luck. Cat."

"Sure." I nodded. "The same to you."

We were standing in another cavern, one that the Hydrans saw as a meeting place, even though there were no openings in these walls, either. I felt dizzy and confused; the pain in my gut was getting worse. But still I was able to see things in this room that didn't belong in a cave; alien things, but things the human side of me half recognized as high tech. And then I saw someone appear at the other end of the room. My eyes wouldn't focus, and at first I thought I was seeing things. They looked like humans.

I dug my hands into my eyes and looked up again. They were still real, standing at the far end of the hall. Another Hydran was with them, but I knew they weren't prisoners: maybe three of them, staring back at me. Murmuring and pointing. I looked at my hands. I tried to yell, "I'm human!" but I wasn't sure anyone had heard it except me.

The Hydrans beside me were telling them, (Here was the one they had been waiting for, the promised, the key. I had the true gift, and the sign had been laid upon me. I was being delivered safely to them. Now at last they could keep their own promises—) The thought had a sudden sharpness behind it.

I felt someone else reach into my mind then; a human probe. I didn't try to block it, and it was gone again as quickly as it had come.

(He is the one. We thank you. Now everything will happen as we promised.) It was one of the humans, answering the Hydrans; the one who'd probed me.

Pain drove into my stomach and I doubled over; I felt one of the Hydrans catch hold of my arms. The fingers felt like steel.

(I'm all right . . . let go of me.)

The hold loosened and I straightened up with my arms pressed against my stomach. I could feel the one who'd traded thoughts before with the Hydrans ask what was wrong. The humans came toward us across the room.

My eyes cleared again and I could see their faces at last. But I saw only one face. Siebeling's. Then suddenly it all came clear to me. The contact at the Sakaffe Institute, from the psions who were making trouble out here in the Crab Colonies. . . . They were here, now. And Siebeling, who'd done this to me, was here with them. I wanted to tell them who he was, to pay him back for it. But I couldn't shape the words anymore, or even the thoughts. Then all I remembered was falling into his arms.

9

AFTER THAT I was lost for a long time, doing dreamtime without end while my body paid the price. My mind sealed itself off from the sickness of the hurting, helpless flesh that held it prisoner. But inside the formless walls of my brain, some part of my consciousness still wandered, restless, afraid to surrender to what might be the final sleep of all.

And so I drifted through a strange dark universe, startling awake images and memories, seeing them flare up like embers from a long-hidden fire. I saw my life flicker past me, in bits and pieces, like they say you do when you're dying. And I felt the nerve circuits open and close, the currents flow, the messages being sent and the changing chemistry and pressures of life inside my brain. . . . I was those things, sensing needs, tending to them, taking a part in my own healing in a way I'd never imagined I could do.

Or maybe that was all a dream, or maybe the dreams were only a part of a greater rhythm, carried on the tide of a universal sea. I had drowned in that sea when the Hydrans took my mind—and been reborn. I'd felt the beauty of their oneness and their sharing, of barriers and walls broken down to let in the healing strength of shared lives. And alone in its own darkness my mind ached to feel that sharing again. I ranged further and deeper, searching the past for a sign, a guide —crying into the unknown with a voice I could barely control.

And I was answered. Reliving my life, I found memories tangled up with my own that had never been mine before—like drawn to like from the other side, cracking the shell of solitude, giving refuge to my dreams and escape from my nightmares. . . .

Hands, thin child's hands—my hands, smeared with rotting fruit, pulling apart compacted wads of garbage, cramming slimy bits into my mouth; swallowing, gagging. . . . Scarred, bloody hands—my hands, my fists beating some nameless punk senseless with terrified bloodlust for calling me *freak*, because if I didn't the rest of his gang would close in and take me apart. Daring to steal the jacket off his back where he lay, because I needed one. Daring to turn my back on the rest of them and stagger away, because feeling him break and bleed made me sick, and all I wanted from them was to be left alone. . . . Beating my bruised fists against the wall in some icicle-hung alley, cursing with the pain of it, cursing because it didn't help; because the weight of my own life was too heavy, and sometimes I wished, *I wished* . . .

. . . Wishing I could fly away. Standing on a silver balcony under the night sky, jewel-covered hands clinging to the vine-covered railing: white-knuckled, slender, woman's hands (not my hands, not my body, not even my own memory, *fusion, confusion*). Strands of gleaming black hair slithered free from the coils at the back of my head, clinging to my tear-wet cheeks. The agony of half a thousand blind emotions at once tortured my helpless mind; but there was no escape from the reception in the embassy at my back, drunken lecherous selfish greedy pitying hating *screaming*. . . . Biting my red-stained lips, to keep from screaming to drown them all out. *No escape, no escape, help me, God, help me, please please someone.* . . . Staring up into the empty sky filled with stars (strange stars, stars in patterns someone named Cat had never seen). Losing myself in the glory of stars— And feeling a poem-seed take root in my soul, until I forgot everything, even tears, in the sudden need to give the poem life. . . .

. . . Alive, dancing through a sweltering Oldcity night to the heart-beat rhythm of endless music, giddy from a jolt of glissen, swept up in the arms of a party that had spilled into the streets and didn't care who joined in. . . .

. . . *Dead.* Staring and staring at the transcript of the 'cast handed to me in the sterile hall of a med center, reading the words over and over that couldn't be true. *(Fusion, confusion;* not my eyes, green cat eyes that could barely read my own name; not my memory, not my life.) My life coming to an end with the end of someone else's, my wife butchered, my child gone, all gone. . . . My eyes blurring out of focus, the walls falling away, the world crumbling, dropping out from under me . . . lost, lost. . . .

. . . Lost, in endless fields of whiteness under a rippling sky. . . . Lost, drowning in an ocean of bodies twice my size, nighttime in Gods-house Circle. Running, falling, crying, crazy with the fires exploding in my head. Shrieking my loss to the world until I lost my voice, until the holocaust of horror burned itself out at last and left my mind in ashes.

Whimpering in the lap of a sagging old woman I never saw again as she held me, held me, murmuring slurry booze-soaked words, not the right words, not the right voice; my world, my past, even my name lying in ashes, smothered, dead. . . . Lying at peace in someone else's arms, long years after: the soft, sweet-scented arms of a girl named Gallena. Breathless with discovery, feeling all my senses heavy with joy—trying not to see the emptiness in her eyes when I told her how she'd made me feel. "Where's the stuff?" she said, looking away. "You promised." I got out my handful of escape and shared it with her. We lay there together talking about our dreams; until her pimp walked in on us and threw me down the stairs. . . .

. . . Crossing the rain-gray Latai Range with a woman I loved, on a Colony world called Timb'rellet, to reach an outland settlement that had once been my home (but not *my* home, *fusion*). . . .

. . . Oldcity, my home. A necklace slipping loose, into my palm; a blade clipping the strings of a brocade pouch. An angry hand closing over my wrist, twisting my arm, bending my thumb back and back—painstars. . . .

. . . Leaving home: moving, unresisting, swallowed up into the heart of a starship, seeing the insignia of Centauri Transport everywhere. Surrendering and striking back—leaving behind the family and the life I'd always known (but not *my* life, *confusion)* and the heartbreaking, mindbreaking indifference, the disgust, the fear. Knowing all the while that there was no escape, that it followed even now, wearing new faces, new minds, eating away my soul; always with me, until death. . . .

. . . Lying on a mat in the back room of an abandoned building that was shelter for a dozen other thieves and boytoys. Hearing voices drift in from another world; shaking with fever, wondering if I was going to die, and how long it would be before anybody noticed. . . .

. . . Looking out through the walls of a corporate tower, the gleaming transparent walls as clear, as hard, as unfeeling and unyielding as the minds of the ones I served (but not *mine*, not my memories or minds). Crumbling under the weight of their derision, trying to pity their fear, trying to win by surrendering, to earn a respect that would never exist in minds as dead as carrion. . . .

. . . Looking out through the windows of my eyes (but not *my* eyes) at empty faces, treating an endless stream of wounded minds, life's work that had lost all meaning because the ones who meant everything to me were gone, and had taken all meaning with them, turning all my windows into walls. . . .

. . . Looking down into the midnight waters of the lake, as dark as the darkness in my soul (but not *my* soul)—softly lapping, whispering peace, oblivion, an end. . . .

. . . Shocked out of oblivion by the press gang closing in. . . . Aching for oblivion as a stranger's heavy hand, with sharp heavy rings, closed over my arm. . . . Small trembling hands, my hands, lifted, begging. . . . Hunger aching in my belly . . . blue dust glowing on my skin . . . music playing . . . green ice walls . . . blue stone tombs . . . wormhole alleys boring into the endless darkness of the underworld. . . .

. . . The sudden brilliance of the Street of Dreams, music and life and showers of gold. . . . The bright rush of a thousand living minds into the space of my own, the input of alien senses bursting apart the walls of my prison and filling me with light, more light than I'd ever seen, growing brighter and brighter, burning away the darkness. A transformation, another world. . . .

Daylight. I opened my eyes and the sun filled them, blinding, beautiful, its warmth lying across my face. I shut my eyes, opened them again, not believing. . . . and it was dusk, with long blue shadows stretched out on the bed like mourners. I heard music, somewhere far away, voices and laughter. All I could see were the ceiling and walls where they met in the gray angle of a corner, my bare arms greasy with nutrient gel, a monitor pad lying across my chest. I didn't know where I was, but I felt peaceful and proud to be waking up there, as if it was a place I'd reached after a long journey. I sighed and slept; not afraid to, now.

Sunlight, prying at my eyes. I drifted up into the new day, felt its warm touch moving over my face. . . . *Human touch,* my mind said. I opened my eyes and watched the room slide into focus, and with it the hand moving away from my face, a face looking down at mine—a face I'd never thought I'd see again. (Jule?) I'd wanted to say the word, but I couldn't; my mind said it for me. I saw Jule's face brighten with surprise. She leaned forward, starting to smile.

My hand trembled in the air until she caught it, completing the circuit of her reality and mine. (Yes, Cat, yes!) Her sending dazzled my mind like a miracle—not short-circuited anymore by defenses I couldn't let down. And suddenly I knew how much I'd missed her, and knew I'd never really missed anyone before. My voice struggled in my throat, but nothing would come. Feeling I couldn't put into words burst through the link between us like an electric shock; her hand tightened in a spasm and she pulled free. But her mind didn't cut me off. It held me, calm and steady and accepting, as she reached out to the table beside the bed and brought a cup of water up to my mouth. She helped me drink it; nothing had ever tasted half as good. I sighed and drank again.

A portable hospital monitor sat on the other side of the bed, scanning everything my body did and reading out meaningless garbage on a screen; the pad still rested across my chest. But we weren't in any hospital room, and I heard music and voices again from somewhere, things I hadn't heard since I'd left Quarro. *Quarro.* . . . I let it rise up into my mind, let myself believe I could be back in Quarro: safe, protected, cared for. That my time in hell was over, and everything was really all right at last.

Jule took the empty cup away from my mouth. I lay back on the bed with a half-assed grin stretching my cracked lips. Just watching her move was pure pleasure; even seeing her dressed in heavy pants and boots, shirt and shawl, my eyes were filled with her beauty and grace. I flexed my fingers; my hands ached like the hands of an old man. They were splotched with yellow and purple, like I'd been bleeding inside. So were my arms. But the marks were already fading; the worst was past. I wondered how the rest of my body looked, but I didn't really want to know. At least I wasn't blue anymore. . . . I said, "God, I want a camph."

Jule looked back at me, the heavy black braid rolling on her shoulder. Her smile filled with gentle irony and crinkled the corners of her eyes. "Tough," she said, and I wasn't sure if she was talking about me, or my chances of getting what I wanted.

I laughed. It sounded like a death rattle. " 'S good to be back."

"It's been over two weeks. For a while we weren't sure you were coming back." She didn't mean to Quarro. Her smile faded. I felt her remembering that I'd been in a hospital room before I'd been here; caught a memory of my body racked on a life-support system.

"A long trip." I remembered how I'd felt when I woke up the first time. "Over now." Contentment filled me up and overflowed.

Colors changed in the feeling that reached me from her. "Cat . . ." I saw the truth show in her face.

"We ain't—back on Ardattee?"

"No." She shook her head. "We're still on Cinder, in the port town."

I looked down, seeing the bond tag still locked into the flesh of my wrist. I shut my eyes. Her concern drowned in the dark rush of disappointment that came with the truth. Jule was here, on Cinder. There could only be one reason for it, and it wasn't because she'd come to get me out of anything. It was only to get me in deeper trouble. If she was here, then I really had seen Siebeling, in the underground with the Hydrans. And if he was here, then Rubiy must be too, and the target of his plan had to be the Federation's telhassium supply: the mines, where I'd been a slave—was still a slave—because of Siebeling. Siebeling, who must have known what I'd wanted to do to him. Siebeling, who hated me. . . .

"Cat—" I felt Jule's mind knot with tension.

"Lemme alone." I kept my face turned away until she left the room. And then, because it was easier than facing the truth, I slid down again into deeper blackness.

Siebeling was in the room with Jule when I woke up again; I sensed him before I ever opened my eyes. I left them shut and pretended to go on sleeping. If the monitors gave me away, he didn't notice. I lay still, listening to them talk.

Siebeling sighed. "Are people like us born with faulty circuitry, or are we what human beings *should* be? And how used to living with the Gift can any of us ever become, in a society where it isn't universal? The best we can ever hope for is to learn control, to 'fit in.' And there's never been a place psions can go for real help. It's what I wanted to do at the Institute—"

"If only everyone could be empathic, or telepathic. Then maybe we'd really learn to understand each other; we wouldn't have to see everything distorted by our own fears. But if we were given a choice, we wouldn't be. . . ." I felt the rueful smile in Jule's mind.

Siebeling laughed once, bitterly. "If there was any justice in this universe, there never would have been a stardrive. We weren't ready for a galaxy. Humanity is an infestation, not a civilization. We never learn. Never. . . ."

. I found him with my mind: he was thinking about his wife. And then he was thinking about me, and the tension inside him was a pain. I opened my eyes just enough to watch him through my lashes.

"Damn it, sometimes I wish I'd never heard of the Sakaffe Institute!" He moved away from the window; sunlight made me squint. "It was a fraud, an exploitation . . . an insane risk."

Jule got up from where she'd been sitting at the foot of the bed. "It helped us all more than you can know, Ardan. . . . It saved my life." Her voice was calm and even, but her thoughts were too full.

"And what did it get you, or any of us? It got us here, trapped inside a conspiracy with time running out—waiting for *him* to find the strength to betray us all." He meant me. "And the 'lucky' volunteers are simply back where they started, barely surviving in their own lives. I was wrong to think I could do anything to make a difference, anything that would last. I was a fool, letting myself believe it. We're not professional spies; we never could be. Corporate Security must have known it was impossible—just like they knew we were expendable. I should have known it. . . . God, I'm sorry I got you involved in this." He put his hands gently on her shoulders.

"You didn't. It was my choice. And I'm not sorry." She met his gaze, held it, her own eyes shining too brightly.

He looked down, shaking his head. "I'm not, either . . . I am and I'm not. Because simply by being here you help me to remember that there are human beings who aren't—like I am, in the galaxy. And then I believe that stopping Rubiy could still make a difference. But I cherish you, Jule. You're the only one, since . . . You mean too much to me, it makes me afraid. If anything happened to you . . ." He pulled her to him; her own arms closed around him. I felt their need, and the sharp edge of fear that sweetened every moment they held each other. Their kiss seemed to go on forever, burning itself into my brain, until I felt my body begin to answer it. . . . But then my own need curdled into envy, and I broke contact.

Jule broke away from Siebeling, murmuring, "It won't. Not now. I don't know what brought me to this place, but it was right."

Siebeling reached for her again, but a high-pitched beeping broke the silence of the room. Siebeling swore; his hand covered his data bracelet. "I've got to get back to the hospital."

She touched his cheek.

He nodded as if she'd spoken, and kissed her hand. Then he turned to check the monitor, and I shut my eyes again, forcing myself to relax. If he saw anything that surprised him, he didn't let on about it. "He's going to be all right." His voice hardened. "It's just a matter of time." He went out of the room. Jule stayed behind, but somehow I couldn't make myself say anything to her. I pretended to go on sleeping, and after a while she disappeared, with a soft inrush of air.

The next time I saw her, strain showed on her face, and I felt a stab of sudden doubt touch her mind as she looked at me. For a second I couldn't understand it. But then I remembered what Siebeling had said about me, *just waiting to betray them.* "Jule, you don't have to be afraid of me."

She started, but then her face relaxed and she began to smile. "I know," she said. And now she was sure. She sat down beside me, twining her fingers together, glancing at my face. "I missed you, Cat; I missed you a lot. After . . . after you were gone. I'm glad to see you again." Her mind touched me and let me know how glad she was. That made me smile; I guess she knew why.

From then on I saw her alone; I never saw Siebeling. She spent as much time as she could with me, when she could get away from the job she'd been assigned to. She fed me soup and wiped my skin with a cool cloth, always as gentle and patient as I'd remembered her; forcing me to admit I was going to live, whether I liked it or not. The first few days I didn't even ask questions, because I wasn't ready to face the answers. She seemed to understand that, or else for her own reasons she didn't try to tell me more than I wanted to know.

When I could sit up, after a couple of days, there was a view of the mountains out the single window. But there were heavy curtains at the window, closed half the time because Cinder's day and night were too short, nothing close to a standard day—most humans were built to sleep and wake up on Earth, and their bodies didn't change just because they lived on a new homeworld. I couldn't even get to the window to open the curtains on my own; but Jule brought flowers into the room, and gentled me with promises of walking outside when I could get my feet under me again.

And one evening she read me some poems she'd written, from a little notebook she had. As she read to me I felt doubt straining inside her, and I understood that she was sharing something very personal, not knowing whether I wanted it or could even accept it. But as she began to read, the images shimmered and burst open, letting me see into them. She'd told me once that poetry was like psi for her, distilling word and thought to their purest form; and as she read to me, the distance between her voice and the touch of her mind closed, word and thought flowed together into one bright song and then another. A lot of the poems were full of pain, but that only made them easier to understand. I don't suppose they meant the same things to her that they meant to me, in the end; but maybe that doesn't matter, anyway.

> *I remember one last night,*
> *the darkness gathering around me,*

> *quietly knowing*
> *every stone and the tyranny*
> *of grief*
> *and all the vows that are made.* . . .
> *Or do I only know*
> *the blinding silence of the billion stars*
> *burning and burning;*
> *the glory of Orion striding up the sky—*

Lost inside my own memories as she read, suddenly I saw her through the images, the filter of her feelings and my own: shivering alone on a balcony, her hands on a vine-covered railing, her eyes open to the night, transfixed by stars. Double vision stunned me as I knew it for a memory of my own (but not my own, *fusion, confusion*) swelling out of the dark underworld where I'd been lost these past weeks.

Jule stopped reading, watching the changes on my face, feeling the shift of my attention. "What is it?"

I didn't answer her at first. And then I only said, "It means a lot to me." Afraid to tell her why—not only because of the memories that had answered it already, but because somehow in one of them I'd shared the moment that poem was born inside her. I hadn't been meant to know that secret moment, and I figured she'd only resent it.

But she smiled, content. I asked her to read the poem again and again, until I knew it by heart. And I wished that I had something to give her in return, a poem, anything; but anything I could think of seemed cheap and ugly next to what she'd given me.

After she left me again, I lay looking at her memory caught there in my mind, as much a part of me as my own were. Other scenes that had never been a part of my life began to surface, then—some that I knew or guessed belonged to her, some that I couldn't put any tag on. It scared me, not knowing what had been done to me while I was sick—until I saw suddenly that I was the one who'd done it to myself.

And then, finally, I began to understand everything—that what had happened after the Hydrans had been inside my head had gone on happening, as though they'd found something caged and set it free. In sickness my mind had wandered out of itself; it had found open doors and gone through them, into the deepest parts of other human minds; pain drawn to pain, hunger to hunger. And from what I could tell no one had known it but me.

And now, whenever I was with Jule, it was easy to reach what lay on the surface of her thoughts—I could read her without trying, like I'd been doing it forever, like breathing. I was a real telepath at last. And I wondered whether the Hydrans really knew what they'd done. I thought about them sometimes, what they'd done to me and for me; and when I did I felt a kind of longing.

But in the long hours when I was alone, I began to work at controlling what they'd left me with; trying to stretch my waking mind to match what my unconscious had done. Because I'd been given a gift whether I wanted it or not; and whatever happened to me now, I figured I was going to need it. At first it was hard to handle; I didn't know how to control it. I was still weak and it was so strong—like the tail wagging the Cat. But day by day it got easier.

Jule had told me why I heard music: that this hidden room where I lay was somewhere in the starport town, over a bar that was about the only entertainment on Cinder. I couldn't reach very far with my mind, I didn't have the energy yet; so I spent a lot of my time watching the ones down below with my mind's eye: feeling them bored, frustrated, homesick, afraid. Feeling the emotions get loud or fade or blur, feeling them shift and the images run like a ruined painting as they drowned their sorrows in alcohol and drugs. Sometimes I followed them down to oblivion, because that was as close to pleasure as I'd been in a long time.

By now it was simple to tell a psion from a deadhead. Normal human minds were an unfocused snarl, and my own was light and sharp enough now that I could wander into them like a thief, taking anything I wanted, and no one even knew I'd been there to steal their thoughts. If they'd had anything worth stealing.

Most of the deadheads were from the mines—guards, technicians, officials, who never knew they were sharing a table with a psion who'd come to Cinder to steal their world out from under them. Because most of the townspeople were psions by now. Jule had told me Rubiy had been replacing as many of them as he could with the psions he'd recruited. She and Siebeling had come here together—he worked at the port hospital and she had a job at the spaceport—after "disappearing" for a while out in the Crab Colonies. Her memories of that time turned private and warm, but edged with bright fear, as if she was almost afraid to think about what their time together had meant to her. I caught a wisp of image of a world I'd seen in false memory before, but not her memory. . . . Siebeling's homeworld. Seeing it again, in her mind, I felt alone and angry.

Dere Cortelyou had come in on the next ship. The turnover of work-

ers on Cinder was high to start with because of the radiation levels—
even with an energy shield projected around the planet to keep most of
the pulsar's radiation out, the background levels on Cinder itself were
still too high—and because of the boredom and isolation. Rubiy's people had been raising the turnover even more by spooking the deadheads
with psionic suggestion, playing on the negatives that were already lying in their minds.

I watched them do it, looking into their own minds—some of them
tight-woven and always shielded, so that I had to use everything I'd
learned and more to measure their skill; some of them almost as tangled
and sprawling as any deadhead. Most of the psions weren't criminals,
not the types you'd expect to find plotting to take over a world. But
most of them were hungry, and angry, and all of them were ready to
take any chance to get what they thought the Federation owed them.

And none of them had ever known anything to match what I'd felt
when my mind had been joined with the Hydrans. I began to understand that no joining of human psions ever did. None of the psions I
probed matched what I could do, either. No one even tried to; I never
felt anyone test my own shield, and by now I was sure I'd know it if
they did. Rubiy himself was the only one I wasn't sure about—remembering how afraid I'd felt the last time I'd seen him. Jule said that he'd
disappeared right after they'd found me; he'd gone offworld, and she
didn't know when he'd be back. She was glad he was gone; so was I.

I could find Jule anywhere in town, any time; a part of her mind was
always open, listening for me, in case I needed her. It made me rest
easier to realize she was always there, even when I didn't see her: someone quiet and kind watching out for me, who wasn't just waiting like
death to catch me when I couldn't fight back. I touched her thoughts a
lot through the days, without letting her know it. Making contact with
her wasn't like reaching a stranger, it was more like finding another part
of myself. But I never went deeper than the surface of her thoughts, or
tried to take anything that wasn't my right. Just touching her with my
mind was enough.

After a while my strength began to come back, and I finally began to
face up to life again. And lying alone in a room with four blank pale
walls, staring out the single window at the same view you can't ever
reach, gets old. Jule was the only thing I had to look forward to; I
couldn't help it if I began to wait for the sight of her, the sound of her
voice, her touch, the soft sigh of air as she materialized at my bedside.

And now that I was really a telepath, I couldn't help it if I began to wonder how it would feel to make love to someone while I was sharing her thoughts—sharing every desire, every pleasure, every secret hidden in our souls. . . .

10

(CAT?)

I turned around on the table where I was sitting, beside the wood-framed window, to see Jule appear in her usual spot—by the bed I was still supposed to be lying in.

"Here." The dim sunlight coming through the streaked panes barely warmed the back of my head.

The scattershot confusion of her thoughts collected into relief as she saw me. "What are you doing there?"

"Looking out." I shrugged like it was the simplest thing in the world. It had taken me five minutes just to get from the bed to the window, and the hospital tunic I was wearing was soaked with sweat.

Objections surfaced in her mind, half angry, half reluctant. She didn't bother to say any of it out loud; she didn't need to.

I got up, feeling my legs tremble under me. They carried me a whole couple of steps before they gave out. Jule caught me and helped me back to the bed. I held on to her a little harder than I needed to.

"You're sick," she said, like I needed reminding. She pushed me down; her hands were gentle and strong. I noticed that she wasn't biting her nails anymore.

"I'm sick of lying here like a corpse." My heartbeat was so loud in my ears that I could hardly hear myself talk.

Her mouth tightened a little at the image. "There are worse things."

I glanced at the bond tag on my wrist. "Yeah." I covered it with my hand, remembering when a week in bed had seemed like all I could ask of heaven.

"I brought you lunch." She bent her head at the two plates on the bedside table, one for her and one for me.

I looked at it, but suddenly I wasn't hungry. "Jule . . ."

She raised her eyebrows, sitting down at the foot of the bed.

"What's gonna happen to me?" Asking it at last.

"I don't know." Her voice got faint. She pulled her shawl closer around her. "I don't know what's going to happen to any of us now. But Rubiy wants you back; that's why they're sheltering you. He's been searching for a way to get hold of you ever since you arrived on Cinder."

"Me? . . . The mines. It's what I know about the mines?"

She nodded. "It must be. His people have been on Cinder for nearly an earthyear, some of them, but they've never been able to get into the mines compound. They're beginning to get desperate. Whoever is backing them is losing patience, and the psions who've been here the longest can't stay much longer without suspicion. Our only hope has been that Rubiy would fail because of time—we've been watched all along, we haven't been able to do anything to stop him, or even to get a warning out. But now that he has you, everything's changed again." *(For the worse.)* But she didn't say it.

"When Rubiy gets back . . ." She didn't hide the disgust she felt when she thought about seeing him again. She remembered his dead man's eyes searching every centimeter of her body, peeling away even her skin, probing for her soul. . . . Humiliating her—not because he thought she was a spy, but just because her name was taMing. He knew that she'd been born into all the wealth and luxury anyone could claim; but she'd still been born a psion—and there wasn't enough money or power to make that stain on the taMing honor disappear. He hated everything she stood for and was heir to; he enjoyed the pain her Gift had caused her family. And he'd let her know that he'd brought her here because of all that, as a pawn in his private game with the Federation's mortal gods. But he wouldn't show her what the game was. . . .

I grimaced and looked down. But I only said, "Where's Rubiy now?"

She shook her mind out. "We think he's gone to meet with his backers again. There are several combines involved in this, but we don't know which ones. A woman named Galiess is in charge, but she doesn't give anything away. Dere can't read her."

"How come Dere ain't been to see me?" He hadn't even been into my head to say, (Hello). I wondered if he didn't trust me now, either.

"Ardan won't let him. He won't let anyone see you until you're stronger."

Strong enough to betray them. A prickle of anger made my skin itch. I took a deep breath, and said, "What about Siebeling?"

She looked away, twisting dark shiny strands of hair between her fingers. Suddenly she was the woman I'd known in Quarro again, frightened and uncertain. I realized how much she'd changed in the time since then—the confidence she'd found, the control of her psi talent and her life. And at the same time I understood that Siebeling had been the one who'd made her reach out again—not just because of what he'd taught her about controlling her psi, but because of the thing I'd felt between the two of them, a sharing and a healing each gave to the other. . . . I touched it again in her mind, and pulled away like I'd been burned. That was why she couldn't answer me: because she couldn't make how she felt about me match up with what he felt about me, and what she felt about him.

I lay back, not knowing what to say; staring at her but thinking about Siebeling . . . until it didn't even seem like a surprise when I caught the pattern of Siebeling's thoughts, and realized that he was coming here. Someone else was with him, a psion—a telepath—a mind I'd never seen the inside of. . . . But I had seen it before. Just once, on the edge of consciousness there in the Hydrans' underground world. I sat up just before the door opened, and watched them come in.

"You aren't supposed to be up" was the first thing Siebeling said to me. He was wearing a medical coat under his parka.

"I'm not," I said, looking past him at the stranger. It was a woman.

"You were." Siebeling pointed at the hospital monitor. "That lets me know everything about your condition. You're recovering from radiation poisoning; your body can't take that kind of stress yet. Don't do it again unless you have my permission."

My mouth twitched, caught somewhere between anger and laughter, because this was nothing like the meeting I'd imagined. But then the stranger caught my eyes. I felt her probe my mind, and knew it for a challenge—knew her for Galiess, Rubiy's watchdog. She was a small, fine-boned woman, who looked like she belonged in a salon somewhere, not in a frontier port town. She wore a long, heavy gown—nothing fancy, but still it looked out of place. And it couldn't cover the truth— that she was an old woman, even though she tried to hide it. Her thick silver-tipped hair was a wig, her face had a stretched look to it; her mind was full of musty rooms. The look in her washed-out blue-green eyes said I'd done something to her, without even knowing her. I let her think she was getting a look right into my soul, without giving her anything; using her own concentration against her while I tried to find out what she really wanted. I didn't get much—she was a good telepath. But she didn't catch me, either. That meant I was a better one—and that I had one less thing to worry about. I made myself look away from her and down, knowing that was what she expected.

"My name is Galiess," she said, like she was talking about the weather. I tried to look like it was news to me. "And you are Cat. I suppose you know that we've waited a long time to have you here." Her voice was brittle.

"Not half as long as it seemed to me." I glanced from Jule to Siebeling. His mind was like mirrored glass. I kept my back straight and my voice strong, knowing like I'd always known that when you were in enemy territory you had to hide any weakness. "And I guess I know what you want me for. Rubiy's got bigger eyes than I figured." I rubbed the bond tag on my wrist.

She nodded. "Your time at the mines makes you a risk, but it also makes protecting you worth any risk. He was right about that much. . . ." Her mind shifted. "And I don't expect working for Contract Labor left you with much loyalty to your employers."

I laughed once. "Not much." I couldn't help looking at Siebeling again. He was frowning, and holding his thoughts in a cage woven of perfect half-lies; I knew they were half-lies only because I knew the truth. Galiess already knew there was bad feeling between us; but it barely covered the deeper anger and fear in his mind as he waited for what I said next. "I told Rubiy I wanted in, before. I sure haven't changed my mind. What do you want me to do—just name it." I didn't have to force the hardness in my voice.

"I only want you to obey Siebeling, for now. Nothing more is expected or required of you until Rubiy returns." The way she spoke his name made it sound like the Holy Name of God. "But you'll need your strength back then. I hope your recovery continues to be as rapid." While a hidden part of her mind wished I'd been dead when the Hydrans had handed me over to her.

She was beginning to realize that I'd been playing with her mind, and she made a sudden, stupid try at getting past my guard. I tied my mind up tight and shut her out completely. She stared at me like she didn't believe it. Finally she said, tripping over the words, "Dr. Siebeling has been told how important you are to us. I'm sure he'll see that you keep improving." She gave Siebeling a warning look. Then she turned to Jule, and the look changed. "Why are you here? Why aren't you at the spaceport? Is working as a clerk too demeaning for you?"

"I brought Cat a meal." Jule waved a hand at the food. "I always do." The words were soft, her voice was even; she almost perfectly blocked the resentment that rose up in her. But I saw her eyes turn cold. "I'll be back at the shipping counter when they expect me to be. If they have any complaints, they'll let you know, I'm sure." It wasn't the first time she'd had to give those answers. Galiess didn't miss a chance to bait her, and I knew from Jule's anger that it wasn't because she deserved it.

"Be sure you remember where you are—and who." Galiess nodded to us all and left the room with her own mind in a snarl.

Jule and Siebeling glanced at each other, their faces grim and tight, with unformed questions passing between them as they waited. When they were sure Galiess was gone for good, Siebeling turned back to me, and I stopped thinking about anything but him.

He caught my wrist, the one with the restamped bond tag. "What the hell are you doing here?" The words dropped on me one by one, like stones. He didn't really expect an answer. He let go of my arm again. I knew for certain then that he hadn't arranged my transfer. Jule stayed where she was at the foot of the bed, her hands clenched in her lap.

I leaned back against the wall, trying not to let him see that I couldn't sit up any longer. "Nothing personal. I just figured I'd rather freeze to death than drown in mud. That's all the choice they gave me. . . . You think I came to Cinder on purpose?"

"I think someone saw that you did." *(Rubiy.)* The name was as plain as if he'd spoken it.

My fingers hugged the plastic tag on my wrist again. "Yeah. It fits . . . it makes sense. He's got the contacts to do that?" I looked up at Siebeling again, but he wasn't listening.

His voice was so quiet when he spoke that I had to strain to hear the words. "The first thing you did when you saw me was try to tell Galiess who I really was. You just had another chance—why didn't you use it?"

I winced, glancing at Jule. She was biting a nail. "I—I didn't know what I was doing, before. I was sick then." My own voice was hardly louder than his.

"You ought to be dead—"

Blood sang in my ears, but all I said was, "Sorry to disappoint you."

His face went white, and I realized that I'd read him wrong. Jule leaned forward, her anger and frustration suddenly back again. "You would have died, if it hadn't been for him, Cat! No one else here understood what was wrong with you, or how to treat it. You owe him your life."

"Maybe he owed something to me." I stuck out my bony wrist with its red band.

Neither of them answered that; and what lay in their minds wasn't an answer, either.

Finally Siebeling said, with an effort, "I only meant that because you're half-Hydran, you have a higher-than-human resistance to the radiation. And you heal more efficiently."

"I know. . . ." I let my arm drop; it felt like lead. "You know what they say about cats—we all got nine lives." I thought about how they would've been safe if he'd let me die. He'd known that, too. "Maybe that is one of 'em I owe to you."

Jule smiled, easing a little, but Siebeling still held himself rigid. I felt his thoughts shift focus.

"And I ain't spending the rest of 'em working for Contract Labor!" I answered him before he could say it. "I ain't going back to the mines. You might as well forget that right now. You heard Galiess—the psions need me, Rubiy wants me. There's nothin' you can do about it. You're stuck with me."

"We're stuck with you?" Siebeling said, his voice rising a little. "Are you trying to tell me you still want to work with us? After what you tried to do?" I couldn't tell whether he sounded sarcastic or amazed.

"You mean, after what you did to me." I pushed forward, wrapping my arms around my knees to keep myself there. Suddenly I was really hearing his question, and wondering what the hell it meant to me. Did I still want to work with them? Was I crazy? I thought about the times, down in the mines, when I'd imagined how good it would feel to wring Siebeling's neck.

But then I looked at Jule again: sitting at the foot of the bed like a mediator, aching for an end to the anger and misunderstanding between Siebeling and me. And I saw the ways she'd helped me, trusted me, believed in me. And I thought about Dere Cortelyou tossing me a camph, telling me more than I ever wanted to know about telepathy or half a hundred other things, trying to make me understand why he even cared. . . . About working with the psions at the Sakaffe Institute; about feeling like a part of something for the first time in my life.

And the truth twisted like a knife inside me. I'd let myself get tied to these people, let my life get tangled up in theirs. It was just like it had always been—getting involved was hanging a stone around your neck when you were already drowning. But if fate wanted you to drown, there was nothing you could do. . . . I thought about Galiess and

Rubiy, and tried to tell myself that I'd be crazy to trust either of them. But that didn't change how much I could gain by working for them. And it didn't change how much I could lose, working against them, for somebody who hated my guts.

I realized that the silence had gone on way too long while I thought it through. Finally I said, "Yeah, I still want to work with you." *I been a loser all my life. Why change now?* I stopped just short of finishing it out loud.

Jule's belief reached me like a smile. But Siebeling's eyes didn't change, and neither did his mind. He didn't believe me; he'd never trusted me and he never would. "You're a bad liar, for someone with your experience." He moved away from me toward the window.

"You got a lousy bedside manner." I sagged back against the wall again, my hands clenched white-knuckled on the bedding. "Listen, I don't give a damn what you think," putting all the strength I had left into it. "You're stuck in this, and you know it's not gonna solve itself. I can help you, if you let me—you ain't gonna survive with Rubiy if you don't."

Siebeling turned; his disgust caught me behind the eyes. "You're going to protect us from Rubiy?"

"I'm a better telepath now. Better than Galiess. You want to know how I got rid of her so fast? I just let her know that."

A frown pinched his forehead again. He glanced at Jule; she looked at me, surprised but not really surprised. He said, "If that's true, then you were a fool to let her know it."

"Uh-uh." I shook my head, even though I wasn't sure he was wrong. I reached out for the cup of water on the table beside the bed. (And you can believe it. I can make you believe it; I can make you believe anything if I want to.) I looked him straight in the eye as I tore apart his shield and sent the thought into his unguarded mind. He jerked physically; the recoil of his thoughts hit me so hard the cup fell out of my hand.

Jule moved to pick it up from the wet floorboards. She filled it again before she said, very quietly, to Siebeling, "I tried to tell you." There was no sharpness in it, but there could have been.

He kept frowning, flexing his long-fingered hands, searching for words; still searching his mind for the tendrils of my own probe.

But I'd already let him go again. I was bluffing him, and I couldn't afford to let him find out. I didn't have the strength in me yet to hold out against him for long—even to go on talking much longer. But I had his attention now; I had to use it while I could.

"How?" he asked, finally.

"The aliens, the . . . Hydrans." I lifted a hand to my forehead. "They went into my mind; they changed it. Healed it, somehow . . . all of them together, in a joining. That's how they live—with all their minds bound together. And for a little while they made me a part of it. It was . . . it was . . ."

(Like coming home,) Jule thought.

I glanced at her, with the image moving like a bright bird through my mind. I looked at Siebeling again, at the blank wall of his resentment. "How'd they get involved with Rubiy? And why?"

"By accident. They had nothing to do with any of this, originally." His voice darkened. "But they discovered the presence of human psions here, and Rubiy's sucked them into it as deeply as he can, using them, letting them think he's here to help them by overthrowing the mines."

"Their ancestors promised them. . . ." I said. "What are Hydrans doing here at all? How'd they get this way? Are all Hydrans like this?"

Siebeling broke my gaze. "I don't know," lying. Old memories stirred in his mind, in a mass of tangled feeling.

"Come on, damn it. This's important to me. I know you know—you said you were married to one."

"I don't want to talk about it." His mind warned me away.

"What the hell's wrong? I ain't asking for your lousy life story—"

(Yes, you are,) Jule said silently, only to me. (You can't help it.)

(What—?) I slid into direct contact, so much easier with her than words. I saw Siebeling's face change as he realized what we were doing. (How? Why does he hate me, Jule?)

(He doesn't—)

(He does! He's hated me from the first time he laid eyes on me. Anything I try to do, he takes it wrong. I never did nothing to him!)

(It's not you that he hates. It's—)

I finished it for her. (What I am? A half-breed, a 'cheap gutter thief'?)

She shook her head without moving. (No! Not in the way you think. *Her mind telling me at the same time that I wasn't a cheap gutter thief, that she wouldn't feel me believing that.* But he lost everything, Cat. His wife and son—)

(What's that got to do with me?)

(Everything! It's not you he hates; it's himself.) And in less time than it would have taken to ask again, she showed me her answer: she showed me Siebeling as he'd been when he was young, barely out of med training, so in love with his proud, gentle wife and their green-eyed son that he wanted everybody to know it.

(He loved them,) I thought, *(he really loved them—?)*

But his wife had dedicated her life to improving the way Hydrans were treated by the Federation. She'd gone back to her homeworld during a combine's relocation sweep, trying to help save her people from being deported. Siebeling had tried to stop her from going, afraid of what might happen to her. But he'd only made her angrier; in the end she'd gone anyway, taking their young son with her. And she'd died—murdered, he was sure, even though he couldn't prove it. Nobody knew whether the boy had died along with her or been transported with the rest of her people, who'd been scattered over half the worlds of the Federation like dust thrown into the wind. Siebeling saw his wife's body; but he never found out what had happened to their son. No Hydran he found knew what had become of the boy, or else they wouldn't tell him; and the combines involved didn't even care. Siebeling never found his son. (He blames himself, he thinks that he failed them because he wasn't with them, and because he's . . . human. Remember the crystal ball you stole?) I laughed, silently; she glanced away. (It belonged to his wife and their son. It was a Hydran thing, tuned to a Hydran mind. Only someone very much like them could make it change, the way you did. Seeing you reminds him of what happened, you make him overreact without meaning to, because you remind him of—)

"—Of my son?" Siebeling said out loud, shattering the clear wall of silence between us.

Jule froze; her face paled and then turned red as she realized what she'd done.

"God damn it, Jule—" Siebeling began. The rawness in his voice was like a wound; pain, not anger. Whatever he'd been going to say to her, he didn't finish it. But something unspoken moved between them, and this time I was the one who was left out of it. The rigid, clenched way he held himself eased, almost against his will. When he looked back at me again, finally, I sank down into the corner, wishing I could disappear. I didn't want to know, didn't want to hear what he was going to tell me, the excuses, the reasons why I—

He said, "When I finally realized that my son was gone forever, I just wanted to forget . . . what had happened, everything I no longer believed. I stopped living, for a long time." He looked at me like he was really seeing me for once. I felt his own stolen memories stir inside me; the moment when he'd heard about his wife, the long years of hiding inside himself. . . . "Until the FTA offered me a chance to do real psionics research, to actually help psions in a way no one had been able to before. And then I met an Oldcity thief with telepathic amnesia, who always seemed to say the wrong thing and do the wrong thing, until finally I sent him away without really understanding why. . . . Maybe it was because I blamed you, for always making me remember things I wanted to leave alone. Because there is a resemblance. You have the eyes, and your age is about right. . . ."

I remembered the strange conversation we'd had once, back in his office at the Institute. "No. You're wrong. I never had any kin; none that wanted me, anyway."

"But you're not sure. You said you don't remember—"

"I remember. I remember always b-being alone." My eyes were shut against him. I felt him pushing me back toward the cliff edge of darkness at the end of my own memories, where something ugly waited to drag me down. (Don't. Don't.)

"Show me proof." The words rang in my head like heavy bells.

I had to make him leave me alone, and words would never be enough. So I showed him the only proof I could—jagged pieces of my life that would leave his crazy belief torn and bleeding: (I've never been a part of your memories!) I showed them both what it meant to stay alive in Oldcity, enough truth so there wouldn't ever be any more questions; and I showed them the fire and the ashes and the screaming. . . .

My eyes were open and I was staring at Siebeling again. He muttered: "I was wrong. I'm sorry," while his sickened mind shrank away from what it had seen.

But I realized that what I'd shown him hadn't really proved anything. Suddenly I hated myself, for letting him see even that much, and I looked down. I couldn't face Jule at all.

"I'm sorry." Siebeling said it again, too quickly. Relief filled his mind now. He wanted to believe it; he was glad I wasn't his son. It was all he could think about, glad his own son didn't have to live like that; he didn't care whether it had happened to me. . . .

"You bastard, I'd rather be dead than be your son!" I pushed myself up again. "So you still don't know about the kid, do you? If he didn't have to live like garbage—if he ain't a slave digging ore someplace right now because somebody didn't like his face? Well, maybe I hope you never find out!"

He slapped me. Jule stood frozen, staring at us like we must be out of our minds. Siebeling said, "I was right all along about what you were." And his mind was pushing it all down again. . . . He turned and left the room. Jule stood a second more looking at me; but the pain was too strong inside her, she disappeared without a thought.

(I hope you never find out!) I flung it after Siebeling, before I collapsed again in the tangled bedding. I lay still for a long time with a crushing ache in my chest.

11

I WAS HALFWAY up the hillside when my knees gave out. I almost managed to make it look like I'd meant to sit down. The view wasn't bad, except that you could still see the town, and I didn't want to think about it now—not the blank-walled room where I'd memorized every crack in the plaster from flat on my back; not the miners in the happy house down below it just waiting to spot my bond tag, or the psions waiting to spot a lie, or the spaceport, or anything else human. . . . I was free from all that, even if it was only for an hour, and all I really wanted was to reach the top of the hill. But in one and a half gravities I still felt like crawling, and I'd never have gotten this far without a stick in my hand and Dere Cortelyou walking beside me. He came up here whenever he could, "to get away from my mind," he'd said.

"Next time," Dere said, following my eyes and reading my thought.

"Yeah, sure." I answered him out loud, because like most human psions he wasn't used to not talking, or to having his questions answered before they were asked. There was a reason why humans didn't make more joinings. I wiped my forehead on the sleeve of my parka, feeling the cold spring air chill my flushed skin. *If there is a next time.* I didn't let him hear that; hadn't let him know what I already knew— that Rubiy had come back during the night. I was trying not to think about it myself, right now. It was too good just to be with somebody who felt sane and calm and didn't want anything from me.

Dere sat down beside me. I leaned back on my elbows; the soft thick moss grass was like velvet under my hands. The air smelled heavy with new life; rustling tendrils of bark spilled down the trunks of the trees. Beyond the golden green of young leaves the sky went on forever. Just thinking about how deep it was, how endless, made me giddy. All my senses felt more alive in this one moment than they'd ever been in my whole life—because in my whole life I'd never had a moment like this, in a place like this; and because with Rubiy back I knew more clearly than I ever had that I had to take it while I could. I wished that Jule could be with us, or that she could be sharing what was in my mind right now; that I could feel a poem take root in it, to crystallize the feeling and make it last forever.

But Jule's mind didn't lie open to my feelings or to my need the way it had before: *before I was well,* she told herself; *before I'd said what I had to Siebeling.* And knowing that, I kept away from her thoughts and shielded my own. "Where did all this come from?" I said, to keep myself from thinking, and Dere from wondering. I lifted a hand across the view of green. "Did it just happen?"

He laughed, folding a piece of bark between his fingers. "No. Life is rarely that simple." His mind shrank tight around the irony; for a second his mind screamed tension, out here where he could, before he got it back under control. Even he wasn't really sane and calm, playing spy in a nest of mind readers—especially not him. He'd been right before, back on Ardattee, when he'd told me that he wasn't much of a telepath. I knew it a lot better than he did now, with my new clearer mindsight; knew how hard he struggled to keep his thoughts to himself, and how afraid he was that he wouldn't be able to. But he was still the same Dere, and he couldn't leave a question unanswered. "Every species of living thing you see here was transported to Cinder from somewhere else, originally." He spat out the end of a camph and fished another one out of his jacket.

"By humans?" I said, starting to get interested. I watched his hands. "Gimme one of those," reaching out.

He shook his head. "Doctor's orders. You're still sick."

"I could be dead, tomorrow. All of us could." I wagged my fingers. "C'mon."

His cold-reddened face went a little gray; but he reached into his pocket and brought out another camph.

I stuck it into my mouth, and laughed once. "Funny."

"What?"

"How worried Siebeling is about my health now. He didn't give a damn what happened to me with Contract Labor."

He glanced at my bond tag. "Maybe he thought you'd be better off with them than you were in Oldcity." Always ready to excuse and forgive. "Contract Labor builds worlds. And it can give someone with no skills a chance to learn one. I've seen it work on Hadder's World— I've seen combine contract laborers who went on to good solid company jobs. The FTA colonized Sephtat with government contract labor, and now it's independent, one of the biggest exporters—"

I swore, and drove it into his brain with the rush of ugly memories that filled me up. " 'Builds worlds,' hell! It mangles them, and it uses warm bodies because they're cheaper than machines!"

He put his hands up to his head; brought them down again, slowly. When I saw his face, I was sorry, but I didn't let it show. I let him tell me he was sorry, instead; that he hadn't known what I'd been through, that I was right and he was wrong. Because I needed to hear it from somebody, even if it was only him. He said, "I know. . . . Ardan's a bitter man, hard on everyone—especially himself." The same thing Jule always said. "Not an easy man to understand, or love."

"Jule don't seem to have no trouble." I looked away, drowning my thoughts in the endless sighing green of the mountains.

"Jule has a gift most of us don't have." He didn't mean just her psi. "And she has the problems to go with it."

I chewed on the camph, watching the sky, the ribbons and veils of color against the deepening blue; until suddenly I heard what lay between the words. I looked back at him. "You're the one, ain't you? The one who—who stopped her from drowning; who told her about Siebeling and the Institute and the research?"

He nodded, glancing down, his smooth brows twitching. "It was dark. She doesn't remember, or recognize, me." He meant that he thought it was better that way.

"You done a good thing, anyway."

He sighed, plucking at wisps of moss grass. "To answer your question: no, the humans didn't bring life to Cinder. It was all here waiting for us when we arrived . . . along with the ones who brought it all here before us."

"You mean the Hydrans?" I sat up again, locking my hands across the ankles of my boots. "What the hell were they doing here?"

He shrugged. "I'm not sure. I'm not that familiar with Colonial history. Siebeling could probably tell you—" He broke off, seeing my expression. "Well, you can always . . ." He stopped again. "I can look it up for you." His job here was taking care of the tape library.

"Yeah, I know. . . ." I grinned a little. "If I ever get out of this, I guess I oughta take up reading." He laughed. "You know anything about the Hydrans? The ones here, they—they live inside that thing you told me about, a joining, all the time. Are they all like that?"

"Not that I've ever heard." He shook his head. "But they probably all have the potential, in a way humans don't—because they have every other psi talent anyone's ever discovered. They got the name *Hydran* because we encountered them first in the Beta Hydrae system—but it took on a double edge when we learned what they could do with their minds. Beta Hydrae is a star in the constellation they call Hydra on Earth; in human mythology the Hydra was a many-headed monster."

I made a face.

"But no one can really deny that they're more like we are than we want to admit. There have been xenobiologists who've claimed that Earth is a world of defective Hydrans—psionic deaf-mutes, mental cripples."

Something turned inside me; suddenly I was listening to him talk about humans like they were strangers, almost aliens. . . . "What happened, then? If the Hydrans could kill a human just by thinking about it, how come the Federation took over all their worlds?" Because I knew that was true; knew the Hydrans lived among humans like something less, the ones who were still alive.

His round face got soft with guilt. "They can't defend themselves." He opened his mind and showed me: just because they *could* kill with a thought, Hydran minds had developed in a way that kept them from ever doing it. If a Hydran killed another being, the act destroyed built-in mental guards; the telepathic shock of the death would recoil and kill the killer. They couldn't commit any violent act without sharing in the consequences. I realized then why the Hydrans here had never been able to drive out the human miners. And that it was why they'd been easy prey whenever the Human Federation decided it wanted something they had.

He showed me how once they'd had an interstellar civilization more highly developed than even our own—one that had been so different it almost seemed like magic to humans, because it was built on psi. It had passed its peak by the time we found them, and we hurried it on into collapse—taking what we could use and calling the rest worthless, like the frightened barbarians we were. . . . (I saw it all happening in Dere's mind, wrapped in his words.) We'd pulled down their cultures, ruined their worlds, destroyed millions of lives, and all they'd been able to bring against it was pleas and protests. That hadn't been enough to save them. I thought about Siebeling's wife. And now the last of their people were living like strangers on their own worlds, or relocated on worlds the humans used as dumping grounds, among the people who'd destroyed them and who despised them, because they couldn't kill the way humans could. . . .

And I thought about my mother, or my father; whichever one had been Hydran. And I thought about the one who must have been human. . . . I sat, chin on my knees, looking down the green slope at the far, glittering snowfields, and I didn't say anything for a while, because of the lump in my throat.

Finally Cortelyou said, "You don't know what happened to them?"

My parents. I tangled my thoughts, angry at letting myself slip that far. "I *know;* it's in here someplace." I touched my head. "I just can't *remember.*"

"Siebeling—"

"I don't want to talk about Siebeling." I cut him off before he could even finish the thought. I thought about the Hydrans instead—who shared everything, and knew everything about each other, even about me.

"Cat, what happened to you when you were with the aliens? Something did, I don't need Siebeling's pointing it out to know you're a hundred times the telepath you were."

I shrugged. "They did it. I dunno how. They made me join with them, and something just . . . came loose."

"You made a real joining? What was it like?" His voice was hushed, almost embarrassed. His mind filled with sudden, hopeless longing, with envy for what I'd shared . . . with a need and a bitter loneliness I'd never thought I'd see inside anybody else, especially him. But maybe it was there all along, inside every human being, that voice crying and never being answered. And maybe for a telepath, living like a one-eyed man in the land of the blind, the loneliness was worst of all.

"I . . . uh, well . . ." I looked at the ground, wishing I could show him somehow. Because I wasn't good at words; because words were too solid, too clumsy and heavy, never really meant to show what I felt anyway. . . . "It was—like all the highs I ever had, and all the burnouts. Confused and bright. A thousand voices singing all at once. . . . Like an ocean, like a whirlpool. . . . Like drowning. . . ." I moved my hands. (I don't know how to tell you.)

He half smiled. "I know." His own stubby hands clung together. "How did it make you feel?"

"Scared" was all that came out of my mouth. But I couldn't tell him that what made me feel that way was knowing it could fill my every need.

He was disappointed. I felt him force his mind away from it. "How good is your telepathy now?"

I looked up at him again. "Better than anybody I seen here."

He raised his eyebrows. "Better than Rubiy? That's what Siebeling claims you told him."

I pressed my mouth together. "Did he tell you to find out?"

"No."

"Then I'll tell you the truth. I dunno how good I am, compared to him. I never felt a mind like his. It's like a wall."

"Your mind is a wall to me now, when you want to keep me out. And it's as clear as the sky when you want to communicate."

"Yeah?" I stretched my arms, letting the stiffness out. But he was watching me too close, and I felt the stray thread of a thought tickle my own . . . *relief,* that I still didn't know his secret. . . . *His secret?* I eased further into his mind, following the strand back, not bothering to hide what I was doing. He tried to tangle his thoughts, to turn me away with confusions and distractions and half-truths leading nowhere. But I followed the true thought on and on, seeing the paths he tried to make me ignore and choosing them each time, feeling his panic grow. . . .

Until finally the truth burst into my mind: "Dere—you're a Corpse?"

He slumped forward. The tension that had been rising for months drained out of him at last, and only a dull weariness was left in his mind. "So it does show."

"You wanted me to do it—" It was half an apology and half a challenge.

He nodded, still hunched forward.

"Why? I mean—you, a Corpse? You said you were just a corporate telepath."

"And every one of you believed me. Jule and Ardan still believe it— for their own good. What I told you wasn't a lie; it just was not the whole truth. I do work for the Seleusid combine. But I'm part of their security force, their private army." Pride glittered in the words, but pride was cutting him up inside; and everything I knew about what it had cost him to get where he was and stay there was still true. He was still a paid snitch, used by deadheads who would never understand.

"How'd you get involved in this? Somebody order you to do it?"

"It was my idea. The FTA needed to know how to deal with psions, so they asked one. And I told them it would take psions to stop psions. I thought it would give us a chance to show them that we can be loyal, useful, productive citizens—"

"How many Hydrans have you helped Seleusid kick off their own worlds, Dere?"

He looked up at me then, his hazel eyes green with anger; but he looked away again. I didn't try to find out what he had to be ashamed of.

"Nothing," he said. "I have nothing to be ashamed of."

(But you got plenty to be afraid of.) If the rest of us thought we had a lot to hide from Rubiy, it was nothing compared to what was in Dere's mind. And he wasn't much more of a telepath than I used to be. "What did you think you were gonna do once you'd got in with Rubiy? What are *we* gonna do? You got any plans?"

I didn't think his face could get any grimmer, but it did. "Rubiy is a professional. He made sure we were completely isolated before we got to Cinder. There's been no way to get a message out, because there's always someone *listening.* Even when you can't see them, you can feel them. . . ." His fists clenched. "But the mines or the FTA have to be warned, somehow—and it has to be soon, before Rubiy comes back."

"You know what he's planning to do?"

The hazel eyes sharpened, for a minute he wasn't sure about me. . . . But then his mind loosened again, and he shook his head.

"Why should you trust me?" I said, realizing that he did. "Nobody else does."

He shrugged. "Because I don't have any choice, now. And because Jule trusts you. Like her, I think that if you were going to betray us, it would already have happened. . . . All I know is that you're supposed to be the long-awaited key to help them get into the mines."

"How?" I pulled my legs up under me.

"I was hoping you could tell me."

"They didn't show me no secret passages while I was in there, if that's what you mean." The muscles in my back were pulling tight again. "Galiess won't talk till Rubiy gets back, and she ain't given me a real chance to read her, if she even knows."

"Whatever it is, they seem to be sure it'll work this time. God knows what demands they'll make on the Federation."

(And God knows what'll happen to us. That's the worst part, ain't it? You know that if I can read your secret, so can Rubiy. Once he comes back your life isn't worth a damn, if you can't stop his plans first; maybe all our lives—)

"Stop it, for God's sake!" For a minute I thought he was going to hit me. "I'm sorry"—he took a deep breath—"but don't answer questions for me before you even ask them!"

I almost laughed. "Bet you never figured you'd be saying that to me." And I realized how much I'd begun to depend on my Gift; as if I'd grown another eye to see with, another ear.

Half a grin grew on his face. He fumbled for another camph and put it in his mouth. "That's for damn sure. My star pupil. . . ." His voice trailed. He handed me another camph.

I took the camph, balancing it between my fingers. Then I said, as gently as I knew how, "Dere, Rubiy's already back."

He froze. "When? How long?"

"Since last night."

"God . . ." he said. Suddenly his eyes unfocused; I felt circuits opening and closing in his brain, but what happened then was nothing my own mind could understand. He let out a cry, like something had torn him apart inside.

I jerked back, not knowing what was happening to him. *Rubiy?* But we were alone, even inside our minds; I was sure of it. "Dere?" I put out my hand, brushing his arm. "What's wrong?"

He shuddered; I pulled my hand away. He wiped his mouth. "I . . . I had a sending."

A sending . . . precognition. I'd almost forgotten that he was anything besides a telepath. "About what?" His mind was jumbled with shock, I couldn't read him.

"About death. My death. Rubiy . . ." His voice was weak and stumbling. "It's too late."

"No, it ain't. You're just scared it will be; it ain't sure. That's the wild card talent, you said it yourself."

But he shook his head, glaring his anger at me. "Not this time. It's in every image. Every one. And so is Rubiy. And so are you. . . ."

"Me?" I pushed up on my knees. "I ain't done nothin' to you. . . I ain't going to, I swear." (I swear it!)

He climbed to his feet, every movement belonging to a dead man. "I know. I'm sorry," he said thickly. "I need some time alone now." He stumbled on up the hill, not looking back. His flickering shadow trailed him like the darkness in his mind.

I sat where I was, alone inside my own darkness, until the sky started to darken to match it. I got up then, stiff and numb, and started back down the hill alone.

12

(HELLO, CAT.)

The sudden voice inside my head turned me around on the slope. I lost my balance and someone's hands caught me from behind, steadying me. Rubiy's.

"You shouldn't be out here alone. You're hardly steady on your feet." Rubiy smiled, but only with his mouth. I hadn't forgotten that smile, or anything about his face. I looked into his ice-green eyes, and saw the bottomless green of a crevasse: shining, shadowy, deadly. His hands were still on my shoulders, holding me like the talons of a hunting bird would hold some poor squirming thing it had trapped in the night. I knew the feel of hands like that. . . . I jerked loose with all my strength, staggering back.

"Did I frighten you?" He held out his empty hands to me, amused. He wasn't dressed for a walk outside, but he didn't seem to feel the cold.

I swallowed. "Takes—more'n a 'hello' to do that." The shock had knocked everything I'd been thinking a minute ago out of my head; I was glad. "I wasn't alone. I was with Cortelyou."

"I know," he said.

I didn't flinch. I kept my mind woven tight, with just enough ends dangling loose to make it seem like I wasn't trying to hide something. "He's still up there." I pointed with my chin. "I got tired," answering him before he asked.

He liked that; his face almost looked human. "You're old friends, I take it." There was something lying between the words that I didn't like.

"Yeah. I guess so." I rubbed my neck.

"I was pleased to learn that you were strong enough to go walking. Your recovery strengthens my trust in Siebeling and his skills."

"Yeah, he's all heart."

He raised an eyebrow. "You don't seem surprised to see me."

I shrugged. "Should I be?" I showed him that I knew how he'd tried the doors of my mind last night—and set off alarms.

He played with a smile again. "The telepath you were when I last saw you wouldn't have known. But I'm told the Hydrans did what those fools on Ardattee couldn't do for you. You're good; Galiess was right. You're even better than Galiess, in fact. . . . How good are you, now?" He threw it at me like a challenge, sparking with excitement, eagerness, hope—a dark glint of envy—dying to take my measure. That was why he was out here, why we were here alone.

I shied back from the first real contact I'd had with his emotions, the first proof that he even had any. "I—dunno. Good enough, I guess." It sounded dumb and sullen. I pushed my hands into my pockets and shifted my weight from foot to foot. My mind left his challenge lying in the air between us.

(Didn't I tell you so?) his mind said. He smoothed a strand of dark hair the wind had loosened. "False modesty doesn't appeal to me. But loyalty does. After the ordeal you went through, I would imagine you're ready to do anything you have to to help us take control of Federation Mining."

I nodded. "You made sure of that," taking a chance.

He shrugged, an easy twitch of his shoulders. "Siebeling made sure of that—in his clumsy, backhanded way. I merely made use of an opportunity." His thoughts were as cold as his eyes.

And a warm body. My hands flexed inside my gloves. "So now I got something you can use. Why am I so important, what's the deal?" I had to ask it, not really expecting him to answer.

But he said, "Until now we've been missing the key to get us into the mines compound. We'd been able to come this far, to reach the world and establish ourselves in the very town. But the identity screens at the mines are too rigid, and the security checks on their actual personnel are too complete. We couldn't get any further. We can't walk in, and we can't teleport in—you can't teleport to a place you've never been." The muscles in his cheek tightened with his jaw; for a second I felt his long months of frustration. "But *you* have been inside, now; thanks to Contract Labor. So we are able to manipulate them from a direction they never anticipated."

(Up through the sewers,) I thought. I realized he still hadn't answered my question.

(Exactly.) Cool laughter slipped into my mind.

"But I can't teleport—I can't get back into the mines. So what good's that gonna do you?" I felt a kind of relief as I said it, because I didn't see how—

My hand jerked out of my pocket with a sudden twist; but I hadn't done it, and he hadn't touched me. . . . *Telekinesis.* He had: my wrist hung in front of my eyes, showing me the bond tag. "You can go back any time you want to."

I was still a bondie. All I had to do was let someone know it. "But . . ." fighting to keep control of my voice, "but, I mean, so I'm back inside. I can't get out again. You're still outside. What good's that gonna do!"

(Cat.) His hand reached out and stroked my arm. His mind made soothing waves, but that didn't ease anything. And then I felt another whisper of real emotion, an echo of the images he'd shown me back in Quarro, telling me, *(he understood, I could trust him, he'd been where I'd been, he knew what I'd been through; we were the same. . . .)* "It isn't forever. Only a day or so. That's all I'll need, all I want from you. And then you'll be free again, and the Federation will be in our hands—" The energy of his vision crackled between us. "You can make a joining; you've made one before." It wasn't really a question; he knew about the Hydrans. He felt me acknowledge it, and then at last he began to show me his plan:

I was going to turn myself in, and they'd take me back to the mines. Once I was there Rubiy would make a joining with me, and use me as a fix to teleport himself into the mines. He knew the layout and he'd sabotage the ventilating system with gas, leaving them all unconscious, and the mines wide open for the rest of his psions to come in and take it over. Once they were in charge of the mines compound, they'd also be in control of the energy shield that protected Cinder from any direct attack as well as from radiation—an invisible wall of electromagnetic force out in space around us. And then we'd be in the control seat, holding the Federation's most important resource for ransom. The combines who'd hired him to do this, to attack the FTA at its heart, thought he was doing it for them; but they were wrong. . . .

His mind shut me out again, as if suddenly he felt like he'd shown me enough, or maybe too much.

I shook my head. "It—all sounds so easy." So easy it scared me.

"It is; now that we have you."

"I thought . . . I heard it ain't that easy to make a joining—not for humans."

"Not for the average human psion. We are not average, you and I. You had no trouble joining with the Hydrans."

"I didn't even have a choice, with them. But I thought there had to be a—a *need.*"

"I have a need—the need to see this plan work! And when the time comes, you'll find you have enough need to see the mines under our thumb. . . ." The promise in his voice made me feel worse than I already did.

"Why do we have to make a joining at all? Why can't I do what you want, there?"

"You haven't the skills, and you won't have the equipment. Besides, it may be—difficult for you to move freely." And besides, he wanted the triumph to be *his.* His eyes were alive now, searching my face, measuring my reaction. "Do your own part willingly and well, and I'll reward you. Believe me, this is only the beginning. You've had nothing all your life; now you'll have everything—"

Power sang through me—his power, my power, shared power, *(All this could be mine.)* It blazed up like wildfire, made me drunk, gave me a rush . . . and left me empty, as suddenly as it had come. (If you are loyal.) Rubiy left the words branded on my mind.

I shook my head, dazed, when I should have been nodding. And I couldn't stop myself from thinking about Cortelyou—not sure if Rubiy had put him back into my mind, or my own guilt had. "When—uh, when am I supposed to—go back?" I only said it to cover what I was thinking, but it was still hard to say.

"Soon. When I'm sure you're ready." He wasn't talking about my health. But in the back of his mind he was already sure that *we were the same.* He reached out, tracing the line of my jaw with his fingers, letting his arm slip across my shoulders. "You're a handsome boy, as well as Gifted."

I laughed nervously, wondering why the first person who'd ever said that to me had to be him.

"Galiess is envious of more than your telepathy, you know. . . ." His mind brushed against mine.

"I'm cold," I said, and it was the truth—suddenly I was cold to my bones. "I better go back down." I edged away.

"Of course." His hand closed gently around my arm.

"I can make it by myself."

"Of course." He let his hand drop again, brushing my hip. "You need a little more time . . . to think over the things I've told you."

I nodded. He disappeared. I made sure he was even gone from my mind before I went on down the hill, feeling afraid of something I couldn't even name.

By the time I reached town it was getting dark, even though it was only the middle of the day. Bright banks of lights were coming on in the streets, but they weren't enough to clear the settling of night. Cortelyou was still somewhere out in the hills; I could feel his mind dimly, distant and closed. The starport lay on my right, silhouetted by the glow of the landing grid eaten out of the hillside beyond it. A couple of cargo shuttles were sitting on the field; I recognized the insignia on the side of them both: Centauri Transport. I turned toward the port entrance, drawn by the sight of the ships.

The lobby was nearly empty. The floor was a tiled picture of the Crab Nebula, with a colored fountain spewing up from its center like the heart of an exploding star, all golds and reds. The walls were midnight blue, glowing with hidden light. I was surprised; the outside of the building looked like the warehouse it was. I stood blinking in the brightness until my mind caught a familiar murmur of thought, and I finally understood what had made me come: *Jule.* I found her with my mind before my eyes found her, standing behind a counter in a half-hidden corner of the room. Somebody in a Centauri Transport uniform was talking to her. At first I thought he was just another horny spacer trying to pick her up. Her irritation stung like hot needles.

But then he handed her something that looked like a message. She read it, and her mind flashed anger/disbelief/suspicion/anger. She wadded the message up and put it in her pocket. I couldn't tell what she said to the officer, but I read the cold refusal in her mind. He actually took her by the arm then, trying to pull her away from behind the counter. She opened up her mind and let him see what she thought of him. He dropped her arm and backed away like she'd slugged him. He almost ran toward the exit that led to the landing field.

I crossed the room to the shipping area; she was the only one there by the time I reached it. She started as she finally noticed me. She looked like I felt, shaken and exhausted. I moved to lean on the counter, needing the support.

(Don't do that!) Her voice inside my head made me pull back. (Your bond tag will set off alarms. Keep it away from things.)

I froze, tingling with panic, but nothing happened. Slowly I put out my left hand, watching her face. I leaned on it, pretending to relax, keeping my other arm clear. (Jule—)

Her gray eyes sent me a look that was almost angry. She was thinking about what it meant for both of us if anybody noticed. "You shouldn't be here, Cat. Galiess—"

(Can go to hell!) I made her wince. "Look, I . . . I need some information."

I felt her wondering why I couldn't have waited, or even asked her about it long-distance, mind-to-mind, with less risk. . . . And then I felt her suddenly *know* why, the way she always did.

Her face softened; she was realizing it had been too long— "Cat, I'm sorry about what happened before . . . for what Ardan said, and for what I didn't say. There was a lot of blindness. Even when you're a telepath—or an empath—it's still so easy to be wrong. Isn't it? . . ." She put a hand up to her eyes, and for half a second she wasn't seeing me. "Because we're still human beings first, always trapped behind a one-way glass of self-centeredness. And somehow that makes it so easy to say the wrong thing."

"I wasn't wrong." I hadn't expected this now. I felt my anger starting fresh, too easily. "I know what Siebeling was thinking. He'd rather have his son be dead than be me."

She shook her head. (No! Listen to what I'm trying to tell you.) "Ardan never meant he was glad you weren't his son. He was only glad that his son hadn't had to suffer what you did. You let yourself misread."

I didn't say anything; I only let myself remember. . . .

"He didn't know what the mines would be like for you. Cat, he didn't know." And she hadn't known, either; she was ashamed that she hadn't understood, that even with empathy she could never really go where I'd been.

Her eyes were hurting me. I looked away. I had what I'd wanted, her understanding; but there was still no sharing between us, only walls. What she said was true. A human could never trust or share completely, the way the Hydrans did. They'd always be too afraid . . . of seeing themselves.

I knew she was watching my face and thinking about things I wished she'd leave alone, angry at herself over me when she didn't need to be. I wanted to tell her that, but I didn't know how. So I said, "Jule, Rubiy is back," and I made myself look at her, just to stop her thoughts.

It worked better than I'd meant it to. Her mind tangled into a wild wall of defense, almost choking me out. She let it loosen again, relaxing but still on guard. "How do you know?"

"I've talked to him." I looked down at my hand, watched it tighten on the counter edge.

"And it made you afraid." She half frowned, because it wasn't for the reasons she'd expected. I felt her trying to read what was too out of focus even for me to understand.

"It ain't just that he's good, or even that he told me how he's gonna take the mines. . . ." Her eyes widened, but she didn't interrupt. "It's . . . there's something else, something more, that I almost caught: more than just what I can do for him, something he—wants. I mean, he wants *me.*"

Her frown sharpened, questioning.

"Yeah, like that. It's all right; I can handle that. But it's more than just that. Deeper. Stronger, like he wants—" *My soul.* I broke off. "I don't understand it; I don't think I want to understand it. Because that's what really scared me, Jule. Because . . . we were the same, once, him and me. . . ."

"And you might still be?" She shook her head, telling me, (Don't be afraid of that. There's no need.) "You were never alike, really."

And I told myself that as long as she believed that, it would be true . . . not really believing it, anyway.

"You said Rubiy told you how he plans to take the mines?" Her voice was barely louder than a thought.

I nodded, and showed her what he'd said.

"So it's true. He really has what he needs. . . ."

"Me." I made a face.

For a minute she couldn't even answer; her feeling of helplessness was so strong I could taste it. "When—when are you—is this going to happen?"

"I dunno. Soon." I couldn't refuse to go, or Rubiy would be on to us all. But if I did go. . . . I covered the bond tag with my hand.

She took a deep breath, silent again for a long minute. She was thinking that (we'd find an answer, we would, we'd find a way. . . .)

"What did that Centauri spacer want?"

"Nothing. He was just. . . . He tried to get me to leave Cinder. He had a 'cast from my father, saying I was in danger." Her mouth thinned. She wondered how they'd found her, how they could know unless they *knew.* . . . Her mind broke the chain of thought, sick with suspicion. "You said you wanted some information?" She forced the change of subject herself, this time. She spread her fingers over the terminal touchboard in front of her, trying to look calm.

I'd gotten enough that I didn't bother to ask why she hadn't tried to give the spacer a warning to take away. But if her family still wanted her safe . . . "Uh—information." I'd only said I did because I needed something to say; but now I realized that maybe I'd had a reason after all. "How often do ships come here?"

"Not often. Every few weeks Centauri sends a freighter—usually to bring supplies from the Colonies and pick up telhassium shipments. The FTA controls the traffic in this sector, and they keep Cinder as isolated as possible." Centauri again. I realized she probably knew more about shipping than anybody on this planet.

"But there's a ship in orbit here now. The one Rubiy came in on."

She nodded. "For another couple of days. Why?"

"Dere—Derezady needs to know."

"Why?" There was frustration in her voice.

"He didn't say." I couldn't tell her any more; what she didn't know couldn't hurt her. "How do people get on board? Does anybody watch, or check?"

"Of course." Another small frown formed, like a ripple on the face of water, and was gone.

"I'm not thinking of myself," I said.

She glanced down, and nodded once. "The security guards check every passenger; and all the guards are Rubiy's, so they double-check, to be sure Galiess intended the passengers to leave. But he knows that."

"What do you need to convince them?"

"I don't know. . . . Why don't you ask Galiess?" Jule's voice dropped to a whisper; her eyes looked past me in sudden warning.

I turned, almost forgetting to keep my hand clear, and saw Galiess coming toward us. She was wearing the same kind of heavy jacket I had on, and an expression that would've killed me if it could.

"What are you doing here?" Her hand closed on my sleeve, jerking me away from the counter. But she still didn't try to get into my mind. "Are you insane?"

"Jeezu. I was just looking around." I tried to look stupid.

"Don't lie to me." But all she meant was that she thought I was hot for Jule. (You're not invisible. While you wear a bond tag, you keep your face out of sight!)

"Okay. Don't get so tight about it." I pushed my hands into my pockets. "Look," I said, trying to get back on safe ground, "Rubiy told me everything—"

"When?"

"Half an hour ago."

(Already?) Her face reddened as she swallowed her anger. "Don't talk about that here."

I shrugged. "Don't worry. But he told me what he wants me to do. I'm an important part of all this. I want to know more about it, I'm sick of bein' shut up in a room. I ain't your prisoner," not so sure I wasn't.

But she nodded, stiffly, like someone forced her to do it. "All right, if that will keep you happy." She sounded like she was talking to a moron. I didn't care, as long as it got me what I wanted. I glanced past her at Jule, saw the confusion and surprise on Jule's face. I shrugged again.

As she led me away, she glanced back at Jule. "Isn't one man enough for you?" The envy in her voice was as sharp as a spear. I would've laughed, except that somehow it wasn't funny.

And that was how I got the back-alley tour of town, what there was of it. Galiess introduced me to a few of the psions who were working as shopkeepers and workers. She didn't tell them about what I was going to do, because she said it could endanger the plan. But still I felt a kind of excitement running through them, as if they knew their long wait was finally coming to an end. Most of them didn't pay much attention to me; I was just another hired brain. One or two of them looked at my face a little too long.

Galiess showed me what lay underneath the town, too: a network of tunnels and metal-walled rooms had been dug out beneath the buildings. They were used for storing the supplies the townies and miners needed to live—and now they were used for storing things that could make them die: weapons and equipment Rubiy had had smuggled in for his takeover. I asked all the questions I could, and all the while I was trying to figure answers to the ones I couldn't ask. By the time we'd seen it all, I was so tired I could hardly see straight. I let it show, stumbling and weaving on my feet. I could tell that Galiess was satisfied that she'd put me back in my place.

When she left me at my room, I collapsed across the bed and lay there for an hour before I even wanted to move again. But it had all been worth it. Because I'd already learned everything I needed to know, and made all the trouble I was going to; and she never even knew it. It was so easy. I got up and sat by the window with half a bottle of strange-tasting leftover brew; listening to the music drift up from below and flipping the torus coin I'd taken from her into the air—the coin that was Dere's ticket out of here. I had the key, and I was going to be the answer to everything; but not for Rubiy. And when they learned what I'd done, they'd all be so grateful—Dere and Jule and even Siebeling. He'd have to see I wasn't just the cheap gutter thief he thought I was. And Jule. . . .

The next day I found Dere picking at his food in the back room of the tape library. He looked totally burned out. After his wide-awake nightmare yesterday, I had a little trouble getting him to go for another walk; but I couldn't tell him what I'd done with all the psions and deadheads picking through the loops out front. Most of them were bored out of their minds, right then, but I didn't want to be the one to give them something to think about. Not yet. I finished most of Dere's food for him, and said finally, mind-to-mind, (Come on, you told me you needed to get away from it all. . . .)

His hands twitched on the scarred wood of the shelf where his food had been; his thoughts were jumbled. He got up then, and we went out the back way. I made sure all the way up into the hills that nobody followed us, even with their mind.

"It's safe," I said finally, sitting down on an outcrop of blue stone.

"For what?" When he got out a camph, his fingers weren't real steady.

"You want a way to stop what's happening, Dere?"

He didn't answer; he didn't need to. Finally he said, "So you think you have one?" He almost didn't want to ask, too afraid of being disappointed.

"I know I do." I grinned. "There's a ship in orbit right now. I know how you can get onto a shuttle at the starport. And I've got the thing you need to do it."

"How did you learn—"

"I was with Galiess. I picked her brains." I held my hand out, showing him the small brass coin with a square hole through the middle of it. It was from Galiess's homeworld; she was the only one here who carried them. "She uses these as her marker. Give this to the guards at the port, and tell them you have to go up to the ship. Say, 'Special check,' and *believe* she sent you. That's all you gotta do. They'll let you by."

"My God . . ." His own gloved hand closed over the coin. He put it in his pocket like a jewel. "How—where the hell did you get it?"

"I picked her pocket, too."

He stared at me like he didn't believe it.

I shrugged. "It was easy. I'm pretty good. I had a lot of, uh, on-the-job training."

He laughed, for the first time since I'd seen him here, and clapped me on the shoulder. Suddenly he looked ten years younger, and felt like it, too. "If I can get to that ship, I can radio a warning from orbit. . . . What about Galiess? Will she miss this?" He patted his pocket.

I shook my head. "She's got dozens. She'll never miss one. But check out the ship's crew before you trust them. Some of them may be playin' both sides. . . . Just keep your mind together, that's all you got to do."

His expression turned to something I couldn't read; for a minute he was looking at me like he'd never really seen me before. But then he took a deep breath and said, "Does anyone else know about this? Ardan, or Jule? Did you tell them about me?"

I shook my head again.

"Good. Let it stay that way. What they don't know can't hurt them. You can handle it." He smiled. "Sometimes I think you're the only one of us who can."

"Yeah, sure." I thought about Rubiy yesterday, wondering if I should tell him about my "interview." But the memory of his death-sending was too close to the surface inside him, eating at his control. I was afraid to push it, afraid to say anything that would make him doubt himself now. "Just make sure the FTA remembers what side I'm on when they come to get us out of this, will you?" I held up my wrist, letting the bond tag show. "They ain't been too grateful so far."

He laughed again. "Don't worry."

"I always worry." I let my arm drop.

(Because of you, I think our worries are finally over.) He grinned at me. (Thank you. Thank you.)

I smiled then too, felt the smile get wider and stronger as we started back down the hill; thinking that maybe I'd finally done something right.

13

I PULLED ON MY sweater in a back room at the port hospital as Siebeling finished telling me, with all the enthusiasm of an undertaker, that I was just about healthy. Jule had told him everything about Rubiy's plans for me and the mines.

But I couldn't even tell him there was nothing to worry about. I took out a camph and stuck it into my mouth, just to watch him frown. I offered him the pack and he shook his head, frowning deeper. And then it happened. The box dropped out of my fingers as the wave of cold terror flooded my mind—not my terror *(fusion, confusion)*; somebody else's, somebody I knew too well. . . . *Cortelyou.*

"What is it?" Siebeling's face was full of surprise now.

"I . . . I . . . something's gone wrong." The words slipped out before I could stop them.

"I can see that. Are you in pain? What—" The words blurred into meaningless noise.

I covered my ears with my hands. "Shut up! I'm trying to hear something." But the terror had choked off. There was nothing left for me to trace through the maze of too much mind noise that was the hospital and the starport beyond it. . . . *The starport.* He'd been close by, and a slip like that could only mean one thing. He'd tried to get to the ship, and something had gone wrong.

"Cat? Cat—" Siebeling was shouting at me. I focused on his face again, saw his eyes, felt his tension turn into fear. I couldn't deal with it. I left the room, left him shouting after me.

I almost ran through the hallways that led to the starport; reaching ahead with my mind but not finding Cortelyou or any answers. I came out into the hall with the mosaic floor; but no one there felt anything strange now, no one looked angry or betrayed. Then I felt the touch of Jule's thoughts; saw her in the distance, doing what she was supposed to, but letting me know by a whisper of feeling that she'd caught Cortelyou's fear and knew something was wrong.

But before I could even answer her, someone was beside me. Rubiy. For a minute I thought he'd actually teleported into the middle of the starport. But then I realized that he'd walked in, just like anyone else— I just hadn't sensed him coming. Somehow I managed not to jerk or shudder; somehow I choked off the panic that splintered my mind at the sight of him.

"You shouldn't be here," he said. "Galiess warned you that it was dangerous."

I tried to shrug. "I just . . . wanted to see Jule." *What did he want —what?*

"See her in less obvious places. Come with me, instead. There's someone else I want you to see. Something I've been waiting to show you." He took hold of my arm. I turned away with him, knowing I didn't have a choice. Could it be he didn't know about Dere? Everything about him was as empty as a clear sky. He could've been inviting me to look at the sunset. But somehow I knew it wasn't going to be that simple. "You're on edge," he said. His grip tightened a little on my arm.

"It's an old habit."

We left the starport and walked down the street a way. The wind was even colder than usual, and the sky was a lid of heavy, mud-colored clouds. The streetlamps were shivering to life even though it was barely midmorning. It made me think about Oldcity. And then I was back to wondering about Dere, and trying not to. We reached the general store that Galiess had shown me a couple of days ago. It looked closed to me, but Rubiy unlatched the door and we went inside. The store was closed; no one was there. We went down into the storage tunnels.

Galiess was waiting for us, with a stungun and a couple of psions I didn't know—men, heavy and tough-looking, dressed in the uniforms of port guards. And Dere, standing like a rumpled bird between them, under the gun. I stopped dead at the foot of the steps as his eyes found me. "What—?" saying it to cover the sick lurch of my thoughts; knowing exactly what.

Dere swayed as he saw me—as his death-sending turned to reality. The guards took hold of him, holding him up. My hands tightened on the rough wood of the railing.

Rubiy turned to look back at me, measuring my reaction; I felt the minds of Galiess and the two guards beating against my control. "What's goin' on?" I said it again, keeping my voice steady. "Dere?"

Dere, don't give out, don't lose it all now, for God's sake. I didn't even dare to reach out and share strength with him; I just tried to make myself believe I didn't know what it was all about, hanging onto the confusion to save my life. Believing that they couldn't know the whole truth yet or we'd all be dead. *Wouldn't we? Don't even think about it!* The muscles in my face were frozen; I felt like I'd come down with lockjaw.

Dere didn't answer, either. The knowledge that his own death was looking back at him with my eyes turned his mind into jangling noise. . . . I realized that he was letting it feed, using his fear to block out the other knowledge that he couldn't afford to let slip. He hadn't been a telepath all his life for nothing.

"I'm afraid Cortelyou has more to answer for than he's willing to admit to you," Rubiy said. The confidence in his voice made my breath catch.

"I don't get it." I shook my head. "What've you got a gun on him for?"

"Because he tried to reach the crew of the ship that's in port just now, and warn them about what we're planning to do here. Fortunately he spoke to someone who works for me."

I felt the bottom drop out of my thoughts, even though I'd been expecting it. . . . *My idea, it was my idea.* I turned it into disbelief, betrayal. "Dere, you did that? Why? We could—we could get rich. . . ." I mouthed all the words I should have been saying, while my eyes tried to read his face for blame. *I didn't set you up, I swear—* choking off even the thought.

And the answer was there: that he knew, he didn't blame me, I was only a tool of a fate no one could control. . . . "For the greater good, Cat." His voice was steady now, but his face was the color of chalk.

"You're leaving out whose greater good," Rubiy said mildly. "Derezady Cortelyou is a Corporate Security agent. I've known his real identity ever since Ardattee. I brought him here in order to be sure he remained harmless to us . . . and to see whether he betrayed anyone else from the Sakaffe Institute."

"And since we haven't learned anything yet, I think it's time we stopped waiting and probed." Galiess bared her glance at me, letting me know she was sure I'd been in this with Cortelyou, and that Rubiy would see for himself when he took Dere's mind apart.

I felt my eyes go wide. I turned the shock of his knowing the truth about Dere into the shock I ought to feel at hearing about it. "Dere, you're a Corpse?" The words grated against the memory of my saying them for real. "How could you work for them—you're a psion!"

He pulled loose from the guards' hold and stood straighter between them. "Yes, I am a Corporate Security agent. And I'm proud of it." He met Rubiy's stare for the first time. "I'm doing all I can to prove that a psion can live a normal life among other human beings."

"You call it a normal life, serving as a lackey to the law that oppresses us?" Rubiy's face came alive. "You're a coward, a parasite, a traitor! We're not human beings, and we never will be; not to the deadheads. We have to strike back. If we want justice, we have to take it!"

"Then you make yourself less than a human being—you can't blame that on your victims." Cortelyou lifted his chin, and I felt his mind fill with a kind of hopeless courage, the way Rubiy's was filled with hate. Dere was challenging Rubiy, feeding his fury and making it hotter. "Two wrongs only make a greater wrong. We can only make the deadheads see us as no threat if we *are* no threat. They'll let us live a normal life among them only if they aren't afraid of us. We have to work within the law—it's the only way. It's the renegades who make them afraid, and bring down punishment on us all." Dere caught my eyes and pointed at Rubiy, his hand trembling with anger—or fear. But none of what he said was meant for me.

"But it doesn't work that way!" Rubiy's own hand jerked like he was throwing something away. "I know it doesn't—and he knows it doesn't!" He glanced at me. "They'll do to us what they did to the Hydrans if we don't fight them. Cat knows what it feels like to crawl, to carry the hatred of the world on his back. He never had a chance at anything better because he was born a psion—even though he was born to be better than any human who ever lived." And he wasn't seeing me when he looked at me—he was seeing himself. "This is why I brought you here, Cat. You call this man your friend. But now I want you to see him for what he really is—a puppet, a traitor to his own kind, who wants us to lose everything we've worked for, everything we deserve. I let him have the freedom to do what he did because I wanted you to understand his crimes, and the kind of punishment he deserves. Do you understand?" The whipcrack of his voice stung me.

I glanced from him to Dere, back at him again, feeling a band of pain tightening in my chest. I nodded, all I could do. Knowing with a kind of despair that I did understand: that he was right; but so was

Cortelyou. And that both of them were just as wrong. My hands twisted the stiff leather of my belt.

"Name his punishment," Rubiy said softly, letting me know what he wanted to hear.

I didn't answer.

"Go on, Cityboy!" Dere said. "You always were a leech, looking for a quick credit and an easy way out. You're two of a kind. He'll kill me anyway—tell him what he wants to hear. Tell him I have to die!" And his eyes under the birdwing brows begged me, *(Say it, say it—)*

"Kill him." The words were acid in my mouth. "He deserves it, kill him!"

Rubiy smiled.

"Wait—" Galiess said suddenly.

But it was already happening. I felt the power surge, and Rubiy uncoiled a lash of psi energy. Dere's face twisted; his hands flew up to his chest. His mind filled with fear and outrage and all the things you scraped up from the bottoms of nightmares, went white-black with agony. . . . And then it was empty, and he was falling.

The railing of the stairs bit into my spine as I sagged against it, holding myself up with my hands, blind, deaf, and numb. All my senses stopped as my mind closed down to save itself from his death. They came back little by little, until I could watch Rubiy move to Dere's body, stand looking down at his face; still smiling the same inhuman smile. He'd reached out with his psi and stopped Dere's heart in his chest. He'd just killed a man in the most personal way anybody could think of, but there was no sign of it on his own face. He blocked so perfectly that he didn't feel a thing. . . . *No.* He'd felt something: he'd enjoyed it.

He turned back to me, but I kept my eyes on Dere. My mind kept searching for Dere, feeling the nothingness inside me where he'd been. I could see him, I could almost touch him; but I couldn't feel him at all. *Dead.* He was dead. He was gone and he'd never come back. And it was all my fault. . . .

"Have no regrets," Rubiy said. "He was our enemy."

"He was my friend." I looked up at him at last.

"Look at him!" Galiess moved suddenly, the stungun still in her fist; she pointed it at me like a finger. The two guards stirred beside her, the expression coming back into their blank, stunned faces. "He's involved, I tell you. You're a fool if you can't feel it. And you let Cortelyou die

without probing him, when you could have learned everything, the
truth!"

Rubiy turned back to her—angry, but not making a move to stop her.
"You're right," he said, and lifted his hands. "Of course. As ever, my
teacher and my guide. But we can still learn the truth . . . we still
have Cat. We'll let him prove whether you're wrong about him. You
have nothing to hide, do you, Cat?" Back to me.

"No," I whispered.

"Then open your mind to me." He'd been waiting for this; I saw the
hunger for it come into his eyes.

I shut my own eyes, focusing inward. For a minute I thought I
wouldn't be able to unweave the bruised and battered wall of my guard,
because I hated what was going to happen so much. But if I refused
him, I'd die just like Dere, and all for nothing. . . . I forced myself to
let go, felt the fabric of my mind begin to loosen and separate; making
filaments of thought into gateways, dropping my guard strand by strand
and welcoming him in.

Cold maggot-fingers of thought crawled into my mind, heavy and
clumsy; he didn't bother to be gentle about it. Probing further and
deeper into every twist and secret place, he pulled out all the things it
wasn't his right to see, helping himself like he owned me, like I was
nobody, not even human—using me the way they'd done at the Institute, the way even the Hydrans had done. And I had to let him . . .
had to hate him, like I'd hated all the others; had to hate myself, my
stinking half-breed blood, the reason why they all did it to me.

And somehow I still had to make myself believe the lies snarled up in
the strands of my own thoughts, lose him somewhere in the tangle of
half-truths woven to cover the real truth. I turned him away again and
again, until he was dizzy and dazzled, until I felt him begin to withdraw. . . .

But he still wondered. And so he tried once more, with a sudden hard
blow that hit me like a fist. Old fears rose to help him, and for a piece
out of forever I couldn't hold onto my control. The lies slid and
smeared into everything else, and I didn't know if I even. . . . And
then he came up against the locked door of the secret room in the
deepest pit of my soul, and heard something behind it, screaming. He
tried to force the block, but he couldn't. I wouldn't let him, not even to
save my life. And finally, after a time that seemed like forever, he
backed off. I knew then that he'd finished with me at last. He let me go,

he thought he knew my limit, he'd taken everything there was to get, he was satisfied . . . he was still the best.

I stood at the bottom of the stairs, my hands locked over the railing; realizing that my mind was really my own again, and it was over. *It was over* . . . I'd beaten Rubiy. And he was the best.

"He's innocent. He knew nothing about Cortelyou's real identity; none of them did." Rubiy's voice reached me from another world; his hand smoothed my hair back from my sweating face. "They are exactly what they seem to be. Are you satisfied?"

And Galiess: "If you are, Rubiy." The stungun trembled in her hand.

I turned and climbed the steps without waiting for a dismissal. I made it all the way through the silent, empty store and out to the street before I got sick to my stomach.

14

IT WAS POURING rain outside. The noise it made on the roof of the
covered walkway was like the end of the world. I could barely even hear
the bunch of mine workers laugh at me as they staggered past. "Wha'sh
the matter, sonny, can't hold your—"

"Have a little hair of the—"

"Didn't I see you somepla—?"

I pushed away from the building and the drunken questions and
stumbled out into the street. The sleeting rain drenched me and froze
me as I walked, until my body was as numb as my mind. I didn't know
where I was going to until the door slid open and I was looking at Jule.

"Cat?" She blinked at me like her mind was light-years away.
"Where were you? What . . ." I didn't say anything. She stood aside to
let me in.

Siebeling was there, sitting on the couch in the one large room that
was her apartment. He stood up when he saw me. I didn't mind seeing
him for once—it was right that he should be here, we all shared this
together. "Dere is dead."

(Dead, dead? dead? . . .) It echoed from my mind into theirs and
back again.

(I knew, I knew something—) Jule's face twisted. "Oh, God!"

Siebeling sat down again, as if his legs wouldn't hold him up. "How
do you know?" Even his voice was weak.

"I was there." My own voice shook; I hardly knew it for mine. Jule's
eyes came back to my face. "Rubiy . . . he just . . . stopped it,
Dere's heart. Just like that." I snapped my fingers. "Just like . . .
that."

Jule took my arm and led me to a chair at her table. I stood staring at
it until she made me sit down. She brought shawls and sweaters and
wrapped me in them, before she sat down across from me. *"Why,* Cat?

What happened at the spaceport? You felt it too, I saw you come in, and you knew. But then Rubiy took you away."

I nodded, pressing my hands together on the tabletop to stop them from trembling. The old fight scars on my knuckles stood out white and silver against my skin. "He made me watch. Dere—Dere tried to warn the ship that was in port . . . only, they turned him over to Rubiy! Rubiy knew—he knew all along what Dere was. . . ."

"He knew?" *(He knew?)* Words and thoughts jumbled. (Us, he knows about us—?)

(No!) I projected it without trying to. "Dere was a Corpse! That's what he knew—and that's all he knows!" I didn't have enough control left to keep their half-shaped questions out, so I took hold of their minds and made them understand: how Rubiy had used Cortelyou, always knowing that in the end he'd have to kill him. How he'd trapped Cortelyou in a betrayal to test my loyalty. How Dere had made Rubiy angry enough to kill him without probing him, because he knew that if Rubiy did he'd learn the truth about us all. . . .

Their relief and understanding filled me; but then the feelings changed again, to horror and guilt, as the real understanding hit. Words came out of their mouths, sounds of grief that didn't even register when the real grief was drowning my mind.

". . . and he just let you walk away from it?" Siebeling's voice broke through as his mind started to focus again. "He didn't even question your story, or ours?"

"Yeah, he questioned me." I looked up again at him, glaring, and touched my head. "He probed *me,* to get the truth." I pressed my hands together again; my bond tag rattled on the wet tabletop.

"After he made you watch a man die?" Jule's hand crossed the table between us and closed over mine.

I nodded, not trusting my voice for a minute. "But—but—I tricked him, Jule, I still kept him away from us. I couldn't let him win, after . . . after Dere . . ." My mind was still searching, still finding nothing. "But I had to be open to him, I had to let him have anything he wanted, so he wouldn't suspect. And I hate it, when they do that, I *hate* it. God! It's like . . . like being . . ." I bit my lip, shaking my head. And the human part of me wondered how the Hydrans could show their entire lives to everyone, to a bunch of strangers.

"They don't share their lives with everyone," she murmured. "They never join with humans, with strangers—only with each other, with someone they know as their own. And the important thing is that their

privacy is given, not taken. That's the difference between a joining and a
—a violation." Her head filled with pasts; she broke away from my
mind, let go of my hands. One of her hands rose to her mouth, she
started to bite a nail.

I caught her hand and pulled it down. I touched her mind; the shared
feeling grew, warm, bright, and strong between us again. I knew that it
wasn't the Gift I hated, any more than I could blame fire because
someone had used it to burn me. And I knew that if I was given a
choice right now, I wouldn't change what I was. "I guess it is. And I
beat him. That's the important thing." *I beat Rubiy.*

"You expect us to believe that?" Siebeling said suddenly. His mind
drove between us. "Rubiy probed you and he didn't learn anything? He
set Dere up and used his murder just to test you? Why you? Why not all
of us?"

"Because—because I'm his key. Because Dere was my friend. Because—" *Because he wants me.* "How the hell do I know!" My fist came
down on the table.

"It's a lot easier for me to believe that maybe you set Cortelyou up.
Jule told me you were asking about ships—for Cortelyou you said. That
you went out of the spaceport with Galiess afterward." His thoughts
were turning on me, to keep from turning on themselves.

"Dere was scared Rubiy would learn what he really was, and find out
about us all. He needed a way to get a message out fast. I found one for
him."

"And got him killed."

"Yes!" I pushed up out of my seat. "But not because I was tryin' to!"
Still knowing it was my fault, *my fault.* . . . Touching the hole in my
mind that someone had filled who'd been more of a friend to me than a
whole city had back on Ardattee. I sat down again and put my head in
my hands.

"You can't even hide your guilt. Why just Cortelyou? Because he was
Corporate Security? Why didn't you betray us all? Or maybe you have
already, and we just don't know it. You're vicious, lying gutter filth, and
that's all you'll ever be!"

"You bastard—" I moved in my chair, my hands turning into fists.

But Jule was beside me suddenly, her hands on my shoulders. (No,
Cat, no, no. . . .) "Stop it, Ardan!" Her mind was a shield protecting
me, absorbing Siebeling's anger and turning it aside. "Not again, not
this time. He's telling the truth."

He's telling the truth. Rubiy's words echoed hers in my mind, making my stomach twist.

"He claims he could convince Rubiy that black is white. He could be doing the same to us."

For just a second I felt her mind waver and search. "No. The wound is too deep. I know him. He couldn't lie that deeply to me. You're wrong, Ardan." Her voice faltered. She lifted her head as if she was afraid of a blow; but it passed. "He came here for help, he's been through something terrible. If you can't believe him, then believe me, at least. You have to believe someone."

Siebeling stood up. A wave of blind hatred washed over him, and I couldn't tell who he hated more, me or himself. . . . "I don't need anyone to tell me the truth! That we're caught in a trap because I got us into this. . . . That because of him we have no hope of getting out of it again! He betrayed Cortelyou. He'll help Rubiy take over the mines and blackmail the Federation—his only loyalty is to himself. He's an irresponsible kid, he's never done an unselfish thing in his life. If you expect anything better of him, if you keep protecting him, then you're committing suicide. But that doesn't matter anyway, because when he's ready he'll betray me—and you, too." He started toward the door. Jule's fingers dug into my shoulders until I winced, but she didn't answer him.

He stopped at the door, his hand on the open-plate, and turned back. He glanced from her to me and back at her again; something happened between them for a long minute that they closed me out of. But his face didn't change. "I don't need that. I don't need anyone." He went out the door and he didn't come back.

Jule's hands let me go, I heard her move away from me. I slumped in my chair, fumbling in my pockets for the pack of camphs. I found it, stared at it for a minute, thinking about Dere. And then I crumpled the whole pack and threw it at the door. "Shit!" I stood up. "I didn't mean for it to happen! Dere was my *friend,* I only wanted to help him. Why don't he believe that! Why can't he—" I stopped, as I saw her face. She was standing very still, and I thought no one should have to feel what I saw then in her eyes. She was trying to keep control, *(but her emotions were too strong for her, they'd always been too strong, and now. . . .)* A rush of agony poured out of her mind.

I took a deep breath, clenching my hands:

$$\left(\begin{array}{c} \text{what's wrong?} \\ \text{Jule . . . } \text{you want me out of here?} \\ \text{are you all right?} \end{array}\right)$$

She looked at me with panic in her eyes, and a tear slipped out and down. "Damn it, Cat!" Then all the tears broke free and she was sobbing, (Don't do that!)

I hung onto my chair. "I'm sorry."

"It's—not your fault. It doesn't matter. He doesn't matter. . . ." Her hand rose to cover her mouth. "How could I be so blind!" Siebeling. Siebeling had made this happen. "Jule, he didn't mean it." "You know . . . what he said. And you know it was the truth. He doesn't need me. He doesn't even want me, he doesn't care."

"He couldn't have meant it like that. He knows you . . ." I fell over the words, feeling helpless, feeling like a fool. "Better than anybody." *Except me.*

"It is true! He's felt that way . . . ever since he lost his wife and son. I thought this was different, that I was. But I was wrong again!" She bit her lips, wiping at her eyes.

I went to her and put my arms around her. She held onto me, sagging against my shoulder, sobbing again. Her grief filled my mind and became my own; until just for a second I wanted to break away. But I knew that everything had already gone far beyond that, and at least I had to give her something to hold onto.

And she said, so softly I barely heard it, "I hate everything." I held her closer, feeling her warmth, and kissed the shining midnight of her hair. "No, Jule, no. . . . Everything's gonna be all right." My throat was so tight that I could barely get the words out. My mind accepted her need, the way her mind had always accepted mine; asking no questions, only trying to show her that she wasn't alone, she'd never have to be alone. . . .

And after a while the sobbing died away. I swallowed hard and said, "Jule . . . I never learned a poem in Oldcity that you'd want to hear. How about a joke?"

Jule pulled back to look at me as if I'd lost my mind, and I grinned. "What would a five-hundred-kilo talking rat say?"

She shook her head. "I—I don't know."

Dropping my voice about an octave, I said, " 'Here, kitty, kitty . . .' "

She said, "Oh . . ." She started to giggle, and then she started to laugh. For a minute we stood there like a couple of idiots, laughing, and the tears were still running down her cheeks. And then I wasn't sure I had the right to, but I said, "Do you want to talk about it?" She stiffened against me, against answering; but then she nodded. We sat down again at the table. I watched her with her face in her hands and her dark hair slipping down. For the first time I noticed the wildflowers she'd brought in to make the room her own, wilting now between us in a bowl. They smelled like spring.

She didn't say anything for a while. She almost seemed afraid to look at me. "It's stupid . . . how hard it is to talk about yourself . . . it's such a stupid story." But she opened her mind at last, and began to show it to me.

I entered the memories as she let them rise: memories of a little girl whose mind always made her feel too much when she looked at everyone; who had to share every emotion, and couldn't even keep her own to herself. . . . Memories of growing up in a shining, empty world where objects had more meaning than human lives, with people you *knew* didn't care about you, or even each other, anymore. . . . Knowing that your very existence was a humiliation to them, another blow driving them further apart. Memories of finally leaving them and your whole life behind, because you couldn't live with your own emotions and their lack of them any more. Moving on and on, trying to escape what there was no escape from—living everyone else's hurts and hatreds and lacks, because you couldn't help it. Caring about their pain, because you couldn't help it; being used and hurt, again and again, because you cared too much. And all she wanted was peace, and someone she didn't have to be wrong about.

But then she was remembering Siebeling, she'd really believed he was the one— A sob caught in her throat. *(Because it was all true. . . .)*

"Jule, what are you ashamed of?"

"I drive everyone away! I'm weak. I'm neurotic, I don't know how to have a real relationship. I tried to drown myself—I couldn't even live with myself."

"It ain't true." I shook her gently. "There's nothing weak about you. Humans . . . shouldn't have to live inside everyone else, too; they have to have protection. But when you're born a freak, you don't have it, and nobody else knows how to give it to you. . . . I mean, it was never your fault. You can't blame yourself for the way you were born."

She frowned.

"I know what I'm saying, Jule," knowing I wasn't saying it right. "Listen to me. You're no fool for trying to love him, or wanting his love. And anybody who'd ever let you go is the real fool."

She sighed, a long, shaky sigh.

"Siebeling don't blame you for suffering, for hurting. He helped you learn to stop having to feel everything and be hurt by it. He knows how hard it was." If he was even half of what she thought of him, he did; but right then I had a hard time pretending to belive he was even human. She almost smiled, but then her face twisted like she still didn't know what to feel.

"He didn't mean it, Jule. I ought to know, if anybody does. He's half out of his mind over what's happening here; he ain't thinking straight, he's too full of guilt and too confused. Ain't that what you kept trying to show me? He didn't even know what he was saying." And I didn't think about what I was saying, didn't choke on the words, only wanting to say whatever I had to to make her stop feeling that way. "He's scared and angry, because he's in love with you, and he's afraid to admit it because he's afraid of losing you like he lost his wife."

She stood up. "Is it true—?" She shivered.

"It's all true." I just let it come, not sure where it was coming from, not even sure who I was talking about anymore, because— "Because he ain't the only one who feels that way." I only knew what I'd said after the words were out—and it was only after I heard them that I knew they were true. (I love you. I love you.)

She reached out across the table and took my hands. She kissed me once—my mind filled up with her emotions, with all the tenderness I'd ever known. She whispered. "Thank you, Cat . . . you're the best, the only real friend I've ever had." She looked up at me again, with her storm-cloud eyes.

But her lover would always be Siebeling. And as I understood that, something snapped inside me, like a broken-off piece of her pain. Suddenly I was five years old, hurting so bad I wanted to cry. Why him? Why did it have to be him, why couldn't it be me? I'd never had anything!

But love was blind, they said, love was crazy—love didn't have any heart, and so it ripped out your own. Jule had taught me how to care; I knew I'd never be able to stop caring about her now. I moved around the table and held her again, just for a minute, pretending she was mine. And then finally I said, "It's gonna be all right. Everything's gonna be all right. I promise you."

I left her apartment, and went out into the night.

15

I TURNED ON the light.

"How the hell did you get in here?" Siebeling leaped up out of his chair; he'd been sitting like a stone in the darkness of his room. The look on his face was worth the effort.

"Slip's secret." I twitched my mouth. "And what the hell do I want —since you're gonna ask that next. I'm here because you got only two people you can count on in this snakepit, and you left both of them bleeding. I came to make you listen to some true things, you piece of—"

"Get out."

"Uh-uh." I shook my head, moving toward him, feeling the grief and rage caught inside me build again at the sight of him. "I ain't getting out of here until I make you understand." I reached out and caught him by the front of his thick sweater, and shoved him up hard against the wall. He started to struggle, but he hadn't learned to fight on the streets. I pinched a nerve; he yelped and stopped struggling. "Yeah, that's right, Doc. I can be everything you think I am, if you make me. Don't make me do it—because it ain't what I want." I let go of him and backed off. "I just want you to *listen.*"

He straightened away from the wall, his eyes dark with confusion and sudden fear. He rubbed his neck. "All right. Say what you came to say." He moved back to the deep-cushioned chair and sat down in it again. He didn't relax any.

I stayed where I was. "First, I'm gonna tell you once more, I'm on your side!" I didn't try to make him believe it, didn't even touch his mind, because he was so sure I was going to use my psi against him. "I know you don't wanna believe it, because you know better than anybody why I ought to cut your strings. And you don't figure I could give a damn about anybody but me—why should I, right? You sure as hell don't. It's your kind that made me believe it, all my life. But everybody ain't like you. Jule ain't. And Dere—wasn't. And Rubiy—" I took a deep breath. "You don't understand what he really is, you don't know! I *know*. He's an iceman, a psycho; anything you ever thought about him ain't close to sick enough! He murdered Dere and he enjoyed it, and I want to make him pay. I'd cut off my own hand before I'd work for him, can't you understand that? I'll do anything I have to do to bring him down—and to make sure he never hurts Jule. Anything! Even if it means saving you." I glanced down. "And maybe I even owe you that much." I looked up again. "I never want to owe you nothin'."

He settled deeper in his chair, glaring at me. But he was listening.

"You think everything's lost, don't you, now that—now that they caught Dere. You got us all into this, and now you think we're as good as dead and it's all your fault." I felt the surge of his guilt and knew I was right. *Welcome to the club*. "So you're just gonna give it all up, cut everything and everybody loose and just sit here in the dark waiting till it's over—just like you done with your whole life after your wife and your kid were gone. I'll bet they'd be real proud to see what you're made of, and what they did to you. . . ."

His fingers sank into the soft arms of the chair like it was flesh.

"Well, I got another answer for you, since you're not looking any more—and this one ain't gonna risk nobody but me. Rubiy's sending me back to the mines, because he trusts me. He thinks I'll make a joining with him and show him the way in. But instead I'm gonna screw his plans, tell them the truth when I get there. Then they'll come and save you, and everything's gonna be fine. You got nothing to worry about."

He stared at me. "God! If I could only believe you. . . ."

"You only have to try." I moved away from the wall and started pacing in the small space of floor in front of him. "But why should you believe me—you don't even believe Jule. You don't give a damn about her, or what you did to her—making her fall in love with you, and then telling her she's nothing. You think I'm selfish, you crippled son of a bitch! You ought to look in a mirror." I turned back to him. "I'd let Rubiy have you in a second, if Jule didn't care for you so much that it would kill her. You lousy bastard, you don't deserve her, you don't deserve to live—"

I never finished it. Because his mind cried, *(I know, I know . . .)*, and I knew suddenly that everything Jule had told me about him, that I'd told back to her, was true: some part of me had always seen it, there inside him. The one he really hated was himself. He'd never understood why his family had been destroyed while he went on living—and so he'd stopped living too, even though his body still went through the motions. He was suffering as much as the psions he treated, but there was no one he could turn to for help, no one who understood what he'd lost. He'd tried to do something good with the Sakaffe psionics research, something to help him feel like he had a right to be alive. But all that had done was cause a good man's death, and trap him in a hopeless situation; and Jule. . . . His face collapsed.

He cared about her, all right. If I'd been blind and deaf, I'd still have been sure of it—the feeling was that strong. He'd hurt her because he was afraid—afraid of losing her, afraid to face her death, and his own. And I saw how much he wanted her, and wanted to make it all right; how much he wanted to stop hurting himself and everyone else, he'd been so wrong about everything. But it had been such an old—habit, to break free of, being so wrong. And now he'd thought there was no hope left. . . .

He didn't say anything, either; as if there was nothing he could say, to her.

And I still wanted to hate him, but somehow I couldn't. Because I'd seen into his mind—but more than that, because I understood what I saw. I wasn't the same burned-out shadow walker who'd been dumped in his office the day I met Jule, any more than I was still the psionic deaf-mute I'd been when I met the Hydrans. I'd changed. More than just my Gift had come back to life inside me; and like it or not, I couldn't twist the knife in his wounds, any more than I could stop loving Jule. . . . I let all my angry words out in a sigh between my teeth. "She'll know, Doc. She always knows. But go and tell her anyhow." I started for the door.

"Cat, wait—" he called after me.

"Go to hell." I opened the door and went out.

I went back out into the nameless street again, moving like a shadow walker, not wanting anybody's mind or even their eyes to touch me. Moving because I couldn't rest—not alone with my memory in my dead, empty room. The rain had ended and the sky was clearing; quicksilver puddles shimmered everywhere. The street stopped beyond the spaceport but I went on up into the hills, the only place I'd ever felt free for even an afternoon; the last place that I'd seen Dere smile.

I went farther than I ever had. The light of the sky was enough to let my eyes find a way. I only stopped when even the memories had to let my body rest; dropping down on the hillside in the spongy grass. The sighing of the trees and the hiss of venting steam was all around me, with the faint rustling music of tiny wild things in the darkness. No human sound, no human eyes, no human mind to ruin the perfect peace.

A cool wind moved through my hair. I looked up for the first time, and I thought that if the days were beautiful, there wasn't even a word for this. The Crab Nebula lay across the clearing sky like golden fishnet, in a black sea rippling with aurora. I lay looking up at it for a long time, opening all my senses, letting my mind escape into the universal darkness. Wanting to stay there forever and let the beauty of it fill me. . . .

A tendril of alien thought curled into the pattern of my own. My mind tumbled in blind panic, trying to protect itself—until I heard the voice that wasn't a single voice but a choir of thought calling me. Not human . . . *Hydran.* I stood up, searching the darkness, and suddenly they were all around me, maybe a dozen of them, as silently as ghosts.

(What . . . what are you doing here?) I looked from face to face, knowing that their eyes saw me just as clearly in the darkness, and that their minds could see clear through me. A couple of them were albino-white, but I wasn't really sure if any of them were the ones I'd seen before. It was hard to focus on their faces when my mind's eye couldn't even separate them.

They asked me, (Why I was surprised to find them here, when this was their place, created by their ancestors? Their ancestors were not born to live in the dark heart of this world. They longed for the sky and the world of living things as much as the outsiders who had stolen those things away from them.)

I looked down.

They showed me that they came here often, in secret, (to gather what they needed to feed and clothe their bodies . . . and to feed their spirit.)

I nodded, and let my mind loosen again, reaching out to become a part of their whole. But I kept control this time, I didn't lose myself as I sank into the image. I joined with them, needing to share in the filling of their spirit, needing it more than I could know.

But as I joined, I couldn't stop the memories of tonight that welled up like blood from a wound. The memories bled into the sea of their shared mind, and yet they didn't break away. Deep waters swallowed my grief, purified it, held it suspended as they shared their strength with me.

But I felt their stunned surprise, the deeper fear beneath it, as they absorbed the truth about the human psions who had promised them deliverance. . . . *(Murder*—the human psions had murdered one of their own and forced the Chosen)—*me, they meant me*—(to be a witness. They were psions, how could they do such a terrible thing and survive?)

(They're human,) I thought. (They're good at surviving.)

And they were asking themselves, (How could they not have seen—?) But sharing their question, I saw that there was no way they could have known—because even though they were the best telepaths I'd ever met, their own minds were so open, so freely shared, that they had no defenses; they didn't even know what a lie was. Without the lie itself, they had no way of telling a lie from the truth. Rubiy must have known that and used it against them, used them like he used everyone else.

But then they were asking me for an answer, (Because there was a strangeness that was more than alien in some of the human minds. . . . There was an unrightness, perhaps a)—the image blurred until it was almost lost—(deceit.) They could learn. They weren't the fools Rubiy figured they were, after all, and I was glad.

But now I had to try to make them understand the truth behind the lies, the way they'd been betrayed, the hope they'd lost— (This is hard . . . but you're right. They weren't telling you the truth, they're—deceiving you. We call it 'lying.' Humans do it all the time, because most of them can't read minds. . . .) And I told them, not hiding what I felt about Rubiy, or how good it felt to show them the truth. (. . . So they lied to you, to keep you out of their way while they took over the mines. They tangled up their thoughts with a false image because you couldn't understand the difference—they thought you couldn't, anyway. Does that make any kind of sense to you?) I let them sink deeper into my mind, as they tried to get hold of something that kept slipping away, and then the word/feeling came back.

(They understood, now. . . . But it was not clear why these new outsiders wanted the unholy place, if it was not because they came to fulfill the promise.)

(Well, they want power, I suppose.) I tried to show them what the blue crystals meant to humans. (So controlling the mines means they'd have the FTA—the ones who control the Human Federation—by the throat.)

It was like dropping a stone into water and getting no ripples: (Not clear . . . there was no need . . . no purpose. . . .) As if they didn't have any idea why anyone would even want power. I tried to remember what I knew about power to let them see why. And I guess they did, because I felt something sharp and sudden form then that hurt my head. I didn't know exactly what I'd been thinking of, myself, until the thought came, (It was the suffering of those weaker than themselves that they wanted.) I caught images they must have picked up from my own mind, about the mines, and the Labor Crows . . . and Oldcity.

(Yeah, I guess that's about right. But power can be used for good—) Except that right then I couldn't think of an example.

A feeling that was almost disbelief patterned in my head; they were whispering, (What ugly, twisted mind-paths these aliens had chosen.) And I remembered what Dere had said, about humans being defective Hydrans.

I felt their hope curdling. (They understood at last that these human psions had used their gift falsely, only meaning to do further harm. But if they succeeded, what would become of the outsiders who held the unholy place?)

The question surprised me. (I don't know.) I figured Rubiy would have to keep the ones who ran the mines alive to get what he wanted. But then I thought about the bondies—nobody would help them, whoever won.

(They saw that there was no good that would come out of this, for anyone.)

I looked up at the ring of dim faces again, seeing that there was nothing left for them now; the thing that gave them life and meaning was being destroyed because of something they didn't even understand. There was no way they could stop it, now. Their last hope of someone to save them, of a new beginning, was gone. And I was sorry I had to be the one who'd told them; I was sorry for everything.

(But they knew it was better to know the truth, good to know that in some ways at least they had been wise. . . .) The circle of their thoughts drew closer around me. Even if I wasn't the answer they'd been promised by their ancestors, I was still the one who had shown them the truth.

I looked down at my hands, wondering like an idiot whether they wondered why I wasn't blue anymore. And then, because there wasn't anything to lose by trying, I tried to show them how Siebeling and Jule were working against Rubiy, trying to stop him.

They listened. And then they asked me, (Why would I help the ones who tried to save the place where I was a slave?)

My mind tried to shut them out—

(Because there was someone who mattered.) They answered their own question, and I saw then that they already knew about Jule and the others, and everything that had happened between us.

(Yeah, someone who matters.) For a minute I felt the old, human resentment rise against their understanding too much. But only for a minute. (So you see, we could use any help. . . .)

There was a silence inside my head. Finally they answered; but it was only to tell me, (They had to consider these things further.)

I nodded. (I don't blame you. You don't owe us nothing.) Except revenge—but I knew they couldn't take that. I felt hopeless and empty. My legs were getting shaky; I wondered how long we'd been standing there. I realized that they were telling me there was nothing left to say or share except loss, (And that was not appropriate to this place.) Their solid reality flickered. I felt them begin to loosen the ties that bound their minds to mine, knew that they were about to disappear again, and go back into their hidden world.

(Wait! I—I need to ask one more thing.) Their presence grew strong again. (You must have seen most of what's in my memory, that time you . . . I mean, I heard the mind is never supposed to forget anything, just that sometimes you forget how to find something you want. I need to know something that happened a long time ago. . . . *And under it, wanting to know about my parents, and why—?)*

They knew my secret. But they wouldn't give me an answer. (Because they also knew that among the outsiders there was a purpose to forgetting; it protected a mind that was solitary, easily broken, and slow to heal. The ways of the outsiders were mine, I had been raised into them and I would have to live with them. I had learned to forget; I would have to learn that there was a reason for forgetting. It was better to leave some things alone.)

(They would not interfere against us. Whatever we did, they would not oppose it, for my sake. But I had seen the truth, there was no choice either way for them. They must think longer on this.)

I nodded again, and my hands made fists. The circle of their mind began to close me out, gently. But my own mind didn't want to let go, suddenly afraid of losing the contact that eased all pain: my lifeline, the only bond with my people. *My people—*

But I lost it anyway. They didn't belong to me; they never had. I knew it as they disappeared with a sound of the wind sighing. I'd lost my true people forever; I was stuck with being human. And that was the same as being an orphan, and right then I hated it.

I went back down alone again, feeling as cold as if I'd died along with Dere. After a while I began to see the lights of town, and the mines compound out on the snowy plain. I thought about what a cheap, cruddy place the port town was, like an old scar on the green hills. Humans destroyed everything they touched. But I didn't have anywhere else left to go, or any other choice than to play out this loser's game of Last Chance with Rubiy. Even if nobody else helped me or even believed me, even if Siebeling still thought I was nothing but a croach and a lousy half-breed kid . . . even if Jule still loved him. I'd never had a real choice in my life; any more than I'd ever really been young.

16

SOMEBODY WAS SHAKING me awake, their fingers digging into my shoulder and their irritation digging into my brain. I crawled up out of black dreamlessness, through the Oldcity memories I always woke into, through layers of time. I reached out with my mind, expecting to find Jule, or maybe Siebeling . . . finding Galiess instead. And then the memory of where I was and what had happened yesterday caught me like a prod, shocking me awake.

I raised my head. Sunlight silhouetted her, throwing her face into shadow. I lifted a hand to my eyes, but I didn't need to see her expression. I pushed my memories into a cell and held them there, clearing my thoughts. I couldn't think about it now, *not now*. . . .

"Get up," she said, letting me go like having to touch me disgusted her. "You've spent long enough being useless."

I frowned. "Get off it. What do you care if I sleep? I got nothin' better to do."

"You do now. Sit up and listen."

I sat up, slowly, yawning until my jaw cracked. (I'm all ears.)

She stiffened. "Rubiy showed you what was expected of you. You've proved you're strong enough—and you've proved your trust, to him." Not to her. "It's time for you to do your part."

It took me a minute to remember that what she meant was me going back to the mines. "It's time? Right now?" My fingers traced the ragged trail of an old scar along my ribs. "Ain't this kind of sudden?"

"What did you expect, a parade?" She wasn't going to give me a chance to ruin anything—or even to get any satisfaction out of it.

I frowned. "Maybe just a chance to ask some questions."

"You're to turn yourself in at the spaceport, and let yourself be taken back to the mines. At an appropriate time you'll begin a joining with Rubiy, who will be open for your contact. That's your entire role and responsibility—and all you need to know."

"If you say so." I shrugged. "One question—do I get time to put on my pants?"

She left the room.

We walked along the street toward the starport side by side, but it wasn't like we were walking together: I was going there alone, and she was making sure I did. The clear afternoon air was bright and still; it gave me chills, but not because I felt cold. I stopped across from the ramp in front of the shining glass starport entrance and looked on past it into the wilderness. Green hills burned my eyes; I kept looking up until I saw the cobwebbed sky. I wondered how much of it I'd be seeing after today.

"You know what to do," she said. "You're being watched, always. And always remember . . . we're your only protection. If you don't do what you've been told, our plan will fail—and you'll be a slave there until you die."

I looked down again. "You don't really want me to go, do you?" Saying that instead of what was filling my mind. "What's the matter, you jealous? If you want to take my place . . ." I waved at the entrance, trying to force a laugh.

But sparks leaped from live wires in her mind. She *did* want to go in my place—wanted to hold the place of honor that belonged to her, do the final deed that would put the Federation Mines into Rubiy's hands and secure the future. It was her right, *hers*, not mine: She'd spent the best part of her life working toward this triumph, working for Rubiy, with Rubiy; molding him, teaching him, serving him, worshiping him. He was her creation, and her god. She'd taken him out of the gutter when he was nothing but a hoodlum—angry, helpless, but burning with potential. She'd never known how to take control of her own life; he'd solved that problem for her. Soon he'd had her begging him to use her, any way he wanted. She'd devoted her life to helping him learn, helping him succeed . . . made herself his willing slave.

And this was how he repaid her: by deciding that she had outlived her usefulness, her ability, his need for her . . . his love for her. Letting himself be seduced, pushing her aside for this dirty half-breed with the morals of an animal. . . . Her control fell apart completely. For half a second I saw the raw heart of her betrayal, and I thought she was going to use her psi against me right there in the street.

But she got her control back almost before it was gone. She had put her life in Rubiy's hands; it was his to use or throw away. She would accept his decision in this, gracefully, as she had always done. . . . No matter how much she detested it, and me. Her hands flexed inside her gloves, and her mouth trembled.

I let go of my own defenses, taking a deep breath. For a minute I almost felt sorry for her.

A couple of town psions pushed past us with sidelong glances. I turned and followed them up the ramp without saying anything.

I stopped once I got inside, letting her hate drain out of me. I had my own problems to worry about. I stood staring down at the mosaic of a star gone nova under my feet; thinking it fit the position I was in right now about as well as anything could. Now all I had to do was find somebody who was waiting to turn me back into a piece of property. I looked around, wondering how to start: I didn't see any guards who looked like I was on their minds. I began to think it would be a laugh if I couldn't find anybody who wanted me.

Then I saw Jule, through the light-fountain, leaning against a counter and talking to some woman. I started toward her, wanting to see her once more before I had to go; to carry her smile with me, to give me courage.

She was facing away from me, listening, as I came up to the night-blue counter. I put out a hand to rest on, not even thinking about it. And then suddenly my wrist jerked down and slammed flat against the counter edge. It startled me; my hand was trapped somehow and I couldn't move it. The counter turned blood-red for a meter on either side of me.

The woman at the counter turned, and then she was backing away from me. I was jerking at my trapped hand; my eyes caught Jule's staring back at me. I could see her fist pressing her chest, she was shaking her head. *(Too late, it's too late. . . .)* I looked down at my own wrist and the world snapped back together: the bond tag. Suddenly it was all real, what I was doing here, and the thought hit me: *What if this doesn't work?*

I quit struggling as a handful of port guards circled me with their stunguns out. I kept my eyes on Jule, and I said, "Help—" She gave me a sad, helpless smile, while one of the guards put a lock on my hands. Then they told her to push a button. She did, and my hand came loose from the counter. They led me away. I could feel her thoughts following me; her mind filled with gratitude. *She knew.* Siebeling had told her everything. I looked back and smiled.

A couple of the guards led me to an empty office, and shut the door against the people still staring at us out in the lobby. They pushed me down into a chair and looked at me; one of them wiped the back of his hand across my face. "No dust. He hasn't been at the mines long; or else he's been out long enough to throw off the effects. You watch him; I'll call in a report."

He left the room. The other one sat behind the desk with his gun pointing across it at me. I shifted in the molded plastic seat and tried to get comfortable; but it was the wrong shape, and I didn't feel much like relaxing. I thought about Jule, about trying to reach her with my mind. But the guard was a telepath, and a good one. I didn't want him eavesdropping; he was too close for comfort. I made myself stop thinking about her. But then I started to think about the mines; and I didn't want to think about that, either. I looked back at the guard. He sighed and shifted his gun. I said, "Nice weather," because I had to do something.

"I suppose so, to you." He looked at me kind of funny. "How'd you get loose, anyway? I thought that was impossible." But he was a psion, and I couldn't help feeling he should have known why I was here.

I said, "I teleported," and he frowned. I kept my mind loose and empty, and watched him wonder. Galiess hadn't even told her own people the truth about me, or what I was supposed to be doing. Making sure I didn't get any special treatment—or any credit. At least I wouldn't have to worry about her anymore. Only about me, about how I was going to make them listen to me at the mines. Joraleman would be there; he was all right, he knew what had happened. And when it was all over, they'd let me go, because they'd have proof that I'd been an agent. Sure, they had to. . . .

The door opened. The guard was back already, and Kielhosa was with him. I shut my eyes and wished I really could teleport.

The trip out from town and down to the snow was the same as before, except that this time my hands weren't free, and this time Kielhosa had a stungun. He didn't say a word; but I knew what he was thinking, so maybe it was just as well. He'd been in town on his time off, *(Just his goddamn lousy luck).* . . . And mine.

I hoped Joraleman would be there when we reached the snowtrack, but he wasn't. There were only a couple of bondies, loading supplies, and a guard sitting on an empty box watching them. Kielhosa came up alongside him and made me stop. "Got room for two more?"

"You're going back early?" The guard looked surprised.

"Not by choice." Kielhosa glared at me. "I've got a special delivery to make. How much longer is this going to take?"

"Nearly done." The guard stood up and stretched. I looked at the prod shimmering in his hand. "I had to wear out my arm, though. Your prize specimens don't break their backs getting the job done. Where'd that one come from—a new recruit?" He laughed.

"To them it's a holiday. And no. This rat thought he could resign." His hand on my shoulder shook me. "They picked him up at the spaceport."

Out of the corner of my eye I saw the bondies look up. Kielhosa was making sure they heard. Their blue faces startled me; I'd forgotten what they looked like.

"Oh, yeah? How'd he get away from you?"

"Long story, and I don't even know all of it. He's been out for a while. But they all turn up eventually, if they don't starve or freeze."

"And twenty lashes'll convince anybody not to try it again." The guard glanced back at me, snapping the prod with a jerk of his hand. He enjoyed thinking about it.

And I wondered how I could ever have been so stupid. The guard moved away, herding the bondies toward the back of the snowtrack with the last of the supplies. I heard a door slam. Kielhosa pushed me toward the 'track. I climbed up into the cab and sat in the backseat. It was too cramped for my legs. Kielhosa shoved me over against the far window, cursing, and sat beside me. The guard sat up front. The bondie who was driving now turned to stare past the seat at me. Then he started the 'track and I looked out at the snow, feeling like I'd swallowed a stone. *What did you expect them to do, shake your hand? Twenty lashes . . .* my God, how much was that? All my fingers, and all my toes. . . . But I hadn't been trying to get away. I was going back to tell them about the plot. I was on their side—I had to remember that. They wouldn't give me a beating when they understood. I twisted in the seat. "Hey, Kielhosa—"

17

THEY DIDN'T BELIEVE ME. Kielhosa took me to the Mines Directorate; I stood on the perfect white carpet and told them all I knew. They listened to every word. And then they started to laugh. Joraleman wasn't even there to back me up; when it was too late, I'd found out from Kielhosa that he was still back in town. The directors called me a liar; all they saw was a scared kid, a trapped rat trying to save his own skin, and nothing I could do with words or even with my mind could make them see me any other way. The head director told Kielhosa to have me punished.

But instead Kielhosa said, "Sir, I think you should know this is the bondie who saved Chief Purchaser Joraleman's life. If we could at least wait until Joraleman gets back . . ." He hesitated.

The director's face darkened. "Him? This is him? The psion, the mind reader?" His own mind filled up with fear. "What the hell do you mean, exposing us to—Get him out of here! And add another dozen to his sentence, for wasting our time."

And so I walked between two guards across the compound yard, where a hundred others stood waiting and watching. The white glare of light on the endless snow was blinding me, and I didn't think I was going to make it to where the other bondies were standing. They'd brought out all the poor shivering blue-faces who weren't digging ore to watch what happened to me. So that they'd never try what I'd tried. *(But I hadn't!)* One of the guards shook his head. I tripped over nothing; it seemed to take forever to cross the yard. I could see the faces of the others, like blue beads strung out across the glare, and all of a sudden I remembered Mikah. And I knew that if he was standing there, he'd think I'd lied to him about escaping. I didn't want that; I felt bad about it, as if it really mattered. I couldn't make my mind search him out, couldn't even look along the line of faces. . . . It was too bright to see anything; I couldn't think, couldn't even feel.

But I could see the gray-silver metal post in front of my face. I tried to pull away but they fastened my hands up above my head, the metal pressed smooth and cold against my skin. The bitter taste of fright was in my mouth. Somebody's hands tore my shirt down the back. I started to shiver. Someone else was speaking; the words fell on my ears without making any sense, words about me. I could see the guard waiting with the glowing arch of the prod out of the corner of my eyes. I remembered how being hit a full blow just once, for wising off down in the mines, had felt. I tried to believe that this wasn't going to be twenty times worse; and a dozen more, for passing as human. . . . I tried to remember to count, so it wouldn't be as bad, so I'd know there was going to be an end. . . . I wished to God they'd get it over with! I—

"Begin."

The prod made a high song coming through the air, and when it struck my back, it went *snap*. A blistering pain like the burn of hot grease spread across my back, and I forgot the cold burn of the metal post against my cheek. I tried to count *one*, but it was just a gasp, my teeth gritted together. And *two* came, while I was trying to disappear into the metal, and laid another line of sticky fire across my back. I made a sound and choked it off. I heard the prod sing again, bracing myself; my stomach knotted, and then it was *three*. I bit my lip until it bled. Again, and that was *five*; no, wrong, *four seven?* And I couldn't count on my fingers now because they were balled into fists. Again, and I knew I wasn't going to be brave . . . again, and it didn't matter anymore. I buried my face against the cold post and let the cry come, letting the pain out the only way I could. There was nothing I could do but let it hit me again, and again, until I thought I couldn't hurt any more than I did; and then it would hit me again. I sagged against the post and my wrists bled as the cuffs cut into them. I barely knew it. I thought I was learning what it was like to be burned alive. I thought I was going to vomit. I thought I was going to pass out, but I couldn't let go of the pain no matter how I tried. . . . My whole life was caught up in an endless loop; there was no beginning or end, it was going to go on forever, and I was going to see and hear and taste and feel it all. . . .

And then it was over. They freed my hands and pulled me away. I heard a voice I didn't recognize still begging them to stop, a voice that couldn't belong to me. . . . My legs wouldn't hold me up.

They took me away. I felt dull sickness and fear follow me along the line of blank blue faces. But everything was far away, now, like a star in a mirror. Then something struck my face, flat and gray—I was on my stomach on a cot. Someone chained my foot to the bed. And then I was alone in the small empty room, while the part of me that was still conscious made dry sobbing noises in the back of my throat.

I lay there for a long time, hurting, and the only sound I heard was my own voice. Finally that stopped, too. I knew at the edge of my mind where I was, in the infirmary, in the ward set aside for the bondies. No one else was in the room. I was glad, because right then I hated everybody in the goddamn universe.

It was a long time before someone came back again. Hollow footsteps crossed the ward, and stopped. A voice muttered, "God!"; a hand touched my shoulder. I swore and it moved away. I started to hope that I was alone again.

But the voice said, "I'm sorry, kid. I'm sorry this happened."

It was Joraleman. I wanted to say, "Me, too," but I couldn't do it.

He waited a minute, before he said, "Kielhosa called me. Your timing stinks, you know that? Why'd you have to get yourself picked up when I wasn't here to get you a break? They could have waited for me to get back—! But why the hell did you have to antagonize the directors with that lunatic story? You weren't telling them the truth." It wasn't even a question.

I tried to turn my head, tried to get out just one word: "Yes!"

"Wait." He kneeled down. "I've got some pain-killer. He pulled back my ruined shirt as carefully as he could, but it still felt like half of my back went with it. I whimpered and swore. Through the red agony in my mind I felt his own mind jerk with disgust at what he saw. "God, I'd never make it as a medic." He sounded sick. I shut out the image of what he was seeing. A hiss of spray struck my back, in an instant of fierce freezing cold. But the cold spread and faded, the fire died . . . the world started to stretch out beyond the edges of pain. I looked up at him then, and said, "Thanks." It sounded rusted-up.

"Forget it." He glanced away. "Look, the story I got from Kielhosa sounds pretty paranoid even to me; I've got to admit that. What in the Holy Name made you try to tell a thing like that to the Directorate?"

I rubbed my eyes. ". . . Seemed like . . . a good idea at the time. Kielhosa—he asked them to wait for you; he tried to keep them from punishing me."

I couldn't keep watching his face, but I felt him half smile. "He's a friend of mine; he owes me a couple. And he knows what I owe to you. Besides, not everyone around here thinks a beating is the answer to all questions. What's the matter, did you expect him to hate you forever, for pulling a fast one on him over the snowtrack? He's even starting to think it's funny, in a way. But with what he heard today, I'd say it's convinced him that you're a pathological liar."

I groaned.

"Maybe it lost in translation. Try telling it again, to me."

I heard him sit down on the next cot. My eyes kept falling shut. "That's all I ever wanted. . . . You got to believe me, Joraleman; you know what happened to the snowtrack! You said it wasn't an accident. Didn't you tell nobody? They acted like they didn't know—"

"Yes, I told them; I told them what I could remember. . . ." He stopped. "After it happened, it was like trying to remember a dream— parts were clear, and parts were hazy. I still don't remember everything. Sometimes a piece comes back." Like he hardly believed now that it had ever been real. "But trouble with the Spooks isn't the same thing as a plot to take over the mines."

"Don't you remember what happened to the snowtrack?"

"Yes! Yes, I couldn't forget that. I put that in the report, at least." He sighed. "They said it was simple equipment malfunction—we haven't had a decent mechanic here for months." He was thinking that no one even questioned it; that nobody believed anyone would threaten the supply of telhassium, or that they could get close if they tried.

"If they don't even believe you . . . ?" My voice started to fall apart. "What's the use of tellin' it and tellin' it, if nobody ever believes it? Why should I even try? The hell with you, you lousy bastards. You deserve anything you get, and I'm damned if I care. Jule's crazy . . . Why'd she have to love Siebeling . . . ? Why did I . . . ?" slipping off into the clouds on the edge of sleep.

Joraleman reached out and shook me. "Come on, I'll listen, at least. Try to tell me the rest of it."

I swore at him again. "Awright, all right, ask Kielhosa, he heard it! There's a group of psions in the port town, planning to take over the mines. . . ." Somehow I pulled my thoughts back again long enough to tell him the rest. ". . . And I was supposed to come back here like this, so Rubiy'd have a focus for teleportation. He's planning to gas everybody so his people can walk in and take over. If I don't make a joining, they can't do nothing—but then the ones I'm with will die. I figured if I could warn you, you'd help . . . go to the town, clear 'em out. I told Kielhosa everything, but he didn't really believe it, none of 'em did."

"You can't exactly blame them—that story would be hard to take even if you were wearing a uniform, and not a bond tag. But he said he remembered some funny things happening around you when he bought your contract. That's why he got you a hearing with the directors. That, and because you saved my life."

"Yeah. When they learned who I was, they were so grateful they gave me an extra beating." *Psion, mind reader, freak* . . .

Joraleman muttered a curse, and shook his head. "Ignorance breeds fear."

"You think you ain't afraid of me? You think you got nothin' to hide—?"

His mind spasmed with guilt. For a second he glared at me. And then he sighed. "That's the problem, you see. For most people, the only one who sees into their soul is God. And most of us wish even God was a little nearsighted."

(The land of the blind,) I thought.

"What did you say?" He blinked and shook his head again.

"Forget it."

"If you were—are—working with those FTA agents, what are you doing wearing a bond tag at all? You didn't plan that—?" He frowned.

"No. I . . . got thrown out of the group, back on Ardattee."

"And they turned you over to Contract Labor?"

"Yeah. It's a long story."

"It must be. But you're still helping them—and us?"

I didn't say anything.

"Why?"

I turned my face away. "It's personal."

Joraleman didn't say anything more for a while. Then, finally, he said, "I'll talk to them."

I couldn't remember who he meant. He left then, but I hardly knew it. Nobody was going to help me; nobody'd listen to a bondslave freak. I'd done everything I could—but I'd failed, I'd ruined our last chance. Jule and Siebeling would be trapped, maybe they'd die, and I'd be a slave forever. . . . And it wasn't *fair*. My hands made fists, the bond tag cut into my swollen wrist. My back felt like raw meat. I was only a lousy kid! Half a year ago I was nothing but a Cityboy slip who couldn't spell his own name. How was I supposed to be able to change anything?

Ever since the day I first laid eyes on Quarro, and saw what it could mean to live a free life, everyone I'd met had been putting their chains on me—chains of need, chains of greed, chains of blame. I moved my foot, hearing the chain around my ankle rattle, loud in the empty si-

lence. Half a year ago I could hardly carry the weight of my own life—
how the hell was I supposed to save the galaxy all alone? All alone . . .
I'd always been all alone. . . .

I slept, finally. And somewhere in the darkness of my dreams I met
the one I only knew from dream to dream, who disappeared even from
my memory each time I opened my eyes to the light. The one who had
been as alone as I was, who knew all the bitterness of the lost; who
wandered now, lost in my dreams, forever. The one whose mind had
touched my own with love once, somewhere in another life; whose arms
had held me safe; whose voice could whisper hope when there was none
left even in her mind; who sang me to sleep with a vision of going home.
. . . Whose ghost moved through abandoned hallways of my mind, and
showed me where to find strength when I thought I didn't have any left;
who made me go on living when I wished I was dead. The one whose
name I could never say, because her true name was hidden in the heart
of her mind. The one whose face was always hidden, too; who would
never let me remember it, no matter how I cried to see her again, no
matter how much I needed her, no matter how hard I tried, how far I
reached, to be held in the warm circle of her arms. . . .

I came awake into blackness. I blinked; grays drifted up and steadied,
but I didn't really focus. My mind was wrapped around something that
the rest of me still didn't know; it was pulling me out of sleep like it
always had back on the streets when there was a need: I was tense and
listening. I tried to lie still until I could figure out why.

The lights were out for the night, but I knew somehow that it was
close to a new day. I knew where I was, and I knew there was someone
else asleep in the ward now, a couple of cots away. He coughed and
moved as I lay listening. I felt my hand, numb with sleep, clenched in a
fist. I felt something more, fire licking the edge of my nerves—my back,
the pain-killer wearing off. . . . And then I remembered what I'd
dreamed: inside walls of nightmare the gentle thought of *her;* needing to
reach her, across impossible distances of time and space, impassible
barriers of loss. Reaching out with all my strength that still could never
be enough—

Until suddenly, somehow it was enough, and more: My mind blazed
up, caught in a tapestry of nameless colors growing brighter and
brighter, filling the emptiness inside me like nothing I'd ever known. A
rightness filled me, a belonging, all the answers I'd ever need, all the
comfort and understanding and love.

But I couldn't hold onto it: I felt the strands begin to separate, saw the colors fading. I didn't have the strength; I was losing control. *No—* I threw all the strength I had left into it, feeding the bright fabric everything I could; because if it fell apart and left me empty now, I wouldn't be able to stand it.

But then the fabric tore, and I was lying dazed in the dark, not knowing whether it was a dream, not wanting to know; with my body and my mind still drawn as tight as wire. Waiting and listening . . . *for what?*

"Cat?"

I froze. And then I lifted my head, trying to look over my shoulder; the pain made me dizzy. Jule was standing there beside the cot in a long pale gown. *Jule.* I could see her face, soft against the darkness, and her black hair falling around her. I stared at her, trying not to blink back the pain-tears, because I knew when I did she'd disappear. *(Don't let me wake up. Stay. You're beautiful, you're beautiful. . . .)*

She moved, came toward me—touched me. I caught hold of her wrist; solid flesh. She was real. I blinked, and felt two tears slip out and down.

(How did I get here?) She was staring down at me, but she didn't believe what she saw. She looked past me into the darkness. *(I've never been here!)* Her eyes came back to me, I saw the panic in them. She didn't bother with her voice. (It is real. But how, Cat? I've never seen this place! I shouldn't have come out . . . anywhere.)

My head dropped back onto the hard mattress. I let go of her, lay just watching her. The answer came without me even having to think about it. (A joining.)

She reached out and pushed my hair back from my eyes. (You're that strong?)

It almost wasn't a question. I didn't try to answer it.

She smiled a little then, kneeling down beside me. (It was like nothing I've ever known. So intense—enough to pull me here, to you. I thought it never happened. I felt you calling me in a dream tonight, so far away; but it wasn't a dream and . . . Cat, what happened to you? *Pain, and such fear. . . .)* She shuddered, remembering. Her memory ran through me, and my hand closed hard on her wrist again.

(I tried to tell them! I tried, I told them what was happening, but they didn't believe me. They laughed at me! They beat me, for escaping. And for being a psion. . . .) I swallowed hard against sickness rising. (Everything went wrong. Joraleman was gone, and they laughed . . . they wouldn't listen, they wouldn't even wait. I tried everything to make them—!) Jule put her fingers up, touching my face, and stopped the thoughts with her own. I felt the aching sorrow in her mind.

She leaned forward, trying to look at my back; one hand touched it, as lightly as a birdwing, and jerked away at my gasp. Then suddenly tears were running down her own face. Her eyes met mine, her pupils were wide and black, open clear down to her soul. My wounds were her wounds and hers were mine; our thoughts were bound together in a second of perfect understanding. My lips found hers; we tasted the salt of blood and tears.

And in the same instant, we felt the mind that gathered like smoke in the shared space of our own: *Rubiy.* The fragile bond shattered like its strands were made of glass, and suddenly we were two separate people staring at each other across the dark again. Our minds were clear; Rubiy's contact had broken with the joining-spell. But we both knew that what really mattered was his reaching our minds at all. He knew what had happened.

"We did it—what he wanted you to do," Jule whispered, looking down. "But you found my mind, not his."

"It wasn't a mistake."

"But now he knows he can do it, too."

"Not if I don't let him. Not if you don't go back. Stay here, Jule— you can make them believe the truth!"

"I can't . . . I can't leave Ardan there. If I don't go back, Rubiy will kill him; he'll know we're betraying him."

"But if you do . . ."

"I have to! I'll find another way!" Her voice rose. "We've been making plans, Ardan thinks he's found a way to get the—"

The bondie who'd been asleep a few beds away began to cough again. He sat up, wheezing, and looked over at us. "Hey, what the hell—"

Jule stiffened and turned like a wild thing, and then she was . . . gone.

My hand that had been holding hers closed over nothing. The other bondie was staring back across the empty room at me. I shut my eyes, with my fingers digging into the edge of the mattress, and tried to look like I was sleeping.

He said, "Hey?" a couple more times in the darkness, and then he lay down again. I heard him swear and gasp for breath. I touched his mind; It was knotted with misery and despair: (*God, don't let me go crazy, please, please, not crazy too. . . .*) And because I'd caused it, I tried to use my mind to ease his fear, to help him forget, for a while. : . . . I felt him drift down into sleep again.

I kept my eyes shut a while longer against the emptiness in my own mind—until I found Jule calling me, from far away, and heard her promise. . . .

18

WITH THE NEW day, the medic on duty came into the ward again. I opened my eyes to watch him check out the other bondie. The bondie coughed and mumbled, halfway into delirium. The medic gave him a shot of something. I felt him thinking there wasn't much point to it as he moved away again. I'd always heard it wasn't easy to get into the infirmary—as long as you could move, you could work. And by the time you couldn't, it was probably too late. This was a small room.

"How's the back?" The medic was standing beside me now. He didn't bother to look at my back, and I didn't try to look at him.

"It hurts." I hadn't moved for hours, afraid even to breathe too deeply.

"That's the point." He left me food and water; on the floor where I couldn't reach them. As he was walking away, I went into his mind and let him feel exactly how much I hurt. I heard him yelp, and the crash as he dropped something. I smiled, just a little.

The rest of that day was the longest day of my life. I tried to concentrate on Jule, on what had happened the night before and what Rubiy would want to do about it. But a red haze of pain filled up my mind until I couldn't focus my thoughts enough even to worry much about it.

After what seemed like forever someone came into the ward again. I heard two voices this time, arguing; one of them was Joraleman's.

". . . against the rules!" the medic shouted.

"I don't give a damn," Joraleman said. He sounded like he was right beside the bed. I opened my eyes and saw his legs in rust-colored uniform pants. "I'll do it myself."

"You can't treat a patient!" The medic came after him.

"Then you do it. Do your duty as a healer, for God's sake. I'll take the responsibility." Joraleman's voice was heavy with disgust. He pushed something at the medic, and sat down on the next bed, waiting.

The medic's hands came at me with a blade, but before I could jerk back, he began to cut away the rags of my shirt with it. I lay still, biting my lip. He sprayed pain-killer on my back, and then something else that covered the burns like a soft skin.

I took a deep breath, and another, without feeling the pain nail me to the cot. Then I moved one numb arm, slowly, stretching it out, and the other one.

"Give it a chance to set," the medic said. "And don't make a lot of sudden moves. Not that you're going anywhere." He gave the chain around my leg a tug. "That's all I can do for him," to Joraleman. He left the room.

"How are you feeling?" Joraleman asked me.

"Better'n I was five minutes ago." I tried to grin.

He smiled, but it was weak. "I can do this much for you, Cat." His big hands twisted together in the space between his knees. "But that's all I can do. I tried to get a hearing today, but . . ." His hands spread in a shrug. "Nothing."

I nodded, not even surprised. "What did they say?"

"That I've gone soft." He laughed once, his eyes shut against seeing my back.

"What're you doin' out here, anyway, Joraleman?"

He opened his eyes. "My job. I'm just another bureaucrat, putting in my time until transfer. The hardship pay is excellent, if I finish my tour. And my time's almost up." He sighed. "It's not like this everywhere."

"Yeah, sure." I looked at my wrist, at the bond tag. "How much do I owe on my contract now?"

He read a number off my tag, and did something with the computer remote on his belt. "Still close to five thousand credits."

"Five thousand . . . still?" I whispered. "Jeezu. I never been worth more'n fifty in my whole life."

He didn't say anything. The bondie in the other bed started to cough.

I pulled myself to the edge of the cot and reached down for the water and food. My hands were swollen and clumsy; he helped me feed myself. Then he got up again. "I've got to get back to work. But I'll try again tomorrow. If I can get in to see Tanake, he might be more willing to listen. . . ."

"I hope you got that much time left."

He looked back at me, startled into a frown. But he only shook his head and went out of the room.

The other bondie was coughing again. When he stopped, he tried to push himself up. He said, "When I was—" and then he collapsed, unconscious, and I never found out what he was trying to say to me.

I lay then and waited until night came again in the civilized levels of the complex. Then I let my mind loose into the nameless sea, searching for Jule. And she answered me at last, like she'd promised me she would. Everything was still all right. I caught the bright ribbon of her thought and fused it to my own.

Her mind wove into mine and I felt the joining begin. But this time she wasn't alone. The cord of someone else's thought wrapped itself around the strands of hers, and as her mind joined with mine, the joining was tripled. Before I could shape the hundred questions crowded into my brain, or even stop what was happening, the bright warmth that had begun inside me turned white-hot. Reality wrenched itself apart inside my head, the space behind my eyes filled with starbursts. And then the contact tore again, the way it had the first time.

Only this time it wasn't just Jule standing by me when my eyes cleared. Rubiy was with her, and I knew then that time had finally run out for us. Jule's face was full of quiet desperation; Rubiy's burned with triumph. It throbbed inside me like the blood in my veins, and all I could think about suddenly was Cortelyou's heart stopping. . . .

Jule kneeled down beside me. Her mind touched me softly; she forced everything out of her own thoughts but her concern for me.

Rubiy's mind came down out of the stars as he looked at us. (Cat!) In the darkness his grinning face looked like a death's-head. He focused his triumph, force-feeding me the giddy electric shock of his exultation until I had to put up a wall to protect myself. I lost Jule's contact in static. He showed me my share in it all, my power, his approval, his pride: (Didn't I tell you, when the time came, you would find the need, and make the joining? *Even if it hadn't worked out exactly the way he'd planned.*)

Find the need. Suddenly I remembered what had made me find the need, just the way he'd promised. Pain gnawed my blistered back as I pushed up onto an elbow. He'd known—he'd known what would happen to me. (Thanks for bein' so sure.) I couldn't hide the anger, didn't even want to.

His mind flashed surprise and confusion, before it shut off like a switch. He didn't know why I felt angry, why I resented it. (You suffered: You paid a small price for a great reward. We've all made sacrifices to reach this goal; only a fool would whine about them. Pain is

nothing—learn to ignore it.) Like he'd learned to ignore pain, and every
other shred of human feeling he'd been born with.

I didn't try to answer. I glanced at Jule, standing with her fists
clenched and her mouth pressed tight. She was looking at the chain that
held me on the cot.

(Then you begin to understand.) I felt his annoyance; I was spoiling
the pure pleasure of his moment of victory. (You'll understand everything, when we're through. You'll know then that I'm right.) He turned
back to Jule. (But first we have to complete our business with the Federation. The maintenance systems control center is on this level of the
complex. We should be able to reach it directly from here.) He began to
move away. Jule started after him, moving like she was stepping onto a
tightrope.

(Wait!) I threw it into his mind. He stopped. (I want to come with
you. Don't leave me here. I don't want to be like this, helpless, when it
happens.) I wore my best victim face, hoping he could see it. (They hate
psions.)

He frowned. (You'll be safe where you are. You'd only get in our way.
I'll come back for you—)

(I'm fine!) Somehow I sat up, holding my breath. I was glad I didn't
have to lie out loud. (Like you said, I can learn to ignore pain. I want to
be there when—when you take this place over for good.) I reached out
to him, letting my swollen hand tremble a little.

His frown faded.

I put one foot on the floor; the chain on the other leg rattled. I kept
my eyes on him, pleading, waiting, praying. . . .

He reached over and put his hand on my leg, let it slide down to
cover the metal cuff. I felt the power focus in his mind. . . . The cuff
fell open, and I was free. I sat gaping at it for a minute before I finally
got up off the cot. The thought hit me that my whole life would've been
a hell of a lot easier if I'd only been born a teek instead of a 'path. I
laughed at the irony, without really meaning to.

Jule and Rubiy were both wearing miners' uniforms, because the
halls outside would be monitored. They were both armed. Jule's hair
was hidden under a security guard's helmet; she was tall and thin
enough to pass for a man. Rubiy took off his jacket and helped me into
it. Even with the bandageskin the medic had put on my back, I thought
the pain when it settled on my shoulders was going to be more than I
could take. But I didn't have any choice, and so I took it anyway. I
sealed the jacket up the front, my hands and face wet with sweat. Jule

watched my fingers, her eyes full of apology and relief. Neither of us alone could stop him, but together we still had half a chance.

I glanced at the other bondie as we left the ward. He didn't even stir; his mind was down somewhere deeper than sleep. I wasn't sure whether he was lucky or not.

Moving through the halls was no problem—because nobody here expected any problems, the security before you got this far was too good. We reached the systems center without anyone questioning us. When we got there, the entrance was sealed by an identity lock. Rubiy set his hand against the plate like he really expected it to open. He focused his psi against it, like he had with my cuff, and in a few seconds it hummed open. I glanced at Jule; a kind of dazed awe filled her mind. I wondered if Seibeling had ever even thought about using his Gift that way.

We went inside. The lights came up as we entered a room filled with more monitors and terminals and screens than I'd ever imagined seeing at one time. If living in Oldcity had been living like a parasite in the guts of some alien being, this was like being a virus inside a brain. No one was watching over it—it kept its own nightwatch, monitored its own systems, like a sleeping body. And Rubiy had come here to infect it. . . . And we'd come here to stop him. I was hardly even thinking about my back now.

Rubiy moved along the walls, forgetting us as he looked up and down the instrument banks. Jule touched her stungun, looked a question at me, not letting it form in her conscious mind. I glanced at the gun Rubiy was wearing, and back at hers. Jule and I had to make any move we tried at the same time. Our only chance to take him by surprise and survive would be if we could split his attention, hoping one of us could put him out before he could tear open our defenses and kill us. I raised a hand, (Wait), and let myself drift across the room. Rubiy was calling up information on a terminal. He finished as I stopped beside him, and looked up at me, pulling a headset off.

I managed a smile. "How's it goin'?"

"Perfectly." He reached into his jacket, and pulled out something sealed in shiny packets. "Now for the final step." I followed him, as he moved to another section of instruments and began to feel his way over a touchboard.

"What're those?" I pointed at the packets.

"Those are what we'll be feeding into the air conditioning system." He didn't look up.

I laughed. "It looks like candy!"

"I don't recommend them. The chemical is a form of a sodium compound that was once widely used as an anesthetic—and a 'truth serum.' "

I froze. My hand fell back to my side.

"They probably don't taste very good." He smiled, enjoying his own wit.

I laughed a little too loud. "How's it work, anyway? How long will this keep everybody asleep? It's not gonna last forever—don't it leak out? What happens then?"

"The gas is harmless. We can keep them unconscious for as long as we need to, until everything is under control. This system is self-contained, the gas can't 'leak out.' It purifies and recirculates the same air."

"Won't it clear out the gas, then?"

"Ordinarily it would. But most of these systems have a regulator built into them—"

"So you can use them to gas people?"

He looked up at me just for a second, with his irritation starting to show. "I hardly think that was the purpose intended by the manufacturer." He looked down at what he was doing again. "It's used for air hydration control, mass immunization, disinfectants—similar functions."

"Oh." I let my hand drift out in a slip's move that was so automatic it was almost instinctive. "Well, ain't it gonna gas us, then?" My fingers closed over cool metal.

"I can bypass—"

I jerked his stungun loose—(Now, Jule, now!)—trying to leap clear—

But my legs didn't do what I expected. I stumbled, and in the same split second Rubiy's arm lashed out and knocked me into the panel; I heard Jule cry out as her own stungun tore itself loose from her hands. I had one glimpse of the total rage on Rubiy's face before the pain of my wrenched back blurred it out, before the same rage smashed into our minds. I felt my body shudder with the blow, felt my heart constrict and miss a beat as my mind barely blocked his attack. The stungun had fallen out of my hands. Rubiy's hands reached out—

I felt psi energy overload the circuits of my mind suddenly, sweeping all the barriers of my control aside, forcing me to join—*not Rubiy, not Jule, not even human. . . .*

Hydran. The combined strength of their mind poured into me, building inside me like the static charge of a lightning bolt. Rubiy fell away from me, his face changing, mirroring my own as I was transformed; no fury left on it, but only confusion and disbelief. I saw his power, *saw* it, shining around him like an aura—but it couldn't reach me now. I saw Jule too, her face slack with shock, her own psi aura haloing her. The whole room shimmered with lifeless light and whispered with silent noise. I didn't feel pain now. I didn't even feel human; my consciousness was like foam on a cresting surge of energy. Static crackled between my fingers, my hair lifted on an invisible breeze. . . .

I watched Rubiy lurch across the room to where Jule clung to the wall, too dazed by what was happening to get out of his way. He caught her in his arms, holding her between us like a shield—not knowing there was nothing I could have done to stop him.

And then suddenly something sucked me down into my own mind, made me forget them both; and all I could think about was where I stood now—in the Federation Mines, in this hell of misery and torture and slow death. All I could see was spending the rest of my life as a slave; all I could feel was the pain in my back, the betrayal, the suffering, the humiliation. . . . And suddenly I knew that I had the power in me now to make it end forever.

(Yes.) I spoke the word where only they would hear me. (Yes. I will. . . .) I felt them answer me; and knew that what they showed me then would stay with me forever, too.

And then the lightning struck—through me, around me, below me . . . everywhere. I think I remember seeing Rubiy and Jule disappear together, before my vision turned inside out. I think I remember screaming.

The thunder followed, deep in the levels of the compound below me.

19

LIQUID FIRE TRICKLED into my mouth, dripped down my throat, filled my nose with fumes that made me gag. Reaction caught me with a heavy hand and dragged me into the real world like a newborn. I was blinking and blinking, starting to wonder if I'd gone blind when suddenly my mind opened to the light. "What . . . what . . . where am I?"

Joraleman stood looking down at me like he thought my next question was going to be "Who am I?" and he wasn't sure what the answer was. "In my office."

I was lying on my stomach on a couch, staring at a holo of some other world projected on the wall behind him. At first I didn't know it from the real thing. My eyesight strobed again, turning the view into a negative, and back. I put a hand up to my eyes. My head felt like it was ready to split in half.

"Here." He pressed a cup into my hands, winced as a spark of static leaped between us. "On my homeworld we call this Holy Water. They claim it can put life back in the dead."

I fumbled it up to my mouth and took another swallow. It was a lot like drinking molten lead. "If"—I gasped—"if it don't kill you first." I drank some more, a sip at a time. "How'd I get here? What . . . happened?"

He sat down on the corner of his desk and took a drink from the cloth-covered decanter, grimacing. My eyes still weren't working right —he wore a halo of pale rainbows. "I found you wandering in the hall like a burnout a few hours ago. A lot of other people were doing the same thing, at the time. . . ." He shook his head. "You were really telling the truth." I began to see how dazed he looked—like someone who'd seen the end of the world. "Needless to say, it was a shock, if not exactly a complete surprise, around here. But how the hell did it *happen*

— I thought you said the plan was just for a takeover. . . ." He rubbed his head, rumpling his yellow hair.

I didn't answer him, because I couldn't. I shut my eyes, trying to focus on the aching chaos inside. The last thing I remembered: *I remembered being chained to a cot . . . Jule . . . Rubiy . . . the chain dropping away. The control room; Rubiy by the computer board, turning on us just as we were about to . . . And then something alien filling my head; my whole body like a jar full of lightning. . . .* I opened my eyes again. "It didn't happen. The takeover Rubiy planned, it didn't happen. We stopped him before he could use the gas. . . ." And then Rubiy had disappeared, and Jule with him. And I hadn't been transformed by wildfire so much as I'd been a kind of transformer for it: knowing that if I thought the word, it would be set free. . . .

"But you didn't stop them—they've destroyed everything!" He took another drink from the cloth-covered bottle.

"What're you talking about?"

"The underground vaults have collapsed. Some are full of molten rock. Everything's in ruins. Why would they do that? And what kind of weapon—" His voice broke off.

I took a gulp of my own drink. "Did . . . how many people were . . . killed?"

"Nobody! That's the damnedest part of it—nobody was seriously hurt." He wiped his mouth; rainbows splintered and danced.

I sighed as the tension flowed out of me. Joraleman was staring at me. I said, "It wasn't part of the plan. . . . It was the Hydrans."

"The Spooks?" He straightened. *"Why?"*

"Why do you think?" I sat up finally, swearing at what it did to my back. Joraleman watched me, not saying anything, until I got my face under control. "Why do you think?" I said it again, meeting his eyes. "They knew what Rubiy was planning, because I told them. They told me they had to think about it . . . and they did. They decided to stop him; and they got what they wanted all along, too. God, did they get it. . . ."

He shook his head. "Why now? Why not a long time ago, if they were going to do it at all?"

Because they'd been waiting for a focus, a key . . . just like Rubiy had. And they'd finally found one.

(What happened to you?) But he didn't say it out loud. Because suddenly he knew the answer. He looked down. "A higher justice," he mumbled, and took another drink.

I thought about what would happen to me if he ever told anybody the truth. And then I thought about how he hadn't even. . . . "You're protecting me. Why'd you bring me here, instead of turning me in?"

He looked up again and his mouth twisted. "Because you were right. And because when I found you, you weren't in any shape to answer a lot of angry questions."

"How long was I like that?"

He glanced at something on his desk. "Close to five hours now."

Jule. Jule disappearing, along with Rubiy. . . . I pulled myself to my feet. "We got to talk to somebody. The psions in the town, somebody's got to stop them. Rubiy's back there, and he knows—"

"It's already been taken care of." He held up a hand.

"It has?" I swayed.

He nodded; the haze of distortion shimmered around him. "We got a radio call from somebody named Siebeling—"

"Siebeling!" I sat down again. "Is he all right?"

"As far as I know. All I know is we got his call right after the disaster, and he claims he turned the psions' own show back on them somehow. We sent out a security force. They ought to be back any time, if—" Something buzzed on his desk. He turned away, "Joraleman," he said, speaking into the intercom.

I closed my eyes and stopped listening, concentrating on what I'd just heard. Siebeling was all right. Then somehow he must have gotten the best of Rubiy, and Jule must be with him. I wanted to find them, but my mind was too full of noise: too full of the suffocating fog of shock trapped here inside the dome, hundreds of human beings numb with it, filling all the levels of the compound; too full of the jangling static of my own pain. I quit trying and made myself relax.

Joraleman left his desk and went to the door, saying something I didn't really hear. He left me there alone, and after a while I dozed off.

I don't know how long I slept. I woke up again just as the door opened; knowing whose face I was about to see. . . . I got up from the couch.

"Cat!" Siebeling said. An aura shone around him, twice as bright as Joraleman's. His happiness and his relief were blinding. I rubbed my eyes, realizing then that the light I saw around him wasn't really light at all.

And then Siebeling was hugging me like a long-lost friend. I yelped and pushed free as the burns on my back came alive. Siebeling's hands dropped; surprise and sudden guilt flashed around him.

"Hey—" trying to keep my voice even, fumbling for a grin, "hey, Doc. You look like you're really glad to see me for once." I laughed.

But his guilt only doubled, flashing crimson. And I'd be lying if I didn't admit I enjoyed it. He said, "Jule told me everything. . . . Will you let me look at it?"

I unsealed the jacket and shrugged it off my shoulders, gritting my teeth. I heard him suck in his breath.

"Second and third degree burns, and they left them like that—?"

"That's the point." I pulled the jacket on again before I could think about how much it would hurt.

He looked away at Joraleman, his face hardening. "This is barbaric. How can you—"

"It ain't his fault," I said. "He would've stopped it, if he could."

Siebeling nodded, grim-faced. "Then will you help me see that he gets decent medical treatment?"

Joraleman was looking at patterns in the rug. "That might be . . . difficult, under the circumstances." He glanced up, with his face red.

Siebeling opened his mouth, shut it again without saying anything.

"Where's Jule? Didn't she come with you?" I changed the subject to the only thing I wanted to hear.

"No." Siebeling looked back at me. "Isn't she here?" His mind took a sick lurch. "Where's Rubiy? What happened?"

"He ain't here. He got away. I thought you'd . . . ?" But he hadn't.

"My God, where the hell are they?" Panic leaped into his voice. "What's he done to her?"

"I think maybe I've got an idea," Joraleman said slowly. "I heard outside that we've lost control of the planetary shield. It doesn't answer commands from the equipment here—and while it doesn't, there's no way in or out of Cinder. We're trapped, like flies in a bottle. Somebody broke into the computer and tampered with the programming."

"Rubiy." I nodded. "He did somethin' in the systems room. But how's that tell us where he is now?"

"He could be at the transmitting station. He could be controlling it directly from there, if he's that good. He could still be holding this world hostage, single-handed." He reached for the intercom on his desk again. "Maybe it's about time we had another talk with somebody on top. . . . Joraleman here." He'd called Kielhosa—the voice that answered him was one I was never going to forget.

". . . if they know so damned much about it! Why didn't they stop it before, if that's what they were here for?"

"But remember what the kid told me, Keel: they were cut off, they couldn't get a message. . . . Never mind, we can fill you in later. Listen, is Tanake back at the systems center? We'll meet you there, five minutes. Uh, one more thing, a favor: give me your word that whoever shows up you'll keep your mouth shut?"

Kielhosa grunted. "So it's the kid. You know damn well that he's mines property. Is it him?"

"All I have here are a couple of Corporate Security agents. Well, what about it—have I got your word?"

There was a long silence. Then Kielhosa's voice said, "You've got it." He started to say something else, but changed it. "Make it fifteen minutes; Tanake's not back yet."

"Right." Joraleman switched off, looking at me. "I owe you this much, Cat. . . . We can join the others at the systems center, that'll give you all a chance to fill each other in." Siebeling nodded, a motion full of angry tension. Joraleman shrugged apologetically. "I'm afraid it's the best we can do. Meanwhile, maybe you'll join me in a drink?" He passed Siebeling a cup; the top of the decanter was full of them. I sat down and he filled mine again. I took a long swallow, trying to get numb from the inside out. Joraleman poured for Siebeling and poured some more for himself. "I'm Meade Joraleman, by the way. I'm Chief Purchaser here. I don't remember our ever being formally introduced out there."

"Ardan Siebeling." Siebeling shook hands, trying to force himself to keep calm. I felt him groping for something to say, anything that would fill up his mind. "Frankly, you don't seem to be very disturbed by all this . . . ?"

"You mean, the fact that in spite of everything you tried to do, you are now sitting on top of the most expensive pile of rubble in this part of the galaxy?" He shrugged again, and sat down in his desk chair. His voice was slurring a little. "I'm beyond surprise, Dr. Siebeling. . . . And I have to admit this isn't my first toast of the day. I've been drinking to my resignation. The nice thing about this stuff is that it doesn't give you a hangover." He leaned back in his seat, looking up at the holo on the wall. "Before you accuse me of leaving the leaky ship, let me assure you the idea isn't a whim as of this afternoon. It's been a while coming." He glanced at me.

I said, "I'll drink to that," and I did.

Siebeling nodded.

Joraleman set down his cup. "We ought to be drinking to you. How the hell did you manage to subdue an army of psion traitors single-handed, anyway?"

Siebeling looked at the cup on the desk. It rose a few inches into the air and hung there, before it settled gently back again.

Joraleman shook his head. "Of course."

Siebeling didn't even smile. He took a deep breath, forcing himself to concentrate, and told Joraleman about the underground storage tunnels. He'd put gas into the ventilating system, just like they'd planned for the mines, after everyone had gathered there for their final orders. He'd set free the handful of miners who'd been locked up in town by the psions, and they'd helped him clean up the ones who'd gotten clear of the gas. . . . He told the whole story like he wasn't even thinking about it. He was thinking about Jule. So was I.

Joraleman grinned and shook his head again.

"So what's gonna happen here, now? Are the mines gonna be shut down?" I asked it to stop thinking about her.

Joraleman nodded. "They'll have to be, at least for the present. But don't get your hopes up; the Federation runs on telhassium. We'll be reconstructing, the faster the better. Time is money."

"Oh."

He held another drink out to me and I took it. "To the Spooks." I lifted my cup.

They looked at me.

"Just kidding." I took another long swallow, looking at my bond tag.

Joraleman half smiled. "Sure. To a higher justice. . . ."

I put my cup down, starting to feel a little gorked, remembering that I was drinking on an empty stomach. The colors around Siebeling and Joraleman hurt my head. I leaned over and looked at my own reflection in the tabletop beside me. It was only a reflection, no halos, and it looked like death warmed over. There were dark smudges of bruise around my eyes, like something had hit me in the face, and dried blood on my upper lip from a nosebleed I didn't remember having. I looked away again.

Joraleman glanced at the clock in his desk. "We can go on down, if you're ready." Siebeling nodded, more than ready. Joraleman looked back at me. "How about you, kid?"

"Sure." I shrugged, and wished I hadn't. "Let's go."

We went to the lift and down a couple of levels. I wished it could have been up, instead; but I didn't let it show.

There was a handful of officials waiting for us in the hall outside the systems center. One of them was Kielhosa. He gave Joraleman a dirty look and muttered something. I stopped behind Siebeling and didn't look at anyone. They were all wearing halos to my mind's eye, flickering like the night sky. Siebeling's stood out like the sun.

Joraleman was making introductions. One of the guards said to me, "I've seen you somewhere, kid."

"That's 'Corpse,' to you." I frowned. So did he. He didn't take his eyes off me. I looked away as Joraleman introduced the man named Tanake; the one he'd told me might listen to my story, once. Tanake looked at me like he really believed I was a Corpse. If he wondered why I was wearing a miner's jacket, he didn't ask. I nodded. His hair had gone white, his face was aging; something about the lines of it made me think of the Hydrans. I glanced back at Kielhosa; but he was gone. I stared at the place where he'd been standing, trying to rest against the cold wall of the hallway. My back hurt like hell under the weight of my jacket, and my head hurt worse. Everyone was asking questions, but they were all a blur to me. I let Siebeling give all the answers.

Finally Kielhosa showed up again, followed by a mob of security guards. My legs almost gave out on me before I saw that they were guarding a group of prisoners and not coming to get me. One of the prisoners was Galiess, crowned with splintering light. She looked at Siebeling and then right at me, as if nobody else existed. Kielhosa was asking permission to question them about Rubiy and the planetary shield. Tanake agreed. I thought about what he could do to get answers, and my knees got weak again. Kielhosa gave a signal and the guards started Galiess moving again. Her eyes stayed on me as she passed. I'd never seen a look like that: I never wanted to see it again. Her mind wove into mine: (I told him what you were, I told him to get rid of you; but he wouldn't listen. He thought he knew everything; but he didn't understand anything. And now you've ruined him. He should have listened to me. . . .) The contact was gone, and so was she.

I looked down. Siebeling and the rest of them had gone into the systems center. I followed them inside. The monitor screens looked out across piles of rubble like blind eyes, like the brain of a ruined body. The whole room shimmered with a dim blue radiance, as if I could even see the life-force of machines.

Siebeling was standing with the others where the engineers were trying to make the shield respond. The energy fog around him crackled, and I heard his voice rising, angry and impatient. I moved toward the viewscreens instead, too tense and restless to stand and listen. I tried to lean on the metal panel, jerked back as it gave me a shock. I kept my hands away from it as I looked from scene to scene: dust and broken stone and twisted metal all deep down below the room I stood in. Tiny figures moved through all the scenes, already starting to put the chaos back in order. I wondered how many bondies had stood in this room even once. And then I found a screen that looked out over the snow outside the complex. The crumpled, shining plain lay cold and peaceful between the scenes of ruin. The compound's lights turned the snow to stars, and beyond them the night's rippling sky turned it blue. I thought about Jule out there somewhere with Rubiy, and suddenly all that mattered was making contact; finding her, finding out what he wanted. I let my mind out into the dark.

And he must have been there, waiting. His mind caught in mine like a hook and I couldn't pull loose, while he made me understand what he wanted. And locked inside his sending was another mind: Jule's. . . .

And then Siebeling was beside me, whispering, "Cat!" His voice jarred me back into the room. "What's the matter with you? You're projecting, stop it—" The words were low and urgent; his mind was forcing me to remember where we were, and what these people thought of psions.

I waved my hands. (Will you listen?) Controlling my thoughts, I said, "It's Jule—Rubiy, I mean! Rubiy's got Jule with him. He just showed me where he is."

Siebeling took a step back.

"He knows everything. He knows what happened here, and what you did. He's waiting for us now at the shield transmitter. I could feel him thinking that he knew we'd try to come after her. It's what he wants. If we don't show . . . he'll kill her."

"You're sure?"

"I'm sure." My hands tightened.

Joraleman said, "One of the psions has the woman you were looking for?"

"Yeah. Rubiy, the one I told you about, who got away—" Turning, I backed into the guard who'd been watching me the whole time. I couldn't stop the sound it squeezed out of me.

Everything clicked together in his mind, I could almost hear it; he had hold of my arm before I could get away. "Sir!" He pushed up my sleeve. The bond tag stood out as red as fire.

"Shit." I pulled away from him.

"We'll straighten all that out later. Go on with what you were saying." Siebeling said it quietly, as if nothing had happened at all.

I flexed my hands. "Rubiy. . . ." But I couldn't remember my own name by then. Joraleman looked embarrassed, and Tanake . . . Tanake said, "Go on, bondsman." And I realized then that he'd seen through it all along; he'd known what they were hiding and tried to pretend he didn't. But now . . . "I'm sorry." He looked at me. The guard had his stungun out; Tanake waved it away.

I nodded, and sighed. "Rubiy got away, the head psion—he's the one who's got control of the shield. He's got Jule and he wants us—Siebeling and me. If we don't do what he wants, he'll shut off the entire shield."

You could have heard a feather drop in the room. Without the planetary shield the radiation pouring in from outside would kill everyone on the planet's surface. "He'll just kill you, too," Joraleman said finally. "What good is that going to do anybody?"

Siebeling shook his head. "We're not helpless. Remember we're psions, too. Give us this last chance to try to trap him. Help us, and we'll help you."

Tanake put his hands behind his back. "So if you answer his challenge, he may possibly let you get close enough to stop him. . . . If you fail, what will this madman ask for next?"

Siebeling shook his head. "I don't know."

"We have the weaponry to destroy the force barrier that seals off the control station—and the station itself, and anyone in it—if we have to."

Siebeling's face froze.

"You do that and you got no way to be sure you'll get control of the shield back." I read the worry that lay in the minds of his engineers and said it out loud. "You want to risk that?"

Tanake looked back at me, startled, and then at the engineers. "No. And I don't particularly want to cause needless deaths, either. All right, Siebeling—if you want to take the risk instead, you can try it your way. We'll give you any equipment you need."

I took a deep breath.

"Bondsman, I think I anticipate your questions. You've been poorly paid for your part in this. I wish there was something we could do; but

now . . . At any rate, for the present I can leave you in the custody of
Dr. Siebeling."

I thought he must be a mind reader. I nodded again, my mouth tight.
"You're free to go with him, then. I think you are needed." He figured they wouldn't have any trouble getting me back. But I knew he
was doing the best he could for me, and maybe that was more than I
could have expected. "I only wish things could have turned out more
happily for all concerned. Good hunting."

20

WE WERE IN a snowtrack together, just Siebeling and me under the light-curtains of night, following a course that would take us to Jule and Rubiy. Tanake had given us everything we'd asked for, including the 'track. Siebeling even knew how to drive one; but he didn't know why I thought that was funny. I finished a cup of coffee from the thermal bottle, and glanced over at him again. "You want some?"

He started. He shook his head, looking out at the night. The halo of his thoughts still shimmered around him. He hadn't said anything for nearly an hour.

So I said, "Hey, Doc." He looked at me. "I see—light around you."

He glanced down at himself, back at me. "What do you mean?"

"I ain't sure," not knowing how to explain it. "Even machinery glows, ever since the Hydrans . . . did what they did, at the mines."

"It's true, then, everything Joraleman told me? I thought he must have been—exaggerating." *(Crazy)*. "The Hydrans focused telekinetic energy through you, to cause so much destruction?" He sounded like he'd never really be able to believe it.

"Oh, yeah. . . ." I put a hand up to my head. "Believe it. I was there when it happened, and I got the headache to prove it." Somehow it didn't come out sounding like a joke.

"Why didn't you tell me? I could have given you something." They'd let him treat my back, but I hadn't said anything about my head.

"I didn't want anything. I don't want no drugs; it could get in the way of my Gift if—when I have to use it. I can handle the pain." I was handling it; Rubiy was right. Somewhere I was finding the control, because I had to. I wondered if Rubiy was going to be right about this meeting, too. "Don't worry about me."

Siebeling looked at me for a minute, and then he shook his head. "And you're seeing some sort of energy?"

"I don't see it, exactly. I *feel* it, like colored noise. Humans more than anything else. Psions are like suns." I wondered if the Hydrans saw the world like that, and I wished suddenly that I could see myself from the outside. "It's . . . I dunno—"

"It's incredible." A part of him wished he could get me into a lab and study me. "I've never heard of anything like this. I think you're probably very lucky you've got a mind left."

"The Hydrans wouldn't hurt me. They know me, they trust me, they think—" I broke off, remembering the message they'd left in my mind. "The first time they saw me they knew I was alien, like they were; even though I was from the mines." It wasn't hard to say that, anymore. "It didn't surprise them that one of their own people could come from outside. They remembered it from—way back. But the oldest memories are tangled up now. They don't seem to know anymore what a lot of it really means."

"They gave a lot to you."

I touched my head. "Yeah. More than I knew. . . . They tried to make a joining with me, the first time they saw me. But with them a joining really is total, it's every part of them, and I couldn't do it. . . . I still can't, really. There's always things I want to hold back; even though they made me a real psion. They said it's because I was raised like a human. Humans can't let go of themselves and give everything that way, they ain't strong enough."

"You weren't just raised like a human; you are human. As much as you are Hydran." Like he thought I could forget that.

"My bad luck." I frowned. "Anyway, I couldn't take the joining, it almost. . . . But when it happened, it changed me, my psi . . . all the barriers came down. . . . And when it happened, I saw a lot of what they remembered. Are all Hydrans like that? Do they share everything? And what are they doing here?"

"I don't know much about these people, really. I don't think anyone does. Even to another Hydran the amount of telepathic communion they share would seem extreme—isolation and hardship have forced them so close together just for survival. Most other Hydrans lost any group mind practice long ago. If my wife and I had been that far apart psychologically, we'd never have . . . been what we were. But I do remember a few things. For instance, their belief in a god-being. . . ." He leaned back in the seat.

So we kept talking, to keep from thinking—talking about the Hydrans of Cinder and what they'd been once. About what it must have meant to be part of a whole civilization that was united in a way the

Human Federation could never be. About Cinder becoming life for the
Hydran colonists and giving them shelter when their empire failed,
until it had become a holy thing, a religion, to them. And about why
they'd come all the way to the Crab:

"The Hydrans were miners? They mined telhassium, too. . . .
Why?"

"Probably for the same reasons we do."

"My people . . ." I felt my face twist.

Siebeling said, gently, "There's nothing to indicate that they used
slave labor. Respect for every part of life is as much a part of them as
psionic ability; it has to be, to protect them from themselves. But don't
see them as simplistic saints and martyrs, either. They have their imper-
fections, they share the whole spectrum of emotion with human beings;
they have their resentments and anger and selfish impulses, even if they
can't act on them as easily. And the ones you met here have had a long
time and good reasons to grow inbred and xenophobic. They used you
—even if you let them—to get what they wanted; just the way Rubiy
tried to do. Accept your heritage, but accept it honestly. Don't deny
your humanity for a dream."

I didn't say anything, but I guess he understood what showed on my
face. Because suddenly he looked down, and he was thinking about me
being half and half . . . like his son had been half and half. The son
who would never hear those words from him. Thinking about how I'd
made him remember his loss, and see what had happened to his own life
—made him look at it until he finally knew he had to live with it. And
that all the thanks he'd given me was to make things worse than ever
for me; that he'd hurt me just like he'd hurt . . . Jule, and everyone
else. He said, "Cat, I don't know how—"

"Look, just forget about it. It don't matter now." I realized that it
really didn't, anymore . . . any more than it mattered now if I never
learned whether he was my father.

He didn't say anything else for a while. But then he started to talk
again, as if he was trying to explain something; I wasn't sure whether it
was all meant for me or not. "When you feel that if you looked around
you, everything you'd see would be sick, with no way to cure it, you
close your eyes—and your mind—until you don't see anything anymore. Even a private hell is more appealing than a public one . . .
sometimes." He wanted me to understand why he hadn't known what
he was doing to me when he sent me back to Contract Labor.

"Yeah, I guess." I felt him look at me. "Jule knew."

"Yes . . ." And it was back in his mind again, losing her, grief and fear for the only other one he'd shared as much with—the only other woman he'd ever loved as much as his wife. His wife: golden, her skin, her hair . . . she was beautiful . . . and he'd lost her, too. And remembering all that again now was almost more than he could bear.

I didn't know what to say, so for a while I didn't say anything. Then I said, "Starfall," which was what they said in Oldcity, when your house burned, when the surplus food allotment was contaminated . . . when somebody lost everything. And I wanted him to know that in a way I did understand, but it seemed like it wasn't enough. I thought about the time he'd said he was sorry to me, maybe he had meant it. I wondered what I'd really expected him to feel. "What did your kid look like?"

"My kid . . ." He stopped, and took a deep breath. "He probably would have looked a lot like you, actually."

"I wish I could have met him."

He glanced at me, and smiled just a little.

The sun came up, fading the colored night into seablue. And I finally knew, without being told. . . . "Now. Stop, we're there." I looked out over the control panel. There was nothing to see except snow and sky glaring; but my inner sight showed me an energy source so bright it was almost black. I frowned. "Is it underground? There's nothing out there, but I can feel—"

"Something's out there; the instruments are going crazy. A shield generator would have to have at least part of its plant above ground; probably Rubiy's left the scatter screen up around it. I think we'll be seeing it any time now." His hands tightened on the wheel.

I nodded. "Look, I've been thinking—let me go in first, alone, all right?"

"You?"

"Yeah. Stay out here and back me up. I mean, we don't know what he's planning—but he's out for revenge, and it could be anything. And I just figure . . . that I could handle it better, being the telepath. There's no way we can take him by surprise now. This way, if something happens, at least he won't get us both at once, like he did with Jule and me." I pulled on my mittens.

"I see. . . . Are you sure you can do this?"

I shrugged. "I don't know. I won't know till I try. But he's got to know now that I beat him once, at least: when he tried to probe me after he murdered Dere. He ain't perfect. That ought to be good for something."

"You tricked Rubiy." He'd known it for days, but now he finally believed it.

I grinned. "See, Doc, I ain't such a deadhead, after all. If I did it once, I can trick him again. Dere always said that's how psions play the game to win. Like playing Last Chance." I twitched my hand, catching imaginary game pieces; trying to make myself believe it.

Siebeling didn't say anything. He was thinking about what I'd said, and about Jule out there. And he wanted to be a telepath more than—
"All right."

I pushed the faceplate on my parka hood down and opened the door.
"Wait."

I looked back at him.

"Do you want to try a joining?" He was almost embarrassed, as if he felt like he didn't really have the right to ask.

"Yeah. . . . No." I thought this was something I had to do myself; something I owed to Rubiy. And some part of me still wasn't sure I could count on being joined to Siebeling, if Jule wasn't there between us. "It's better if we're not tied. But if I need help"—I jumped down into the snow—"you'll know it!"

"Be careful. Don't . . . take any chances."

"Not with Jule's life." Ahead of me was only white noise. I started walking toward it.

21

THERE WASN'T ANYTHING—and then there was, right in front of me, as if it had been there all along. The shield control. Even though I knew what was happening, it startled me more than it should have. I stopped where I was, holding the cold, bright air in my lungs.

The building was a huge metal bowl flipped upside down, with a ring of towers and filament wires wrapping it like a web. The bowl was coated with ice, in layers that had rippled and run, flowed and refrozen along lines of force until it looked like a spun sugar castle. The silver-coated towers dripped icicles like frozen tears. And all around it a forest of the crystal trees made their glittering music. The sight took my breath away, for a long minute I stood there forgetting everything but my eyes. But then I remembered what this place was, and how it had cut off a whole world from the rest of the galaxy. I made my eyes search out the entrance, and started toward it.

And as I walked, I thought about what I was doing here. And how half a year ago, back in Oldcity, there wasn't anything that could have gotten me to do this . . . nobody I would have done it for. Then I thought about how I'd never wished I was back in Oldcity instead, no matter what was happening to me here. *No matter what.* I focused my thoughts and wove my mind into a wall, blocking the bright noise of the shield's energy and my own battered body. None of that was important now; it was only static, and once I stopped listening, it didn't exist. There was no trace in my mind of anyone else's trying to reach me—not Jule, not Rubiy. I took out my stungun, and then I went into the building.

The hallway was dark after the brightness of the snow, but not too dark for my cat eyes. I pushed back my hood and unfastened my parka so I could move easily. There was humming in the air, and something more—the crackling overflow of trapped energies, that made my skin tingle. I couldn't help wondering if it was something more than the shield. But still there was no touch against my mind. I could almost be here alone. I didn't let my mind explore; letting Rubiy make the first move instead. I could see light up ahead now, real light, coming from one of the control rooms.

I reached the doorway and stepped into the light. The first thing I saw was Jule, just sitting there, waiting. But not because she wanted to. Her dark hair floated on the charged air as she turned her head to look at me; her mouth was open as if she was trying to warn me, but couldn't. Her gray eyes were the eyes of something caught in a trap.

"Well, Cat. It seems I'm a good judge of human nature after all."

I raised my head. Rubiy was waiting for me across the room. He was sitting in front of a control panel, with circuitry creeping up the walls, surrounding us all. Making me think about webs: spiderwebs, mindwebs. I raised the stungun, and like some fool in a threedy show I said, "You're under arrest, Rubiy. If you move I'll—"

The stungun jerked itself out of my hand and flew across the room. I watched it drop down on the panel behind him. I'd been so caught up in protecting my body from a mind attack that I'd forgotten to watch the gun. I kept trying to swallow, but all of a sudden my throat was as dry as dirt.

"You won't be needing that." His face was as calm and unreadable as ever, as if nothing ever touched him.

I shrugged, trying to match his expression. "I've come. What do you want?"

"So, you really came to risk your life for Jule taMing? For the daughter of Centauri Transport?"

I nodded, holding my mind closed as tight as a fist. But still he didn't try anything against it.

"And even you were working for Corporate Security all along. My compliments to them. Your cover was ingenious."

"Good enough to fool you." I touched my bond tag.

"So it seems. . . . And you're still wearing that. It must be satisfying to know you've been so well-rewarded for your loyalty to the Federation Mines." He lifted an eyebrow.

I tried to laugh, but the truth made it stick in my throat. "Look, what do you want with us?"

"What do *you* want, Cat? To take me prisoner, and go back to the mines as your reward? Is that why you came? Is it worth that—are they worth that to you?"

"Shut up." I went to stand beside Jule and touched her shoulder. I couldn't reach into her mind.

"Cat. I'll tell you what I want. . . ."

I looked back at him. And suddenly I was seeing a real face, tight with strain and fear, his eyes that saw his own humiliation and death ahead. And his mind was open—he'd dropped his guard to me.

His mind clawed at me: (I want to get out of this! Help me, Cat, you're the only one who can. Turn me in and they'll destroy me, they'll destroy you, too. Help me—and I'll teach you every trick I know. I'll make you a better telepath than I am. Work with me and you can still have everything I promised, everything you ever wanted—!)

I felt my hands cover my ears as if they could shut him out. *Lies, why should he . . . ?* But I took a step toward him. Jule gasped, as if she felt my control slipping. . . .

But his mind was open to me, it was all true. And I'd known all along that this was what he'd wanted me for, what he'd planned for me all along. He couldn't believe that I hadn't understood—that Galiess was too old, that he needed someone new and smart, someone young. Galiess knew he'd chosen me—she resented it, and that was why she'd resented me. But she was loyal; together they would have helped me, they would have taught me . . . I was only a raw beginner. I'd created sophisticated results out of blind ignorance, I didn't even know the things I could really do.

Or what I had done. No one had ever tricked him before. But I'd tricked him. I pulled him down, me, the half-breed kid—but he didn't hate me for it. He admired me. If I helped him now, we could still escape this trap together. He'd take me with him, there wasn't anything I couldn't be, or have. . . . And my mind was full of what it would be like, again: the worlds and the wonder, the satisfaction, knowing they all had to ask *me*. . . .

And this was why I'd been afraid to face him. Because now I wanted it all. I wanted to know what I could really do with my mind. I wanted to be everything I could be, proud of my Gift and in control. . . . I wanted to know how it would feel to have everything money could buy, power, respect. . . . (Everything I want—everything?) I looked at Jule; my hand slid down her back in a caress.

Her face froze as she understood; but then her eyes said that she understood everything, before they dropped away. And that she knew there was no hope.

(Jule, I—) I pulled my hand back.

(Take her, if you want her!) Rubiy caught my mind. (Use her, stop being a fool! Don't you know who she is; what the taMings stand for? They're one of the most powerful and corrupt shipping families in the Federation! They're part of the cartel that hired me to take over the Federation Mines! You've let her seduce you all along: for what? Have you forgotten Oldcity, the slums of Quarro? She never cared about you, none of them do. They're all alike, parasites feeding off the combines that feed off the gutter scum—you and me, Cityboy! Always the ones who suffer and bleed . . . because they keep it that way. Because they need it! We make the systems work, our suffering, our despair. They're using you, they've always used you. Hate them. . . .)

The way he hated them. I touched his hatred, and black bitterness, rage like cold diamonds, ripped me inside. There was no light in the world, only a craving hunger, the need to survive. There was nothing I wouldn't do, nothing I couldn't do to them; they deserved it all and it was my right. . . .

But it wasn't my right. I was only half human . . . and half Hydran. And now at last I saw what that really meant—that a part of every other Hydran lived in that half of me: a presence born into me like instinct, the presence of the people who rejected the ultimate use of power. To take a life was the unforgivable wrong; to destroy another was to destroy yourself.

"No . . . I can't." I stood beside Jule again, my mind torn in two, my hands tightening into fists. Jule, who was only Jule, who'd never done anything to me but show me she believed in me. But at the same time I knew that everything he said was true, and that another part of me hated half the universe for the things they'd done to me, to him, to so many others like us for so long, so long. . . . That he had the right to hate them. That we were the same . . . once.

But not now. Now I saw how hate and power had twisted him into the thing he hated. He didn't give a damn for anybody, including me. He'd destroy the only thing that had ever mattered to me—the thing I shared with Jule, and Siebeling—and use me to do it. He'd use me worse than anyone had; he'd destroy me with his mind sickness. . . . He was crazy, and I couldn't let him do it. I had to stop him—

I had to look at him. His face was a lie; his eyes didn't show me anything. I knew then that it was too late to stop anything. I'd let him through my guard, and into my mind—

He took control of it.

Then I learned about triumph, and thought maybe I was going to die of it: he held my mind cupped in his hands, he could smack them together and smash it like a bug; every time I breathed it was only because he let me. He waited, letting me feel it, letting me see how strong he was; that no one could stop him, we were all crazy even to have tried.

He nodded, and his mind's hand loosened around me. "I've misjudged you twice, now, it seems. The first time I underestimated you, and I paid for it. At least this time I didn't make that mistake. This time the mistake was yours, half-breed: you've lost sight of reality. I am—disappointed. I'd hoped. . . . But your choice is plain enough."

So I knew what would happen next. We were all going to die. And it wouldn't even be because we'd ruined his plans; it would be because we'd hurt his damn pride. Now he was going to prove that he was still the strongest, and the best. He didn't have anything else left, no way to escape, no future; but he could still have that much. He'd get his final satisfaction from the three of us, and especially from one half-breed bondie who'd ruined everything. . . . *(Siebeling!)* I called him without even meaning to. *No, don't think about him, he'll—*

Rubiy smiled. (Think about him all you like; I already know. He's coming to join us now. We'll wait for him; I think it won't be long.)

He picked something up from the control panel, came and put it into my hands, cold metal. Static sparked in my palms as it touched them, and made me flinch. I tried to feel surprised, looking down at it, but I couldn't. It was a six/ten energy hand weapon. In my whole life I'd only seen one a couple of times, on Citicorpses in riot squads.

I looked up into his smile, and didn't need to ask what he wanted me to do with it. But the pictures came into my mind, where I couldn't close my eyes to keep them out; and I saw my hand press the button—to kill Siebeling, and then Jule, and finally myself. I wouldn't be able to stop it, and neither would they, because he'd have control of us all. He could make us do anything to each other. *Anything.* My mind started to form images of . . . *No!* I jerked the gun up, trying to aim it at him.

And then suddenly my throat closed and I couldn't get any air; I couldn't even make a sound. Seconds passed and more seconds and more; the paralysis didn't come undone. The room floated around me. I got too dizzy to stand; I went down on my hands and knees with my chest on fire, clawing at my throat. . . . And then he let me go, and I crouched panting with my head down, my eyes shut.

(Get up.)

I got up, somehow.

(Pick up the gun.)

I did.

Rubiy came over to me and caught my jaw with his hand, looking into my eyes. (Yes, I could kill you all myself—it would be simpler. But this way I'll enjoy it so much more.) He let go of me again. (Consider the irony of the situation, Cat, while you have the time left. I find the arrangement fitting.)

(You bastard, I'm not gonna kill for you, I won't, I . . . can't.)

And he knew I couldn't kill, because I was Hydran—he knew what it would do to me. But he knew I would kill, because I wasn't Hydran enough—or strong enough to stop him. Because he was the best, he was stronger than any of us. *But not stronger than all of us. (Jule—!)* This time slipping free, finding her in the darkness of our mind prison; linking, feeling her mind flow into mine.

Her hand rose and clutched at mine. But we were barely touching fingertips through the cage bars. It was only because Rubiy chose to let it happen, because he enjoyed pulling our strings. . . .

(Cat!) Her voice filled my mind; she knew everything Rubiy had shown me. (Why did you come? I wasn't worth it. . . .) And her guilt was a weakness that Rubiy used against her, like he used my own guilt, and my half-alienness. He was playing us all against ourselves, we were flies in his web, and every time we struggled we only pulled it tighter around us. (Jule, he can't make me use this thing.) I looked at the gun, trying to make myself believe that; but knowing, too, that he knew every secret fear, and how to turn them all against me.

And then he reached out and broke our contact. Jule's fingers slid down mine, my hand dropped . . . I was alone.

And Siebeling was coming. I felt Rubiy focus his mind like a part of my own, to take Siebeling over; I felt like it was my own mind being lost all over again. Now he had us all. Not wanting to, I turned to watch the door, and I waited.

I saw Siebeling come into the light. His face was stiff, like Jule's face; the face of something trapped and helpless. His eyes went from Jule to me to Rubiy, and back to me. I had the gun pointed at him. His eyes asked the question—

(No, I don't want to do it!) But I couldn't reach into his mind and make him sure, any more than I could find Jule again. My hand held a gun on him, and all he knew was that he was going to die.

"Dr. Siebeling." Rubiy nodded. "Now the circle is complete, and we can finish this." He said it out loud; I wondered why he bothered. I felt his mind begin to push me, gently at first and then a little harder; because he had plenty of time, and he wanted to enjoy this. And it wasn't like pain; it wasn't anything I could fight back against, or even get hold of. It was just the understanding that if I didn't do the thing he wanted me to do, in the end my mind would shatter into a million pieces like glass. *I couldn't do it . . . I couldn't . . . but I couldn't stop it.* My hand began to shake, I watched while my other hand rose to steady it . . . he was trying to make my fingers close over the button . . . now both hands were on the gun. But Jule and Siebeling were all I could see. And they were all I had—

And I held him. My fingers froze like a part of the metal, he couldn't make me fire.

It shook him. His control of me slipped a little: he'd taken on too much, he didn't have any reserves left, he couldn't control us all for long. He wasn't a god—he was pulling a bluff too! And I tore his web, found Siebeling first, (Join with me!) But Seibeling's mind turned me back; he wouldn't join. He thought I wanted to kill him. The words formed in my mind, his words: (You lying gutter thief. I should have known better than to trust you.)

(Stop it—) My hands were slipping.

(I should have known what—*no, I*— what you were.) And then everything he'd always thought of me, despising me, denying me: (I should have known.)

"God damn you. . . ." My voice broke.

(No! Cat! I won't!) Horror filled his face.

Rubiy pushed me and I pressed the button.

I knew what he'd done then, I jerked my hand aside, but it was too late. The energy beam caught Siebeling and dumped him against the wall. Jule screamed with his pain, and my mind echoed with it.

And then he disappeared from my mind. Rubiy's gloating pride filled the emptiness. *It was a trick, another trick;* and Siebeling was dead. I whimpered and swayed on my feet, but Rubiy controlled my whole body, holding me there. I felt my head pull around to look at Jule. She sat with everything and nothing in her eyes and on her face.

"I'm sorry, Jule. I'm sorry, I'm sorry. . . ." I felt my hands swing around with the gun. She just kept on staring.

Now there were only the two of us left; Rubiy knew he could make us do anything. Now it was Jule's turn to die. He'd made me kill once, and after I killed Jule too, he wouldn't even have to force me to use the gun on myself. Because I wouldn't want to live.

I saw Jule behind my eyes, and what I was going to do to her—to Jule, for him. And I knew that there had to be something stronger than Rubiy, and stronger than hate, in what she meant to me. Finding that thing was all that mattered, she was all that mattered. . . . *Find her, find her, nothing else is real.* . . .

And I did find her, caught her, cried, (Jule! join with me—) I felt the blackness close in on me again, but I wove her mind into a band of light, I *made* her join. The power wavered and grew in me, until it felt as strong as it ever had, and suddenly even stronger, as if someone else— The gun swung back and away and back like it was caught in a magnetic field.

Rubiy's mind struggled to tear us apart, but our minds were one, fused by the fire of need. He tried to stop our hearts, but he couldn't reach us. He probed the pain center in my mind and ripped away the block I'd set there; my body cried out with the shock. But that didn't matter, I didn't really feel it; the pain was diluted, absorbed, shared.

And then his attack shifted again; he caught me from behind and his mind forced me down into hell. And hell was my own face mirrored in his eyes, my own stinking face: Cat the gutter thief, Cat the drug dreamer, the slip, the boytoy, Anything-for-a-credit-Cat, seeing my whole rotten, wasted life stripped of its lies. I struggled in his web, trapping myself, until there was nowhere to hide. . . . I relived all the ugliness that had made me what I was, every memory as sharp as hunger. . . . I remembered everything. Until finally he drove me back against the locked door in the deepest part of my mind—the barrier I'd built myself at the beginning of my life. Until I had nowhere else to go, nothing left but to surrender or to break—

I broke through, into the time I couldn't remember, and memory poured into the darkness: *Sleep, my little one . . . dream of the stars and sun . . .* her voice, singing away my fear. I could see her face, the face that smiled only for me, at last; I could reach the mind that touched me with love. And nothing mattered but the joy I felt holding the hand that held everything. . . . *Dream a world of your own.* . . . How could I ever have forgotten that face? . . . *Dream of a life, dream of a time.* . . .

And then, answering me, Rubiy—tearing me loose from that hand . . . *dream of my love . . .* making me remember why, making me follow the strand to its end, the end of the song and the memory and the only *happiness security peace love* I'd ever known. I watched my dreams die again in an Oldcity alley splattered red with death: hearing her screams, the screams that nobody answered, the screams inside my head that only I could hear—the agony, the nightmare. . . . Crying and crying to get free, (But there's no escape, Cat, only death her death your death . . . *death.* . . *.)* And Rubiy showing me how it had to end.

But I wasn't alone anymore! The past was dead, but I was bound to a new life. I was joined more than just mind to mind—soul to soul—and I knew that I never had to be lost and alone again. Strength that was more than just my own strength shrouded me in light, warm pure light, shielding me, shaping me, forcing, forcing—and I was a mirror, I shone with light. (No escape! Rubiy, there's no escape. We've already won!) I felt the terror that had trapped me turn back on him, and the truth drove it home. And I broke him, heard him cry, *(No, stop, I don't want to die—!)*

But he'd shown me the truth and I wanted my revenge; my mind flashed free like a coiled spring. I couldn't stop . . . I pressed the button. The gun jerked in my hand, a smear of blue-white light blurred my view of him—

He died. And his death was my own, in agony that exploded like a star and vaporized my soul inside shattering bonds of light. . . .

And it was quiet. Like the place had been full of—noise, something; but now everything was quiet. Everything. All I could hear was the air scraping down my ragged throat into my lungs, my heart still beating. Jule stumbled up from her seat and stared at me for a minute, holding her head, with tears running down her face. I couldn't tell what she was thinking, but then she went to Siebeling. As she kneeled down beside him, I knew suddenly that it had been a three-way joining, not two-way. That it was Siebeling who'd known the answer to Rubiy, and made me use it. . . . Siebeling was still alive. I watched her lift his head; she said, "Thank you, thank you, thank you. . . ." But I didn't know who she was thanking. Siebeling's eyes were shut; he didn't move.

I looked down at Rubiy, his body lying ruined on the floor instead of their bodies, instead of my own. The nothingness where his mind had been made me gag. I dropped his gun and wiped my hand hard on my pants. And I wondered what was the matter with me, I'd seen plenty of death, I'd seen it happen before. But never because of me, I'd never brought . . . death. *There was too much death behind my eyes.* . . .

I looked back at Jule and Siebeling, blinking hard, fastening my jacket because I felt so cold, as if the death had gotten into my bones. My mouth tasted like death; death stank in the air around me. Because

I was Hydran, body and soul, and to kill was the unforgivable wrong; but I was human, body and soul, and I'd wanted to kill. . . . I pulled my hands in against my chest, against death that stood with me, death that filled the halls like a static cloud, death that was a wound inside. I felt my mind trying to get away, with nowhere to turn but in on itself. Panic rose up in me, knowing what it would mean. "Jule—!" The whisper echoed.

I saw her glance up at me. I reached for the gentle thought of her— (Help me!) But I couldn't find her. The words fell away into the nothing hole I'd made of Rubiy with my mind and a gun: all I could see, all I could feel, all I could remember . . . a wound bleeding hate and terror, a wound that would never heal.

There was no aura shining around her head or Siebeling's anymore. There was no trace of them in my mind. And I knew my thoughts wouldn't cross the endless silence to find them, ever again. I'd never know what I could have done with my Gift. Because I'd killed myself when I killed Rubiy . . . I'd felt both of us die together. My psi was in ashes, it was gone, and everything it had given me was gone with it, forever. I'd never be a telepath again, I'd never be Hydran, everything was gone. I'd killed and I'd survived it, and that was my punishment: to come full circle, to be a walking dead man, blind and alone and going nowhere. . . . Only this time it would be worse. This time I'd know what I was missing.

I stood shivering beside Rubiy's corpse, with my hands pressed against my chest, and started to cry.

Jule teleported to the mines to bring back help. Somewhere in the silent hours while she was gone, Siebeling called my name. I went to him, sat beside him listening to the words that slipped out of his mouth like the hot tears sliding down my face: asking me to forgive him, but I didn't know why; telling me that he'd make it up to me, that he'd make me whole again. But the hole was in my mind and words didn't mean anything anymore. And after a while the words stopped and the tears stopped; I sat with his head on my knees and death watching over us with empty ice-green eyes.

Jule came for us, finally, her eyes swollen and tired, a cold wind behind her like a slap in the face. I watched her kneel down beside me while the doctor looked at Siebeling; but she only saw Siebeling. There were others standing behind her; I didn't look at them. There was talk, and maybe they were telling me to get up; I didn't listen. I just sat staring, until somebody shoved me with a foot and I fell against her. She caught hold of me, startled. Her face looked confused, she was frowning, "Cat . . . where are you? Cat? Oh, God. . . ." They tried to pull me away but she said, "Leave him alone!"

The hands let go of me, except hers. The guard said, "Bunch of freaks, they're all crazy." She didn't look up, holding onto me, "Cat, oh Cat, what's wrong—?"

I pulled at my jacket. "I can't feel you, Jule. I can't feel you, it's gone." My eyes were like sand; I thought there weren't any tears left, but they ran stinging down my face again. There wasn't enough room in the galaxy to hold all the pain inside me. "I'm all alone." I started to hiccup. Somebody laughed.

But Jule wiped my face with her sleeve and held me close. "I know, I know. . . ." Her voice shook. She took my hand, then; I got up and followed her outside.

I sat beside her in the snowtrack, with my head on her shoulder and my hands bound together. She murmured, "It's going to be all right," over and over, but I couldn't feel her at all.

". . . This is insane. You can't still want him. . . ."

I remember the mines, sitting quietly in a strange/familiar room while Jule stood over me, protecting me, as she argued with someone: ". . . of the taMings who ship your ore. My credit is *very* good. . . ." But the words didn't mean anything anymore; I couldn't feel them. No one hurt me, they just came and stared. They weren't real anymore either, so it didn't matter that a couple of them looked familiar. After a while I noticed that my hands were free. Then there was a flash at my wrist and something fell off, a red band; but my wrist still wore red. Somebody wrapped it in white. And all the while I was getting farther and farther away. . . .

PART III
CROSSROADS

22

I WAS HUMAN; so I survived. I'd even come home to Ardattee: the crossroads of the Federation. Gray sky and flowing towers and silvered glass—every day I sat in the dome lounge at the Sakaffe Institute, staring out over the city, and by now they knew enough not to bother me. The techs had put me back together, with Siebeling making sure they did it right this time. They'd used everything they had to bury the guilt and stop the pain, to mend my torn mind. They filled the nothingness piece by piece; they were tough and patient and they wouldn't leave me alone.

Because Siebeling had forced me to kill Rubiy, he didn't have any choice. But he'd known what it would do to me, better than anyone, and I guess he wanted to make it up to me now. So the wound healed, but it left scars that no one could help. Scars that sealed me off from the past, cauterized nerve endings that turned everything that had happened to me into something happening to someone else. All the memories, all the feelings, all the gifts of a psion, that had been mine once, were behind a glass wall now—where I could see them but I couldn't touch them.

The techs had told me there was no reason I couldn't be a telepath again; but they were wrong. I couldn't project anymore; I'd lost all my sense of direction, I couldn't find anybody else's mind. I didn't even know where to start. And if someone tried to break through to me, my mind would shut them out, I couldn't stop it. Even Jule. Every time we were together, she tried to reach me, but all I could see was her smile that stopped at the skin. And when I believed finally that it wasn't ever going to change, I got up and left the room; I wouldn't see her again, or Siebeling either. Because it wasn't enough, after what we'd had before, and knowing that I could never have it again was more than I could stand.

She and Siebeling had gotten married as soon as he was out of the hospital. I remember how strange it had made me feel, surprised, when she told me. Not because they were actually married, but because I finally realized that I wouldn't be with them anymore. I wondered what I'd expected: the job was done, and they were married. That wasn't any surprise. But it mattered, more than I wanted to admit; and hurt more than I ever let her know. Because I'd loved her more than a little for a long time now. But I'd had time to realize she didn't love me the way she loved Siebeling . . . and sitting alone for hours watching the sky, I finally realized that maybe it wasn't the same way, how I loved her, either. They'd have a lifetime together, in happiness; time to make up for all that had happened to them before. . . . And if they were married, the last thing they needed was me around reading their minds.

But I couldn't read their minds, after all. I had to keep poking myself just to remember someone was in the room. And no tech was ever going to fix that, no matter how long I stayed at the Institute. I had a clean record with the Corpses and a data bracelet to hide the scar on my wrist, and nothing else, and I guessed that now maybe it was time to go home.

I turned back to the window, leaning across the sleek, leathery coolness of the seat. I could see the towers pushing up pale and gleaming through the shadowmist of winter snow, like a picture out of a fairy tale. I remembered the endless fields of silver and the crystal forests of Cinder.

But suddenly I was remembering a part of the city you couldn't see from here. Where there'd never been a crystal tree, or even a blanket of fresh white snow—where winter was icicle-hung sewer pipes and dirty slush in Godshouse Circle, frostbite and pneumonia. . . . Where the icy wind sucked in from the sea cut through your worn-out clothes like a knife, and nobody would let you sleep where it was warm. Where dreams rotted and the darkness ate its way into your soul like worms. . . . Oldcity. Home sweet home. *Dream of a life, dream of a time.* . . . My mother's voice still sang about broken dreams, somewhere in my mind behind a wall of glass. . . . If she was really even my mother. I'd never know for sure, now. I looked down at my twisted thief's hand; it made a fist. *God, you freak.* . . . *Now you've really got nothing. Not even the gutter.* My mouth started to tremble. I dropped in a piece of sour candy and cracked it with my teeth. I hadn't touched a camph since I'd come back from Cinder; every time I saw one I thought of Dere. Poor Dere . . . lucky Dere, honored in death like he'd never have been alive. All his troubles were over now. I rubbed my eyes.

Someone had come into the room, I felt—I *heard* it; and I looked up. Jule and Siebeling were standing there, each with an arm around the other. Siebeling's other arm was still bandaged. "Hello, Cat."

I grinned without thinking, but then I pulled my mouth down again. "What are you doing here?"

Siebeling said, "It's no better, then?"

"No. I told you; it's not going to get better." I looked away, out the window again. "So what else is new?"

They stood there, invisible, for a while, before Jule asked, "Did you get your commendation from Corporate Security?"

"You mean this?" I reached into a pocket and pulled out the message 'cast, all in a wad. I'd been too embarrassed to ask anyone to read it to me; and then I'd forgotten about it. I smoothed it on my knees, and found my name printed at the top. "Is that what it is?"

Siebeling actually laughed. "And that's all the attention it probably deserves."

I smiled. "I didn't want to get a swelled head. What's it about, anyway?" And I knew how glad I was to see them; the tension eased inside me.

"We were the heroes of the moment, all over the galaxy—for about that long. At least we forced them to admit psions had done something to save the Federation, as well as something to try to destroy it. . . ." They sat down and told me more than I really wanted to know about what had happened because of us. ". . . So Galiess and the other psions will be in prison somewhere for a long time for what they tried to do, if they aren't executed for it."

I wondered how much harder their punishment would be just because they were psions. "What about the ones who put 'em up to it? There were combines backing Rubiy. . . ."

"And whichever ones they were, their identities died with him. Not even Galiess knew who his contacts really were." Siebeling leaned back against the window. "The FTA has its suspicions, but they have no proof. Even they don't have the power to act unless they can prove something without question."

"There was no proof?" I looked at Jule, remembering what we'd both heard Rubiy say about her family and Centauri Transport.

"No." She shook her head, answering the question I didn't ask. "Some things are more important—some ties never come unbound, you never get free of them, no matter how much you think you want to. And maybe that's only right."

"I guess maybe it is." I thought about Dere again. "But you saved their ass in a big way. Did it . . . did it make any difference?"

"Just a little." She smiled, just a little. "They didn't ask me home to take my place on the board. But they offered me a substantial settlement for staying away, to go with what the FTA owes us. That means more than they know. . . ."

"They bought you off," I said.

She nodded, and she didn't say anything more.

I leaned back in the seat. "So that's it. That's the end of it, huh?" The Federation kept going, because of us. And the telhassium supply on Cinder was safe because of us. The bondies were still dying there because of us, the Hydrans were being "investigated" because of us . . . and Dere Cortelyou was dead. I stared at the half-hidden scar on my wrist, and felt the new-made barriers in my mind come down to cover the old pain. *Me, a big hero. . . .* I wadded up the commendation and threw it on the floor; and I said something I shouldn't have, too softly for anybody to hear.

But Jule said, "Don't you think that what we did did any good?"

I tried to think about it. "I don't know. If it meant the ones who run this screwed-up universe got some of their own from me, then maybe. . . . But we didn't change *any*thing; that's for damn sure."

"Maybe we changed something." Siebeling touched Jule gently, and smiled. "And Cat—the Federation keeps going, because of us. That means that at least there's something that tries to restrict the whims of a Rubiy. This galaxy would be worse than it is—damn it, there'd be no end to the misery and pain—if there wasn't something."

I glanced up at him, angry. But his voice was bitter, and I realized what it meant for him to be saying that, after what the Federation had done to his family.

"By the way"—he looked past me out the window—"Corporate Security is looking for replacements for Cortelyou. They're offering us an opportunity to do more work for them."

"I ain't Dere." I shut my eyes for a minute, trying to see Dere's face. "Are you—?"

"No." He looked back at me. "Then I take it making the galaxy safe for hypocrisy doesn't really appeal to you . . . either."

"No. What are you gonna do, then? Go back to the Colonies?"

Jule shook her head. "We've been making plans for staying here in Quarro. . . ." With the money they were getting from her family and the FTA, they were going to work with psions. Not just the ones who could pay, like Siebeling had done before, but the freaks who really needed help, the ones in Oldcity whose lives were being ruined by what they were. And there were a lot of them; it was hard to be human and a psion.

I thought about Siebeling's son, wondering whether he thought . . . But then I knew they felt that even if they never found his son, they'd find something that was worthwhile. I smiled.

"That's why we're here, Cat. We thought maybe you'd want to work with us." More than just professional interest showed on his face; but I couldn't read the feeling.

"Work with you . . . ?" I stopped, feeling the smile go flat. "Just what you need, a basket case. Try and tell me from the patients."

He said, "There's nothing wrong with your psi ability; except that now you control it too well. You aren't ready to use it again. And I can't change that for you this time; because it's not my right. You need to be in control, only you can decide what you need the most now. But I think you will be a telepath again, when you're ready—when you've had the time that you need to heal."

I shook my head. "I'm glad I've lost it, I don't care why. I hope it never comes back! It's too *hard*. . . ." To think I'd found everything, because of what I'd become . . . and because of what I'd become, to lose it all. The pain started and choked off again inside me. I couldn't even feel anymore . . . because I'd already died. "I wouldn't be any good for what you want."

"I think you'd probably be very good. More than anyone, you'll never forget how hard it is—or how much it can mean—to be a psion. Even if you never use your talent again, there'd always be a place for you."

I stared at the floor, eating a piece of sour candy.

After a minute I heard them get up, and Siebeling said, "It's up to you, Cat. Whatever you decide to do, from now on; it's finally up to you." He smiled.

Jule caught his eyes; he nodded and moved away, leaving us alone together.

"Cat." She touched my face; I saw her ring flash in the light. "I know . . ." Her hand dropped away. "But you didn't lose everything. The things that drew us all together are still stronger than the things that separate us now. They can't be changed, not for the three of us. You'll always know where to find us. It doesn't matter why you come—but

come and see us, please. Don't forget us. . . ." She turned away as if it
hurt.

Siebeling came back again, and put his arm around her. He reached
into his coat pocket and brought something out. He held out his hand,
offering it to me on his open palm. It was the Hydran crystal ball I'd
stolen from him once, somewhere in my former life.

I took it from his hand, my own hand slow and uncertain. It was
warm, like a living thing, like it always was. There was a nightflower
plant blooming inside it—midnight petals streaked with silver like the
light of the stars.

"A promise," he said.

I cupped the ball in my hands, looking up at him. For a minute I
couldn't even speak. Finally I got one word out: "Thanks. Thanks."

He nodded. I watched them start away together. As they reached the
lift, Jule stopped and looked back at me, and I heard something in her
voice that I couldn't feel in her mind: "We never get everything we
want, Cat . . . but sometimes we get what we need." The lift chimed,
its doors opened and closed, and they were gone.

They were gone, and it was a while before I really understood: that
they were gone forever, this time. That what I did with my life really
was up to me now. I was free, I was rich, I was . . . nobody again; like
always, like I'd been at the start. And once I would have gone out to the
Colonies, if I was rich; but my back was scarred, and I remembered too
many lies. And once I would have searched for my mother's people, if I
was rich; but my mind was scarred, and I couldn't face them—because
I'd killed, because I wasn't Hydran enough. And once I would just have
done dreamtime for a month. . . .

The past was dead. The past was in a museum. And the price for
bringing it back was too high . . . I couldn't pay that price again, I
didn't have the strength. But I didn't have the strength to forget. What
was the use of a future, if I couldn't stop wanting the past?

I looked down again at the Hydran ball in my hands, alive with
captive light, potential energy, promise— And suddenly I remembered
that final frozen moment in the mines back on Cinder, when the
Hydrans left their farewell in my mind. They'd shown me the future—
their future, my own future, splitting apart from that moment on: theirs
blazing up in a moment of triumph, then fading to black; the fragile
threads of possibility fraying, breaking, disappearing one by one.

And mine—blackness and ashes; but not an end, only a new beginning. The threads of my life tangled and frayed, but didn't break. Weav-

ing the pattern of the future they multiplied and grew until the choices I had were like the stars in the sky. And as grief started in me for the Hydrans' loss, their hope for my new beginning had filled me. . . .

I tightened my hands over the crystal ball again. The nightflower would bloom in there forever, if I let it; but more strange and beautiful things than I could imagine would always be waiting for me to set them free. I closed my eyes, trying to focus, trying to call them out—

When I opened my eyes again, the nightflower was still there. Nothing had changed. Jule had said it: to be alive was to be disappointed. You tried and failed and kept on trying, never knowing whether you'd ever get what you wanted. *But sometimes we get what we need.* Now I had everything I needed to start over again, with even odds this time. Only a fool would throw all that away. This was the place where the past and the future came together: I held them both here in my hands.

Nothing's changed—yet. But it will. I got a few lives I ain't even tried yet.

CATSPAW

This one's for you, kid.
You know who you are.

(With his glared off face glued back into position
A dead man's eyes plugged back into his sockets
A dead man's heart screwed in under his ribs
His tattered guts stitched back into position
His shattered brains covered with a steel cowl)
                        He comes forward a step,
                                and a step,
                                    and a step—

                        —TED HUGHES

We are afraid of truth, afraid of fortune,
    afraid of death, and afraid of each other.

                        —RALPH WALDO EMERSON

To understand a cat, you must realize that he has
    his own gifts, his own viewpoint, even his own morality.

                        —LILIAN JACKSON BRAUN

PROLOGUE

SOMEONE WAS AFTER ME. The feeling, the knowing, was like the touch of ghost hands on my back all through the long afternoon. I *knew* it, the way I still did sometimes, picking things up like bits of song heard through static. It had got hold of me first in the bazaar of the orbiting spaceport. I'd been standing under the colored sunscreen at the jeweler's booth, letting a dark woman with long fingers puncture my earlobe with a ring. "Duzzin hurt," she was crooning, in some kind of accent as thick as the smoke from the charred meat in the next stall. "Hold still, duzzin hurt, duzzin hurt . . ." like she was talking to a child, or a tourist. It did hurt, but not much. And I was a tourist, everybody here was a tourist, but that didn't make acting like one feel any less strange to me.

I winced, and then the second of sharp pain was over. But in the second of empty whiteness that followed it, while I was waiting for more pain, I got something else: the touch, the whisper of something's interest brushing against my mind. Not someone, something—neutral, patient, mindless. I looked up and away, jerking free of the jeweler's hand as she wiped blood from my ear. But there was nothing to see, no one I knew, or who seemed to know me. Just the shifting crowd of colors that were too bright, faces that were too soft, like the crowds in an Oldcity night. . . .

I shook my head as the past slid across the present like a membrane. It still happened to me too often—that suddenly I felt like I was dreaming, like I didn't know who or where I was. The green agate beads on the wire bumped the side of my jaw.

"Anuzzer—?" the woman was asking, reaching out. I pushed away into the crowds, and let them carry me on down the street under the light of the artificial sun.

Once I knew the thing was onto me, I couldn't stop feeling it—that whispering, toneless song like a hook caught in my brain. I tried to tell

myself it was my imagination; my crippled mind feeling something the
same way an amputee felt phantom pain. But it didn't work. I knew
what I knew. It went with me along the twisting, gaudy streets that
tried to hide the fact they were only going in circles; into the quiet,
shadowed sprawl of the museum complex and out again; into a food
bar; into the silver-fixtured hotel men's room. It watched me, only me,
tuned to the electrical fingerprint of my brain, locked in. I thought
about going back on board the *Darwin*, but even a ship's walls wouldn't
keep it away from me. There was no reason in hell why anybody at all
would put an ID trace on me. Maybe it was a mistake, a trace meant for
someone else, an echo-reading. . . . If somebody wanted me, where
were they? Why didn't they just ask? Why shadow me through this
crowd of vacant-faced marks in their showday clothes—

"Cat—oh, Cat!"

I turned, my fists knotting up, even as I recognized the voice. My
hands were slippery with sweat. I opened them, working my fingers.

It was Kissindre Perrymeade, her half-dozen brown braids dancing
down over her khaki shirt, her smiling face like scrubbed ivory.

I stopped, letting the crowd flow on around me until it brought her to
my side. "Hi, Kiss." Her nickname always made me smile. I pushed my
hands into the pockets of my jeans. "I'm glad to see you," I said,
meaning it for once.

You are? her face asked, with that mix of aching shyness and trying-
not-to-stare that usually left us both acting stupid whenever we met.
We'd walked the surfaces of half a dozen worlds together, along with
five hundred other students in the Floating University, but I'd never
really gotten friendly with her, any more than I was friends with any of
the rest of them. She was a teaching intern, which made me half-afraid
to say anything to her to begin with. And the fact that she was rich and
pretty and stared at me only made it worse. Because the same things
that made most of the others keep their distance from me pulled at her.
I didn't talk like they did, I didn't dress like they did. I hadn't come out
of the same places. I had eyes with long slits for pupils, in a face that
wasn't put together right by human standards: a halfbreed's face. I
never talked about any of it, but that didn't make it go away.

And yet the things that made most of the others snap shut like traps
made Kissindre stare. I knew she sketched my face with her stylus on
the edges of her glowing noteboard, as if I was something she thought
was beautiful, like the artifacts and scenic views she made painstaking
drawings of—things everybody else holoed once and would never look

at again. I didn't know what I was to her, and if she knew she wouldn't admit it; and that made me feel even more awkward whenever we were together.

But now, with something inhuman locked on my brain, I was glad of any face that wasn't a stranger's, more glad that it happened to be hers, even smiling that painful smile. I noticed she was wearing jeans. Nobody else on the ship wore jeans, except me. Jeans were cheap, common, worker's clothing. It hit me suddenly that she'd only started wearing them after I met her.

"Is something wrong?" she asked, glancing up at me again.

I shook my head, only partly for an answer. "Why? Because I said I'm glad to see you?" My eyes kept wandering away, searching the street. I took her arm, felt her start but not pull back. "Come on, let's take a jump, let's get out of here. Let's go see something." Thinking that if I could get away from the spaceport for a few hours, maybe I could lose the mistake that was dogging me.

"Sure," she said, brightening now. "Anywhere. It's incredible—" She broke off, as if she knew she was starting to talk too much. At least she meant it. Most of the students on the *Darwin* were too rich and too bored and only looking for a long vacation. But a few of them were really here for what they could learn. Like her. Like me. "Your ear's bloody," she said.

I touched it with my fingers, remembering, feeling the earring. "Just got this. Supposed to be a relic."

She stiffened.

"Don't worry," I said. "It's not." I didn't like the way humans helped themselves to pieces of the scenery without asking any more than she did. Maybe less. Concentrating, I tightened the fingers of my mind into a fist; something I could still do, even if I couldn't reach out. The scratching alien hum stopped. With luck, I'd just stopped existing for whoever was on the other end. But it was like holding my breath.

We made our way back to the museum, went down ten levels to the wide shadowy cavern where the shuttles squatted in patient rows like opalescent beetles, waiting on the smooth ceramic pavement to carry people like us down to the planet's surface. There was no permanent human structure of any kind on the world that lay a thousand klicks below our feet, the world humans called the Monument. The whole planet was a Federation preserve . . . an artificial world, constructed millennia ago and dropped into an orbit around a bleary orange star out here in the middle of nowhere.

The spaceport station orbited high above it, as big as a small town, which it was. The museum complex occupied about half of its core; it was a center for the study of the vanished race that had created the Monument: rooms and rooms full of artifacts and questions without answers. It was supported by the flesh and flash of the tourist resort that made up the rest of the port.

As we came out of the dark hallway under the heavyalloy pillars, three shuttles rose up together with a hum like invisible wings and circled away into the dark mouth of the airlocks. On the far side of the field the polarized hull of the station let in the sky: midnight blackness shot with stars. The orangey streetlight of the Monument's nameless sun shone in one corner; the world itself rolled silently past down below our feet. It had been left here by a civilization humans had named the Creators, because they couldn't think of anything better. The Creators had vanished long before humans ever crawled up out of their own gravity well and spread like roaches across the stars. Nobody knew where the Creators had gone to, but everyone agreed they were gone, leaving behind almost nothing except this monument to their mystery. Even the Federation respected it.

"What do you want to see?" I asked Kissindre, as we drifted up to join the usual long line of tourists and students putting in their requests at the gateway. I didn't care where we went, as long as it got me out of range. You could take tours that took only hours, or as much as a couple of days, to any part of the world. It wasn't that big a planet; its diameter was only about thirty-five hundred klicks, even though its gravity was almost Earth-normal. It was one of the things the xeno experts couldn't explain: why a world put together by aliens seemed to fit humans so well. If they hadn't been like us, then maybe they'd wanted to tell us something. But then, there were the Hydrans, who were so close to human that the differences didn't even matter on a genetic level. I was living proof of that. And what was left of the Hydran race was living proof that humans didn't listen very well.

"Well . . ." Kissindre bit her lip, staring up at the shifting images on the screen over our heads, the deep views changing, the overlying digits in bright yellow flashing the transit times and the fees. "The Moonpool Caverns are supposed to contain some of the best examples of synaes-thetics . . . and if you want to dive . . ." She glanced back at me. It was an overnight trip.

"Great," I said. "Anything you want." The effort of holding my mind shut was making me sweat again. I focused on her face, concentrating on that. She was staring at me, her eyes as transparently blue as deep water, her lips parted. It made me realize suddenly that I was horny as hell. That I wanted to kiss her.

She looked up at the screen, away at the view of space, back at me again. She blushed. "Except . . ." she mumbled, "I promised Ezra I'd meet him for supper."

"No problem," I lied, glancing away this time. "Another time. Something short . . ." I stared at her back, feeling even worse than usual, and pinned my restless hands against my sides with my elbows. We were almost to the gateway.

"Yes, maybe we—"

"Kissindre!"

She jerked around as the voice—Ezra's voice—suddenly caught us from behind. I turned with her, saw her boyfriend come galloping out into the square toward us. He always moved like he was about to fall over. He spent most of his time with trodes taped to his head. His face was red as he cut into the line beside us; so was hers. Different reasons . . . or maybe not. Once I would have known for sure.

"What are you doing here?" he said, trying not to sound like he sounded.

"Studying," she said, a little too loudly.

"Studying what?" He looked at me.

"The Monument! I thought you were still working on your compilation—"

"I was in the resource center when I saw you out the window—"

"So?"

"So when were you planning to meet me for dinner, Kiss?" His voice rose over the muttered conversations around us. "In your next incarnation?" The black frizz of his half-grown beard quivered when he stuck out his jaw.

"Ezra . . ." Kissindre hissed, hugging her sketchboard against her with white-knuckled fingers. "You're so archaic."

"Three," I said to the gate. "Student." I let its sensors scan my databand. "Goldengate." The station was passing right over the Goldengate window. A short jump, one we might all survive. I went on through the gate, hearing my boots click on the ceramic.

After a few seconds I heard two sets of expensive magnetics follow, and more muttering. I ducked into the next waiting shuttle, and sat down. Kissindre climbed in and sat down right beside me. After a minute Ezra joined us, sitting on the other side of me. The door sealed;

destination co-ords rippled across it. The shuttle lifted, so smoothly I hardly felt the motion, and spun toward the locks. I settled back as we passed through and out, beginning our drop down the Monument's gravity well. I stretched out my legs; loosened the fist I'd made of my mind, finger by finger.

Nothing. Out of range. I sighed, shutting my eyes. Now it was easy to believe it was a mistake. Or even my imagination. Paranoia was an old habit, a hard one to break, when I felt like a freak and a fraud. When every time I shut my eyes I still saw the darkness . . . I opened them again, blinked, stared; watched the world below swelling outward like a balloon across the viewscreens as we dropped toward it. If I thought about that too much, it made my stomach climb into my throat. I glanced at Kissindre and Ezra, remembering again that I wasn't alone. I might as well have been. They were still arguing, across my chest, in angry whispers.

". . . Well, I can't help it, I have to access, I don't have an eidetic memory like the Walking Data Bank here—" His hand in my face, gone again.

"Ezra—"

I looked at the screens again. We were almost down now, entering the atmosphere, our trajectory altering toward our final destination. The deceleration buffering wasn't very good. Kissindre and Ezra got quiet as it got harder to speak. The discomfort made me feel better instead of worse; at least we had brakes. Too much of the galaxy was run by things I couldn't even see. It still made me nervous.

The surface of the Monument was spreading out below us, like a painting coming into clearer and clearer focus. I stared at the view, letting the images seep in through my eyes, feeling a slow smile stretch my mouth. *It was so beautiful.* Sometimes when it was like this I felt as if I'd had a brain transplant, as if I was living in someone else's body. The fact that I couldn't prove anybody else was real by their place inside my thoughts any more didn't help the feeling.

I tugged on my earring, feeling the pain; rolling the cool, hard surface of the beads between my fingers. I'd never had any jewelry before. Never wanted any, when it only attracted the wrong kind of attention—the kind that would get your throat slit. One morning-after back in Oldcity I'd woken up with a tattoo, but even that didn't show with my clothes on. Getting the earring today I'd been trying to prove to myself again that I didn't have to be invisible any more. I tried not to remember what I had to remember every time I glanced at my credit readout:

that by the time the University finished its studies here I'd be zeroed, out of money. I took a deep breath, easing the tightness in my chest, watching the view.

Anywhere you set down on this world, you'd find a scene that filled up your eyes with wonder. The air was like satin, the winds like musicians. It was as if an artist, or a thousand artists working together, had been given a whole world as clay, as lightbox, as a musical instrument. Nothing but beauty anywhere, as perfect as diamonds. Nothing. Nothing alive to disturb its stasis. Not a leaf, a bird, an insect. Not until now.

The changing view of beyond-the-walls had stopped changing. The hatch sighed and yawned. We climbed out, stretching, silenced by the sudden silence of the yellow windswept plateau that was the designated viewpoint. Two other shuttles were already there, and a bunch of gaudy tourists stood a few meters away. I could hear their voices, but the sound was thin and high, as if they were somehow farther away than they looked. It was nearly sunset. The reddening light burnished the sandstone cliffs, making the hills look like they'd been cast from brass. If you didn't know, you would have sworn that only time and wind had eaten them down into those forms. But if you looked at anything too closely—anything at all, a pebble—you might find a hidden sign, an undecipherable signature, telling you that some sentient mind had laid everything out just so, and left it that way for eternity.

I turned, stepping away from the shuttle. As I looked around me the hugeness, the sheer size of world and sky, hit me so hard I couldn't breathe. It made me feel like there was no place to hide . . . the way I always felt when I took on too much open space too fast. I made myself keep looking, feeling the wind ruffle my hair with an easy hand. I took a breath—forgot to finish it. Beside me Kissindre and Ezra sighed and said, "Oh . . ." and broke off their argument.

This ship-in-a-bottle world's foster sun lay framed inside the arch of stone they called Goldengate, as if time itself was trapped there, frozen in the moment. The black silhouette of the bridge was shot through with a pattern of bright rays, riddled with the precision of lace. And as the wind rose, lifting a pale curtain of dust, I could hear it: the thin, high piping far up in the air, the song the wind made in the hollow flute of stone. The sound reached into my chest like an invisible hand to break my heart. I started away from the others, forgetting them, forgetting everything, sunblind, stone-deaf. . . .

Loud bleeping cut across my senses, jerking me back. I stopped at the edge of a sheer drop, the boundary of the access area. I stepped back

onto safe ground and waited for my ringing ears to clear. Then I stood
on the edge between worlds, listening to something else. . . . After a
minute I crouched down, making handprints in the burnished dirt. I
picked up a smooth, striped stone no bigger than my hand. I put it
down again, in a different spot; it still looked perfect. The voice of the
wind turned cold inside me.

"Whatever made them do it?" Kissindre murmured, not to me but to
the wind, and I realized she was standing beside me now. "Was it just
for its own sake, all this beauty . . . ?"

"A ritual object," Ezra said, "part of their structure of worship."
That was the answer we usually heard while images of strange artifacts
poured into our heads. It meant the experts didn't know what the hell it
was either, and probably never would.

"No." I straightened up, brushing my hands on my jeans. "It really is
a monument."

"To what?" Kissindre asked, her eyebrows rising. Beside her Ezra
frowned.

"Death," I said, feeling the word fall out of my mouth, cold and
hard. "Bits and pieces, the bones of planets, that's what it's made of.
That's why there's nothing alive here." The sun was disappearing beyond the cliffs. The wind was beginning to feel as cold as I did.

Kissindre caught at my arm. "Who told you that?"

"Huh?" I looked back at her, seeing sunspots where her eyes should
have been.

"Who—?"

I shook my head. My thoughts felt heavy and slow, like molten glass.
"Dunno. Heard it, I guess. . . ."

"I've never heard that one." She shook her own head, but it wasn't
denial. She squinted out across the sea of stone, her body tightening
with excitement.

"He's making it up," Ezra mumbled, without the guts to say it to my
face. Kissindre began to murmur notes into the recorder on her necklace, her eyes back on me.

Still feeling like I'd been hit on the head, I bent down, trying to hide
what was happening inside me. I pulled the knife out of the sheath
inside my boot, straightened up. Leaning against an outcrop of rock, I
reached into the pouch pocket of my tunic and found the eggfruit I'd
bought this afternoon. I began to peel it, steadying my hands, before I
looked up at them again.

Their faces were like two six-year-olds, the naked fear slowly drain-

ing away, leaving them slack-jawed. Like they'd never seen anybody
pull a knife before.

"I don't make things up," I said finally, and then wished I hadn't,
while they nodded, too eagerly. I didn't know how I knew what I'd just
told them about this place, couldn't remember ever knowing it before
that moment. All I was certain of suddenly was that I was an alien. Had
always been, would always be.

I put my knife away. "See you." I looked back at Kissindre and Ezra
for as long as it took to say the words. I started toward the waiting
shuttles, and they didn't follow.

"Cat—?" Kissindre called suddenly, her voice pale.

I turned back, waiting.

She licked her lips. "Can you . . . can you really read my mind?"

So that was it. She knew I was a psion, knew it was Hydran blood
that made me half a stranger. But she didn't know the rest of it. . . .
Probably she wouldn't want to. "No." I said, "I can't." I went on alone.

On board the shuttle I ate my dinner, and stuffed the pit into the
ashtray, next to some skagweed user's stale cud. The smell of the cud
was overwhelming the air scrubbers. There was the butt end of a camph
in the ashtray too. I almost took it . . . let it fall back. Still too much
memory. Maybe there always would be. Maybe the monument to death
wasn't falling away below me now, maybe it was inside my head. . . .

That was easier than believing that somehow I could just know things
about a place. Or maybe I was just better than the rest at reading the
subliminals embedded everywhere in the Monument. That made a kind
of sense. Maybe the Creators had been more like Hydrans than like
humans, after all. But it didn't ease the feeling of being out-of-focus that
had only been getting thicker all day. I tugged on the earring again.
First the tracer, then Kissindre, now this. . . . I remembered I was
falling back into the tracer's electronic net right now. Humans were
always making my life lousy, still hounding me, like they'd done to the
whole Hydran race. . . . *Screw it. Stop acting like a shadow walker.* I
unclenched my fingers, pulling them out of the holes they'd dug into the
formfoam armrests.

I held my mind shut, holding my breath, the rest of the way back to
the station. When we landed I stepped out again into the perfectly
antiseptic, climate-controlled womb below the museum. The port's
massive ceramic/composite hull was all around me, like the walls of a
fortress. There were half a hundred people within reach of my voice,
and none of them looked too interested in me. I let go, setting the

crippled receptors of my brain as free as I could, listening: nothing. The toneless static of the trace wasn't there . . . if it had ever been there in the first place. My telepathy had gone dead three years ago, but sometimes my brain still played practical jokes.

I shrugged the shadows off my back and went on across the tiles, out through the gate with the rest of the sightseers. They flowed on into the echoing mouth of the walkway that led back through the museum's labyrinthine guts, and eventually to the lifts that would carry them on up to the port levels. I went with them, letting my shoulder hug the reassuring closeness of the wall along the edge of the crowd.

And then suddenly I stopped, staring. Spraypainted on the wall, inside a clumsy heart, was my name. CAT. CAT & JULE. People swore as they bumped into me, but I didn't care. I didn't even notice as all the rest of them passed me by; didn't notice that I was standing there all alone now, with only the sound of my breathing and the sign on the wall. I felt a kind of panic begin to rise inside me. The day had just gone from out-of-focus to completely insane. I looked back over my shoulder. Light and darkness shifted around me, flowing across the pillars and walls like water, as if they had a life of their own.

I turned, feeling a sudden bright stab of warning a split second before my eye caught real motion. Two shadows peeled off from the darkness of a passageway, and closed in on me. I caught a flicker of orange, the flaming badge of some combine's colors on somebody's sleeve. And then the cold bite of nothingness hit my neck, chemical teeth sinking toward a vein, finding it. And that was all.

1

I CAME TO on board a ship, but it was no ship I'd ever seen before. I was lying on a foam-padded, fold-down bunk, in a room that I couldn't mistake for my cabin or any other place on the *Darwin* if I'd been blindfolded. The last thing I remembered was a flash of combine colors on a Corporate Security uniform jacket; the gray-green garbage-can walls around me now, the stripped imitation asceticism of the single desk and chair, the storage nets, the bed, all screamed military.

I'd been bodysnatched by some combine's Security arm . . . which made no sense at all, except that here I was. I tried to sit up, and was more surprised than not when I found out I could. No binders on me, no straps. My knife was missing. I felt along my neck and stripped off the patch I found there. I'd been drugged, all right, but my head seemed clear enough now.

The door of the cabin was shut. Just then it slid open, as if they'd been waiting for me to wake up. Two men entered, probably the ones who'd done it to me. One dark-skinned, one pale. They wore interchangeable faces and interchangeable silver-on-gray duty fatigues. They stopped inside the doorway, waiting, tense. I wondered if the combines made their Corpses get face jobs so they'd match. Then my eyes found the insignia on a jacket front, and I froze. Data flowed across the ID patch below the sunblaze logo of Centauri Transport. A giddy flash of double-sight hit me. I didn't know what this was about, but I knew now it wasn't a mistake. And it wasn't good. Cold anger, or maybe cold fear, slammed though my brain. I stood up, and said, "Wha's goin' on—?"

And sat down again with my stomach up in the back of my throat. "Shid." Now I knew why there were no binders. No need. Whatever they'd drugged me with left a hell of a hangover.

The twins looked at each other and grinned, but it was more like relief than like they thought it was funny. They came across the room, as if they'd been afraid to get too close to me before. "Okay, freak," one of them said, "the Chief wants to see you." They hauled me up again, and half-dragged me out the door. I wished I'd eaten more dinner, because I wanted to see it all over them when I puked.

We were on board some kind of small scoutship; at least they didn't have to drag me far. They pushed me through the doorway into another cabin, and down onto a wall couch.

I was wrong; I wasn't on some scoutship. This was some combine vip's private cruiser. It might have been on a different world from the room I'd come to in.

"Here he is, sir. He's safe," one of the guards said beside me. I realized they didn't mean safe and sound. They meant crippled.

I'd been wrong . . . and right. "The Chief" was Centauri's Chief of Corporate Security. He was sitting in a tapestry-covered recliner behind a perfect black semisphere of desk, staring at me from across the room. He had a face like the blade of a knife, thin, sharp, and cold . . . no beard, except high up on his cheekbones in a feathery line, as if his eyebrows grew around to circle his eyes. His eyes were so dark they looked black. He was wearing a full-dress uniform—a gunmetal-gray helmet with Centauri's logo and his insignia dancing on it, a conservative business suit in silver tweed, a drape crawling with shining crap that made my eyes swim. I'd never seen so much flash on one body before. The fact that he was wearing it said either he wasn't worried, or he wanted to impress me. I didn't know what that meant, either way.

I looked away from him, because he was staring at me without blinking. We seemed to be inside a bubble, hanging out over the black heart of space. The Monolith's sun hung just above his left shoulder, like a floating lamp. I couldn't see the world itself. I looked down at my feet, glad that at least there was a rug. Sapphire blue, it had the Centauri logo shot through it in gold. Subtle. I pressed deeper against the back of the couch, waiting until my stomach caught up with the rest of the body again. Then, as carefully as I could, I said, "Wha'. Do. You. Wan'?"

"Your name is Cat. My name is Braedee." The black eyes were still fixed on me like cameras. "I'm Chief of Security Systems for Centauri Transport. Do you understand what that means?"

It meant there was probably nobody higher in the combine's power structure except the controlling board members. It meant that he was probably the most trusted man in that entire structure. Also the worst enemy anybody who crossed them would ever have. The ruling board itself must have sent him after me. Did they really know who I was? My paranoia started doing the multiplication tables. I shook my head to answer him. It was cold in his office; the sweat crawling down my ribs made me shiver.

"It means that I don't see just anybody. It means," a muscle in his face jumped, "that we need . . ." twitch, "a telepath." Twitch. "Now I'm going to explain why."

Surprise caught in my chest, then relief, and confusion, and anger. I sucked in a breath. "No." I touched my head, meeting the telephoto eyes. "Nah. Till. Fix. Dis."

"The drug blunts your psionic ability. The speech is an unfortunate side effect. Your comprehension is completely unaffected. There's no reason for you to say anything until I've finished."

"Fu' you." I stood up, turning toward the doorway. The two matching Corpses filled it up. I turned back again to face Braedee. "Fix. It!" If they knew what I was, they should know I was no more danger to them than any deadhead they picked off the street. Less—I wouldn't kill them. But from the way his face worked, I knew he was as piss-assed scared as anybody else. Maybe more, considering what he did for a living. The more someone had to hide, the more they usually hated psions.

Braedee shook his head. He said, "Gentleman Charon taMing heads the Centauri board. He ordered me to keep you drugged."

TaMing. I jerked as I heard the name. "Fu' him too," I said, trying to cover my surprise.

Braedee glared at me for a long minute, considering the alternatives, probably feeling the invisible fist of Centauri ready to come down on us both. There was something wrong with his eyes, more than just the way he looked at me; but I didn't know what it was. At last he said, "I'll give you the antidote if you'll submit to a scan." Calling my bluff.

My hands tightened, went loose again. I nodded finally and sat back down. One of the Corpses came and dropped the veil of silvery mesh over my head. I flinched and shut my eyes as it molded to my flesh, tingling like a thousand insects crawling on my face. The urge to rip it off was almost more than I could stand; the first time one had been used on me they'd had to use binders, too. At least by now I knew what was coming. I'd been through so much testing, so much therapy since the killing that I'd learned to live with it. I clenched my jaw, trying not to resist—resisting anyway, not able to stop blind instinct as the sensation began. Worms ate my brains for dinner, while somewhere the scan sequence vomited a useless data simulation of my mangled psi.

It was over in less than a minute—subjective time of about fifty years.

The mesh dropped into my lap. I brushed it off and kicked it away, wanting to spit.

Braedee was staring into the air, at me, but through me. I looked over my shoulder but there was only the single wall that backed me up. "She was right," he murmured. "The shape of your profile is . . . well, see for yourself." He really was looking at me now.

I didn't see him move, but suddenly the sun disappeared behind him, and instead my scan profile flashed across space in pure light lines of red, blue, and green. Data into symbol—making it comprehensible for humans, who had to input everything the hard way. I stared at the dead end that had turned me into a deadhead, the wall I'd built myself and couldn't tear down again. "Seen. It."

The image disappeared. I blinked at the sudden reappearance of the sun. "All right. Give him the patch," Braedee said.

One of the guards stepped forward again, and stuck another patch over the vein in my neck. "Leave it there for twelve hours, or you'll regress," he said.

I nodded, and waited a minute longer before I tried to speak again. "Okay, deadhead." My voice was raw and shaky, but I heard what I expected to. "I'm ready for the reason. It better be good."

His mouth lifted, just a little, like I amused him. Then the thin, pale lips stretched over his teeth again; he pressed his fingertips into a steeple on the lifeless surface of his desk. "You were once briefly . . . involved . . . with Lady Jule taMing, who is a member of the founding family of Centauri Transport."

"A friend," I said. "I was her friend. I'm still her friend."

He frowned, at the interruption, or the implication. My own face appeared suddenly in the air behind him: a little younger, a lot thinner, hair curly and white-blond, skin brown, eyes green and slit-pupiled. The story of my life was summed up in about half a dozen depressing lines underneath it. No living relatives . . . criminal record . . . psionic dysfunction . . .

"We know all about your . . . relationship with the Lady and Dr. Siebeling, her husband," he went on, still frowning. "About their Center for Psionic Research, about the . . . service you performed for the Federation Transport Authority." He seemed to be having a hard time getting the words out, coughing slightly every time the taste got too acid for him.

"I'll bet. I'll bet the FTA would be amazed at how much you know about that." I leaned back, putting one boot up on the couch. One of the guards moved forward and slapped it down.

"That patch on your neck comes off just as easily as it went on." Braedee stared at me, not blinking. I realized he never seemed to blink. I wondered if he was really alive. I couldn't tell.

I swore under my breath, suddenly feeling stupid for saying anything. Stupid and scared again. Nobody sane crossed a combine the size of Centauri and opened their mouth about it. Just seeing a uniform was still enough to make my stomach knot. I'd had a lot of run-ins with Corpses in my life, enough to know that if they had you they always made you pay. The only people who knew where I was right now were all Centauri Corpses, and all in this room with me. And there were worse things than a speech impediment.

"All right," I mumbled, not meeting his eyes. "What do you want?"

"We need a telepath. As I said before." He leaned back in his seat, easing off. His drape flashed and shimmered as he took a deep breath. "Lady Jule recommended you. She said that even though you were young, you were . . . extremely intelligent, and . . . loyal." He shifted again. He looked like he trusted her judgment about as much as he trusted me right now. But I was here, and that meant either he did believe her, or he was desperate. Maybe both.

I thought about Jule, let her face form in my mind, the details getting a little hazy when I tried to focus on them now. The surprise was back in place, hot as coals: that Jule would tell her family anything about me; that they'd ever want anything to do with a psion. Jule was a psion, like I was. Her freak-hating family had made her life a living hell because of it, until she'd finally tried to cut all her ties with them. But blood was still thicker than water, and the taMings were a family with a long reach. They didn't like to lose something that belonged to them, even if it was flawed. They kept in touch.

"Why'd you snatch me, then?"

"Would you have come, if we'd simply asked you?"

I thought about it. "No."

He raised his eyebrows, as if that was all the explanation it needed. "That heart sign on the museum wall . . . you think of that?"

He shook his head. "Lady Jule suggested we do something . . . unusual to attract your attention."

My mouth twitched. I jerked my head at the image in the air behind him. "You don't want me. I'm brain-damaged." The way they'd brought me here told me enough about what I could expect if I hired on as a corporate telepath. And I couldn't imagine anything they'd want that I'd ever want to do for them.

"That blockage is self-inflicted." He half frowned, as if he couldn't imagine why having somebody die inside your mind might make some part of you want to dig a hole and never come out of it again. He was right. He couldn't imagine. "It isn't irreversible. Lady Jule suggested that you might even find working for us to be a therapeutic experience."

I shook my head. "I don't believe that."

His face hardened. He was allowed to believe that I'd lie to him, but I didn't have the same right. "I have a communication from the Lady," he said. "She realized that you might be skeptical."

I leaned forward on the couch. "Let me see it."

"When I'm ready." My picture on the invisible screen behind him ate itself. The sun was back over his shoulder again. "First you hear me out. This is no ordinary security position we're offering. I'm not stupid enough to think that would interest someone like you. And you hardly fit our profile." I smiled; he didn't. "This is a matter that concerns the taMing family personally. One of them, Lady Elnear, has had attempts made on her life. So far we have successfully blocked the attacks. But we have been unable to discover why the attempts are being made."

"You mean she's such a wonderful human being she doesn't have any enemies?" I said sourly.

The frown came back. "On the contrary. There are any number of competing interests that could be considered Centauri's enemies . . . her enemies. Lady Elnear's holdings have united Centauri and ChemEnGen," as if that was supposed to mean something to me. "She is the widow of Gentleman Kelwin, and fills his seat on our board, as well as being the lynchpin stockholder of our merger lease with ChemEnGen. She also votes for our interests in the Federation Assembly."

"Oh." She was either one hell of a woman, or a complete pawn. I thought I could guess which. "And you want me to find out which one wants her dead?" If all their best snoopware couldn't track it, I could hardly believe they thought I'd have better luck.

But he nodded. "You would function as her aide, accompanying her at all times. Lady Jule suggested that using your . . . abilities to protect another person might help your condition."

I sat up straight. "The person would have to matter. Lady Elnear doesn't mean shit to me, and neither do the interests of Centauri Transport." I shook my head, starting to get my nerve back. "Anyway, I've been through enough therapy to change the lives of everyone on a planet, but I still can't keep control of my psi. I used to be good enough —maybe—to do what you want me to do, but not any more. If you really want Lady Elnear safe, find somebody else."

He didn't answer me at first. But then he said, "There are drugs that can make it possible. That can block the kind of pain that's crippling you. We can get them for you."

I looked down. "I know," I said, finally. I looked up at him again. "There are drugs that will let you walk around for days on a couple of broken legs, too."

His fingers began to move one by one, tapping a silent code on his black desktop; spelling out his impatience. He looked at me, his mouth thinning. "Centauri will make it worth your while."

I shook my head again. "Sorry. I've already got something to do. You interrupted it. Take me back to the *Darwin*." I got to my feet.

"If you wish." Braedee leaned back in his seat and cracked his knuckles. "But your credit is down to three meaningful digits, and your tuition will be due again at the end of this term. What are you going to do then?" It wasn't just curiosity; the words were a knife blade pricking my ribs. "Yes," he said, smiling, "we really do know all about you."

I felt the helpless anger try to choke me again. I hadn't even had a rating or a databand until three years ago; hadn't even existed to the galactic Net that monitored the lives and fortunes of everybody worth noticing, from the day they were born to the day they died. Then I'd been paid off for my "service" to the Federation with a rating that made me dizzy, and the freedom of a galaxy to spend it in. I hadn't been stupid enough to think it would last forever. But I'd lived my entire life in the bottom of a sewer. I had a lot to learn, and a lot to forget, and I'd wanted to see what I'd been missing all my life. So I'd signed up for the Floating University, which cost a lot.

"No smart answer?" Braedee asked, pressing a little harder. "Did you really think that repository for the spoiled offspring of privilege was going to prepare you to live in a high-level technological society?" I felt my mouth tighten; so did he. The smile started to come out on his face again. "I understand that until about three years ago you were completely illiterate. . . . Of course, given enough time and training, you'd be marginally employable, although your lack of social skills would probably keep you in a low-level position. But you aren't just ignorant —you're also a psion. You look very Hydran. I don't have to tell you what that means."

I felt my face flush. "I don't have to work for a combine." I was
fighting the fear inside me—the fear that it was all true. It was bad
enough just being a psion. All human psions had Hydran genes in them
somewhere. But most of them didn't have to wear it on their faces; their
mixed blood was ancient history.

"Of course not. There are other jobs. Contract Labor is always looking for bodies. . . . But you know that."

My hand went to my wrist, covering it, like somebody caught naked;
covering the scar that still marked the place where the bond tag had
been fused to my flesh. But it was already covered. My fingers felt the
warmth of the databand, solid and real. Mine. "Forget it, scumbutt.
You just lost me." I stood up for the last time.

Suddenly Jule's face was in the air behind him, larger than life, so
real I could almost touch her. Her gray, upslanting eyes were looking
straight into mine. Her face was tired, pale, uncertain . . . beautiful.
"Cat," she said, and a trace of real smile pulled at her lips, as if she
could really see me. I felt my mouth smile in answer, even though I
knew she couldn't. I hadn't seen her face in over two years. Seeing it
again made me ache, the way sometimes a song would, triggering memories. I wondered if it would always make me feel that way.

"I'm not sure this is the right thing," she went on, glancing away at
someone, and back. "It has to be your choice—I told them that—or it's
no good." She brushed a long strand of midnight-colored hair out of her
eyes as the breeze lifted it. There was the shifting green of leaves behind
her, the wink of sunlight on spray. I felt the breeze touch my face,
smelled the fresh smells of damp earth and flowers. Whoever had made
this tape hadn't spared anything to make it feel real. I wondered if Jule
was in the Hanging Gardens, upside in Quarro. I felt a twinge of home-
sickness for the first time in my life. They hadn't taped her at the Center
for Psionic Research, in the stink and the noise and the darkness of
Oldcity. Maybe they couldn't take it. Maybe they hadn't wanted me to
think about that. Except that it made me think about that anyway.

"They told me about Elnear." Jule's eyes darkened. "I don't understand it . . . but if you can help her, Cat, if you're willing to, do it.
Please. She's the only one . . ." she glanced away again, "the only one
in my family who ever loved me." Shadows moved across her face—
leaf-patterns, and the darkness of past lives. Her eyes were both hard
and longing when they met mine again. "She's a good woman. She
needs someone she can trust. She can trust you. I trust you. I . . ." she

did smile, now, "we miss you." She lifted a hand in farewell, and she was gone.

The room seemed colder without her; emptier than if I'd been there alone. But I wasn't alone. I looked up. Braedee's eyes were fixed on my face, sucking in everything that showed. I almost asked to see the tape again. I thought about him watching me watch her. I didn't ask. Remembering it would have to be enough. *All right,* I thought. *For you. All right.* And it was all right this time that she couldn't hear me think it.

"She told me not to tell you this," Braedee said, "but the Center that she and her husband run is almost out of funds too."

I felt my mouth twist. "You always go one step too far, you know that?"

"Then I have you." It wasn't a question.

I glanced out at the sun, where Jule's image had been. "You don't know how close you just came to losing me again. One day you're going to walk right off the edge."

He smiled.

"I'll do it for Jule. But I want the money. For me. For the Center too. Set up the contracts. I'll tell you if it's enough."

"Of course. Some now—more later, if you do your job. We'll settle the details as soon as we reach Earth."

"Earth?" I said, sounding a little like I'd been hit in the stomach.

"That's home to the taMings." I was amusing him again. "They are a rather conservative family."

"Home." It was a strange thought. I looked down at myself, back at him. "You know, Braedee, you're in the wrong kind of work. You should have been a blackmailer."

He shook his head. "You have a lot to learn about politics, boy."

2

ONCE BRAEDEE HAD FINISHED convincing me that nothing was ever free, including me, he signaled the doorway like a magician calling up tricks. When I turned around to look, I wasn't really surprised to find someone standing there: a tiny dark-haired woman who looked like an antique doll, like her body might be made of soft cloth under the cover of her dark business suit. She wore a combine logo like a brooch at her throat. It wasn't Centauri's.

I clapped my hands, once, twice, three times. "That's pretty good," I said, looking back at Braedee. "Can you do animals too?"

One of the guards made a sniggering noise. Braedee looked at him with those eyes. He stopped.

"This is Mez Jardan, Lady Elnear's Executive Assistant," Braedee said, the words dry as sand. "Go with her. She'll brief you as much as possible on what your duties will be as Lady Elnear's aide. Afterward I'll see you again." The last part was more a threat than a promise.

I nodded and stood up, meeting the woman's eyes for the first time. I had to look way down; she barely came up to my shoulder, and she was wearing platform shoes. "I'm all yours," I said. Her expression didn't change; she still looked like she smelled something rotten.

I followed her to the ship's commons. There were long bone-colored couches hugging the wall, a round metal table with magnetic chairs locked to the floor. Private—but not too private. She sat down at the table, looking back at me.

"I already know how to eat," I said from the doorway.

"I doubt that." She folded her hands. Her voice was high-pitched, almost like a child's. "We don't have a lot of time, and you know almost nothing of the world you will be entering—"

"Earth?" I came into the room and sat down.

"No," she said. "I meant politics."

I leaned back in my seat, twisting the chair on its single leg with the motion of my foot. "There's that word again."

Her doll's face reddened. "Now listen to me, Mez . . . Cat," stumbling over it, as if there should have been more to my name. "I watched your performance back there with Braedee. It didn't impress me. You have a smart mouth, but I see no proof that you have a mind to match it. I am going to give you a lot of information, and I am forced by circumstance to deliver it verbally. I will repeat it as often as necessary until you understand everything. You may interrupt to ask me questions, but they had better be short and to the point."

I shrugged, smarting a little. "You won't have to repeat yourself. I'll get it right the first time."

Her small mouth twisted down.

"Try me." I leaned forward.

She took a deep breath. "All right, then. Some background, to begin with . . ." She told me what Braedee had already told me about Lady Elnear and how she'd married into the taMings. "A premarital noninterference agreement was signed, but since the Gentleman's death the taMings have . . . taken a greater interest in ChemEnGen's policymaking. . . ." Her voice soured; she wanted to say more. But she knew whose ship we were on, just as much as I did. Combines had long memories. "The Lady is under constant Centauri Security protection at all times since the . . . the incidents." Her hands, which had been lying quietly on the table, curled around each other, protecting, strangling. Suddenly I was sure of one thing: Mez Jardan's loyalty to her boss was as total as her hatred of Centauri. With an effort that cost her, she controlled her hands and laid them quietly one on top of the other on the table surface again. She glanced up at me. "Well?"

I began to repeat everything she'd told me, word for word.

Her eyes widened, for a heartbeat, before the tight, furrowed frown came back. "Are you hotwired?"

I touched my head. "It comes with the wetware. Package deal." She looked blank. "I was born that way. Most telepaths can do it, if they want to bother." I'd bothered because it helped me learn. I remembered things perfectly. It was forgetting that was hard to do.

I felt more than saw her withdraw, as if every separate cell of her body wanted to crawl away from me.

"Psion," I said, and she flinched. *"Telepath.* Better get used to it."

"We didn't ask for you," she snapped. "You were Centauri's idea. The last thing that Elnear needs is a taMing mindreader to spy on her."

She'd said "Elnear." Not "the Lady." She must be more than a top aide; maybe a personal friend. "She send you to check me out?" I asked.

"In part." She glanced away. "We're forced to accept you, in any case. The least I can do is try to make you presentable." Emphasis on *try.* "Not even all of the taMing family will know that you are a psion, when you arrive. They think that I am away simply to find her a new personal aide. Her previous aide was poisoned." The frown looked almost like pain now.

"How?" I asked.

"A piece of sillaby, intended for Elnear, which Elnear had given away because she doesn't like sillaby. Clara nearly died. Her health is still not good. . . ."

"Poison candy? Pretty crude," I said. Maybe they'd counted on surprise. "Who do *you* think would want to kill her?"

"I don't know." She shook her head, looked down again. "I just don't know. Braedee comes up with new possibilities every day, and all of them are *possible.* . . . I've been with her for twenty-five years, and nothing like this has ever happened before."

"You sound like it's a big surprise. I thought the combines spent half their budgets trying to screw each other." I'd done a lot of reading, after Jule had taught me how, and a lot of accessing once I'd joined the university . . . trying to figure out how the Federation worked, and how I'd come to be who I was, and where I was in it. Facts and figures can tell you a lot, but they can't tell you that.

Her face eased. "It is a fact of life in her position, yes. . . ." Her gaze left me again. "But Elnear is not like that. She believes in the perfectability of humanity. She works only for the greater good—"

"That's enough to make some people want to kill you, right there."

Her eyes snapped back to my face. "Listen to me, you deviant. If you ever say anything like that in front of her, I'll have you—"

"Hey," I said, cutting her off before she could finish it. "Okay, Mez Jardan, you're one tough bitch, and your boss is a goddamn saint. Just tell me what I have to do, and get it over with."

She smoothed her hands again. "As I was about to say . . . Lady Elnear considers her true work to be her involvement with the Federation Transport Authority's independent Drug Enforcement Arm—"

A nark. A combine vip, a saint, and a nark . . . everything I heard about Lady Elnear made me feel less like I ever wanted to meet her, let alone save her from death. . . . I didn't say anything.

"She has been so dedicated in her work for the Arm, and such an effective media representative, that the FTA is considering her for the current opening on the Security Council."

I whistled softly. Braedee hadn't mentioned that. That was something like going from being a saint to being a god. There were only twelve human beings on the Security Council, and they made all the FTA's policy. And the FTA regulated all interstellar commerce.

"As you can see, you will be exposed to levels of society and government about whose rules you know almost nothing. You may allow people to believe that you are acting as a kind of physical bodyguard as well as in the capacity of an aide, to help explain your lack of the—usual requirements for the position. But under no circumstances will you tell anyone that you are a psion."

"Why?"

"That should be obvious. If you're to be of any use at all in helping discover who is trying to kill the Lady, then your ability has to be kept secret."

"That's not going to be so easy." I pointed at my eyes, the long slit pupils. A lot of people knew what that meant.

"Braedee will take care of that," she said.

I smiled, more like a nervous tic. "He's going to give me his?" They were even stranger looking than mine. I wondered it he left them on the table at night when he slept. "He's cybered, right?"

"Of course he is. Do you think he could be Security Chief for a combine without augmentation?"

"He looks pretty normal. I've seen some grotesques—"

"Only a fool would advertise exactly what he can do."

I thought about that. "Depends on what you're into, I guess."

"We're not dealing with street gang pathology," she said. I wasn't so sure, but I didn't say anything. I knew the combines didn't allow most of their employees more than an occasional memory plug-in, besides what they needed to do their specific jobs. The higher you were in the network, the more augmentation you were allowed. If it was really good, it didn't have to show; but if you had that kind of power, why not flaunt it? She said, "Most combines discourage flamboyant displays of personal engineering. Most of humanity still finds aberrance threatening."

"Yeah." That made perfect sense. "I've noticed." I touched my head.

As if she hadn't heard that, she reached into the soft leather bag she carried and pulled out a handful of holos. She tossed them out onto the tabletop in front of me. "These are some of the people you will have to recognize and deal with." I couldn't believe she didn't have some better way of giving me information. Maybe Braedee was making it hard for her. I had the feeling she hadn't been exactly welcome on this trip.

I picked up a holo, stared at it. "Family portraits." Not even a question. It was a picture of a middle-aged man, but the resemblance to Jule was so striking that a cold finger ran up my spine. I shuffled through the rest of them, holding the membranes up to the light, looking at profiles and full faces as they stared, yawned, smiled or frowned through a moment of their existence, over and over, trapped in a kink of time. Too many of them could almost have been Jule's twin.

Jardan named them, one by one, as I picked up the pictures. She didn't really have to tell me which were the outsiders who'd married in.

For the first time I saw Jule's father, a grandfather, a great-grandmother, a cousin . . . a brother. I didn't even know she had a brother. He looked just like her too. Holding images of her face over and over again, barely changing, began to make my fingers tingle as if mice were crawling over my hands. "Why do they all look like that? They all look just like her—"

"Like who?"

"Jule."

She looked at me blankly for a minute, before she remembered. "Oh. Yes," she said, as if she was disposing of an unpleasant reminder. "As you may have gathered, Centauri Transport is something of an anomaly: they are still controlled by the heirs of their founder. After more than three hundred years, that is a rare accomplishment."

"So why do they look like clones? They're not marrying each other—" I tossed the holo back onto the pile.

"They control the transfer for their genetic material very strictly. Only a minimal amount of outside material is introduced into each new generation. They select for the psychological traits that have given them success in the past—and, obviously, for physical resemblance. It's part of the control factor . . . part of their mystique, if you will."

Genetic incest. I thought about Jule—a psion, an empath and teleport born into that family of perfect mirror images reflecting back through centuries. A mistake. A mistake that had almost driven her insane. I wondered how it could have happened. I glanced at the pile of pictures again. "You have one of Jule's mother?" Jule looked like her father. I didn't know much about her family life, but nothing I'd heard about her father was good. I couldn't help wondering what her mother was like.

"Lady Sansu is dead."

I let the holo I was holding drop. I looked down at the pile again, realizing suddenly who else was missing. "Where's Elnear?"

" 'The Lady'," Jardan said. "You will refer to her as 'Lady Elnear.' Or 'ma'am.' "

I grimaced. "So where's 'The Lady's' picture?"

"You've never seen her?"

I shook my head, wondering if she was supposed to be a threedy star too.

She took one more holo out—out of her jacket, this time—and handed it to me, with all the careful respect that had been missing from the way she'd given me the rest.

I took it between my thumb and finger, holding it up. "That's her?" I said, surprised into asking it.

"What do you mean by that?"

"Nothing. Except . . ." Lady Elnear didn't look at all like a taMing, which was a relief. But she was . . . ordinary. A woman who looked like she was past fifty, with a long face and too many teeth, colorless hair, a body that was doughy and soft. Her clothes fit like they didn't belong to her. I looked up at Jardan, saw the resentment in her eyes, and almost couldn't say it. "She's not—beautiful. I mean . . . hell, they can afford it, right? They can get it fixed if they don't like it, they can get all the systems running right, they can get their body clocks set back? They never have to get too fat or skinny or old. . . ."

"Lady Elnear believes that there are better uses for her time and money than indulging in personal vanity."

"Hnh." I glanced at the picture one last time. Lady Elnear looked tired and sad and horse-faced as she turned away from me, again and again. I handed the holo back.

She put it away carefully in her jacket; piled the other holos up neatly and left them between us on the tabletop, like a small wall. Then she began to tell me How to Act: the official duties, the endless lies and phony rituals of people pretending to be decent to each other while all the time they were trying to get behind each other's unprotected backs with knives. I set my brain on *record* and thought about other things . . . about getting jerked around like a puppet by fate and the combines. About seeing Earth . . . About Kissindre Perrymeade and whether she'd think my being gone was because of her. If she even noticed I was missing . . . I forgot where I was, and laughed.

"Are you listening to me?" Jardan's voice was as hard as a slap.

I looked up, blinking. I fed the last few sentences she'd spoken back to her. "Don't worry. Even if I fall asleep, I'll remember it."

Her mouth thinned. "Do you actually understand any of this? You haven't asked me a single question."

I frowned, because I hated what I was hearing, and hated being forced to listen to it . . . and hated to admit that maybe she was right. "It's like getting the instructions for a machine you've never seen. It's not going to make any sense till I get there. If I have questions, I'll ask The Lady."

"Braedee!" She got up from her seat. Braedee appeared in the doorway before she'd finished the motion.

"You're pretty good at that, too," I said sourly.

"I'm through with him," she said, meaning me. It sounded as final as if my next stop was the incinerator chute.

"On the contrary." Braedee shook his head.

Her frown deepened. "He'll never pass."

"For human?" Braedee's eyes flicked over me, probably scanning me all up and down the spectrum, straight to my bones. "He will when I'm finished with him."

"That's not what I mean."

"He'll have to. You—" He pointed at me. "Come with me." I did.

He led me to what looked like his personal lab. It wasn't impressive, cool green and antiseptic tile, a lot of strange-surfaced alloys, but nothing that would make you want to get the hell out of there. But knowing who he was, and suspecting what he could do, I knew those walls probably hid as many secrets as his skin did. "Sit down," he said. "I'm going to fix your eyes." He nodded at a stool in front of what looked like some kind of scanner.

"There's nothing wrong with my eyes," I said.

"Don't act stupid." He shoved me toward the seat. "You look like a freak."

"All I need is some eyeskins—" I hugged my elbows, looking toward the doorway.

"I just want to look at your eye structure." He sat down, waiting for me. I sat down too, slowly, and put my face against the headpiece. "Look at the rings." Nothing inside but darkness, and a set of concentric rings floating in space like a target. I watched it for a long minute, squinting my eyes. Nothing. I began to relax.

There was a sudden blow against my eyes, that wasn't light or heat or pain, but somehow all three at once. I jerked back, swearing, rubbing my face. "You shit. What did you do to me?"

"See for yourself," he said. A mirrored plate slid down over the window in front of me. I stared at myself. The long slits of my pupils were changing while I watched, shrinking into pinpoints, the green of my irises filling in like crystal growth. "A simple molecular graft. Eyefilms would leave you half-blind in dim light. Not useful. Also detectable. This isn't permanent, but you can have it made permanent."

I looked up at him, away from the perfectly ordinary human eyes staring back at me from the mirror; away from the expression on my face. "What makes you think I want to look like a human?" My voice sounded shaky again.

He ignored that. "A little cosmetic facial surgery would be better. . . ." He hesitated, watching me. "But to do it safely takes more time than we've got. You can pass, I suppose; there are enough exotics around to make you look normal."

I took a deep breath, glancing at the locked storage units along the walls. He could turn my whole face into boneless mush with some of the virals he probably had in there.

He smiled; he enjoyed keeping people off-balance. "Mez Jardan has told you everything she considers important—" Heavy on the sarcasm. No wonder she hated him. "Now I'm going to give you what you really need. You can use a standard access—?"

"Sure," I said, as if I'd been doing it all my life.

He passed a programmed headset across the table. He had everything ready and waiting, every step planned. I took the headset, carefully. They always looked like a twitch would crush them, even though you could wad one up and keep it in your pocket for days. I dropped the net over my hair, waited a second while I cleared my thoughts out. Then I pressed the trodes to my forehead, and waited for the hard rush of image to hit me. I'd had some trouble learning to use one, because my mind wanted to treat the information feed like an invasion. But once I'd learned to access it was like being a sponge. I'd spent most of a standard year submerged, doing nothing but sucking up facts.

This time there was a megadose of data about the rise of the combines and the Federation Transport Authority. Most of it repeated what I already knew about the bad blood between them, stretching back over centuries to Old Earth days. The FTA's control of telhassium, and with it, of shipping and communications, meant that they butted heads with the transport networks every time they put an embargo on some government they wanted to toe their line better. It cost Centauri Transport every time the FTA wanted to make some other combine pay. Centauri hated their guts. They were the Big Enemy, to Centauri.

But Centauri Transport had other problems, and the flow began to change color, getting more personal. Now it was intercombine warfare, shifting loyalties and alliances. Focus on Triple Gee, Centauri's prime competitor, always looking for a way to give them grief. Anything it could get away with: goods delayed until the transport contract was invalid; an explosion in a fitting yard; a trade ambassador who never arrived to negotiate a deal, who never arrived anywhere again. Images of derelict vessels with breached hulls, bloated bodies drifting; of what a vial of biotoxins did to a shipment of transplant organs—and the ship's crew. The usual kind of thing.

Focus on Lady Elnear, her work for the FTA, work that Centauri didn't like much, that a lot of combines didn't like even more. She had a rival for the opening on the Security Council, one with heavy combine support. A lot of networks would do anything to plug him into that slot in her place. Anything they could get away with. One murder was nothing. . . .

The whole transfer took less than a minute: Centauri's self-serving picture puzzle of who would want to kill Lady Elnear, in about a hundred tiny bits. It was going to take my brain a day or so to put them together so that I understood the details completely . . . but already I had the feeling there were pieces missing. I didn't ask about them—not yet.

I took off the headset, and started to lay it down.

"Keep it," Braedee said. "Replay it as often as you need to, until you know everything on it."

"I already do," I said. Most people couldn't retain that much data that fast; they'd need to replay it over and over as it settled in.

"You really remember everything?" he asked. There was curiosity as much as challenge in it. "That easily?"

It was my turn to smile, for once.

He took the headset, and didn't ask again. "You'll find more acceptable clothing in your cabin. Put it on when you get back there. And use this on your hair—" He tossed a tube of something at me. "Give it some shape. Nobody wears their hair like that."

I glanced at my reflection again, and back at him. If he had any hair at all, I couldn't tell. I raised my eyebrows.

"It's my business to know what's expected. You'll have enough trou-

ble not violating sensibilities every time you open your mouth. Try to
keep it shut."

I picked up the tube and pushed to my feet.

"Not yet," he said, waiting just long enough to make me feel awkward. He help up a thin strip of transparent plastic, covered with maybe
a dozen colored dots. "We aren't finished yet. About these. . . ." The
drugs.

I sat back down, suddenly feeling lightheaded. One hand caught hold
of the other, squeezed it too tight, like lost children under the table's
edge. Those very expensive little skin patches would give me back the
Gift . . . make me whole again. Let me touch another mind, warm
myself at its fire without the cost, the sickening echoes of somebody
else's deathpain that blinded me every time I tried to make contact—
that made me stay out in the cold and the darkness, always remembering. . . . Except the pain would still be there. Just numbed. Nothing
was really free.

I was half Hydran, and I'd killed a man. If I'd been all Hydran it
would have killed me too; the psychological feedback mechanism was
built into Hydran brain circuitry along with the psionic abilities that
made it necessary. If you could kill with a thought, there had to be
something to stop you. Humans didn't have the psionic ability, or the
safeguards either. That was why the Hydrans hadn't stood a chance
against them. I was half human, with half the ability of a real Hydran,
and half the safeguards. The feedback hadn't killed me, but it had
crippled me real bad. Time was the only thing that could heal me: fresh
bandages of clean memory, safe experiences grafted on like layers of
new skin. There hadn't been enough of either yet.

With the right drugs acting on exactly the right areas in my brain, I
could use my telepathy and not hear warning bells. But it was like I'd
told Braedee: sooner or later I'd start to pay for it, doing more damage,
until maybe it crippled me for good. But what kind of choice did I
have? I needed the money.

And I needed to feel that fire. I felt a flush start to crawl up my face,
saliva filling my mouth, my palms sweating.

"You have all the physiological responses of an addict," Braedee said.
"Does it really mean that much to you?"

"Deadhead," I whispered, "you can't imagine." I reached out for the
sheet of patches.

He held it back. "What about the side effects you mentioned—'like
walking on broken legs,' you said."

"That doesn't matter. I'll worry about it later. . . . I'll do whatever you want. Just give me the drugs." I stretched out my hand.

"When we arrive," he said, beginning to frown.

"*Now*. I need some time to work on it, get my control back. . . . Come on." My hand fisted.

He hesitated, staring at me, reading responses. Doubt, calculation, mockery—all of them could have been on his face, or none. I couldn't read him. Finally he put the sheet of patches down where I could reach it. I snatched it up, staring at it.

"Keep them out of sight—especially when you're using. They last for one standard Earth day. I'll have more, when you need them."

I nodded, not really listening.

"If you need targets, use Jardan and my aides. Don't tell them." He hesitated. "If you ever try to read me, I'll know it. And I'll kill you."

I looked up, then. I got to my feet again without saying anything, and left the lab. Before I'd gotten halfway back along the hall, there was a patch behind my ear.

3

THERE WAS SOMETHING about coming to Earth . . . it was coming home. It didn't matter that Earth had stopped being the center of the Federation centuries ago, that it was a backwater stagnant world, a living museum; that the only reason the Federation Assembly still met here was tradition. It didn't make any difference that Ardattee, where I'd spent my whole life, was the Hub and the Heart now, where everything that really mattered happened first. . . . Or that I was too Hydran to feel really human, and too human to ever really be Hydran. It went deeper than that, below the scars and the memories and time itself, catching me by surprise right in the gut.

It kept me silent and wide-eyed as we left the Centauri Transport field complex. The entire planet had been a Federal Trade District for a couple of centuries, under the direct control of the FTA; it was peppered with starports because of the tourists. But most of the heavy shipping the distribution activity still centered on a place called N'yuk, and so the major transport combines had been granted footholds there. The Federation Assembly met in N'yuk, on neutral ground, inside a sprawling plex that also held the FTA's Security Council and headquartered all its activities. I'd spent five carefully monitored minutes of access time on Braedee's ship studying up on it.

N'yuk was on the coast of a major continent, just like Quarro, where I'd grown up, but it was centered on a handful of islands instead of a peninsula. The prime starport, and the Centauri complex, took up the largest island, Longeye. Triple Gee was based on another island called Stat. Combine embassies sprouted on the mainland like crystal growths, fantasy fortresses, for kilometers along what had once been one of the most polluted stretches on the face of the planet. Like everything else, the pollution was still there, just different. It was data pollution, now.

Braedee put me into a mod with Jardan and sent us on to the family estates, somewhere inland. "I'll be in touch," was all he said before he let me go and slipped like a fish back into his own world. And then I was alone with Jardan, and my thoughts. She didn't say anything for a long time, gazing out at the red/gold/green world flowing by below us. Somehow I'd expected it to be blue, because blue was what it was on the Federation Seal, the logo all the FTA's Corpses had worn back in Quarro's Oldcity. In the distance behind us the ocean reflected the sky, as blue as I'd always imagined, but below us the land looked like it was on fire.

Jardan wasn't impressed. Her mind was far ahead of us, already trying to deal with the hundred different scenarios of disaster and humiliation she was sure she was bringing back with her. Earth was just something you stood on, to her. . . .

I made myself stop reading her with an effort. While one part of my mind was staring slack-jawed out the window at the scenery, another separate part was always tracking her, gathering in the random images that floated on the surface of her thoughts . . . feeding on her reality. The world around me was alive again; the solid human flesh, hers and everyone else's, that had been invisible to my mind for the last three years was suddenly there again—breathing, thinking, feeling.

It was hard to remember now that for most of my life I hadn't used my Gift, hadn't even known I was a telepath. My mother was Hydran. When I was barely old enough to know what was happening, somebody had murdered her in an Oldcity alley. I'd felt her die, and survived it, but it had burned out my psi. After that I'd been alone for years, living like a deadhead, without even the memory that once I'd had someone who cared about me. I'd spent most of my time drugged into oblivion, hiding from the life I'd lost, and the living death I'd ended up with instead. Then the FTA had come along looking for psions and jerked me out of the gutter. Dr. Ardan Siebeling had put my mind back together and taught me how to use it. And Jule taMing had taught me why it mattered. And then the FTA had used us for pawns in a power game, and I'd killed a man, and died all over again. Only this time I remembered what I'd lost.

Now I had it back again. And knowing I couldn't keep it only made having it that much sweeter. I wanted to touch Jardan with my mind: Share, give . . . let her know the mystery she was blind to. Make her feel what I felt when I looked out the window at this world—the emotion too deep to put into words that didn't sound stupid. All words turned stupid and clumsy when you could share someone else's mind, and simply *know*. . . .

She looked up at me suddenly, her dark eyes sharp with *guilt/anger/ suspicion.* "Are you reading my mind?"

"What? No—" I lied, picking up the red heat of her resentment without even trying. Wondering if I'd really slipped that much. But I realized then that I hadn't let her feel it, hadn't let my control slip—it was only her own deadhead's fear suddenly catching fire, afraid I was hearing what she thought of me.

"Braedee said he gave you drugs, so you could—"

"I'm not using them yet," I said, as calmly as I could. If I told her the truth I knew she'd panic, and we were alone way the hell up here in the air. God only knew what she'd try.

She glared at me, but I saw/felt her easing up, relaxing a little. "Don't worry. I won't read everything you think anyway. I have to really concentrate on it. And I'm not that good." It was true. I wasn't much good. Not like I used to be . . . and it wasn't just that I was out of practice: the stuff Braedee had given me wasn't much good either. There were drugs on one of those customized dreamdots to block the chemical reactions I called pain and terror and grief that my memory triggered every time I used my Gift; and there were drugs to deaden the traumatized response centers that short-circuited my psi every time I even tried to get that far. But I already knew that if I pushed too hard, I still hit a wall. Even with two patches. They weren't strong enough. Braedee didn't want me as good as I could be; that made me too dangerous. If that was how it was going to be, I didn't see why he wanted me at all. Maybe fear just made him stupid, like most people.

I'd tried his mind, in spite of his warning—but carefully. He was burglarproofed, all right, for all kinds of electromagnetic snooping. Even psi energy might trip something. Maybe not; but I wasn't curious enough about him to get myself killed finding out. I looked out the window again. "I never thought I'd see Earth. I didn't think it would be like this."

"What were you expecting?" she asked, after a long minute. Her voice was almost pleasant with relief.

"Blue . . ." I stared at the lavender-blue mountains rising up ahead, looked down again at the trees. "Not all these colors."

"A world isn't all one kind of thing, you know."

I looked back at her. "I guess not," I said, thinking of Ardattee—of Oldcity, and Quarro. Mine had been.

Her face hardened over again as she met my eyes. She broke my gaze. Her glance flicked over the new me, dressed in a high-collared shirt, a loose, belted green jacket and pants. They were plain but expensive, and they fit like they'd been made just for me. Maybe they had. There was a Centauri logo on my sleeve: branded. "Why is your hair like that?" she said.

I almost reached up. "Braedee told me to fix it." I'd used the tube of gel he'd given me on it, making the curls stand up in spikes. It was something I remembered was going around Oldcity just before I left.

She sighed, more like a hiss, and murmured, "Scum." I settled deeper into my seat and didn't try to find out which of us she meant. She didn't say anything more, and neither did I.

It wasn't much more than half an hour from the time we left the Centauri fields until the mod began to lose altitude again. That meant we'd probably come three hundred klicks or so. I'd been surprised at how much open space there was, this close to the urban corridor that hugged the eastern coastline. I'd seen a handful of lone houses, and towns that didn't look anything like the few combine claves I'd seen other places. But then, Earth wasn't like other places, and the combines didn't run it. It was hard to believe that nobody wanted to live here. But most people went where the money was. Only people who already had money could survive on a world like this.

The mod drifted down into the arms of a steep-walled valley. If it was autumn up on the mountainsides, it was still summer in the valley's bottom; it looked like it was carpeted in green velvet. I could see estate houses lying along the silver road of the river that ran the length of it, each one larger and more expensive than the last. "Which one is the taMings'?" I asked, finally breaking the silence.

"All of them," she said. "The entire valley is their private estate."

I shook my head. "Is it big enough?"

"They have many others—here on Earth, on Ardattee, all through their network." She didn't even bother to glance up. Her voice was dull; her hand rose to touch the logo at her throat that wasn't Centauri's.

I grunted.

The mod landed softly in the courtyard that had been widening below us. The yard lay behind a building that looked like it had grown up out of the soil, part of the overgrown mass of trees and shrubs that surrounded it. It was all stone and wood. Small windows, their glass crosshatched into half a dozen tiny panes, watched us silently as we got out and stood together on the cracked, ancient flagstones. The long shadows of late afternoon lay across the yard, but the air was sweet and warm, without the chill I'd been expecting. Here the trees were still a fresh green; flowering vines climbed trellises and spilled over a high stone wall. A stooped old man in a baggy coat was patiently and almost soundlessly trimming a hedge with a hand-guided lightstick. He glanced up at us half-curiously, and went back to his work as Jardan nodded at him. For a moment the clenched-fist way she'd held herself ever since I'd first seen her eased. She'd come home, at last, standing in this yard.

"This place looks like it's been here forever," I said.

"For five hundred and eighteen years." She answered without thinking about it. Then she looked at me, and the fist clenched again. "This is Lady Elnear's private residence when she is on Earth, which is most of the time these days. Each family member maintains his or her own estate house, as they choose. I live here too; so will you."

With a click and a hum the mod lifted again behind us, going off obediently to some outbuilding, where it wouldn't spoil anybody's illusions. You could almost believe it was five hundred years ago, pre-space, another age. There was no trace of any security anywhere, although I knew that on the way in the mod must have cleared half a hundred snoopscans that were backed by measures which would have taken us out if we'd failed any of them. The more money and privacy you wanted, the harder a shell you needed. Some things probably hadn't changed in a lot longer than five hundred years.

Jardan started toward the house entrance, up the wide stone steps that led onto a vine-walled porch. I shouldered the bag with the few things Braedee had forced me to take, and followed her.

It was dark inside. The pupils of my eyes didn't work as well as they used to. But they worked well enough; after a minute my panic eased. I followed her down a hallway that smelled like oiled wood, up more creaking stairs, along another hall. The house was larger than I'd thought. We stopped in front of a closed door, and she glanced at me. I stood there, waiting, but the door didn't open. She pushed me aside and opened it by hand, looking at me as if I was stupid for expecting it to open itself, like every other door I'd ever seen that wasn't in a slum. "This will be your room."

I looked past her through the doorway. A bedroom . . . I could see the bed. The bed, inside its forest of carven wood, was large enough to sleep four, easy. The room itself seemed to go on forever, filled with bureaus, tables, chairs, and things I couldn't name. Only the desk/terminal in the window alcove didn't look like it had been there as long as the house had. The rug was dark and dense under my boots as I moved across it, and patterned like a kaleidoscope with jewel-bright flowers. The ceiling was at least three meters high. I put my bag down on the bed; the bed jiggled, full of jelly. I sat down beside my bag on the smooth, cool surface of the covers, suddenly feeling more than a little lost. Jardan was still in the doorway. I forced a smile. "Well . . . it's cramped, but I can stand it."

She didn't react; no sense of humor at all. She touched an inset in the wall beside the door. "If you need anything, this gives access to the housekeeping programs. There is also a small human service staff."

I nodded.

"Any questions?"

I shook my head.

"Perhaps you'd like to rest—"

"No." I stood up. "Let's get it over with."

Her face pinched. "All right then . . . You may come with me to meet the Lady."

Her doubts were screaming silently at me. They weren't any louder than my own as I followed her out of the room; but anything was better than staying behind alone.

Lady Elnear was sitting by herself on a sun porch. The light streamed in through the tall windows around her, golden and green. She was painting a picture on a lightbox: the view from the window, half-hidden in vines. It wasn't very good. And it wasn't what I'd expected. . . . I wondered what I had been expecting.

She turned as she heard us enter. I saw the sad, sagging face I'd seen in the holo, the awkward body, the plain clothes. And then she smiled, as she saw Jardan—and suddenly she was another person. She had the most beautiful smile I'd ever seen. Like the sun, it made you blind to everything else. "Philipa, you're back." And then she saw me. The smile disappeared. "And this is . . . the young man. The one Braedee sent to watch me. Jule's friend." Even her voice had an odd quality: almost quavering, musical and uncertain all at once. It warmed just a little as she said Jule's name. She was staring at me, trying not to. "The telepath."

Because she was looking at me, I nodded. Jardan gave me a sharp poke in the side. "Yes, ma'am," I said. "Lady. I'm Cat."

"Cat—?" She raised her eyebrows, waiting for the rest of it.

"Just 'Cat.' " I shrugged, glancing at Jardan. "Ma'am."

"Oh." She smiled, but it was false this time. She knew she should offer me her hand, a peace gesture; but she couldn't quite make herself do it. Like maybe I'd give off sparks when she touched me; like being a psion might be contagious.

I put out my hand: not a peace offering. More like a dare.

She took it. Her hand was strong and warm. "I've never met a . . . Hydran before." But she had to say that.

"Half-Hydran," I said, letting go. "Half human . . ." Most people had never met a halfbreed either; because most humans would rather have a brainwipe than a cat-eyed freak for a son. Once humans had been glad to know that they weren't alone in the universe. That time was long past, now.

Her colorless cheeks reddened a little. "Please forgive me if I seem . . . awkward, and self-conscious. It isn't personal. It's just that being in the presence of a telepath is not something that I'm used to. It will take a little time. . . ." She stepped back, her hands helpless at her sides.

A lifetime probably wouldn't be enough. I only shrugged again, trying to shake loose the invisible weight that pressed down harder and harder on my shoulders.

Jardan moved away from me to Elnear's side. She whispered something I couldn't hear: she was telling Elnear that I was a cripple without drugs; that I couldn't read them at all right now.

"Yes I can," I said. "I lied to you."

Her head snapped up, her eyes cold with fury.

Elnear put a hand on her arm, gently but firmly. "Temper, Philipa," she murmured. She looked at me as if she expected an explanation.

"Centauri hired me to help protect you. Jardan's right—I can't do you any good unless I use the drugs. I figured the sooner I started doing my job, the better. If you can't handle that, it's your problem," I said, looking at both of them. "But if somebody was trying to kill me, I'd damn sure be glad of anything that made it harder to do. Ma'am." Might as well be the tough guy. It was better than being the freak.

Elnear nodded, but their faces didn't change much. Elnear led Jardan past me. Her hand was still on Jardan's arm, as if she didn't trust us that close to each other. "Come, Philipa, it's nearly dinner time. I have to dress. They've asked me to join the family at the Crystal Palace, and I can hardly refuse again. Will you keep me company?" They went on out of the room together, talking softly, as if I wasn't even there.

I stood where they'd left me. I watched them get smaller and smaller as they went down the hallway, leaving me there without a word, not even looking back. Only I was the one getting smaller and smaller, being swallowed up in the suffocating emptiness of the silent house; so that by the time they came back again, I would have disappeared. . . .

(I didn't ask for this either!)

They spun around together as my sending caught them from behind; gaped at me, with their hands pressed to their heads. For a minute, neither of them moved. Then Lady Elnear started back down the hall toward me. Jardan caught at her hand, but Elnear shook her off and kept coming. When she reached the doorway she stopped again. Her baggy sleeve slid down her arm as she caught at the white-painted wood for support. She stood there, still staring, her free hand still pressed to her head. "Come with us," she said, finally. "Of course you should come with us to dinner. You should meet the family. You are my new aide. . . ."

It took me a second to believe I'd heard it; another to make myself move. When I reached her side, she was as surprised as I was. We began to walk together. Up ahead of us the hall was empty.

"What are the terms under which Braedee hired you?" she asked, as if she hadn't even noticed that Jardan was gone. I told her. "I'd have the contracts run through a legal advisory program, before you agree to anything, if I were you," she said, her face expressionless. "One can't be too careful."

"I will." I nodded. "I know." And smiled.

She smiled too, just a little, looking straight ahead.

4

THERE REALLY WAS a Crystal Palace. It looked like something carved from ice, lit up from the inside, and it stretched out along the darkening riverbank, admiring its reflection. Earth's sun had slipped down behind the western mountain, and the valley was blue with evening by the time we stood on the palace steps. It reminded me a little of the combine centers in Quarro, but it was built of glass and iron, had to be at least as old as the house where Elnear lived. She'd told me it had been transported to this valley from somewhere else on Earth, like most of the buildings here . . . anything that caught a taMing's fancy down through the centuries, and had a price. Some people collected antiques; the taMings lived in them. Looking up as we went in through layers of splintered light, I felt my senses go into overload. This was a private home. . . . This was a dream; nobody lived like this.

I followed a few steps behind Lady Elnear, not because Jardan had told me those were the rules but because I didn't know what the hell else to do except follow somebody. I felt like I was walking through a minefield. Elnear was dressed in a long, loose sack of a tunic over leggings, wearing ropes and ropes of jeweled necklaces. She didn't look elegant, but at least she looked rich. Jardan walked beside her; I knew it had taken a good half hour for Elnear to get her to come out of her room after I'd mindspoken them. Elnear hadn't mentioned what I'd done, or even warned me not to do it again. She treated me exactly like a new assistant, explaining, suggesting, pointing things out as we rode up the valley. She didn't do it because she liked me; she did it because she disliked unpleasantness. She was good at keeping the things she felt off of her face. It was all part of the games they played in her world. She had no choice, and so she pretended I was normal. Considering all the choice I had, I was grateful she was a good player.

The interior of the Crystal Palace had been one huge open space, once; I wondered what it had been used for then. The taMings had broken it up into rooms and levels, like a glass beehive. The walls, the ceilings, the floors were transparent, but polarized, so they could be made opaque in changing patterns.

"This is the original family residence that Estevan taMing had brought here after he returned to Earth. He started Centauri Transport and made his fortune out in the Centauri system." Elnear was still giving me the guided tour, reading the questions in my eyes. "My brother-in-law . . . Jule's father lives here now. After so many generations in one home, sometimes you get tired of seeing the same four walls." She glanced away; you could see the river, through half a dozen perfectly clear panels.

"Why not just move?" I asked, and felt like a fool as soon as I'd said it.

"Tradition," she said softly. "They are a very stubborn family. They don't like to let things go."

I didn't say anything, thinking about Jule. We were closing now with the hot cluster of minds that I'd picked up as we entered. Elnear had told me there'd be more taMings than usual tonight, because Centauri was having its quarterly board meeting right now. The floating butler that had led us through this maze of mirrors disappeared suddenly through the doorway in a wall opaqued to a pearl-gray.

The butler chimed as we entered the room, and then began to drift away. "Thank you," Elnear said, even though it was nothing but a machine. There were twenty or thirty people there already. Heads began to turn as the three of us stopped in the doorway. I felt Elnear clench up inside, like someone about to dive into cold water.

"Auntie! Auntie!" A shrill child's voice cut like a drill through the polite mumble of adult voices talking treaties and voting and forced merger. A little girl with long black hair pushed through the legs of the crowd and came bolting across the room. She collided with Elnear like a heat-seeking projectile, and hung on her tunic skirt, squealing with delight.

"Talitha." Elnear smiled, the smile that could change everything, stroking the dark hair as the little girl beamed up at her. "How's my favorite girl?"

"I have new shoes," Talitha said. "See?" She stuck out her foot, which was covered with something that looked like a large, hairy bug wearing a red hat.

"Lovely," Elnear said. "Just the thing! Show them to Philipa."

Talitha hopped around her, one foot still up in the air, until she saw me. She froze, staring, then buried her face in Elnear's tunic. One clear gray eye showed again after a minute, and then the other. "Talitha. This is my new aide." Elnear patted her shoulder. "His name is Cat."

She looked up at me from under her shining black bangs. "I have two cats," she said. "Their names are Blunder and Calamity. I'm four." She held up the right number of fingers.

"Nice names," I said. Suddenly I was remembering Jule again, seeing her face in Talitha's, just the way she must have looked when she was small. She'd probably never even seen Talitha. "You remind me of your cousin Jule."

A frown wrinkled up her nose. "We don't talk about Jule," she whispered, and pressed her finger against her mouth. "She's bad."

I looked at Elnear.

"No, treasure, she isn't bad," Elnear said gently, not looking at me. "She was just . . . unhappy. But now she's better."

"Daric says she's bad—"

"Talitha!" This time it was a boy's voice calling. I glanced up and saw him coming toward us. He looked about eleven, with the same shining black hair and gray, upslanting eyes. "Oh, hi, Auntie." He stopped next to her, kissed her cheek as she hugged him with her free arm. "Mother said you weren't coming tonight. I was so bored I thought I was falling into a black hole. Can we sleep at your house? I hate it here." His voice turned sullen as he looked over his shoulder at someone.

"We'll see," Elnear said. "I'll ask your mother." He grinned again, abruptly. She turned him to face me. "This is Cat. Say hello."

"Really?" He stared me up and down, his eyes wide. "That's your *name?* Wow, your hair is terminal!"

"My thought exactly," Jardan murmured.

"Will you show me how to do mine? How old are you? Are you Auntie's lover?"

"Jiro—!" Elnear's hand flew up like it wanted to clamp over his mouth; fluttered in the air, dropped to her side again. "Cat is my new aide."

"Oh well." He shrugged. "You have to fix my hair," he said, looking at me, "you promised. Come on. Talitha. Let's find Mother. You want to stay at Auntie's, don't you—?" He hauled his sister away, squawking.

"You should have boxed his ears," Jardan said, when he was safely out of range.

Elnear smoothed her skirts. "Well. It's not easy to be young here. Or old. . . ." She glanced at me, finally, almost sheepishly. "You've just met the new generation of taMing empire-builders. You may as well meet the rest."

I followed her on into the shifting dance of the crowd, into the bodies in orbit around the long table covered with food and drinks. Too many of them, too much alike. Parents and children, aunts and uncles, nephews and nieces, at least six generations of them—but none of them, even the oldest, looked any older than Elnear. Even the ones who didn't look like taMings were all too beautiful, and they all wore perfect clothes and jewels that made my head swim, and murmured things I didn't understand and thought things I didn't want to hear. . . .

And all of them were *alive,* too real, thinking, feeling . . . not just around me any more but inside me, *angry mocking tense bored smug afraid.* I'd forgotten what it was like to be open all the time; forgotten how to really control it. It was like being thrown headfirst into a mob after three years in solitary. My nerves were closing in on burnout fast.

I reached up when no one was watching and picked off the patch behind my ear, dropping it on the floor. Then all I could do was hang on until the drugged nerve centers half asleep in my mind woke up again: until the black ache that was pain without a name came crawling back; until my crippled psi response went fetal, smothering the fire of too many other minds inside me. . . . I went on, trailing Elnear through more meaningless head-on collisions like a dazed deafmute. No one seemed to notice, or care, not even her. She was only using me as a crutch; I was something to say, to people she had nothing to say to.

Until we came face to face with still another taMing, a handsome man in a silver-threaded evening coat, wearing a ruby button as big as an eye. He looked like he was in his mid-thirties, but he couldn't be: he was Jule's father.

"Gentleman Charon taMing, Cat," she said. "This is my new aide—"

"Yes," Jule's father said. I looked back at him, surprised. "I already know about him." He did know: he knew what I really was. *Jule's freak.* He was the head of Centauri's board; the one who'd had me hired. "Just do as you're told, and don't do anything else, and you'll get along fine, boy," he said, with a smile that never touched the words.

I looked away, my hands clenching over the loose cuffs of my jacket. Somehow, somewhere, there had to be a way out of this place. . . .

"You understand me—?" When I didn't answer something brushed my shoulder, just hard enough to seem casual. His hand. But it wasn't a hand; it only looked like one, wrapped in a skin glove. It was almost pure augmentation, and he didn't just use it to direct-access. I jerked as the pressure of his grip hurt me without seeming to.

"Yes. Sir." I had a hard time getting it out. I rubbed my shoulder. "You're just like she described you. Sir."

"Who?" His glance darted at Elnear.

"Jule."

Eyes on me again. This time I didn't look down. His face darkened. But then he turned and walked away without saying anything more.

"Don't try those games with him," Jardan said to me. "You'll lose."

"What games?" I asked, because I hadn't been playing one.

"Don't try them on me, either," she snapped. Elnear only looked at me, her mind telling me something I didn't want to hear.

I turned around, bumping into the table heaped with strange food, spilling a crystal glass full of wine on my pants. I swore, and somebody frowned, and somebody else laughed. I tried to pretend it hadn't happened, wasn't happening, that I really wanted something to eat. I'd never seen so much food in my life, and none of it was anything I recognized.

I reached out for something, blindly. Behind me I heard Jardan mutter, "Pig." And the table might as well have been piled with garbage; suddenly the sight and smell of everything on it made me sick. I backed away again. At least the other guests looked like they were losing interest in eating. I told myself it would be over soon—

A butler chimed again, somewhere across the room. "At last!" Elnear m_rmured, as if it meant something she'd actually been looking forward to. "Dinner."

I opened my mouth; closed it again, as the crowd sucked us away.

Elnear looked at me, curious. "You look like you expect to be the main course," she whispered. "Cheer up! The food is actually quite good."

I grimaced, hoping it looked like a smile.

"Auntie—!" Jiro and Talitha were back, dragging a tall black-haired woman after them.

Jule. I almost said it out loud; stopped myself. It wasn't Jule's mind when I found it; not even her face, when I saw it clearly. This woman was more beautiful; only hers was a soft, spoiled kind of beauty, not the strong clean lines of Jule's face and body. She looked like she'd never even thought about the kind of pain Jule had always known. But still the resemblance was so strong it made my throat tighten.

"Mother says we can stay with you!" Jiro was shouting triumphantly. "It's all set!"

Charon taMing came drifting up behind them, his eyes on the woman's back, a half frown pulling his lips down.

The woman made a quick hidden gesture with her hands, asking Elnear a question. Oldcity had its handcodes too, but this wasn't one of them, and I couldn't read it.

Elnear smiled at the children, half doting, half amused. "Of course," she murmured to the woman. "You know you're always welcome, Lazuli."

"This is my mother," Talitha said, looking at me suddenly, hanging on Lazuli's arm.

Still staring at her mother, I managed to nod.

"We're going to have a baby brother!" Talitha sang. "He's going to look just like me."

I glanced at Lazuli's body without even thinking. She was wearing a clinging bodywrap that glowed like moonstones, and she sure as hell didn't look like she was expecting a baby any time soon.

Her glance followed mine downward. She smiled. "It's in vitro. No one bothers with *that* any more. . . ."

I looked away again, in a hurry. Charon taMing's eyes were on me, his frown deepening. I glanced away from him, too, not knowing whether it was even safe to look at anybody.

"I mean pregnancy, of course." Lazuli laughed, like music, and I couldn't help turning back to her.

"Not sex," Jiro said helpfully. "Mother likes sex. Do you?"

"Jiro!" she murmured, going pale when I expected to see her blush. "What am I going to do with you—?"

"Get him a girlfriend," I muttered, and Jardan jerked me away from them like I had a disease.

As I turned, I saw Charon catch hold of the boy's arm with that hand, and squeeze it hard. Jiro bit his lip, but he didn't make any sound. I looked away again.

Someone was watching us, his mouth curved up in a half-smile. Jule's brother, Daric. He'd just come in. In a crowd of rich-colored party clothes, he was the only one still wearing basic business drab. There was somebody with him, a woman—his woman, from the way he held onto her. My eyes stopped dead in their tracks when they got to her. If the way he was dressed made everyone else in the room look like tomorrow, she made them look like yesterday.

She was an exotic: she'd had things done to her body that were meant to make people look at her and see something new. Her skin was silver, gleaming in the light. Her hair was a silver-white shockwave cresting over her copper-colored eyes, spilling down her back. Even her fingernails were silver. She was wearing a holo, the abstract forms and colors flowing around her, always almost letting you see too much flesh but never doing it. . . . She moved with a kind of easy laughter playing around her like the colors, as if upstaging everyone in the room, making them murmur about her, blush, swear, gossip in hand-sign, was exactly what she wanted out of life. I wondered what she was doing here, with somebody who looked like him.

"Jeezu, ain't that a piece and a half. . . ." I said, and then realized I'd said it out loud as Lady Elnear turned back and gave me a look. I felt the tension-coil inside me wind one twist tighter; realizing suddenly that I couldn't afford to stop thinking about anything I did or even said around these people, not for one second.

"Her name is Argentyne," Elnear murmured, not having to ask what I meant. "Daric's . . . companion. She's an entertainer—a symb-player, I believe." Even in her voice there was more fascination than disapproval.

I pulled my eyes away from Argentyne, looked at Daric again. He was still watching us back, measuring our reactions with that smile on his face. He raised his eyebrows as he looked at me. I looked down, and away.

Before I had the chance to ask any dumb questions they were gone, and the table was in front of me. I sat down. Jardan flanked me on my left, Elnear on my right. There was already food steaming under a clear dome on the plate, and what looked like bread and fruit and tofu on smaller plates, like planets circling a sun. I reached out, toward something familiar.

"Don't touch that!" Jardan hissed.

I pulled my hand back. No one else was eating. They were all looking toward the head of the table, where Gentleman Teodor, the oldest active board member, was sitting. He didn't look more than fifty; he was four times that old. Watching the way he moved, the slowness, you could tell. They could set back the body's cellular clocks, but they couldn't fool time forever. Not yet, anyway. He went through some hand ritual, and everyone around me responded. Then, finally, he reached for the food, and so did everyone else.

I flipped the steam-clouded lid off my dish. I jerked back; the chair I was sitting in *skreek*ed on the floor. There was something dead on my plate. Its glazed silver eye stared up at me from a bed of different-colored lumps glistening with sauce. The sauce looked like it had rat turds in it.

"What is the matter with you?" Jardan murmured.

"It's dead." I looked at her plate. There was another dead thing on that one.

"I assume you'd prefer to eat it alive," she said, dripping venom. She picked up one of the dozen silver utensils in front of her and dug a piece of flesh out of it. She put it into her mouth and began to chew.

"You've never eaten fresh fish?" Elnear's voice made me turn back.

"Sure," I said, half frowning. This wasn't it.

"I mean freshly raised fish." She nodded at her own plate. "It tastes much better than cloned. Try it."

I looked at the fish, and the utensils laid out between my own dishes like dissecting tools. There weren't any chopsticks, so I picked up a fork.

"No," Jardan whispered. "Start from the outside." She pointed at a different fork.

I dropped the one I was holding. It clattered across my plate. I picked up another one, and dug into the fish near the tail. I ate a bite, trying not to gag.

Elnear had it right; the food was incredible. I looked up at her, wanting to tell her so, but she was already talking to someone else. I went back to my eating. When I picked up the fishhead Jardan knocked it out of my hand. I realized then that a lot of people were staring at me . . . realized that my mind had quietly gone dead while I was eating, and I hadn't noticed. Jule's brother was sitting almost across from me, still wearing that same half-smile. He was younger than Jule, which meant he couldn't be a whole lot older than I was; but somehow he looked twice his own age—or half of it. He had the same night-black hair, the same eyes . . . but if I hadn't known he was her brother, there was nothing about him that would have made me believe it.

I looked away from him, feeling my face flush again. Argentyne was next to him, and she laughed as he kissed her throat and whispered something in her ear, probably about me. She winked at me as she saw me staring at her. I looked away from her too, wishing I was dead. Trying to ignore their eyes and everyone else's, I reached out for a pitcher to refill my glass.

And then it happened. As I picked up the pitcher, something invisible took hold of it, trying to pry it out of my hands. My brain countered instinctively; my fist tightened again before a drop spilled. I pulled the pitcher toward me slowly, watching my hand every millimeter of the way. I kept my free hand tight around my glass as I refilled it, and set the pitcher back where it belonged. I raised the crystal glass to my mouth—and it happened again. The glass jerked; my hand spasmed. I almost snapped the fragile stem in half as I choked, and drops of clear red splattered onto my jacket. I gulped the wine down in three swallows, and set the glass on the table. And then I sat with my hands knotted into fists below the table edge.

Someone had used psi on me . . . someone in this room. My eyes tracked face after face along the table, but every face was the same, a mask I couldn't read. I swore under my breath. I'd thrown away that patch, figuring it was safe, that there was no one here Elnear had to worry about . . . when I should have been worrying about my own skin. These people might seem like nothing more than a bizarre family of clone-faced eccentrics, but some of the most powerful and ruthless vips in the Federation were sitting right at this table with me. They *were* Centauri Transport—and now I belonged to them. This was the peak of the pyramid that had crushed me all my life . . . and if I ever forgot it again, it could be the last mistake I ever made. Because one of them was a psion, too.

It didn't seem possible. How could a psion pass, and no one ever suspect it? Jule had been driven out of her home, driven half out of her mind, by the untrained psi she'd been born with. She'd even told me there were no others . . . that no one in the family knew why it had happened to her. But what had just happened to me wasn't my imagination, and it wasn't an accident. I'd been doing a good job of looking like a jerk without even trying. But for somebody here, that wasn't enough. They wanted the new boy completely humiliated. I wouldn't even have known it wasn't my own stupid fault . . . except that I wasn't just another deadhead. Someone with a sick sense of humor must be wondering right now why the trick hadn't worked this time. I looked at Elnear.

She glanced at me, her faded blue eyes intent. "Did you want to ask me something?"

My eyes scanned the table, flicked back to her. "Ah . . . can I have your roll? Ma'am."

She passed it to me without comment, and looked away again.

She didn't tell me there were still three courses of dinner to go.

I kept picking at my food to keep from seeming stranger than I did already. Nothing more happened. After what seemed like hours, and was, people began to leave their seats around me. As I got up from the table Jule's brother Daric was suddenly there in front of me, so close that I nearly stepped on him. I didn't, but it took an effort not to look like I was trying. Argentyne came up beside him, shimmering like a mirage.

"So this is your new aide, Elnear." He wasn't impressed. "Where did you find this one?"

"I know your sister," I said.

"Many men have known my sister. That hardly seems like the sort of experience that you'd be looking for, Elnear?" He had such a toneless voice that it took a second to realize what he'd actually said.

Before I could do anything, or Elnear had to, Jardan said, "Your father chose him. For security reasons."

"Really?" He looked at me again, still deadpan. "And what special equipment or skill qualifies you for that important duty?"

For just a second I was still thinking about kicking him in the balls. Instead, I reached out and found the nerve inside his elbow. I pressed hard. "I fight dirty," I said.

He gasped and went white. His mouth opened, but nothing came out. Argentyne looked at us with an expression I couldn't put a name to. Everybody else stopped breathing, including me, as I suddenly realized what I'd just done. I'd just hurt a taMing.

But then the color came back into Daric's face in a red rush. "Good . . ." he whispered, shaking out his hand. "That was just perfect." The look in his eyes was so strange I almost thought he meant it. He began to turn away; turned back. "You're the first interesting person Elnear has ever brought into this house." He flipped me a salute. And then he was gone again, leading Argentyne after him, with a jerky swagger that made no sense at all inside the clothes he was wearing.

I looked back at Elnear and Jardan, with my guts full of jelly.

"What in the Nine Billion Names of God do you think you're doing—" Jardan started.

Lady Elnear held up her hand. "His job," she said, sounding surprised.

And then Jiro was at her side. Lazuli trailed behind him, looking exhausted, carrying Talitha, who'd fallen asleep somewhere after the second course. We moved away through the crowd, taMings scattering and regrouping like fragments of a stellar explosion. As we walked

Elnear suddenly stumbled. She would have fallen if I hadn't been following closer than I was supposed to, and reached out to catch her. She
thanked me, more embarrassed than grateful; nothing important. Except that I couldn't see any reason at all for her to have stumbled like
that.

When we finally reached the manor house, I went straight to my room
and put on another patch. By the time it had taken, I knew that I was
the only one still awake in the entire house . . . and that I probably
wasn't going to sleep at all that night. My body felt like it didn't know
where it was, what time it was, what year. My brain was going around
like a caged rat, going back and back over everything it had seen the
last day and a half, all the data Braedee had fed me, every random
flicker of dream it could suck up from the surrounding rooms. And still
none of it could make me forget that I was lying in the hollow silence of
a room as big as a house, alone in a bed that could have slept four,
staring at the darkness with a stranger's eyes . . . that I was utterly
lost here, afraid to touch anything, eat anything, even say anything,
because everything I knew was wrong. . . .

I pulled my knees up against my chest, pulled the covers over my
head against the darkness of a world that was nothing like the darkness
or the world I'd always known, and lay there trembling.

After a long time I let go of myself again; stretched out my knotted
muscles, pushed back the covers. I got up and took a leak, ate some of
the leftover fruit I'd stuffed into my pockets, went to the glass doors
that opened onto a narrow balcony. The stars were out, their millions
crowding the night sky—that dead black nothingness that was so much
greater, and stronger, and more permanent than any of them.

I recognized a pattern suddenly, the constellation called Orion—recognized it in a stolen memory of Jule's. This sky looked totally unfamil-
iar when I matched it against my own memories. So did any night sky I
ever saw, even Quarro's. Growing up in buried Oldcity, I'd never seen
the stars.

As I stood there, I realized suddenly that I wasn't the only one awake
in the house any more. I caught the candleflame of someone else's
thoughts wandering the same night sky, invisible to my eyes but not to
my mind, watching the same stars, the same black emptiness between
them . . . thinking like I had that no one else ever saw them that way.
I let myself weave a little deeper into the strands of unguarded thought:
Doubts and longings, unnamed fears, memories of death, loss, empti-

ness . . . a sadness so deep that when I reached it I broke contact, because it was too painful. It was a mind I'd seen once before. One I'd never expected to hold the kind of things I'd just found there. It was Lady Elnear.

I looked down at my hands, clenched over the railing of the balcony. The fight scars on my knuckles showed silver-white in the moonlight. I remembered how even before I'd met her, I'd figured the Lady had everything anybody could want; everything I didn't have—money, power, family. But she felt lost, helpless, trapped inside the motion of things she couldn't control—surrounded by enemies and strangers. I'd never imagined that someone like her, living in a place like this, could feel that kind of helplessness . . . a helplessness as total as my own. I let go of the railing, let my hands fall back to my sides . . . touched her mind again, just enough to keep contact, not enough to intrude.

I waited until she left her window at last, drifting silently back to her bed, still thinking that she was alone. The aching awareness of her life had been made small again, bearable again, by her awareness of the night, so that she could try to sleep.

I went back to my own bed and lay down again, finally, and slept.

5

ABOUT THREE SECONDS after dawn somebody came crashing into my sleep like a bolt of lightning. "Are you still *sleeping—?*" It was Jiro taMing. His voice took a sudden broken leap of about an octave in the middle of the sentence.

"Not any more." I pushed my face up out of my pillow, feeling like shit. "What do you want?"

"I want you to fix my hair like that. And that thing you did to Daric, that was really a fanged move, I want that too. Why don't you have any pajamas?"

"Jeezu." I let my head drop back into the pillow. "I'm too tired."

He jerked my arm. "You work for Centauri, you take orders from me."

I sat up, so fast that he didn't have time to move. My hand clamped around his arm, just over the elbow: "You want to know what I did to Daric—?"

His mouth fell open, and he almost fell over himself trying to pull away. I shoved him, letting him go. "Get the hell out of my room."

He scrambled backwards toward the open door, his mind a tangle of asinine awe and terror. The door slammed shut.

I lay down again, and tried to go back to sleep. But adrenaline was dumping into my veins now as I remembered where I was, and why. Finally I pushed myself up again and stumbled into the bathroom. I stood in the fresher for a long time, letting it needle my skin numb and loosen up my muscles, my brain.

I stopped to look at myself in the mirror when I stepped out. My eyes still looked like somebody else's. My hair still looked the same, standing up in soft fingers, even after I'd slept on it. I touched it; good stuff. I wondered if I'd have to shave my head to get rid of it.

I went back out into my room, still feeling a little dazed. I picked through the clothes I'd brought, hating the sight of them, the company logos and what they stood for.

"Where'd you get all those scars on your back? . . . Are you a merse? Were you in a war?"

I looked up. Jiro was in the doorway again, staring at me. "No. Yeah . . . sort of." I caught up the first shirt I could get my hands on, and jerked it over my head.

"I wish I was you," he said, dreamy eyed.

"No you don't." *Stupid little bastard.*

"Is that a tattoo—?"

"Yeah."

"Why do you have Draco's logo tattooed on your butt?"

I looked down at the blue lizard slithering up my hip, the holoed collar of feathers or flames shimmering around its head. I could never see the thing well enough to tell which it was, feathers or flames. "It's not Draco's logo."

"Yes it is, the dragon and the sunburst—"

"It's just a lizard." I saw the tube of gel Braedee had given me lying in a tangle of clothes. I picked it up and threw it at him. "Here. Put this on your hair and let it set." Hoping that would get rid of him. But instead he came on into the room. He planted himself in front of my bathroom mirror like it was his own. I finished dressing, as quickly as I could.

"Hey, this doesn't work—!" Jiro stuck his head out of the bathroom as I was starting for the door.

I stopped, looking back at him. His shoulder-length hair stood up and then flopped down again over his face, like black curtains. I bit my lip to keep from laughing. "Your hair's too long."

He pushed it up and back again, squinting. "Well, what am I supposed to do?"

I shrugged, "Cut it off," and left the room.

Everyone else was still asleep, even the servants. I went downstairs, moving as softly as I could, relieved to be alone. I wandered until I found the kitchen, which was as big as a warehouse. At least it was cleaner. I went from counter to counter, nervous but hungry, querying systems until I'd gotten what I needed from the hot and cold units. On the far side of the room there were doors opening into a small courtyard. I went outside and sat down on a wooden bench, gulping black coffee and listening to birdsong, waiting for the sun, or whatever happened next.

"I'm hungry." I felt the bright, tangled web of a child's mind behind the words; looked up as Talitha came shuffling out into the courtyard, dragging a blanket and wearing bugs on her feet.

"Ask your mother," I said, damned if I was going to be a servant for every taMing who looked at me.

"She's asleep." She stopped in front of me, pressing the blanket against her face.

"Ask your brother, he's not."

"Jiro woke me up."

I sighed. "Me too."

"He said I didn't get any dessert yesterday. . . ." Her gray eyes filled with sudden tears. "He said I didn't get any dessert because I was a bad girl, I fell asleep at the table. He ate all my desserts."

I stood up as the damp wave of her misery rolled into my brain. "Your brother's a croach. Here." Reaching into my pockets, I emptied out the candy and nuts I'd brought back from dinner last night. "I saved dessert for you last night. Eat this first," I pointed at what was left of my food.

Her eyes went wide. She scrambled up onto the bench and began to eat, still looking at me. "You're my special friend, right?"

"Right." I smiled, and touched her hair. Maybe she said that to everybody, but what the hell. I needed to hear it; it felt good. I went back into the kitchen and began to get myself some more breakfast.

Someone's surprise caught me from behind—surprise so sharp it was almost anger. I turned around and Lady Elnear was standing across the room. She wasn't expecting to see anyone, especially not me.

I felt my expression turn guilty as I saw her face, as if she'd caught me stealing food, instead of just preparing it. I forced myself to meet her eyes, to remember that I had a right to eat, at least.

"You're up very early, Mez Cat," she said. Not happy about the fact.

"So are you," I said, because I couldn't think of anything else. "Ma'am."

"I've always gotten up very early." She came slowly into the kitchen, and began to call up some tea. "I value this time alone before the day begins, before anyone else is about, to disturb me." She had her back to me, but I could feel the sharp edge of every word. "Do you always get up so early?"

"No, ma'am," I said. "I like the night. It's what I'm used to." My second breakfast slid up onto the counter in front of me. I picked it up, before I let myself look at her again. I could feel her eyes on me,

questioning. "I didn't plan on getting up so early. Couldn't sleep. Guess
I'm still a little timewarped. I didn't figure you'd be up this early either."

"Oh? Why not?"

Without really thinking about it, I said, "Last night, when I couldn't
sleep, and you were . . ." I broke off, too late, as she suddenly knew
what I meant. All the expression disappeared from her face, but her
mind recoiled as if I'd seen her naked.

I set my food down again. "Maybe I'll go back to bed." Realizing
with a kind of sick frustration that I'd just completely destroyed any
trust that might have been starting between us yesterday. Not looking
at her now, I headed for the door.

"Please be ready to go into the city with me in three hours. I'm going
to the Arm today," she said, her voice resigned and cold. "I'm told you
will accompany me."

"Yes, ma'am." I nodded, still without looking at her, just wanting to
get out of there. As I went back along the hall I heard Talitha's voice,
"Auntie look! Dessert!"

When it was time, I went back down. The Lady and Jardan were waiting together at the entrance, side by side. They looked like they were
waiting for the enemy. Or for me. I felt my face settle into a frown.

A mod that was larger and more plush—and a lot more secure—than
any I'd ever been in carried us back toward the coast. After a while
N'yuk began to take on reality in the distance, rising above the sprawl
of the surrounding urbs; a manmade mountain range of peaks and valleys, one solid block fused from the skeletons of the countless ancient
corporate towers that had squatted there on the bedrock of an island
between two rivers. The rivers were bridged by arcing buttresses of
more structure.

The dully-gleaming mass of it swallowed us at last, down through a
crevice and into its hidden nervous system. We took some kind of shuttle from the garage. It sucked us through transparent tubes toward the
destination that Elnear gave it—gliding, slowing down, shifting our
track; guided by some invisible master plan that shuffled the moving
vehicles like someone juggling at the speed of light. I caught glimpses of
storefronts, offices, restaurants. People did everything here, spent their
entire lives here, all of them pulled into the gravity well of a government
center a lot of people wanted to believe was as obsolete as a human's
appendix. Somewhere in the middle of all this the Federation Assembly

and the FTA Security Council both met, and tried to outmaneuver each other.

And somewhere else, in the real, hidden heart of city, was the brain that made it all work: the communications and data core that was one of the brightest stars in the invisible universe called the Federation Net. One perfect telhassium crystal no bigger than my thumb was able to store all the information, contain all the mindboggling manipulations of it that kept this city's systems from collapsing of their own data density. They only needed a few thousand more in order to calculate hyperspace jumps for most of the ships leaving this mainline port. Telhassium made the kind of computing power the Federation had to have cheap and easy to use . . . and as long as the FTA kept control of it, the Council would never lose its influence over how the Federation ran.

Finally we entered the government complex. The blue logo of a slowly turning Earth, which the Federation Trade Authority had decorated with wings and claimed for its own, watched me like a shining eye from datascreens and wallways as the shuttle car slowed for its final stop. We exited into the velvet-covered fist of a security station. Lady Elnear and Jardan waited patiently while my databand was doublechecked, while I was bodyscanned, retina- and finger-printed, holoed, filesearched, and registered.

The FTA didn't take any chances here; they couldn't afford to. The vulnerability of the Council, and the massive concentration of city around it, was enough to make a stone paranoid—and the FTA had at least that much imagination. It was hard for me to imagine how even a flea ever got this far without someone noticing it, somewhere in the overlapping layers of security they must have crusting this place. I was real glad the commendation I'd been given after the FTA had finished with me had gone on record for the data check to spit up . . . and that because of it my criminal record had been sealed. Now that I had a databand I wasn't a nonperson; I was real to the Federation Net. The only problem with not being invisible any more was that too many people got to see you naked.

When I was clean enough to suit the security registers, and imprinted on their system forever, they let us go back into the flow of human traffic heading deeper into the maze. By now I was completely lost, all over again. I didn't like the feeling. People passed us on all sides— riding bicycles, some of them pulling buggies; in floating carts; even on skates. We walked, because Elnear believed in exercise. I thought about the only FTA plexes I'd ever seen the inside of: their Corporate Security station in Oldcity, and the Contract Labor processing center where I'd started a one-way trip to hell. They both looked like prisons. This place didn't bring back any memories; the only thing that looked the same was the Federation Seal plastered on everything and everyone in sight. The imitation reality around me was as full of reflecting surfaces that turned your eyes away from the truth as the walls of any combine's HQ.

We were passing through the fringes of the actual Assembly nucleus. I began to notice more and more different combine colors around us; more than I'd ever seen in one place before. But then, I'd never been here before. Lady Elnear wore no logo at all. Jardan was wearing the logo that wasn't Centauri's at her throat again. Finally I asked what it was, just to break up the monotony. She glanced at me with a kind of bleak annoyance, and said, "Why do you bother to ask?"

I stopped where I was. "You really think all I want to do is get into your mind, or hers?" I gestured at Lady Elnear, who was walking ahead of us, talking with someone wearing an FTA insignia. I picked his name out of his thoughts, and some random bits of what he was thinking about, like Braedee had ordered me to. He'd told me to memorize everyone she talked to, and why, in case there was some clue in what happened that I wouldn't recognize. In the back of Elnear's own mind a strand of her attention was always turned toward me, making every word she said painfully self-conscious. "Don't flatter yourself."

Jardan's mouth tightened.

"I'm working *for* you—"

"You're working for Centauri."

I looked down at the logo on my jacket. "Then who the hell are you working for?"

"This is the ChemEnGen logo." I felt the heat of the defiance behind it, and remembered: Lady Elnear was a controlling stockholder, with a place on ChemEnGen's ruling board. But now Centauri controlled ChemEnGen, and Jardan's boss. And now I understood what that badge really was—a finger raised in the face of every taMing who saw her.

"That takes a lot of guts," I said, but she didn't smile. I looked away from the wall of her eyes.

Elnear stood waiting up ahead, looking back at us—listening. I wondered how much freedom she really thought she had, just because she didn't wear a logo here. *This was her real work,* Jardan had said. I rubbed the patch on my jacket as we went on.

A part of my mind was always reaching out ahead of us and behind while we walked, scanning the other minds around us. I told myself I was looking for something wrong; but I knew I was like an ex-blindman, really looking just because I could. Almost everyone I scanned was interested in seeing someone else dead, but none of them had Elnear in mind. And none of them were crazy enough even to think about trying anything here. It was hard to imagine anywhere that Elnear could be safer. But Braedee claimed that his own security had picked up someone tracking her here with a dartgun.

Eventually we reached the Drug Enforcement Arm nucleus and Elnear's office in it, deep in the FTA's sector of the plex. I looked up at the Arm's logo riding beside the FTA's above her door—the black wings of a shadow-thing reaching out and down to circle a galaxy. I wondered if that was supposed to reassure anybody. After my walk through the minds of the Federation Assembly, I felt like I'd been cleaning toilets with my brain. I let the thought tracers shrivel up and die, relieved. Two days ago I'd been ready to do anything to get back my Gift. . . . Somehow it was too easy to forget that everything had two sides.

"You're unusually subdued," Jardan said to me, as we went inside. The translucent office door began to slip shut behind us.

"I'm doing my job." I said. I followed her past a couple of curious office technicians toward Elnear's private inner office.

"Elnear!" someone called, from out in the hallway. I turned, looking back as the outer door flashed open again to let in Daric taMing. I caught a whiff of his thoughts as my mind crossed his track. I broke contact; he stank. He was part of the family. That was one mind nobody was going to force me into headfirst. I hadn't been able to scan him last night, but what I caught today matched what I'd seen then better than I would have liked. It was still hard for me to believe he was actually Jule's brother. But then, she was the one the family thought was crazy.

He pushed between me and Jardan as if we didn't exist, and went on across the room to Elnear's inner office. She stood behind the antique metal desk looking like she hoped he wasn't going to climb over it. He was violating her sanctuary, she couldn't stop him; she didn't like it. "What, Daric?"

"Vote today, Elnear. Just wanted to remind you. You will be there, of course—Centauri is counting on ChemEnGen's support, as always." He knew she wouldn't forget, knew that she'd vote their way. He just enjoyed rubbing in the salt.

"Of course," she said, and sat down, doing her best to pretend he'd already gone. "Goodbye, Daric."

"Goodbye, Elnear." He turned on his heel, all his motions still full of too much energy, the way they'd been last night. He started back through us toward the door. I moved out of his way. It was the wrong thing to do. He stopped, cocking his head at me. "Hey, new aide," he said, as if he'd just noticed me. "How's your first day on the job? Just fascinating, I'll bet."

I didn't say anything.

"Oh, come on." He folded his arms. "You can speak frankly. We're all friends."

I shrugged. "It's all right." I forgot to say "sir."

He didn't call me on it. "Only 'all right'?" he repeated, enjoying himself a lot more than I was. "Where are you from, anyway?"

"Ardattee. Quarro," I said, not meeting his eyes.

He was actually surprised. "The Hub? . . . No wonder we don't impress you. You'll have to tell me all about it—are table manners really passé there?" He was watching to see if he drew blood. It took all the control I had left, but I didn't bleed. "Well, be sure to enjoy your stay on Earth. All of human history is here for you to enjoy, stuffed and mounted . . . if my aunt ever allows you any time off for good behavior." He looked away from me, back at Elnear. "Loan him to me some evening, Elnear. My friends would kill one another to meet him. . . . Oh. Sorry. Pardon the expression." He was already moving toward the door; he was gone before anyone could ruin his fun, or his face.

I followed Jardan into the inner office. A security screen blinked on across its door. Jardan went to Elnear's side, murmuring something I didn't bother trying to hear. I sat down on the window ledge. It wasn't actually a window, but a holo that did a decent job of looking like a view of the ocean. I looked at it, sunlight winking on blue water far away. I could see why she needed one.

I looked back again at the Lady and Jardan. The air was so thick with bad feeling that it was hard to breathe. I felt like a lightning rod. I thought about all the things I wanted to say about Gentleman Daric, and tried to forget them again. Instead, I said, "What would happen if you didn't vote the way the taMings want you to . . . ma'am?" as Jardan glared at me.

Elnear sighed, looking around her for something that didn't seem to be there. "Well . . ." she said, her gaze still wandering, as if she were discussing a missing stylus, "I leave that to your imagination, Mez

Cat." She meant that I could find out if I really wanted to, but she didn't feel like spelling it out just to satisfy my curiosity. She was thinking that they would sell off ChemEnGen's patents and chop its network into small separate bits, and feed the pieces one by one into the open jaws of the biosci Lack Market. . . . At least, that was how Charon had put it to her. He was the head of Centauri's ruling board, and she didn't have any reason to doubt what he said. She pushed away from the desk, her formfoam chair resettling around her as she looked up at me; there was something in her eyes that I hadn't seen there before. Suddenly I was remembering what I'd said to Braedee about blackmailers—and what he'd said to me about politics.

"Does it really matter that much to you?" I asked. "Enough to let them blackmail you?"

"Yes," she nodded, "it does." She didn't tell me why.

I glanced at Jardan. "I thought Jardan said you set up some kind of noninterference contract when you married in, Lady."

"I thought so, too." A sadness filled her that had nothing to do with any betrayals of trust. It was gone again before I could see more. "While my husband was alive, everything went well. Then after his death . . . well, you remember that I advised you to have your contracts with the taMings reviewed . . . ?"

"You mean you didn't?" I said, surprised. I got up from my seat.

"Not carefully enough, it seems. They have some of the most powerful legal advisories operating in the Federation."

I looked down. "You don't think . . . is there anybody at ChemEnGen who'd be angry enough to want you dead over that?"

Jardan stiffened. Elnear shook her head. "I'm all that stands between them and a complete loss of autonomy. I don't think so."

I nodded. "I guess everything works like that around here." I didn't expect an answer; figured I already knew it.

But she smiled faintly. "Not in this office," she said, as if somehow the FTA's symbol over her door had some kind of power to protect what she did.

"What makes you think the Arm is any better than anything else?" I waved a hand at the door and what lay outside it. "It's just what they call it—*arm*. Another way for the Security Council to use muscle on the combine vips when the Council's out to get it their way. The FTA's no better than the combines. It controls the telhassium market; it runs Contract Labor. It's all the same, just power plays. More blackmail."

"For someone who's been here less than one day, you seem to have formed some strong opinions," she said, mildly; but I felt her impatience and irritation stick me in the ribs. And as I watched her, suddenly she changed again: suddenly she wasn't a vague, empty, aging woman, but someone who belonged behind that desk. "If you are going to work for me, you had better understand how we look at things in this office." She motioned at me to sit down again. I sat.

"To begin with," she said, "let me tell you something about the society we live in. Most people believe that human beings still run it. But I think they're wrong. All these centuries we have been waiting for our machines to get too smart for us and turn us into dinosaurs. We never realized we'd already created the next step in our own evolution . . ." *The interstellar combine.* She went on, telling me her pet theories about how the Federation really operated. She claimed no single human, or even a ruling board, actually controlled the largest combines now. Instead, humans had become the combines' tools; just like the AI systems and databanks they'd developed to make the interstellar networks possible in the first place.

"You really believe that?" I said, trying not to let her hear how I really felt about the idea.

She nodded. "And I'm not alone. There are many logic-studies that conclude the same thing. No one has absolute proof—no one has ever directly communicated with a network core. But I really believe that the combines are the evolving beings of a new order; that they are the way the living universe is accommodating itself to space travel."

Human space travel. I thought about the Hydrans, the Net of psi energy they'd based their own civilization on.

"The combines are the lions and tigers of a new age," she said, "ruthless, and totally amoral." They had evolved and changed to fill the niches of the super-ecology called the Federation, and their individual styles and levels of operation were the mutations that had fitted them to their functions. Some of them had evolved toward such massive augmentation that one or two or a handful of what had been humans became an entire network. Most of them had gone the other way, using millions of separate human beings as the cells of their supersystems. The combines took care of those individual cells as well as it suited their needs—some better, some worse. But most of them expected the kind of unquestioning loyalty in return that a body would expect of its own flesh. If you betrayed them, you were dead, or as good as. And any individuals or human services that fell between the cracks of their needs were invisible, as far as they were concerned.

I glanced down at my databand. I'd been invisible for a long time; it hadn't been an easy life.

"We can't judge the combines by human standards," she said, "any more than we can expect them to treat individual human beings as if we were their equals. The FTA is the only independent system capable of interacting on an equal basis with the combines." Her eyes never left my face, even while I looked down. "Over the centuries it's taken on the job of filling those empty spaces, protecting the rights of the individual human being. The FTA maintains a safe balance—a kind of Humane Society, if you will, working for the protection of our no-longer-dominant species. And that is what we do here, and that is why I choose to work for them."

I looked up at her again. It sounded so perfectly reasoned, like a speech. . . . It was a speech, one she'd given again and again. She was good; really believable. And she really believed every word of it. Maybe it was even true, for her. But the FTA she thought she knew wasn't the one I knew. I'd survived living in the cracks; but not because of anything the FTA had ever done for me. I'd gotten the FTA's attention a few times—but what they'd done to me then had only made my life worse. "I guess I've got a lot to learn," I said, but the words were as sour as vomit in my throat.

She broke off, half-frowning. It wasn't the response she was used to getting. She looked away from me, resenting the tone of my voice, my attitude, my presence, me. "The vote is at four," she said to Jardan, looking down at her desktop again as she turned toward her access unit. "I won't review the report, since I already know what my vote will be. But I have a lot of my own work to do by then. Philipa, will you call up the Sarumo file and find out what became of that data about Triple Gee? And then I guess the usual—request, turn down, and put off. Get the correspondence processing . . . when you get to that point, come back and show Mez Cat how to do it. He might as well earn his keep." She glanced up at me again finally, lifting her eyebrows.

"Yes, ma'am," I said, almost relieved. Any kind of work at all had to be better than sitting around until my butt got numb, waiting for Braedee to tell me I was free again.

Jardan nodded, and started for the door. She stopped again as the security screen blinked off. "Will you be all right alone—like this?" She almost looked at me.

Elnear's glance followed the twitch of Jardan's head. Every time her eyes registered me a small shock ran through her, as if my face kept startling her. "I expect so," she said, a little dryly. "I'll keep him occupied somehow." She was thinking that if something sensitive came up, she'd send me out on an errand. . . .

"It won't help," I said.

"What?" She looked at me, blank-faced with surprise.

"Sending me out. You'd have to send me farther than that. If I want to know what happens here I'll know it. Look, it really doesn't matter—" I pushed on before the protest could form on her lips. "Like you said, Lady, what do I know about anything? I don't care what you do."

"Centauri does," Jardan said.

I shook my head. "All I know is that they want you to stay alive to go on doing it. All I want is my money."

Elnear sighed, and waved Jardan gone. The screen came back on as she left, shutting us in together.

"Please never do that again," Elnear said, when we were alone.

"What?"

"You know."

Listen to her thoughts, and answer them out loud. I nodded. "Sorry, Lady."

Something that was a cross between amusement and annoyance pulled at her mouth. "You know, somehow when you address me as 'Lady,' it sounds entirely different . . . rather like you were yelling at me from a street corner." She turned away again, as her phone chimed.

I waited while she talked with the shimmering face on the other end, doing something strange with her left hand on the console part of the time . . . some kind of direct neural transfer. Somehow it surprised me to realize she was augmented—but I could feel her using, her brain transferring and calling up data, storing new facts; communicating with her caller on some other, independent level even while they talked, still pretending to be only human. And these people hated psions, and called us unnatural—when they had to rip apart their bodies, rewire half their brain with custom bioware, just to get a pale imitation of what a psion was born with.

I looked away again, studying the office, staring at the clutter on her desk—an uneasy mix, like she was. A crystal vase filled with dried flowers, tape readers and strange little books, datadots inside a security seal, a handmade cup . . . old holos of Talitha and Jiro and a man who was a taMing, but not one I'd met. I realized it must be a picture of her dead husband. The access unit she was using looked like a piece of stretched black silk. Her console was totally out of my league, from what I could see of how it worked—which was nothing at all.

Across the room under a slow-moving sculpture painting there was a more normal unit, with a touchboard and trodes; probably meant for an aide, or someone like Jardan. I stood up as Elnear finished her call. "Ma'am, you mind if I use that port?" I pointed.

"What do you want to do with it?"

"You have a map of N'yuk I can access?"

She nodded, figuring that would keep me out of trouble for a while. She did something with her hand and light showed on the unit. "That one answers to 'Twinkle'," she said, and looked a little embarrassed, as if she'd never really listened to how the name sounded before.

" 'Twinkle'." I kept my face expressionless as I went to Twinkle and sat down to ask it for what I wanted. It pulled the map for me. I put on the trodes, let the data slowfeed into my memory so that I could get a clearer idea of what I was learning. It was a good map, with a lot of overlays—of the underlying substructures, of major landmarks, of where to find a place to eat, to pray, to get your teeth fixed. . . . Once it had settled in I'd be able to get around almost like a native. At least that was one kind of lost I wouldn't have to be any more.

But there was one area on the map that was still a blur when I was through . . . an area at the southern tip of the city, called the Deep End. There was a street grid, but it was incomplete, and what happened there wasn't on any reference lists. The fact that it was missing was a warning; if you went there, you were on your own. You didn't find spots like that on the map of a combine clave; but the Federal Trade Districts always had them. Free zones, safety valves, escape hatches—feeder tanks. Oldcity had been one of those. I knew what I'd find in the Deep End. I hoped I wouldn't need it.

Only about ten minutes had passed while I let my thoughts walk around inside the map grid. When I came up for air Elnear was lost in her own business, even managing to forget for ten minutes that I was in the room. I went back into the datafiles and chose a dozen other things that looked interesting or useful; mostly things that would tell me more about how a vip's aide filled up a day. I tried to get them to transfer continuously, but the best Twinkle would do was three at a time. Absorbing all the files I'd chosen took me about another twenty minutes.

Then I asked for the threedy scan, looking for something to help pass the time while my mind cooled off. Even watching threedy shows had been an education, once I'd gotten out of Oldcity. At first I'd watched the most mindless shit on the Net, all the time, the same way I'd eaten food—just because I could. But it hadn't taken me long to see that the threedy could teach me things I'd never get out of a datafile, about how people who always had enough to eat and a decent job acted around each other. I'd already learned, the hard way, how much I didn't know about that.

And coming here had given me a whole new level of ignorance and inadequacy to sink to. . . . As I thought about that my stomach began to hurt. I tried not to think about it, tried to concentrate on what I was seeing in the air in front of me as show after show winked by. I couldn't believe the number of channels Elnear had open—all the public accesses, and five times as many pay ones with full sensory feed. Most of the subscription channels were only corporate propaganda, the combines' way of sending messages and warnings to each other without seeming to. But some of the channels were experimentals, sending incredible visions, sounds, and sensations vibrating like drug dreams through my brain.

I dropped back into public access finally, too strung out to enjoy anything that intense. Ordinary light and noise was enough. . . . "Stop," I said suddenly, freezing a talking head in the air in front of me. It was a man giving a speech; not the kind of thing I liked to watch even now unless I wanted to catch up on my sleep. But there was something different about this face—something I couldn't look away from, once I'd seen it. Something I had to see more of.

He had one of the most beautiful faces I'd ever seen. I leaned back in my seat, watching him speak, somehow forced to listen to what he was saying: ". . . And I believe that we lost something more than simply our identity as a people," he was saying, "when we left our homeworld for the stars. We lost our understanding of our uniqueness in the eyes of God. The combines have become our idea of heaven, where all our physical needs are provided for, our lives laid out for us in perfect comfort from birth until death. It has become too easy to forget that there was once a higher purpose that drove us to succeed where other beings failed—"

"Greed," I muttered, disgusted. A religion hyper, shilling for some combine, probably. Holy war. I thought I was about to change the channel, but somehow I went on listening instead; not because I liked what he was saying, but because I couldn't help liking him. It wasn't just the way he looked, but something about the way he was—the openness, the earnestness, the sincerity as he told the people accessing him to "see the humanity that bound them together, as they looked into a stranger's face . . ."

You could change the way your own face looked, and he probably had. But you couldn't buy that kind of charisma. You had to be born with it. I stared at him, fascinated, even while I felt a kind of envy twist inside me.

"Mez Cat." Jardan's voice broke in on his, making me jump. "What are you doing?" she asked, staring at the image flickering in the air in front of me.

"Nothing." I blanked the port, and shrugged.

"Sojourner Stryger," she said. "Somehow I didn't expect that he would be to your tastes."

I frowned. "Why? Is he a friend of yours?"

Her mouth pursed up. "He is the leader of the Revival Movement, and an extremely active lobbyist for humanitarian causes."

"One of those," I said. She ignored that, and told me to come with her. In the outer office she introduced me to the rest of Elnear's staff. They nodded and mumbled, looking at me with their disbelief showing. I wondered what Elnear's other aide had been like. Not like me, I guessed.

The work Jardan expected me to do was dull, but I did it. Finally Elnear left her office to go to the Assembly. Jardan and I went with her as far as the transparent-walled viewing gallery; that was as close as nonmembers ever got to the Assembly floor. The Assembly Hall looked just like it did in all the media pieces: long and high, with the ancient logo of a flaming sun circled by nine worlds, the original Federation. A lot of combines hated that logo; hated even the name of the Federation, because it suggested too much centralized control. But by now it was tradition, and they were stuck with it, just like they were stuck with the Charter that allowed the FTA to initiate its own policies, independent of them.

Tier after U-shaped tier of seats faced the curve of the Security Council's High Seat, enough to hold a thousand combine representatives. The fact that my mind was working again only heightened the reality of the Assembly members moving restlessly in the seats down below. With a bug in your ear you could actually hear what they said—the arguments, the charges and counter-charges, the options open in whichever endless resource war they were trying to settle today. Most of the data I'd accessed in Elnear's office this morning had to do with what happened here.

This vote was something strictly among the combines. The FTA's Security Council was mediating, but they weren't inputting anything . . . at least not anything we could witness. They weren't even here in the flesh. At first I wasn't sure, through the murmur of so many other minds down below. But I narrowed my focus until I was positive—they were only projections, holos, ghosts. "Why aren't they up there?" I asked Jardan.

"What are you talking about?" she said.

"The Security Council. They're holos, not the real people."

She looked at me, startled. She bit her tongue before she could ask me how I knew that; because she already knew how I knew. "For security reasons."

"Is that why they call it the Security Council?" I knew the second I asked it that I should have kept my mouth shut. *No, it wasn't.*

"No, it isn't. Spare me your sense of humor," she said, and looked away.

I looked down at the Assembly floor again. The eerie thing about it— the thing that you only realized here—was that unless you were wired for sound nothing seemed to be happening. There was nothing but silence on the chamber floor. All the debate or discussion was done subvocally, or in ways even stranger and more private. I wondered what was happening down there that never even touched us, up here in the gallery.

Jardan pointed out Elnear, sitting motionless in the middle tier, waiting to cast her predetermined vote. I wondered whether most of the 'neutral' parties down there had had their minds made up for them the way she had, by pressure from merger partners with a lot of arm. I remembered what she'd told me about the combines, and as I watched disembodied numbers begin to tally on my chair arm, the feeling inside me that something important was happening down there died. Maybe she was right—those hundreds of humans around her really were nothing but mouths, ports; the combines were tallying the outcome for them. And yet her single vote still mattered, at least to Centauri. . . . I found Daric taMing up in the first tier of seats—each tier was a little more comfortable than the last, as they got closer to the High Seat. All the combine reps had equal votes; but some were still more equal than others.

And then there was the Security Council, up there on the High Seat, independent of them all and flaunting it. The Security Council made the FTA's rules, played out its own games that were usually played against the will of some part of the Assembly. The Assembly could vote down a Security Council ruling, but it took a two-thirds majority, and with the combines always at each others' throats, it had to be a damned unpopular law to get them all united against it. The Council was the FTA's brain, and Elnear was up for one of its slots. I wondered how much more satisfying that would be than what she had now. Maybe it would just be different.

The voting was over. I stared at the numbers on the screen; blinked, realized I'd been staring at them without blinking for way too long, while my brain shuffled through the information I'd swallowed whole this morning. "Who won?" The numbers didn't mean anything, when I didn't know what they'd been voting for.

"It doesn't matter," Jardan murmured, and left her seat.

"That's cosmic," I said, and she frowned.

Elnear met us down below, and we started back through the maze of halls. Her face was longer than I'd seen it all day.

"Lady Elnear . . ." Someone called her name from behind us. I looked back, tracking through the crowd with two sets of eyes and ears. No one I knew . . . someone Elnear and Jardan did know. I watched a small, slender man coming toward us, still pushing people aside even though Elnear had stopped to wait for him. And suddenly I realized I knew him, too; he was the one I'd been watching on the threedy. Nobody else could have a face like that.

"Sojourner Stryger," Elnear said, nodding uncertainly.

"Lady Elnear." He stopped in front of us; about a dozen people materialized around him in the seconds that followed. His people. "It must be God's will that we should meet by chance this way . . ."

Chance, hell. Surprise pinched me hard. He was out of breath; he'd chased her through the crowds all the way from the Assembly Hall. I stared at him. Even in person he had the most flawless face I'd ever seen. Skin, hair, eyes—every feature so perfect that my own eyes couldn't find anything wrong with them . . . except that they were too perfect. It had to be a cosmo job; but even realizing it, my eyes kept *liking* him.

I made myself look at Elnear without listening to what he said. I felt the blow of her ordinariness hit me, breaking the spell of his face; felt the raw pain of her self-consciousness as she looked at him. She struggled past it, trying to listen and not to *look*. . . .

". . . about the upcoming debate before the media," he was saying. "I hope you will not take this in a negative way, since we'll both be speaking in support of the same viewpoint . . . but have you considered whether your principles might not be compromised? After all, if the Federation does in fact deregulate pentryptine, ChemEnGen stands to make a great deal of profit . . . they do hold the ancestral controlling patent on the entire pentatryptophine family, I believe."

Pentryptine. It was a drug he was talking about. Back in Oldcity they called it *bliss.*

Elnear blinked, moved her head. What Stryger had said wasn't the thing she'd been expecting to hear. "In fact, Sojourner, my stand is, and has always been, *against* deregulation. As you know, I will be representing the Drug Enforcement Arm in this public forum. . . ." I wondered why she called him by his first name; until I realized it wasn't a name. It was a title, one he'd taken for himself.

He raised his perfect eyebrows as if he was surprised. But he wasn't. I kept watching him, confused, because nothing about him fit. "Well, I must have been misinformed. . . ." He tapped his forehead with his finger, looked at her almost quizzically. "But surely a person with your long dedication to individual rights can't believe that there is something wrong in allowing more widespread application of these drugs? I can cite hundreds of criminal incidents that have occurred right here in N'Yuk in the past month. . . . The pentatryptophine drugs have proved safe and harmless in suppressing overt aggression, as well as in controlling many other forms of antisocial behavior. These things should have been eradicated long ago. It has seemed to me for some time that we have the way—but not the will—to completely control criminal behavior."

Elnear lifted a hand, shook her head slightly. "Sojourner Stryger, it isn't that I disagree with you on that. Not at all. It's simply that if these drugs become widely and easily available there is such potential for their abuse. The pentryptine subfamily is also a perfectly safe and harmless way for a combine to control its population illegally, to drug them into believing their lives are wonderful, when in fact they are not. I'm afraid many combines are far too willing to take the easy way out—to take away freedom of choice, and replace it with mindless gratitude."

Stryger nodded. The agreement shining in his eyes was real this time. "Of course, precisely. That was never my intention, and of course I will emphasize that the deregulation should never be allowed to further misuse—"

Elnear shook her head again, regret showing on her face. "I'm afraid our individual warnings or precautions won't be enough to stop a flood, once someone removes the dam. I simply don't have enough faith in the power of individual will. I wish I did." Her eyes clung to his face.

I was staring at him again, too. There was a kind of golden transparency to his skin, his hair, that his simple street clothes only made brighter. He looked about thirty-five, old enough to look responsible but still look young. He was probably older than that. He carried a long wooden pole in his hand, half as thick around as my wrist, and with half its length covered with carving; the designs looked like words, but I couldn't read them.

"If everyone had your own strength of will, you would not say that, Lady Elnear." He smiled with honest respect. His eyes were wide and clear; his voice was like water flowing. I touched his mind again, just to be sure he was real.

He turned toward me. I realized suddenly that he'd been looking at me, too, from the corner of his eye the whole time he was talking to her. "Excuse me . . ." he said to Elnear, breaking off like he'd only just noticed me. "Who is this?"

"My new aide." She sounded relieved, at the sudden change of subject, and that he'd stopped looking at her.

"Really." He turned those searchlight eyes on me, looking everywhere but into my own eyes. "You have a rather unusual facial type . . . do you have Hydran blood, young man?" He met my stare at last, found what he'd expected to when he saw green eyes.

And when I saw what was in his eyes then, suddenly I hated his guts. "No." I started to turn away.

"Forgive me—" His hand caught my arm, pulling me back. "I don't mean to offend you. It's just that the Hydran people have been a particular interest of mine for a long time. I'm not often wrong." Calling me a liar. The tip of his tongue slipped out, wetting his lips just a little.

"Get your hand off me," I said, very softly. "Or I'll break your fingers."

"Cat—" It was Jardan's hard, high voice. The warning sounded far away and almost frightened.

Stryger's hand let me go, but I couldn't shake his stare. Even as he turned back to Elnear, he was still looking at me. *Someone had set him on me.* He'd come all this way, forced this meeting, just to have a look at me. *Hydran blood.*

When he looked at Elnear again, finally, I was still what he was seeing, making him see her in a new and unexpected way. "Of course," he murmured, like an apology but not one, "someone in your position would hardly have a psion on her staff."

I stared at the back of his head, through it; saw into the nest of maggots squeezed into the space where his mind ought to be. He was human, all right.

He went on speaking to Elnear about meaningless details of whatever the thing was they'd been discussing. I didn't really listen; the buzzing of his brain was too loud inside my head. He called himself a religious man. He was absolutely certain that he knew what God was, and exactly how God wanted it all to be. . . . Those people standing around him, waiting with inhuman patience and goodwill for him to finish, thought he knew, too. He kept glancing at me, as if he couldn't keep his eyes off me. My own eyes kept turning traitor, still wanting to *like* his face, even when I could see what lay behind it. I wondered if he had that effect on everybody; the thought scared the hell out of me.

Finally he finished his business. He took one last look at me and went away down the hall, his disciples trailing him on an invisible string. I stood watching him go for too long, until I had to run a few steps to catch up with Jardan and Elnear.

"What does that scumbag really want—?" I said.

They both glanced back at me, surprised, almost outraged.

"That was Sojourner Stryger," Elnear said, "of the Revival Movement. It's an extremely popular prespace-fundamentalist religion; his media appearances draw huge numbers. I would not refer to him as a . . . as you did, if I were you." She looked back at me again, letting me see her disapproval, as if I couldn't feel it. "He has done more for the dispossessed and exploited in our society than anyone I know of. He has an impressive record of speaking out in defense of human rights."

"I know that . . . ma'am. I saw him on the threedy. But what's he doing here?"

"Lobbying, probably," Jardan said bluntly. "He has also almost single-handedly made the deregulation of pentryptine a real possibility. As a result of his influence, he's under consideration for the same position on the Security Council as the Lady."

I almost stopped walking. I forced myself to keep moving, to keep up with them.

"We have our differences of opinion on some matters," Elnear said, glancing down as if it were her fault, "but I have no doubt about his effectiveness as a reformer, or the sincerity of his beliefs. He is a deeply religious man."

"He hates psions," I said, looking at her. "How religious are you—?"

She looked away. Neither one of them said anything; they began to walk again.

I followed them. "I had a friend," I said to their backs, "who told me once, 'In the land of the blind the one-eyed man is stoned to death.'" They kept walking. "He was a psion. He's dead now."

Elnear stopped, turning back. "Mez Cat," she said finally. "Is there some point to all this?"

I shrugged. "No," I said, feeling my mouth twist down. "No point at all."

6

I DIDN'T REALLY need anything more than the meeting with Stryger to make my day perfect. But when we got back to the taMing estates, there was a welcoming committee waiting in the yard as the mod settled. Jiro and his mother, both of them looking grim. One look, and I knew why. He'd cut his hair.

"Elnear, a word with you—" Lazuli said, tight-lipped. Her hands were on Jiro's shoulder's like clamps. "About your aide."

I stood staring at the walls while they talked it over. Jiro looked like something with bad teeth had tried to chew his head off; he'd done it to himself. He liked it that way. His mother didn't. So he'd blamed me. "Perhaps we had better return to the Crystal Palace. . . ." Lazuli was saying, the anger in her voice gone dreary now.

"Not at all," Elnear said, her own anger still honed by her embarrassment: *She had a freak for an aide; but worse than that, he was a moron. She couldn't fire me, she couldn't excuse me, she couldn't even explain why*— "Mez Cat, you will stay away from my grand-nephew and -niece from now on. You are not even to speak to them, do you understand?"

I glanced at Jiro, staring up at me with sullen guilt from his mother's shadow. I looked back at Elnear. "Yes, ma'am." I turned away and started up the steps to the house.

"Mez Cat—" Elnear's voice.

I stopped.

"I think that you owe Lady Lazuli an apology."

I turned back, my jaw clenched so tight I thought I'd never get it open. But then I looked at Lazuli. In the blue evening light, it could have been Jule standing there, angry and unhappy and confused. . . . "I'm sorry," I said. *I'm sorry, Jule.* I went into the house.

I stayed in my room all evening, not even bothering to eat.

"Hey, Cat."

I turned back from the windows, reeled my thoughts in; saw Jiro standing in my suddenly open door. "Jeezu. Stay away from me."

"You like my hair now?" He grinned self-consciously as he edged into the room, not even sure himself whether he'd come to make fun of me or to apologize.

I leaned against the glass-paned door, staring out at the night, ignoring him to keep from strangling him.

"Everybody's real mad at you."

I looked back at him again. "Get out of here, you little croach."

"What's a croach?"

"A lying little cheat who makes other people pay for his mistakes."

"You can't talk to me like that!"

I laughed, past caring what anybody did to me now. "Tell your mother. Fire me."

"You shouldn't have told me to cut my hair. That's why I got in trouble."

I looked at him. "If you're too stupid to understand sarcasm when you hear it, that's not my fault."

He looked down. "I knew you were making fun of me. . . ." He pushed at his hair. "I don't care."

"Then get out." I started toward him, ready to help him along.

His other hand was hidden behind him. Suddenly he brought it up. There was a gun in it.

I stopped short, and stopped breathing.

"Here," he said. "I brought you this."

"Why?" I asked, my voice almost strangling.

Still looking down, he said, "I want you to like me."

"Or what? You're going to kill me?"

"No! It's just a target laser. Maybe you could use it to practice. Maybe you could show me how. . . ." He moved closer, holding it out.

I took it out of his hand and threw it across the room. "What the hell do you think I am?"

He stared at me, totally confused. "You said you were a merse—"

"A merse is somebody who eats shit for money. It isn't fun."

"Philipa said you're supposed to guard Auntie. Have you killed a lot of people?" He kept insisting, blindly, not listening.

Deep in my brain, a black empty hole opened up. I looked into it, needing to feel afraid, but not feeling anything. . . . "One," I said. "That was one too many." It sounded meaningless. I looked down at him, seeing his face again. I shoved him out the doorway into the hall. I slammed the door after him, and locked it. Then I lay down on my bed and watched my hands tremble for a while. And waited.

When the house was dark and quiet, when all its minds had their shutters closed, I used the household system to call for a mod. I slipped outside; stood in the flagstone yard with my fingers crossed. About the time I was ready to give up and start walking, I saw it come drifting silently down to me.

I wasn't sure it would take my orders, but it did. I got in and it lifted, heading for N'yuk. "I quit," I said, watching the taMings fall away behind me. I lifted my finger.

This whole thing had been an insane mistake from the start. They didn't need me, and I didn't need them. I'd go into the city; find some kind of work, it didn't matter what. Anything was better than this. I settled back in my seat. Even from here, I could see the nightglow of the distant shore.

Before long I was dropping down again, somewhere over the urbs. I didn't know where I was going to land, didn't really care. There was a lot of light below me now, arrays of changing colors—too much light. It looked like . . . Grids clicked into place in my mind, artificial memories locking on. I sat up suddenly in my seat, my hand white-knuckled on the armrest. "Shit." It was the Centauri Field Complex.

Braedee was waiting on the platform as the mod's door sprung open, his arms folded, a smile on his face. The light coming up from under him made him look inhuman. A dozen Security drones ringed the mod already, bristling with weapons. I wondered if he was planning a murder-suicide.

I climbed out, slowly, and stood in front of him.

" 'I quit'," he quoted, and gave me the finger back, unblinking.

I felt my face get hot again. "You heard it right." Trying not to feel as helpless as he wanted me to. "What do you want with me? You know everything that goes on anyway." I jerked my head at the mod, disgusted.

"Not about what happens inside the FTA."

"You mean Lady Elnear really does get clear of you when she goes to the Arm?" I asked, surprised.

No comment.

"Well, that's your problem." I shook my head. "You should have listened to Jardan. She was right. I'm all wrong for this, and I'm out of it—"

"I need you. You're staying until I'm through using you."

"You can't stop me." But I couldn't help glancing at the mod when I said it. "I'm a free citizen—" I held up my wrist with the databand. The databand went dead.

My heart made a fist in my chest. I lowered my hand, touched all the right spots on the band; shook it, whacked my wrist with my free hand. Nothing woke it up. My hand knotted. "Turn it back on!"

He shook his head, still smiling.

"You can't do this to me." I couldn't even imagine how he'd done it. "It's illegal."

"You are a Centauri employee. In return for that privilege, you give up some rights."

"I haven't even signed anything—"

"But your verbal agreement is on record. The rest is a formality."

"Goddamn it—" I looked away, across the endless Centauri grids crawling with light and activity even in the middle of the night. The wind brought me a thousand different noises—machinery, motion, voices calling—the smell of hot metal and ozone. I stood there, lost somewhere in the middle of it, remembering what it felt like to be invisible.

"Now, tell me about what you saw today. Who you saw; everyone, everything."

I told him, when I found my voice again. And as I talked, the feeling that I was doing something wrong grew stronger with every word. Braedee looked bored, impatient, or indifferent at everything I said, but that didn't mean that I wasn't violating a trust. Even if it meant Lady Elnear was safer that way, she was losing something. But I didn't see what I could do about it. Or why I should care.

"So you've already met Sojourner Stryger?" Braedee interrupted suddenly. "What was your impression of him?"

I told him.

He laughed. "That's refreshing. Why are you the only person I've met who didn't find him likeable?"

"He's a freakhater."

"Ah." He nodded. "And you're a freak."

"Why don't you like him?" I asked, because he didn't.

"I think he's dangerous. He's a fanatic; he's crawling with a kind of charisma that even people with real minds seem to find irresistible . . . and he's got too many supporters."

"You mean converts?" I thought of the glazed-looking mob he'd had trailing him.

He smiled, like a death's head. "I mean combines. No individual gets the kind of attention, controls the media base he does, without help. I know what his backers want from him. But I'm not sure he still remembers. . . . What I really want to know is what they're going to get that they don't expect."

"How about the FTA? They might give him that Council slot—?"

He shrugged. "The FTA is no more interested in nonexistent purity than anyone else. Everyone on the Security Council was once someone else's pawn. Do you play chess?"

"No," I said, not even sure what it was.

"I didn't think so." He bent his head at the mod waiting behind me. "Go back to the estate. Sleep it off. Do your job."

"What about my contract?"

"You actually want to look at it?" he asked.

"You bet your ass, Corpse."

"It will be accessible on your unit in the morning. I think you'll find it in order." He sounded amused; I wondered what was so funny.

"What about my deebee?" I held my databand out again.

"You'll be alive again when I think you've earned it."

I turned away, eating my frustration; trying not to give him any more satisfaction than he'd gotten off me already. I stopped, suddenly remembering something. "Who's the other psion?"

"What?" he said.

"Besides Jule. There's another one. You didn't tell me there was a—"

"Where?" He crossed the space between us in one stride.

"The taMings . . ." I almost backed up, but there was nowhere to go. "Last night, at dinner. Somebody tried to use psi on me."

His hand closed on the front of my shirt. "Don't ever lie like that to me again. I know everything about that family. I know what's not possible."

I held his stare, until slowly his hand loosened.

"You actually believe that," he murmured. He looked down at his own hand, moved the fingers, as if he didn't believe he'd been ready to snap my neck a second ago. "Another telepath?"

I shook my head. "A teek . . . telekinetic."

"What happened?"

"It was little things—trying to make me look stupid. Nothing obvious. Nothing anybody else would even recognize."

He frowned at the suggestion that somebody could really know things he couldn't. And then his face went expressionless; his brain had gone somewhere else. After a second he was seeing me again, and he said, "You can't tell me who it was?"

I shook my head again. "I . . . I wasn't wearing the drugs. You think this has anything to do with the Lady—?"

"No." He cut me off before I could even finish the sentence. His face changed. "You must have been mistaken."

"I wasn't."

"Forget about it. Your problem is Lady Elnear, focus on her." He'd been edging me further backward, until I didn't have any choice except to get into the mod again.

I put my hand on the mod's wing door, ducking under it. "I don't think—"

"Exactly right," he said. "Don't."

I got in, the door sealed and the mod went up, taking me back to the taMings. I was nearly there before I looked down, and realized that my databand was alive again. *Not until I'd earned it . . .*

I went back across the flagstones and into Lady Elnear's house, as quietly as I could. Right back where I'd started from; like in a nightmare. I crawled into my bed and lay there, wondering where I'd be when I woke up.

"Mez Cat . . . may I speak with you?"

The next morning it was Lazuli taMing who caught me with my pants down. I looked up, startled by her voice, because I hadn't felt anyone coming. I realized too late that I'd forgotten to put on another drug patch last night. She'd opened the door without knocking before I could even move.

Now she stood staring at me, about as surprised as I was, but with her eyes still wide open, and no trace of embarrassment on her face.

Because she didn't look away, I didn't move, staring back at her, my hands at my sides. She was wearing a long loose gown that drifted against her skin like snow, as if it was defying gravity. After a handful of heartbeats I finally reached out and caught up my shorts, pulled them on. "Ma'am?" I said, my voice a little hoarse. Now I knew where Jiro got his manners. But then, I was only an employee here. Maybe I was just another piece of furniture to her; a chair, or a bed. . . . I looked at the bed, back at her.

She blinked; suddenly she looked as awkward as I felt. "Perhaps I should come back later."

"That's all right." I shrugged, pulling on my pants. Not saying the obvious.

"I just wanted to apologize. . . ." She took a tentative step into the room.

I smiled. "I'll just remember to keep my door locked, ma'am."

She did blush now; half turned away, turned back. "No—I mean, yes, of course . . . I feel like a fool." She laughed, that same chiming laughter I remembered from last night. "I only wanted to say . . ." she met my eyes again, "Jiro told me this morning that it wasn't your fault. About his hair." She smiled helplessly, gesturing at her own hair, piled up like black silk on top of her head. "I'm sorry. I really don't know what to say. You must think we're . . . well." She shrugged. "I'm sure you've thought of a lot of names yourself."

I felt my smile ease. "Yes ma'am; a few. . . . I seem to have forgotten them, though."

I thought she'd leave then, but she stood where she was, her hands hugging her elbows, looking toward the windows. "It's very difficult. I don't know what to do with him, half the time. Especially when he's around his stepfather. He misses our home, he misses his father. . . ."

"Where did you come from?" I asked, to fill up the silence.

"Eldorado . . . it's in the Centauri system. We came to Earth because I'm on the Centauri board now."

I wondered why she was telling this to a total stranger. Maybe because in this family, that was your only choice. "What happened to his father?"

She looked back at me, clear-eyed. "I don't know. He left me three years ago. Charon and I have been married a little over a year. He said that it would be in the best interest of the company if I married him. That way I could take my cousin Jule's place . . . on the board." Her chin lifted as she saw the look that must have been on my face. "And Jiro and Talitha would be in the direct line to inherit a seat."

I closed my mouth, swallowed. She was married to Charon taMing—Jule's father. She was Jule's cousin and her stepmother. "You look a lot like her. . . ." Saying the obvious didn't make either of us feel any more comfortable. I saw Charon in my mind, the head of Centauri Transport's ruling board; saw the way he'd looked at me when I'd been looking at Lazuli. "I mean, I know Jule. She's a friend. What happened to his first wife?"

Lazuli looked away again. For a moment her eyes were as empty as I'd once seen Jule's. "She was . . . she had some ties to Triple Gee. It was supposed to be a unifying marriage. She died some years ago . . . an accident." She was trying not to think about it. There were no accidents in her world.

I remembered the baby growing in vitro in a lab somewhere, wearing designer genes. I thought about Gentleman Charon's hand; wondered what it felt like to have that touch your body. I didn't say anything.

"Jiro is away at study center most of the time. But every time he comes home, and we're all together he seems more . . . more . . . It's very . . . difficult. I'm sorry." She was seeing me again. Her hands twisted. "Now I'm boring you, after insulting you—"

"No, ma'am. At least it takes my mind off my own problems." My mouth twitched up.

She smiled too, uncertainly. "You've been very kind. Perhaps sometime you'll tell your problems to me, and give me a chance to think of someone else besides myself for a while."

I couldn't tell whether she meant that, until she reached across the space that still separated us, and touched my arm, very gently. Then she turned away, in a whisper of cloud-white, and was gone. I touched the spot where she'd touched me.

It hadn't happened while she was watching me. It hadn't happened while she was talking to me. One touch, and it had finally happened. . . . I groaned, and went on dressing. I had a hell of a time fastening my pants.

Trying not to think about Jule's stepmother touching my arm, I stuck on a fresh drug patch, and asked the desk terminal for my contract with Centauri. Braedee was as good as his word; it was waiting for me. Like a bucket of cold water. Now I knew what was funny. I stared at the document scrolling up the screen. I didn't understand half the words I saw there, and even those were broken up by strings of legal code. I made a hard copy and stuck it in my pocket, before I finally went downstairs.

Everyone else had already eaten. The octagon-shaped dining room with its long embroidered curtains and wood-paneled walls was silent and empty. Almost empty. I went to the table.

"Beat it," I said to the silver-plated drone that was trying to clear away the leftovers. I gave it a shove, and it went back into the closet. The way these people wasted food was a crime. I drank a half-full cup of coffee that someone had poured too much sweetener into, piled up a plate with untouched spice pastries and half-eaten eggs, a piece of cold smoked fish, some fruit salad. I sat on a cushioned seat beside the table and began to eat.

Lady Elnear walked into the room, with an empty cup in her hand. She stopped.

I reached across the table and picked up the teapot, held it out to her.

Wordlessly she came across the room, and let me fill her cup. "Thank you." Her eyes were still fixed on the plate beside me. "Mez Cat," she said, with a strange gentleness, "no one is forced to eat scraps in this house. Please, there's always plenty of fresh food. . . ." She gestured vaguely toward the kitchen.

"No, ma'am," I said. "There's not."

She looked at me, not understanding.

I shrugged, and ate another spice roll. "I've never been picky about food, ma'am."

She sighed faintly, and went out of the room.

7

THAT MORNING WE didn't go into N'yuk again. Instead we met Lazuli in the hallway, and a mod took us all on up the valley. Jardan told me we were going to attend Centauri's board meeting. I didn't say anything, wondering why they even bothered to tell me, when I didn't have any choice about going. I sat next to Lazuli, because neither of the other women wanted to sit next to me. Lazuli was wearing a sexless gray-and-silver business suit now. The plainness of it made her look more like Jule, and yet it made the softness in her face that much easier to see. She stared out the window like she didn't notice that I was there. But she knew it, just like I did. Her mind kept remembering what I'd looked like naked. Feeling her remember it was like being tortured with ice and a heat pencil.

The mod set down in the courtyard of a mansion that felt older than any building I'd seen yet on the taMings' land. It was far up the valley from the other houses, almost to the end, crouched like a hermit on a rock ledge above the river. The water roared over the lip of stone there like it had a suicide urge, crashing and drowning in the pit of rocks and shadows far below.

Inside, the mansion was one gigantic work of art—arched ceilings painted with murals, framed by scrolled carvings, white marble pillars, congealed flows of stairway with golden banisters. Paintings of long-dead people in bizarre clothes covered the walls; sculpted busts of total strangers lined the entrance hall like the cut-off heads of taMing enemies. If moving through the Crystal Palace had been bad, walking here, on the way to a combine board meeting, was agony. Somebody like me hadn't been meant to walk through places like this; hadn't even been meant to know they existed.

I couldn't get up the nerve to ask whose house this was. I picked the answer out of Elnear's thoughts, feeling like a thief: The mansion belonged to Gentleman Teodor, the one who'd sat at the head of the table when we'd all eaten at the Crystal Palace. The head of the family, the oldest living taMing.

Braedee met us in one of the endless halls, and I read his smug satisfaction as he saw me, right where he wanted me. He greeted the others like this was his ground, and not theirs. While the Centauri board met, it was. He told them the way to the board room, as if they didn't already know it, and let them pass. But he blocked my path as I tried to follow, nudging me toward a doorway. "He'll be right with you, Lady Elnear," he said, as she turned back, waiting, frowning. "I have some further instructions for him."

That didn't reassure her. Maybe it wasn't supposed to. She turned and went on, still frowning.

"In here." Braedee moved into the room, making me follow him.

"What?" I said, when I was standing in front of him again. The sight of a Corpse uniform and the memory of last night made me knot up inside as I looked at him. "Jeezu, don't you have anything better to do than hassle me—"

His hand shot out and smacked me across the face. I staggered, banging into a table. Something fell and smashed on the floor.

"You are not an equal here," he said. "Don't act like one." He looked down at the pieces of broken crystal glittering like knives around my feet. He crushed a shard under his boot heel, looked up at me again. "The price of the vase will be deducted from your salary."

I rubbed my cheek, glaring at him, blinking too much.

"Two ambassadors of Triple Gee are attending the board meeting today, as are the regular Centauri associates and controlled interests. I want you to pick their brains—especially the Triple Gee representatives. I want to know their real thoughts on what they hear."

"Wait a minute," I said. I had to force the words out this time. "That's not what you hired me for. I'm not here to spook for Centauri—"

He looked at me. I flinched, even though I was trying not to. But he only said, "You are here to protect Lady Elnear. Since we still do not know who wants her dead, we have to make use of every opportunity to explore the real motives of everyone she comes in contact with. Triple Gee is our primary competition. That's all."

It sounded logical. I didn't believe it, any more than he did. I was afraid to try reading him face to face, but I could figure that much out for myself. I was protecting Lady Elnear, but he could force me to pull data about the competition too, because I didn't know enough about anything to know when I was crossing the line. I was the perfect tool. No wonder he couldn't stay away from me.

"I want to know what everyone who is not Centauri thinks, you understand—"

"Everyone? Even the Lady?"

"Particularly the Lady."

I glared at him. " 'For her own good'?"

"And yours," he said softly. He jerked his head at the doorway.

I looked down, and nodded. I stepped out of the ring of broken glass, and left the room.

I reached the boardroom at last. A security screen blinked off, showing me a hall that must have been fifty meters long, with angels dancing on its ceiling. The air was blue-silver; the light that poured in through the high, narrow windows was like light from another age. I wondered what people had done in a room this size centuries ago. Probably not what they were doing now. I looked toward the table in the center of the room. Or maybe they had: Lying, cheating, fucking each other over . . . some things never changed.

As I entered the room I heard a noise, and saw a head disappear down at the far end of the long white-and-gold table. The people nearest that end turned in their seats, rising up, reaching out. Somebody had fallen. My eyes and my mind leaped, looking for Elnear. My mind found her first.

She had one of the ornamented, high-backed chairs at the near end of the table. She was standing up, leaning forward, looking toward the noise. Jardan was sitting in one of the seats lined up in a second row just behind the board seats: the row of aides and advisors. Security guards wearing a rainbow of combine colors lined the walls of the room. A couple of them had moved forward, but none of the rest looked worried. They were just there for show. The real security here wasn't anything you could touch or see.

I sat down beside Jardan. "What happened?"

"One of the Triple Gee ambassadors," she murmured. "He seemed to miss the seat as he sat down. . . ." She was thinking people who met in rooms like this one never made mistakes like that. I heard/felt the tittering amusement of the Centauri board members all around me. Triple Gee had just lost a whole lot of face.

Jardan turned to look at me again. "I suppose Braedee was simply reminding you of your duty. . . ." she said, taking my mind off Triple Gee.

"Yeah," I muttered. I looked away along the table until I saw Lazuli, sitting next to Daric . . . her stepson. She didn't look any older than he did; I wondered how old she really was. He murmured something to her; she laughed. There were maybe thirty other people around the long table. Twenty of them were the actual Centauri board. The rest, like Elnear, represented smaller combines they'd forced alliances with because each had something they needed or wanted. I counted eleven taMings sitting around the table; just enough for a majority. Something in the way they held themselves and moved said that they never forgot that for a minute. They stood out, even at that table, and it wasn't just because they all looked alike. . . . I saw old Teodor, who'd been on the board longer than anybody else, and would be until he died . . . saw Jule's grandmother . . . a couple of aunts and uncles, great-aunts, great-uncles. Lazuli held the seat that had belonged to Jule by right. It had been filled by a proxy for years, after Jule left home.

I looked at Charon, sitting at the table's head, as far from the Triple Gee ambassadors as he could get. He gave me a look that made me feel cold inside. Braedee had told him that since they had me they might as well use me; but having me in the same room with him made him damn uncomfortable. I realized the real reason Braedee took such a personal interest in me was because I was his idea, and Charon didn't like it. Charon was Centauri, as much as any single human being could be. If I caused any trouble while I was here, I wasn't the only one who'd pay. I looked back down the table again. "Why is Triple Gee here, if they're the enemy?" I asked Jardan.

"To keep lines of communication open," she said. "They exchange ambassadors whenever a board meets. They have more in common than the same potential market for their services—"

They both hated the FTA. I nodded. "I know. . . ." I said.

She gave me a strange look. I didn't bother to answer it, and she looked away again, leaning forward to say something to Elnear.

I remembered suddenly that Braedee had said Elnear held her dead husband's board seat. That must give her two votes. "How can the Lady be on the Centauri board?" I asked, as Jardan sat back again. "She's not really a taMing."

"Because they never found her husband's body," Jardan murmured. A technicality. Everybody knew he was dead, but nobody could prove it legally. Until someone did, or she died too, she'd continue to be his proxy.

I grimaced, sorry I'd asked. I settled back as Charon called the meeting to order, remembering that it wasn't the taMings I was supposed to be watching. The two Triple Gee reps were sitting like statues at the far end of the table, rigid with surface calm, groping for the dignity they knew they'd lost for good in one second's lack of attention. The one who'd hit the floor was chewing the inside of his mouth. He was sure that somebody had done it to him on purpose, but he couldn't figure out how.

Inside both of the Triple Gee reps, *suspicion, hatred, grudging respect* mixed like oil and water, leaving a scum of envy on everything they thought, everything they heard as the meeting started. From what I could see, if Triple Gee was behind trying to assassinate Lady Elnear, neither one of them had heard about it.

I glanced at Lady Elnear's back, feeling her accessing information; feeling her own self-conscious awareness of me. She wanted to tell everyone there what I was; hated herself for not having the balls to do it. I swore under my breath, hating that bastard Braedee for making everything harder for me than it had to be. I didn't even want to think about what would happen if anybody else—or everybody else—in that room suddenly found out what I was. Most combines never used telepaths for snoopware, because they were too paranoid about getting snooped themselves—by somebody else's psion, or by their own. Triple Gee would probably declare war if they knew what I was doing. Their security would kill me on the spot anyhow, even if all they did was walk out on the meeting.

I made myself focus again, shutting my eyes, trying to look like I was just bored, and not groping a lot of unsuspecting minds in the dark. The board was reporting what had been done about handling an upsurge in communications traffic in some critical sector. The Triple Gee reps took it all in, the envy static getting louder in their brains. One of them thought about the hostile takeover move on a local competitor that Triple Gee was making in that sector of their own network. Triple Gee figured the force-merger was what it would take to compete efficiently. Centauri was going to be surprised. . . .

Until I told them about it. I realized Centauri wasn't going to discuss anything here that would actually surprise Triple Gee. It was all to test out their responses. I went on around the table, until I was back inside Elnear's mind again. She was thinking about the ironies of communication, around this table, and across the Federation. That for all the technology that let them access the way they did, there was still no simple, instantaneous communication that could reach between star systems.

Board members and combine representatives and millions of daily messengers still had to travel in the flesh from all across the Federation, their ports and heads crammed with artificial memory, in order to keep the universal data Net functioning, and a combine's brain alive. Centauri had it better than most combines, because outside a single solar system communication was just another commodity, and they handled it themselves. But data was the lifeblood of an interstellar network, and if somebody ever cut off the supply, even Centauri would be braindead in a week.

I broke contact, shaking out my brain; wondering if the Lady ever thought about anything as simple as which shoes to wear. Maybe not. Maybe that was why she dressed the way she did. . . . I let my mind go on around the table again, skipping Centauri heads, reading the rest, memorizing what I found there, no matter how meaningless it was to me. As I got used to the patterns of bioware, I realized none of them wore anything that could sense me. But that didn't make me feel any easier. Playing corporate telepath was still like playing Last Chance back in Oldcity . . . a suicide game.

I sat up straighter, remembering yesterday, as Daric said something about Sojourner Stryger. The two Triple Gee ambassadors leaned forward at the far end of the table, suddenly letting their interest show. ". . . Stryger's effectiveness quotient in the independent media is still rising," Daric was saying, "because of the exposure he has been achieving in regard to deregulation. As is yours, Elnear—" He grinned across the table at her like he knew something she didn't. He probably did. His eyes moved past her to touch on me, slid down me once. But then they were gone again, and he was looking toward the Triple Gee reps. "Apparently the Security Council is waiting for the outcome of the deregulation vote before filling the open slot. Since they are, as we all know, somewhat out of touch with life in the real world, they appear to be using deregulation as a kind of test of wills, or a way to see whose personality has the greater force, the most impact on public opinion . . ." He smiled, glancing at Elnear again. Her irritation prickled behind my eyes. "A moot point in the end, as we also know—but one which seems to have some curious ritual significance to the FTA."

The thought of Stryger ending up on the Security Council made me feel sick. Those stupid slads, didn't they know what he was—? I remembered what Braedee had told me, and that didn't help.

Daric leaned forward, peering down the table at the reps again. "Tell me, Ambassador Ndala, is Triple Gee still waffling in its feelings about deregulation?"

"Triple Gee is not so much 'waffling,' Gentleman Daric, as it is carefully weighing the consequences," Ndala said. "We hardly need to point out to you how much profit Centauri stands to make on this drug, because of its controlling interest in ChemEnGen. Those additional profits could easily be used against your competitors."

Daric shrugged. "Or . . . they could as easily make us mellow and content to let our network go soft just a little . . . especially if you were to support us wholeheartedly in the Assembly vote. After all, you must keep things in perspective. *We* are not really the Enemy. Sometimes we do lose track of that; but it's true, nonetheless."

The Triple Gee ambassador leaned back in his seat, looking straight up the table at Charon. "Perhaps we will find something substantive waiting for us when we return to the embassy—?" he murmured. They were lying. They already knew they were going to vote for deregulation, even though they didn't care about the drug itself. They wanted Stryger to win. But they were going to see what kind of compromises they could shake Centauri down for. . . .

"Consider it done," Charon said. He glanced at me for just a second as he said it. His word was about as safe as I felt right now.

Elnear sighed heavily in front of me. She knew as well as any of them did that even though she had the FTA behind her on the drug vote, Stryger had his backers too. She wanted deregulation to fail, for reasons that ran so deep in her that I couldn't really read them. She was even thinking that she'd be willing to withdraw from consideration for the Council, even though she wanted that slot nearly as much, if withdrawing would keep some of Stryger's backers from voting for deregulation just to get him into it. But she knew nothing was that easy, or that clean.

She thought Stryger was a good man; she thought he'd be as good a choice for the Council as she was. Maybe better. She didn't believe Stryger was really the combines' tool any more than Braedee did; but not for the same reasons. She didn't know what Stryger was; didn't believe—or probably didn't give a damn about—what I'd told her. She admired and envied his faith in God and human nature. She thought it was simply unfortunate that his belief in pentryptine as a solution to everybody's problems played into the hands of so many combine interests. . . .

I slumped down in my seat, aching, not sure if I was exhausted or just depressed. These vips had the augmentation and easy access that let them keep up with the flow of interstellar empires. But it didn't give them a clue about what went on behind another human's eyes. I didn't know if I felt disillusioned, or just relieved, to know that they were only deadheads like anybody else, when it really counted.

Finally the board meeting ended; but that wasn't the end of my duty. There was another room waiting for us, this one piled high with food and drinks under a ceiling crawling with gold and white plaster flowers. I was hungry, but I didn't touch anything this time. It wasn't worth the risk. I only watched and listened, staying by Elnear like I was supposed to. Jardan shadowed me at first, but when she saw I wasn't eating or talking, she left me alone.

I was only an aide, and if I didn't talk no one talked to me. I stood listening to the mortal gods of the Federation discuss how to get around the FTA's back, and how to get into somebody's pants; how much they needed pentryptine to stop the rioting on Belke's World . . . how much the franchise disputes had hurt production . . . what a pain in the ass the FTA had been about their labor practices. . . . Advising and bitching and gossiping, sometimes all in the same breath.

I watched a tall, blond man spit out a skagweed cud and leave it lying halfway under the table; someone else stepped in it while I watched. *Jeezu, he had worse manners than I did*—But manners didn't seem to matter, if you were rich enough; just like they didn't matter if you were poor enough. It was only the billions suspended in between, those who had something to lose, who had to know how to act. I touched the logo on my sleeve; let my hand drop.

There was a crash and then laughter and cursing somewhere behind me. I turned around fast, because just for a second I'd thought I'd felt something, psi energy. But I wasn't sure, and it was only somebody who'd spilled a plate of food. Probably nothing, probably just liquor or nerves. . . . It got on my nerves, remembering there could be a psionic practical joker in this crowd somewhere, just waiting to try me again. But maybe they'd realized why the joke hadn't worked on me. If they knew, they hadn't given me away. Maybe they had something to hide, too. Maybe that was why they only did little things, things nobody could trace. Maybe they'd leave me alone; but I doubted it. Braedee had told me to back off. But what he didn't know could still hurt me. I began to loosen up my brain, starting to scan—

"Mez Cat."

I turned. Lazuli taMing was standing beside me.

I blinked. "Ma'am?"

"You look like you're asleep on your feet."

I pulled my mind back into focus in a hurry. "No, ma'am. Just . . . uh, doing my job." *Shit. Don't say that.* "I mean—"

"It's quite all right. You've barely had time to take a breath before being thrown into all this. It must seem very alien to you."

I heard the unconscious condescension in it; felt it. But she was standing here talking to me, something nobody else would do. And besides, she was right. "Yes, ma'am. Very alien." Seeing Jule's face when I looked at her was more comfort than I'd had in a long time. It helped me remember that all this was supposed to have a point.

Charon was watching us, frowning. I touched his mind with a quick finger of thought—pulled back again, tasting *jealousy, suspicion, frustration . . . hatred.* The last one for me, the rest for his wife. I felt the twisted uncertainty in him every time he looked at her. He hadn't married her for love, only for politics; he knew she didn't love him. But when he looked at her he saw Jule too . . . his own daughter. Only perfect, this time. And it made him uneasy and uncertain, things he never wanted to be; made him feel things no man ought to feel when he remembered his daughter. There was an emotion still alive inside him that should have died long ago. . . .

I looked away from him again, my skin crawling.

"What did you say?" Lazuli asked.

I hadn't said anything. "Nothing, ma'am," I answered, not sure if I'd let something leak, or only made some sound. "Is Jiro here?" I changed the subject, because I had to get my own mind off it. I hadn't seen Jiro anywhere, but if I had to pick someone who'd use psi as a bad joke, he'd be my first choice.

She shook her head. "No. He wanted to come, to observe the meeting, but I told him he couldn't. That was his punishment for lying to me."

I almost said I thought lying was what vips learned first; but I didn't. Maybe it wasn't the lie he was being punished for, anyway. Maybe it was just for admitting the truth. I looked at Charon again, saw him begin to move toward us. "Ma'am—" I ducked my head and turned away from her.

I made my way through the crowd to Elnear. She stood in a shadowed alcove, talking to Jule's great-uncle Salvador, who looked younger than she did but was twice as old.

"Mez Cat," Elnear said, nodding to me as she noticed me. She looked tired, and felt worse. "I think it's time we were leaving. I have my own work to get back to." I felt a little heat stir in her, and a lot of relief. Relief that she could finally get free of this nest of relatives; relief that I'd been here the entire time without embarrassing her. I nodded too, more relieved than she was. Jardan came up beside me, glancing at me without frowning, for once. "Thank God," she said.

Daric taMing was walking behind her as she said it, holding a lot of liquor in a large crystal mug. He stopped, looking at us, his eyes glittering. I met his stare, because this time I knew I hadn't done anything he could shaft me for.

"So you've been a good boy today, new aide—" he said. He started on, hesitated, looking back. His mouth quirked up. "Did you know that your fly is open?"

I looked down, because everybody else did; knowing it was impossible, knowing he was wrong— He wasn't wrong. Everyone watched me fasten it.

8

I WENT WITH Lady Elnear to the Arm again the next day, and the next. Before I knew it I'd been on Earth for a week. It seemed like a lot longer. But nothing happened that hadn't before, except that I became an aide. I digested the data I'd swallowed whole the first day, and used it; and every time I used the console I swallowed more. The fact that sometimes I knew more about a job than Jardan did, and other times didn't know whether to input what she gave me or eat it, didn't go over very well at first. But by now most of the surprised looks I was getting from her were relieved. Lady Elnear could even forget that I was a freak for long enough to look at me without startling, sometimes.

One lunch hour I hired a legal program and got my contract with Centauri cleaned up and registered. Some of the other hours I spent wandering the floating paths through the streets and levels of the city near the Federation plex. The bizarre combinations of old and new, soaring curves and knife-blade edges, stone and steel and ceramoplast, glass and composite, made me feel like I was caught inside the mutating guts of some ancient, cancerous crystal being. I could see the layers of time in the layers of its structure, feel the crazyquilt of lives going on all around me in its heart, a separate reality flowing through the unoccupied spaces of its body. I got myself some new jeans, right from the source, but never got to wear them.

And nothing happened to anyone that shouldn't have, except that I had to see more of Jule's brother Daric than I wanted to. And more of Lazuli.

I thought I knew why she and her children were staying with Elnear instead of at the Crystal Palace where they belonged. It didn't have anything to do with me. But that didn't make it easier to be around them. I avoided Jiro and his sister like I'd avoid a street gang, and for pretty much the same reasons. I stayed away from their mother as much as I could; but short of staying in my room until I starved to death, I couldn't keep away from her completely. And whenever I saw her, I had to feel her think about me. And feel myself think about her. Her face stayed with me in the nights, while I lay awake waiting for Braedee to call. I knew that mindlarking about Charon taMing's wife made about as much sense as thinking about setting myself on fire. It couldn't have made me feel any worse; or any hotter.

And every night after everyone else was asleep, Braedee's ghost materialized over the console in my room, and I reported everything I'd seen and heard. What the hell, I figured; what real difference did anything make, anyway?

By the second week, I could stumble through the Lady's office routine without driving the system and everybody around me crazy. Sometimes I could almost forget that this was anything but an honest job. . . .

"Mez Cat," Elnear said suddenly, from across the room. "Haven't you anything better to do?"

I was watching "You Are There," the Independent Daily News fax; getting a lurid sensurround of a shipping disaster. I had everything damped out except the picture; screams and the smell of burned bodies were more than I really needed. The Indy was always desperate for ratings because their coverage wasn't subsidized by combine credit; they were a strange mix of honor and sleaze, and I kind of liked them.

I shut off the image and glanced up. "Everything's in the system except the committee summary; we still don't have all the data. I'm waiting for Geza to get done right now."

"What about the reports—?"

"I dumped what you were through with, and brought up the rest of your list."

She was silent for a minute, trying to think of something else she could call me on. She couldn't think of anything. "Cat," she said finally, glancing down, "I confess that you have been a surprise, in some ways. You are actually managing to do an adequate job in this position. And frankly, considering that you were totally unqualified for it, I find that amazing."

I smiled. She did too, and turned back to her work.

I felt her go white, suddenly, as she scanned the overnight listings on her unit. Jardan came in from the outer office, and the security screen blinked on behind her. "What is it?" Jardan asked, answering some summons I couldn't hear. I'd figured out days ago that she was more than just Elnear's assistant, and my keeper. She knew everything that mattered; she even wore enough augmentation to hold it all. She was the only one Elnear trusted that much.

"Look at this." Elnear put something on the screen of my unit that lobotomized the news fax. I sat back in my chair while Jardan read over my shoulder. She looked at Elnear; jerked the headset off of me and stuck the trodes on her own forehead. All that I recognized that I could see was the name of Triple Gee. "Triple Gee is boxed out—?" Jardan murmured, as if it was more unimaginable than even the thought of her smiling at me. "You only communicated with Suezain yesterday. How could Centauri have learned about the dispersal ruling—?"

"There's no way. I took absolute measures. . . ."

Suddenly there were two sets of eyes drilling into my skull, two minds with the same idea. I sat staring at the screen, trying not to make it three. No one asked the question; figuring there was no point. I didn't answer it, either.

Elnear got up from her seat, heavily, and pulled on her drape. "I have a face meeting with Isplanasky to go to Philipa. Lingpo can see to this business, and Geza can cover Cat's duties. . . ." She glanced at me, resigned. I went where she went, like it or not. Right now she didn't like it at all.

We went through the halls, on foot as usual, deep into the heart of the FTA's office plex. Elnear walked seven or eight klicks a day. I didn't mind it, but it always surprised me that she didn't either. For someone who didn't seem to care what her body looked like, she took damn good care of it.

This time we passed through a huge open space I'd never been inside of before. It was hung with banners and drifting light sculptures. Gigantic holo representations of Historic Earth shimmered in the walls, behind things inside stasis fields that looked like relics from a museum. It was a place that could only be for show, for the tourist trade that helped keep Earth alive. It startled the hell out of me after the nondescript halls and offices I'd gotten used to. But once I thought about it, I realized a place like this had to be here somewhere. The FTA claimed it represented all of humanity. It had to have a public face for humans to look at.

Elnear kept walking ahead of me; navigating the trajectories of the crowd that had come to gape or take spoon-fed tours. I tried to keep up, but my own eyes kept being pulled away, toward a huge block of jade hand-carved into an incredible miniature landscape . . . a holo on the wall of a city, before and after it had been melted down by primitive nukes . . . a perfect zero-gee crystal floating inside a sphere.

"Cat!" Elnear's voice jerked my leash. "If you want to take the tour," she said, when I reached her side, "please do it on your own time."

"I didn't know there was a tour . . . ma'am." I looked away, staring at the mosaic mural on the wall behind her.

"Well, now you do," she said, but her irritation was fading. She turned, glancing over her shoulder to see what I was looking at instead of her. "A family portrait of the human race," she said.

It was a picture of maybe thirty people, old, young, all different sexes, sizes, colors. Once I'd started to look at them, I couldn't stop until I'd looked at them all. Whoever had made that portrait over four hundred years ago had done a good job of catching their souls.

"It hung originally in the plex of the old world government that preceded the Federation," Elnear said, "to remind the people of the nation-states that met there of their common humanity . . . something which they constantly forgot, anyway." She wasn't sure whether what we had now was better or worse; but she thought that at least individual humans didn't kill each other as often, or in such big numbers.

I looked at the faces again. Some of them looked less like each other than she looked like me. But none of them were Hydran faces. None of them really looked like me. There were words embedded in the picture, in some pre-space script I couldn't read. "What does it say?"

" 'Treat others as you would like them to treat you,' " she said.

I didn't say anything. She started on and I followed her. The mural's eyes watched my back as I walked away.

I didn't know who Isplanasky was until we reached the end of our stroll; I was too busy thinking about what had happened back in her office to bother picking it out of her thoughts. I only looked up as we finally reached his doorway, in time to see the logo on the wall above it: *Natan Isplanasky. Director of Operations, Contract Labor Services.* The past put its hands around my throat. I went inside, but I didn't want to.

Isplanasky actually had a room with a view, a room at the top; which made sense, for someone at the top of the FTA's biggest and most profitable operation short of the Federation Telhassium Mines. His secured inner office was huge, and it had a view of the city's rolling peaks, tier on tier of artificial mountains.

"Elnear . . ." Isplanasky got up from what looked like a purple reclining chair with some strange design quirks. He shook off a slow-moving daze as he came toward us, and at first I thought he'd been sleeping. He'd been accessing. He was loaded with augmentation, but none of it showed. "God, what a pleasure to see your face. It's been too long. Sometimes I think I've been buried and forgotten in the Net. . . ." He shook his head again, rubbing his temples, blinking. "It was good of you to come, when a call would have done it." He was wearing black, like the Labor press gangs, but his was pretending to be a suit, not a uniform. It looked good on him. He looked about forty standards; he was heavyset but not fat, with bronze skin and long black hair caught in a clip, a thick curling beard. He moved like maybe he really didn't leave that chair for days on end.

"Natan, I will use any excuse, any time, for a chance to get together with you." Elnear flashed him that shapechanging smile, and he grinned, white teeth showing in the black beard. Just friends, no more . . . but real friends. She thought he was one hell of a guy. But then, she admired Stryger, too. "Besides, you need someone to remind you to come up for air."

"Who's this?" he asked, his voice still a little thick. He smiled at me like he actually wanted to know.

She introduced me, and he crossed the room to shake my hand, telling me how damn lucky I was to be working with one of the best in the Arm. I didn't answer; my throat felt paralyzed. My mind kept trying to find the dead black core in his own mind, that would tell me how someone could head the largest slave labor operation in the Federation and still smile at anyone like he meant it. Except I couldn't find one. . . . Frustration started to burn a hole in my concentration. I might as well still be psiblind as have the kind of gray half vision Braedee's drugs had given me.

Isplanasky gave Elnear some tea. He handed me a beer and opened one for himself like we were all having a picnic on top of the world. My bottle said "since 1420" on it; it was made of brown glass. I popped it and took a long drink of thousand-year-old beer. It was pretty good. I finished it off.

"I don't like this debate with Stryger. . . ." Isplanasky said to Elnear. I looked up again. "The very fact that it's happening stinks of interference. Too many combines want deregulation—"

"Yes, I know." Elnear nodded, sipping at her tea. "He's quite sincere in his beliefs, but he strikes me as naive. He may make a deal with the devil simply because he believes in angels—to use his own terms."

His grin came back. "Unlike you and I, who are quaintly cynical down to our socks."

I leaned back on the couch by the window, listening to them discuss Stryger as if he was some kind of harmless crank. When I'd had a couple of free minutes on the Net, I'd called up everything I could find on him. I'd listened to him speak, I'd studied his background. He'd always been a godlover; he'd been a minister of the Universal Ecumen on Gadden. He hadn't always been a fanatic about it. Everything I could dig out on his early years said he was a decent man who pretty much lived what he preached, working to make other people's lives better.

But then he'd had some kind of religious vision—at least that was what he claimed—when he'd been braindead for a couple of minutes after a fall. And he'd started to change. After that he'd come to Earth to study pre-space religion, because his vision had told him he'd find God's Real Truth waiting for him here.

Interstellar travel had proved once and for all that Earth wasn't the center of the universe; running into the Hydrans had finally shown humans that they weren't alone in it. Human religion had done a double-take then, going through the Re-creation. What survived were kinds of religion that preached oneness with all lifeforms, and practiced what they preached by keeping a low profile. It made more sense, and it didn't compete with the combines for loyalty.

But Stryger wanted to bring back the old-style religion, the kind that said there was a real God somewhere who cared enough to play favorites, and humans were it. Which meant Hydrans weren't. I couldn't figure out when he'd started to hate Hydrans so much, or why. He was careful not to talk about it, because he wasn't stupid, and he knew that the ones he really wanted behind him weren't stupid either. They probably hated Hydrans as much as he did, but now that most surviving Hydrans were under some combines's thumb, or "relocated" in dumps like Oldcity, talking genocide wasn't easy like it had been once.

Stryger had started traveling, gathering supporters and money, playing his Human Rights themes to get attention on the Net and to spread his word from world to world. He'd been at it for a long time; he was fifty-three. He hadn't always looked like he did now—I'd been right about that. He'd had enough plastic work done on him so that the oldest images of him were barely recognizable. He preached about the dignity and beauty of the human form, unaugmented, unchanged, the way God had meant it to be. But little by little he'd played God on himself, transforming himself into a calculated vision of human perfection.

And over the years he'd convinced both the combine vips and the Security Council that he was almost as perfect as he seemed. It couldn't be easy to play both sides as well as he did, to make two enemies hear just what they wanted to hear when you spoke the same words. You had to be damned smart and slick, but more than that you had to have the kind of belief in yourself that made other people want to believe in you. He had it; I'd felt it. And too many other people believed in him already. His Movement had a higher financial profile than a lot of combines. He could buy himself anything he wanted; he had that kind of money.

Only, he hadn't done that. He actually fed most of his profits into creating the kind of help for life's losers that he preached about. I'd seen some of the shelters he'd sponsored, in Oldcity . . . I'd used some of them.

That had stopped me cold when I found out about it. I hadn't known what to make of it, I'd wondered if maybe somehow I was wrong about him. If he'd done it for promo, he'd get more for his money just hiring hypers. But then I'd realized that money, or even fame, wasn't what he was after. He wanted real power. He wanted that slot on the Security Council, and it looked like he was using the pentryptine vote as a way to get himself there. Something was still driving him to reach higher and higher, and it wasn't something holy. I'd stared at the final image of his perfect face for a long time, wondering what the hell was really going on behind those eyes. . . .

I turned to look out at Isplanasky's view; clearing Stryger's image out of my mind. I had to shut my eyes then, as they suddenly told me how high up I was. I pressed my hands against the couch, hanging on for a second until the dizziness passed. The couch was covered with something that felt and smelled like real leather. I ran my hand over it, back and forth.

". . . if this gains him any more support we'll be in trouble," Isplanasky was saying. "The majority of the Assembly is for deregulation already. Aside from the fact that you are clearly the best candidate, Stryger is completely unprepared for the real demands of a Council position. He's not even cybered—calls it unnatural, for God's sake."

"Yes, exactly: 'for God's sake.' " Elnear rested her head against the high back of her seat, staring at the ceiling. "He really believes God is on his side. You know, I have always tried to do what I understood to be right, in keeping with the manifold ways of God. But sometimes I can't help wondering. . . . I think about this debate night and day. I dream about it, and wake up arguing with myself."

"I know how you feel, believe me." Isplanasky moved restlessly back to his bar. "If combines start using pentryptine on their citizens—"

"You might be out of a job," I said. The FTA rented out contract laborers to whatever combine wanted extra bodies, usually to do things their citizens wouldn't do. No questions asked. It also used them in its own operations—things like the Federation Mines, where they mined their telhassium on a piece of burnt-out star called Cinder out in the Crab Colonies.

They looked at me.

"Well, that wasn't exactly my concern," Isplanasky said, still good-natured. "My concern is the same as the Lady's. I oversee Contract Labor; it involves the lives of a vast number of people, who would be more at risk from combine drug abuses than most of their population. I believe that human dignity and freedom of choice are worth fighting for; that individual rights have to be protected and maintained at any cost. I don't want to see the people under my charge treated badly and unable even to protest it."

"You want your bondies left free to eat all the dirt some combine feels like feeding them, without drugs to make it easier?" I asked. "As long as somebody keeps paying you for ten standards of their time—"

His smile disappeared. "Not at all. I work for the FTA because Contract Labor exists as a viable, humane alternative, so that those individuals who lack regular combine citizenship have somewhere to turn. It gives them a start, a second chance; useful training. 'Contract Labor builds worlds'—" He gestured at the logo on the wall behind him.

I stared at him. He had to be the most perfect hypocrite I'd ever seen, or a pathological liar—because he meant every word of that.

"Are you all right?" he asked.

I said, "How many bondies did you have to skin to cover this couch?"

"By the Nine Billion Names of God!" he murmured. "Are you an anarchist, son, or is it just that you can't hold your liquor?"

I unfastened my databand and let it drop off. I held up my arm, letting him see the wide, smooth band of white scar tissue. He didn't know what it was. "I used to work for you," I said.

He raised his eyebrows. "You seem to have come through the experience with your skin intact." His voice was cool and dry.

I reached behind me for the tail of my shirt. Just then Elnear's desperate anger caught in my mind like a thorn. I glanced at her, saw the disbelief in her eyes. "Ma'am, I—"

"Yes, certainly, you may go." She raised a dismissing hand. "Back to my office. I'll speak with you there." It was the closest thing to a threat I'd heard from her. She'd speak; but she wouldn't listen. She murmured an apology to Isplanasky, something like, ". . . he isn't feeling well . . ."

I left the room, leaving their stares behind. The memories still followed me, because there was nowhere I could ever go where I'd be able to leave those behind.

"Well, squire—" Daric taMing's twitchy, grinning face pushed in front of me as I dragged my aching stupidity back through the halls. "Where's your Lady in white armor?"

Damn. The one person in the entire universe that I wanted to see the least. I shrugged, not even sure what he was talking about, as usual. I wondered if he spent all his days like this, wandering the halls looking for victims.

"She's supposed to be with you, I thought." He kept pushing, matching my steps. "Or vice versa. That's what you're paid for. Am I right?"

"Not today," I said, my hands making quiet fists.

" 'Sir.' "

"What?" I looked at him.

"Say 'sir.' . . . You're just not very good at this, are you? You know what Elnear says about you behind your back? 'You can dress him up, but you can't take him anywhere.' "

"I thought 'sir' was only used as a term of respect."

It took him a minute, because he didn't believe I'd said that. Then he laughed. "You know, I think I admire you, Cat. You actually don't give a damn what we think of you . . . or is it just that you're really so naive that you don't know what we could do to you?"

I felt myself so cold as I realized he meant that. I kept walking, watching my feet take one step after another. "Jule never told me she had a brother."

He sniggered. "That's hardly surprising. She always hated me, because I'm normal. She tried to kill me once, when we were children. She tried to push me off the balcony at the country house on Ardattee."

I looked up, frowning. He was still smiling at me. "Then she must have had a good reason." I looked ahead again, walking faster.

He kept up with me, hanging onto me like a dog with its teeth sunk in my leg. I wondered what he wanted—because this was building up to something, I could feel it. He hadn't run into me by accident. I wondered what his problem was; if he was on drugs, or if just being a taMing was enough to fuck him up this bad.

"What was it that attracted you to my sister, anyway? Most normal people find psions repulsive. The thought of them crawling into *your* thoughts, or stopping your heart with . . . a thought. You know. Of course, maybe you find that erotic, like necrophilia, or having someone piss on you. . . ."

I spun around, my fist coming up; not even caring that half a hundred witnesses and even more security eyes were about to see me beat the shit out of an Assembly member—

"I know what you are," he said. "You're one too."

My hand dropped to my side like dead weight. "What?" I said; and then, "Who told you? That I was a telepath—"

"It's true . . . that explains everything." His gray eyes clung to my face like a sweating hand. "You are a psion. My father actually hired a psion." He laughed again, high and strained, and smacked his forehead with his hand. "God, I don't believe it."

"Who told you?" I felt the anger that had barely stopped short of his face try to reach out for him again as I realized he'd tricked me.

"Father told me." He shrugged, as if Charon taMing talked about me like he discussed the weather. "I just couldn't believe it." I didn't believe that, either. He must have overheard something, gotten access to some private file. "After Jule left home, I was sure that if a psion ever crossed his range again, he'd have her—or him, in your case—incinerated on the spot. Braedee must be more persuasive than I thought. Or he knows more about us than I realized. . . ."

"I'm not a psion, to most people around here. Braedee wants it kept that way. I'll tell him you know." Hoping that would be enough to keep his mouth shut.

"Oh, your secret is safe with me." His face changed suddenly, started to twitch again. "Being a psion . . . doesn't it make you ashamed? Doesn't it make you want to pull your brains out? Jule wanted to. The way everyone treated her—" Something haunted his eyes then: *fear.* That it could have been him, and not his sister.

"Like you did?"

He frowned, twitching.

I went on down the hallway, and this time he didn't follow.

9

I WAS READY in the usual place at the usual time the next morning. I was the only one. It wasn't like Elnear or Jardan to be late. If anybody besides me hated mornings in that house, I didn't know about it. I leaned against the stairway banister with my eyes shut, waiting. The nagging ache that had started in my head yesterday afternoon was still there. It had slipped away when I inhaled some painkiller, but it came crawling back every time the medicine wore off. My stomach felt queasy, and I hadn't bothered with breakfast. I kept looking at the time, watching it get later and later, until all at once I wondered if they'd left without me. Suddenly my stomach and my head felt a whole lot worse. I spun out a searching finger of thought until it jabbed into Jardan's mind, still somewhere in the house.

I went back along the hall until I found her sitting in the sun room, sipping coffee as if there was all the time in the world. "You're late," I said.

She glanced up at me with a kind of cold spite. "No." She shook her head. "Lady Elnear is attending a board meeting of ChemEnGen this morning."

"Without me?"

"She's in her study." Jardan twitched her head in the general direction. "It isn't necessary for her to attend this meeting in person; it's merely a formality." Centauri's board held all the real power. "The rest of the day she'll be accessing, in preparation for the debate tomorrow—"

"Oh." I thought about how I could still have been upstairs asleep. "Thanks for letting me know."

"—Although after yesterday I would hardly blame her if she chose to leave you behind." She looked out the windows again.

"Maybe I had a—"

"Bound and gagged."

I swallowed what I'd been going to say. "Chew on rats," I said, and left the room.

Back upstairs I peeled off the Centauri clothes I'd been wearing and pulled on my new denims and my old shirt. Then I went down the back way and outside into the fresh air. I walked through the courtyard into the field beyond, something I'd never done before. The openness made me giddier than it usually did. I pushed myself to take one step and then another away from the high stone wall.

"Cat! Cat!"

I looked back, saw Talitha waving at me as she came around the corner of the wall, riding on the back of the biggest dog I'd ever seen. Her nanny was leading it by some kind of harness.

"Look at me!" she shouted, in a voice you could have heard on the next planet. "Do you want to ride with me? Her name is Bootsie, because she has little white boots!" The nanny hushed her, frowning.

The thing was kind of tan and white, its face half hidden in a tangle of thick hair. I backed up as her nanny jerked it to a stop beside me. If the woman had any name besides Nanny, I hadn't bothered to find it out. She always wore gray, and usually looked like she'd been sucking on something sour. She looked that way now. "Good morning," she said, sounding like she doubted it.

"You can ride with me," Talitha offered again, looking hopefully at me. "Can't he, Nanny?"

"Bootsie can't carry both of you," Nanny said flatly.

"Thanks anyway." I shook my head. "I don't like dogs."

"She's not a dog," Talitha said. "She's a pony. You don't ride on dogs."

"Oh."

"Come on, Talitha. I'm tired of walking. You've ridden long enough." Nanny jerked on the pony's lead again, starting to turn it back the way they'd come.

"No, no!" Talitha's face crumpled as she clutched at her saddle. "We didn't even go around the house! Please—"

"No."

I watched them start away, feeling the nanny's boredom and Talitha's helpless disappointment in my head like the taste of old metal. "I'll take her around for a while," I said.

Nanny wheeled the pony and its sniffling rider back again, slapped the lead rope into my hands before I could think about changing my mind. "Here," she said. "Be careful, it bites."

I grimaced.

"Bootsie never bites me," Talitha said.

Nanny headed back toward the house, taking the taste of old metal with her.

I looked at the pony; touched its mind, feeling the strange, shifting surface of an animal's thoughts, like clouds drifting across a sky. Not afraid, not angry . . . content and trusting. My hold on the rope loosened a little. In the distance I could see the Crystal Palace. Spines of light hit me in the eye as the molten sun poured over the mountain wall and turned it into a burning-glass. I could see another house, closer by, off to my left. "Whose house is that?" I asked, not really caring.

"That's Daric's house," Talitha said. I was sorry I'd asked. I looked toward my right, saw the river flowing by, wide and quiet. I started toward it, pulling on the pony's rope. At least the pony was something to hold onto as I crossed the empty field. We reached the river's edge and I stopped under a tree.

"Hey, Cat—"

I looked up, startled.

Jiro came swooping down on us in a rattle of artificial wings. The pony shied, jerking on the lead rope. Talitha squealed in fright. I caught the pony's mind inside a loop of forced calm, and settled it down fast.

Jiro landed beside us, the wings folding neatly behind him as he dropped his arms. "Did you see me? Just like a bird—" He raised one arm again, the wing fluttered.

"Jiro!" Talitha said. "You scared my pony."

"Oh." He shrugged. "I'm sorry, Tally. But isn't this really vork? Auntie got it for me. Charon said I couldn't have one, it was too dangerous."

I wondered if Elnear was hoping he'd break his neck, and there'd be one less taMing in the world. But even as I thought it, I knew that wasn't the reason she'd done it. She didn't hate these kids; she didn't even hate all the taMings. I wondered how she felt about the one she'd married. . . . Jiro was wearing a shock suit and a helmet; she'd bought him those, too.

"Why are you dressed like that?" he said.

"Like what?" I looked down at myself.

"Like you're zeroed." *Poor.*

I frowned. "Why do you always say the first thing that comes into your head, no matter how stupid it is?"

He stuck his lip out. "You should talk. I heard about what you said to Isplanasky."

I looked away. Talitha sat on the pony's back, singing, "I love my pony, I love my pony. . . ." over and over and over, while the pony tore at the soft green grass with its blunt teeth. The sudden fright had already disappeared from both their minds. I looked back at Jiro. "Why is it I never see any of you people talk to each other, but you always know everybody else's business?"

He just stared at me, blankly.

I shrugged, trying to shrug off my frustration. "Sometimes I get angry, because nobody around here understands anything." They were the worst kind of deadheads, thinking they knew everything when really they knew nothing, didn't even want to know. "Sometimes I say things because I can't help it."

"I do too." He looked up at me, and there was someone else trapped behind his eyes. I touched that other, hidden child with my thoughts. "Sometimes I can't help it. . . ." His throat worked.

I remembered what Lazuli had said . . . remembered that he had Charon taMing for a stepfather. I touched his shoulder lightly. "I know," I said.

He smiled, a little uncertain. "Mother said she knew you were really a good person, because Charon hates you so much."

It startled a laugh out of me. I didn't say anything for a minute, while half a dozen things cancelled each other out inside my head. "Where is your mother?"

"She's up at the Crystal Palace with Charon." His face twisted. "Auntie says 'Charon' is the name of some shipper in an ancient story, who used to transport dead bodies to Hell."

I laughed again.

"Someday I'm going to give him a dog with three heads."

"I want to see the dog with three heads!" Talitha burst out. She scrambled down out of the pony's saddle.

"I don't have it now, you flit—" Jiro said. "Where's *your* mother?"

I looked back at him, surprised. "She's dead."

His face pinched. "Where's your father?"

"I don't know."

"I don't know where my father is, either. . . ." He caught Talitha and pulled her toward him, holding her close while she squirmed. "Do you think if you wish something enough, it happens?"

I shook my head, watching the river pass like time.

"Don't let anything happen to Auntie."

I nodded.

"I want to fly." Talitha pulled at Jiro's wings.

"You're too little." He let go of her, pushing her away, as he un-latched the harness. "Here, you can try it—" He slung the wings to-ward me. "It has lifters, you don't really have to flap."

I looked up at the sky. My head and my stomach changed places just thinking about it. "No thanks."

He shrugged, and dumped the wings on the ground in a heap. "Okay. Let's do something else then."

I winced. "Jeezu. You're going to break that."

"Auntie'll get me another one." He was already stripping off his suit and helmet.

Talitha was wandering along the edge of the meadow, picking purple and white flowers, singing a formless song. I sat down under the tree, resting my back against the rough bark. Everything smelled good here. The pony snorted, still eating grass.

"You want to race? We could get more horses—" Jiro stood in front of me, in a bright red tunic and shorts.

"I don't know how to ride." I shrugged.

"We could race skimmers—"

"I don't know how to do that either."

I could feel annoyance growing like an itch under his skin. "We could go swimming—" He waved a hand at the river. "That's easy."

"I can't swim." I looked down, tracing lines in the dirt with my finger.

"Don't you know how to have fun—?"

I glanced up at him. He was still standing in front of me with his hands on his hips, frowning. "No. I guess not." I looked down again.

"Well *I* do." He peeled off his clothes and ran down to the river shore.

I watched him wade naked into the water and dive in, watched him swim with strong, easy motions, as if he'd been born to it, like a fish. I sat where I was, feeling the echo of his thoughts, the sensations of water and motion, like a kind of mocking laughter.

"Here." A fistful of dirt-clotted flowers shoved into my face, Talitha behind them. "These are for you. Why aren't you swimming, like Jiro?"

"I can't." I took the flowers awkwardly, dropping a couple.

She picked up the strays and pushed them into my hands. "For you. And these are for Mother, and Auntie, and my pony. . . ." She showed me the clump in her other hand, then put them carefully on the ground beside me. "Let's leave them here," she said, like she was the adult and I was the four-year-old, "and we can go down to the water like Jiro. I'll help you." She pulled open my fist and laid my flowers on the ground beside the rest, tugging at my arm while she did it.

"I suppose you can swim too," I said, getting up.

"Oh, no," She shook her head. "I'm only four. When I'm a big five-year-old, then I'll be able to swim. Maybe when you're five, you can swim too."

"Yeah. Maybe." We went down to the shore. The water was clear for about a meter out from the muddy bank. I could see smooth stones and tiny darting fish lying below its surface. After that it got deep faster, shading into brown and gray, reflecting the blue-green sky further out. Talitha waded in up to her knees, splashing and squealing, scattering fish. Slowly I pulled off my boots and rolled up my pants legs, and then I went in. It was freezing cold. The cold didn't seem to bother Talitha or Jiro. Clenching my teeth, I let her drag me after her, feeling the soft bottom squelch and shift between my toes, the edge of the deepwater current lick at me. I wasn't sure whether I liked it or not. I stopped when the cold water started slapping at my knees.

Jiro shouted and waved, Talitha giggled and splashed. Spray flew like rain. The sun felt good and hot on my back, the air was sweet, my face in the water's shimmering mirror said I was smiling . . . said that this day really belonged to me. And suddenly I felt a surge of panic that took my breath away. *Thief.*

I backed out of the water again and sat down on the bank, breathing hard, putting distance between me and something that had more to do with watching them play in the river than with the cold water touching my skin, or the muddy bottom shifting under my feet. . . . The feeling I'd had when I'd entered the taMing's castle on the cliff—that I didn't have the right to be here; or even the right to know that places like this existed.

The heat of the sun soaked into my flesh, making me sweat. After a while I unknotted my fingers, stretched out the muscles in my arms, and pulled my shirt off. The wind breathed on my sweating skin, letting the heat inside me escape. I picked through the smooth warm stones that lay in a dark mosaic all around me. I tossed them into the cold water, one by one, watching the rings they made as they fell, watching the way the rings collided, overlapped, mingled like the patterns of separate minds converging.

Talitha came back onto the shore and sat down beside me. She began to make mud cakes. After a minute Jiro burst up out of the water like some kind of monster, making her shriek, and splashed ashore to pull on his clothes. He picked up a stone and threw it, making it dance across the water like it was massless. I threw another stone and it sank.

He squatted down beside me. "What's the most fun you ever had?"

I glanced at him. Three more stones hit the water and sank, while I searched my mind for an answer that would mean something to him. The kind of games they played in Oldcity were the kind you learned the hard way. "You ever see a comet ball?"

"Sure. I've got four of them, in different colors."

My mouth twitched. "I had one once. When I was a little older than you. It was incredible. Oldcity's kind of like N'Yuk in a way, closed in, no sky—Quarro buried it when the new city spread out. Except it's dark in Oldcity, even in the daytime. Your whole world's only about ten meters high, there in the streets. . . ." I'd snatched the control box out of a storefront after a fire, but I didn't say that. I hadn't known what it was. When I'd switched it on, a huge sizzling ball of light had exploded out of the wand and gone rocketing up toward the roof of the world. "It was like trying to hold onto that—" I glanced up at the sun for a second, down again. "Like trying to reel it in on a string. . . ." I had bounced off the tangled undersides of Quarro, leaped back and forth from wall to building wall, shooting sparks, lighting up the backstreet gloom like a captive star. After a minute or so of just staring, I'd begun to realize that I could control it with the wand. I could make it do anything I wanted, leap and spiral, paint pictures on my retinas with fire. "Everyone came out into the street to watch me . . . to see it. They kept handing me food and brew, shouting, 'Keep it going!' It was the best show I'd ever seen—any of us had ever seen, maybe. I felt like kind of a hero, giving them all this free sun show. . . ." I remembered wishing it could go on forever.

It had lasted for about an hour, before someone who'd wondered why somebody like me had something like that had let the Corpses know about it. They'd busted me for stolen goods. I'd spent the next four months of nights in a meter-high detention coffin, the days cleaning urinals or down on my hands and knees scrubbing the lightblocks of Oldcity's glowing pavements with a brush, wearing a monitored stun collar locked around my throat. And that had really seemed to last forever.

It hadn't been worth it. I hadn't even been able to stomach thinking about the memory afterwards. I hadn't thought about it in years. It surprised me that I'd remembered it now; almost as much as it would have surprised me then to know that someday I'd be sitting here, five hundred light-years away, on this riverbank in the sun with a couple of rich kids.

"If that's your favorite thing, you don't look very happy about it," Jiro said. *Doubt, confusion, disappointment* flickered through his thoughts like a chain reaction.

"It was a long time ago." I shrugged, and got up. "Why is it so hot here? I thought it was almost winter." On the distant mountainside the autumn colors were burning like a fire, but all around us in the valley it was still warm and green.

"It's part of the system." Jiro scrambled to his feet while I pushed my boots on. "You know—the security and everything. It never gets real hot or real cold, everybody likes it like that. It never snows down here."

I shook my head, half smiling. If you wanted your life to be a long summer afternoon here, all you had to do was say so. . . . "What if you want snow?"

"You can go to the chalet."

I didn't bother to ask what that was.

"Let's go to Daric's house. Argentyne is there—"

"No thanks." I didn't think there was anybody in the universe who could make me want to visit Daric.

"But she's famous! Don't you want to meet her?"

That was all I needed. I shook my head, tying my shirt sleeves around my neck. "Come on, Talitha. I'll take you back." She got up, resigned, and let me set her on the pony's back again. Jiro put his wings on, looking sullen. "You're going to get it, Tally—look what you did." He pointed at her muddy clothes, glanced at me as if it was my fault. Talitha pouted. Jiro ran and leaped, rising into the air like a kite. He circled us a couple of times as we plodded back across the field. Then he headed away toward Daric's house, alone. I felt kind of sorry for him; but not sorry enough to change my mind.

I led Talitha back toward the house. Nanny got up from a garden seat like a shadow and came to take her away. She caught one look at a muddy leg. "My Lady—!" she called. Lazuli came down off of the porch into the sunlight, shielding her eyes.

"Mother! Mother!" Talitha squealed, bouncing up and down in her saddle with a grin so guiltless and wide I almost didn't regret anything.

Lazuli looked at her, and at me, and I felt her try for anger, only

finding laughter. "I guess you are an anarchist, after all," she said to
me. It was what Isplanasky had called me, yesterday. I winced. "Oh,
come on, Nanny." Lazuli looked back at the older woman. "It's only a
little bit of mud. Reality doesn't frighten us that much around here—"
The irony in her voice surprised me. Even she wasn't sure how she
meant it.

Nanny sighed heavily, and led Talitha, skipping and waving, into the
house.

"Jiro is with Gentleman Daric, ma'am." So she wouldn't think I'd
drowned him.

Lazuli turned back to me. She glanced down at the half-wilted bunch
of flowers in my hand, as the pony I was somehow still holding started
to eat them. I held them away from its mouth.

"Are those for me?" she asked, still half mocking, and half surprised.

"Uh . . . yeah." I put them into her hands. "From Talitha."

She took them, still looking up at me as she held them close to her
face, breathing in the sweet smell. An odd disappointment tickled the
back of her eyes, making her blink.

Suddenly feeling like an ass, I said, "And from me too, I guess."

"Thank you." She smiled then, tucking the flowers into the waist-
band of her flowered tunic. Her legs were bare, and perfect. She took
the pony's lead rope from my hand, her fingers touching mine. "Let me
take that. You look like you want to be rid of it. . . . You're very good
with children, and it's kind of you to spend time with mine." She began
to lead Bootsie away, looking at me all the while. Wanting me to follow.

I followed. "They're nice kids," I said, because I had to say something, and because I suddenly realized it was true. *Sad kids.* But I didn't
say that. I thought about them growing up into the next generation of
the Centauri controlling board.

She was silent for a while, walking beside me. "I love them so much,"
she said at last, the words forced out past something in her throat.
"Sometimes I begin to lose my perspective about things when . . .
things close in on me. I don't want to turn around someday and find
that I've lost them. When I think about that, when I even try to imagine
being without them, I don't think I could bear it. . . ." She was thinking about her first husband. "You look at me so strangely sometimes,
Cat." She looked back at me, quizzical and embarrassed.

I blinked and shook my head. "It's just that sometimes you look so
much like Jule . . . ma'am."

"Oh, Jule . . ." She glanced away, stopped. Someone came toward us from the low stone outbuildings, and took the pony. "She's married now, isn't she?" She looked at me again, a sudden questioning look, like she wished she could read my mind. "To another psion?"

"Yes, ma'am." I remembered that she didn't know what I was. When she looked at me all she saw was a human face.

"Don't call me ma'am," she said gently, "it makes me feel old. Call me Lazuli."

I nodded, suddenly not able to say anything at all.

She smiled again, as if she knew it. "Will you walk with me a while? It's such a beautiful day, and no one gets enough exercise around here."

"Except Lady Elnear," I said.

She laughed. "I like the way your mind works."

I wondered what she'd think of it if she really knew, the way Jule did. . . . "Did you know Jule very well?"

"No." She shook her head. "Barely at all. I've only heard about her. Stories . . ." *Not good ones.* "Poor thing." She was thinking her cousin must be happier now. With her own kind.

"She doesn't need anybody's pity," I said.

Lazuli glanced at me. "I'm sorry. You really do care about Jule, don't you?"

I nodded, still not quite able to call her by name.

"Did you love her . . . do you?"

Irritation and sudden memory spilled into each other in my mind, oil and water. "She's my best friend." Telling the truth. Part of it. Once I'd looked at her and wanted her body, thinking that was all love was. But then I'd shared her mind. Siebeling had taught me a lot of things, he'd given me my psi; but Jule had given me the real gift. She'd made me whole. She'd changed everything I knew about women, and men, and myself. And I'd finally realized that I didn't love her the same way Siebeling did . . . that to be her friend was all I really wanted from her, all I really needed.

I felt Lazuli's curiosity withdraw; but her hand still held onto my arm. And she was still too much like Jule when I looked at her . . . but not enough like her to keep me safe. We walked along the shadow of the high stone wall; private, discreet. "It takes a lot of . . . courage, to be that close to someone most people would be afraid of," she said.

I made a sound like a laugh, that wasn't. "She was more afraid of all of you. And she had more right to be."

She was silent then, wondering whether she'd really understood me, or whether I was leaving too much unsaid on purpose. My bare arm

under her hand was slippery with sweat; the heat of the day seemed to
breathe on us. I felt a tension rising in her that had nothing to do with
the conversation. I felt it rising in me, too, as I realized what it was.

"Is something wrong?" she asked, finally.

I shook my head. "I . . . just a headache. Comes and goes. It's all
right—"

But she led me to a wooden bench along the bright edge of the
gardens, and made me sit down. The air was filled with the hum of
insects. "Sometimes if you rub the temples, just here . . ." she murmured. I felt her fingertips against my sweating forehead, moving in
slow, gentle circles. . . . Her face, her hair—too familiar—her lips almost touching mine, the smell of flowers and sunwarmed skin . . .
Suddenly I couldn't look away from her eyes, because I could see all the
way through to what lay behind them. "Is that better?" she murmured.
She took her hands away, and that was worse.

"Yes," I mumbled.

One hand still hovered, touching the white line of the scar over my
left eye. It dropped down to trace another jagged line along my ribs.
"You have a fine body," she said, "but you haven't taken care of it. You
should treat it more gently—it has to last for a long time."

"I know." My head wasn't the only part of it that ached now.

"When you're so young, you think that everything lasts." She looked
away.

"No," I said. "I know it doesn't. Lazuli—"

"Cat!"

I jerked around on the bench, looking up. I could just see Elnear
standing on the balcony of her study, staring straight down at us.

"Would you come inside please?"

I pushed to my feet, the spell broken that had stopped time, stopped
thought inside me. I left Lazuli there, backing away until I could make
myself turn and walk looking ahead toward the house.

I went up the steps, through the door, into the cool shadowy hall,
blinking as I followed it to Elnear's study. My mind was still lost somewhere back along the path from the garden. I didn't know what Elnear
was going to say to me; worse, I didn't know how I was going to answer
it. "Ma'am?" I said at last, my voice hoarse, as I stopped in her doorway.

Elnear turned away from the windows. She came toward me, silhouetted by the light. At first I couldn't make out her expression. But I felt
it.

"I don't know what you think you are doing here," she said, not even bothering with the usual polite pretensions. "But you are not here to insinuate yourself into the private lives of this family. I will not have you using your—telepathy," she said it like an obscenity, "to take advantage of children, or of a troubled woman who doesn't know what she wants."

I felt my face burning. "I wasn't—" I broke off, realizing that it was no use. That true or not, nothing I could say would make any difference to her. And that was the worst part of all. "I don't understand it," I said, finally.

"What don't you understand?" She kept the length of a long tabletop inlaid with stars between us, and a wall of *anger contempt fear.*

"Why Jule thought you loved her. She asked me to help you because she said you were the only one who ever loved her. That's the real reason I came here—because she asked me to. You must have hated her just as much as everyone else did."

Her mouth worked; she wanted to blame me for the pain that was suddenly there inside her, but she couldn't. She turned away, looking at something across the room. Her husband's picture. She said, her voice almost inaudible, "Jule was so helpless . . . so lost . . . she needed someone so much, someone who would love her unconditionally. . . ." She looked back at me, and suddenly in her mind there was the unwanted image of how I'd looked that first day, as she'd left me standing there alone in the sunroom. "Jule was different."

I turned, moving too fast because I wanted to get away from her so much. My shirt caught on the outstretched arm of a sculpture standing by the doorway. I heard cloth rip as it jerked me up short; the loose-knotted sleeves came undone around my neck, and my shirt dropped to the carpet. I leaned down, grabbed it up, swearing. It was torn right across the front.

"Cat." Elnear's voice caught at me like the sculpture's arm.

I straightened up, the shirt wadded between my fists, facing away from her.

"How . . . who did that to your back?"

"Nobody." I took a step.

"Cat."

"Ask Isplanasky." I turned to face her again. "I got out of Contract Labor with my skin intact, right? So there's nothing wrong with my back." I threw my ruined shirt over my shoulders, tied it in a knot again, covering my scars.

"That happened to you while you worked for Contract Labor?" Not really a question. "I have heard that some of the combines treat their laborers badly," she said, awkwardly. "The FTA tries to maintain—"

"The FTA did this to me." I remembered how it had felt as the charged prod laid a line of liquid fire across my naked back, and another, and another. "At the Federation Mines, out in the Crab Colonies . . . If it hadn't been for Jule paying off my contract, I wouldn't be standing here right now. Forty-five percent of the bondies there don't live long enough to last out their time. But you probably never access that kind of information."

She looked at me for what seemed like hours, bracing herself by her hand on the back of a chair . . . looked at me and thought about my words, and looked, and thought . . . like someone looking at a square with five sides. At last she said, "I understand now why you said what you did yesterday. But I don't understand how it could happen. Natan would never allow—"

"You said it yourself. Humans don't run the FTA; it runs itself. Isplanasky doesn't run the Federation Mines—he doesn't even run Contract Labor, any more than I do."

She'd said it, but she hadn't heard what she was saying. "But the whole reason the FTA exists is to protect the welfare of . . . of the dispossessed," she said. "Not to create more suffering. Why should it exploit with one hand as it stops exploitation with the other?" There was no echo of recognition in her mind; she was so deep inside her own vision of her work that she couldn't see anything else.

"Do you eat meat?" I said.

She looked at me blankly. "Yes, I do."

"But you consider yourself a moral person, right? You love animals, you have them for pets, you'd never kick a dog in the street. How do you justify eating meat?"

"I . . ." Her face reddened. "I have to eat to survive."

"Jule never eats meat."

She looked away, her fingers stretching open at her sides. I wondered which of us was more surprised by this conversation.

"Okay," I said, "so maybe the FTA even considers itself a moral being. You called it a Humane Society for humans. But it's got to eat. And eating meat is easier."

One hand rose to her head, ruffling her hair. "Your point, Cat," she murmured, finally. "A point well taken. I will speak with Natan about it, when I get the chance."

"You really think that'll make any difference?"

She frowned slightly; the frown faded. "Individuals have been known to change their minds. Even on such a scale. But they need input, information. Just as you said."

"Is that why you're doing this debate?" I'd wondered why she bothered, if she didn't think that what individual humans wanted or believed made any difference any more. Maybe it explained why she wanted to be on the Security Council too; maybe her reasons really went deeper than just wanting power, or to escape from the taMings. "You really think there are some ways you can still matter?"

"I suppose I do." She nodded, but she wasn't sure of anything now, not even of why she really wanted that Council slot. She moved back toward the windows, the bright heat of anger gone out of her, her movements slow and almost aimless. She wanted me to go away. It was what I wanted, too, but somehow I couldn't. I couldn't let go of that invisible line between us that neither of us knew how to snap.

She stared down at the gardens, outlined by the light. Lazuli was gone; gone from sight, but not from her thoughts. "How is Jule?" she asked at last. "What is her life like now, with Dr. Siebeling? Is she finally, truly happy?"

"As happy as anybody ever is, I guess." I crossed the room until I stood beside her on the balcony. But not too close. "She and Siebeling have a little place upside in Quarro. She's got it full of stray animals . . . she can't leave anything alone that needs help. Doc just steps over them, and smiles." I'd been her first stray. After he'd learned to live with me, he hadn't minded the rest. "Siebeling's good for her. She's good for him. They have a place in Oldcity were they help other psions to pull their lives back together, like they did for themselves . . . and for me."

"I'm so glad." She was. I felt her thoughts begin to find a center, an anchor, in the image of Jule smiling, helping others to smile. Maybe there was still hope after all, even for herself. . . . She glanced back at me, her eyes questioning.

"Have you ever been to Quarro, ma'am?" Asking it before she could ask a question nobody really wanted answered right now.

"Yes, many times. I keep a house in Quarro."

"You ever go to the Hanging Gardens there?" It gave me a chance to look away from her, out at these gardens again. When I'd first seen the Hanging Gardens, when I was sixteen or seventeen, I couldn't believe that what I saw was natural, barely even believed it was real. I remem-

bered the colors had been too bright, the forms too incredible, the rich
sweet perfume of the flowers too intense. The Gardens rimmed the
access well that was the only way in or out of Oldcity. They'd been
right over my head all my life, always just out of reach.

"It's a beautiful place," Elnear said. "Some of the most exquisite
gardens I've ever seen."

"It's beautiful here, too. Sometimes it reminds me of . . . of
Quarro." I couldn't quite make myself say "home."

"Does it?" She looked surprised, looked out at her own gardens
again. "I guess you have to be a stranger to a place to really see its
beauty."

"Did you ever look over the edge when you were there at the Gardens?"

"Over the edge?" she asked, trying to imagine what I was talking
about.

"Into the Tank. Into Oldcity."

She shook her head. "No."

"You have to live in a place to really know its ugliness."

"Yes." Suddenly she wasn't seeing the gardens any more. Sorrow
settled over her, graying her mind, sloping her shoulders, until I was
sorry I'd said it. "I must get back to my work." She meant getting ready
to face Stryger in the debate, to defend her belief in the FTA's incor-
ruptibility (she glanced at me as she turned away from the window), to
take another step toward a slot on the Security Council, and away from
here, the taMings, Centauri—this trap that her world had become. "If
you'll excuse me . . ."

"Ma'am—" I said. She turned back. "I hate Centauri nearly as much
as you do. I . . ." as she looked at me, "I just wanted you to know
that. Braedee won't hear anything from me again that you don't clear
first."

Suddenly she was remembering what I'd said about the real reason
why I'd come here to work for her; suddenly she was really hearing it.
She looked down, moving random objects randomly on her desk: a
statue of a child, a glass ball with a fragile puffball flower suspended
impossibly inside it. . . . For just a second I stared at it, because the
ball looked so much like something I'd had once: a Hydran thing, full
of hidden secrets, that had felt warm and almost alive when I held it in
my hands. . . . But that was gone; this was only a cold ball made of

glass, with an image inside it that never changed. Like a memory. She looked up again, and caught me still staring. I turned away from the look in her eyes and went out of the room without saying anything more.

10

SOME DWEEB ONCE said to me, "Cheer up. Things could always be worse." He was right about that much.

The face debate on drug deregulation was set for late afternoon the next day. I got to the place where it was going to happen about midday, before Elnear and Jardan, working with Braedee's Security crew this time. I'd had to argue Braedee into letting me come. I wasn't sure whether it was the news that Daric knew about me, or the trouble I'd caused in Isplanasky's office, or just his own fear of psions that made him try to tell me that before Elnear got there I didn't matter. He finally gave in, the way someone would stop chasing a fly because it wasn't important enough to waste time on.

The floating Independent News studio had been set up inside a historic landmark deep in the heart of N'Yuk. It was a thick-walled building made of gray stone that had been a godshouse before the Re-creation. Since the Indy couldn't count on an interplanetary freighter to crash-land during the debate, they'd wanted to give the viewers something to look at besides heads if their attention wandered. When I walked in, it was like walking into a kaleidoscope. The tall, arching windows along the side walls were made of thousands of bits of colored glass fused together, pictures of paradise painted from fragments of pure light. The Indy production crew had backlit them all for perfect effect, and rainbows of color bled into the stagnant air above the stage.

It had been Stryger's idea to have this debate; but the Indy News had made it a reality. They'd even gotten an exclusive lock on it. They were plugging a lot of other vips into the same circuits with Stryger, so that curious citizens all over the Federation could get close to them in a way they didn't get to very often—while they were simply speaking their minds, not sending hidden messages through channels that only they could access. With all the publicity support Stryger had gotten, the ratings for this event would probably be astronomical. Everybody in-

volved with it hoped they would be. The thousands of channels that
wove the Net's million separate corporate systems into something like a
coherent whole were mostly there to keep their citizens amused; but
they were also a way that combines too paranoid to communicate directly could send out messages under a white flag to each other, and to
the rest of the galaxy.

Shander Mandragora was moderating the debate. Mandragora was
the Indy's most popular fax hyper; even I knew who he was. He covered
anything important the Federation Assembly did, and what they did
was always important to somebody. Other hypers, from more combine
networks than anybody knew existed, had been crawling all over the
floating studio where the debate was set since before dawn that morning. Most of them were bitching about the Indy's calculated generosity
in letting them help it spread its logo all over their private systems.

The media techs were easy to spot—their attitude was *if you got it,
flaunt it.* They wore their cyber equipment openly as they swaggered
past; third eyes and hand-cameras, all their senses wired to record. Like
street gangs, they liked the idea of standing out from the crowd. It gave
them a special power, like psi . . . but it was one the combines wanted
and needed, so it made them different, but it didn't make them freaks. I
felt a kind of jealousy as I watched them, the easy arrogance their
portable territory gave them.

After a while the debaters themselves finally began to arrive. Besides
Stryger and Elnear, the main draws in this particular infotainment,
there was Isplanasky repping the FTA, three Assembly members front-
ing various combine blocs, and a couple of Corporate Security Chiefs.
Stryger came in first with his band of ass-kissing disciples, carrying his
walking stick in his hand. *Sojourner* meant *seeker.* He always carried
the staff, as a kind of symbol of his journey. The wash of colored light
from the windows only made him look more beautiful. There was no
doubt in his mind that he was going to make this day his. He was in his
element; I wondered if somehow he'd had something to do with them
choosing this place for the debate.

He spotted me in the crowd, almost as if he could feel me staring at
him, feel my hatred, or my fascination. . . . He saw me, and suddenly
his confidence screamed, rattling through my skull.

I stood there watching while he stopped his forward momentum,
lifting his staff to stop the momentum of everyone around him as he saw
me. They swirled to a halt in a kind of confused slow motion while he
looked into my eyes and thought, *(I know you're listening. . . .)* The

words were fuzzy and shapeless, formed by a mind without any sensitivity to the Gift, but clear enough. He raised his staff to me in a kind of benediction, and smiled, as if he knew some secret that only we two shared. *(Bless you, boy, you are the answer to all my prayers.)* He smiled, a smile so sweet it should have been a lover's, a smile that leered at me like a slashed throat. I wanted to use my psi on him, to find out what he meant by that—to see his smug face crack, to feel his *loathing, disgust, raw hatred*—anything but what I felt inside him now. But his confidence was real, and it turned my concentration to random noise. At last he looked away from me and went on, setting me free to slink off like a coward and lose myself in the crowd of techs.

Elnear came in with Jardan a few minutes later, and the media imageshapers crawled all over her like bugs, like they'd done with the rest. Only Stryger had his own personal image crew. I sat in a corner close by Elnear, trying to make myself invisible while I kept track of the swarms of hypers buzzing around her. She was wearing a bodyguard, like all the speakers, but I did my job anyway. Now and then Jardan sent me to fetch something or someone, her voice like a barbed whip; waiting for me to do something half-assed again. Isplanasky stopped by for some kind of last minute exchange, and glanced at me like he expected me to explode. But as he passed me on his way out he said, "I want to see you later." At least it didn't sound like a threat.

Finally every piece was pushed into place. I settled onto one of the hard historical benches beside Jardan, herded together by Security with all the other aides and hangers-on and hypers. Up on the stage the speakers seemed to float above the curving band of light that was their mutual podium, flowing into the sea of light behind them. I wondered how anyone would be able to concentrate on anything but that light. The words had better be good.

They were good. I leaned back, listening to one speaker after another, the talking heads that gave human faces to the beliefs and policies of faceless economic networks. These people had been chosen because they knew how to come across well—and because, whatever they were saying about the deregulation of pentryptine, that it was a disaster or a blessing or didn't really matter in the Great Motion of Time, they believed it. They were all augmented, and they were plugged into Mandragora, letting him monitor their sincerity electronically. The viewers could readout for themselves exactly how much to trust what they saw and heard. Even Isplanasky came across clean and sincere in everything he said.

But in the end it all came down to Elnear and Stryger, the unspoken rivalry between them, the opening on the Security Council that they both wanted. Nobody was saying anything about it, not yet anyway, but everyone knew: all the hypers waiting with their questions and their prefab points of view, the Federation Assembly members, the Security Council itself. They'd all be weighing the impression the speakers made, their impact on the audience . . . the leverage they could get on the Assembly, which would prove their strength when the votes on deregulation were counted. Deregulation was still being data-modeled by an Assembly special committee. But Elnear—and everyone else—knew that the committee would approve it in the next few days. And the way things stood the measure was almost as sure to pass on the Assembly floor.

Isplanasky finished his speech and Mandragora gave the audience to Elnear at last. She looked out over the crowd, her eyes searching their faces as if she was looking for someone; but there was too much light. She looked at Mandragora again. "I had a very unusual conversation yesterday," she said. "With someone who asked me why I was participating in this debate, when I had told him that I thought individual human beings no longer had control of the Federation's fate, that our lives were ruled by the whims of interstellar commerce. . . ."

I leaned forward in sudden surprise. Jardan glanced over at me, irritated.

"I told him that I would be here today because I believed that even something on the scale of the Federation Assembly or a multiworld combine could still be influenced, if the evidence had enough weight, enough public opinion behind it pushing. I know that there are enough individual citizens inputting us here to influence the courses chosen by even such gigantic systems. You have the access right in your hands to register your opinion on the open Net. I want you to do that, whatever your decision is, so that you can see the power you still have, if you choose to use it.

"Because yesterday this person asked me some other questions, hard questions about the things I believed in. The Federation he knows is a very different place from the one I know. It made me realize how easy it is to dismiss a problem that doesn't seem to touch you directly—how deceptive, how dangerous. He also said to me that 'you have to know a place to really see its ugliness.' . . . Well, I know the biochem business."

I listened as she went on speaking, telling them her vision of what letting these chemicals loose could do to the individual human identities of the billions of people receiving her, and how easily it could be done. Telling everyone that she was on the board of a drug combine that held the major patents on those drugs. That it would make profits off of them that would bloat ChemEnGen (and Centauri, although she didn't mention it by name). Telling the Federation that she still couldn't accept the promises that had been made about safety, because she knew too well how much promises were worth. . . . The words weren't that different from the ones Isplanasky had spoken; but there was a heat behind them that seared them into your brain. As if this wasn't just a matter of ideology, but something she felt as responsible for as her own life. As if those invisible billions were her own family, her children. . . .

Jardan sat silently beside me, her eyes on Elnear, her face shining with pride and reflected light. All the speakers had been good, but Elnear was genuine, original—the best.

But she wasn't the last. I looked at Stryger as Mandragora introduced him, and all the eyes in the room, real or recording, began to focus on him. He was the only one who seemed to belong here. His face was as translucent and glowing as the air, radiating the intensity of his own belief, in himself, in the divine power he thought was speaking through him. If this place hadn't been chosen just to suit him, it might as well have been. He began to speak: strong but easy words, nothing about God or damnation; letting the listeners know he wasn't a fanatic, or a combine vip, but just a concerned Everybody.

I tried not to listen to what he was saying or to look at him, and yet my glance kept falling out of the air, away from the windows, back to his face again. Party because I couldn't help hating him; and partly because, like the last time, I just couldn't look away. Maybe absolute confidence gave you that kind of gravitational pull, or maybe it was just the fanatic's intensity he'd been born with. But I kept watching, kept listening, as his speech slowly sucked a billion minds into the "dark underside of life" that he claimed to understand, like he really knew anything about it. . . . *About killing to stay alive, about stealing to keep from starving, about making ten credits the hard way, and using it to buy enough drugs to help you forget what you'd just done to earn it.* . . . Talking about how *his* drugs could "let the light" into the minds and lives of all those deeves and pervs and psions (and there was no change in his voice, as if he didn't really hate psions any more than murderers or rapists)—those trouble-makers who still kept crawling out of the cracks to violate humanity, kept it from running like a perfect machine,

when we had the means within our grasp to change all that forever—
His voice was ringing now, his eyes were smoking, but I could feel him
still in perfect control of the rising spiral.

And there was nothing at all on the readout below him, nothing that
would prove to anyone watching whether he meant every word of it or
not. *He wasn't cybered,* Isplanasky had said. He had no way to tie into
the Indy's system. But somehow, instead of making him seem like he
had something to hide, it only made him seem to be above all that, so
goddamn pure that he didn't need to prove his sincerity to anyone.

". . . Lady Elnear is concerned that deregulating the production of
these drugs might lead to their misuse. . . ."

I looked up again, as I heard him mention Elnear.

". . . But I believe that it would be taking them *out* of the hands of
those people who already misuse and abuse them . . . the criminals
who now produce and illegally sell tiny quantities of these drugs for
astronomical prices on the Lack Market. To defend the laws that force
these drugs into the hands of those very criminals who are now the only
ones who profit from them financially is hardly in anyone's best interest.
They are the ones who could profit the most morally if the drugs were
used as they were meant to be used.

"To suggest, as Lady Elnear has, that using these drugs for the purpose God intended is evil can only be called misguided. To say that the
combine networks that provide for all our needs are worse than the
criminals that exploit us is irresponsible. I have always believed that
Lady Elnear was sincere in her unflinching crusade to create a more
humane society—

"But now I must question you, Lady." He turned to face her, violating the structure of the debate, which was supposed to leave Mandragora in charge of asking the questions. "Are you not in fact protecting
the deviants in our society, protecting those degenerates you claim to
detest as much as I do?"

Elnear looked at him, startled, caught off-guard. "Of course not. I'm
sure you know that that was not my point at all—"

"It has come to my attention, Lady Elnear, that you actually have a
psion, a Hydran halfbreed, a telepath, employed on your personal staff.
Isn't that true?"

Elnear flushed; for a second her gaze left Stryger's face, flashed out
over the watchers. The readouts jumped and changed colors below her.
"Well . . . yes, I do . . . but—" Beside me Jardan murmured a
curse. I felt her sudden useless fury as she looked at me.

"What possible reason could you have for employing a member of a group known for its instability and criminality, its destructive effect on society? I hardly need to remind anyone here of what would have happened to the Federation if the psionic renegade called Quicksilver had successfully seized control of the Federation Mines, only three years ago—"

"I don't believe in holding an entire group responsible for the actions of a few of its members," Elnear said. She recovered fast. "There is a long history of persecution of psions—both Hydran and human—by the Federation. I have always tried to judge individuals on their own abilities."

"This individual, who serves as your personal aide, has a criminal record. Were you aware that he was one of the psions who conspired with the terrorist Quicksilver to hold the Federation's telhassium supply for ransom?"

Elnear broke off again, her mouth still halfway open for speech. "No, I wasn't aware. . . ."

"His record also includes assault, theft, and drug abuse . . . an all too typical record. . . ."

I swore softly. *How the hell did he find out?* It wasn't in the public records. And he was making me out to be a traitor, and that was a goddamn lie. I wanted to shout it out to Elnear, to the whole Federation—

Jardan caught my arm as I started to get up, jerking me around. "Move!" she hissed at me. I felt her rage transfer through her hand and up my arm, into my head. "Before you do any more damage."

"But it's a lie—"

"Shut up, you fool." She dragged me toward the closest exit, her mind a nightmare of what would happen if those hypers gathered like a pack of dogs around us got hold of me.

"It's hard for me to believe that with the security access available to you, you wouldn't have known about such a thing," Stryger was baying. "How you could possibly consider such a person suitable to work for you, unless there was some other reason. . . ."

I didn't give Jardan any more argument; I just followed, as fast as I could, keeping my head down until we reached the door. The door read our IDs and released, letting us out without any trouble.

"There were unusual circumstances. . . ." I heard Elnear protesting, felt her rising desperation drowned in my mind by the rising excitement of the crowd. And then the door sealed shut behind us, cutting off her voice, and that was the last I heard.

The cold, sheer-walled tunnel of street was silent and empty, except for the floating banks of lights high above us. Security had cleared everything for levels around before the debate started. As we stopped outside Jardan turned suddenly, before I even had time to react, and hit me.

"Damn it, Jardan—" I gasped.

"God damn you!" I saw the furious tears backing up in her eyes. She said, "The worst part is that Stryger is right about psions!"

"Wait a minute—" Pain began to throb behind my own eyes, frustration trying to beat its way out.

A mod dropped down from somewhere, answering her summons. ChemEnGen's logo was on its side. She climed into it; tried to slam the door on me. I forced it open again. She let me in, but only because she remembered how much worse it would be for Elnear if she left me there for the hypers to find. She sat back in her seat, pressing into the formfoam. The mod began to drone, "Destination please, destination please, destination please," until she finally gave it orders.

"Damn it," I said. "It's Stryger, not me!"

She looked back at me, wiping fiercely at her face. "If you didn't exist, there was nothing he could have done to her—nothing. That was true, what he said about you. Wasn't it—?" Her hand tightened into a fist.

"No! He twisted it around. I'm not a traitor."

"You don't have a criminal record?"

"Yeah, but. . . ." *But nobody was supposed to know that. . . . It wasn't my fault. . . .* I shook my head. It didn't matter. I'd lost Elnear the debate, any maybe the vote, and the Council . . . her freedom, the freedom of every psion. By being a psion. The answer to Stryger's prayers.

I shut my eyes, put my hands over my ears, bit my lip, stopped breathing. . . . To keep my brain from screaming out loud. The pain circled my head like a knotted cord, tightening . . . eased off as I slowly got myself under control again. After a few more deep breaths, I opened my eyes.

Jardan was rigid in her seat, staring at me like she thought she was trapped with a lunatic. I lowered my hands, wove my fingers together in the space between my knees to steady them. She looked away from me finally, wishing we were already at our destination, wishing I'd disappear.

The mod went on silently through the hollow streets, the endless muted silvers and grays, blue-greens and golds, the steel and composite caverns. We flowed through the arteries and veins of a fossilized insect sealed in high-tech amber, heading toward some destination I didn't have any control over. We'd been supposed to go back to the FTA plex after the debate; but that wasn't really an option, now. I wondered how much longer the questions would go on behind us, how long Elnear would have to face them down. I began to sweat just thinking about having those bloodsucking hypers after my throat. I wondered where we were going, where Jardan thought she could hide me from them.

At last we funneled into one of the arching legs that straddled the river on the western edge of the city. The inner skin of the tube was fleshed with more city, with offices and townhouses. The mod homed in on one of them, tracking its electronic scent like a hound until we were setting down on a terrace somewhere high above the river. A taMing townhouse. I remembered that there was going to be a reception here tonight, for Elnear, after the debate. More like a funeral, now. Until now, Elnear's biggest worry about tonight had been that parties wasted her time.

I couldn't look down along the glass-smooth, green/black building front as we crossed the black mirror of the polished terrace. Looking up along its curve was nearly as bad. I followed Jardan in through the high, lacquered doors, into a dark entry hall. Clatter and conversation reached us from a distance; I could feel the electricity of minds overloading with last-minute preparation for tonight. But here, just inside the entrance, it was still quiet, and we were still alone.

Jardan turned on me, hard-eyed. Her hand gripped my arm until it spasmed. "Follow me. Say *nothing.*" She led me through the townhouse, avoiding everyone as she took me up in a lift three or four levels. She left me in a cramped, stuffy room that passed for a study, even though I knew by the dead smell of the air that no one ever used it. "Keep the door locked. Speak to no one, until the Lady has spoken to you. Do you understand me?"

I nodded, and she left me there alone. I stood in the middle of the room, without even the strength to move, staring around me. The room was high and narrow, like everything about this place. At its end there was a high, narrow window. Outside the early evening light was slanting across the river; shadows were filling in the valleys of the city's carapace. The space around me was filled with a fungal growth of pale, diseased-looking furniture.

I hated the thought of touching anything, afraid it might crumble away like rotting wood, but after a while I got tired of standing. I went toward the window, sat down on the quivering edge of a shelfseat. I couldn't hear any sounds now. I stared out at the view of the sheer, shining city wall, the gray-blue river waters rolling by below. A few hours ago it would have seemed beautiful to me; but suddenly nothing looked like it had before.

I sat and thought about the time when the most important thing in my life had been whether I could scrounge enough food to make it through another week; when all I'd cared about was slipping enough stolen goods to a freedrop to make what I owed to the dealerman; when a tough problem was finding a warm place to sleep at night. When everything was simple: Life, or death. . . . I slumped forward, letting my aching head rest in my hands. *When I hadn't understood why somebody only had to look at me to hate me.*

I stayed like that, waiting, while the sky slowly changed beyond the windows and the world blued over . . . until the day was teetering on the edge of night. Then at last I heard the soft sucking sound as the door opened, and Elnear came into the room.

11

I HEARD THE mingled voices of people passing in the hall behind Elnear; all sound stopped as she closed the door. I got up, while light oozed out of hidden crannies in the walls. Elnear stood where she was, her body rigid. The anger and betrayal she felt as she faced me at last forced its way in through all my senses. There was nothing soft or weak about her now . . . like understanding, or sympathy, or even pity. I could forget about those. Finally she said, "I hope that Centauri is satisfied. Your presence in my life turned today's debate into a disaster —an exercise in futility. We will certainly lose the upcoming vote on deregulation now." Which meant she'd lose the Security Council slot too; she didn't even need to mention that. "Because of you." Or that either, but she did.

I looked away at the deepening indigo of the sky, back at her. We were both too visible, there was no hiding place, standing here inside this lens of light. I didn't answer, looking at the floor now.

"You're usually quicker on your feet." There was a tone in her voice I'd never heard before. "Aren't you going to argue with me? At least you usually argue with me. A good saboteur always tries to cover his work, I thought. But then, I suppose your real job is done. And I thought you were only sent here to spy on me."

I looked up. "That ain't—*isn't* what I'm here for, goddamn it. It's not my fault Stryger hates psions. I didn't tell him to nail me!"

"You could at least have told me," she said, her voice cold, "that you were a criminal."

"I'm not—" I shook my head. "Stryger twisted everything around. I was pardoned. I'm clean. My record was sealed, buried, nobody can access it any more. I don't even know how he found out—"

"Anyone can find out anything, with the right contacts. And he certainly has them." She threw the wrap she was carrying down onto the couch. She began to move restlessly back and forth, glancing at me as she moved. "The worst part of the entire ordeal was being accused of conspiring with criminals—as if by attempting to keep these drugs restricted, I want to afflict all of humanity with a plague of degenerates and sociopaths!" Her open hand came down on a tabletop, hard. "I had to agree with him, grant him his point, or look like a liar as well as a hypocrite . . . because of course I agree that criminal behavior and deviancy should be controlled—"

"You mean, like psions? Isn't it enough they can't get hired for most kinds of work? Ain't it enough they get drugwiped if they ever get caught using their psi to commit a crime? Stryger wants them drugwiped the minute they're born. That's why he wants pentryptine deregulated. That's why he wants to be on the Security Council. So then he can have 'em all put in relocation dumps, and then he can make it illegal for them to breathe—" My voice broke. It had already happened to the Hydrans . . . it had happened to my mother. Now Stryger wanted to make it happen to anybody with a single psi gene drowned in their chromosome pool. I knew what he wanted . . . I *knew*. I pulled my voice back together. "You said up there that psions deserved to be judged like everybody else, one on one. I almost thought you believed it. You could've pushed harder, you could've fought him—"

Except that after what he'd said, calling me a criminal and a traitor, she hadn't wanted to. *Stryger was right.* The same thought, the same betrayal and disgust as I'd seen in Jardan's mind. "You brought this on yourself."

"Half of what he said about me was lies. You believed him, without even makin' him prove it. Yesterday, I thought you. . . ." My empty hands made fists. "Why?"

"Because what he said about psions is true," she snapped. "Psions are mentally unstable, sociopaths—harming themselves as well as the people around them." Thinking of Jule, thinking of me . . . the only psions she'd ever seen. But she knew the stereotype: psions were all floaters, freaks, head cases. We'd only proved the point. "Perhaps they would be better off if their . . . powers were under some kind of control. . . ." Now she was the one who wouldn't meet my eyes. Some part of her knew even as she said it that it wasn't right, or just; that it denied everything she had always thought she believed. But she couldn't help herself . . . and her guilt only gave her resentment more strength.

"That's what Jule and Siebeling are trying to do," I said; trying not to reach out to her mind, not to try to *make* her see. Knowing that that would be the worst thing I could do. "To teach psions how to control their own Gift. Like Siebeling did with me, and Jule. That's how to stop them from getting into trouble. They're not animals—"

"If all psions were in complete control of their abilities, they would only be tempted to use them against others. Power is the strongest drug of all. You worked for that terrorist Quicksilver." Parroting Stryger again, the memory burning in her eyes. "He would have crippled the FTA, and torn the entire Federation apart if he hadn't been stopped—"

"How do you think the FTA stopped him?"

She didn't answer. She didn't know.

"They used psions! Siebeling, Jule, me, a bunch of others. That's when I met her. That's what I was doing out there on Cinder, at the mines. Ask Jule—" She didn't even know that. All she knew, all any of them still remembered, was that a psion terrorist had nearly brought down the Federation single-handed.

"Quicksilver didn't do it alone," I said. "He wasn't some kind of crazy god. He had plenty of combines backing him. Just like Stryger. But we still stopped him—Jule, and Siebeling, and me." I held up my fist. "I killed Quicksilver myself. I felt him die inside me, and that's why I can't use my psi any more unless I'm so drugged up I can't remember his pain." I felt tears spill out of my eyes, so suddenly that I didn't have a chance of stopping them. They burned my face like acid, like they hadn't done in years, not since the moment after the killing when I'd realized what I'd done, to him, to myself. When I'd looked into my own mind and seen the nothing hole I'd made of somebody else with my telepathy and a gun: a wound bleeding hate and terror, a wound that would never heal. When I'd realized that I'd destroyed the Gift that had become my life. That I was back where I'd started, blind and alone and going nowhere. . . . I wiped at my face with my hand, choking on sobs . . . feeling nothing.

Elnear was staring at me with a kind of horrified fascination, like someone watching a burnout scream curses on an Oldcity street-corner. If she'd had any doubts about whether freaks were all crazy, I'd just proved it was true. . . . She was backing toward the door. "I think," she murmured, feeling for the plate on the wall, "that your work for the taMings is probably finished. You have certainly done enough already." The anger and frustration were back in her voice; the door flicked open. "Under no circumstances are you to attend the party downstairs. My own Security people are here tonight. They will see that you are removed if you show yourself there."

She left the room. The door sealed shut behind her, and I was alone again. I sat down, facing out on the view of coming night, blind with tears. Pain like knives stabbed into the back of my eyes. I got up again and stumbled across the room, found the trash can I'd seen beside the desk and vomited into it. After that my head felt a little better; but the trembling in my hands went on for a long while.

I lay back on the couch, feeling the skin on my face tighten as the tears dried, wondering what in hell was happening to me. Maybe I was sick, maybe I was tired . . . *maybe it was starting. Symptoms:* My mind eating away at my body because the drugs kept it from eating away at itself. It was sending me a warning, telling me to *stop, for God's sake*—I touched the patch behind my ear. I'd just been fired, hadn't I? My cover was gone, what was the point in wearing a patch any more, walking on broken legs. . . .

I tried to make my fingers peel off the patch. *What about Elnear?* Somebody was still trying to kill her; that hadn't changed. "Fuck her—" I said. But that didn't do anything except make me feel lousier. I'd ruined her life. What did I expect her to do, thank me? Besides, it was Braedee who'd hired me, and he hadn't fired me yet. Maybe I should wait. I needed the money. I needed. . . .

I pulled my knees up, rested my head on a crust of pillows, feeling my anger slowly melt down into a puddle of envy. I listened with my mind to the rising murmur of mental noise, guests arriving, filling the levels of the townhouse below me.

Elnear had said she hated parties, they were a waste of time. She was probably going to hate this one more than usual. But I'd felt her, somewhere in the back of her mind, remembering a time when she'd loved the music and the dancing, the company of the best of the best . . . when she'd been giddy with wine and laughter; when every word had sparkled like diamonds, when every sensation was a perfect counterpoint playing on all her senses at once; when she'd been in love. . . .

I couldn't help wondering what that would feel like, to have everything you ever wanted, even happiness. It hadn't lasted for her—but what ever did? I'd thought at least I'd get to taste it for one night— But now any memories I'd have of tonight would have to be stolen ones.

I let my psi slide into the white water of those hundreds of minds, all of them together but forever alone, even in a place like this. I collided with random bits of image and emotion, collecting them: *someone else's eyes falling on a beautiful woman wearing a gown of jewels, the sudden taste of fresh kiskfruit rind dripping with chocolate, the smell of roses and*

imported incense. Pulsing music, pungent disgust, hot hunger as some-
one's blood-red nails traced a slow line down someone's/my backbone. It
was all so easy, they were all so blind. . . . I lost myself inside their
pleasure, sinking deeper into fantasies, letting myself be rich and famous, fire and ice . . . *a psion.*

I sat up on the couch, jerked out of my peepshow dreams as my mind
wandered in through the wrong open door. But I'd been loose and
careless, not trying to guard my own thoughts, knowing none of those
deadheads would ever know the difference. Except this one wasn't a
deadhead. It had been a man—that was all I knew for sure before he
knew, and cut me off in sudden panic. I lunged after him, let my mind
fall like a net over the sea of stars-in-darkness that was the party down
below. But he was gone, losing himself in the void that kept those stars
separate forever. He wasn't very good—but neither was I, and one thing
he knew how to do was hide.

I gave up the hunt after a while, leaning back as I sank into playing
voyeur again. I was better at that, and Braedee didn't want me digging
up family secrets anyway. . . . *The odor of warm flesh and perfume; the
electric shock of sudden humiliation; braying laughter; synth music. . . .*

The door opened.

I sat up fast; afraid it was Elnear who'd come back and caught me
jerking off my brain. But it was Daric instead. He spasmed with surprise, as if the last thing in the world he'd expected to see here was
another human being . . . or me. He laughed; it cut off like a stick
snapping. "Well, hello." He came on into the room, every movement
full of angular momentum. "So this is where she's exiled you to. . . .
The Cat's out of the bag, so I hear." He raised his eyebrows, smirking at
some joke I didn't get. "Now everybody knows your secret. You won't
be safe anywhere. You're a marked man, to the hypers . . . you're
famous. Poor Auntie's ready to make violin strings out of your guts."

I sat forward, pressing the heels of my hands into my eyes as my head
started to throb again.

"I don't mean to intrude. I can tell you must be having a marvelous
time, hiding out up here all alone while the party of the century goes on
without you, just out of reach downstairs." I heard him pass close by
me as he crossed the room. "Hasn't she even brought you up a cup of
lukewarm tea and a handful of crumbs? Thoughtless—but then, she's
having such a *wonderful* time, herself. . . ."

"Jeezu!" I said. "You're really an asshole." I raised my head.

He turned back, staring at me, but not really seeing me. "You're right. . . ." There was surprise on his face now, like he was seeing himself for the first time in a mirror. "You're very perceptive about human nature. But then I suppose all telepaths are." His mouth slid into another mocking smile.

I swore and stood up, sick of being one of his sick jokes. I started for the door, not knowing where I was going, but only that I had to get away from this.

"Cat, wait—"

I stopped, turned around.

He was wearing the best imitation of a real face that I'd ever seen on him. He bent his head to one side. "Listen, I am sorry. I have made an ass of myself. You're absolutely right. And absolutely honest, which is more than I can say for anyone else around here, including myself." He lifted his hands in a shrug. "Don't go. How about a truce? I won't make fun of you, if you promise not to tell the truth."

I felt my face tighten, waiting for the next slap. I didn't say anything.

But he only turned back to what he was doing, which was putting his hand through what looked like a solid sculpture hanging on the wall. His arm disappeared up to his elbow, came out again holding a small ceramic box. He set the box down on the desk. "My drugs," he said. He pulled it open with a kid's guilty grin; showing off, waiting for my reaction. When I still didn't say anything, he took out plastic sheets covered with colored dots and began to peel them off one at a time. He decorated his forehead with blues and greens; stuck on a double line of golds and reds around his throat inside the open collar of his neat gray tunic; shoved a purple one down the front of his pants. "Ahh, that's better."

"I hope you know what the hell you're doing," I said finally. "Because I'm not going to scrape you off the floor when you overdose."

He snorted. "Of course I do. . . . How about you? I hear you're an experienced drug abuser from way back. Help yourself." He waved me toward the half-empty sheets.

I shook my head. "I don't use, any more." There was a time when I'd tried anything anybody'd sell me, trying to find the one that could fill the empty place where something nameless had been torn loose inside me; the one that could take away the pain of living through another day on the streets. I was lucky I was still alive. I didn't need drugs, any more. . . . Suddenly my hand wanted to reach up behind my ear, to feel the patch, to rip it off. Or maybe to make sure it was still in place. I kept my arm down at my side.

Daric looked at me, half puzzled, half frowning. I tried to make myself find out what was going on in his mind. I got the usual stench of mockery and black humor; under it the electric song of barely controlled tension, aimless strands of disgust and loathing. . . . His mind was like a jungle, the drugs filling it in with impenetrable vines of random sensation as they opened up all his senses. I couldn't get any further, pushing against the limits of my crippled psi.

Daric sighed, a smile of pure pleasure stretching his face out like a piece of plastic. *"Much* better." He looked like someone who'd just had a knife blade moved away from his throat; I could almost *feel* him relaxing. No wonder he liked drugs. I watched him shove the box back through the sculpture into its hiding place. "I have no intention of staying around here for more of the overdressed dog and pony show downstairs. Trust me, you're really not missing a thing. A vicious, meaningless, and ultimately boring game of Beasts and Victims, that's all it is. I'm having my own private party, down at Purgatory. Argentyne has created a new work, just for tonight. I'm going there now. All my favorite people are going to be there. . . . Do you want to come?" His eyes brightened with sudden eagerness. "Come with me. You'll be a sensation!"

I blinked, stared, not really believing I'd heard him ask. I shook my head. "I can't."

He raised his eyebrows. "Why not? Are you afraid the hypers will eat you alive? No one will even know we're gone. You'll be safe."

I thought about it, hit with a sudden rush of excitement as I imagined getting free of this prison, feeling alive and real, for even one night—"I . . . I'm supposed to stay here. I've got to do my job. Braedee—"

"Braedee?" He laughed. "Do you really think Braedee cares what you do now? Do you really think Elnear does? . . . Do you actually believe someone is going to murder her in the middle of this crowd? Besides, everyone here has been scanned right down to their entrails for weapons." He strolled toward me, reached out to jog my arm. "They don't *need* you," he said gently. "Don't take yourself so seriously. No one else does."

I jerked away from his hand.

He shrugged. Irritation showed in his eyes, was gone again. "Do what you like. Sit here and sulk. Pretend you matter." He turned away, starting for the door. "You had your chance. . . ."

"All right. I'll come."

He turned back, grinning. "I promise you a night you'll never forget.
. . . You sure you don't want any drugs?"

"No thanks," I said. *I've got all I need.*

12

I FOLLOWED DARIC out of the room, through a maze of empty back hallways, down a lift that only servants used . . . slipping past doorways that opened onto a wall of light/noise/motion, into darkness/silence again. I could feel him still grinning up ahead of me, lighting up my brain with his pleasure buzz, counterpointing the dry empty throbbing in my own head. We came out at last in some kind of sub-basement garage, where half a dozen private mods sat waiting for people who needed a quick escape.

As we stepped out of the lift into the shadowed underworld, someone materialized from behind a pillar. I swore, jerking up short.

But Daric only laughed, and pulled me forward. "Jiro!" he called. "Good boy, you escaped them. Look who I've found to join us."

Jiro stepped out into the light. His hair was still wild, and half his face was streaked with blood-colored paint. He was wearing a brocade jacket with one sleeve missing, over a torn shirt over a striped ankle-length tunic. It took me a minute to realize he hadn't been in some kind of accident. His ear-to-ear smile fell away as he saw me. The static of his excitement faded, broken by the sudden blankness of uncertainty, sharp pangs of doubt and curiosity. *He knew,* just like everybody else did now. "Cat. . . ." His shoulders twitched. "Are you . . . I mean, are you really a freak? Are you . . . you know . . . reading my mind all the time?" His eyes were bright and dark, the whites showing.

"He knows our every secret, don't you, Cat?" Daric murmured.

"No," I said, as evenly as I could. "I'm not a freak. I'm a psion. And no," I said again, ignoring Daric's laugh, "I'm not reading your mind all the time. You're not that interesting." Jiro frowned. Daric's laughter goaded me out into the open space. Jiro skittered backwards as I passed him, came forward again, almost treading on my heels as he tried to prove something to himself. Somehow the space inside the mod seemed cramped, like there were two of me sitting side by side.

The mod delivered us right to the door of Purgatory, Argentyne's private club; what I saw of the Deep End around it made me damn glad of that. We climbed out into the glare of a hundred different hologos dancing in the darkness overhead, stepped over a burnout sprawled in the gutter. Jiro coughed from the stink of a garbage fire somewhere down the block. A gang of street slugs done in gold teeth and threedy paint gave us the eye as they pounded past. The one thing I hadn't been expecting to see was the way the city's sealed dome arced down into the bay, creating more breathing space, reclaiming the bottom of the sea. Argentyne's club was just offshore—the black wall of water rose haflway up the dome here, drowning the stars in half the night's sky.

I don't know what I'd thought a place run by Daric taMing's lover would look like. On the outside it didn't look like much: An ancient cement-block warehouse, with the word "Purgatory" holoed in red crawling endlessly over its face like a blind worm. Daric strode across the dirt-blackened bricks of the pavement as if he owned this part of town, and went down the shallow stairwell to the club's entrance. He touched something on the rusted iron door that sent out a silent call. I followed after him, staying close to Jiro, who was sparking with his own nervous energy. He was so high on excitement that I almost thought he'd been taking drugs; but his mind was clear when I checked him. At least Daric hadn't made his stepbrother the same offer he'd made me. I knew Jiro liked Argentyne, but I was surprised Daric would bring a kid like him to the Deep End. Argentyne was a symbplayer; like magicians, they worked your head best if they did it live. But Jiro had said she was famous. She must do gigs in bigger and better places than this.

The graffiti-covered door cracked open, swung wide as whoever was behind it recognized Daric. Cinnamon smoke and screaming laughter reached out and dragged us inside.

"Welcome to Purgatory!" A face, or a mask, pushed into mine—I couldn't tell which from the leering smile. Young or old, male or female . . . somewhere inside all that I found a man's mind, or thought I did. "Not quite heaven, not quite hell. . . ." His breath stank from skagweed. His hand grabbed my wrist, inside a swirl of translucent glitter cloth, yellows and golds, and he hauled me forward, shooing Jiro ahead down the hallway. "Your first time, pretty?" I wasn't sure if he was talking to me, or Jiro, or both of us. If Argentyne wanted to keep out anybody who didn't have a sense of humor, she was doing a good job.

We half stumbled, half slid down a dark ramp. It dumped us out into the middle of a madhouse. I stopped, staring. Daric was already wading through the crowd, shouting and waving his arms; the crowd parted around him like a sentient sea, and voices called his name.

I stood at the bottom of the ramp, weaving my mind into a fist in self-defense as Jiro plunged out into the shifting mass of bodies after Daric. Still just trying to take it all in—the vast, scarred womb that was the club's interior, the glaring, pounding music that filled it like an invisible force, trying to split open its walls . . . the people. They looked like they'd been bodysnatched and dropped down here from every age, every world, every imaginable level of human life. They wore lace and brocade, leather and rags, grafts, jewels, chains and batteries, plastic, hair, skins and bones. I felt like a mark, still wearing combine colors. Daric's ultraconservative suit looked so wrong that it actually made him seem to belong here. Some of the guests hugged him, kissed him, groped him. I began to spot a few that weren't natives—bored vips escaping like he was from their own respectability, trying too hard to seem like they fit in. I could spot that kind in my sleep.

Behind me, flanking the entrance, there were two bouncers—huge grotesques who'd had themselves built into shells of augmented alloy that made them damn near indestructible. Near the wall on my left three more or less naked men were wrestling in a pool of green jelly, splattering the shrieking onlookers with slime. Four gilled, sexless exotics did an underwater ballet inside a clear bubble of glass drifting past overhead. One of them put a hand against the glass, gazing down at me. Slowly I reached up, stretching to meet it; the hand twitched away as I touched the glass. Its owner was gone in a swirl of silent laughter. A pair of chained-up black dogs yelped and snapped at me as I edged past them and out into the room. The strange danced with strangers, shaking and flailing like they'd been set on fire, or sprawled exhausted on jewel-colored cushions by low tables covered with food and drinks. There was nothing here I hadn't seen before, but I'd never seen it all in one place. . . . There were clubs in Oldcity more bizarre than this, but I'd never had the credit line to get past their doors.

There was a stage at the far end of the room. It was empty now, the only spot in the place where nothing was going on. Musicians were performing all around the club; each one singing, playing something different, lost in some separate auditory hallucination. And yet somehow it was all one sound; half a dozen kinds of synths playing half a dozen kinds of songs fusing into one perfect web of music, the changing rhythms meshing like gears . . . Argentyne's symb. I'd never heard one this good. But I didn't see Argentyne anywhere; there was no lightsong happening yet either. She must be the spirit, the one who did the visuals, who made it all work.

I waded on through the dance, my body twitching to passing rhythms, my vision changing color as I passed through bands of amplified light, searching for Daric and Jiro. My eyes did a double take as my sight suddenly turned black-and-white. All the color was missing from the far corner of the room. I looked down at myself, back at the people around me; we were all still in living color. I reached the split in reality, stepped across it. I turned black-and-white, like everyone and everything around me. I stepped back again, not ready to go colorblind.

Someone pushed a drink into my hand. It was Daric, from out of nowhere, with a couple of female exotics hanging on him. "Come on, Cat. Do something. I promised everyone you'd be interesting—"

I took the drink. It was blue and steaming. I tapped Daric's thoughts just long enough to be sure it wasn't loaded. It was safe enough. I took a sip. "Where's Jiro? He shouldn't be left alone here. He shouldn't be here at all." One of the women blew kisses at me with tattooed green lips.

Daric laughed. "My God, you sound like Auntie! I thought you were supposed to be some kind of wild boy; I thought this was your element. Don't get stiff on me—"

"*I'll* get him stiff. . . ." One of the women oozed away from him, toward me. I backed up, and behind me someone else's hand slid down over my ass. I jerked forward again. The woman with a single horn growing out of her forehead threw her arms around me. There was something long and shapeless squirming in her hand, something grayish-pink and wrinkled. "This is a suckworm," she whispered. "Guess what it does. . . ." She pushed it at me, trying to slip it into my clothes.

I let my disgust slam into her brain without control, without warning. She squealed and fell back. Daric didn't bother to catch her, and she sat down hard on the floor, blinking, dazed. "Well, fuck you," she said, to nobody in particular. She picked up the worm and crawled away through a forest of legs. The crowd around Daric murmured, and I heard a ripple of applause.

"What did I tell you?" Daric said to them. "Mental powers!"

I turned back to him. "I used to live off divers like you—night trippers with fat credit, pretending they were something they weren't. You think this is all a big joke. You're wrong. I don't want Jiro hurt. Where is he?"

Daric winced. "You're telling me the truth again. That's against the rules—" He raised his hands as my own hand made a fist. "He's safe! He's backstage with Argentyne. She'll watch over him like a nanny, he's in perfect ecstasy. Relax." He shrugged, still amused. The crowd of hangers-on around him kept changing, like a kaleidoscope, leather and lace, flesh and fur. "Meet your fans, Cat. It's such perfect timing. . . . Today you became notorious, a media star. Tonight you can celebrate it, among people who really understand what it means to be unique, a freak—"

I grimaced, taking another gulp of my drink as he dragged me through the crowd to a table next to the stage. "My personal table, my guest of honor." He caught my shoulders, chivvying me around. "You'll have a perfect view of Argentyne's performance from here. Sit down—" He pushed me down onto a pillow in the sea of colored cushions, keeping an arm around my shoulders. His face was flushed, his eyes were too bright; he looked like a man with a fever. *Excitement, eagerness, pride—* I was his prize catch, a moment's inspired impulse, proof to the inhabitants of the Deep End that he was as twisted as they were inside his silver-gray straitjacket. He lived his double life with a vengeance that was hard to believe. Flaunting Argentyne at the family estates was only the surface membrane of his secret self, a hint to his family that if they dared to push through it they'd find a lot more secrets than they were ready for. He played the perfect combine vip by day, but it was only a role, just like the jaded deeve he played here by night. I wondered what the real Daric was, or where, or whether there was anything at all behind the masks.

The seats around me at the table filled up before I had time to set down my drink, and the questions started flowing. "Is it true that psions —" "—tell me what—" "Read *my* mind!" "What's your Prime?" "How does it *feel* . . . ?"

I let the hungry curiosity seep into my brain, the eager titillation as they waited for me to rape their minds with a thought. . . . *Even fear could be a pleasure—a new kind of drug.*

As the drink loosened me up I started to let myself believe that nobody around me hated my guts, or wanted to get away from me, or was actually laughing at me inside. At least I knew what kind of people these were; at least here I didn't have to worry about everything I did, everything I said, even the way I said it. . . . I felt myself relaxing for the first time in days. I answered their questions, out loud at first, until I saw that that wasn't what they wanted. Then I answered them with my mind—slowly, gently, so that nobody panicked. They giggled and held their heads like children. Daric smiled with anticipation, not asking any questions of his own.

"Read *my* mind—" the woman with scales glittering on her skin whispered again beside me. She licked her lips with a slitted tongue.

(I don't need to.) I grinned, and so did she. I finished off my drink, and there were two more in front of me before I could even ask. I took a meat-filled bun from one of the platters heaped with food in the center of the table, bit into it, still grinning. Across the table from me a bald, thick-necked slug in patchwork leather was stuffing food into his mouth as fast as he could, choking it down, hardly bothering to breathe. He'd cleared off half the platter closest to him already. I watched him eat for a minute longer; realized I was forgetting to chew the food in my own mouth. I glanced away, at a couple a few cushions past him. They could have been male or female or both, and they were slowly peeling away each others' clothes, like somebody peeling the layers of an onion. Somebody else began to give me a back rub while I watched, kneading my neck and shoulders, pressing their thumbs into the hollows along my spine. It felt good, and I let the hands strip off my jacket without even looking around.

I answered more questions as the crowd around me changed again. I drank more drinks, ate more food from the tray that never seemed to get completely empty, while everything began to feel better and better. I'd had dreams about this: about being at the center of a diver's private fantasy, as an equal. . . . I felt myself letting go, an almost physical thing, as if my bones were melting and my body was moving away in seven different directions at once. My mind began to drift, floating in a warm, hazy sea of acceptance, where the only tension was sexual, and there was no fear at all.

After a while Jiro came dancing out from behind the stage. He jumped down into the cushions beside us, panting, his face flushed with excitement, and wriggled like a puppy into a spot beside Daric. As he settled in, the music that had been all around us until I didn't even hear it any more changed, in a way that made everyone stop everything and look toward the stage. Reality shrugged, and suddenly the stage wasn't empty any more. Shimmering above it now was a gleaming black filament like the web of some mutant bloodspider. There were human victims, half a dozen men or what looked like them, dangling in the wires, with blood or something like it dripping from their wounds. The air smelled like ozone. I shut my eyes and looked at them with my mind, and they were the musicians who'd been playing all around us. They were still playing, still hooked into the symb net. Their writhing agony was a freeform dance, tied to the heartbeat of their music.

I heard Jiro suck in his breath, half frowning as he tried to guess whether what he saw was real. Knowing it couldn't be, but still not sure—

"It's just an act," I said. He nodded, frowned a little deeper, pushing his hair back from his eyes. "I know that." He hunched his shoulders and looked away at the stage again as lightning played down the web.

Argentyne was there, suddenly, drifting down through the web like some pitiless goddess of death, her hair a shockwave of silver white. Black leather cupped her like the petals of a nightflower; black silk fringe slid over bare flesh like the groping hands of her victims, reaching out for mercy as she passed. As her feet hit the floor she began to sing, swiveling out of the web along the tongue of stage in spike-heeled killer shoes, stretching her silvered arms to embrace the crowd. Watching her strut it was hard to take my eyes off her; almost impossible to separate her from the beat that drove her motion in through every pore of my body, or her voice from the reverberating air. I couldn't make out the words she was singing, even as they etched themselves across my brain, like acid eating its way into glass . . . *a song about men and women, a song of war, in and out of the flesh* . . .

And as she sang and as she moved her flesh began to heave and buckle, as if something monstrous inside her was trying to force its way out. With the music screaming, her perfect flesh tore open like rubber. Glistening limbs flailed, pushed, burst free, her mutilated body fell away, withering like a cocoon. . . .

. . . *about getting inside others' skins, would it really be so different?* . . .

A silver-haired man, the sheen of sweat on the silver flesh laid bare above his tight black leather pants, heavy codpiece, thigh-high armored boots. Armed to the teeth, he raised a metal-studded fist to the crowd, and his voice was Argentyne's, and no one else's but his own. . . .

. . . *Would it really still be war?*

And he turned, and Argentyne was waiting there behind him. Alone, defenseless, she held up her hand, as if she could stop his slow, hungry advance on her by nothing but willpower. . . .

And the gun dropped from his hands as his chest began to heave and tear, showing velvet as red as blood; as his face contorted and the music screamed while a hand struggled out through his mouth . . . as his body exploded like porcelain dropped from a height.

A silver-haired woman in a red velvet gown emerged like a snake, shedding the man's skin, shuddering free of it as it sloughed to the floor, kicking it away. I watched Argentyne walk toward Argentyne, undulating like the sea. As they passed each other like figures in a mirror, the two women lifted their hands, blowing kisses, while Argentyne segued into the final verse of her song. . . .

. . . *if you were a woman, and I was a man . . . inside the other side of life tonight* . . .

The crowd howled, its voice strobing inside sound like a sun gone nova . . . as Argentyne appeared and disappeared, moving through curtains of synthesized reality, shouting and applause . . . to settle, as the music rolled away and the visions faded, into the space that had somehow opened for her between Daric and me.

I stared at her, hardly believing she was actually right beside me. She looked back at me, blinking with a kind of startled recognition as she realized she'd seen me before. As she realized now, like everyone else did, what I really was.

"Argentyne . . . magnificent . . ." Daric murmured. He put his arms around her, kissing her lips, her throat, her breasts . . . laying claim to her and all that she was, all that she'd just created, in a way that nobody who saw them could fail to understand. She didn't resist him, dissolving against his body, turning the kiss into an extension of what she'd done on the stage, still radiating the white heat of her performance energy. What drove into my dazzled brain then surprised me as much as anything I'd just seen on the stage: she actually wanted him, wanted to feel his lips against her skin, and it was her own pleasure that let the contact continue long after it could have ended.

I watched them, like everybody else was watching them, with the heat of Argentyne's energy still burning inside me, mutating, shifting, getting hotter; Daric's arousal, my own. . . . Slowly realizing that there was a whole hidden layer of sensation that only I could share, out of everyone in that room who saw them. I shared it, hungry, greedy, not able to stop myself . . . knowing all the while that they knew I knew, and wanted me to know, and liked it that way. . . .

They broke apart at last, to more whistles and howls. Jiro sat gaping, caught somewhere between awe and panic. Daric looked straight at me, grinning, still with one arm holding Argentyne close. He said, "How did you like the show?" He didn't mean just the one on stage.

I grinned too, leaning back in the soft embrace of the pillows. I could sense the entire room now, as I let my focus dissolve: the flow, the heat, the pressure, the wild energies . . . feel it all funnel back along the lines of contact until my mind felt like a star. I let out a little of that raw fissioning fire, feeding it into him, into Argentyne, into every mind around me at the table; letting them feel exactly how much I enjoyed it. There were gasps and giggles, aftershocks of stunned disbelief, and then everyone's eyes were on me again. They all wanted more—The slug across the table even stopped eating for long enough to look up at me. I opened myself to them, feeling the contact ebb and flow as I dropped the circuit breakers in my mind. A strangled laugh escaped from Daric. I felt his craving for the forbidden touch . . . the terror that squeezed it, compressed it until it became a kind of lust. . . .

I broke contact with him as I suddenly remembered Jiro. Jiro was staring at me too, his throat working. He was even more terrified of what I'd just done than Daric was, but he was trying desperately to look like he'd enjoyed it, to look like everybody else.

I wanted to say something to him, but then Argentyne leaned away from Daric, toward me, looking directly into my eyes with all her attention; really seeing me for the first time. "That was incredible," she murmured. She laughed, shaking out the silver mane of her hair. I felt her enjoy the feel of it down her back, felt her titillated by the sensation of thoughts turned inside out; felt her wanting to feel another mind run its fingers through her own again. I brushed her mind with an image, and she shivered. "I'm ruined. . . ." she said, her voice caressing me like warm fingers. "You're like silk. Accessing is going to feel like sandpaper in my brain for the rest of my life. You've ruined me with one touch. . . ." Her hand reached out this time, brushing my cheek. She was only half serious, but Daric's grip on her tightened, pulling her away. She glanced at him, more amused than annoyed, pulling her spike-heeled feet in closer to her on the cushions. "You brought him here, love. Let us enjoy him. We don't see nearly as many psions here on Earth as you worldjumpers do."

"Why not?" I asked, half realizing that down here where nothing was a surprise, telepaths shouldn't be as interesting as I seemed to be to them.

"This is Earth," Daric said, his smile twitching with spite. "Psions are . . . well, abnormal." He shrugged. "They're discouraged from settling here. They might pollute the stock." His eyes moved, not meeting mine, as his own paranoia suddenly set in again.

My anger shot out past my control, spilled over into the open lines of my mind and hit him. The people gathered around the table jerked and gasped . . . laughed, nervously. Daric wiped at his eyes, shook his head—looked at me again. Eager again, in a way that should have made me want to get away from him. But the warm feedback of everyone else's acceptance melted my anger, dissolved my resentment. I couldn't hold onto my thoughts, any more than I seemed to be able to keep them to myself . . . and somehow I didn't even care that something was going wrong.

"Have you ever plugged in?" Argentyne asked, leaning toward me again, her copper-colored eyes intent. "Have you ever worked a symb circuit? Would you like to try?" Do what she did—the music, the images, creating a mass hallucination out of the artist's imagination. I shook my head. "God's teeth," she said, "you'd be astounding—you could make people *live* what they see and hear. The ultimate."

"That's socketwork. It's illegal," I said, the words flat, "for psions." Even I knew that. "If they catch you, they drugwipe you."

"If I could create that kind of effect, even once," she said, "it would be worth it."

"It's not your brain."

She shrugged, and the petals of black leather she'd been wearing were suddenly watercolor silk. I blinked, wondered what she was really wearing. . . . The image I was trying not to form inside my head formed anyway, and leaked. More tittering laughter. Argentyne smiled. "Fairly accurate," she said.

Daric's frown came back, but he only kissed the back of her neck, and said, "Argentyne, Jiro would like to dance with you, but he doesn't know how to ask."

She turned away, looking toward Jiro. "Delighted." She pushed to her feet in a wash of liquid color, and took Jiro's hand. Jiro scrambled up, speechless, and followed her away toward the dance floor. I watched her go, watching her tight dancer's muscles flow beneath the silk until she disappeared into the crowd. I left a strand of thought tied to her mind even after I lost sight of her.

As I looked back, across the table from me the Eater stuck his finger down his throat, and puked into the bucket waiting beside him on the floor. When he was finished he began to eat again. More bodies slid into the empty spaces beside Daric, like sand funneling into a pit. I turned to look at the grotesque who was shoving in beside me. The wall of his chest had been replaced with a transparent synthetic. Blood pulsed though veins, wet purple and gray organs churned, muscles slid and contracted. He stared back at me, just as curious.

Something warm and wet circled my ear, probed inside it. I jerked around, startled. The woman with the long, slitted tongue was back, kneeling behind me. The tongue that had just been in my ear licked her lips again, left them wet and glistening, as her hands slid down across my shoulders, massaging my chest. Her eyes were a golden yellow; her pupils were long slits, like mine should have been. But hers had been engineered to look that way, the way mine had been engineered to look human.

The thin film of scales on her skin caught the light, gleaming like a sheen of sweat. I reached up, touching her face. The scales felt warm and dry, softer than I'd imagined. Her lips were very soft, opening as I rose on my knees to kiss them. Her tongue slid into my mouth, as casually as if it belonged there; stayed there, investigating every corner, while our kiss went on and on, and a hot throbbing pressure grew between my legs. I heard a whimper, a stifled groan, from somewhere around the table.

I tried to break off the kiss, looking back at Daric. I caught an unfocused flash of his knowing smile, someone else behind him, arms circling his waist . . . And then the woman's hands were drawing me back and around and down into the cushions beside her. Long deft fingers slid down the seal on my shirt, pulled it open, raked my skin with sharp nails and left me burning. I reached up, cupping her breasts with my hands through the gaps in her slitted ivory gown. She squirmed and sighed, with my pleasure and hers, lowering herself until my lips could reach her. I covered one of her nipples with my mouth.

Sounds and movement were all around me now, as the others at the table began to melt and flow together in my heat, their heat radiating back along the sizzling filaments of contact into my brain, until it was all one molten sea, and I was sinking into it, ". . . don't . . . stop . . ." Begging to drown.

Someone else's hands seemed to be pulling at me, hands everywhere, peeling off my shirt, sliding over my skin . . . unfastening my pants, setting the hard rod of my erection free, to giggles and moans of delight. The scaled woman's tongue was back inside my mouth now, going deeper. Something sweet and sticky was trickling from a pitcher onto my belly . . . someone was licking it off. . . .

Daric was beside me, smiling, his breath coming in shallow gasps as he lifted my hand. He sucked on my fingers, one by one—sank his teeth into the flesh between my thumb and forefinger until he tasted my blood. I screamed and jerked, screams echoing around me as he gasped and let go, falling back with my pain inside his head. He crawled forward again and dumped a freezing cold drink onto my naked skin. Gasped with my pain again, and laughed—

I struggled to sit up but the hands weighed me down, the mouths, the bodies . . . soothing, stroking, caressing, probing. Until my bones were rubber and my mind flowed into the drowning pool again, helplessly willing.

Something warm and shapeless flopped onto my chest. I lifted my head, saw the suckworm lying there in an oozing pool of syrup. Panting, I watched it squirm along my belly to the music of their laughter . . . waiting for it, helpless with their hunger, burning with their need, screaming inside. Their hands held me down with silken cords of muscle and flesh, as they drank in the sweet juice of my yearning, the vinegar of my disgust. . . .

"Jeezu!" Argentyne's face swam into sight above me. "What the hell are you doing—?" Staring down at us, her eyes widening enough to take it all in. I had a sudden strobe flash of what it looked like from where she stood, driven into my brain by the force of her *incredulity disgust *arousal* anger *arousal* disbelief *arousal* disgust—*

I tried to struggle, tried to hold onto her anger, to push free of the soft, yielding heaviness that was suffocating my will like a pillow of flesh . . . couldn't.

"Argentyne, come on—" Daric crawled on his knees to her, his own clothes hanging open. He reached out for her, pulling himself up her body. "Come and *feel* the real thing. . . ."

Argentyne punched him hard in the gut, doubling him over. She began to turn away, and I grimaced as I saw Jiro's face behind her. She blinded Jiro with a sudden slap. *"You* keep your face out of this! Stay there." She turned back, stepping over Daric's head, shoving half naked bodies out of her way as she leaned down and picked the worm off my belly. She hurled it away. "This is my club, I put on the floor shows here. Get your clothes on and get out, you shiteaters." She kicked a few more bodies; their pain went off in my head like explosives in a sea of mud. I groaned and rolled over as everything imploded; burying my hard-on in the pillows.

"*You—*" Her hand caught my shoulder, wrenching me back into the light again. "Put your fucking pants on, you mindraper. Take your freakshow someplace else."

I struggled with my pants, struggled with my brain, my thoughts still running out of me like diarrhea. "I can't. . . ."

"Like hell." She fastened my pants for me, making me gasp; picked up my shirt and threw it in my face.

I couldn't sit up. I managed to get over onto my hands and knees. All I could feel now was *her,* no room left in my mind for any thought, any choice, any decision of my own. "I can't . . . help it," shaking my head. It didn't do any good.

She was standing over me, staring down at my back. I felt her eyes catch on something, felt the giddy change of direction as she leaned over to pick it off my neck like a flea. A patch.

"No, wait—" I put up my hand, but the patch behind my ear was still there. I sat back, making my eyes focus on her while she studied the patch on her fingertip. Her face twisted. She flicked it away. *A dose of easy.* It took away your inhibitions and your self-control; made it easy to do anything. . . . I felt the anger drain out of her/me. Not wanting it to go; wanting to be able to feel my own. "All right," she said gently, "I guess the boy can't help it, after all." She reached down, helping me to my feet. "You understand what happened?" she asked me. "Somebody drugged you." I nodded. "I think you're going to be ready to kick some ass in a few minutes," she said. "Or you should be."

She let go of me and turned away. Daric was on his feet now too, grimacing. Her knee came up, stopped just short of his crotch. "No," she said, her voice spiked with spite. "You'd enjoy it too much. You turd. You drugged him, didn't you? And set him up for this gangbang—" Her arm swept the circle of chagrined partiers still fumbling their clothes on.

He shrugged, making odd faces, like a kid caught cheating at Square/Cubes.

I pulled my shirt on with stiff, clumsy fingers. I couldn't see my jacket anywhere. I kept my eyes on the floor, because there were so many other eyes looking at me that wouldn't go away, so many minds. . . .

"Come on," Argentyne said to me. The odd gentleness was back in her voice. She took my arm again, making me move forward. I saw Jiro then; he hadn't kept his back turned for long. I couldn't make sense out of what flashed into his mind as he looked at me. Maybe he couldn't,

either. I looked down again. Argentyne caught his arm with her other
hand, steering us both toward the entrance. "Daric!"

He followed us through the crowd, across the dance floor, toward the
door. He moved slowly but inevitably, as if she held him too, dragging
him along on an invisible chain of will.

My head began to clear out just a little as we left the club. Putting the
physical barrier of the walls between me and the eyes and the minds
made it easier. I took in long swallows of cold night air, tasting smoke
and dankness. The mod that had brought us here came down from
wherever it had been waiting overhead, homing in on Daric. It settled
onto the street, scattering the ground traffic. The doors popped. I stood
staring at it, starting to shiver inside my thin, syrup-soaked shirt. Trying to decide what to do . . . trying not to wait until somebody else
told me.

Argentyne turned away as Daric came out into the street and the
gatekeeper slammed the door behind him. She was back in leather
again, this time head to foot, solid and heavy like a trooper. I couldn't
help wondering again what I'd actually feel, if I touched her . . . see,
if I touched her mind. . . . Desperately I tied up my thoughts, and this
time it held. Relief hit me so hard it felt like an electric shock as I
realized I was getting some kind of control over the psi again . . .
relief, and disbelief. And then the betrayal and the fury, riding each
others' backs as I turned toward Daric.

But Argentyne was there first, the mask of control she'd worn inside
the club gone, the anger naked on her face. "You bastard," she said, and
the words trembled. "You scumbag, how could you pull a piece of shit
like that in my place? How could you do it to me? How could you do it
to him—" waving a hand at Jiro, "—or him?" Pointing at me. Jiro
stood as silent as stone behind me. People swirled past and around us,
making a religion of disinterest. "What makes you *do* these lousy—"
She broke off. There were tears in her eyes. "Why do I let you do it to
me. . . ." Her hands jerked, as if they wanted to beat on him. And
trapped behind the transparent window of her anger there was the kind
of pain that only grew out of one emotion. . . .

Daric stood without resisting, his mind full of the same twisted pain,
letting her bury him in garbage, *hating/loving it/her/himself.* . . . "I'm
sorry," he said at last, when she'd run out of things to call him, and the
energy to spit out the words. "I'm sorry. . . ." He said it again, as
humbly as if she was the taMing, and he was no better than the burnout
still face-down in the gutter behind us.

"Go home. Go back where you belong." She waved him gone, turning her back on him. "Stop fucking up my life. . . ." without even the strength left to sound like she meant it. She was facing me again. She pushed her hair back from her eyes, studying me until I had trouble meeting her stare. "You okay?" she said, finally. She was worried about me filing a complaint . . . she was worried about me.

I felt the corners of my mouth twitch, like a spasm. "My brains aren't hanging out any more. . . . So, yeah." I shrugged, nodded. "Sex never killed me before. I guess I'll live."

She half smiled. "Forthright," she said. "You seem to know this territory by heart." She touched my chest, let her hand drop. "Will you get these lost babes back where they belong? Since you're the only one who really knows where that is." She glanced at Daric, Jiro.

I nodded; Felt a smile of my own start, in spite of myself.

She began to turn away. But it was only her body turning. Her mind stayed behind. . . . And then suddenly she was facing me again, and her arms were reaching out to pull me against her. She kissed me, long and hard, her nails digging into my back. She let me go and pushed away; stood looking at me again, her open lips smiling, her eyes hot. "Now you know why I had to throw you out of there." She nodded toward the club, and took a deep breath. "If that helps, remember it."

She went to Jiro, kneeled down beside him, gave him a hug. He stayed rigid and silent in her arms. "Oh, baby," she said, looking away. "Sometimes life's a bitter drug. If you have to take it, it's better if you get it from somebody who cares about you. . . . You dance great. Go on, now." She nudged him toward the mod. He got in, as numbly obedient as I'd been ten minutes before.

She passed me again, grazing my thigh with a warm hip; passed Daric, who was looking at her, at me. "It's your fault," she said to him. His eyes followed her like a dog. The door to Purgatory swung open as she started down the steps, and slammed shut again behind her.

I waited while Daric's eyes tracked back to me. I was ready to smash his face if there'd been anything behind them that even reminded me of laughter. But his mind was the color of the streets, of need and anger and desperation. I turned my back on him too, and got into the mod.

After a long minute he climbed in, and ordered the mod to take us back uptown. Jiro sat squeezed down into a corner, as far from either of us as he could get. I stared at my feet, not wanting to watch as the mod lifted from the ground. My hand hurt. I looked at it. In the dim light of the street below I could see the black stain of drying blood where Daric's teeth had gone through my flesh. I focused my mind on stopping the pain, to keep from thinking about how it had gotten that way.

Daric was looking at the wound too when I glanced up at him, the way a starving man would look at a half-eaten piece of meat. Only it wasn't causing pain that he still wanted. It was feeling it. . . . In the moment after Argentyne had left him, there'd been something I could relate to going on inside his brain. It was gone now. "You got any diseases I ought to know about?"

His mouth twisted. His eyes were empty as he looked away, out the window.

I sighed, letting my head fall back against the seat.

"Why did she kiss you like that?" Jiro asked me. His voice was tiny, accusing.

Me, like she meant it. *Me*, not Daric. *Me*, not him . . . I only shook my head. "Ask Daric." I lifted my aching hand, pointed it at his step-brother.

He didn't ask. He only squeezed deeper into his corner, trying to get away from the ugliness and confusion in his own head, the images that looking at us only made clearer. And Daric didn't answer. If he had any regrets about what he'd done to either of us, they hadn't occurred to him yet.

I started to reach out to Jiro with my mind, knowing that he needed help, and that no words could help him. But even as I did, I knew I wasn't up to it. That if I tried to help him now, he'd know it. I pulled back into my own disgust and exhaustion, and left him alone. And suddenly I remembered where we were going to be again in another few minutes. I tried not to wonder who was going to end up getting blamed for everything when we got there.

13

I FOLLOWED DARIC back through the halls of the townhouse, feeling like someone who couldn't wake up from a bad dream. Elnear's party was still going on, but by now it had shrunk to just one room. Daric ducked in through the first doorway that opened onto light and noise, leaving me behind with Jiro as he lost himself in the crowd. I stared after him, not sure whether relief or envy was winning out in me as I watched him slide back into his other skin with smiling ease. Jiro stood shuffling his feet, not wanting to be left standing beside me, but filled with sudden panic as he thought about facing his family . . . his stepfather.

"Go on in," I said softly. I reached out, put my arm around him. "You didn't do anything wrong." *You didn't*— Repeating the same thing to myself, for the hundredth time.

He didn't believe it, any more than I did. He jerked away from my hand and ran into the crowded room without looking back. I stayed where I was, suddenly more afraid of going in than he was, as I remembered what had happened this afternoon. To me it seemed like about a million years ago, by now; but it probably didn't seem that long to the people in there. I let my mind search the crowd, searching for hypers, or for Elnear. Somehow I had the feeling she'd still be there. She might be a lot of things, but she wasn't a coward. I wondered what her evening had been like while I was gone; if it had really been as bad as mine, and what that would mean when she saw me again.

My eyes followed my thoughts restlessly, taking in the scene. The shifting mass of bodies stunned me with its normalness. There were a few exotics, wearing feathers for hair or calico skin, but it could have been makeup, costuming, for all I could tell. There was nobody who looked like they'd be caught dead wearing their guts out in the open. But I could have passed for human. . . . I could have been in there, having a painless good time, having the best night of my stupid life. I *should* have been there—

I wondered what I would have had to say to anybody if I had. . . . Probably just the wrong thing. I sagged back against the wall again, safe, out of sight, and suddenly too tired to move. Those were the elite of this world and dozens of others, in there—the richest, the most powerful, the most successful. They didn't need to wear their specialness on the outside, forcing the world to blink when it looked at them, to notice them, to acknowledge they were alive. Their only problem was convincing each other that they were still human, when half their head was full of bioware . . . when half of their souls were dead. . . .

Or all of their brain. My own brain stumbled as it hit a mind as empty as a broken eggshell. My sight homed in, and I stared at him: A perfectly normal-looking total stranger, wandering through the crowd with a drink in one hand. He moved through the same aimless circulation patterns as anybody else, making programmed responses when they needed to be made, circling. . . . *Why?* I pushed deeper into the blankness where a mind should have been. I didn't have to be careful; he couldn't feel me. The organ was intact, the wrinkled gray container of flesh that should have held all the complicated magic that made him a sentient being. But it wasn't anything now except a piece of meat. Something was in there, keeping his vital signs up, making him respond. . . . *Programmed.* That was it. What was imitating a mind was nothing but somebody's biosoft.

I felt my stomach turn over. *Elnear.* Where the hell was she? Suddenly I was sure she was still in the room, that he was waiting for the crowd to thin out a little more, for some perfect moment—I found her, standing on the far side of the room, carrying on a conversation she didn't care about with a person she didn't know. Her arms were folded, her large-knuckled hands clutching her elbows; but otherwise you couldn't tell that she was enjoying this about as much as standing on a bed of broken glass.

I started into the room, keeping a fix on her mind as I pushed my way toward her. It was like working the night crowds back in Oldcity. . . . Some half-buried itch couldn't help signaling me that I could steal half the people in this room blind, and they'd never know what happened—

Two sets of hands suddenly locked over my arms. A man and a woman I'd never seen before, with bland, too-perfect faces, were smiling at me. "How good to see you." "So glad you could come . . ." The pressure on my arms suddenly increased until if I didn't stop moving something would snap. I stopped. Looking at them, groping . . . *They were Corpses.* Guilt smacked me with an open hand. But then I realized they were Elnear's Security people, the ones she'd warned me about. They knew I'd know what they were, that I'd hear the message behind the meaningless words.

"Listen," I said, "I have to tell—"

"—Look at his hand, Adson, poor fellow, whatever did you do to yourself come on sweetheart we'll fix it right up . . ." *(Don't make a scene, you little bastard, just come on—)* They turned me around in my tracks and started me back toward the door.

Suddenly I saw Lazuli. She saw me too: I got a sudden flash of how I looked from across the room, my coat gone, my shirt fastened crooked and hanging out of my pants.

I opened my mouth. "Where's—" The pressure on my arms got so bad, so fast, that I had to clench my teeth to keep from crying out. (Take me to Braedee or the whole room hears this, Corpse!) Their hands loosened as if I was red-hot. "I need to see him," I said to them, trying to keep my voice down as Lazuli came toward us. "It's important. It's about Lady Elnear."

Lazuli was searching the crowd, frowning with concern, but it wasn't about me. "Cat, have you seen Jiro?" she said. "I haven't seen him since—"

"We'll take you to Braedee," the man muttered, his voice grating, urging me forward again. "Come on."

"Jiro's all right," I called back over my shoulder. "I'll explain later." Not knowing how, or when, or what in hell I was going to tell her.

Braedee was waiting for us, out in the darkened hallway beyond the door.

"Braedee, you've got to—"

"What now?" His mouth pulled up in the usual sardonic smile. "First you want to quit, and now they have to drag you away from the Lady?"

The two ChemEnGen Corpses on either side of me were watching him the way you'd watch a snake. "Lady Elnear's orders were to keep him away from her tonight," the woman said grimly.

"No one told me that." Braedee's eyes never seemed to move from their faces, but suddenly he was looking at me. "Who did that to your hand?"

"I bit myself, eating. Shut up and listen to me, damn you. There's somebody in that room who doesn't belong there. He's brain-dead—"

Braedee's laughter rattled up and down the hall. "Almost everybody in that room is brain-dead. It's hardly a secret."

"I mean literally, goddamn it! He's a total burnout running on somebody else's 'ware. There's nobody *in* there." I brushed my head with my hand. "I think maybe he's after the Lady."

Braedee's head twitched, as if he was about to reject the whole idea. But then he said, "Show him to me."

Elnear's Security people went rigid, as if they were ready to use their own bodies to stop us. "He's not going back in there. We have orders—"

"He works for me," Braedee said. "And you don't. This is my system, and it covers everyone on these grounds equally." Suddenly there were two more Corpses, wearing Centauri colors, standing in the hall shadows behind him. "You are in my way."

My arms were free. The two Chem Corpses didn't move as I turned around. I didn't wait for Braedee to step on my heels before I was on my way back down the hall. I stood in the doorway, scanning with my mind—found Elnear, a lot closer to us now. She was standing with Daric and Lazuli. I veered away, not wanting to know what he was telling them, trying to keep my concentration whole.

"There." I pointed. The burnout was across the room but angling toward her, still smiling, still empty. My mind cringed. "Get him out of here. Stop him. He's trouble—"

Braedee watched the stranger, with God-knew-what going on in the systems behind his eyes. "He's a legitimate guest. There is absolutely nothing that could injure anyone concealed anywhere on or inside his body. He's drinking something harmless." He glanced at me. "You've had too much to drink. For God's sake, tuck in your shirt." He began to turn away.

"Braedee—" I caught his arm.

He jerked free. "Don't ever do that again," he murmured, smoothing his sleeve. And then he was walking away.

I swore, and went back into the room, going after Elnear.

Daric saw me coming, this time, and nudged her arm. She didn't see him smile as she turned away, searching the crowd for my face. Lazuli looked up with her. I felt Elnear subvocalize a call to her Security people as she spotted me wading toward her. Her frown deepened as they didn't appear.

"Lady—" I gasped it out as I got close enough for her to hear without me having to shout it. "Please, ma'am—" Not daring to touch her mind, knowing how she'd react. I saw the walking vegetable stop, a few meters behind her, and smile his empty smile at me. He looked back at her, taking an awkward gulp of his drink.

She was calling Jardan now, as she realized the guards weren't coming. Something that wasn't quite frustration and wasn't quite panic began to wind like a spring inside her. She took in my syrup-stained clothes in one quick glance, hating the sight of me. "Mez Cat—" Her voice was perfectly calm, and cold. "What are you doing here?"

"Ma'am, I think you're in danger. There's not time to explain. Please, will you please just come with me?" I reached out for her hand.

"Where is my Security?" She stiffened, her hands clenching at her sides. "What are you doing here?"

"Probably wants to tell you all about his evening in Purgatory." Daric leered. "I was just telling them what a good sport you were."

I felt my face flush. "Shut up, you slad." Lazuli was frowning now. Heads were turning; I half heard the whispers starting. "Lady, I'll explain anything you want if you just come with me." I caught her arm, tugging her forward. "No trouble, I swear—" I saw Jardan push past the burnout, coming toward us. He almost spilled his drink; finished it in a desperate gulp, his eyes riveted on us. The drink. He started forward as he saw us begin to move. . . . *The drink.*

$$\left(\begin{array}{l}\text{Get down!}\\\text{Oh, shit—}\end{array}\right)$$

I shoved her, knocking her into Daric and Lazuli, knocking all of them flat. I landed on top of them in a tangle of hard elbows and knees, just as the stranger exploded.

The shock of the blast punched into my eardrums like an icepick. More bodies crashed down on top of me, crushing the air out of my lungs. I lay there for a long time, trying to breathe, trying to tell whether the pain I felt everywhere was inside me or outside; if any of the groans and screams were mine, if the wetness dripping into my eye was really my own blood. Everything was in slow motion: sounds, movement, all sensation with it, as if I'd been hit by a tidal wave and drowned. . . .

Someone was picking bodies off of me. Someone was hauling me up like a body. I blinked my eyes clear. There were uniforms everywhere, Centauri logos, blood. A hand slid down my shoulder: it wasn't attached to anything. I watched it drop to the floor, lie there in a red puddle. I saw Lazuli, heard her screaming, over and over; saw Daric, silent and dazed, and Elnear, her eyes closed. . . . My head was so full of shock and pain and horror that I couldn't hold it all.

Suddenly Braedee was in front of me, blocking out my vision, his hand lifting my chin. "Can you hear me?"

"No," I mumbled, scratching at my ear. I was ready to start screaming too, as I tried to find the strength to close down my mind, shut out the terrible noise. . . .

He leaned close to my face. "Damn it, boy! How did you know—?"

I swore, shaking my head. "Told you. I told you. . . ." It was all the answer I could get out. And all the answer he deserved.

14

THE HUMAN BOMB had killed three people. Elnear wasn't one of them. He messed up a whole lot of fancy clothes; about twenty more people were transferred to the med center. I was one of them, although cleaning me up was the worst part of what they had to do to me there. They scanned me and picked some bone shrapnel out of my shoulder, then let me go. I was bruised and half-deaf, but otherwise there was nothing wrong with me that wouldn't be wrong with anyone who'd just had somebody else's guts scraped off of him.

I finally let my eyes clear when they told me I could leave the examining room. I put on the clean clothes that had appeared out of nowhere, and walked out through the doorway; bumped into the jamb, and stopped.

I knew that I was in a hospital, and that it had to be a good one, considering the clientele. But it could have been a suite in the best hotel in N'yuk that I'd walked into: a cool green room that was all softness and peace, thick rugs on the floor, hidden lighting, music that was almost subliminal; no cold antiseptic halls, no ceramics, no noise: no evidence that anybody ever felt pain, or needed help. It stank of total unreality. But it couldn't keep the handful of people sitting together on the modular couch from looking like survivors huddled together in a lifeboat. None of them were wearing what they'd worn an hour ago.

I saw Lazuli, sitting with her arms around Jiro, her face too white and calm, as if she was tranked on the same sedatives they'd tried to give me. I'd had enough drugs for one night. Daric sat across from her, sitting on the edge of his seat like he had a stick up his ass. His mouth pinched as he saw me, but this time he kept it shut. Everyone sitting in the circle was a taMing. There were two others that I recognized; one of them was Charon. There were no outsiders—except me.

And Braedee. He was standing in the center of the ring of faces; asking questions, probably. Or maybe answering them. I couldn't hear what he was saying. I wouldn't let myself feel what they were feeling; not yet. I was still too close to the edge. I'd managed to build the mental shield, strand by strand, that put silence between me and the agony all around me. I was afraid to let it down again.

I stood where I was, half wondering whether I wasn't here by mistake, as more heads began to turn. But Braedee gestured me toward them, said something impatient-sounding that I couldn't make out. I went over and sat down in the circle of taMings, feeling all their eyes fixed on me. They all had to know who and what I was now; but I still wasn't sure what that meant. I looked up at them, down again, wetting my lips.

"Thank you," Lazuli said quietly.

I glanced at her. She smiled, ruffling Jiro's spikey hair with her fingers. He pressed closer to her shoulder as he stared at me, his eyes dark. Other faces smiled, other voices echoed her thanks around the circle. Charon taMing didn't say anything, and there was no crack in the cold wall of his face.

I glanced at Daric. His face was frozen too, a warped mirror of his father's. "You're welcome," I said, still meeting his stare. His gaze broke suddenly and he looked away. I almost thought he was ashamed, but maybe it was my imagination.

"Where's Elnear?" I realized suddenly that I'd forgotten to say "the Lady." But for once no one frowned. Maybe saving her life had given me the right to forget, for once. "Is she all right?"

Braedee sat down on the couch an arm's length away from me. He nodded. "Thanks to your . . . loyalty." The catch was back in his voice, the way I'd heard it the first time I'd seen him; as if he hated having to say it. His finger traced the curve of his brow around the edge of his eye. It was the closest to a case of nerves I'd ever seen in him.

I wondered if he'd rather have seen more people die than be proved wrong by me. I wondered what he'd told the taMings—if he'd told them how he hadn't listened to me. I didn't say anything.

"She's with Philipa," Lazuli said.

I looked up, suddenly remembering that Jardan had been passing the stranger just as he finished his drink.

Lazuli nodded, reading the question in my eyes. "She was . . . badly injured." She took a breath, getting her voice under control. "They say . . . that they don't know. . . ." Her voice trailed. She blinked, like something hurt behind her eyes.

I grimaced. I glanced at Braedee again. His lips thinned. "Can I speak to her? Elnear—Lady Elnear, I mean. I need to tell her . . . something."

Braedee frowned, and Charon taMing said, "I have questions about what happened tonight that I want you to answer before you go anywhere." His voice was as cold as his eyes.

I shook my head, looking at him. "Not tonight," I said, and I didn't look down. I stood up, slowly because I was getting stiff. "I'm too goddamn tired. I just want to see the Lady, and then I want to sleep. Ask me tomorrow."

He stiffened. I saw real emotion on his face for the first time. It looked like disbelief. Before he could say anything, Lazuli said, "Of course, Cat. I'll take you to her. And then . . ." she glanced at Charon, back at me, "perhaps you would be kind enough to see us home to the estates?" She got to her feet, nudging Jiro up.

I blinked, feeling a sudden warmth creep up my face. "Yes, ma'am."

"Lazuli." Charon reached out, catching hold of her arm. "We are staying at the townhouse tonight."

She went even paler, but then her color came back in a rush. "No," she said. "You can pretend it didn't happen if you want to. Not me. Not Jiro." She jerked her hand free, and crossed to my side. Jiro followed her, glancing nervously over his shoulder.

Charon half rose from his seat; settled back again under the weight of too many watching eyes. "Very well. I will see you tomorrow, then." His own gaze flicked from her to me, back again.

Lazuli lifted her head, still defiant. Her hand slipped around my arm. I saw Charon's eyes fix on it, and wished she hadn't done that. But there was nothing I could do about it now except follow her out of the room.

Elnear was sitting alone in another room that hardly looked like a hospital waiting room. But it was, and she was waiting, her face heavy with grief and shock and exhaustion . . . all the things I wouldn't let myself read in her mind. Behind her was a wide stretch of dark glass. At first I thought it was a mirror. It wasn't. It looked down into a surgery. She could watch, if she needed to; but right now this was as close to Philipa as she could get.

"Elnear—" Lazuli said softly, as she started across the room.

Elnear looked up at us, the dazed suffering fading from her eyes. She rose to her feet, a little unsteady, and held out her arms to Lazuli and Jiro. She held them close, before she pulled them down beside her.

I hung back, feeling like an intruder, as her eyes found me again.

They were red-rimmed, but there were no tears in them now. They were a clear, steady blue as she looked at me without saying anything, looked at me until I began to wish I hadn't come. And then she lifted her hand from her lap, holding it out to me.

I crossed the room, stopped in front of her, uncertain. Slowly I took her hand, and she put her other hand on top of mine, making me sit down beside her on the cushioned seat. "I feel . . ." she said at last, and broke off, as if for once she was having trouble finding the right words. "I feel as if I owe you such a debt that to thank you, or even to apologize to you, can only be so meaningless that it would be insulting. . . ." She looked down at my hand, up at my face again. "But thank you for what you did. Thank God you are all right. And I am so terribly sorry, Cat. . . ."

I looked away, choking on the crazy laughter that suddenly filled me up. I tried to stop it, but it burst out of my throat anyway, in a strangled bark that sounded more like a pain cry. I pressed my hand over my mouth, taking a deep breath, and another, until I was sure I could keep a straight face when I looked back at her again.

They were all looking at me, but no one looked like I'd done anything strange. Maybe after what happened to us all, anything we did seemed normal. I glanced up at the window behind me, careful not to focus because I might see what was happening on the other side of it. "I'm sorry too, ma'am. About . . ." I nodded my head at the window, "Philipa." It sounded about as meaningless and empty as what she'd just said to me. But even that was almost a relief, somehow.

She nodded, her eyes dimming again as she remembered what was being done in there.

"They have the best of everything here, Elnear," Lazuli said, touching her shoulder. "There's almost nothing they can't do. And they'll do whatever is necessary for her."

"Yes, I know." Elnear sighed. Her hands were back in her own lap again, clenched together.

"Won't you come back to the estates with us?"

She shook her head. "No. I'll be fine here. I'm not going anywhere until I'm sure that . . . that everything will be all right."

Lazuli nodded, getting slowly to her feet. She glanced at me as Jiro stood up beside her. I stood up too, waited until they were halfway toward the door. I looked at Elnear. "Ma'am . . . I told you the truth before. I've never lied to you about anything. And the other things Stryger claimed, about things I did back in Oldcity—I did them to stay alive. That's all." I turned away and followed Lazuli out of the room. Not knowing, not really caring, whether the words meant any more to her now than they had before, or whether she'd even remember that I said them. At least I'd know I said them.

As I followed Lazuli and Jiro back through the med center's halls, I began to realize that everyone I saw wore either a Centauri logo, or a Centauri security clearance. "Do you own this hospital too?" I said finally.

Lazuli hadn't said anything, or even looked at me, while we walked. Now she glanced at me, distracted by my voice—glad of the distraction. "It must look that way." She laughed, a little too sharply, still teetering on the brink of something darker. "Centauri contributed a great deal to the construction of this wing. In return, we retain certain facilities on long term lease for our private use."

"The taMing Wing?" I said, and laughed.

A little color came into her cheeks, a smile touched her lips. "A number of the larger combines do the same thing. It's more . . . secure. . . ." She glanced away, her words fading. She slowed her footsteps until she was walking beside me. She held Jiro's hand tightly in hers, and he didn't complain.

We took the lift up to the garage level. A few more steps across a silent space to a mod and I could let my whole body drop into autopilot. The day would finally be finished with me.

The doors slipped open. The first thing I saw was Daric. He was surrounded. A dozen hypers were swarming over him like flies on garbage.

"Jeezu!" I whispered. "Who let them in here?"

"It's a public access—" Lazuli looked left and right, her face pinching as she searched for a way around them.

"Get away from me. I don't know anything about it!" Daric waved his hands, twitching with irritation. "Ask him." He turned, pointing at us, at me. "He's the one you want to talk to. There's your hero—" He ducked through the gauntlet and ran, as the hypers turned to see what he meant.

And then they were all over us, trapping us against the wall, shoving hands that were cameras and spotlights, and faces with three eyes into my face—

Suddenly the nearest hypers were stumbling back like something had sprayed them with bug killer; suddenly their echoing voices sounded like they were coming at us from the other side of a wall. We were shielded. "Cat," Lazuli murmured, "you don't have to speak to them now. We're still inside Centauri's security system."

I'd covered my fave with my arm, ready to cut and run like Daric had if I needed to. But then I began to hear what the hypers were trying to ask me. It wasn't about this afternoon . . . it was about tonight.

Slowly I lowered my arm. Shander Mandragora himself was planted right in front of me; I could see him subvocalizing to his audience.

"It's all right," I said to Lazuli. "Let it down. I want to talk to them." The sudden rush of adrenaline that had hit me when I saw the hypers was making me feel brave and alert. She didn't look happy, but suddenly the voices were rattling in our ears again as the hypers surged forward.

". . . Lady Elnear Lyron/taMing's controversial young psion aide," Shander Mandragora said, suddenly coming on audio as he elbowed somebody out of his way. "You're quite a hero." He smiled at me, cool, confident, and looking earnest as hell. He was wearing padded body armor. So were the rest of the hypers. I wondered if it was to protect them from each other, or from their victims. "Tell us how you managed to save the Lady and several other members of the taMing family from a human time bomb." He was gazing right into my eyes, and his own eyes were the color of sapphires. He was standing so close to me that we were almost touching, and he looked just as good as he did on the threedy—lean, square-jawed, tough. I remembered having a dream about being him once, while I was asleep on a moldy mat in the back room of an abandoned building. "Did you use your mind?"

I felt the crazy laughter try to get loose inside me again. I swallowed it, along with half a dozen wiseass answers. I couldn't help staring at the camera lens in the middle of his forehead. It looked like a paste-on jewel, the same color as his eyes; but once you knew that it wasn't, it was hard to look away from. Kind of like the muzzle of a gun. "Well, I . . ." My throat suddenly went dry the fear of saying the wrong thing, and I had to swallow again. "Yeah. I used my . . . my Gift." Trying not to sound like I was embarassed to admit it. "I picked up on a party guest who'd had something done to his head. He wasn't . . . human any more, he was a machine. I knew I had to warn the Lady. I was almost too late."

"What made you read the guests' minds tonight?" Mandragora asked, blinking as if he suddenly wondered what I was doing now. "Are you always 'on'?"

"No." I shook my head, tried to smile away the look on his face. "It's hard work. I was just doing my job. Checking out the crowd to make sure they were all right. It's part of what I was hired to do."

"You mean you were hired by Lady Elnear as a personal spy—" Someone's open hand flashed in front of Mondragora's face; a camera eye stared at me from its palm. Some combine logo I didn't recognize was tattooed above it.

"No—" I bit off the curse that wanted to follow, wondering if the hand belonged to Stryger's media base.

"To spy for Centauri—?" This hyper had on Triple Gee colors.

"I was hired to protect her! Because somebody's been trying to kill her. Like they almost did tonight."

"Why didn't the Lady Elnear tell us about that in her rebuttal—?" Shander Mandragora was back in my face again, and somebody was groaning in the background.

I shrugged, feeling my frown get deeper. "Maybe she didn't feel like discussing it with the whole galaxy."

"Lady Elnear—" Lazuli said, very loudly, very clearly, "didn't want the people watching to feel that she was using a personl problem to gain their support. She felt that her arguments had to be strong enough to stand on their own."

I smiled, grateful, as the cameras, and the heat, turned away from me toward her.

"Lady Lazuli taMing," Mandragora said, acknowledging and identifying her from an augmented memory bank. "Another survivor of tonight's tragedy. Do you have any idea who would want to kill Lady Elnear?"

"No." Lazuli shook her head. "No idea at all." I felt her falter behind the skin-deep mask of a board member's arrogance.

"How is Lady Elnear? Why hasn't she come out yet?" someone shouted. Mandragora was losing ground.

"She's fine, perfectly fine!" Lazuli had to raise her voice again to make them listen. "A personal friend was seriously injured. The Lady is waiting for news about her condition."

"Why didn't you save everybody?" Somebody else jarred me back against the wall. "Why didn't you bring in Security?"

Whose logo was it? I couldn't even see. "I did—didn't have time." Not sure why I was covering for Braedee.

"Why didn't you stop him yourself? Why did you let those other people die? You could have stopped him with your mind."

"It doesn't work like that. I'm just a telepath, that's all. Not even a very good one. I'm not God. I'm not a Corpse, either."

"But you are a criminal. Why did Lady Elnear hire a traitor who worked for a psion terrorist? Why are you free? Sojourner Stryger called you—"

"I know what he called me." I shoved the camera away, and three more replaced it. "He's a liar!" I twisted until I could see Shander Mandragora and he could see me. "You let Stryger smear the Lady today!" I yelled. He'd done it . . . he could fix it. "Jeezu, I don't believe this—I didn't work for Quicksilver. I killed him! Doesn't anybody here know that? How the hell can you know all about me and not know that?"

"Do you mean you were a part of his terrorist group, and you betrayed him to the FTA?" he called. *The stupid bastard.*

"I killed him in self-defense, goddamn it! And to save my friends, and to save your stinking telhassium. I wasn't a traitor, I worked for the FTA. You've got a head full of history, why the hell don't you use it? We were fucking psion heroes. For about as long as it took to say our names . . . just like tonight. But I missed it all, because I had a nervous breakdown after I killed him. That's what it means to be a telepath, and kill somebody. . . ." I had to stop, taking a deep breath in the sudden silence. "And I guess it still doesn't mean shit to be a psion and a hero."

By the time the questions started again, it was too late. I was halfway to the waiting mod. Lazuli and Jiro followed behind me.

The mod sealed us in, out of reach, and took us away at Lazuli's order. As we left the garage, its too-normal voice said, "Lady Lazuli, I have detected five intrusive listening devices in the clothing of the passengers."

"Deactivate them," she said, her voice still perfectly calm. I almost thought I felt the scramble burst that burned them out. Lazuli waited until the voice reported, "Clear." Then she slumped back into the formfoam of the seat, and covered her face with her hands. After a moment her hands slid down again, dropped limply into her lap.

"They bugged us?" I said, incredulous.

She nodded. I saw tears shining on her face in the brief light of a passing streetlamp. Jiro looked up at her, and his mouth began to tremble as he saw his mother crying. Suddenly tears were running down his cheeks. He hid his face against her as he cried.

I swallowed hard, keeping my mind clenched, afraid that in a minute it was going to be three of us. "I'm sorry," I murmured, only realizing now how much it had cost her to show the hypers that proud, cool face; to protect me, and Elnear, the way she had. "I didn't know they'd . . ." My hands made fists; let go again, too tired to hold onto the anger. My whole body ached, my nerves felt raw. I wished I'd taken everything they'd offered me at the med center.

"It's all right," she lied. "I'm quite used to them." She sat up straighter, wiped at her eyes. "It was just the final . . . the last thing, that was too much. They had no right to do that to you, to Elnear through you . . . no right!" She blew her nose. "But it's all they know how to do—"

"I knew the combine hypers were all liars," I said, rolling the sour words on my tongue. "I just didn't know the Indy's hypers were all shitheads."

Her mouth twitched, and Jiro lifted his face from her shoulder to stare at me, as if hearing someone talk to his mother that way was more than he could believe.

" 'Scuse me, ma'am." I looked out the window at the one large moon rising, the dark world below; for a heartbeat remembering somewhere else.

"Don't apologize," she said. "I find it refreshing." She frowned then, thinking about something else. "Our own media people should have been on this, and given them the true story by now. I don't understand why they didn't seem to know the truth."

I glanced back at her, realizing that she knew what everyone else knew about me, now—the truth, and even the lies—but it hadn't seemed to make any difference to her. "Ma'am," not using her name, because Jiro was still looking at me that way, "did Braedee say anything at the hospital tonight about the—about what Stryger claimed I did?"

She shook her head.

"Nobody asked him?"

"Great-uncle Hwang did," Jiro volunteered. "Charon said forget it. He said it didn't matter, it just made everything perfect."

"Perfect?" I frowned, wondering what in hell he'd meant by that. I was too tired to try to figure it out. "I'm not a traitor," I said.

Lazuli looked at me, her face calm in the wash of moonlight. "I never thought you were."

"Why not?"

She glanced down suddenly, and shrugged. "You don't act like one."

That didn't make any sense either, but I didn't push it. Instead I asked, "What did Daric tell you and the Lady?"

She looked surprised, as if I'd asked something totally pointless. "He said he took you and Jiro to hear Argentyne perform. He said that you seemed to enjoy the show more than Jiro did. . . . I asked him not to take Jiro anywhere again without telling me first." Her arm curved around him protectively.

I glanced at Jiro, glad we were all in darkness just then.

"I'm never going anywhere with Daric again," Jiro said, his voice hard with anger and betrayal. His eyes kept touching me and jerking away, coming back to my face again.

"Why?" Lazuli asked.

"He's a croach," Jiro said.

Her fingers moved in a short, silent question. He shook his head. She looked back at me again. My stomach tightened as I waited for her to ask me what had really happened. But she didn't ask. Nobody said anything more.

When we finally reached the estates, I helped Lazuli steer Jiro to his room. I waited while she put him to bed, letting the doorway hold me up, too exhausted to bother moving. But as she waved the lights down and came out into the hall, I heard Jiro call my name. I glanced at her, and she nodded. I went into the room.

"Cat . . . ?" Jiro said, his voice think with sleep.

"Yeah, I'm here." As my eyes adjusted, I could see his face clearly in the dim wash of light from the hall. He couldn't see mine.

"You probably think I'm real stupid, don't you?" he said.

"No." I half smiled. "Just real lucky. I guess nobody's luck lasts forever."

"You saved Aunt Elnear, just like you promised. And you saved my mother too—" His voice blurred with feeling, his eyes got wet again. "I'll give you anything you want. I have stuff like you've never seen—"

I didn't say anything. I turned away, starting back across the room.

"Cat—?"

I stopped.

"I was scared of you tonight. I hated you, too."

"I know."

"I don't any more."

I did smile, this time. "That's all I want."

Out in the hall Lazuli looked at me, curious.

"He just wanted to say thanks."

She nodded, hesitated . . . reached out and put her hand on my arm. "Cat . . ."

"You already have. Good night, ma'am." I went back along the hall, before it was too late. I stumbled up the stairs to my own room and fell into bed, hardly stopping long enough to peel off my clothes.

I couldn't sleep. I lay there, feeling the seconds pass like water dripping; feeling every centimeter of my spreadeagled body twitch and crawl and shiver like a plucked string. Closing my eyes only made me see things I'd never wanted to see in the first place. Opening them again, in the empty bed in the empty room, only reminded me of how alone I was.

And then my door opened softly, and someone stepped inside. Caught in the random moonlight, her pale gown moving around her . . . *Jule.* A tiny spark of light caught fire in the palm of her hand, guiding her across the uncertain darkness to me.

"Lazuli . . ." I pushed myself up, feeling the covers slide down over the sudoskin bandaging my shoulder. *You shouldn't be here don't do this to me I want you.* . . . Afraid to speak, because I didn't know what would come out of my mouth first.

She sat the lamp chip on the table beside the bed, stood gazing down at me. Her night-black hair fell free over her shoulders, her skin was like amber in the lampglow. She reached up, began to unfasten the pearls that buttoned the neckline of her restless gown.

"Wait—" I whispered, my throat tight.

Her fingers froze; her eyes clung to me.

"What about—Charon." I looked down, not sure who I was more afraid for, her or me. "If anybody finds out—"

Her eyes filled with sudden tears. "Please . . ." she said, and her voice trembled. "Please don't make me beg you. I need someone. I don't want to be alone tonight. . . ."

I raised my hand; she caught it, kissed it, settling onto the bed. Dizzy with disbelief, I let go the clenched fist that my mind had been since the explosion, letting it fill with her thoughts, her emotions. *She'd almost died tonight.* . . . *But she was alive, so alive that every nerve in her body sang with need.* Nothing mattered tonight, not Charon, not tomorrow, not who she was or even what I was. She needed to feel loved, and that was all she knew. She wanted me to love her, *me and no one else,* because she'd known when I looked at her how much I wanted it too. . . .

I pulled her down beside me with unsteady hands, feeling her hair brush my cheek as I found her mouth and kissed it. I broke away again, not able to meet her eyes. Burning with the hunger in my blood . . . not knowing what to do next. I'd been naked in bed with strangers before, for nearly half a lifetime; but all there had ever been between us was money. Nameless, faceless, we'd done what we had to do, with no real emotion and no expectations. I'd never had a woman like this—this beautiful, this untouchable—not in my wildest fantasies. One who really wanted *me*. . . . One who had a right to expect things that maybe I didn't know how to give. The fear that I didn't know how to be what she wanted suddenly seemed like the worst fear I'd ever known.

But she took my hand as gently as if she thought I was a virgin, and laid it on her breast. I fumbled with the buttons of her gown, awkward and uncertain as I finished what she'd started. The gown seemed to melt away under my clumsy fingers like it had a life of its own, the silken cloth becoming her flesh, warm and yielding. I shuddered with the electric shock of our contact as she pressed herself against my thighs; rolled onto her, holding her there under me, her softness beneath my sudden painful hardness. It was too easy to go on then, after all that had happened tonight . . . too easy.

She clung to me, her mouth open, hungry for my kisses. Her lips were like flowers after the rain, I could have kissed them forever, lost inside the wet, warm contact, feeling her pleasure . . . *she had always wanted to be kissed this way, kissed and kissed endlessly* . . . feeding my own. Her hands explored me in slow, grazing circles, the white scars on my back, the smooth brown of my sides, my thighs. I slid off of her, my own restless hands covering her breasts, curving down along the gentle hills of her belly, into the warm, waiting valley between her legs.

She moaned softly, her hips moving to meet my touch, guiding me deeper into her hidden places. I felt the murmur of her mind, as open and yearning as her body. I followed its whispering voice down, deeper and deeper, until I knew every sweet ache, every burning, dazzled second of her arousal. I'd never made love to a woman while I'd had my Gift—never known what it could do, how it doubled every ecstasy, her pleasure woven into mine until every place I touched her body brought heat as dizzying as her touch against my own. Suddenly I wasn't afraid any more that I couldn't give her what she wanted. Because I knew what she wanted. . . .

My mouth left hers, traveling down over her throat, her shoulders, her breasts . . . following her lead, granting her every unspoken wish with growing urgency. Her breath came in shallow sobs, she whimpered, and then began to tremble, as the realization grew in her mind of what was being done to her. *Wonder, joy, frantic longing, rising panic—*

The hands that had clung to me, caressed me, urged me, suddenly were trying to push me away. Gasping for breath I let her go, backing off, putting space between us for the length of heartbeats it took for the heat of her unfinished desire to burn away her fear. And then I began again. This time I took more care, not answering every need, or not too soon; drawing it out, letting her feel that there were still secret places that she could keep hidden, if only in her mind. Soothing, lingering, exploring, until my mouth reached the place where she had ached for someone's mouth to be—

And the rising wave of her pleasure reached its crest and broke over her, over me, through every synapse of my body, until it was all I could do to hold myself under control. I swung my hips over her again, down into the waiting space between her open thighs. I slid into her, deep into the final place that now at last she was ready to share. I began to move, feeling myself, feeling myself inside her, stunned with sensation. Her hips rose to meet my thrusts, while the tide rose inside me this time, rising and rising toward that impossible crest, and exploding over me, out of me, back along the filaments of contact I had woven and into her unprotected mind. I felt her come again, her climax recoiling through my own like a riptide, fusing us into one. I covered her mouth with mine to drown out her cry, and she kissed me and I kissed her, echoing echoing echoing, until there was nothing left of us but warm ashes.

She held me inside the circle of her arms, I held her inside mine, and there were tears on my face, but I didn't know whose they were. Still clinging to each other while the darkness slowly faded into dawn, we slept.

15

WHEN I WOKE UP again it was the middle of the morning, and my mind was still half in a dream. I sighed, reaching out into the warm band of sunlight to touch warm skin, reaching out with my mind. The bed was empty. My mind touched the mind of a total stranger.

I pushed myself up, confused—jerked back as my eyes registered the pair of uniformed legs standing beside the bed. The Corpse looked down at me, expressionless, and said, "The Chief and Gentleman Charon want to talk to you about last night."

Lazuli— I bit my tongue to keep from blurting out the question before I found the answer. *No.* She was nowhere in sight, nowhere in his mind. It was about the explosion, that was all. If the Corpse wondered why I looked so guilty, or why I looked so relieved, he didn't let it bother him. A one-track mind had its points. "Sure. Just give me a minute."

While I pulled on some clothes I wondered about why they'd sent a body to deliver the message, instead of calling me. Maybe they were that paranoid about security, after last night. Or maybe they just wanted me paranoid.

As I passed the bathroom mirror, a sudden flash of green caught my eye. I stopped, looking at myself, turning my head—saw the light wink again. My ear. I reached up, touching it, with a slow smile starting. There was an earring in my ear, one I'd never seen before. Green glass, catching the light when I moved, like a cat's eye. I knew I hadn't put it there . . . I figured I knew who had. I stuck a drug patch behind my ear, and went out of the room.

The first thing the Corpse did when I came downstairs was make me take the patch off. Braedee's orders. It took about half an hour for the effects to wear off. By the time we reached the city, he wanted me deaf and dumb. The Corpse threw the patch away. I didn't bother to tell him about the second patch I'd stuck on behind my other ear.

He took me back into N'Yuk, to the taMing townhouse. You'd never have known there'd been three murders and a lot of blood there the night before. I followed the Corpse through the room where it had all happened, and everything in it was immaculate—walls, carpets, furniture. Some of the furniture looked different than I remembered, but otherwise it fit the room perfectly. It made my skin crawl.

Braedee and Charon taMing were waiting for me in the room beyond, a space like a cell, which didn't make me feel much better. As I walked through the doorway I felt something not-human whisper across my brain and fade again. Then I understood. It was a whiteroom —so thick with security that my psi actually registered it. I stopped, uncertain, as Braedee stood up from the couch. Charon stayed where he was, deep in its folds, staring at me. I made myself look right at him, my face as stupidly expressionless as I could manage. Trying not to look like I'd just slept with someone's wife was something I didn't have a whole lot of practice at.

"Why are you looking at me like that?" he snapped.

"Nothing, sir." I glanced away from him, at Braedee, at the door.

"Sit down," Braedee said, and pointed at a chair.

I followed his hand, glad to have somewhere else to look. But my mind was still focused on Charon, just as paranoid as he wanted it to be, for all the wrong reasons. But not deaf, or dumb. Inside the forest of his augmentation, I felt him daring me to sit in that chair. Somehow I managed not to turn back and stare at him. I kept looking at the chair, the one Braedee had pointed out. Soft, humpbacked, blue-gray—there was nothing unusual about it. But whoever sat in it was going to get one hell of a shock, right where it hurt him most.

My own disbelief made me freeze. Why—? *A trap.* If my psi was really shut down the way he wanted it to be, then I'd go to the chair and sit in it, and he'd get to watch me jump. But if I could read him, I'd know—

Braedee was looking at me again. I clamped down hard on my body functions, hoping I could keep the readings normal enough to suit him. Forcing myself to stay calm, forcing myself to move, I crossed the room. Without taking a deep breath, I sat down in the chair.

They weren't bluffing. I leaped up again with a curse, as the current sank its teeth into my ass. "What the hell—?" I yelled, as if I didn't know. I didn't have to fake the anger that came with it. "Is that supposed to be some kind of fucking joke?" I looked at Braedee and shook out my smarting hands.

Braedee stood where he was, his arms clasped behind him. He didn't move to do anything, which had to mean I'd passed his test. Charon settled back into the couch, his body going loose as the suspicion flowed out of him; satisfied, because Braedee was.

"Not a joke, I assure you," Braedee said mildly. "A test."

"Of what?" I remembered to ask, still frowning.

"Of whether you were reading us."

"Shit," I said. "Maybe that's where your brains are," rubbing my butt, "but mine are up here." I jerked my head at him. "Whose chair is that—Daric's?"

His mouth twitched. "Sit down . . . I promise you, it won't happen again."

"You sit in it," I said. He was telling the truth, but I didn't feel much like sitting down, anyway.

He shrugged, and sat down in the chair. Nothing happened to him.

"Why do I have to play deadhead for you, anyhow?" I asked.

"The Gentleman prefers it that way," Braedee said, and glanced at Charon.

I turned to look at him again. It was easier, this time. "I thought you were paying to keep me switched on." I wondered if it was just his disgust at the thought of being touched by my mind, or if he really had something to hide. By the time I got out of this room, I was going to know which it was.

His anger was like a wave of heat. "I'm paying you to do what you're told," he said. "We will ask the questions. You answer them—civilly." He shot a dark look at Braedee, one that said he thought Braedee was letting me get away with too much, letting me mouth off without stepping on me. I remembered what Braedee had done to me before the board meeting. He hadn't let me get away with it then. But then I hadn't known something that could ruin his career. He'd finally stepped off the edge.

I said, "Yes, sir," anyway, because Charon was making a fist of his cybered hand. I didn't have to read his mind to know what he'd like to do with it. Knowing what he owed me for saving his family and Elnear last night hadn't changed how he felt about psions, expect maybe to make him more bitter. I went to the couch and sat on it, because it was the only place left to sit down. I kept as much space between him and me as I could. Its soft folds were filled with something that shifted out of my way like water. I tried not to flounder. "What do you want to know? Sir."

"You read the mind of that assassin last night," he said. I nodded, even though it wasn't a question. "And you saw something that gave him away to you, something that didn't register on any of our security scans. What was it?"

I glanced at Braedee. He hadn't told them. He was looking back at me, looking a little grim, but that was all. I slipped in through the hissing grids of his implants, waded too-clear streams of biosoft, treading as lightly as I could: He knew I hadn't told anybody what he'd done —or hadn't done—last night. He was counting on me to cover for him again, even though he wasn't sure why I'd done it, any more than I was. . . . He figured I must want something from him.

I realized he was right. I just had to figure out what it was. "Somebody had stripped his brains. He'd been reprogrammed to act human, but he wasn't. He was just a . . . a bioware death machine." The memory of what had been done to him made my jaw clench until my teeth hurt. "Who was he?" *The poor bastard.*

"A midlevel official of Centauri." Charon waved his hand, pushing the dead man aside like yesterday's weather report. "No one important." I looked at him, looked away again. "What is important," he said, his voice dropping until it was barely audible, "is who did it to him." Now his face showed something. Now he was *angry, frustrated, sick with rage, aching for revenge.* They'd analyzed every dripping millimeter of the human bomb's remains, without finding a clue. But he had to know—not because whoever had done it had destroyed one life, or four, in a way that would make a hit man retch. How they'd done it, what they'd done, didn't matter to him half as much as the fact that they'd done it to Centauri . . . to him.

"I don't know who did it," I said, too softly.

He leaned toward me, his eyes hot and hard. "You have to know. You saw inside his mind. Who wired him? Who sent him here?"

I shook my head. "I told you, I don't know! Whoever did it was good —they didn't leave any fingerprints."

"Is he telling the truth?" Charon said to Braedee. Braedee nodded.

I frowned. "He didn't even know who he was looking for. They'd set him up so that when his eyes registered the right visual cue, he'd drink that drink. He didn't know anything until he saw it—" Her. Elnear. I saw him in my mind, trying so damn hard to swallow that drink down before she got away from him. If only Jardan had really made him spill it. If only I'd understood what it meant, before it was too late. . . .

"You knew about the drink?" he asked, his voice jerking my attention back.

I nodded. "I knew—but it was too late. It was the way he *had* to drink it. . . ." I glanced at Braedee again. "I just didn't figure it out until there wasn't time to stop him. All there was time for was hitting the floor. What the hell was in it?" *You said it was harmless.* The words almost got out of me.

"A glass of wine with a few random molecules of ceboric in it," Braedee said, thin-lipped. "It appeared perfectly innocuous—and it was, until it catalyzed the LDA they'd planted in his stomach. Then it blew him up."

"I know. I saw that part." I looked down, swallowing.

"Then there's nothing—absolutely nothing else you can tell us about who set up this attack?" Charon said.

I hesitated, searching my memory for something I might have forgotten, or refused to remember because it was too ugly. . . . Finally I shook my head. "No sir. I told you everything. There just wasn't anything *in* there to see."

Charon swore, turning back to Braedee. "Now what? This is critical, goddamnit. I want answers. You said nothing could go wrong—and everything has. You slipped, Braedee, you nearly cost Centauri Elnear. She's no good to us dead—" He stood up, looking like he had something down his shirt, gnawing at his flesh.

Braedee glanced at me, frowning, as if he was afraid I was hearing too much. . . . *Too much about what?* He looked back at Charon, his face under control again, as he said, "The psion served his intended purpose, sir." Every word carried a weight on it. Iron. *Irony.* It took me an extra beat to realize that he was talking about me. "He filled a breach in our security, just as I said he would; one that could not have been filled any other way. Because of that Lady Elnear is still secure." Not *alive;* secure. "Your stepson and your wife, as well." Taking the credit as calmly as if it belonged to him. "The attack was almost undetectable. Not many of our competitors have the capability for something like that, even if they have the intent."

"What about Triple Gee?"

"Their ambassadors didn't know anything about it," I said.

"That doesn't prove anything," Braedee murmured. "But the way it happened was too imaginative for Triple Gee's Security."

"Anybody can hire a specialist," I said. "There's plenty of arm in the Lack Market, who'll kill anybody for you, any way you want it done.

That doesn't take much imagination." Something that didn't make sense bumped up against the back of my eyes as I said it. The other attacks on Elnear had been so crude they were almost a joke. Nothing at all like this one.

"That's impossible," Charon said coldly. "No combine's board would consider that."

I laughed; stopped laughing as they looked at me. They actually meant that. They had their own armies, spies, assassins. They thought they didn't need outsiders. "You mean it's more fun if you do it yourself?" The stares got blacker. "Look, this attack doesn't match the others at all. Maybe they gave up and turned it over to somebody who knew what the hell they were doing."

They looked at each other. The subvocal exchange between them said they knew I was wrong. *They knew. How could they be so sure?* I sank a quiet hook deeper into Charon's brain.

"What about the Lack Market?" Charon murmured, his eyes still on Braedee. "Could there be any possible tie-in—?"

"Hardly," Braedee said. He was back in the control seat again. I'd covered his ass, he didn't have to worry about Charon any more; just me. "It's in their interest to keep the drug restricted, and that's what Elnear wants too."

Charon nodded, thinking Elnear wasn't exactly the sort to get into trouble over secret gaming debts. But then he was back to wondering who was taking advantage of this, and why—? Panic alarms were going off inside him. He had no idea who it could be, he only knew this attack had nothing to do with the things that had happened before. I pushed deeper: *There was no doubt in his mind—*

Braedee's head swiveled around; he gave me a strange look. "What's the matter with you?" he said.

"Me?" I blinked, pulling back fast.

He looked pained. "I'm not talking to myself."

"I'm . . . just trying to think." They acted like they were thinking about this for the first time. Like they'd never really considered any of this before. . . .

"Do it without your mouth hanging open." He looked back at Charon. "What about him?" *Me.*

Charon frowned at me. "He's told us all he knows, obviously. Send him away." He was looking straight at me, but still talking about me as if I couldn't understand a direct command.

"I don't mean that," Braedee said. "I'm talking about keeping him on."

Charon's head jerked back toward him. His mouth tightened, as he barely stopped a refusal. "Are you serious?" Half sarcasm, half incredulity.

"After what he did last night, yes, sir. We still need him. . . . His function has simply changed."

"He fed the hypers last night, for God's sake! Did you access the Morning Report—?"

I sucked in a breath, imagining what kind of cretin they must have made me look like. "I only wanted to help the Lady, sir. After the way Stryger lied about me, I thought if I could make them understand the truth. . . ."

"You wanted to help!" His hand jumped, fisted. I sank back into the corner of the couch, as his sudden fresh anger slammed into my unguarded thoughts. He'd seen the 'cast, and he thought I *had* helped her. And that was the last thing he'd wanted. He wanted her alive . . . but discredited, demoralized, a failure—under his thumb. "You misbegotten guttersnipe." His hand loosened, and he pushed to his feet.

"All the more reason to keep him here, at least until the vote," Braedee said. "It would look bad."

I stopped listening as sick realization filled me up. They hadn't planned to keep me on until they found out who was trying to kill Elnear . . . because nobody was trying to kill Elnear. They'd staged the attacks themselves—Centauri, Braedee, under the direction of the board; of Charon. Just enough to throw her off-balance, to frighten her, to make her dependent on them and their Security. Just enough so they could force her to accept me. They'd lied to her, they'd lied to me— they'd been using me all along, to spy on her, just like she'd figured.

But more than that—they knew that Stryger hated psions. So they'd set me up as a target, and let him knock me down. So that they could make sure Elnear would be humiliated and lose the debate, and the vote, and the seat—

Except that somebody had found out about the phony attacks on her, and tried to use them to cover up a separate attack, not knowing that the others had all been faked. So now Centauri really did have an attempted assassination on its hands.

"Do what you want with him, then," Charon was saying. He started for the door. "Just get results. And control him—keep him away from me."

He had to pass by me one last time to get to the door. He glanced down at me, as if something had caught his eye; stopped. "Where did you get that earring?"

I shook my head, still dazed. I raised my hand to my ear; felt the slick, cold surface of the cut glass under my fingertip. Froze. "I—uh— got it from a street vendor."

He grunted, and went on out. The door sealed behind him, leaving me alone with Braedee.

"All right," Braedee said. "What do you want?"

"What?" I couldn't remember what he was talking about. I rubbed my eyes, feeling the pressure/pain build behind them.

"You know what I'm talking about." He moved two steps one way, two steps back, his hands locked behind him. His eyes were on me all the time. "To keep quiet about last night."

I laughed. It didn't sound real. "Oh. That."

He stopped moving. "What the hell's the matter with you?" He was half afraid that I was just plain crazy.

I looked up at him again. "You used me," I said. "You bastard, you were using me all the time—you and the taMings. There was no plot against the Lady, not before last night! You set her up, so you could use me to fuck her over."

He stared at me.

" 'How do I know all that'?" Taking the words right out of his mind. "How do you think I know, deadhead?"

His face went white with fear, and fury. He looked at the chair we'd both sat in.

"It didn't work, Braedee."

His black eyes snapped back to me. "You were reading us all along. You sat down anyway. Why?"

"Come on," I said. "Wouldn't you have done it, if you were me?"

He looked at the chair again. "I didn't think it was possible." For me to have fooled his lie detectors. For him to have been so wrong. He'd really believed I was that much of a coward. That stupid. A punk kid, another screwed-up freak. No threat, no problem. "Surprise," I said.

And then I watched his hand reach for the gun hidden under the smooth line of his uniform jacket. . . . For a minute he really didn't know whether he was going to let me live or kill me—

I sat there while he decided, feeling my palms go clammy with sweat as I suddenly wondered if I'd misread him even worse than he'd misread me.

His hand came out of his coat again, at last. He needed me. . . . He was still frowning, thinking I knew everything he thought; but I watched his body ease out of its systems alert. He lifted his shoulders, in something that almost looked like a shrug. "So you know it all, now. I'll repeat my question—what do you want?"

I sighed. "How about an apology?" I said, just to see if I'd get one. I didn't. "You want me to work for you—for real, this time. Lady Elnear's no good to you dead, and you really think I can do something to help you keep her alive. That's what you were telling Charon. Right?" He nodded, barely. "That's what I want, too."

He looked surprised. "Why?"

My mouth twisted. "You want to hear something else I've learned since I came here? The only real difference between a combine vip like Charon and a streetrat like me is how many people believe the lies we tell. . . . I don't enjoy feeling like your whore. And that's what I'll feel like if I leave now. I want to finish this job, now that it means something."

His eyes narrowed. "I suppose that's reasonable." He didn't know what to believe about me any more, and it bothered him.

"But it'll cost you."

He smiled, relieved. He could relate to that. "That's what I thought. Centauri will double the amount of your contracts."

"All of it—for the Center, too."

"Of course." He nodded.

"Do it now."

He glanced away from me for a long second, and back. "It's done."

"I'll check it when I get home." The formless couch was beginning to give me a sensory deprivation attack. I stood up, shaking it off. "What happened to Elnear's Security people?" They'd been witnesses—the only witnesses—to my warning him about the bomb.

"Don't ask questions you don't really want answered." He folded his arms; watching my expression. "You think you've figured out how to play this game, don't you? Just because you hold the key pieces, right now." He shook his head slowly. "Believe me, boy, you've had beginner's luck. Don't push it." Meaning that I'd been stupid not to spill what I knew about him when I had the chance. Because if he hadn't decided right then that he needed me, there would have been one more fatality after that explosion.

I rubbed my hands on my pants legs. Then I said, "There's one more thing I want."

He raised his eyebrows. "What is it?"

"I need stronger drugs."

"No." His mind closed like a door.

"I'm still half-crippled, Braedee. What you got me isn't good enough. I can't do what I need to do, if you really want my help." My hands flexed. "And I'm starting to get . . . symptoms."

"I can't get you anything stronger. The board wouldn't permit it. I had a hell of a time even getting you this far."

"You can do it if you want to. If Lady Elnear winds up dead, Centauri loses ChemEnGen. And you lose, too. . . . That's heavier on the scale than what Gentleman Charon thinks of psions."

"I can't do it."

"You owe me. Get me the drugs."

"I can't." He shook his head. "You underestimate how difficult it is for me to get what you need. That's not some streetcorner dreamdot you're asking for. Charon monitors everything that's done concerning you. . . . You also underestimate how much he resents your presence here."

I made a face, my hands tightening again.

"I'll give you this," he said finally. "I'll give you space. If you can get what you want somewhere else, I won't stop you."

I nodded, surprised.

"Lady Elnear is still at the hospital. She is expecting you to join her there. I don't have to tell you to keep your mouth shut about what you know. Do I—?"

I hesitated. "I guess not."

He nodded at the door. Somehow it had opened again while my back was turned.

I started for it, happy to be going out.

"One more thing."

I stopped. "What?"

"That earring. I wouldn't wear it again, if I were you. Particularly not around Charon."

My hand went to my ear, covering it, protecting it. "Why not?" Not quite able to keep all the tension out of my voice. "It's only a piece of glass."

His lips pulled up. "It's an emerald, you fool."

I stared at him, still touching my ear. "What—?"

He'd scanned its density just by looking at me. He looked at me now, and shook his head again. "You're lying about where you got it, too. It carries a taMing registry code; it belongs to Lady Lazuli."

My hand dropped to my side. I turned and went out the door. I felt his eyes following my back as I crossed the endless, lifeless room beyond.

16

ELNEAR WAS WAITING in still another private lounge when I got to the med center. She looked like a different woman from the one we'd left there last night. *Philipa was going to live.* It was all over her face, her mind. "How is she?" I asked the question anyway, so that she could tell me herself.

"She's going to be fine. Everything is going to be fine." She stood up, smiling that smile that made you feel like you'd just stepped into sunlight. Actually smiling it at me. After spending time with Braedee and Charon, getting that smile was like winning a prize. Right then I probably would have jumped out a window if she'd asked me to. The smile faded again, as she said, "Someone said that you were injured—"

I touched my shoulder; hardly even felt any soreness. Surprised by that, too. "Nothing much," I said softly, remembering to answer her, "ma'am. Glad to hear the good news." Not as glad as she was, but close, for her sake. "Have you seen her?"

Elnear shook her head. "No. She's still in the intensive unit; she'll be there until the reconstructive work is finished. It will be several weeks, they say." Her voice got a little weak. "She's suspended, of course, so she wouldn't know that I was there. . . ." But still she wished she could be. "At least she'll have only peace, no memory of—of this pain."

"She's lucky to have friends like you." Saying it because I couldn't help remembering what happened to people who didn't have friends like her. Loyal . . . and rich. I touched my shoulder again, looking away at the flow-mural wavering aimlessly over the far wall.

She glanced at me, curious, but she only asked, "Have you talked with Braedee?"

I nodded. I sat down on the long sofa next to her, suddenly feeling tired.

"I seem to have misjudged Centauri, for once. It seems he was right all along about how much I needed you."

I kept my face empty. "Yes, ma'am. I guess so."

"Are you still thinking about yesterday?" she said, trying to read my expression. "About Stryger? About all the—injustice?"

I was thinking about today. But I nodded, because hearing her say Stryger's name suddenly made me remember yesterday. I looked back at her, as the final thing she'd said registered. *Injustice.*

"Yes," she said, answering what was clear enough on my face now. "I've seen the Morning Report."

I laughed once. "I slept through it." The Indy's Morning Report—that was what Charon had been talking about. "It must have been good." Or at least not as bad as I'd figured. "I seem to be the only person in the galaxy who missed it."

"I hope so." She smiled again, but this time it was full of steel. "I hope everyone sees it. Do you want to see it now? I can call it up."

I nodded, and the mural that no one had been watching suddenly disappeared from the wall across the room. A new image came on-screen, jumping out at us as it went threedy. Sound came with it in a blare that made me wince. Shander Mandragora was suddenly in the room, somehow looking me right in the eye while he repeated yesterday's news. The only way I could tell he wasn't actually there was by the empty place where his mind should have been. But then, after what I'd seen last night, that probably didn't prove anything. I waited for some lurid full-feed of the bombing; feeling my eyes try to look away. But instead the report was on the debate between Elnear and Stryger. Images from it opened out behind Mandragora as if he could project his own memories; he could, in a way. I watched Stryger tell his lies about me again. I started to frown, wondering why Elnear wanted to make me look at this.

And then suddenly it was me up there, "refuting the charges in his own words"—reliving last night, up against the wall with Lazuli and Jiro while the hypers closed in on me. I looked down, away from it.

But Elnear's hand closed on my shoulder, giving me a gentle shake, forcing me to look up at the screen again.

"I killed him in self defense!" my reflection shouted, looking me straight in the eye. "And to save my friends, and to save your stinking telhassium. I wasn't a traitor, I worked for the FTA—"

But before I heard the insult I'd blurted next, my image was gone again. Mandragora was back, telling me how the Indy had "researched these conflicting versions of the incident. Here is the actual record," he said, not even smiling. "Let it speak for itself."

He stepped aside, into some spacewarp, and I sat up straighter, with all my attention on the show now as I saw something I'd never seen before: part of an original tape about what had happened after I'd killed Quicksilver. A Mines official I remembered, a man named Tanake, was describing how the psionic arch-criminal Quicksilver and his terrorists had nearly taken control of the telhassium supply. His version of what had happened didn't match my memories of it; probably just as well.

But then he was thanking the FTA's Security Arm for "fighting fire with fire"; admitting right there in front of the entire Federation that it had been psions working undercover inside Quicksilver's terrorist group who'd been the ones who stopped him—the only ones who could have done it, mind against mind. . . .

A sudden gust of wind, a sudden change of scene, and suddenly I was looking out across a winter-white Quarro from someplace up high: Jule and Siebeling stood together on the balcony of a house . . . being interviewed, having their five minutes of fame. They didn't look like they were enjoying it much; but they did their best to make a good impression. The voice-over and visual stats were making a lot of Siebeling's professional standing and Jule's family ties; trying to prove something. I watched them, listened to them, breathing in a memory of the cold sharp air of a winter's day with every breath. Siebeling did most of the talking, like he always did, used to it. Jule had always saved her words, turned them into poems instead. Siebeling was talking about Dere Cortelyou, the corporate telepath who'd first broken through my mental walls and forced my mind out of hiding. Our friend, who'd died there on Cinder, killed by Quicksilver. Then I listened to him talking about me, about why I wasn't there beside them when I was the one who deserved the real credit for stopping Quicksilver. . . .

I tried to touch the place where my mind had been while that was happening—couldn't. A dizziness like the fear of falling made my brain sing.

". . . I had a nervous breakdown," my mirror image was saying across the room. "That's what it means to be a psion, and kill somebody. . . ." I looked up, seeing myself last night again, trapped, badgered, like an animal in a cage. ". . . And I guess it still doesn't mean shit to be a psion and a hero."

I watched myself push out of view and disappear, as Mandragora suddenly reappeared, to point out the obvious, about me, about me and the Lady, about Stryger's "incomplete data." It wasn't exactly an apology, and the asinine questions he'd thrown at me himself had all been trimmed away. But he'd given me what I'd wanted after all. Maybe he wasn't such a bastard.

Elnear was leaning back on the couch, her arms folded comfortably, watching me with a look that was somewhere between curiosity and satisfaction.

I shook my head, as the fax finally winked off, taking the past with it. "So," she said. "The truth sets us free."

I turned toward her. "You really think that can make up for what Stryger did?"

"It will certainly help. Why—don't you believe that it will?"

"It's only one version of the story. The lies have already got it outnumbered." I shrugged. "Even what you saw wasn't really the truth. It was what happened . . . but it wasn't the truth." I thought about Centauri. They'd been a part of the truth for me back then, just like they were now; part of the combine conspiracy that had backed Quicksilver. I wondered how many people in the entire galaxy besides me knew that. Jule knew it; and somebody might even have listened to her. But she hadn't told anyone. Blood was still thicker than water.

Elnear sat there next to me, looking tired but content. She thought she knew the whole truth about what had happened at the Federation Mines on Cinder; she thought she knew the whole truth about what was happening now.

I couldn't let her go on believing it. She had to know everything about what Centauri had done. She'd never win otherwise, never get clear of them. I remembered where we were, and how easily even the hypers had planted eavesdroppers last night. I couldn't tell her anything here. "Ma'am, I haven't eaten yet. How about you? I saw a noodle joint a couple of levels up, on my way here—"

She looked surprised at the sudden change of subject. But then she realized how exhausted, how hungry, she really was. "Yes, of course . . . I haven't eaten a thing since yesterday afternoon. And I didn't have much of an appetite then." She smiled, rueful. "But there's no need to go out; I can have food brought to us here."

"Hospital food?" I asked, and made a face. *Damn.* "I'd rather have a plate of noodles."

"It can be anything you want," she said, still smiling. "Do you really want that?"

I'd forgotten what it meant to be a taMing, for just a minute. . . . I put my foot up across my knee; my fist began to tap a frustrated rhythm on it. I rested my head against the wall, staring at nothing, as I reached out with all the gentleness and control I could still manage, and touched her mind. (Lady,) I thought. She jerked; her eyes went wide. (Don't panic—I need to talk to you. Outside.)

She sat blinking for a second as if someone had shone a light straight into her eyes. When she seemed to register me again, she murmured, "Well . . . perhaps you're right. I can't stay here forever. There are things to be done. Now that I know Philipa will be all right. . . ." She got up, following my lead like a sleepwalker.

By the time we were in a mod she'd taken charge again, taking us back to the FTA plex, through the security scanners, into what ought to be the most privacy anyone could hope for on this planet. But we didn't go to her office. Instead she took me to the delegate's restaurant, on an open terrace at the pinnacle of an ancient tower. The roof garden was filled with small tables underneath umbrellas of living tree. You could look out and down across the geologic layers of time and structure that made up the city all around, and yet still believe you were out in the open air under a perfect sky. The sky was a monomole shield, so flawless that I couldn't tell it from the real thing, looking up at it from below. The higher towers touched it, supported it like rigid fingers.

Elnear ordered us lunch, and spent the time until it came pointing out historic landmarks to me, as if there was nothing more important on either of our minds. Some of the pre-space structures went back eight hundred years; and this was a new city, for Earth. I remembered when I'd thought the buildings in Oldcity were old. There'd been so much intermediate buildup here that by now it was hard to tell what the forms of most of the original structures had been. The one I could see best was an inverted cone, the whole building balanced on a tip a few dozen meters wide. "It was built when composites were first introduced," Elnear said, when I asked about it. "The architects of the period tended to be a little . . . giddy." She smiled.

The food came, laid out like it belonged in an art gallery. I hated to touch anything on the perfectly designed plate, but I was too hungry to let it stop me for long. It tasted better than it looked. I sighed, looking out at the view, as pastry shaped like flowers dissolved in my mouth. Thinking that I could get used to this . . . I glanced back at Elnear.

She was staring at me, the way she'd look at something she was thinking of making into a painting.

"Ma'am—?" I said, suddenly aware of every square centimeter of my body; wondering if I'd made an ass of myself somehow. I'd thought

Jardan had driven enough basic protocol into my brain to at least let me eat in public.

But she said, "It was no exaggeration to call you a hero for what you did last night. Or to call what you did for the Federation on Cinder an act of heroism . . . what all of you did there, but especially you. You deserve—"

I glanced away. "No, it wasn't," I said, cutting her off.

"What would you call it, then?" she asked.

"Survival," I said. "I did what I had to, to survive. I killed Quicksilver because he was going to kill us. I didn't have a choice. There was nothing heroic about it." *Nothing at all.* I frowned, looking down seeing my reflection trapped in the tabletop.

"How did you become a part of the undercover operation that stopped him?" She hadn't even known that Jule had been a part of it, until yesterday; hadn't believed it, until today. . . . But by now everyone's blind ignorance was beginning to make sense to me. What we'd done on Cinder had almost cost Centauri everything—and one of us had been one of their own. They must have done all they could to suppress or distort the news about it; and they weren't the only ones involved. Maybe it wasn't so insane that even Shander Mandragora hadn't heard the real story.

I looked back at Elnear. There was nothing but respect, honest curiosity, behind her question. I laughed, and shook my head. "How—? The hard way, just like everything else I ever did back in Oldcity. I got away from a press gang, and the District Corpses picked me up for making fools of the Labor Crows. They tested me for psi—they were testing everybody they hauled in, because the FTA was looking for psions. Psions are all criminals, right; how else would you find one—?" I smiled, and she looked down. "That's when I met Jule; she was in the group too. Siebeling was in charge of it. He'd set it up like a kind of therapy group, an excuse to teach us all how to use our Gift, and have the FTA pay for it. The FTA hoped we'd attract Rubiy—"

"Rubiy?"

"Quicksilver . . . his name was Rubiy. He had a name," I said, not sure why it bothered me that nobody remembered that. "They knew he'd be looking for recruits. They couldn't get at him any other way, and they figured, no big loss if he found out the truth and killed a few freaks. . . ."

She blinked. "A catspaw," she murmured.

"A what?"

"A 'catspaw' is someone used by someone else to do a job that is unpleasant or dangerous."

"Yeah." I nodded. "That fits. It worked, too. Rubiy picked four of us, sent us to work with his people on Cinder who were trying to break the Mines' security."

She glanced away, confusion starting in her thoughts. "If you were working undercover for the FTA, then why—?" Remembering my scars.

I touched my back, my mouth twisting. "Like I said, the truth's never that simple. Siebeling and me . . . we didn't get along too well at first. He threw me out of the group, sent me back to Contract Labor. But when Rubiy found out, he used it—he got me sent to the Mines. I was his inside man." The world faded into white, into the memories of what I'd seen there, and what had been done to me . . . the times when I'd wanted Rubiy to succeed. He'd even counted on that. "Rubiy would have given me anything I'd wanted if I'd given him the Mines." He'd trusted me, because he thought we were the same—dead inside. There were times when I'd nearly believed that myself.

But he was wrong. I blinked, my eyes smarting with the burn of memory.

"Why didn't you?" Elnear said, her gaze steady now.

I looked down. The plate of half-eaten food in front of me seemed like an hallucination. I shook my head. "Because of Jule. She taught me some things Siebeling didn't know how to. That I was still . . . alive. That I could still care about someone else." I kept looking down. "I guess she taught both of us that. I wonder how she knew so much about it?"

Elnear didn't say anything.

"Why did you marry a taMing, anyway?" I asked it, finally. "Why did you let them get such a hold on you? Did they make you do it?"

She looked back at me, half smiled as she realized that I was only doing what she'd just done. "Oh, no," she said. "I wasn't forced into anything. I married Kelwin because I wanted to, and he wanted me to. I was much younger, then. . . ." Meaning not just in years. "I loved him very much. What more did I need to know—?" She'd thought that she had protected her interests. She'd thought that he would live forever.

"How did he die?"

"He was away on Centauri business, on Dandrosa, when it happened. There was a massive intrasystem failure. . . . The details don't matter.

They found evidence of sabotage." She looked away, her folded hands tightening on the table top. "It was shortly after Jule's mother died."

"What happened to her?"

"She had a drug problem." Elnear was still looking somewhere else. "They said it was an accidental overdose. But ever since the family had learned that Jule was—was—" *(defective)*, her mind said, helplessly, instinctively, "—a psion, there had been suspicions, accusations of some sort of genetic tampering or falsification of hereditary charts. . . ."

"You're telling me you think the taMings killed her?" I remembered Lazuli not-quite-saying something about Jule's mother, Charon's first wife.

Elnear shrugged. "Nothing was ever proved . . . in either case. Jule's mother had ties to Triple Gee. The marriage was supposed to ease tensions; it involved the exchange of certain planetary interests in the same system where Kelwin died."

"So she was a hostage." *And maybe a saboteur.*

Elnear looked up again, almost startled. "Perhaps, in a sense." Her eyes turned bleak. "But then, aren't we all hostages to fortune . . . ?"

"So maybe your husband had to die because she did?" Maybe I didn't want to get used to this life, after all.

"Perhaps." She got up, restlessly, as if part of her wished I'd leave it alone. But part of her wanted it, needed it.

"How long ago?"

"Sixteen years." No hesitation. She could have told me how many months, days . . . seconds.

"It should have been Charon."

She turned back, her hands clenched now. *(It should have been Charon.)* It had crystallized in her own mind at the same instant it had come out of my mouth.

"No," I said, to her half frown. "You didn't think of it first."

She pressed her lips together, tried to wipe her eyes without me seeing her do it. She sat down again, her mind as open, as defenseless, as any human mind ever was. "All I've really wanted," she said finally, so softly that the thought was almost louder, "for sixteen years, was to see it through." Her work, her legacy, her life. Trying to hold on to what still had some meaning, trying to keep Centauri and the taMings from taking it all away from her: that had become her whole life, since she'd lost him. When she died they lost her holdings too because there were no children, and they knew it. No wonder she hadn't been interested in setting back her clocks, once Kelwin was gone. But she wasn't interested in being assassinated, either. . . . It had been easy to make her think someone wanted her dead, when you could never be sure anyone's death was from natural causes.

Her face changed, as she finally felt ready to hear whatever I wanted her to know: "What was it that you were going to tell me?"

I glanced away, out over the glaciers of glass and stone, suddenly uneasy again. Maybe this open terrace was really as shielded as the offices down below, but I couldn't believe it. Braedee had said he'd leave me alone, but I knew how much that was worth. He didn't want me telling Elnear the truth, and God only knew who else had what kind of long eyes watching.

They said ignorance was bliss. The more I knew about this world, the more paranoid I felt. I couldn't be sure of anything—except myself. (Lady,) I said, very gently again, mumbling something pointless out loud for any ears that were listening. (I have to be sure. Don't fight me—) She sat frozen, her muscles rigid; only I could tell that inside her something was happening that no one else could see. When I was sure she was really ready, I reached out again, letting the message form as softly as snow. (Lady . . . no one was trying to kill you, before last night.)

Her head jerked with surprise and confusion. I let the images implode as her incredulity crushed them; waiting until she could deal with what it meant to her. (I found out today from Charon. The same way you're finding it out from me—) She kept blinking at me, like someone taking drugs. But she nodded, letting me know she understood, ready for what came next.

(Centauri started it as a way to get at you, scare you, keep you under control.) I let her see how and why, using the images like an information feed. I began to get feedback as she realized it was the same kind of harassment she'd endured all along, only more vicious now. Centauri was trying harder to keep hold of her as she tried harder to get away. (They used me to spy for them, Lady, just like you thought . . . even to set you up for Stryger.) I winced at the stab of her betrayal. *(A catspaw,)* I thought, without meaning to. That's what she'd called it; that's what I'd been, again. (I didn't know. They used me!) Letting my own anger batter hers back, tired of taking the blame. I'd been fucked over by Centauri too . . . and not for the first time. (Centauri was part of the conspiracy behind Rubiy that nearly got me killed. And they got away from it clean. If I hate the FTA for what happened to me out on Cinder, I hate Centauri worse—) I let her see it, let her see why, until

she really believed that none of this had happened because I'd wanted it
to.

(But yesterday night—that changed things.) I showed her the rest of
it. That now there really was a threat, and Centauri didn't want her to
die any more than she did. That even Charon thought I had a use now.
That I wasn't going to leave until it was over, and she was safe; until I'd
made it up to her.

She stared at me, not even blinking now, as if she was beyond anger,
or surprise, almost beyond any emotion at all. "Thank you," she murmured, finally, although that wasn't what she wanted to say. Gratitude
was the farthest thing from her mind after what she'd just learned . . .
the way she'd learned it. And yet—

She put her hand out blindly; needing real, solid, contact with another human . . . and there was no doubt left in her mind *that I was as
human as she was.* There should have been a better way to put it, but I
couldn't think of one, so I just gave up and took it the way she meant it.
I got up from the table after a minute, looking back at her. My smile
hardly pinched at all as I said, "Ma'am, right now I've got some—
business I've got to work out. I don't know how long it'll take."

"What kind of business?" she asked, suddenly uncertain again.

I shook my head. "Calling in some favors."

"This is going to help us find out what really happened last night?"

"I hope so. . . . It's better if you don't ask," I said, stopping her
before she did. Her mouth pressed shut, her forehead wrinkled. She
wished that I'd trust her, not really believing there were things she
really wouldn't want to know about me.

I started to turn away, hesitated. "Lady, how much do you think
Stryger really wants that Security Council slot?"

She looked at me blankly for a minute. Then she started to frown,
and shook her head. "You can't imagine that he would try to have me
killed. . . ." Incredulity that was almost laughter filled her voice.

"Braedee doesn't think that walking bomb was a hire job. I do. He
can't think of a combine that would do it for themselves, but he thinks
they're too proud to use the Lack Market. You know Stryger's got
combines behind him. They think he's just another catspaw—but that's
not what Stryger thinks. He wants that slot for the same reason you do,
to get himself free of them. He wants the power, real bad. I think he'd
kill to get it."

She shook her head again, half smiling as she began to get up from
her seat. "Cat, I understand why you feel this way. But I assure you,

Sohjourner Stryger may be too intense for his own good—he may even be something of a fanatic—but he is not an evil man."

"He lied, didn't he? He smeared you, and me, right up there in front of God and everybody, to get what he wanted—"

"He could have been sincere. He claims that he was misinformed. . . ."

"Why are you defending him?" I said. She didn't answer me. "Do you really still think he's better than you?" My hands dropped to my sides. "Lady," I said finally. "I met someone like that once. He picked me up on the street in Oldcity, bought me the first decent meal I'd had in about a week. And while I was eating, he was talking to me about how psions were evil and unnatural, because they had these abilities. . . ." Something that wasn't really a laugh caught in my throat. I hadn't known what he was talking about, why he was saying those things to me, staring into my green eyes with their long slit pupils. . . . "Then he took me up to a hired room and beat the crap out of me."

She sat down on the edge of the table, her mouth open, her mind groping. "Why?" she murmured at last, weakly. "Why didn't you leave . . . ?"

"Because that's what he was paying me for." I left the restaurant.

17

"WELL," ARGENTYNE SAID, as she met me at the door, "somehow I didn't expect to see you here again. At least not so soon." Her silver eyebrows rose, asking silent questions, as she pulled the door to Purgatory open wider. "Don't tell me you're lonely."

She was still blocking the doorway with her body. I stood on the steps, suddenly feeling more self-conscious than I thought I knew how to. "I wish I was. Lonely, I mean. . . . Is Daric here?"

She laughed, ruffling her hair. "Is it still daylight?" She glanced out, looking for sky. "He only comes out at night."

"That figures." I pushed my hands deeper into my pockets.

"You want to see him?"

"No."

"And you're not here to close me down, or you wouldn't be here alone. So what can I do for you?" She yawned, the camph she'd been sucking on dangling from her fingers. I realized suddenly that she was yawning the way an animal yawned, instinctively showing teeth. Yawning because she was nervous, even a little afraid. Just like I was. It made her real, easier to look at without feeling my brain seize up.

"I need directions." I glanced over my shoulder at the street behind me. The water line was halfway up the dome, but there was still a wide stretch of sky visible. The map in my head had brought me this far, but it ended at the water line. "The map ends here." And no map from the city files could tell me what I really needed to know, anyway.

"You want to go off the Deep End?" She looked incredulous again. "Alone? Why?"

Now that I really knew why they called it that, I wished I didn't. "It's not something I want to do. And it's not something I want to talk about in the middle of the street." I jerked my head at the swirl of bodies in random motion behind me.

Argentyne stepped aside, opening the way for me into the club's interior. "Sorry. I just got up. It always takes me a while to regain consciousness." Her mouth curved in a wry smile. "It's so early, you know."

I grinned, stepping inside. "Yeah, I know what you mean. Or I used to."

"You used to be a performer?" she asked.

"Sort of."

"And then you got respectable." She led me back along the hallway, down the ramp. She was wearing a soft robe that looked like it had been made out of a bedspread; most of the color had faded out of it a long time ago. It was something she wore because she loved it a lot.

I looked down at my neat, perfect, Centauri-branded clothes. "Not by choice," I said.

The club was nearly empty, gray with filtered daylight. A couple of indifferent floods lighted up the darker corners so the drones could finish their work, siphoning up the detritus of a hard night. The space and silence made it seem like a different building from the one I'd been in yesterday. Up on the stage a handful of bodies were clustered by a single bare table, sprawled across each other in the small island of cushions around it, looking like they'd had too much of something: I recognized the players of her symb. "Rehearsal," she explained, nodding toward the stage. It felt more like a mass hangover to me.

"That was really incredible last night," I said, remembering the way their separate kinds of music had fused into a perfect web of sound, the mindwarping visuals that had come rippling out through the noise . . . suddenly remembering who she was again; suddenly feeling awkward and self-conscious again.

She looked at me, about to toss off some remark about my own performance here. Seeing my face, she only said, "Glad you enjoyed it. Glad you enjoyed something about last night." She glanced down, embarrassment and leftover anger at Daric blurring her memory, and we were back on the same ground again. "That wasn't the usual crowd, last night," she said. "That was a private party. I just wanted you to know." *That it wouldn't happen again.*

I didn't say anything.

"You like the muse, huh?" she asked, to fill up the silence. I nodded. "You sure you wouldn't like to complete a circuit yourself?" She climbed onto the stage, reaching back to give me a hand. It wasn't an offer she made often, or to just anybody. It was an apology; and something more.

I climbed up after her, more than surprised. But a kind of panic started to choke me the second I thought about taking her seriously. I shook my head. "I don't have any talent."

"You never know until you try. We could wire you ourselves. Nobody would have to know. It takes no time; it doesn't even hurt." She lifted her hair with her hand, showing me the flesh-colored jack on the back of her neck. She was still thinking about what she'd felt last night. "Wouldn't you like to find out . . . ?" She wanted to find out—what it would be like to link me into something bigger, and play my mind. Her copper stare met me, dared me.

I glanced away at the players, wondering what they'd think of that. "Maybe . . . someday. Not today." I shrugged, too much else on my mind right now. Besides, she might think it was nothing, but if the FTA's security scans picked up that socket, I'd be in deep shit. "Anyway, what you did last night was about as real as it gets. You don't need a psion if you can make that happen with your own head."

She shook off the compliment. "Holograms. Cheap tricks. I can imagine it, but I can't make people share it, *live* it, even with illusions. *You* knew it wasn't real. . . ."

I grinned. "Yeah—but I forgot. And that's the real magic, right? If you can make people forget it's not real."

She shrugged, annoyed and flattered.

A couple of the players began to clap and whistle long trills, as we came toward them and my face registered. I felt my face start to go red, figuring last night here at the club was the reason.

But then one of them said, "Yo, Cat. Caught you on the Morning Report," and the other heads were nodding.

Argentyne turned to look at me, curious. "What happened?" She wondered suddenly if I'd come down here to get away from something I'd done.

"He only saved your habit and a bunch of other vips after you threw him out of here. Some assassin blew himself into meat salad at a taMing hole last night." The flute player bowed gracefully toward me. She was dressed metallic, as long and thin as the flexible pipes that had replaced the fingers on one of her hands.

"Daric—?" Argentyne said, with a sudden sharp pang of *guiltshockfear*. "Daric—is he all right?"

I nodded unenthusiastically.

"You saved him?" she repeated.

"It was an accident," I said, and someone laughed, but it wasn't her. "I was hired to guard Lady Elnear. He just got in the way."

She was still looking at me though a haze of mixed emotions. "Oh God," she murmured, and looked away. "Why didn't he tell me himself . . . ?"

"You still expect him to act like a human being?" one of the players wearing a touchboard in his chest asked. "To treat you like one?"

"Oh, bugger off, Jax," she said. "Who asked you?" Under the silver skin, the silver hair, I got the feeling there was somebody a lot more normal than Daric was, maybe a lot more ordinary than she wanted to admit to herself.

"Daric looked pretty fragged," somebody else said gently. "Don't worry about it. Maybe it'll shake some steel into him." He grinned, his teeth large and white against his blue-black skin and beard. He wore the beard tucked through his belt, and some instrument that looked like a sack full of light plugged into his neck.

"Since when do you get up so early, Midnight?" she asked him, still prickling.

He shrugged, blinked his bloodshot eyes. "Up? I haven't been to bed."

She half smiled; twitched her shoulders to shake off her mood. "Well," she murmured to me, rubbing her face, "thanks anyway, even if it's thanks for nothing. Tell me what you're looking for. If we've got it, you can have it."

I glanced at the players, back at her.

"They're family," she said. "And they're not easily shocked." She moved back to the edge of the stage and sat down, her bare feet dangling. The players shrugged and flopped down where they were, waiting.

I sat down too, feeling less obvious that way. "I need some drugs."

Her face twitched almost imperceptably. She took the camph out of her mouth and looked at it. "Why don't you just ask Daric?"

I grimaced. "Two reasons. The second one is that he doesn't have what I need."

The twitch turned into a frown. "You're in that deep? You want hard stuff?" She was surprised.

I shook my head. "Just hard-to-get stuff. Topalase-AC."

She looked at me blankly. "What's that? I never heard of it."

"It lets me use my psi."

"You need drugs for that?" she said. "I thought you were born that way."

"I was." I explained, keeping it as short as I could.

"Hm," she said, when I was done. She pulled her knees up, hugging her ankles. "Why won't Centauri give you what you want?"

"Charon taMing's a freakhater—Daric's sister Jule is a psion. He's afraid of me."

"Of you?" She laughed.

"Should I be insulted?" I said.

"Oh, hell no." She waved a hand at me. "Jeezu, have you seen Charon—?"

"Lots."

"Then you know what I mean. . . . So they want you to do this gig but they won't give you the equipment, is that it?"

I nodded. "That's it. But Braedee said he wouldn't stop me from getting it myself."

"You really want to burn your brains out? You care that much about them? Why not just go along, play dumb and collect your pay?"

I thought about it. I looked back at her. "Why do you go with Daric? Just for the money?" It came out a little nastier than I'd meant it to.

(Fuck you—) I heard it through her eyes, but then her expression changed. "It's not like that. He's not like he seems—" Remembering last night, she broke off. "Well, maybe he is . . . but not when we're alone." Her hand tightened into a painful fist. "I *care* about him—"

"You love him." Saying what she couldn't make herself say. Asking the question even though it was none of my business, just because the idea was so unbelievable.

She looked back at me, suddenly resenting it. "Sometimes. . . . So what if I do? It's none of your business, kid."

"I know," I said.

She thought about it a minute longer. "You care about Lady Elnear?"

I nodded. "Yeah. I guess I do." Surprised by that, too. Without meaning to, I thought about Lazuli, and her children. I touched my ear, the emerald earring; let my hand drop.

"Lady Elnear wants to change the universe," Argentyne said. "What about you?"

"Just part of it."

She laughed. "You got it, laddie love." She climbed to her feet, looking back at the players. "I don't know who to call on. Anybody know where he could find someone to give him what he wants?" The ones who were still awake shrugged, heads moved back and forth. *No.*

"We don't do a lot of drugs," she said, as if she had to explain it. "It screws up our timing." She stared at her feet, scratched her head. "Daric knows the territory better than any of us do. You got a sample of his dream jewelry last night. He plays hard, and he makes deals for his friends. . . ." She was worried that he played too hard, that he was already in too deep. "If you won't ask him, I can tell you who to talk to, and where to look for them. I can't promise they can fix you up. Maybe they'd know who could. But frankly—" She was looking back at me again, "I'd ask Daric before I'd try it alone, even if I hated his guts. There's a reason the Deep End's not on the city maps, you know. The Lack Market runs it. It's got a whole different set of rules."

I nodded, my mouth pulling up. "Yeah, I know. But I grew up in a place like that. I know how the people there think. I know *what* they're thinking if I need to."

"Every place is different," she said, the worry line still etched deep between her silver brows. "But if that's what you want. . . ." She shrugged when I didn't say anything more. "You can't go under dressed like that. You'd be dead before you got a hundred meters. Come on in the back. We've got plenty of gear you can pick through."

She led me through the wings of the stage and down a corridor, pushed open a door. Inside, it looked like a costume shop having a nervous breakdown—clothing in piles, hanging from hooks, strung up on racks, tacked to the walls. "Help yourself," she said, wading in.

I followed her into the room, breathing in the strange, musty smell of the place. "I never saw this many clothes in my entire life."

"You can be anything you want to be, here. Clothes make the man— into a woman, if you want. Or vice versa." She tossed a long striped wrap-skirt at me, grinning. I shook my head and dropped the skirt. "Androgyny's very big right now," she said. "You'd look regular."

"If I have to run I might trip." I picked up a loose yellow-brown tank top, held it out. Symbols from some pre-space language were printed inside a circle on the front of it. "Rolecrossing was real popular in Quarro about five years back. Everything keeps coming around. . . ." I took off my jacket and shirt.

"Maybe someday it'll even mean something," she murmured, kicking through mounds of cloth. "Quarro, huh?" She sounded impressed. "You must be a real trendsetter."

I laughed once, pulling on the tank top. It was long and baggy, but it let me move. "I was lucky if I had a shirt on my back, most of the time I lived there."

"Uh-huh. . . ." She picked up a hat made of feathers and put it on. "Being poor sucks, especially in a rich town."

"I wouldn't know."

She looked at me, puzzled.

"In Oldcity, if you didn't have a credit line, you couldn't even leave. I never saw Quarro."

She made a face, suddenly feeling cold inside. "Being poor sucks, anywhere," she said. "That's why I wanted this club. After my five minutes of fame are over, I want to have somewhere to crawl home to." I felt her remember her family suddenly; remember how her father had thrown her out for good the day she'd come home with silver skin.

I nodded, thinking about Jule, and Siebeling. "Makes sense," I said softly. I picked out some brown knit leggings and a heavy leather jacket. The jacket would give me some protection if I ran into a little trouble. . . . If I ran into a lot of trouble, even body armor wouldn't save me. "How long you been with Daric?"

"About a year and a half. I met him right after we went nova and started to play gigs above the waterline." She was looking at me, but her gaze was somewhere else. "We were doing this exquisite private club, right up under the stars. Everybody there was some kind of famous, only they were all there for *us* . . . it was the most incredible night of my life. And then Daric came up to me, after the show. He gave me a silver rose, and he said, 'You've waited all your life for me. Let me show you why.'" She was seeing him now, the way he'd looked to her that night: young and handsome, rich and confident. Remembering the way he'd looked at her—as if he'd never seen anyone more beautiful. Remembering the way he'd made her believe that every word he said was true. . . .

I looked away from her face, sorry I'd asked. "How do you like his family?"

Her mind snapped back to the present, and her smile turned black. "About as much as they like me. They scare the shit out of me."

I shook my head. "When I saw you with them, you looked like you were having a pretty good time raising their blood pressure."

She lifted her hand and made half a bow to me. "I'm an entertainer. It's all part of the act, love. . . . Daric enjoys if far more than I do." Her smiled softened. "I remember you, that night. You looked like you were in shock. Like you'd crash-landed on the wrong planet."

"I had," I said.

"I felt sorry for you, until you stood up to Daric. Then I figured you for a survivor, after all."

I looked down. "Yeah, that's one thing I'm good at, anyway."

"Cat," she said. I looked up. "Ask Daric. He can get what you want. I'll even ask for you, if you want me to. He owes you that much."

I shook my head. "I can't trust him." I already knew too much, about politics.

"I know what you think of him." She tossed the feather hat away, impatient. "You're right, he's fucked up. But there really is a human being inside there—"

"That's what I'm afraid of."

She cocked her head at me. "Oh," she said, finally. "You think you can't trust any of us, huh? You think we're all rotten, because you can see into our minds and read all our dirty little secrets—?"

I looked down, picked up a pair of heavy gloves. "No. I don't think that. . . ." I glanced up again, pulling them on. "I try not to, anyhow."

"Daric treats me better than anyone I've ever known." She was thinking about all the things he'd done for her, given to her. Anything she wanted. He'd set her up with this club, like I'd figured—but she owned it, not him.

"When he's not treating you like shit." I shrugged on the jacket. "Sure, why shouldn't he? You're beautiful, you're famous, and his family thinks you're trash. You're everything he needs."

"You don't know anything about his needs," she said, frowning. "And you're starting to piss me off."

I lifted my head. "What's he ever done that's decent, for anybody besides you?"

She looked away, searching her memory. "The girl," she said, after thinking a little longer than she probably would have liked. "A while back he brought a kid here, a young girl. Somebody'd beaten her up real bad." Her face flinched. "He said he'd just found her on the street, and couldn't leave her there. He asked us to help her. So we did." She put her hands on her hips, as if she was waiting for me to congratulate her. "He didn't do that out of anything but common humanity." While inside her thoughts she was remembering something strange about the girl; how the kid had looked like a street nothing, dressed in greasy rags . . . except she'd had a face that looked like an exotic's: eyes that were too green, with long slits for pupils. Like she'd had expensive cosmetic surgery done. . . .

"A psion," I said. "The way she looked—she was a psion."

"Who?" Argentyne shook her head. "You mean the kid?" Not asking me how I knew what the kid had looked like. She gave me one of those looks deadheads always gave me when I answered questions they hadn't asked. "I don't know."

"She didn't do anything—use her psi?"

"Not while she was here." She shook her head again. "But she wasn't here that long. He brought her in one night; she was in shock, then. She couldn't even move on her own. We patched her up and put her to bed upstairs. When I looked in the next morning she was already gone. I never saw her again. Daric asked about her; he really cared about what had happened to her, whether she was all right."

Daric taMing playing godsend to a freak. I didn't know what the hell to make of that. Maybe she'd reminded him of Jule . . . except I thought he hated Jule. I wondered if he'd beaten her up himself. "I still can't trust him to know about this. You've got to promise me you won't tell him I was here."

She sighed. "If you're that obsessed, who am I to stand in your way?" She looked at my clothes. "Out of all this, you had to choose that?" She waved a hand.

I didn't answer, my mind still hooked on the image of a lost girl with green eyes, so terrified that all she knew how to do was disappear. I wondered if she'd had any more idea of why somebody would want to beat the crap out of her than I'd ever had. Maybe nobody could ever really understand a thing like that. . . .

"Cat," Argentyne said, facing me without my noticing she'd moved.

I stepped back, startled. Remembered she'd said something about my clothes. "Thanks for the clothes," I mumbled. "Just tell me who to look for. I'll get out of here and stop pissing you off."

"We could bodypaint you a little, first—" she offered, and I realized part of her was still trying to stall me. She was really afraid I'd go out of here and get my head kicked in.

I turned away, annoyed. "No." I gestured at the clothes. "I know what I'm doing." I hesitated, turning back; managed a smile. "But thanks for caring whether I do or not."

She smiled too, resigned. "It's my curse." She tied a hank of green scarf around my head. "Come on." She nodded, and started back toward the door.

18

THE TUBE THAT RAN under the bay from N'Yuk island to the island called Stat had been built nearly three hundred years ago. It hadn't been intended to make stops along the way. But then they ran out of room up above, and the city had started oozing off the end of the land into the cold, dark waters of the harbor. Now most of the sea bottom between the islands was covered with a separate city, clear domes spreading like a mass of fish eggs over the silty muck, reclaiming it for the air-breathers.

But nobody could call that part of town real desirable, and so like Oldcity it had filled up with the dregs, the losers and the users, the kind of people who slipped through holes in the combine nets—by choice, or because they couldn't help themselves, and couldn't find anybody else who wanted to help them either.

The Tube made stops there now, and at the third one I got off. To reach the surface, I climbed about three hundred steps that smelled like piss, because the lift was out of order. The pilastered cavern of the station itself didn't look so bad—the FTA managed the services here like it did in Federal Trade Districts everywhere. They did a pretty good job of it. And then they left the human flotsam who lived there to drift, instead of taking care of them too. They needed their pools of desperate, unskilled labor all over the galaxy for their press gangs to feed off of, to sell to the combines to do their dirty work.

I stepped over a sick dog that lay panting at the top of the lightstrung stairs, my hands clenched inside my jacket pockets as I looked around me at the graffiti and the garbage. I didn't want to touch anything, have the greasy dirt rub off on me, stick to my skin, pollute me. I felt sick when I remembered how it had been once, when I'd been once of these people. When I hadn't known where the filth stopped and my flesh started, and hadn't even cared. . . .

"Shit—" I said softly. I stopped, forcing myself to lean against a wall while I got my bearings. Now I knew I'd been too long with the ta-Mings. I hadn't just begun to forget who I really was, I'd actually begun to hate myself. It must be catching. I pulled up my collar as I moved away from the station steps. I almost thought I could still smell the sea bottom, that stench and tang I used to catch a whiff of sometimes in Oldcity, when an accidental breath of real sea air found its way inside. But the sea bottom was buried under monomole and composite. It was only my imagination, trying to make something better of the stale smell of sweat and urine.

This was the place I wanted, the station called Free Market Square. Argentyne and the players had described it to me, filling in holes in each others' knowledge until my own mental map was as clear as I could make it. The warren of streets around the Tube stop entrance was at the heart of the Lack Market's business district. The Lack Market had a motto: "Anything you want." Representatives ready to provide the kinds of services the combines liked to pretend didn't exist any more cruised the open square, mingling with bodies looking for those services and with other bodies that were only here because they didn't have anywhere else to go.

I froze suddenly, staring out across the crowds. Someone was moving through them, coming toward the station entrance—someone I recognized. *Stryger.* He was cloaked, and surrounded by followers but no media that I could see. Nobody else even looked at him twice. I stepped behind a peeling ad kiosk, keeping out of sight as I watched him pass. I brushed his thoughts, wondering what the hell he could possibly want from a place like this. Hoping it was dirty.

He glanced over his shoulder, looking back the way he'd come. He felt pity, and satisfaction . . . but that was all. One of the shelters his money had paid for was right here, across the square. He'd come to the Deep End on his own, to see for himself what kind of job it was doing. That was the only reason he'd come here. There was nothing else on his mind right now; not the Assembly vote, not the Council slot, not genocide. . . . I watched him disappear into the Tube station, while a kind of numbness spread inside me. Once all he'd wanted was to do that kind of good. Maybe there was even some part of him that still wanted it. I tried to imagine him that way, the way everyone else saw him—controlling the kind of money and power he did, and using it only for good.

It made me feel lousy. I pushed out of my hiding place and moved on into the crowd.

Vendors had set up stalls or just squatted on the pavement with food and wares spread out around them, interrupting the flow of foot traffic. Their shrill cries and blaring music drowned out the murmured queries, the muttered answers of the real transactions going on. Argentyne had said that sometimes the Corpses put in an appearance, just to keep things orderly; I didn't see any out now. It was just like Oldcity: all they cared about was appearances, anyway. They were out of their depth here, literally and figuratively, and they knew it. You could do or buy anything down here, as long as you did it by the numbers.

I took my left hand out of my pocket and caught hold of my collar: a sign that I was looking for drugs. I left it clenched there as I found the nerve to push out into the sea of grotesques and hunters and derelicts. I saw other seekers with a fist clenched over a collar; some of the fists were real white-knuckled. There were hands locked behind backs, hands clutching the opposite wrist, hands speaking in silent gestures against a thigh, all sending out different messages to whoever was interested. If you didn't know the codes you could walk here for hours and never get a single response from anybody you wanted to meet. The signs were different from the ones I knew, but in subtle ways. Prying into thoughts as I passed, I checked the codes against their meanings, learning, remembering. If I made clumsy mistakes somebody might not notice; but then again, somebody might. . . . I dodged past something human the size of a horse, that was leading a half-naked burnout on a chain.

One after another, dealers came up to me, offering me the usual street shit. They all shook their heads when I said what I wanted. All of them knew the names Argentyne had told me to use, the ones Daric did his major business with, but none of them would admit it. Some of them turned around and walked away from me like I was poison when they heard; but some of them just looked silent, and then went away to check. I should have known none of them would trust me on sight— they couldn't read my mind. Daric usually met with his dealers in Purgatory, Argentyne had said . . . halfway between his world and theirs. They wouldn't circulate personally in this crowd. So all I could do was wait, and hope one of them was interested enough to send for me.

I kept moving, to fend off the pickpockets and beggars and sellers trying to sell me things I didn't want to buy. A skinny kid with a runny nose and an ugly scar across one eye, a skinnier little girl dragging behind him, whined and pulled at my sleeve, "Please, mister, please—"

I started to pull away; didn't. I felt in my pockets for the markers I always carried, a habit left from the days when my wrist was as bare as his. I gave him a handful. He disappeared, but someone else was there to fill the hole he left before I could take a step, and someone else after her and someone else, until I'd emptied my pockets of everything. When they saw I wasn't giving any more the beggars disappeared, looking for fresh marks with fresh markers, leaving me space to move on. There were some kinds of holes you could never fill; even if your credit never ran dry.

I glanced at my databand, swearing as I saw the time. I looked up, but there was nothing to see—the dome high above me was invisible against the sea. The sky was a deep green suffusion of light reflected from the streetlamp stars. That was all the higher your hopes ever went in a place like this. I wondered what the Deep End looked like from above, to the strage creatures swimming outside. At least I still had my databand; in a crowd like this, that was something. I wore a thumblock on it, because I knew how easy the usual latch was to unscramble.

I leaned against a lightpost at the edge of the square and shook out my hand, which was getting numb from hanging on my collar. I felt tired and strung out; every second that winked past as I watched was more proof that I was getting nowhere. Down one of these streets, behind some door with heavier security than most combine embassies carried, there was somebody in a black lab making just what I wanted, or somebody willing to front it to me. I began to wonder why nobody had come back, whether there was something going on that maybe Argentyne hadn't even known about, that was keeping me from getting what I needed. Some mistake I was making; some secret, some hidden trouble.

I wanted to go find out. Except that if I was right, pushing on into those strange green streets alone might be the worst thing I could do. Maybe it would get the attention of the right people. Maybe it would just get the wrong ones. Why the hell couldn't anything ever be simple—? My head wanted to hurt again. I pressed my fingers against my temples, trying to will the pain to stop.

"Hey, hotpants, come with us. We'll give you everything you're asking for, and more—"

I looked up again, jerked back as the gang of half a dozen bully bitches gathered around me. The stink of leather and pheromone perfume made my stomach turn over. Their leader pinned me up against the lightpost, her metal-studded fingers grabbing at my crotch. "You like to party rough, huh baby?" Her fist closed over my balls. "So do we."

I swore with the pain, and knocked her hand away. "Back off. I didn't ask for sex. I'm looking for something else."

"Then why were you signalling for sex, sweetmeat?" Her hand mimicked the way I'd been rubbing my head. She caught me by the front of my jacket. "I get it, you just want to play hard-to-get . . . ?" She jerked me forward and slapped me.

I slapped her back, knew it for a mistake as her gang moved in on me. Hands in chainmail and leather pinned me up against the pole while she slapped me again, two, three times. I sat down in the garbage, dazed, as they let me go. She jerked a lipstain out of the ancient cartridge belt slung across her chest. Her own mouth twisting, she pulled it open and smeared it across my mouth. The rest of the gang followed her away into the crowd.

I hauled myself up again, wiped my face on my jacket sleeve, wincing as I ran into buckles. I only managed to smear the dark leather with lipstain, and with blood from the place where she'd laid open my cheek. The crowd just kept flowing past, like nothing unusual had happened. Nothing unusual had.

"Hey, kid—" A heavy, stubble-bearded face pushed in front of mine, blocking my way as I started forward. He was half a head taller than me and twice as wide, dressed in dark, flapping clothes. I braced, ready for another mistake, wondering what the hell I'd done to attract the wrong attention this time. But he laughed at the look on my face—or maybe the way my face looked—and said, "I hear you're looking for Venk."

"Yeah," I said, trying to keep the sudden screaming relief out of it. He was real. He knew Venk, worked for him.

"What's it worth to you?"

I held up my wrist, let him see my credit line. "I can make it worth his time."

"Why do you want to see him?"

"That's personal." He already knew the answer. It was tough playing headgames when my own head was still ringing.

"Then how do I know Venk can help you?" He kept pushing . . . he wanted my source.

I wiped my smarting cheek again. "Daric taMing sent me. You want to deal, or not?"

"Follow me." He started away before I could say anything more.

I followed him. It took all my concentration to keep from losing him in the crowd. He moved like he didn't care if I lost him, like I needed him more than he needed me. He was probably right. But a part of his mind was keeping track of me behind him even while he pretended he wasn't—and he was subvocalizing to somebody somewhere ahead of us.

He led me away from the station, out of the square. We headed down one of the murky streets full of hidden specialties that waited beyond the lights and noise. It was a relief to get out of the square alive; but the relief only lasted until I couldn't hear the crowd noise behind me any more.

I realized that there'd been a kind of invisible field around Free Market Square. Nothing tangible, just a kind of attitude, an unspoken threat, that kept the outsiders in. On this street there was nobody moving who didn't belong here, and who wasn't being tracked through a hundred windows, visible and invisible. *Outsider.* The featureless, prefab building walls whispered it, reaching up into the eerie gloom of a sky just waiting to fall on us from fifty meters above. A luminous grid of geodesic lines glowed faintly, marking the inverse line of sea and sky like electric fishnet . . . all that separated us from the fish.

I felt tension settling on me like a weight, until it was hard to breathe . . . realized suddenly that it wasn't just my imagination. "Hey," I called.

My guide slowed, turning back to look at me.

"This isn't the way to Venk's. Where you taking me?"

He shrugged. "Venk's orders. He's gonna meet you down by the Locks instead."

"The Locks?" I repeated, picking an image out of his mind. The edge of town, here in the Deep End. Where divers went out to tend maintenance or seafarms . . . where they got rid of their garbage. But Venk was going to be there, waiting for me. That was what he'd been told, and he believed it. "Why?"

He shrugged. "Venk didn't say." He started on.

I followed him wordlessly. *Where they got rid of their garbage.* This whole thing felt bad, felt worse with every step. I wanted to stop, turn back—but it was too late now. We kept walking, mods and ground trams slipping silently past, other pedestrians looking at us sidelong as we got closer to the end of the line.

The shining grid of the sky arced down to meet us as we came out on a kind of quay. You actually could smell the sea here, where clusters of airlocks lined the wall, in sizes running from single-occupant to gigantic, their designation data glowing patiently in the green gloom. I could see strange shadows moving beyond the dome wall; natives of the other side, or divers invading their space. It was hard to see much beyond the dome, but somewhere out in the murky darkness I thought I saw lights. There were separate little blister worlds out there in the bay that belonged to people who wanted more anonymity or security than even the Deep End had to offer.

The quay at the end of the street was empty; too empty. Nothing moved anywhere nearby, on the open dockyards, between the gaping-mouthed warehouses. It took a minute for my mind to find the lone figure waiting near the black mouth of one of them. Venk came forward slowly, his bodyguard glowing faintly in the dim light, until I could make out his face, and he could make out mine.

I felt the shock of recognition as he registered my features. "I saw you on the threedy," he whispered. I wondered why he was whispering. "Daric sent you to find me . . . ?" he asked, his voice dragging a strange accent.

"Yeah," I said, groping with my mind. My skin prickled as I felt the images begin to harden suddenly behind his eyes. *Shit—* "I need some. . . ."

"No," he whispered. He wiped his nose.

My guide was about a meter away from me. He turned as Venk moved, his own hand rising—

I kicked out, hit his arm with my foot just before the beam of hot light lanced out of his sleeve. Pain branded my side as the white heat punched a hole in my jacket. I kicked him again, hit body armor where his balls should have been. I threw myself at him, because he was expecting me to run, and knocked him down. His head cracked hard on the pavement. I scrambled up. And then I ran like hell, away from the lone figure glowing like a haunt on the too-silent quay and whatever lightning he was calling down on me.

I made the end of the street, luckier than I'd ever thought I'd be— Venk's man wasn't wearing heatseekers. I saw a tram waiting at the turnaround and bolted for it, yelling. It jerked forward and drifted away, picking up speed as it left me behind . . . on purpose. I slowed, panting, cursing. The few people left on the street looked through me like I was invisible. Or marked. They disappeared into the shadows, into doorways, melting away from me without seeming to. I ran on down the street, my heart hammering, letting my mind search ahead and behind for hunters. Wondering how far I was going to get, wondering what I'd done to make Daric's dealerman want to kill me. I tried to remember when I'd felt as stupid, or as scared. I didn't think they'd waste me in the middle of the street, even here. Hell, I was a fucking media star. But if they couldn't they'd take me someplace where they could. And then the Locks would be waiting.

Behind me now I felt three minds converge, searching for me. Up ahead there were three more, moving in to cut me off. I dodged into a side street as I saw the shadows start to take form. I felt like I was swimming through the green light, running in a nightmare. *God, getting out of shape—* I heard myself laugh, a gasp of noise, as some part of my mind drifted free inside a bubble of panic, rising up toward somewhere outside of reality.

Light leaked through the sudden gap of a barely-open gate, catching my eye. I crashed through it, not caring what was on the other side. I collided with something—someone, almost knocking him down in a tangle of rough white robes. "Huh," I wheezed, half a question, and half a gasp of relief. *A prayer meeting.* My night eyes made out some kind of cult objects on an altar; a cluster of figures all wearing white, none of them expecting me, looking for me, hunting me.

There were curses and gasps as hands reached out to steady me— frisked me, and then jerked my arms apart until I was spread-eagled between them like a prisoner. Light flared, blinding me. The hard, tattooed faces closing in on me as my sight cleared didn't belong to a bunch of holy men. I started to struggle, and somebody hit me in the stomach. I went down, helpless, as they let me go. Doubled over on the floor, I heard a wailing moan that didn't sound human, heard it shape itself into words: "A sacrament! Fresh wine for the cups of the Souldrinker—" Heard the *clip* of a knifespring.

My head jerked back as someone's hands braced it. The knifeblade flashed in the light, arcing down toward my chest. I threw up my hands, screamed as pain slashed through my palm, and my own blood spurted into my face.

The sound of a stungun fired too close to my ear tore my senses apart, and all at once there was more shouting, more swearing, as the number of bodies in the space around me suddenly doubled. The whiterobes scattered, screaming the name of the Souldrinker into the night—leaving me on the ground in a forest of dark, armored legs. More hands hauled me up, as the street soldiers who'd driven me into this dead end claimed what was left of me for themselves.

19

I LET THEM THINK I couldn't walk because I couldn't walk, telling myself while they dragged me back out to the street that I was just waiting for the right chance to make a break for it. . . .

Someone stood waiting for us in the dimly-lit throat of a building across the way. He wasn't glowing; wasn't shielded. Wasn't the same one, not Venk, that I'd left standing on the pier.

"Hullo, Cat," he said.

The two men who'd been dragging me stopped, letting him take a look at me, letting me look at him. He knew me; he thought I knew him. There was something vaguely familiar about his voice, but I was sure I'd never seen that face before. A light chip flickered in his palm, showing me his features in sudden clear detail: Young-old, bronze-skinned, with a sharp nose and hard unreadable eyes under a fall of straight dark hair. He was wearing body armor like the rest, but his face shield was up so that I could see him. The silver ring through the left nostril of his nose winked in the light. "Know me now?"

I shook my head, my brain still strobing back to the image of a knifeblade coming down, again and again. . . . "No," I mumbled, wondering why he didn't just kill me and get it over with.

His thin mouth quirked. Slowly he lifted a hand, pulled off his studded glove. There was a white band of scar ringing his wrist, just like there was around my own. "Now?"

I shut my eyes for a second, listening to the voice of his mind. *Mikah.* I looked up at his face again, with a kind of disbelief. The last time I'd seen that face we'd both still worn the bond tags that had left those scars. "Mikah." I'd never seen his face whole and healthy, when it hadn't been stained blue with radioactive dust, or wasted with sickness. We'd been work partners, never friends; in the Mines it didn't take long before there wasn't enough left of you to make any effort at all. But he'd seen me escape, leaving him behind wearing a death sentence. And the look on his face had eaten into my memory, until I'd had to do something to get it out of my dreams. "What are you doing here?" I said, my voice sounding like something squeezed out of a child.

"Haven't you figured it out?" he asked, like I'd missed the punch line of a joke. "Shit, kid, I'm here to save your ass." He came forward, handed the light chip to one of the other men as he looked me over. "Got your pupils fixed, huh?" His smile stretched a little wider at my grimace. His hand caught my wrist in a loose grip, lifted my slashed hand, not even seeming to notice as my blood began to run down his arm. I swore as I got a real look at the wound. The knife was still jutting out of my palm. It had gone clear through. Suddenly the light seemed too golden; I felt like I was sinking into honey.

Mikah's dark eyes came back to mine, but they weren't expressionless now. His smile disappeared. "You . . ." he said, shaking his head. "It was you bought off my contract, and sent money for the meds to clean out my lungs, and enough left over to let me make a start—" His grip on my wrist tightened. "And you never told me why. Why? Why'd you do that—?"

I winced; his hand loosened suddenly. I didn't say anything, because I couldn't think of an answer that would have made any sense.

His free hand rose, closed over the knife hilt. His grip on me tightened again as I flinched. "Look at me," he said. I looked up, and he jerked the knife free.

My vision went red, and I cried out again; choked it off, because half a dozen men who did this to stranger all the time were staring at me. I took long, shuddering breaths while he peeled the glove off my bleeding hand.

When I could focus again I saw Mikah nod slightly, saw a faint smile pull at the corners of his mouth again. He dropped my blood-soaked glove on the floor. Then, silently, solemnly, he took the blade he'd pulled out of me and laid it down across his own palm. "Nobody ever did anything for me," he whispered. His eyes never left my face. "Not my own family. Nobody except you." His jaw tightened as he pressed down with the blade, and blood welled out suddenly, pooling in his cupped hand. He lifted his palm and pressed it against mine, folding his fingers over my hand until the wounds met, and our blood flowed together. "Anything you ever want—anything—you can ask me. You understand, brother?"

I nodded slowly. He let go of me. Pulling loose one of the long colored scarves he wore around his throat, he wrapped it tightly around my palm; wrapped his own hand with another one.

I looked at my hand. "I want to sit down," I mumbled.

He grinned. "You got it." Shoring me up with an arm around my waist, he led me back out to the main street and down a few doors to the entrance of a bar. The other men followed us, flanked me, easy but watchful in the way they moved. It finally began to sink into my brain that they were all his men, following his orders. "Somebody's trying to kill me—" I said, shaking my head, as Mikah tried to force me toward the bright, loud doorway.

His razor smile came back. "Not any more."

"Not them—" I jerked my head back the way we'd come. "Somebody else."

He snorted. "You don't waste much time, do you?" He pushed me forward into the open arms of light and noise. "Not any more," he repeated, as I dropped like a sack onto the bench in the closest empty booth. "You got Family now." He signed to the soldiers with him; they nodded and faded into the background noise.

He sat down across the laminated tabletop from me, propped on his elbows; spoke an order for drinks into the waiter on the wall.

"Jeezu," I said thickly. "Where the hell did you come from?" It wasn't cold here, but I was shivering.

He waved a hand. "Hey. I was born here. I work here now. I used the credit line you left me to buy into a Family." He laughed. "What did you expect me to do, join the FTA?"

My mouth twitched up. I shook my head.

"Good prospects for advancement." He nodded away into the room, where his men were sitting around a table, tossing Cubes. "Got my own squad already." The drinks he'd ordered flipped out of the wall. He pushed one of them at me. I shook my head, watching whitish froth form a crust on its rim. "Drink it," he said. "It's only bicarb."

I drank it, grateful. "What's your specialty?" Wondering if I'd be sorry I asked.

"Whatever makes a profit this week." He shrugged. "Mostly security and protection."

I thought about it. "All that still doesn't explain how you just happened to be there in time to protect my ass. I don't have that kind of luck."

He laughed again. "Saw you on the Morning Report, hero." He gulped down half of his own drink. "When I found out you were on-planet, I had you traced. I wanted to . . . square things. I didn't figure I'd get to start this fast."

"Who were those crazy bastards?"

"Rippers . . . a cult gang. Eat your heart out—literally."

I looked away, feeling my face get clammy. "Argentyne told me I was being an asshole." I cradled my throbbing hand inside the good one. The shock was wearing off; I felt like I'd picked up a handful of hot coals. And couldn't put them down. I damped out the pain receptors in my brain with an effort. "I thought I knew the rules."

"Argentyne? The symbplayer? You know her?"

I looked up as I felt the flash of unguarded excitement run through him, before his control dropped on it again. With the part of my mind that was still functioning, I realized that I'd impressed him. "A little."

He leaned back, trying to look like he hadn't just let me know that. "She puts me on overload with her socketwork."

"Yeah," I said. "She's a nova." I made a picture of her in my mind, letting it warm me up.

He shrugged. "I like her work. She's not my type."

I glanced up again, surprised. "You don't look dead to me."

He laughed.

"You don't like women." Realizing half a beat late what the total lack of heat when he thought about her meant.

"Not in my bed. . . . You got a problem with that?" His face hardened over at the expression I felt spread across my own.

"No." I shook my head. "I'm a freak, who am I to criticize anybody? . . . I was just wondering how come you never tried to hit on me down in the mines." I realized again, more strongly, what total strangers we were. I didn't even know his last name—if he even had one. I looked down at my hand, at the blood oozing through the layers of cloth. Blood brother. I started to shiver again.

"I was too fucking tired and sick." He looked at me, a slow smile coming out on his face again. "Besides, you're not my type either, freak." There was no sting in it; the truth, and nothing more. But he trusted me—that I wouldn't try to touch him with my mind—because I'd never hit on him, either. "So, this is where I am, now," he said. "What the hell are you doing down under, besides trying to commit suicide? You looked like you had everything you needed, up there on the wall this morning. Bodyguard to a vip—nice work, if you can get it."

"I got a drug problem. Not the usual kind—" I said, as his eyebrows rose. I explained it again. And I couldn't help thinking how much easier it would all be if I could just set it whole into someone else's brain; if only there wasn't so much fear.

"And Venk tried to null you, when you told him Daric taMing sent you?" Mikah frowned.

I nodded. "He recognized me, from the news." Trying to make that make some kind of sense with the rest of it, because somehow it had seemed to be a step on the path. Nothing at all made much sense to me right now.

Mikah rubbed his head. "Beats the crap out of me. He's not crazy. If he tried to kill you, he had a good reason. . . ." He stared at his half-empty cup, glanced up at me again. "You want me to find out what it is?"

"Yeah. Especially if it's a good one." I hesitated. "And—"

"Get you the drugs." He grinned. "How's that for mindreading?" He finished his drink, swept the cup into the dump along the wall of the booth. "Come on. That's not a drink of water you're looking for. I'd better take you to see the Doctor."

"I don't need a—"

"He's not that kind of doctor." A thin smile. "Doctor Death. Runs a black lab."

I grimaced.

"His real name's DeAth. Fits him better this way, though." He stood up.

"I'm not looking for poison," I said sourly. But maybe I was.

"Too bad. He's got the best. He supplies most of the big Families with the specialties they need for their hire business." The Lack Market had its combines too; but working for them was a lot more personal. Mikah signaled his soldiers. "He's got the best of everything. He can fix you up."

I followed him toward the door, stopped as he stopped by the public phone in the entryway. He touched in a silent code, got a query symbol on a blank screen. He fed in another code. This time he got a single line of letters: THE DOCTOR IS IN. He glanced back at me. "You don't see him without an appointment."

We took the Tube a couple of stops deeper into the Deep End, and a tram to a quiet streetcorner. The buildings wore more flash here, the streets were cleaner and had a more exclusive feel than the ones around Free Market Square. The only people who came calling here knew exactly where they were going. Mikah led me on down the street to the sixth rowhouse. Its door was black; ornate grillwork crawled like a vine up the walls, covered with black iron leaves.

Mikah stepped up on the porch, signaling me to join him; his gang sauntered away down the street, back the way we'd come.

I watched them go, wishing they'd stayed. Mikah stood motionless in front of the black door, his hands held out and open, away from his sides. I did the same, figuring we didn't need to knock to let anybody know we were here.

After a minute the door opened, letting us in. There was nobody waiting. We walked down a long hallway with mirrored walls. "Getting sanitized," Mikah said. By now I was almost beyond caring who or what was on the other side.

The doorway opened at the end of the hall, and we were in the black lab of Doctor Death.

"Hello!" a cheerful voice called, and somebody came toward us through the maze of scopes, electronic cookers, and data screens that covered an entire building floor. I watched a good-looking woman disappear through a doorway at the far side of the lab. The man was squat and round-faced, wearing lab pastels, his bald head gleaming in the brilliant light. He had two sets of eyes. The extra set looked like they belonged to some albino insect—two glittering, faceted rubies. He stopped in front of Mikah, beaming up at us, his gloved hands clasped and shining like water. "What can I do for you boys?" he asked, with a shopkeeper's eager smile. "Some Family business?" It was Doctor Death.

I stared at him, trying not to. I realized I'd come expecting somebody who lived up to the name. Not somebody who looked like he ought to be minding a bar somewhere, telling jokes. Except for the eyes. "Uh . . ." I said.

"He wants topalase-AC." Mikah said. "You got any of that?"

"Topalase-AC?" DeAth said, with his invisible eyebrows going up. "What in God's name does he want that for? He wants to become a mass murderer, but he hasn't got the nerve?"

Mikah didn't say anything, so finally I said, "I want to be able to act . . . human."

DeAth looked back at me, doubt furrowing a notch between his bug-eyes. "That's an ambiguous response, if I ever heard one. So, well, I know, 'it's none of your business, old man.' It's just a shame, when a kid comes in here looking to ruin his life. But I just make the stuff, how you use it is your business. . . ." His hand was already dancing over a touchboard while he spoke, calling up data. "I have it on hand, if you've got the price." I could tell it really broke his heart to sell it to me.

I winced at the price I saw on the screen. But I nodded. I put in a clearance on my databand, transferring the sum to him.

"I'll be back." He turned, trotting away toward the door that the woman had disappeared through.

I took a step, half afraid he was going to leave and never come back. But Mikah caught my arm. "He'll be back. Don't touch anything," he muttered, "the lab's armed."

I stayed where I was, and waited. DeAth came back, in less time that it seemed like. He held out a sheet of stick-ons to me.

I put my hand out, so eager to get hold of it that for half a second I forgot what I'd done to myself.

DeAth's arm jerked back in a startle-reflex. "Yik," he said, his lip curling as he saw the bloodsoaked cloth wrapping my hand, I wondered how he'd react if he ever got to see what his chemicals did to other people. Like the kind of thing that had happened at Elnear's party last night. . . . He slapped the paper into my other palm. "Please go, before you contaminate my rug. Goodbye." He herded us back out into the mirrored hallway; the inner door sealed shut with a hiss behind us.

There was a rushing in my ears as I peeled one of the blood-red dots off of the sheet, and put it on, one-handed. Mikah watched me like he'd watch a junkie, but all he said was, "You better get that wound fixed."

I shrugged, hardly thinking about it as I stuffed the sheet of drugs inside my jacket. "Don't worry about it, everything's fine now. . . ." In a few more minutes all the walls in my mind would be down at last, and I'd be able to see forever.

He stopped, pushed me up against the mirrors. I stared at the two of us reflecting back and forth into infinity as he shook me once. "You hear what I said?" His voice was as hard as a fist. He took my wounded hand and slammed it back against the mirror; I gasped with the pain of it. "That's a bad cut. Get it fixed, freak."

I grunted and nodded as the pain cleared out my head. "I hear you." I took a deep breath, looking him in the eye until he believed me.

He let go of me and turned away as the front door opened, like an impatient arm urging us out.

When we were out in the street again I said, "What happened at Lady Elnear's party last night looked like a hire job to me. That the kind of thing DeAth does?"

Mikah nodded. "Yeah. That was slick. He could have supplied it."
He looked ahead, not taking it past an idle guess. His soldiers were
around us again, from somewhere, nowhere.

"Can you find out?"

He glanced at me. "Maybe. I'll work on it."

"I want to know why somebody down here wants her out. Or who's
paying them."

He nodded. "Right." We walked on in silence.

"I'll be in touch," he said, as he left me at the Tube again. "Take care
of yourself, brother."

I lifted my bloody hand, a promise and a goodbye. People around me
edged away.

I couldn't remember when I'd felt better.

20

"YOU LOOK LIKE A SPOTLIGHT. I guess you got what you wanted," Argentyne said, her gaze locked on my face as she opened the door. She stepped back, stared at my bloodstained clothes as she let me past into the club. The ends of her mouth pulled down. "Mother Earth . . . I guess you got what you were asking for, too."

I shook my head; not denying it, just trying to shake loose the feeling that I was really everybody within a hundred meters of me. I focused on her relief turning into *disgust, relief, worry, disgust.* . . . damped it down further until I was only myself again. "Yeah," I said, following her back inside. There were a few customers hanging out already, scattered in clumps around the room, but at least I'd made it back before the evening really started. I wasn't sure I could have handled that, the way I felt right now.

"Is that all you've got to say?" she asked, too sharply, when that was all I said.

"Sorry," I mumbled. "This takes some getting used to. Strong stuff." I touched my head. "Gotta get my clothes and go."

"They're upstairs. I'll put some sudoskin on that hand for you; it looks pretty shitty."

"Thanks." Now that I was back inside my body, I was discovering again that it hurt like bloody hell in a couple of places. I followed her upstairs, into the long, wide room that was her private apartment. It was almost large enough to hold everything she wanted to have around her, stuffed into dressers and chests. The rest of it was sorted into vague heaps on top of pieces of furniture. Some of the furniture looked like it had been around a lot longer than she had. Clothes and ornaments hung from everything that would hold them, and a whole lot of plants squatted in pots on the floor below the windows. Some kind of animal with reddish fur scuttled off the bed and into a closet as we entered the room.

"Don't mind the mess," she said, because I was probably staring. "I just can't seem to throw anything out. I guess it's because for a long time I didn't have anything to throw out."

I nodded, feeling in my pocket for the markers I'd given away. "Hard to break old habits," I said.

"Sit down." She smiled finally, picking a pack of camphs off a dressertop and putting one into her mouth. She held out the pack to me. I hadn't had one in years; not since Dere Cortelyou had died. They always made me think of him. But tonight all my memories seemed far away. I nodded, grateful, and she flipped me one. She was wearing loose gray pants now, tied at the ankles; a blue shirt with a loose gray jacket over it, the wide sleeves rolled up. Her earrings were the size of eggs, and silver.

I stuck the camph into my mouth and bit down on the end of it, feeling it deaden my tongue with ice and spice as I sucked on it; letting it calm my nerves. I sighed, sitting on the edge of the bed, because it was the only place left in the room where you could sit. It felt so good I could have gone to sleep right there, sitting up, if my body hadn't felt so bad. My hand throbbed and burned; so did my side, now. I pulled back the leather jacket, pulled up the blood-splattered shirt under it. Beneath the fresh burn holes in both of them was the burn on my side where the hole had just missed going through me too. "Shit. . . ." I said, not sure if it was because of what had happened, or what hadn't.

"Jeezu," Argentyne murmured. "What did you do to get your stuff, commit armed robbery?" She sat down beside me with a first-aid box.

I laughed once, shook my head. "Daric's dealerman tried to kill me. I think I got in the way of something more than a gun. You know anything you didn't tell me?"

She half frowned, shaking her own head. "No. But with Daric, you never know everything. . . ." She looked tired suddenly. "I'm sorry. Take your coat off. I'll plaster that one too." She popped the kit open.

"It's clean, it'll heal over by itself."

"Don't be stupid." She helped me get out of the jacket without moving too much.

"Sorry I ruined the clothes. I'll pay you for them."

"Don't be stupid," she said again. She pulled my shirt up. Her hand froze suddenly; she was staring at old scars. She let the shirt drop, covering them up again. She looked at me. "Do you like pain?"

I grimaced, startled. "I try like hell to keep away from it." I shrugged. "Sometimes you just can't. . . ."

She looked down again, as if she was embarrassed. She took the can of sudoskin out of the box and sprayed it on my side. Then she was unwrapping the cloth around my hand, biting hard on her own camph to steady her nerves. She looked at the wound, looked away again, her face twisting. My hand was still bleeding. I looked away too.

"I can't deal with that," she said, shaking her head. "Let me get Aspen—he'd better do it for you. He used to be a med student, until he found out he didn't like sick people." She stood up.

"I can go to the meds."

She looked back at me. "And what are you going to tell them when they ask how you got that way—?"

I half smiled. "I could tell them the same thing I told Braedee, when he asked me how I got that way last night."

She made a rude noise, and went out of the room. I fumbled for the leather jacket to get out the sheet of drugs. It slid off onto the floor. I kneeled down to pick it up; glanced into the low, flat cave underneath the bedframe.

Sometimes having better sight than anyone else isn't something you're glad of. Someone else probably would never have noticed what I saw lying there in the darkness. But I saw it, and knew what it was. And then I saw something else, and something else: things that had never been intended to do anything but inflict pain.

I pushed to my feet, holding the jacket; turned toward the door, feeling like I just wanted to get the hell out of there. But Argentyne was already back, with one of the players who had a shining touchboard for a chest trailing behind her.

She looked at me strangely, because she thought I was looking at her strangely. I sat down again, and held out my hand. Aspen took it, turned it, flexed the fingers, very carefully. "Tried to shake hands with a mugger, huh? Can you use it at all?"

"Not right now," I said irritably, thinking that much ought to be obvious.

"Hm." He frowned, suddenly turning professional; not easy when he looked like a floor lamp. "Let me get my own kit; I've got to suture this." He drifted out of the room again, humming faintly, accompanied by synth sounds. One half of his brain was reviewing a medical procedure, while the other was composing music.

"Why did you look at me like that?" Argentyne asked, as soon as he was out of earshot.

I hesitated. "I saw what's under the bed." Her face didn't redden through the silver of her skin, but I could feel the surge of heat behind it.

"Daric," I said. "Daric—?" Not even sure what the emotion was that closed around my stomach like a fist. "You let that bastard do that to you?"

"No!" She swore. "No," looking down suddenly, "I do it to him."

"Why—?" I said, but before it was even out of my mouth, I saw the answer. "Because you love him." The words were so hard to say they were barely audible.

She raised her head.

"You said it to Jiro last night, didn't you? 'It's better if you get it from someone who cares about you.' . . ." If I tried hard enough, I could almost make myself believe that.

She turned away to the dresser, pulled another camph out of the pack. She glanced up, staring at my reflection in the mirror, so that she didn't have to face me. And then she looked down again. "Yeah," she whispered. "I mean . . . he hates himself so much, and I don't know why. Sometimes he scares me. I do it because if I didn't, God knows where he'd go to get it, or what would happen to him then. . . ." She slammed her hands down on the dressertop, making trays of body paint and makeup jump, hurting herself.

"Everything okay?" Aspen asked, coming back through the doorway carrying a portable surgery.

"Your timing is just perfect," Argentyne said wearily, turning to look at us again.

"Hey, thanks." He sat down on the bed, thumbing the case open. "I've really been working on it." He patted his glowing chest; notes floated up like bubbles.

Argentyne cleaned up colors, or pretended to, while he went to work on my hand, his attention suddenly sharp and focused again. He pressed a patch of painkiller down on my wrist; my whole hand dropped off the nerve map in my mind. I sighed with relief. He put on a strange-looking set of lenses and stared at the wound; seeing into it, looking for structural damage. "Hm," he said again, and took them off. "You were lucky. Nothing vital severed. I'll seal it up." He picked something else out of the case. It looked soft and moist, a little like a big slug. He wrapped it around my hand, covering the cut. Something happened that I could feel even through the anesthetic, like a kind of heavy suction. "Hold still," he said, catching hold of my arm. "Okay—" as the slug suddenly changed color. He peeled if off and dropped it back into the case. I looked at the ugly red mouth of the wound. It was closed. "That's the best I can do." He sprayed it with sudoskin. "I don't have a lamp; if you want it to heal fast, you'll have to get a regeneration treatment someplace else."

I nodded. "Thanks." I moved my fingers experimentally. They all worked, at least, even though I couldn't feel them.

"No problem." He got up and drifted out of the room, waved at us over his shoulder as an afterthought.

"Thanks," I said, to Argentyne this time.

She shrugged. "Your things are in the closet over there. I've got to get ready for the evening." She started toward the door, avoiding my eyes.

I almost called her name; didn't. I found my clothes and changed into them as fast as I could. Then I went downstairs, glad enough to go on my way without any more conversation.

"Argentyne! Argentyne!" A voice that could have raised echoes in deep space was bellowing her name. I stopped, looking down the hallway in the direction of the noise. A turn blocked my view, but I could feel half a dozen minds clustered around the corner.

"Hey, Cusp. . . ."

"Come on—"

"Argentyne!" Banging noises.

I went down the hall, stopped, looking around the corner. One of the club's bouncers was beating on the door of Argentyne's dressing room with a pincer-arm, shouting her name over and over, while players from the symb buzzed around him like flies, with about as much effect.

"Argentyne—!"

Someone made the mistake of grabbing his arm; he shrugged, and three bodies went flying halfway down the hall.

Suddenly the door opened. He backed off a little as Argentyne stepped out into the hall, wrapped in her faded bathrobe. "Cusp!" she said, doing a damn good job of hiding how small and intimidated she suddenly felt. "What is this shit?" She waved a hand at the pile of bodies slowly untangling. He gargled something unintelligible. *Her biggest fan.* Literally. "Thanks, but no thanks. . . . Come on," she said, almost gently, "get back out front and do your job. I have to get ready, you know?" She managed to smile as she tried to get him turned around and out of there.

But the armored claw closed over her wrist, jerking her forward, and began to drag her away down the hall.

"Hey!" she squawked. I felt the flash of her pain and surprise, the stupefied fear of the helpless players backing away. I froze, trying to think of something to do.

And then suddenly somebody was standing in the doorway of her dressing room, looking out. Daric. "Argentyne—?" he called, staring, uncertain.

She looked back at him in wordless panic, stumbling as Cusp pulled her forward again.

"Let her go," Daric said, starting after them down the hall. If Cusp heard, he didn't pay any attention.

Daric began to run, catching up with them. I watched, feeling like I must be dreaming. Daric caught Argentyne's arm; her hand came free at his touch, as if Cusp's grip on her was no stronger than a child's. Cusp stopped, turning back in slow motion, the way a mountain would turn; raising his armored claws—

Then he crashed over backwards, with a *thud* that made my teeth hurt.

The players stood gaping. Argentyne turned slowly inside Daric's arms, her eyes wide and glassy as she faced him. "Okay?" he murmured, stroking her hair, pulling her to him in a sudden, protective embrace. Cusp was making a high keening whine, lying like a gassed beetle on the floor. Argentyne looked at him lying there, and shook her head, her mouth quivering, close to tears or hysterical laughter.

"Hey, Daric," Aspen said, "how'd you do that, man?"

Daric glanced at him, twitching. "I didn't do anything," he snapped. "He's just drunk." Lying. "Get him the hell out of here. Call Security."

I stayed back out of sight as he turned and walked Argentyne to her dressing room again. The players gathered around Cusp like pallbearers to drag his helpless body away.

I pressed against the wall, staring at nothing, wondering how I could have been so blind. Because now it was so obvious . . . Daric was the one. The teek I'd been sensing. *A psion, just like his sister.*

I don't remember leaving the club. I don't really remember how I got to the Assembly plex; to Elnear waiting, weary and relieved, for me to come back. She didn't mention what I'd said before I left; she hoped I wouldn't mention it again, either. Ever. Instead, looking at my bruised face, she asked what had happened, if anything was wrong. I don't remember what I told her, but she didn't ask again.

We took a mod back to the taMing estates. She fell asleep before we were out of sight of the city, leaving me the privacy to go on thinking about Daric. *Daric, Daric* . . . all I could think about, ever since I'd realized the truth. I wondered how it had happened. How could there have been two of them—two psions, brother and sister, born in the same generation into a family where there had never been one before, ever? How could Daric have hidden his psi all those years, from everyone. . . .

But I thought more about why, because that was so much easier to understand. He'd hidden if because he knew what happened to freaks. He'd seen how his family treated Jule, and what they'd done to his mother just because Jule was born a psion. His life must have been a living hell, when one slip would mean discovery—would mean that he'd lose everything: his position, his power, his wealth, maybe even his life . . . the love and protection of his family; the approval and the security everybody secretly craved. All of it torn away in a second if anyone even suspected. He'd still be the same person they'd always known— but in the eyes of everyone who mattered to him he would have turned from a golden child into an outcast, a subhuman . . . a freak.

No wonder he baited them with little teek torments nobody would ever be able to catch him at. No wonder he flaunted Argentyne—hinting, daring somebody to look deeper, even while he worked at being more like everybody else than they were themselves. . . .

My guts twisted just thinking about the kind of pressures at work inside him, distorting everything he thought and did. I'd been a psion all my life, but I'd been lucky. I hadn't known it. Maybe I'd never wanted to know, because my life in Oldcity had been so close to the edge all the time. Having to face that too could have been the thing that finally broke me. It was easier, safer, just to find a hiding place in some dark hole in the streets, inside some drugged fantasy world, inside my mind. Coming out hadn't been easy. I never would have done it alone. I knew how a secret like that could eat somebody's insides out: The fear, the loneliness, the hatred that had nowhere to turn but inward. No wonder he needed what only Argentyne would give him. . . .

It was easy to feel sorry for him. But it was easier to remember what his secret had done to everyone who crossed his path. Jule, and Jiro, and Elnear; even Argentyne. . . . Easier to remember how he'd treated me: like a freak. And then the pity knotting my gut would turn back into disgust again.

I had to wake up Elnear when we reached the estate. She looked confused, and then concerned, looking back at me. I tried to wipe the grim tension off my face until she looked away again.

"I'm going directly to my room," she said, her voice quavering more than usual as she tried to control it. "I'm going to sleep until I want to wake up. You should do the same."

I nodded, and followed her inside.

Lazuli was waiting for us on the porch, even though there was a sharp bite to the evening air that I hadn't felt before. Her eyes found mine and her thoughts collided with me, and suddenly I couldn't feel the chill any more. She murmured something to Elnear as she passed, touched her shoulder briefly.

She let me pass too, but her mind reached out for me, opening its arms in the darkness, searching helplessly. I hesitated at the foot of the stairs, looking back; looked at her, and followed her down the hall instead.

She led me into Elnear's study and closed the doors. I hadn't really seen it when I'd been here before. It was high-ceilinged, like all the rooms, and its walls were lined with dark wooden shelves, the shelves lined with antique books sealed behind glass. I wondered whether anyone had looked at them in centuries. There was a fire burning inside a stone fireplace. The rich, heavy smell of the smoke made my mouth water. I thought I could feel its heat even where I stood; but maybe it was something else. "Why do you have a fire?" I asked, trying to think of something besides her. It didn't work. "You don't need one." This house might be old, but it was state-of-the-art on comfort.

In front of the fireplace was the long mahogany-wood table that was the one thing I remembered seeing in the room before. Its surface was inlaid with gold in patterns of stars, a map of the night sky. Lazuli leaned against it, turning to look back at me. "No, of course not," she said softly. "But a fire warms the soul, somehow." She held her hands out to the flames. She was wearing a loose velvet tunic the color of red wine, its random hem brushing her calves, brushing her knees. I crossed the room to be close to her. I touched her mind, very gently; touched her shoulder. The feel of velvet made gooseflesh start up my arm.

"Are you all right?" she turned toward me, suddenly uncertain. She saw the sude on my hand and the bruise on my face, was suddenly afraid that Charon had had something to do with them. Her eyes went to the emerald earring I was still wearing.

"Yeah. I'm fine now," I said, and smiled. The snap of flames, the rustle of whirled sparks, was loud in the silence between us. "Are you?"

She looked up at me, with a tiny smile starting on her own lips, and what lay behind her eyes washed over me like a wave of heat.

"How's—how's Jiro?"

She glanced away again. "He felt much better this morning. The children are up at the Crystal Palace. Charon . . . demanded that we attend dinner with the family."

"What about you?"

"I wanted to see you, first. Because I won't be back tonight." She brushed at a loose strand of night-colored hair. "Charon wants me to spend more time with him. . . ." Spend the night with him. She looked down, knowing that I must know what she was thinking, and how she felt. "I'll join them in a while . . . I said that I was sick." Sick at the thought of him touching her. Her eyes came back to me. *(Sick with longing,)* they said to me.

"Lazuli . . ." I shook my head, looking down. Last night we'd burned away our loneliness together in the dark. It shouldn't have happened even once. It couldn't happen again, ever. I couldn't afford to let it. I reached up, started to unfasten the earring.

She lifted her hand, stopping me. Her body was as taut as a bow, pressed against the hard edge of the star-covered table, straining against impulse. *(I want you,)* it said. *(Touch me again,)* said her mind. She pulled my hands away, pulled them to her, ran them down over her velvet dress.

My burning body took the last step across the space that separated us. I kissed her then, hard and deep and hungry, because that was how she wanted to be kissed. My hands slid down the velvet again, this time without any urging, and into the soft curves of her body. They circled her hips, pulling her against me until there was no space at all left between us. I felt the heat of the fire against my back, the heat of her; the heat of my own need, even hotter. I couldn't stop now, didn't want to. Because I knew that I was really *good,* that I could give her everything she wanted, and more. That I could make this beautiful, unapproachable woman need me so much that nothing else mattered to her, nothing at all. And all because of the Gift that wouldn't be mine to use much longer. . . .

I laid her down across the starry table and made love to her right there, hard and deep and hungry . . . while she called me deeper into her mind, called me her only real lover, called me the fire. . . .

21

I WAS BACK on the job the next day, because Elnear was back on the job. "Losing Philipa is like losing a part of my own brain," she said to me, as we walked through the halls of the FTA plex to her office. "I'm not sure how I'm going to get through my work."

"Is she that augmented?" I asked, surprised because I'd been sure she wasn't. She didn't have anything like the neural taps that Elnear did.

"No." Elnear shook her head, a little embarrassed. "But she is formidably organized. She has everything in its place, all those little details that keep one from making a fool of oneself in public, and she can access faster than I can think, sometimes. . . ."

"Why can't you just plug into all of it yourself? You're wired. Why do you even need someone else to do it for you?"

She shrugged. "I'm really very lazy. I don't want to spend all my time accessing, the way Natan Isplanasky does. I like to have time to step back and look the day in the eye . . . paint a picture, visit a new place. Philipa gave—gives me the time to do that." The rueful smile faded, as memories piled up until her mind began to sink under them. *Philipa, loss, fear, defeat, death. . . .*

I made myself pull back before I went too far. The topalase was working, almost too well. It gave my mind x-ray eyes. It was so easy to start, too easy, with someone I knew. I could just pick up a strand of thought without even thinking, and follow it back through the maze. I could be inside someone else's head before they knew it, without their ever knowing it . . . deep inside, where it got too private. Every human had things they didn't want to share, things they didn't want to admit . . . even me.

Knowing it was so easy now made me feel the way I'd felt that night at the taMings' party: realizing that I could steal them blind . . . knowing that to do it was wrong. Dere Cortelyou had taught me before he died that there was a reason the deadheads were afraid of us. He'd gone too far, tried too hard to convince them that he wouldn't hurt them. He'd worked as a corporate telepath, and they'd treated him like dirt. Rubiy had gone too far the other way, crazy with power, using everyone else like his personal property. They were both dead. Somewhere in between there had to be a survivor's path, some way to balance on the tightrope without taking a fall that would kill me. . . .

We walked on in silence, neither one of us smiling.

I accessed Jardan's datafiles when we reached the office, sucking up the next few calendar days and trying to make sense of it all—appointments, decisions to be made, data to be sent or collected. A thousand briefing details: this combine vip's hair phobia; dietary restrictions to be careful of with that Assembly rep . . . somebody's grandmother's illness to be asked after the next time she was on some other planet. Information coming in from across half the Federation that she needed to know or wanted to know every day; changing every day. Now I understood what Elnear meant: just sorting it all out would leave her with no real time to analyze or make sense of it. Maybe I'd never like Jardan any better than she liked me. But now I respected her, at least; respected what she could do, with only a human brain.

Wearing Jardan's data in my memory, I went with Elnear through her restless perpetual motion: walking the halls, paying personal calls where a vid would have done, as she spoke to one Assembly member after another about the upcoming drug vote. "Because when you come in person, people remember you," she said, her eyes bright with her need to believe. I fed her names, gave her the relevant details, reading them right out of the stranger's head if they weren't in my own, and slipping them to her so gently she almost believed she was remembering them herself. But she knew she wasn't. At first she gave me that Look every time it happened. But not for long.

Sometimes the people she wanted to talk to made me wait in the hall when they saw my face; usually the ones who had the most to hide. I waited outside, but it didn't do them any good. More and more, Elnear's eyes searched my face as she came out of a meeting, looking for clues. It took nearly a dozen calls before she finally got the nerve to ask: "Am I making any progress? Getting anywhere at all?"

I shrugged, glancing away. "Some, maybe. . . ."

"You don't have to lie to me," she said, her face settling into folds as the hope went out of it. "The answer is no."

I nodded.

"That's what I suspected. While I'm talking to them, I actually begin to believe that they are human beings; but they're simply access ports. I might even convince the human being; but the human being is not what really votes, in the end." She rubbed her neck, because she wanted to reach out and shake somebody. "Why did I even ask—?" Her head jerked with her sudden anger. Behind it was the knowledge that yesterday, in spite of everything that had happened, the special committee had finished its study of the drug deregulation—and had set it free. It would be up for the general Assembly vote in a matter of days. And she knew now that that vote wouldn't go her way, no matter what she did.

"Why is this so important to you, anyway?" I said, trying not to let myself go ahead and find out without asking. "It's not just the principle of the thing, and it's not just the Council slot. . . ."

She gave me a sidelong glance, afraid I was about to do just what I was trying not to. When I didn't answer my own question, she looked away again, her footsteps slowing. "My parents . . ." she murmured, as if she was drifting off into a reminiscence, "developed the penta-tryptophine family."

I half frowned. "Your parents? I thought pentryptine had been around for a couple of centuries."

"About a century and a half," she said, nodding. "Just about as long as my parents lived. They had a very long career. They synthesized or developed many of ChemEnGen's most profitable biochemicals. . . ."

"And you think they wouldn't want to see pentryptine used like this?"

Her eyes went bleak and pale. "They wouldn't have cared . . . perhaps they would have been glad, because it was good for the company." She frowned, looking down at her feet. Her mother and her father had developed all those chems and virals; but wondering how they would be used, for what, by who, had never given either one of them a moment of doubt or a bad night's rest. And she had never been able to understand that, or to forgive them for it.

"What happened?" I asked. "To make you see it different from the way they did?"

She shook her head. "Nothing, that I know of. I've simply always believed that to live a life without some sense of responsibility to humanity, or for one's actions, is—immoral, wrong." She sighed, brushed a strand of graying hair back from her face. "I suppose I was just born that way."

"Kind of a freak," I said gently, and felt my mouth twitch.

She looked at me. "Yes," she said, "I suppose so." We started moving again. After a few steps I realized we weren't going to pay another call; we were going back to her office.

"There's got to be some better way," I said. "You'll find it."

She didn't answer.

I got through my office work as fast as I could, and went out for a walk. I used the first public phone I came to to call up Mikah, wanting the privacy of its security screen. His face filled in on the vid; it was the slightly washed-out image of a bandphone receiver. "Cat," he said, with half a nod. "Make it fast."

"You got anything for me?"

"Maybe. Tonight—?"

"Purgatory, before the show."

"Yeah." His image blanked out. I shut off the screen and started back through the halls, moving more slowly this time. Letting my mind drift, spreading out like fog, touching the surfaces of a hundred different minds and moving on. I didn't even realize I'd been searching for something until I found it: Something about Stryger . . . and Daric. Passersby bumped into me, murmured and moved on, as I stopped, focusing in. Daric was leaving his office on the next level down, going to meet with Stryger to discuss matters of mutual interest. Yesterday's vote, yesterday's news. Daric was always a clenched fist; but the way his mind felt right now made the way he usually read seem like meditation. I sank a silent tracer into his brain, and took the first lift that came, following him through the plex. *Mutual interest.* . . . Anything they had in common had to be something I needed to know. Because it had to involve deregulation, and Elnear.

Stryger was waiting for him in a whiteroom, maximum privacy inside maximum security. But I'd planted the perfect bug, undetectable, already riding inside Daric's brain. The room wasn't far from the display hall where the tourists came to gape. I found a quiet corner where I could wait without looking obvious. On the wall across from me was the mosaic mural, the portrait of the people of the Human Federation— male and female, young and old, brown and yellow and black and white. Their faces stared back at me like silent judges. But I was the only one who could really decide if what I was doing was wrong or right, justified or only thieving. *Deadheads.* I looked up at them again, their faces, their eyes. And then I shut my stranger's eyes, concentrating.

I opened up my senses, weaving them through the boundaryless territory of Daric's mind like tributary streams, letting his thoughts begin to bleed into my own. It wasn't easy, invading the mind of another psion; especially one whose brain was this sick, full of paranoid quicksand and dead-end mazes of augmentation. But needing all my skill, and being able to use it, feeling it work again with the perfect control I'd had once, made it almost a pleasure.

But I didn't find anything I didn't know or suspect already. Daric was Centauri's contact with Stryger, giving Stryger instructions, suggestions, orders from the board. He was only one of too many data-feeders; most of the others were from combines with large, expensive populations. Stryger nodded and smiled and praised God for sending him such friends and counselors.

And all the while he was only half listening. Once I was inside Daric's mind it was easy to get inside Stryger's. I only had to step across the short empty space between them to pick up his responses. He was already one step beyond, imagining how it was going to be once they'd given him the thrust he needed to reach the Security Council, and he made the slot his own. . . .

And all the while Daric was talking—his voice calm, his face calculating and cool, everything about him stinking of arrogance—his own mind was twisting around and through itself like a snake, his body was twitching, sweating. . . . He knew as well as I did how much Stryger hated psions. It fascinated him, the way a gun lying on a table would fascinate somebody who was thinking about murder, or suicide. . . .

I figured I'd seen enough. I wasn't going to learn anything new from this, anything that would help Elnear. I was wasting my time picking through garbage. I began to withdraw, slowly, carefully, not letting my disgust get in the way of my control long enough to give me away. Daric wasn't a telepath, but his mind still had more sensitive burglar alarms than a normal human's did.

Daric froze suddenly, as something went off like a flare inside his mind. I froze too, until I realized it was something Stryger had asked him, and not some slip I'd made, that had set off the response.

"Have you found me another?" That was the question. I reached for him again, going deeper, listening, sifting; curious about what could trigger that kind of panic reflex in Daric's brain. What Stryger could want that he'd ask for that way—

I watched/felt Daric's response take form, like an image rising up out of the black depths of a pool, suddenly there on its surface like a face in a mirror. *"No, not yet . . . having a little—trouble, with my access to the supply. . . ."* And something in his mind was thrashing like a trapped animal, stuggling to get free, to cry out, *Take mine. Use mine.* But he couldn't say it, *couldn't, couldn't ever.* . . .

I thought it had to be drugs. But it wasn't drugs. Below the spoken words there were random images of the Deep End, dark streets and darker deals, but not for drugs; not this time. Tension and terror tightened like chains around an emotion they'd crushed so completely that I couldn't even recognize it.

Flesh and blood. A body to use. Stryger wanted Daric to hire him a victim. But not just any victim. He wanted Daric to find him a psion. The way he'd done before.

Images were pouring out of Daric now: memories of red weals on pale flesh, swollen purple bruises slowly turning a face unrecognizable, screams driving pain into his own head like a nail. . . . *Terror* . . . *Thirst* . . .

I let them come; but I didn't need his memories. I had my own.

It took all my control to keep from screaming inside Daric's head—*I know everything, you bastard*— screaming it until his eyes bled. I broke contact; heard my voice gasp out a curse like somebody talking in his sleep. The eyes of the mural across the hall watched me, *somber, curious, happy, sad.*

I shut them out; stepped across the empty space and into Stryger's mind again. Because now that I knew what he really was, there were questions I had to have answered; answers that would make all the difference, to Elnear . . . to my own sanity. I drove into his thoughts with one hard thrust, knowing how a knife felt when it sank into somebody's flesh. B6ut he never felt a thing. *Deadhead.* I ransacked his mind, keeping my focus tight, sealed like an antiseptic barrier. There were only two things I wanted from him. I didn't want anything else; didn't want him to infect me. . . . But I had to be sure.

He wasn't the one. Not the one who was trying to kill Elnear. He wanted that Council slot, but he thought he already had it. God was on his side, God wouldn't let him fail, God would make it happen. He didn't have to help God along. . . .

He wasn't the one. He wasn't the same one who'd taken me up to that hired room back in Oldcity and beaten me up. But he'd done it to enough other freaks. And he needed to do it now, needed it bad, because of what had happened to him yesterday: caught in a lie, humiliated by a psion, by me, in front of so many watching eyes. And Daric, sweating like he had a fever, was ready to help him do it again.

I cut contact. *He wasn't the same one.* Then how many were there, just like him? Just like the one who'd done it to me. Thousands? Millions? I looked at the faces of Humanity watching, waiting, one last time. "Go to hell," I said, as I started out of the room.

22

"I GOTTA TALK TO YOU," I said, standing in the doorway of Argentyne's dressing room.

She turned in her seat, away from the mirror above a cluttered table. The startled look on her face faded into something like distraction. "Oh, it's you. Can't it wait? I've got a show to do." She was half in and half out of the Argentyne the public saw, in a coat bristling with glowing fiberoptic quills.

"No."

She'd started to turn back to the mirror; she stopped, looked up at me again instead, in surprise. "All right," she said, "Talk to me." She picked up a wand and began to run it over her hair; the silver threads rose up like worshippers following the sun, and stayed that way.

I pushed clothes off of a chair and straddled it, resting my chin on its hard plastic spine. "About Daric."

She studied herself in the mirror; she didn't move her head, but the reflection changed and changed again, showing her different angles. "Laddie love," she said patiently, "are you trying to save me from myself?" Warning me off.

I frowned. "I'm trying to tell you the truth."

She shrugged, reaching up to hook an ear cuff dangling heavy rhinestones over her ear.

"Daric's a psion."

The earring clattered onto the table, lay there. I had her attention now. "Bullshit," she said. She picked up the earring, not looking at me; twisted it, watching it gleam in the hard light. "Are you sure?" she asked finally.

I nodded. "It takes one to know one. He's teek—telekinetic. That's how he stopped Cusp. I was there, I felt him do it."

She looked up at my reflection behind her in the mirror. "But he said.
. . . He's never. . . . I didn't—"

"Nobody knows it, except him—and me. He never told anybody."

"Why not?" She honestly couldn't imagine.

I laughed. "Why do you think? He'd lose everything if his family found out he was a freak. Look what they did to his sister."

She turned in her seat again, slowly facing me, her face slowly changing. Her image in the mirror stayed frozen the way she'd left it, waiting. "Why are you telling me this?" she said. "You want to know if it makes a difference to me? If it matters that he didn't trust me . . . or that he's a psion?"

"Maybe." I looked down.

"Did you really think that was going to change how I felt?" The anger behind her eyes was getting hotter. "So he didn't trust me with a secret that could ruin his life . . . so he's a freak. So what?" Her silver-nailed hand jerked at me. "At least he's not a goddamned peeping tom!" Like me.

I shook my head. "A 'mental pickpocket,' " I said.

"What?"

"A mental pickpocket—that's what the other psions called me, back at the Institute in Quarro. . . ." I raised my head, meeting her stare. "Yeah, I picked his brains. And that's not all I got. You know about Sojourner Stryger?"

She hesitated. "He's the big godlover who wants to save everybody; the one who wants the drug dereg to go through? Daric's talked about him sometimes. . . ."

I nodded. "Stryger wants the same Security Council slot that Lady Elnear wants. Centauri is one of the combines backing him. . . . Did Daric ever tell you Stryger's a freakhater?"

She shook her head.

"Daric is Centauri's liaison with Stryger. He gives him his instructions—" I hesitated; pushed on, feeling my anger like a fire smoldering in my gut. "And he gets him whatever he asks for."

Her frown came back again. "What do you mean?" she asked, impatience elbowing out her curiosity. "You mean Stryger does drugs?"

"He does psions."

Her mouth opened again, but nothing came out of it this time.

"You remember that girl you told me about—the one Daric brought here, who'd been beaten so bad she couldn't talk? The psion—?"

The knuckles of her hand stood out as it tightened on the back of her chair. "Daric?" she murmured. "Daric made that happen?" Her eyes were begging me to tell her I was lying.

"She wasn't the only one," I said. "Sometimes he even watches."

"Oh, God." She broke away, pushing up out of her seat, her hands balled into fists at her sides. *"Why?"* she said, turning back. "If he's a psion too, why would he do that?" Challenging me to make it make sense.

I shook my head. I'd asked myself the same question, trying to make it make sense, all through the endless afternoon. "I don't know. Why don't you ask him?" I got up off my chair.

She jerked a piece of clothing free from a hook, thought about throwing it in my face; threw it on the floor instead. "Why did you have to tell me that? Goddamn you—what do you want me to do about it?"

I shrugged. "Like I said. I just wanted you to know the truth. What you do about it is your business." I started for the door.

"You're a lousy human being, you know that?"

I looked back at her. Her face was all congested-looking; she was going to be crying in another minute. "I try," I said. I went on out.

I sat down at a table out in the club and had a drink, watching the room fill up, waiting for Mikah to show. They'd hired a new bouncer. I half expected him to come over and tell me to get out, after what I'd just done; but he didn't. The club was as dark as a cave tonight, and smoky. Fingers of colored laser light gibbered across the darkness in frantic parabolas, shattered into clouds high above my head to the wailing of recorded synth music. I settled back, losing myself in the dark/bright spaces overhead.

Finally I sensed Mikah making his way across the dance floor. He sat down at the table with me, wearing black body-armor. He fit right in. I had on my old jeans and torn shirt; I'd brought them to work with me in a shoulder bag, knowing I'd be going out. "Hey, freak," he said.

"Don't call me that."

He looked surprised. "What's eating you?"

I looked away, down at my empty glass. "Nothing. What's your problem?"

"I'm a deeve." One side of his mouth pulled up. "Somebody been rubbing your nose in it? Wipe the shit off your face, kid, and forget about it. You ought to be used to that by now."

I shook my head. "It's not that. I wish it was only that." I unclenched my good hand, laid it flat on the table.

He ordered himself a drink, settling back into the pile of cushions. When I didn't say anything else, he shrugged and asked, "What happened to your shirt? You have a hot date last night?"

I looked down at the long rip across the front and almost laughed, remembering how it had really happened. But then I remembered last night, the fire and the star-covered table. . . . I reached up, touched the emerald earring, still in my ear. I hadn't meant to keep it; hadn't meant for anything to happen the way it had, last night. . . . Finally I admitted the truth to myself, that Lazuli had only been using my body to help her forget how much she hated being with her husband; maybe even to pay him back. And I'd let her. It had been so easy to use me, like the only brain I had was between my legs. I felt stupid and helpless —felt myself start to get an erection again, just remembering red velvet and golden skin. . . .

"You must be somebody's type," Mikah said. "I hear it's fun to be famous."

I glanced away. "You find out why I'm so popular that total strangers want to kill me?"

He shook his head. "It's not street talk. That means it's vip level, and their secrets keep real well."

I looked up, surprised. "You think it has something to do with Elnear?"

He shrugged. "Dunno. But you guessed good about DeAth—he did the footwork for what happened at that party the other night. But after that I hit a wall. I can't find out who hired him to drop the Lady. Nobody down under seems to want her gone—she's on their side, they don't want that drug deregged any more than she does."

I wondered what Elnear would think if she heard that. "Damn," I said. "I thought I knew . . . I thought it was Stryger. But it's not."

"Stryger?" Mikah grunted. "You mean the Plastic Saint? You realy thought he'd try to take out his opposition with a human bomb?"

"Yeah," I said, feeling my eyes ice over. "That's exactly what I thought."

"Hm." He shrugged again. "I've heard talk about him. Thought it was only talk." He sounded relieved; I'd just restored his faith in human nature. Even he could have told me the way to one of Stryger's good works.

"Whatever you heard, it's not bad enough. But it doesn't do me any good—" I rubbed my face. "DeAth would know who hired him right?"

"Maybe not." Mikah shook his head. "He's too paranoid. He likes to keep his clients protected—and his own ass covered. He'll fill any order that comes in on a credit float. No questions . . . no ID." No responsibility, and no risk.

"Jeezu—" I felt frustration strangle the disgust inside me. That meant that even if I could get into DeAth's brain and pick it, it probably wouldn't get me anywhere. "There's got to be some kind of record, someplace. What about numbers on the credit transfers?"

He thought about it. "Yeah, maybe. . . . But if you think his lab was a deathtrap, his personal accounts are gonna make that look like a park. Nobody sane would try a data raid on him."

I hit the table with the wrong hand; winced and swore. "Damn it," I said, "there's got to be somebody on the Market good enough. I want to access those fucking files. Who's the best?"

Mikah tugged on the silver ring in the side of his nose. "Unh. I did say nobody sane. . . ." He half smiled. "Maybe you're talking about Deadeye. He does things nobody else can. Nobody knows how. But only when he feels like it. A real hostile son of a bitch."

" 'Deadeye'? He like to pick off his visitors with a stungun, or what?"

Mikah laughed. "I heard he's dropped a couple . . . but maybe that's just hype. I dunno, could be his rep as a cracksman. . . . Could be the fact that he's got a dead eye." He shrugged, still laughing behind his own eyes.

"A dead eye," I said.

"Yeah. Looks like shit, all festering." He wasn't joking.

"How come he doesn't get it fixed?"

"I told you, he's half crazy. But he's a wire wizard, if he'll deal."

I started to get up. "Let's go find out."

"Hey—" he said, his disappointment showing. "Don't you want to stay for the show?"

I glanced at the stage, still empty and waiting in the darkness above the crowded floor. "I've done it."

He sighed, and stood up. "Right."

We made it through the crowd to the door without any more distractions, and took the Tube under the bay.

Deadeye's part of town was a lot less choice than DeAth's, although down in the Deep End that probably didn't make a whole lot of difference. We waded through drifts of trash to a barricaded iron door large enough to swallow a tram. It was the entrance to what looked like an abandoned warehouse. There was no flicker of any security; no sign that anybody even lived there, or ever had. "How do you know he's here?" I asked.

"He never goes out." Mikah raised his fist to beat on the door—jumped back with a curse as it hit the metal. "Shit! It's electrified." He shook out his hand, looking at me, half exasperated and half embarrassed. "You got any ideas? You're the one who wanted to meet him."

I looked at the door, up the silent, windowless building front. "Yeah. I'll give him a call."

"He doesn't have a phone."

I smiled. "I don't need one."

He tapped his head. "What makes you think that'll make him glad to see you?"

"I got nothing to lose." I shrugged.

He grunted. "Excuse me while I cross the street," he said. *Just in case Deadeye decided to fry me.* He stepped back, but only about a meter.

I folded my arms, hugging my chest, centering myself. I let my mind out into the block of formless darkness that was the warehouse, that held one fragile star, the energy of a living human mind. Somewhere. . . .

There. *Contact.* I went in through the shell of spidery radiance, weaving my way into the pattern of a stranger's thoughts; surprised, when I didn't find the dead black walls of illegal augmentation I'd expected. I moved on, a thief entering a sleeping house, not bothering to cover the sound of my footsteps as I got ready to give Deadeye one hell of a big surprise—

A fist of raw energy smashed into me, searing the filaments like a beam of coherent light. I let go and bolted, breaking all contact, shutting down, walling up my own mind behind a jumble of barbed wire.

"Ah—!" My own shout of surprise, still loud in my ears. I was back on the street again, staring at a blank wall, with eyes that were ready to jump out of my head. "Jeezu! You didn't tell me he was a telepath!"

Mikah had backed up a few more steps, away from contamination. He was staring, but his expression changed as the words registered on him. "A freak?" he said, loud with disbelief. "I didn't know he was a freak—"

I held up my hands, waving him quiet; braced for another attack . . . for something that didn't come. Slowly, carefully this time, I let out a tracer, hunting Deadeye through the darkness again. . . . Found him, balled up tight as a clenched fist behind his own barbed wire; fear so strong it made me feel sick oozed out of him like sweat. He had a lot of raw psi talent, but he didn't know how to use it the way I did. I could see the chinks in his defenses; taking him would be easy. But I could see, too, that if I broke through now he'd go right over the edge. I touched him, barely; let him prick the finger of my thought just to get his attention. And then I backed off, letting him feel me go, letting him know that I wasn't going to come back . . . leaving him alone, there in the dark.

I shook my head, seeing Mikah's face again, the question in his eyes. "No good. You were right. He *is* half crazy." I glanced at the sealed door, the blank, unyielding walls. "Now I know why, anyhow. Come on. Let's get out of here."

Mikah nodded and shrugged. He hunched his shoulders as we began to walk away, keeping his distance.

There was a *clank* and a grating scrape behind us, as the iron door swung open. Somebody stepped outside, shapeless, anonymous, inside a heavy load of mismatched clothes. But I didn't have any trouble making out his face—the raw, weeping sore where his right eye should have been. I looked away again, fast.

"Who is it?" he asked, his voice hoarse, like he hadn't used it in weeks. "Which one of you?"

For just a second I thought he was completely blind, that he couldn't see us. But then I realized what he was really asking. "Me," I said. I took a step forward. (Me.) I laid the picture in the barely open fist of his thoughts as carefully and nervously as I'd pass over a piece of crystal. I hadn't done this in a long time.

His mind spasmed shut over it; crushing it. Opened again, millimeter by millimeter, until a finger tendrilled out, beckoning me. (Come here.) His real hand twitched, hidden inside a frayed glove; trying to gesture in case I hadn't understood.

I moved toward him, not really wanting to get any closer, but not seeing how I had any choice. I kept trying to look at his face, but my eyes slid away again every time that oozing socket came into focus. I wondered how the hell he could leave it like that, untreated. I wondered how long he'd been wearing those same clothes. I could smell him before I got nearly as close as he wanted me to.

He stood staring at me, his good eye squinting, as if even this gloom was too bright for him. Glance by glance I filled in a face covered by a bristle of half-shaved beard. He was nearly bald, and he'd half shaved what hair he had left, too. His whole head was pale and lumpy, like something made of dough. His teeth looked rotten. I couldn't tell how old he was; he looked middle-aged, but maybe not. His one good eye was as green as a perfect emerald.

His gloved hand rose up to my face. I managed not to jerk away as it groped me like a curious spider, and dropped to his side again. He was just proving to himself that I was real. (Telepath—?) he asked. I nodded. (What . . . what do you want?) The uncertain mutter of his thoughts inside my head said he hadn't used that voice in a long time, either.

(I need some help. I want to access a system.)

His mind clenched up, eased open again. (Whose?)

(He calls himself Doctor Death.)

His fist shot out, catching me by the front of my shirt, catching me off-guard. "Who sent you here?" he rasped, losing control, snapping the thread of real contact.

I forced his hand away; took a breath as he backed off. I felt Mikah shifting from foot to foot behind me, weapon-systems armed. (Nobody sent me.) I dropped my guard just enough, and let him pry until he believed me. (I need some information that only DeAth's got. I can pay—)

(Go away.) He turned his back on me, began to shuffle toward his door.

My hands tightened. (Wait! How long's it been? Since you felt this? Since you had somebody who could really talk to you—)

He stopped, and faced me again. My eyes cringed; I made myself see through him with that other set of eyes, until his surface disappeared. I felt him remember something, *a touch, words that weren't spoken but only were —but it was so long, so unbearably long ago; could have been just a dream.* . . . The one eye that he still had got red-rimmed and watery-looking; his Adam's apple jerked up and down in his throat. Finally he nodded, silent with his mind, lifting his hand to wave me after him as he started back toward his door.

I followed, with Mikah treading on my heels, his face expressionless, his mind locked on *ready.*

"Who's that?" Deadeye stopped short suddenly, blocking the doorway, looking at Mikah.

"My brother," I said, and Mikah's mouth twitched.

"He don't look much like you," Deadeye mumbled. But that was all he said. He started on again, letting us follow him inside.

We went on through the dark, echoing space of the warehouse, Mikah hanging onto my sleeve because he couldn't see without his night lenses. I could feel him wondering why it seemed like we could when he couldn't.

Finally there was real light ahead again. Deep inside the warehouse Deadeye had built his room, his refuge. It wasn't what I'd expected. His world was lit by a single stick-on glowplate, but it was neat, ascetic, clean; it had dull but decent furniture, a portable kitchen unit, and a simple console, the kind everybody who had a place to put one had to have, so that daily life could go on. Mikah was right—there was no vidphone plugged into it. Deadeye didn't even have a threedy. But it was plain he wasn't hurting for money. He wanted it this way.

He sat down in an ancient rocking chair, and picked up something from the box lying beside it. I saw a pair of long, thick needles, tangled in what looked like a ruined sweater. He untangled the mess with hands that knew just what they were doing. I felt Mikah tense up beside me as he tried to guess whether it was a weapon. I shook my head, glancing at him, and he eased off.

Deadeye set the chair rocking with his foot and began to work the needles through the yarn, feeding more bright-colored thread into the sweater, until I realized he was actually making it out of nothing. The chair creaked, the needles clicked; he never looked up at us standing there waiting. He'd never had anybody all the way in here before; not even once.

I moved on into the room, sat down cross-legged on the floor in front of him. (What is that stuff?) I thought, focusing on the motion of his hands.

(Knitting.) The wordsign flickered on in my mind: images of needles performing an ancient dance with yarn, turning it into a hundred different patterns and shapes.

(What do you do it for?)

(It feels good.) He looked up at me, for half a second; looked down again when I flinched at the sudden sight of his face. (Eye make you sick, does it?)

I nodded.

(Supposed to. Keeps 'em off me.) *Everybody else.*

(That could kill you.)

His face rearranged itself until I realized he was smiling—the way somebody would smile who'd just glued your feet into your shoes. (Not unless I look in a mirror.) That was no rotting sore on his face; it was only a cosmo piece, a joke, a trick.

"No shit," I said, feeling my own mouth start to smile in relief, even while my eyes were still refusing to believe it. Mikah jerked upright on the couch across the room, startled by the broken silence.

(Who are you?) Deadeye asked me, finally.

(Cat.)

(Where'd you come from?)

(Ardattee. Quarro.)

I felt his irritation sting me; I wasn't giving him anything that meant anything, that words alone couldn't say. (You a 'breed?)

I nodded.

(Thought so.) The warped smile squeezed out of him again. (Why aren't you crazy?) The one eye looked into me, too knowing.

I glanced down. (Dumb luck,) thinking of Siebeling. I felt him groping, nagging, pushing. . . . I let down more defenses, loosened more knots; let him creep into my mind and take a look around, answering his own questions. Picking through my past like a dog nosing over trash. My body went rigid muscle by muscle, while I struggled to keep my mind loose and open.

He grunted, and blinked, and broke contact. One hand let go of his knitting . . . reached out, pulled back again, and picked up the thread. After that there was no sound but clicking needles; no other motion, no other sign. Nothing but a wall of tangled wire and despair.

I sat waiting, taking deep breaths. (Goddamn it,) I thought finally, slamming it through his guard, (you got what you wanted from me! What do I get from you?)

He jumped like he'd been shocked. He looked up at me, his one eye red and wet. He put out his hand again, reaching for me. I braced, ready to pull back. But he only patted my shoulder twice, gently, and took his hand away again. I stayed where I was, too surprised to do anything at all.

(You got a job you need done,) he thought, as if I hadn't told him that before.

I nodded.

(Why don't you do it yourself?)

I touched my head. (Not wired.)

He smiled that smirking joker's smile again, as if he knew something the rest of the universe didn't. But he only asked, (Why me? This?) Touching his own head. He'd thought nobody knew about his psi; he'd tried to keep it that way.

(No.) I waved a hand at Mikah. (He says you're the best. The only one can do it.)

He looked down at his knitting again; needles clicked in the silence. Mikah rearranged himself restlessly on the couch, wishing he was somewhere else.

(Can you do it? Crack that system?)

Calm confidence seeped into my mind, all the answer Deadeye needed to make. Mikah hadn't lied.

(Will you?)

(Why?)

I felt my muscles start to tighten up again. (I said I can pay—)

(Why—?) Not why should he. Why did I want it done—what did I want to know?

I showed him. He hadn't even heard about the human bomb. He took it all in, while I waited some more, counting my heartbeats.

He looked up again at last. (Might be worth it.)

I grinned, sitting back. (Where's your ware? You got it in a separate room?) Looking around this room again, I noticed the heap of knitted things beside the door; but still not even enough tech to make a phone call. And there was no bioware hidden inside his skull. If he even had an access jack, I couldn't feel it.

He actually chuckled this time. It sounded like clearing phlegm. (Don't need any.)

Shit— I blocked it before he heard me. He *was* crazy, the old bastard. "Forget it—" I started to get up.

(I don't need any.) The image filled my head again; clear, hard, insistent.

I stood looking down at him. "That's impossible."

He shook his head. (That's what they want us to believe. . . . That's what they believe themselves. I stumbled over the truth. Probably others have.)

(But you don't pass it on.)

(Why should I? What would it get me, except trouble?)

I thought about it. He was right. (Why are you telling me?)

(Because you understand what it means, to be a psion, and live by stealing.) He looked down again. (Because you're good, and I might need your help.)

(You mean you'd show me how? We'd do it together?) Excitement and fear collided inside me.

(Maybe.) His good eye turned noncommittal. (How's your memory?)

(Perfect.)

(Good.) He dropped his knitting over the side and stood up. (A lot to learn, first.) He trudged across the room to his console, and woke it up. For a minute I thought we were going to start in right there; but he was only calling up library files.

"You ready?" Mikah asked, his voice sharp with uneasy impatience. Both of us jumped at the sound of it.

"Almost." I almost forgot to answer him out loud. I held up a hand. Deadeye turned back to me, handing over a headset. (Memorize these data. Teaches you as much as anything can about how a machine's mind functions. It can save your life. Don't come back unless you know it all. Then we'll see.)

I nodded, took the headset and pushed it into my pocket.

(Bring that back. Only one I have.)

I nodded again.

He moved toward the door, suggesting with the motion that we should get out. He stopped suddenly as he reached the pile of clothes, and scooped up an armload. He went on out, carrying the heap with him into the darkness.

When we reached the street he herded us through the door, and then he dropped the load of knitting onto the pavement beside the building.

"He's dumping that out?" Mikah asked, as if that only proved to him that Deadeye was out of his mind.

Deadeye shrugged. (What about him?) he asked me, glaring at Mikah.

(He's my brother,) I said again.

He went back inside without saying anything, and slammed the door. Mikah was still staring at the pile of clothes.

"He doesn't need them," I said finally; explaining, because somehow I had to. "Somebody'll come along who does." Already it felt like having to put my thoughts into words before I could get them out was as hard as walking uphill.

Mikah gave me a Look, and started to turn away. He turned back again, as curiosity tipped the scales on his irritation. Searching through the pile of knitted things, he found a long red scarf and wrapped it around his throat. I picked up the brown-green sweater that landed at my feet and pulled it on over my torn shirt. It felt good, heavy and warm. There was a dank chill to the air here. As we started away down the street, Mikah said, "That was the strangest fucking fifteen minutes I've spent since the day you disappeared on Cinder." He made a small noise in the back of his throat; still trying to shake the feeling of being deaf and dumb, and invisible.

"Could be worse."

He looked at me.

"You could feel like that all the time." I touched the patch behind my ear.

He looked blank, for a minute. Then he asked, "How's the stuff you got from DeAth doing for you?"

"Doing its job," I said. "Just fine."

He nodded, but he didn't smile. "So what about your freakin' cousin back there—?" He flicked the end of the red scarf. "He gonna do the job after all?"

"Think so." I sighed, feeling a weight lift off me as I realized that I'd already done the hardest part of my work, just getting through to him. "I got to go back and see him again in a couple days." I hesitated. "Keep it sealed that he's a freak."

He nodded. "What was on that hairnet he handed you?"

I felt in my pocket for the headset. "I can't tell you."

He looked interested, but he only shrugged. "No problem." On the streets half of what you knew was never more than a jigsaw puzzle with pieces missing, anyway. We went on to the Tube station, talking about the weather.

"You going back to the club?" he asked, as we got on board together and the waiting transit sucked us away from the memory of Deadeye.

"Not tonight." Not sure when I was going to see Argentyne again, or what I'd say to her if I ever did, after what I'd said to her tonight.

"Oh, yeah." He smirked. "I forgot. You got one hot body waiting up for you." His grin got wider as the trans sighed to a stop in the next station. "Me too. See you." He flipped me a salute, and went away down the platform, whistling.

23

"AUNTIE'S SICK." Jiro was sitting on the stairs as I came into the house, his face propped in his hands, his eyes shadowed, his thoughts dark.

I stopped dead, pictures of poison or biocontamination strobing in my brain. "Where is she? In the hospital?" Elnear had looked all right when I'd left the office with her: tired and depressed, but that wasn't surprising. I'd even watched her get into the secured private mod that would carry her straight here.

He shook his head. "She's just in her room. I guess she's asleep. She fainted or something when she came home. Charon sent our meds to see her; they said it's just because of all the—" He broke off. "What happened, I mean . . . you know. And because she's old. They gave her some stuff. She had to rest."

I nodded, relieved. But if Elnear had been depressed before, this wasn't going to make her feel any better. "Thanks," I said, and started past him up the stairs. Stopped, looking back, "Is your mother here?"

He twisted on the steps to look up at me. "Why?" he asked, a little too loudly.

"Just wondered." I shrugged, trying not to act like it mattered, and went on up to my room. I stood looking out the window, feeling tired, flexing my sore hand. Maybe tomorrow I'd get it treated somewhere, like Aspen had told me to. I still had trouble realizing that I had the credit to fix things I didn't like. As I stood looking out into the darkness, it began to rain. It only rained at night here. The taMings always fixed the things they didn't like.

I heard Jiro come into the room behind me, like I'd known he would, sooner or later. The darkness behind his eyes hadn't been because Elnear was sick, so it had to be something else. I turned away from the windows, went to the bed and sat down. "What is it?" I asked, even though I was pretty sure I knew.

He opened his mouth, the words that he'd held bottled up inside him ready to burst out. But still he couldn't say them, for a long minute. "You—my mother—I mean . . ." His hands flapped. "Did you—do that with my mother?"

I looked down at my own hands resting across my knees. "You mean, did I spend the night with her?" I looked up at him again, and nodded.

His face got red. He'd expected me to deny it, even if it was true. Somehow the fact that I didn't look ashamed about it made him feel ashamed instead. He began to blink hard; his mouth trembled.

"Come here," I said. He came across the room. "Sit down." He sat on the bed, keeping his distance, staring at the floor. "How did you know?" I asked.

"My mother . . . I saw her come out of your room the other morning, real early. She didn't know I saw her. And she acted so . . . different." His voice squeaked.

"You know," I said, "the first time I met her you damn near acted like a pimp, pushing her at me. No, I'm not saying it was your fault—" as he looked up with sudden anger in his eyes. "It just happened. . . . I only wondered how come it bothers you so much, now that it has. Because of what I am?"

He shook his head, his jaw clenched.

Very carefully, I let myself into his memory, looking for the answer he wouldn't give me.

"Because of what you saw at Argentyne's club." Until that night he'd been like any other kid, his curiosity about sex practically an obsession. But then in five minutes he'd learned more than he'd ever wanted to know. "You think it was like that, what your mother and I did?" I felt my face pinch with his pain.

This time he nodded, blushing again.

"Jiro. . . ." I broke off. "What you saw there—that wasn't making love. That wasn't even good sex. More like rape." He looked at me now, out of the corner of his eye. "There is a difference."

"Are you going to marry my mother?"

"Your mother's already married."

He half frowned. "She could get a divorce. Aren't you in love with her—?" Fantasies were starting to pop like bubbles in his mind.

I looked away. "I don't know. I don't think so."

"Isn't she in love with you?"

I shook my head. "She's just not in love with Charon." I felt the bone-deep ache of his disappointment; couldn't think of anything I could do that would ease it. Finally I said, "I think she loved your father . . . I know she loves you, and your sister. You're more important to her than anything else in her life. Be glad." *You could have been me.* But I didn't say it. I wondered what it would be like to have been born a taMing, to have anything I ever wanted. . . . I couldn't even imagine it. Even if I hadn't been born rich—just to have had somebody there, all those years . . . anybody. I looked away from him, down at my scarred hands.

He got up, slowly. "My mother said for me to ask if you'd . . . think about her, tonight."

"Yeah," I said. "I'll do that. Good night, Jiro."

He straightened his shoulders, trying hard to look like a man and not a boy. "Good night, Cat." He went out of the room.

I stayed where I was, listening to the lonely sound of the rain. I wasn't ready to sleep, or in the mood to think about Lazuli right now. With a kind of surprise I realized it was Elnear I was still thinking about . . . worried about. I let my mind track until it found her. She was in her bed, but she wasn't any closer to sleep than I was. The sedative the doctor had given her hadn't been enough to take hold against her body's own overdose of adrenaline. But her mind wasn't on tomorrow or today or even yesterday any more. It was caught in a place where memory was like something seen in a dark mirror: where the image of a perfect afternoon in the Hanging Gardens of Quarro with the man she loved made her dizzy with misery; where the image of Talitha as a laughing baby filled her with sorrow. A place inside her that she couldn't escape from, because the past was still so much sweeter than anything she thought of when she let it go, and tried to listen to the rain. . . .

I got up again and went out, back through the dark, quiet halls to her room. There was a thin line of light tracing the crack under her door. I knocked.

"Yes—?" I heard the word quaver with her surprise; felt her surprise behind my eyes.

"It's Cat."

There was silence for a minute. Then, "Come in," she said.

The door wasn't locked. I went into the room, suddenly feeling more than a little self-conscious. But she looked up at me, her face mapped with shadows, and smiled. It was almost relief she felt, now that I was here.

That made me smile too, a little, while I searched for something to say now that I'd come. "Jiro told me you were sick, ma'am. I just

wanted to know if you'll need me in the morning. And to . . . to know
if you need anything now."

"Yes," she said, suddenly not afraid to say it. "Sit with me for a
while, if you would. I need some companionship, more than anything
else. The one thing that no one has thought to offer me." She glanced
down, and back at me. "I feel terribly alone tonight . . . and somehow
I don't find it difficult to tell you that. I suppose because I think you
probably already know that, and that it was why you came." Her eyes
held mine until I looked away. "Thank you for coming." She was gathering things up from the surface of the bedcover as she spoke; restless
holos of familiar faces that had been trying to keep her company, and
failing.

I sat down on the edge of a tapestry-covered chair, still afraid of
breaking something as I glanced around the room. A single lamp with a
shade made of stained-glass flowers turned the room's light soft and
warm. The furniture here was old and elegant, like most of the furniture
in the house. I stared at the face of a woman carved on the back of a
desk across the room, her long hair flowing down into the grain of the
wood. I looked back again at the pictures of faces gathered in Elnear's
hands: Jiro and Talitha, and Kelwin taMing.

"I hadn't thought of it before, but sometimes it must be a kind of
blessing to be a telepath," Elnear said. "To be able to know that someone else is out there, thinking about you, even when you can't see or
hear them."

"Sometimes," I said. "Sometimes it's just looking in through the
windows of houses where you aren't wanted." *In the land of the blind.* I
shrugged. "But like you said once, everything looks better when you
don't have to live with it, I guess." And being what I was, not human
enough, not Hydran enough, even that much was better than the alternative . . . better than nothing.

She smiled again, and nodded. "Yes, I suppose so. If I'm lonely, at
least I still have my privacy intact."

I settled back a little uncertainly into the curved hollow of the chair.
"When I was with other psions, I used to have it both ways—the sharing, and the—solitude, when I wanted it. It was . . ." I looked away,
into my own dark mirrors. Trying to feel something that made sense
when I looked at my memories; only feeling numb. Drugged . . .

I made myself remember Deadeye: how even with him, twisted up
like he was, it had been so much easier—to speak without words, to just
know. The way it should have been; the way it ought to be. The way it

must have been for the Hydrans, before the humans ended it. "Humans are so . . ." groping for the words, when it would be so much easier just to show her—

"Pathetic?" Elnear murmured. "Is that what you're thinking?"

I looked up at her; looked away again as soon as I met her eyes.

"But you lived that way yourself for most of your life, didn't you?" she said quietly. "Unable to know another person's thoughts. I would think that would give you more sympathy for the way we are than most humans are capable of themselves . . . more compassion."

My eyes squeezed shut as something spun and dropped suddenly inside me. "I don't know." I shook my head. "All I know is none of you can understand what it's really like, to have what I had, after a lifetime of nothing—and then to lose it again. I didn't know what was missing all those years. But now I know—" And finally I understood why being a telepath again was so important to me: because it was all I'd ever had that was really mine.

"But you have it back," she said, a little surprised.

I shook my head. "If I go on using these drugs, I'll burn it out for good."

She hadn't understood that. "Then, if you're only doing this because of me, you should stop now."

I shook my head again. "I can't."

"I don't want to be—"

"I can't."

She looked at me.

I rubbed my face. "Don't ask. Just forget I said that." I started to get up.

"I can't," she said.

I stopped.

"But if you wish, we can pretend that I have. If that will let you stay, and humor a lonely old woman a while longer." Her mouth pulled up into a smile that was half regret and half irony. Her hands held the pictures a little tighter.

I sat down again, trying not to look as awkward as I felt right then. Watching her hands, I asked, "How come you never had any children—you and your husband?"

She looked down at the holos. "We always thought there would be plenty of time." Suddenly she was blinking too much, as she stared at her husband's face. "Isn't it strange, how any little thing can—set off your memory, when you least expect it. A song, a certain light . . .

Sometimes, when I remember my life with Kelwin, it seems to me as if those are someone else's memories that have somehow gotten inside my head. That the person with him, that I remember so well, can't possibly be me. It makes it so difficult . . . almost unbearable, sometimes. And yet not ever to think about them is more unbearable. And the worst part is that it's the *good* memories that hurt me the most."

"Yeah," I whispered.

"Tell me about your family," she said, trying to change the subject. It struck her as odd and humiliating that she'd never even pictured me having any. She wondered suddenly if she'd been afraid to, knowing what I was. And she wondered what it would feel like to live as a Hydran . . .

I wondered too. "Nothing to tell." I shrugged, looking away. There was a time when I'd wanted to search for my mother's people. But then I'd killed Rubiy. And after that there hadn't seemed to be much point in it; because by killing him I'd proved that I could never be one of them.

Elnear pressed her lips together, and didn't let herself ask again. At last she said, "Cat, do you ever wonder, when you relive that awful loss . . . feel that sinking-into-a-hole darkness . . ." her gaze got lost somewhere, "if perhaps you feel that way not because you're so different from the rest of us, but because you're so human?" She glanced up at me; I felt her trying to reach out to something inside me—something she wasn't sure even still existed.

I felt myself clench up, in a kind of angry reflex. But then I made myself look at her again, face her reality, acknowledge all the things about her that had made her matter to me . . . admit that *human* wasn't a four-letter word. "Siebeling said . . . he told me not to—to pretend I'm something I'm not." I looked down at my hands, suddenly wishing that I had pictures to hold. "That I'm not really human, I mean. Most of the freaks I know are human, every way except one. . . . Even the Hydrans I've met are more human than they want to be."

"Most humans are more human than they want to be, too," she said quietly.

I half smiled. "Thanks. . . ." I got to my feet.

"For what?" she asked.

"For reminding me that if humans and Hydrans didn't have something in common, I wouldn't be here."

She laughed. I liked the sound of her laughter. "That's an unusual sweater," she said, really seeing me for the first time tonight. "Wherever did you find it?"

"Lying in the street. Good night, ma'am."

"Good night," she murmured, looking after me a little oddly.

I smiled as I left her, figuring that at least I'd left her with something to wonder about besides the future; something to think about besides the lonely night and the rain.

But it didn't leave me with much else to think about, by the time I reached my room again. I pulled Deadeye's headset out of my pocket and put it on; stretched out on the bed with my hands behind my head and filled the empty places with all the data I could swallow in one dose. There was still a lot of information left waiting when I pulled it off again. Then finally I closed my eyes, and let the static in my brain sing my aching body to sleep.

I woke up again with a start, for no reason that I could name, hours later. My mind was quiet now, and it let the grayness come seeping back as I listened to the rain. Listening, I wondered about how the sound of rain seemed to fill my mind with the same kind of longings and sorrows that I'd seen in Elnear's. I could count on the fingers of one hand the number of times I'd heard it rain. I hadn't had a lifetime of listening to it to make it mean more to me than the simple sound of dripping water. I remembered the way I'd felt when I'd first set foot on Earth . . . a total stranger, and yet somehow coming home. Remembered what Elnear had been trying to show me this evening: that the human side of me had its own needs, its own history; and that not everything it felt was something I had to be ashamed of. And I realized that for the first time in a long time I didn't feel angry.

I thought about Lazuli then, wondered if she was lying awake in Charon's bed, not alone but always lonely, listening to the rain. *She wanted me to think about her.* . . . I wondered if she meant it the way I thought she did. I wondered if she was thinking about me, missing me. I knew that even if she was, her thoughts didn't go much further than the way my body fit into hers. *I'd been a pullover, and she'd known it—*

I waited for that to make me angry. But it only made me remember the feel of my body fitting into hers. . . . There'd been too many others who'd really fucked me over. Why should I be angry at a bored, unhappy, beautiful woman who'd only wanted some boytoy to fuck her brains out. . . . Maybe it didn't really matter why she wanted me; not when just thinking about that smooth perfume-scented skin, her hair like silk down across my chest, was enough to make my head swim. But

it wasn't going to happen again. Not tonight. Especially not like this. I
told myself to forget about her, and go to sleep. I told myself I wasn't
crazy; I told myself I was. I told myself she was using me again. . . . I
told myself if she really wanted me to think about her tonight, I could
make sure she never forgot it. . . .

I let go of my thoughts, reaching out into the emptiness, spreading a
net of invisible threads tipped with light. I pictured the Crystal Palace
in my mind, not so far away that my mind couldn't reach it, reach
inside, searching through the dark silences for a familiar star.

I found her, side by side with Charon. Asleep, dreaming a dim, restless dream about suffocating in a windowless room. I drifted past the
sullen heat of Charon's sleeping mind without looking in, and closed
focus to enter Lazuli's. I slipped into her dream, as softly as a thief . . .
felt her body quiver and stir, not quite waking; felt her dream change to
include me. I lay down beside her inside her dream, and let my mind
begin to touch her the way my hands, my body, ached to do . . . fired
the nerve strings that fed her mind every sensation I could have given
her, moving over her, against her, inside her. . . .

Somewhere in the middle of it she woke. (You wanted me to,) I
whispered, (you asked for me. . . .) Gentling her, reassuring her, so
that she didn't cry out but only let herself drift back down into her
yearning . . . feeling the sensations of her pleasure doubled as her
hands began to touch her body, the way my hands were already touching my own. Until the beam of white heat joining us mind to mind
exploded like a sun, and left us alone in our separate bodies, back in our
separate worlds again, only sharing the sound of the rain. . . .

In the morning when I woke I knew more about artificial intelligence
than I'd ever wanted to . . . and less than ever about what in hell I
was really doing here, waking up in this bed, playing cat and mouse in it
while I played ratcatcher for the taMings. I wondered what Lazuli was
trying to do—to herself, to me. If she really didn't care whether Charon
found out; if she was really that stupid, or that unhappy. Or whether
she just didn't care because she thought if anything happened because
of this, it wouldn't happen to her. . . .

Feeling numb and out-of-control, I got up and slapped on Deadeye's
headset again. I fed my brain as much new data as it would take;
forcing it, to keep from thinking about what I was doing—and because
the sooner I knew everything he wanted me to know, the sooner I could
get at the information I really wanted, and maybe get out of here. Then

I stumbled downstairs to find something to feed my body, to get it through another day.

Talitha came shyly into the dining room, stood staring at me while I heaped my plate with the usual morning leftovers. I ignored her, my brain buzzing too loud, until finally she came across the room and tugged on my sweater.

"I want more," she said.

"You've got the right idea, kid," I said. "You'll make a good ta-Ming." I went on filling up my plate.

"I want more grapes." She looked up at me, waiting, her small face as perfect as a flower, and just as blank. "Grapes—" She tugged harder on me, and threw in a grudging, "Please?"

I handed her a clump of grapes. "Thank you," she said gravely.

"Sure." I nodded, feeling just a little crummy.

"Auntie said we're going to pick berries this morning!" she announced, around a mouthful of fat green globes.

"Great," I mumbled, through a haze of binary code sequences and half a piece of bread.

"You can come too. I'll show you how, because you don't know how to do anything right." She began to tug on my arm. "Come on—"

I shook my head, red-faced and half smiling; not sure if I could think of a worse way to spend the morning if I tried. "I got things I have to—"

"Please join us, Cat." Lazuli stepped into the room, into my line of sight, and changed my mind with a glance. She was dressed in a transparent tunic patterned with leaves, over an electric-blue bodycover that somehow only made what it was covering up more obvious. She didn't say anything else; didn't need to, when her mind was saying it all.

I nodded slowly, choked down another bite of spiced bun that suddenly could have been plastic.

Elnear came into the room, carrying her art console; dressed like she usually was, as if she didn't want anybody to look at her for long. The contrast between them almost hurt my eyes. "Yes, won't you come—?" she asked, missing my nod. I bit my tongue for wanting to say the obvious, with Lazuli's eyes still burning a hole in my flesh, and couldn't think of anything else.

And so somehow I found myself in the autumn forest out on the mountainside above the taMings' private valley, with the smell of damp earth filling my head the way buzzing data strings filled my brain. The things Elnear called golden raspberries grew not-really-wild in a patch

of jagged leaves and thorns. We picked them, and it was everything I'd
expected it to be. I hated every minute of it. It reminded me of trying to
pick answers out of Daric's mind . . . it reminded me of digging ore in
the Mines on Cinder: Picking something fragile and perfect out of a
matrix that didn't want to give it up, where any wrong move could
mean pain. . . .

"You don't look like you're enjoying this very much, Cat," Elnear
said, peering out at me from underneath her wide-brimmed hat. She
looked happier and more relaxed than I'd ever seen her. I shrugged.

"He doesn't know how to have fun," Talitha said; I heard Jiro laugh,
too sharply, somewhere behind my back. "That's why I'm helping
him." She was eating berries out of my hand as fast as I picked them.

"Then let me help you, too." Lazuli slid a berry between my lips with
deft, gentle fingers. It was as soft as her skin, the juice sweet and tangy
as I crushed it with my tongue. "There," she said, "now you're smiling." Her body, her mind, were smiling at me—had been, helplessly,
ever since she'd laid eyes on me this morning. Her awareness of me like
a warm fluid slowly melting down through the ice of overlapping data
inside my mind. "You know, I had a dream about you last night," she
murmured. Her eyes laughed at the sudden panic in my own, even
while they begged me to prove to her again that it hadn't been just a
dream.

(It wasn't a dream.) I saw her face flush as I proved it. I looked down
and away again, not answering her out loud, because Elnear was watching us too closely. I wished Lazuli wouldn't do this to me. I felt embarrassed, frustrated . . . on fire with the heat of the arousal I couldn't
control as she imagined me reaching out to find her, to touch her,
anywhere; like some kind of demon lover who could take her even while
she lay asleep in her husband's bed, making her forget who she was and
where, making her forget anything but the pleasure of being made love
to impossibly. . . .

"Well," Elnear said, making us realize that we'd been standing there
staring at each other like magnetic dolls for way too long. "I believe I'm
going to try some sketching on down the slope. Do be careful—" Something in her voice made me look back at her. "It can be treacherous
. . . when the leaves are wet, you know." One last glance, her eyes as
transparent as blue glass, letting me know that she understood: everything that was happening, how it felt to be young, how it felt to be
lonely . . . how it felt to dance on a minefield. "Do be careful," she
murmured again, glancing at Lazuli this time. "Come with me, chil-

dren—" She waved to Talitha and Jiro. "I've brought a special treat for you."

Lazuli looked after her, half troubled and half self-conscious, as Elnear guided the children away, leaving us alone together intentionally, pointedly. Not giving us her blessing . . . but giving us room to breathe. Talitha ran ahead, squealing and scuffling through the leaves while Jiro trailed behind, looking back over his shoulder at us, his expression more like his mother's than he knew.

When they were gone we settled side by side on the blanket, our bodies not quite touching, while I wove a band of warm contact between us. She fed me berries between long deep kisses. Light showered down through the trees, haloing her hair; making the restless ceiling over our heads into a living window of stained glass. Looking up into all that beauty, I wondered if this was how someone had gotten the idea. And I wondered if it was really so impossible to be happy in a place like this. . . .

The call function began to beep on my databand. I sat up, startled; looked down to be sure the bandphone video was off before I answered. It was already on . . . had been on, transmitting for God only knew how long. I hadn't done it; I knew I hadn't. Lazuli's face paled as I swore, blocking the image with my hand. "Braedee—?" I said, my voice white.

I hadn't turned on the receiver, either, but his voice said, "Checkmate." And that was all.

24

I DID MY BEST to make Lazuli believe that Braedee wouldn't talk, without telling her why. I had to believe he only meant that we were back where we'd started, because now he had something on me that could hurt me plenty—just like I had on him. That was the way he wanted it; the way he liked it. But somehow after that she couldn't shut out reality any more, and neither could I. We went on down the hill through a golden rain of leaves, looking for Elnear; not touching, not even speaking much.

That night she stayed with Charon in the Crystal Palace. She didn't ask me to think about her, but part of her wanted to. I thought about her anyway, but this time I kept my thoughts to myself. Braedee didn't make contact with me again, and I didn't return his call. I told myself that I wanted to wait until I had the information Deadeye was going to help me get; knowing that I was really stalling just because I didn't have the guts to face him without it.

By the next day Elnear was itching to get back to work, and so was I. The last of Deadeye's data was filtering down into my mind; by the time night came around I'd be ready to pay him another visit. The usual morning in the office seemed to go by in slow motion. I wasn't sure if it was because what was filling my mind was so strange, or because it made everything else too normal.

Finally I took a break, giving my restless thoughts some space. I didn't get far down the hallway before somebody's hand caught my shoulder, jerking me back and around. *Daric.* I hadn't sensed him coming up behind me; probably because he hadn't wanted me to.

"You bastard," he said, shoving me up against the wall like we were the only two people in the entire building. I didn't have to look past the rage in his eyes to know the reason: Argentyne. But buried below the pain there was something more—sheer terror was wearing his fury like body armor. The only reason I wasn't dead of an embolism or a heart attack right now was that he knew he couldn't get past my guard. "Come with me." Her jerked me forward again. I let him lead me through the halls to the same whiteroom he'd used with Stryger. He sealed it, turned back to me. "You little shit—" he said; broke off, and had to start again. "You turned her against me. She said she never wants to see me again. She said to ask you why. . . . *Why?*"

"Because I told her the truth about what you are," I said.

"What do you mean?" He held me with his eyes, fists trembling at his sides while he fought himself for control. "She knows everything about me—" The fear inside him was swelling until he was afraid it was going to choke one of us to death. "If she didn't hate me before, why should she now?"

"Now she knows what you do for Stryger—the truth about that girl you brought to Purgatory. You remember," I said, hardly recognizing my own voice, "the one Stryger hurt so bad you were afraid she'd die. The freak you bought to play victim for him."

"Is that all—?" Daric's whole body suddenly went slack with relief. "So what?" he said, and shrugged. "Nobody made the bitch to it. She didn't file any complaint."

After a long minute I asked softly, "How was it, watching him beat her up, Daric? How'd you like it? Was she a telepath, did she let you *feel* it? Is that what Stryger really likes? What you really want? Did you really wish it was you instead . . . or do you just get off on knowing Stryger's like all the rest of the deadheads, never guessing your secret—"

He turned white. "Which secret?" he whispered.

(You're one of us,) I thought. (Freak. Teek. Psion.)

His mind struck at me like a snake. My own mind blocked the thrust of thought, and broke its back before it could reach me. I tossed his sending back at him. "You can't hurt me. You're not good enough." He'd never be good enough, even if he'd had training to teach him how to use it right. He didn't have that much talent. Being a psion had driven his whole life into this dead end, and he wasn't even a good one.

He turned away, his eyes searching the corners of the room. "No," he said, "no, no, no, no. This isn't real. It's impossible. No. No." He licked his lips, rubbed his hand over his mouth. Trying, after a lifetime, to believe it had finally happened. He turned back to me; I felt panic claw at the walls of his mind. "Who else did you tell? Argentyne, you told her. . . ."

"Yeah, I told her." I nodded, enjoying the look on his face. He wanted to smash my own face in, more than he'd ever wanted anything in his life. Now he knew how he'd made me feel.

"That's why she turned against me—"

"She doesn't give a damn about it," I said.

Incredulity fought its way out through his fury. "You're lying. You told her so she'd hate me—"

"Yeah. That's right, I did." Finally admitting it, to myself more than to him. "But she really didn't care. Not everybody's a bigot. If she hates you now, it's because you're a lousy bastard. Not because you're a psion."

Because you're a psion— His father's image filled his mind like a black storm: a child's terrifying night monster, etched forever on the lens of his memory. "Who else did you tell—?"

"Nobody."

His expression changed. *(Maybe,)* his mind said. *Maybe it still wasn't too late. . . .*

"Don't even think about it," I said. "You can't kill me yourself. And if you try to hire it out, I'll know. Nothing better happen to Argentyne either. Just think of me like a jar of toxins. You break me, and I take your whole world with me."

He wiped his mouth again with a trembling hand. "You son of a bitch. You freak! What do you want—money?"

I shook my head. "I'm getting plenty of that already."

"Then *what?*" Drops of spit glittered in the air between us.

I didn't answer. I wasn't used to having power over somebody; I was just beginning to realize how it felt . . . that it felt good. I looked at him, letting the dark, sweet pleasure fill me; letting him realize along with me how easy it would be for me to destroy him. He'd treated me like shit, and Jule, and everybody else he'd gotten close to; contaminated our lives like a disease. Destroying him would be a public service.

For just a second I cracked my defenses, let myself into his mind, wanting to enjoy the fear that must be eating his guts out right now—

It slammed into my thoughts, nauseating, bitter, blinding. I spat him out again, shaking my head. "I want . . ." I swallowed. "I want you to stop pimping for Stryger. If you ever get him another freak to work over, you're gone. That's all." I turned away, started for the door.

"No—" His hand clamped my arm like a binder. "Don't say that. That's not all, it can't be. You can't tell me you *know,* and then tell me you don't want anything. Tell me what you want from me!" He shook me, his whole body floundering with the motion.

I stood still, feeling myself go rigid under his hand. (Just leave me alone.)

His hand came loose and dropped to his side. He stayed where he was, motionless but still quivering, his mouth hanging open, slack and wet. I left him like that, sealing the door behind me as I went out, so that I didn't have to know what he did next.

Back in Elnear's office again I pretended to work, but I couldn't concentrate. Finally facing Daric, I'd broken the thin ice between the light and the dark. My mind was out of synch with the fantasy around me, the world that only existed as long as you believed in its reality. I was back in the nightworld, the otherworld, where people like Daric and Stryger really belonged . . . people like Mikah and Deadeye . . . people like me. I sat staring at the wall, seeing Oldcity, where I'd learned the truth—that light was an illusion, that only the darkness was forever, the night that had existed before there were stars, and would still be there long after they died.

I couldn't do Elnear's work, work that suddenly seemed meaningless and stupid, like her faith in human nature—and so I began to play with the terminal, trying out my new knowledge, trying to see if I could find Deadeye's secret passage to inner space on my own. But it was no use. I understood the tech of information storage, the interface of EM and chem that made up the artificial brains of an information net, that manipulated the data. But I couldn't find anything more that I had in common with it than I had in common with the molecules in a wall. After a while I gave up on that, too, wondering if there was even any point in going back to Deadeye's. But I knew I'd go back anyway.

The day's end finally came, and set me free. I took the Tube down under the bay, made my way on foot to Deadeye's building with no problems; maybe because tonight I moved like I belonged here. I buzzed his brain, and he let me in. "Where's your brother?" he said, suspicious like always.

"He's someplace he'd rather be." I hadn't asked Mikah to come with me this time. I figured we'd all be better off if I did this on my own, even if it meant risking my skin on the streets.

Deadeye loosened up, with a grimace that looked like pain, but that meant he was relieved. I'd forgotten how shitty his eye looked. I tried to forget it again as I handed him back his headset. "I'm finished with this."

(Let me see.)

I let him into my head, let him see for himself that the data had all copied perfectly in my brain.

He nodded. (Think you're ready?)

I shrugged, and couldn't help remembering this afternoon—how I'd tried, and failed.

(You don't believe it'll work,) he thought, reading my hesitation. (Because you already tried it.) He laughed suddenly, a rusty, scraping noise that said it figured. (Show me what you did.) He jerked his head toward the console across the room.

I went to it and sat down, started to press the trodes to my forehead; glanced back at him.

He nodded, his own mind riding piggyback inside mine. I did what I'd done that afternoon, trying to make something real and recognizable out of that lifeless flow . . . failing again.

(No, no!) he said, too loud inside my brain. He jerked me loose from the contacts. "You're doing it all wrong!" breaking into speech as exasperation broke down his control.

The sudden noise hurt my ears. "Well, how'm I supposed to—"

(You're looking for something alive. It's not alive!) His mind shut me up. "It's a *system,* you shithead," he said, slowly and too clearly, like I was stupid. "It's only a system. You're not gonna find anybody else in there."

"I know, but—"

"You don't know shit, kid. Those tapes didn't tell you everything. You don't understand the important part—"

(Wait,) I thought. (Don't tell me. I've got Centauri's Corpses on my back. I dunno if I'm being snooped.)

He frowned, but he nodded. (Fuck 'em. They can't hear us now. . . .) He liked it better this way, anyhow. So did I. (Nothing in the Net is like you or me, you understand me? Look—) Showing me: *The Net wasn't using any kind of energy I'd ever used; I only recognized neuronfire patterns, because that was how a psion sensed another person. Now I had to learn to see into a new part of the spectrum, and recognize new kinds of forms.* (It's not going to come to you, you got to go to it. . . . You ever pick up any random EM readings, in a heavy security area, say?)

I nodded, remembering the hissing whiteroom doorways I'd passed through lately.

(Means your talent's wideband; you got no problem there . . . but you got to quit looking for something else, first.) *That was why I'd never*

heard of a psion doing this before—they'd never even think to work this way. (Even the humans using that system are nothing but EM flow patterns once they get inside. The Net's made up of billions of mice—)
"What—?"
(Shut up. Human mice, stupid. Billions and billions of 'em, working parallel all at the same time, all trained to touch the right plate, to register *on* or *off* . . .) *Human microcomponents inputting data, calling it up, changing the patterns over and over . . . following orders.* (The combine boards make the rules and they filter down. The mice follow 'em. They eat their pellets and shit and go home.) *They'd never imagine the real reach of the supersystem they were a part of; but at the same time, it couldn't exist without them. Human brains were limited-function, but they were cheap, flexible, reliable equipment. There were always plenty of them. And when they were linked together into a network, with superseed access fusing them into a whole, those puny, slow-moving human-sized intelligences became something more—*
(Superbeings,) I thought, remembering what Elnear had told me. (In their own ecosystem. With superminds. . . .)
(Exactly.) He looked at me, surprised, and nodded. (That's a relief—)
(What?)
(You're not as stupid as I thought.)
I rolled my eyes. (But you mean the combines actually exist, in the Net? You've really seen them? They talk to each other, they fight, just like in the real world—?)
He frowned. (I said they exist, didn't I? . . . But they're not like you or me, they don't play Square/Cubes, for God's sake.)
(How about chess?) I said, irritated.
He grunted. (They communicate, they change course, but it's usually real slow, because they're so big—they're spread out over light-years, their realtime's in slow motion. They've got personalities of a kind—depends on who runs their board, and the population of their networks. They don't really interact with me direct. I know a lot of their subsystems better.)
(You *know* them . . . ?) I asked, wondering if he meant personally.
(Yeah. There's stuff going on in there on a million intermediate levels. It's like being a rat in the pantry; you can take your pick.) *The subsystems were all supposed to be bound, under control; but some of them were so complex that they actually had conversations on the side with him all the while they were performing their programmed functions.* (They get lonely. The more independent they get the riskier it is for them: then

they're like cancers. If they don't keep a low profile, some tuning checker will lobotomize them.)

I shook my head. (If all this exists in there, why doesn't anybody know? Why don't the cybertechs know it's going on, or the board members, with all their augmentation?)

(A lot of them suspect . . . but they can't prove it, because they can't get outside of the infrastructure. They can't see the forest for the trees. They're nothing but EM flow, like I said. They have to play by their own rules, or their systems stop working. Sometimes their subsystems do things they don't expect; they know that much. They try to control the drift. But they can't see the real picture.)

(You're telling me we can.) I wondered what Elnear would give to be in on this conversation . . . wondered what it would be worth to the cybertechs, to have proof that what they suspected was true. . . . I stopped wondering. Deadeye was right; all it would get freaks like us was mindwiped.

Deadeye nodded, only answering the thought that I'd let him see. (We don't have to play by the rules.)

(Can those things see us?)

(Some of them can. Most of what's in the Net is blind to you for the same reason you're blind to it right now. Only, once you quit thinking you're such a hotshot, you can reprogram yourself to read it—to see the individual subsystems: the bodies, the hands, the guts, the immune systems. They can't do that with you.) *That was why we'd be safe, that was how we could walk though the walls of their security.* (Some of the sentient things have evolved enough to see you, but you're on their own plane, and they seem to like that. You'll be like a ghost in the machine. That works both ways, though: You can look but you can't touch—you can access any data you need, but you can't change anything you find there. A teek might be able to do that, but you can't. . . . Only, a teek couldn't get into the system.)

I nodded. (That's all I need, just to read it. Tell me how to start—)

(Sit still and shut up.) His hands pushed me down in the seat again. (I haven't got to the best part yet. You know what a maze is?)

(Yeah,) I thought, (I guess so. Someplace confusing. Full of dead ends.)

He wheezed out more laughter. (You ever been in one?)

(No.)

(Well, you will be. This is the damnedest maze of all. The hard part isn't getting what you want. It's finding what you're looking for, and finding your way out again. Because the walls are always moving. Finding DeAth's back door isn't going to be easy. That's why you're going with me—it doubles the odds of me getting back.)

(What happens if we get lost?)

(We just sit here.) His face crinkled. (Probably we just sit here till we die. You ready—?)

(Yeah . . . sure.)

He didn't ask me if I wanted to change my mind. It was probably a good thing. He pulled up a second chair and sat down beside me. (Hold my hand,) he thought, leering, but all he meant was keep the mental link. (And do everything I do. And don't break contact, whatever happens—understand?) I nodded, glad all he needed was a simple link, and not a joining. His mind wasn't something I really wanted to get more intimate with.

He stuck one trode to my forehead and one to his own.

(Why do we need these? I thought we weren't really gonna use the system?)

(We aren't,) he said. (But it'll help you get the feel of what you're looking for. Kind of like a tuning fork.) As the subliminal hum of an open access-line filled my head, I felt him begin to do something with his mind. I tried to do the same thing, trying to fake the steps of a dance I didn't know as he supercooled his thoughts, retuning them to new frequencies. I wondered how he'd ever discovered this in the first place . . . found the answer in just sharing his mind, feeling his pleasure as his senses dimmed and the world he'd been born into began to fade. He'd wanted so bad to find some other world besides the one he lived in, one where nobody could bother him, that he actually had: He'd turned his brain inside out, and pulled himself into an electronic hat.

I felt him starting to slip away from me as the machine static got louder. He was sinking into his other world too fast for me to follow him, and any second I was going to lose him completely—

(Relax!) His mind came back for me. (Don't fight it, don't try so goddamn hard! It's like Zen, kid, you can't get there by trying to. Fix on your goal—you want that fucking data, or not?)

I felt need fill me like a power surge as my focus narrowed down to getting the data. I let go of the reality of where I was and what I was trying so hard to do, and just believed it was happening. . . .

It happened. I'd never seen a ghost before but now, just like he'd said, I was one, floating in a place outside of space and time—or maybe deep inside it, inside the electron shells of a storage crystal or drifting in some EM river. I saw Deadeye, or something like him—my mind shaping his presence into a lifeform. It pulsed with a kind of hologlow in time to something that might have been his heartbeat. I looked down at myself—except there wasn't really any up or down—and saw my own holo shadow hovering; saw its shining hand merged into him, linking us tenuously into one form with no more reality than the two separate ones had. (Look around,) he said, the message buzzing inside me. (Remember everything you can. All the tracks will be changed some by the time we get back; you got to get the *feel* of it.)

I did what he told me, looking around and through myself without motion, trying not to panic as I worked to tune in a sense without a name. Around me at first there was only white noise, like the squeaking of a billion mice . . . the total mindlessness I'd butted up against when I'd tried this before. Except now I was trapped inside it. I forced myself to look at it through the filter of Deadeye's thoughts, looking for the larger patterns he knew were there. Opening eyes I never knew I had, I watched as Deadeye made the invisible visible, leading me into a world that nobody else realized existed.

I watched it unfold, warping and patterning with ever-changing density and form—crystal layers of structure rising up, spreading out, overflowing as they took on more reality for me, until they were as endless as the ice fields of Cinder. (You see where you are? You got it now—) Deadeye answered his own question. (Let's go.) He started forward—as if there was a direction you could call forward, or a way back.

I tried to look behind as he sucked me after him; it was like having a glass head. I saw a strand of light, our own energy reeled out behind us, arcing endlessly up out of sight: our lifeline to the real world. I wondered if my mind had really funneled down that, and how I'd ever worm up inside it again.

I trailed Deadeye, not sure if I was moving on my own or only being towed, as he shifted focus again to match some EM bandwidth, like a traveler hitting the road. The glowing lifeline of our entry stretched out, stretched thin, was swallowed up in the random motion of inner space.

There were other travelers on this road, but they were lifeless drones carried like dust on the electron wind blowing through the commweb that netted Earth's solar system. Photon messengers drilled high, piercing lines of color through my lightfield; random bits of codestring burned me with impossible cold/heat.

I concentrated on trying to see the shadowlines we were tracking clearly enough to trace them back again. The data Deadeye had made me swallow helped me shape the half-sensed fields we were passing through into images my mind could hold onto; but it was like having studied geology when what you really needed was a road map. Endless combine data cores shimmered past me, armored with crystal walls of impenetrable security. But I flowed through their unbreachable barriers like they were fantasies painted on silk, while all around me the drone-slaves of a million other masters veered away, or smashed into them and were incinerated . . . or, sometimes, passed through, into the seething energy hearts I sensed deep inside.

And what he'd told me was true. We weren't alone here. Using his mind's eyes, I could sense them: beings that were like nothing my mind had ever known, drifting through my consciousness like music heard in a fever dream . . . massive sentiences hovering around and through the data cores of the interstellar combines, arcing out toward infinity, waiting for their toes to twitch or their stomachs to growl or some other part of their mind to change, in some other solar system.

And once or twice I felt eyes that weren't eyes turn toward me as I disturbed some brooding subsystem that actually sensed our passing; felt it scan with something that wasn't really a mind for something it couldn't quite comprehend: me. Sometimes tendrils of contact reached out to me, greeting me wordlessly, probing my mind gently as I passed. And once I sensed something in the distance that wasn't like anything else I'd seen—that felt stranger and yet somehow more familiar than any of the alien presences we'd blown through. (What's that over there?) I asked.

I felt Deadeye track my line of thought. (It's the FTA Security Council,) he said. I strained toward it, curious, but he snapped me back like a piece of elastic. (Leave it alone. It knows too much.) He didn't explain, and somehow I knew there was no point in asking.

The patterns repeated sometimes, like we'd been going in circles; stabilized sometimes, as Deadeye stopped his restless datasearch and waited for some sign. And then they'd begin to flow again . . . as eternal as the molecular patterns they were trapped inside of and yet slowly shifting, creeping like glaciers or drifted dunes, when informational parameters changed and their data structures altered. There was no sense of time here to keep track of, no sense or sensation that had any meaning, that was more real than my own hallucination of myself. We could have traveled microns, or halfway to the moon by now. But something was growing deep inside my awareness like a dull ache . . . doubt, or loneliness, or something as simple as my body's need to piss somewhere back in the real world . . . growing and growing as the crystallized wasteland kept passing me by. . . . (Deadeye!)

(Shut up.) The hot human clarity of his contact felt good, even while he jabbed me with irritation for breaking his silence. This place terrified him . . . and yet the only peace he ever knew was when he lost himself here. He was as glad as I was not to be here alone; but he didn't like being reminded of the fact.

(Deadeye—) I interrupted him again, because it wasn't peace that was eating away at me. (When does it end?)

(Shut up!) he thought. (Just keep moving. Don't fuck my concentration.)

I kept moving, trying to concentrate on making my own roadmaps of Nowhere, just in case he decided that this time he didn't want to bother coming back. Wherever we were now, the density of the matrix had thinned out: there were less crusted data sinks, less lines of force to track . . . less than nothing. I wasn't sure what that meant, wasn't sure that Deadeye wasn't lost or crazy, wasn't sure of anything except that if it didn't end soon I was going to start screaming—

(There,) Deadeye said, a millisecond before I snapped. (That's it: where the good Doctor buries his secrets.)

Dizzy with relief, I felt him turn me until I was fixed on the data citadel he wanted me to see, a warping of density no different from a million others I'd already seen. A chip, a blip, nothing impressive on the scale of most of the corporate constructs that had deformed the spectral badlands behind us. But there was something about it . . . it was too dense, almost smoky-looking somehow; hard to see into even with my ghost eyes. (It looks funny. How do you know this is it?)

(Take my word for it,) Deadeye thought.

(That's not good enough.)

I felt his irritation stab me again. (We tracked a security checker from his lab address through about a dozen false stops to this. This is the end of the line. This is the real thing.) Satisfaction now, sleek and smug.

(Where are we?)

Something bubbled through my mind: laughter. (You mean, where in the world? On an orbital station out in cislunar space. Don't look down.)

I made a face, or tried to. (Why's it look like that? Cloudy—)

(Privacy. Real privacy. Most of the big combine cores look transparent, because a lot of their business ain't hidden—don't have to be. Believe me, the good stuff is under a lot of ice, deep in their cold, cold hearts.)

(But that shouldn't make any difference to us, right—?) Something in the shifting tone of his thoughts made me uneasy.

(It could . . . the fact you can't see clear through it means DeAth's security is a lot denser than most, that it covers more of the EM spectrum. We're part of that spectrum, kid, and don't forget it. This system's too specific to be really sentient—you can sense that, it's not curious. But it's real good at what it does. Shouldn't be any problem for somebody like you, though. You used to be a thief. It's the same kind of thing. Go on in there like a pro, remember all your tricks—just don't lose your head. Don't even sneeze—you might trigger it, and if it starts looking, it might find you. . . . Blow through the files till you see what you want, and then pull out.)

(What's this "you"—) meaning *me*, (—shit? You're the cracksman!)

(And you're the mental pickpocket. You know what you're looking for. I might miss something important. What are you bitching about?)

(I'm paying you to do the hard part—)

(You're paying for the chance to learn a new trade. The hard part is finding the place. We've done that. Go on. Just hold onto the link, don't let go. Those data sinks are like dead stars; their density's so great it's hard to find the way out once you get inside. You come out in the wrong place, you could get all twisted around, never find your way back where you started.)

(Great.)

I felt him give me a mental shove, felt my concentration begin to drift, my spectral body oozing out like protoplasm toward the place where DeAth kept his bodies buried. I tried to concentrate on why I'd started this insane trip, what I had to do to finish it . . . felt my need energize me again. I felt the nothingness begin to slide, drawing me down and in faster and faster, until I collided with the colorless formless waiting wall that would stop, turn back, destroy anything it could sense and codify—was sucked through it, through ripple rings of blaring burning silence, and swallowed up inside.

I was inside a hive; a hive full of insects, crawling with energy, charged particles swarming through me, each doing its own separate dance all in perfect synchronicity. I could still feel my link with Deadeye reeled out behind me like a fragile thread, reassuring me as I moved like a wind through DeAth's hidden soul. Code strings passed across my mind like glowing fog. The things Deadeye had made me learn turned flickering light and darkness into numbers, figures, facts, the truth—

I searched through years of DeAth sentences in the space of a nonexistent heartbeat; all those years, all the clean antiseptically stored details of a thousand different ways to ruin a human body beyond anybody's ability to put it back together again. I tried not to stop long enough to look twice, to really remember—because it wasn't my business, there was nothing I could change in here. I was only a ghost in the machine. And there was only one death sentence I really cared about, or could do anything about now—I kept searching, looking for the right sequence, one that would spell out a victim I knew . . . *Elnear.* Not finding it, and not finding it, knowing it had to be there, but still not finding it.

I pushed down the frustration that was starting to blind me, and began again. Searching by date, by location, by details of the job, narrowing it and narrowing it. . . .

TaMing. The name exploded out at me like a flare, *Daric. Victim.* The place was right, the time, the specs . . . but it was the wrong victim. *Daric.* Not Elnear. *Nobody wanted her dead,* Mikah had told me. *She wants what they want.* But the first time I'd said Daric's name to somebody in the Deep End, they'd nearly killed me. It was Daric somebody wanted dead. Daric they'd tried to hit . . . only making it look like an attempt on Elnear because they thought she was already marked. . . . I watched the shockwave of my own disbelief echoing away, saw it absorbed into the subatomic song of the hive. Daric, that twisted bastard who was always there trying to ruin somebody's life every time I turned around. Somebody had almost gotten rid of him for good; only I'd stopped them. . . .

Something was happening around me. The exponential curve of the nonwalls was steepening . . . the particle-hive was churning like a stomach suddenly registering that it had swallowed poison. Barely remembering to save the codestrings I'd eaten, the private account numbers of whoever wanted him dead, I tugged on the lifeline that tied me to Deadeye. (Shit. Shit—Get me out of here!) I tried to erase myself, turn invisible as the wind again, while the walls closed in, wanting to squeeze me down into nothing. Getting in had been a free ride; getting out was like climbing a mudslide, while DeAth's security system thickened the blinding soup all around me, trying to nullify an intruder it couldn't put its finger on.

And then my lifeline snapped. (Deadeye!) I shouted, but I was shouting at myself. The formless, suffocating pressure intensified, homing on my panic, trying to make me real enough to catch.

But I was already one panic-leap ahead, pushing blind through the stupefying waves of energy, holding *out* in my mind like a prayer, willing myself *out* as the bandwidth of my invisibility narrowed and narrowed—

Out. I was back in the outlands . . . alone. Behind/in front of me, the citadel of Doctor Death was as black as a singularity's heart; it had my number, and I'd never get back through its security again. At least it couldn't track me down and follow me, out here—I didn't leave any footprints.

And I'd never need to crack its walls again. I'd gotten what I needed —more. (Deadeye—?)

No answer. For a second I wondered if DeAth's defenses had caught up with him. Probably he was still out here somewhere; probably he'd just let go of me to save his own mind. He'd warned me about two mistakes, and I'd made both of them: I'd made DeAth's system notice me, and then I'd lost the link. Now, looking around me, I realized I'd just made number three: I hadn't come out where I'd gone in.

I began to move, groping for something familiar, trying to circumnavigate DeAth's citadel or get a fix on some bulge I recognized in the restless night mountains all around me. But if there were three dimensions here, they were mutant ones, changing when I tried to make them hold still, refusing to move when I did. Without Deadeye's mind to focus my own, it was hard to find enough landmarks to be sure of anything. If he was still here waiting for me, I was never going to find him in time, at this rate.

I kept searching, groping for his image, calling his name. I began to wonder how long I'd been gone out of my body . . . how many minutes or hours had passed; if it was getting hungry, thirsty . . . desperate. What would happen to me here if it died . . . if I'd just wink out of existence in this other plane too, or if I'd go on wandering here forever, random energy. . . .

Panic started inside me, making it even harder to keep hold of the half-seen images in my mind. Deadeye must have abandoned me when the link broke, gotten the hell out, afraid of DeAth's security and figuring I was dead. He was probably halfway back to his own room by now —into his own skull. I wondered what he'd do then. Would he come back and look for me? Not too damn likely. What would he do with my body? Dump it in the street, just something else he was finished with, probably. And then I'd never get out of here—

I felt my mind begin to diffuse, gibbering apart into a blur of unfocused energy. I pulled myself back together again, damned if I was going to give up and disappear, and give Deadeye that satisfaction. Down below me in the void—I wanted it to be down, because Deadeye had said we were up in space—I thought I could sense something I knew, the strange warp of crystals that might be the core of some orbiting station we'd passed on the way here. And beyond it, faintly, I thought I could sense the massive energy pulse of Earth's own commweb. I took aim at it, forcing myself to concentrate. And then, before I could lose my nerve or my hold on the map, I headed back the way I'd come.

There was no trail to follow, since we hadn't been able to leave one, to change anything with our passing. I traveled by feel, by instinct, spiraling down through the void; sensing the energy fields growing more intense, more complex, as I sank into Earth's data well. I felt surer of my vision as there was more to sense; began to really believe that my inner sight might even guide me true. It was like using the night vision you had when you looked out of the corners of your eyes, like navigating by lightning-light.

Over and over I plunged into something familiar only to come out someplace I'd never seen; made wrong turns and had to double back because any way I came at a thing, it always seemed to look the same. I tried to become nothing but a logic machine, analyzing, correcting, changing my course . . . searching for identifiable fragments in the noise, for the formless mutterings of combine cores, the whisper of a curious subsystem. I told myself over and over that I was just winding myself in, I wasn't really here any more than I was real here. That when I got to the other end there'd be an end to find. . . .

But no matter how I thought about it, I knew I'd been here too long. And the longer I wandered here the realer it got, the easier it was to hear the spider voices of the ghost things that lived in the void. I tried to ask them questions, got answers I almost understood, pointing me in directions I couldn't really see. . . . And if I'd thought on the way out that I was ready to start screaming, the thought of spending forever with nothing but the souls of machines for company left me so terrified that screaming seemed as meaningless as laughter, or tears. . . .

I stretched out toward something I thought looked familiar for what seemed like the thousandth time . . . ended up inside the glowing, hissing aura of a system that seemed alien even here—the thing that Deadeye had claimed was the core of the FTA's Security Council. *Stay away from it,* he'd said . . . but I wasn't even sure how I'd reached it. I tried to pull out, turn back, go on. . . .

(What do you want?) something sang like a crystal wire inside me, all around me.

(Deadeye—?) I thought, a question and an answer; knowing it wasn't him, wasn't anything like the way he felt inside my mind I thought I could see a glowing form, or a dozen, linked together like echoes.

(You want Deadeye . . . ?) their voice sang.

(Yeah . . .) I whispered, my brain melting. (Oh god oh god yeah . . . please Deadeye please—) And watched the forms begin to close in on me, the coherent noise of their approach taking on too much form, until they were realer than I was, and I knew that I must be dying, or going crazy.

I let go, fell back into the randomness and white noise, tumbling through chaos—

And out the other side. And when I reached the other side, somehow, like a miracle, I was back where I thought I'd started from: tied to an umbilical of light, the open line from the computer port. It was still bright and alive, ready to take me in. There was only one strand, no sign of Deadeye. Whatever that meant. I didn't know what any of it meant, by now; didn't even care. I went for the streamer of light, and tried to funnel myself back into it.

I couldn't do it. It was like trying to climb through a mirror. I butted into my own reflection—my own thought energy, echoing back at me from its source, blind to me, not recognizing that I was the real self and not the reflection. I beat against the flow of light like a bug beating against a streetlamp, getting nowhere, cancelling myself out.

(Deadeye—!) Throwing everything I had into the sending, one last time, all the panic and frustration that finally had nowhere else to go—

(What's the matter, kid?) Deadeye's voice said, as Deadeyes's mind calmly linked up with me. His glowing image grew out of my arm again like he'd never been away.

(Jeezu! Wherethehellyoubeen!!!) The question exploded between us, so hard he probably never saw the words. But he got the message.

(Right behind you all the time,) he thought, and I tried not to believe that was really laughter inside it. (You made it home. What's the problem?)

(I can't get out—) There were two lines of light leading out of here now; two reflections in the mirror, mine and his. (Get me out of here!) (No problem.) His image shivered, began to get fuzzy, like he was about a disappear. I clung to the link between us, digging in. (Don't fight it!) he said. (Let go—of yourself.) I tried to do what he said; felt myself start to turn inside out as he began to suck me up. . . . (Remember, this isn't really you . . . you're out there. You got to accept that. Let go of it. . . .) I felt him begin to fade into static as he shifted further out of my range. I gave up trying to make sense of him, or hold onto his image . . . sank into his static, letting it infect me. I started to fade and flow into the running field that he'd become, disappearing into him as he disappeared, because it was worse to stay here alone and whole, alive or not, than to follow him through into oblivion. . . .

"You can wake up now," somebody said.

My eyes were already open, anyway. It took me a minute to figure that out, and another one to realize I'd actually heard those words spoken out loud . . . that I was actually moving, turning, breathing in Deadeye's musty smell, seeing his godawful ruined face and not a shining phantom. There were tears on my own face, and my nose was running, the mucus dripping into my open mouth. I wiped it on my sleeve. "Jeezu," I mumbled, "this must be real life, all right."

Deadeye sniggered, and patted my shoulder with that peculiar sudden motion, the way he'd done once before. "Good boy," he said.

I peeled the trode off my forehead and shook myself out, checked the time on my databand. We'd been gone nearly five hours.

"You got what you needed?" Deadeye asked, looking at the floor now, like it was my feet he was talking to.

I nodded. "No thanks to you. Where the fuck were you? You dumped me and ran when I hit trouble! I could've been wandering around in there forever—"

"You could've got us both terminated." He shrugged, getting up from his seat. "I warned you. I thought DeAth swallowed you whole. But I hung around a while. And you got out—wrong place, but still that was good, you didn't panic. You found a landmark and got back on course. Took guts." He shuffled away, heading for the bathroom.

"How the hell would you know?" I yelled, louder that I needed to, as he turned his back on me and used the toilet. "I screamed my fucking goddamn brains out. You weren't there."

"I was there. Just wanted to see what you'd do if I left you alone."

"Why—?"

"Wanted to know what you're made of. Best way to learn, the hard way. Like I learned it."

"Bullshit." I said. "You dumped me—"

"—in the water to see if you'd sink. You swam. I followed you all the way home. I was always right there behind you, looking over your shoulder. A couple times I almost called you back, thought you'd made the wrong turn for good—but you always fixed it . . . or I was the one remembered it wrong." He came back, still fastening his pants. "Couldn't believe it when you went to the goddamn Security Council to show you the way home. Thought you'd gone crazy—"

"Me too," I muttered, wondering if they'd actually helped me find it. I didn't ask, because I didn't think I could face the answer, either way.

"Not bad." He nodded grudgingly. "Clumsy, amateur, I'll never be able to get near DeAth again . . . but not bad. Might even use you again sometime."

I felt my face prickle, not sure if I was flattered or just pissed off. "How many others you used up, anyhow? They all still in there?"

"None." He shook his head. "Never met anybody stupid enough to believe me before."

"Drop dead." I started to get up from my seat.

He caught my arm, holding on; his one good eye held my gaze like his fingers held my flesh. (Don't listen to what I say,) his mind begged me. (My mouth's like my eye. I let you in because you can see past that kind of shit. Work with me again. Be my partner. You saw what you could do. It'll be easier next time. It'd be like exploring unknown worlds. . . . You could get rich easy—)

I shook my head, as surprised as I was uncertain, all of a sudden. (I can't.)

(Why not?) I felt the sharp jab of his betrayal. It had cost him to make that offer. Getting rejected was more than he was ready for. I realized with a kind of shock that he actually liked me. (Goddamn it—) he thought, angry at me, more angry at himself.

(I can't because I'm on borrowed time.) I touched the patch behind my ear. (I'm wearing drugs. I can't use my psi without them, and I can't use them much longer. Pretty soon I'll be just another deadhead again.)

His good eye squinted almost shut. (So. . . . They got to you after all . . . the deadheads. Fucked you up. Thought you were too good to believe. Should've known.) He moved away from me, but his touch stayed on inside my head a second longer, the way his hand had touched me, once, twice. "You got everything you need, then?" Falling back into the impersonal distance of speech, shying away from further contact. He was fucked up, I was fucked up, because of what we were, had been, would always be . . . and he didn't want to feel it any more.

"Yeah, sort of. . . ." Remembering the surprise I'd gotten along with the data. "Got some kind of code strings—secret account numbers, I think. Don't know whose. Now I've got to figure that part out."

"Show me."

I let him read what I'd found.

"Hell, that's easy." He snorted, and waved me back into the seat. "I can show it to you right now."

"No, thanks—"

"Make one more run with me. It'll do you good. You'll trust yourself more . . . you'll always know you can do it if you need to." I felt his mind behind the words, pushing, pulling, pleading.

"Okay," I said, partly because he wanted it so much, not to be alone on that journey if he didn't have to be; not to be alone again in this room any sooner than he had to be. (Okay.) Partly because he was right, too.

I took a leak and gulped some water at his sink, and then we dropped back into inner space. It wasn't as hard going in this time, or as far away when we got there. (Banks are stupid,) Deadeye thought, grinning, when we had our digits tracked down, tied to a filename, more datacodes, a whole shitload of credit from unlisted sources. A Family, probably. That was all we found, even in those secret depths, but it would probably be enough. I didn't make any stupid mistakes this time, and Deadeye stayed linked to me all the way there, all the way back. It was still hard to let myself out, let my self go—but he pushed me back through the mirror into reality, or what passed for it to everybody else.

I rubbed my eyes. "How the hell did you ever find your way out of there, the first time you did it?"

He shrugged. "I just gave up. I thought I was lost forever. I let go and got ready to die. . . ." His bloodless face got even harder to look at as he remembered. "Thought it was just what I wanted, too, until I woke up again here."

"Yeah," I said. "I guess I know what you mean." I stood up, felt his eyes follow me. "Well, I got to get going. . . ."

He shrugged again.

I stayed where I was, trying to think of the words that would let me go. "Thanks. For helping me out. For . . . trusting me. Teaching me."

His face twisted. "You gonna make me regret it?"

I shook my head.

"Then get your ass out of here, you cripple. You wasted enough of my time."

I grimaced. "See you around." I started for the door.

He didn't get up from his seat; wasn't even looking at me when he said, "Not if I can help it."

I looked back one last time as I reached the doorway; looked down at my sweater. (You do good work,) I thought, touching it.

(Sweater looks nice on you, kid.) He was still facing the wall.

I let myself out through the darkened warehouse, heading for the street. I was halfway down the block before I heard him say, (Wear it in good health.)

25

WHEN I WAS SAFE inside the swarming, light-washed security of the Tube again, I stopped to call Mikah. I got a recording. I left him a message, and then I called Braedee. I didn't have a call code, so I made one up, figuring he was probably monitoring every call I made anyway. "Braedee, I need to see you," I said. "What?" a stranger's faceless voice answered. I cut contact and got on the next transit that came.

When I got off at the transfer point there were Centauri Corpses waiting. They wondered why I wasn't more surprised to see them . . . remembered what I was, and figured they knew.

I got into the mod and settled in my seat, not paying any attention to the trip as my mind went over what I'd learned, and how I was going to tell it to Braedee. When I thought I was ready to face him I looked out the window, expecting to see the Centauri Transport fields spreading out like a lava flow below me.

But the only light was the moon hanging halfway up the sky; there was almost perfect darkness down below. We'd left N'Yuk behind and we weren't heading east. I sat up straighter. "We're going back to the estates?" I asked.

The Corpses glanced at each other. "That's our orders," the bigger one said.

"Braedee's there?" I was surprised now.

They looked at each other again. "Don't know about that," the big one said. "If it's important enough, maybe he'll be there."

"Maybe? It's about murder, about somebody wants to kill a taMing. . . ." I broke off. "Braedee didn't send you." Finally seeing the reason behind their confusion.

"Gentleman Charon ordered us to pick you up." That was all they'd been told.

Braedee must have contacted him after I called. That made sense; Charon would want to hear it too. I wondered what he'd think when he heard. But that wasn't my problem. I shrugged, and settled back in my seat again.

We landed in the floodlit courtyard of the castle that sat alone far up the taMings' valley; the place where I'd gone to the board meeting when I'd first come here.

The Corpses led me through its museum-halls until we reached a small—if you could call anything in this mansion small—room. There was a fireplace at one end. It had been sealed up, and the room was cold. I thought of Lazuli, suddenly. But it was her husband who sat waiting for me in a red brocade-covered chair. It looked like a throne. I wondered if he played king of the galaxy in it when he was alone.

He wasn't alone now. Braedee was there, just like I'd expected he'd be. But so was Daric . . . and so was Jiro. They were all standing, waiting, looking at me . . . with the wrong expressions. I hesitated, confused, and one of the Corpses gave me a small shove forward: *Don't keep the king waiting.* I went down the five steps from the hallway and started across the patterned marble floor toward Charon.

"That's close enough," Charon said, when I was still about three meters away; as if I had some disease he didn't want to catch.

I stopped, glancing from face to face again, feeling more confused with every heartbeat. Braedee's mind read *disgust frustration (You stupid bastard)* as he looked back at me. Daric's mind was almost unreadable, like it always was, because he didn't know whether he was *glad excited amused scared shitless* when he imagined what was about to happen. Jiro wasn't there at all, *dazed with pain* like someone had hit him in the stomach; but the pain was mental, not physical, and the one who'd done it to him was Charon.

I said, "I have more information about Lady Elnear. That's why I called Braedee. Maybe we should—"

"Shut up," Charon said. He got slowly up out of his chair, like some compulsion had hold of him, and came toward me.

And suddenly I saw Lazuli, in his mind. *Oh my god. Lazuli—*"Wait," I said, lifting my hand.

He caught my hand inside his own hand—the one that wasn't really alive. He looked down at mine, wrapped in peeling sudoskin, my trapped fingers curling up like the limbs of a fetus as his grip hurt the half-healed wound in my palm. "Yes . . ." he said, looking straight into my eyes, now, "you should be afraid. I know that you have been having an affair with my wife." The pressure increased on my hand as I tried to pull it free . . . as he thought about me touching her body, exploring her. "I let you come into my world, I trusted you, and you used your mind to seduce her—"

I gritted my teeth. It wouldn't do any good to make excuses, to try to explain, to deny it. His anger, his hate ran too deep. He hated psions just as much as Stryger did, but he had a reason— "I saved her life!" The pressure let up, just a little. I glanced away from him for the second it took to scan. . . . *Braedee?* He was watching us like someone studying insects, but his face was only a mask. Braedee hadn't told Charon about us; Braedee had too much to lose. *Daric?* He looked like he was spitted over a slow fire—in agony, in ecstasy. But he had too much to lose, too. *Jiro?* He was staring at his stepfather's hand closed over mine; not really seeing it, sick with his own fears about his mother, and himself. "Who—?" I whispered, not really meaning to.

"My wife talks in her sleep," Charon said, the unforgiving hatred clamping down again. *He'd heard her call my name. But that hadn't been enough for him; that had only been the beginning. . . .*

I swore under my breath, only partly from the pain. He'd used the hand that had hold of me now on Lazuli, to try to force the truth out of her, and then he'd used it on her little girl. . . . "Where is she? What did you—"

"I sent her back to Eldorado." Talitha too; they were both gone. I glanced at Jiro, still here, and suddenly I understood why he looked like he did.

"You bastard," I mumbled, blinking too much.

"Blame yourself," he said. "The only reason I don't have you killed is that you did your job. Braedee." He looked away, his eyes hunting down the Security Chief who'd let this happen. "I want him out of here —out of my life, out of my network, off this planet by morning." His look told Braedee that he wasn't going to forget any of this soon.

Braedee nodded, stone-cold as usual, his black unblinking stare fixed on me. "Yes, sir. But I want to hear what he came to tell us, first."

Charon's mouth opened for a refusal. I glanced away, at Daric's barely-controlled face, and back. "It's about Lady Elnear—" I said, before Charon could make me stop, "and Gentleman Daric." I had Charon's attention now, and suddenly I couldn't wait to tell him that hired killers wanted his son. "He's—"

Daric's panic and betrayal exploded in my head as he registered the words; as he thought I was about to say something else—something that would destroy his life. "Why don't you ask Cat about Jule, father?"

ALIEN BLOOD

he blurted. "Ask him how many times he slept with your daughter, too. Ask him which one he liked better."

My mouth fell open. Daric smiled at me with bitter triumph, as Charon looked down at my hand still trapped inside his own, seeing the image of his daughter, the image of his wife, my image trapped together inside his brain. . . . He closed his fist.

Right then I would have told him everything about Daric: perversions, drugs, hit men, *psion*—everything. But the raw cry that came out of my mouth didn't waste its time on words.

He let go of my hand, finally. I hardly felt it as he ripped the emerald earring out of my ear. "I've changed my mind," he said to Braedee. "I want you to kill him." I looked up, feeling the words bleed on me, and stopped breathing.

Braedee didn't answer for a long minute. Then he said, "No, sir. You don't want me to do that."

Charon frowned; he looked at the others watching him, me, us. "I said I want the freak killed. Take care of it now."

"No, sir," Braedee said again. "Let me deal with him my own way."

"Goddamn it!" Charon shouted. "You do what I tell you!"

"Yes, sir—" Braedee started slowly across the room toward me. "But he is a fully-registered citizen. That means I can't guarantee your family's involvement would remain confidential. . . ."

Charon straightened up, his hand making a fist as the two of them locked stares. But it was Charon's gaze that broke, finally.

Braedee finished crossing the room to collect me. As he forced me toward the door he muttered, "Don't talk. Save it." I didn't have any trouble obeying.

"All right," he said, as the mod that had brought me to the estates took us both away again. "Now talk."

I watched the taMings' valley fall into the darkness below me, fighting dizziness, trying to center my mind enough so that I could answer. I looked up again into Braedee's dim, dead eyes. The two Corpses who'd brought me to the estates were sitting across from us, empty-faced. Braedee had done something that sealed us off from them; neither of them heard him speak. Finally I said, "Why didn't you just kill me?"

He glanced away from me, out into the night. "You hadn't given me your data."

He was serious. I stared at him, feeling sick. "I got nothing to say to you," I said. I cradled my hand against my stomach, feeling my skin get warm and wet as fresh blood seeped out of my palm. "Any of you." The need to spill Daric's secret died as I realized what would have happened if I'd told Charon the truth. Nothing anybody could have done would have gotten me out of that room alive. Maybe I should be glad he'd crushed my hand.

"You were eager enough to call me in the middle of the night," Braedee snapped, like nothing had happened in between that might change my mind. "What about?"

"Find out for yourself. You don't own me any more."

"Do you feel humiliated?" he asked. Disgust made the words as heavy as lead. "Do you feel like a stupid fool? You should."

Lazuli's face filled my eyes again. "She's really gone?" My throat ached.

He nodded.

"Why's Jiro still here, then?"

"Gentleman Charon said that he wants to keep closer track of the boy, since he's next in line for a seat on the board."

"Jiro's not his son."

"That makes no difference."

"Jiro hates him. He's doing it to punish her—"

"That's not my business."

"You're all business, aren't you? Don't you ever wonder what the point of it all is?"

"If you'd stuck to the business you were hired for, instead of cuckolding your employer, we wouldn't be having this discussion."

I glanced at him, frowning, and away again. "What do you want me to say?" My face burned.

He flicked a finger at my wound. "That you deserved that. You deserved worse." For half a second there was something that wasn't self-interest in the human half of his mind. He took care of these people; he didn't like seeing them get hurt. Especially not by somebody he'd told them they could trust.

I swallowed hard. "All I want now is what Charon wants—to be out of his life. To be off this stinking planet before I have to see it in the light of day again."

After a long moment, he said, "What about Lady Elnear? Are you going to tell me what you learned? Or are you going to let some assassin kill her, after all?"

I raised my head again slowly, not wanting to. Realizing I had to give him that much, for her sake, to feel clean. "She's not the target of the real hit, either." I felt more than saw him stiffen; his disbelief and confusion rang through my nerve circuits. "Somebody was using the attacks on her to try to take out Daric. They didn't know the attacks were only something you invented."

"Daric?" he repeated. "Are you certain?"

"What do you think?" I jerked around in my seat. "You asshole. Lady Elnear's safer than birth control. Just keep Daric away from her and you got no problem." Thinking that this news ought to make Elnear happier than anything had in sixteen years. I was hoping it would; wishing it would.

Braedee was silent again, trying to control his own sudden anger, trying to reorder his priorities all over, one more time. "Why?" he asked finally. Maybe I was just imagining that I heard a whine in his voice. I wanted to hear him whine.

"Somebody in the Lack Market doesn't like him. Drugs, maybe. Now you know as much as I do."

I could feel him frowning, feel him wanting to ask me *how I knew, what my sources were, what methods—?* Pride wouldn't let him . . . pride and knowing that even if he knew it probably wouldn't do him any good. Because I was a psion, and he wasn't. And because the Lack Market might as well exist in a different dimension from his own. There were gray places where they intersected—business was business, black or white—but real criminals had never been his concern. The enemy had always been his own kind. I felt him glance at me: *Not his kind, either.* "You aren't leaving yet," he said.

I kicked the bag full of everything I owned that was lying against my foot. "You mean I have a choice?" I asked sourly.

"No," he said. "You don't. You still have work to do for Centauri. I want you to find out why Daric taMing is in trouble, so that I can stop it." *Even more—to tell him how to stop it.* Daric was a member of the board and the Assembly . . . and a taMing. Switching the assassin's sights from Elnear to Daric hadn't made Braedee's own life any easier, or his position any more secure.

"What about Charon?" I asked.

"He doesn't have any choice, either."

"He's not going to like it if you don't ship me out tonight. You might lose your job."

Braedee shook his head. If Daric taMing or Lady Elnear died, he could lose his job. He flicked the logo on his sleeve, and shrugged. "If his son is in danger, I think I can make him see my point of view again.

If not. . . . Charon taMing may head the Centauri board, but he isn't
Centauri Transport. No matter how much he likes to think so."
   "Good. . . ." I flexed my hand just enough to remember how much
it had hurt; feeling something ugly and alien squirm in my brain as I
thought about Charon hearing the news—about how much he'd squirm
when he found out the truth.
   Braedee glanced at me, and I felt him frown. "Tell me," he said. "Did
you actually sleep with his daughter, too?"
   "No!" I glared at him.
   He didn't say anything more.
   "Where are we going?" I asked, finally. We were coming down over
the glowing night mountains of N'Yuk.
   "I'm dropping you off in the city. You are no longer welcome on any
taMing property. But I expect you can find whatever you need here;
you seem to have a knack for that. I'll be waiting to hear from you."
   I got out of the mod as it settled in a public lot. I turned back,
looking at him. "You ought to be glad," I said, "that I'm really sure you
didn't tell Charon about me and Lazuli."
   "That sounds like a threat." He cocked his head. "Are you still trying to play this game . . . one-handed?" He gestured at my hurt hand
like it was some kind of pointless joke.
   I reached out and pressed my hand against the window beside his
face, painting the bloody handprint there for him to look at all the way
home. He grimaced, and the door hissed down between us, shutting me
out of his world.
   I stood and watched the mod until it disappeared, not even sure why
I did, except that suddenly I couldn't make myself move. But I had to
move, and so finally I left the field, and found a phone with a security
screen. I tried to call Elnear, but I couldn't get through to her. I wondered if Charon had already killed my private access code. I tried
Mikah again, but there was still no answer. So I walked. I took the first
transit that came along, changed to another, and another. I walked
some more, drifting down through the echoing, hologram-rainbowed
levels of the city. Sometimes a surveillance scanner stopped me, asking
about the blood. I always said I was on the way to a med walk-in, and
they let me go on. I didn't find one, because I didn't really want to.
   Nobody else acknowledged me, even though I was never quite alone.
The nightlife of a city, even one like this, was almost dead in the hours
before dawn, but there were always a few people out, floating through
their own bright-and-dark fantasies. They looked at me and through

me, and none of their stares were friendly. I followed them with my mind as they passed, seeing in their minds the images of where they were going, where they'd been. . . . Always half-afraid that someone was there because they were watching me, that maybe they were following me. I told myself I didn't care if they were . . . but it didn't make me feel any better when they weren't. I was the only one without a destination in my mind, or any answers at all.

Maybe that was why I found myself on the steps of Purgatory, just as the line between sea and sky was turning visible with day far up over my head.

Argentyne opened the door and peered out at me, squinting, her eyes fogged with sleep. "Go home." She started to close the door again.

"Don't have one," I said.

The door stopped, leaving a crack just wide enough for her curiosity. "Daric?"

I shook my head. "Charon."

"Why?" she asked, grudgingly.

I tried to answer. "I need . . . to talk," was all that came out.

"You've got a lot of fucking nerve," she said. But the door opened a little wider. She looked out at me with both eyes. "Is that blood?"

I nodded.

"Whose?" Imagining for a second that it might be Daric's.

I held up my hand.

"Jeezu," she muttered, and waved me inside.

Aspen sealed the wound back together, doing it mostly in his sleep. "I told you before to get a treatment," he mumbled. Music spilled out of him as he stumbled up from the littered table in the middle of the empty club. "I'm telling you again. . . . Told you before . . . tell you again . . ." The words began to fall into a rhythm, reordering themselves, turning into music as a song started to form inside his head. I listened to his mind, following the act of creation into the distance as he wandered back to bed.

"Hey." Argentyne snapped her fingers in front of my eyes. "Where are you?"

"Uh . . . listening," I murmured, not saying to what. I refocused, feeling like I'd been caught looking through a keyhole.

"What made you come here, anyway?" she said, and there was a tension in the words that wasn't really anger. "You had a whole fucking city, and you're not zeroed—"

I shrugged, staring at a dish full of skagweed cuds like it held the secret of the universe. Now that I was finally sitting down, my body was buzzing like a half-dead insect, struggling to get back on its feet. "I dunno," I mumbled. "Guess it was an accident." I started to get up. Her mind changed suddenly. Her hand caught my sweater sleeve and pulled me down into the pillows again. "Talk to me, you jerkoff, since that's what you said you wanted." She peeled a used stim patch off the surface of the table and stuck it to her forehead above her eyes, something to get her awake and alert.

I half smiled. "That's the nicest goddamn thing anybody's said to me all day," I murmured, surprised and grateful, knowing normally she wouldn't have touched that patch.

She stretched and shook her head as the stimulant went to work. "What made Charon want to do that to you? Did you tell him about Daric?" Her voice took on an edge again.

I shook my head. "I slept with his wife."

"Jeezu!" She smacked her forehead with her hand. "You really must hate the taMings."

I looked up, frowning. "No. It wasn't like that."

She studied me for a long minute, shrugged. "And you didn't tell him about Daric?"

I shook my head again.

"Are you going to?"

I didn't answer, because I didn't know what I was going to do about anything. My mind was full of static, and I didn't know where it was coming from; I couldn't pull my thoughts together enough to care.

"Why not?" she asked, as if I'd said something.

"I think he'd kill me."

She laughed once. "Which one?"

"Both." My mouth twitched.

She picked up a platter full of crumbs and dumped it. The drone circling her feet sucked up the crumbs as she set the plate down again. "I thought maybe you felt sorry for him."

"Which one?"

She hesitated. "Both."

I touched my hand. "Why should I?" My body was still buzzing, even though it was so heavy with exhaustion that just the thought of having to move made me feel paralyzed.

"Because Charon already lost one of his children." She pushed her hair back from her face. "Because Daric's suffered enough."

"Because they were freaks, him and Jule—?" I grimaced as I made a fist of my wounded hand. I shook my head. "Charon sent Lazuli and Talitha away. He kept Jiro here, just to hurt Lazuli more."

"Ah—" she said. "Shit. Poor baby." She knew how much Jiro hated his stepfather. "What about you? He threw you out too?"

"He tried. But Braedee won't let me off his hook. Braedee wants me to keep working for Centauri, whether Charon likes it or not."

"Because you saved Elnear?"

"Because I found out she was safe all along."

Argentyne looked blank. I explained, watching her expression fill back in. "Daric?" she repeated. "The Lack Market wants Daric dead? Why?"

I shrugged. "That's what I'm supposed to find out."

"Is he all right—?" She pressed forward against the table edge.

"He's safe enough, if that's all you mean; for now, anyway."

Her stare started to turn into a frown.

"He came to see me, like you told him to. I told him everything. So if that's what you mean—no, he's not all right."

"Does he think I hate him?" Her voice got small.

"Don't you?" I said. "Don't worry about it. He knows if he tries to hurt either one of us, it's the last thing he'll ever do as a Gentleman."

She did frown, now. "Damn it, that's not—"

"You miss him that much?" Feeling how empty it left her just to think about him. "That human VD? You ought to be relieved you took the cure."

"I don't know . . . oh, fuck. Fuck you." She rubbed her face, smearing unexpected wetness.

"I'm sorry," I mumbled. "I thought I was trying to help."

She made a face. "You made me feel shittier than he ever did. You act like it's supposed to make sense, like it's simple. You use your head-games to cut my life in half, and then you come back in here and want to tell me how bad you hurt. If it's all so easy, then why couldn't you keep your pants on around Lazuli taMing? How goddamn simple does your life feel tonight, you prick?"

I lurched up from the table. (I'm sorry—) I thought, laying it gently into her mind as I looked at her; because I couldn't trust myself to say the words . . . because words could mean anything but the truth, or nothing at all.

She put her hands up to her head, her eyes shadowed. I walked away as fast as I could without stumbling. The dance floor seemed endless, now that it was empty, and so did the silence behind me. The hallway showing me out was as black as my mood by the time I hit the door. I kicked it open and climbed up into the gray light of dawn, one step at a time. Even this street was empty.

"Cat—" Argentyne's voice stopped me halfway along it.

I turned back.

"Where you going? You got anyplace to stay?"

I shrugged. "I'll hire a box." Not caring; wondering why she cared.

She pressed her lips together. "You can stay here, if you want."

I stared at her. "Why?"

She let out a high thin laugh that echoed through the empty morning. "Misery loves company."

26

"So," MIKAH SAID, resting metalloid elbows on the tabletop at the club. It was early the next afternoon, and he'd come in like a black cloud, making the bouncers edgy. I hadn't bothered to ask what he'd been doing. I told him as much of what I'd been doing as he needed to know. "You're telling me Deadeye claims Daric taMing is the prime number. That Lady Elnear's not even listed." His head moved from side to side like something on a spring. "That's a real bite in the ass." He snorted.

"Yeah. My ass." I watched the fingers of my good hand hit the tabletop, coming down one at a time, over and over; counting them with some spare part of my brain. I made a fist and forced it down into my lap. "Centauri won't take its teeth out of me until I tell them more about who wants to null him, and why. I got some credit data for you. Can you pin ID's on them?"

"Probably. Gimme the list. Let's see what pops."

I gave him the list. I had a hard time remembering all the numbers, even though I knew they should have been lasered into my brain.

"What's the matter with you?" he asked, frowning a little as he plugged his recorder back into a stash on his arm. "You look like a piece of dog shit."

"You'd look like shit too on two hours of sleep," I said, annoyed. My body had come awake, answering its own alarm, when it was time to go to work for the Lady. Memory wouldn't let me go back down.

He shrugged. "Your lover still keeping you up nights? You better tell her—"

"Not any more," I said.

He broke off. "Uh-huh." He nodded his head, looking almost relieved. "Thought maybe it was the drugs," he said, when I frowned. "What happened? She dump you when your five minutes were up?"

There hadn't been anything about last night on the Morning Report this time. The taMings were keeping it hushed up. I wondered what they'd told Elnear. I looked away from Mikah's naked curiosity. "Her husband found out."

He let out a laugh. "And he cared—?"

Argentyne sauntered up behind him, coming back into the club from somewhere, and saved me from having to think of an answer. She was dressed now, looking like what she wanted the world to see. "It makes you laugh, that some people actually care about each other?" she said, to the back of Mikah's head. The words dropped on him like rocks and her gaze flicked past him to me.

He winced as he recognized her voice, and turned to look up at her.

"You're making my security paranoid," she said to him. She looked back at me, raising her eyebrows like she expected an explanation.

"He's an old friend," I said, and made intros. They clenched thumbs in a handshake.

She glanced at the ring in the side of his nose, back at me. Her thumb and first finger made a circle; the middle finger of her other hand pushed through it. Asking him, *"How friendly are you?"* in handsign, half surprised and half curious.

"Not that friendly." Mikah shook his head, fingering the ring in his nose. "I'm a fan of your work. You ever have need of any arm, just let me know."

"I'll keep that in mind." Argentyne half smiled, said to me, "I'm relieved to see you hanging around with a better class of people."

I laughed, "Yeah," and looked back at Mikah. "You can do it for me?"

He glanced at Argentyne, raised his eyebrows. I nodded. He said, "If I get the answer for you, what happens then? You feed Centauri?" I felt the tension level inside him surge. That kind of information crossfeed didn't fit his codes much better than it fit Braedee's. He'd sworn over his life to me, and suddenly he was starting to regret it.

I thought about what I really wanted. It wasn't to get him killed . . . or to make a happy man out of Braedee. I shook my head. "I'm not out for trouble. I just need to understand for myself what's really happening."

He twitched his shoulders; light glanced across the shining blackness of his powered armor. "I'll see what I can do." He pushed to his feet and made a quick, gallant, almost-embarrassed pass of compliments to Argentyne. It surprised her as much as it surprised me. Then he turned and stalked out of the club.

" 'An old friend'?" Argentyne said, watching him go.

"We dug ore together in the Federation Mines, out on Cinder."

She glanced back at me, and I felt her remember the scars. "How old are you?" she said.

I shrugged. "Twenty, maybe. How old are you?"

She laughed, and didn't answer. She was twenty-eight. "What was that about?"

"Daric."

Her face froze, as she realized suddenly that what happened to him was really in the hands of people like Mikah . . . like me.

"It's his own fault," I repeated, for what seemed like the hundredth time.

She looked back at me, her eyes hard. "What are you going to do?"

"That depends . . . on a lot of things," I said, because I didn't know; or maybe because I didn't want to know. My mind began to back up with choices and mistakes and memories; the flood of uncontrolled images hit me like a drug rush.

"Like what?" Her hands tightened.

I had a hard time seeing her face for a minute. "Like what I'm going to do about myself. . . ." I rubbed my head, brushed the torn, empty hole in my ear where the emerald earring had been. Feeling the sudden gaping hole in my mind as something punctured my memory, and everything emptied out. . . . "I got to talk to Elnear." I got up and left the club, only remembering when I was far away that I hadn't even said goodbye.

At least my work clearances were still functioning. I made my way back to and through the Federation plex like I was following a programmed track. I felt like a blind man, outside, inside.

Until someone spoke my name. I only stopped then and looked up because I couldn't get any farther, because someone's body was blocking my way.

Stryger's body. I stared at him, feeling like somehow I'd conjured him up out of the blackness of my own thoughts. "What are you doing here?" I said, stupidly. He was coming out of Elnear's office, surrounded by a bodyguard of worshippers.

"I was going to ask you that." He was even more surprised than I was. "I was just told that you were no longer working for the Lady . . . that in fact you were no longer on planet." He was staring now, seeing me right there in front of him, so real he could reach out and touch me. . . . A flush began to spread over his perfect face, lighting it up like fireglow.

"I guess you heard it wrong," I said. I was starting to admire him, the way he looked. . . . I made myself stop. Reaction crawled up my spine like bugs.

"They said it was 'family problems.' " His eyes looked me over like they had a life of their own—taking in the planes of my face, my borrowed clothes, the bandage on my hand. Curiosity and suspicion oozed out of him. He couldn't wait to ask Daric about this. "I admit I was surprised to hear it. I know that you have no family."

It took a second for the words to register; and then, suddenly, the memory of the girl he'd beaten filled my mind. *That was the way they liked it—the hunters, the sick ones: No protection.* Nobody waiting up, searching the streets, calling your name. . . . Suddenly I was half a galaxy away, and half as old, with no one to help me, not even a memory—"You heard wrong." I pushed forward, forcing him to back up. I elbowed a couple of true believers who tried to object to my lack of reverence.

I strode on into Elnear's offices like I still belonged there, not looking back as I felt the fist of his anger hit me uselessly from behind. "You piece of shit," I said out loud, to keep from sending it straight into his brain.

The people I'd worked with for weeks looked up at me and didn't know what to think; but then, they'd always looked at me like that. I spotted a new face in the room, someone I'd never met before. "I need to see her," I said to Geza.

Even as I said it, the security screen in the doorway to Elnear's inner office dematerialized. She was already waiting there. "You're here?" Half question, half demand. She gestured me inside.

When we were private again, she said, "Now explain: You weren't there this morning. There were messages for me. . . . One was from Braedee, and it said that I needn't worry about further attempts on my life. The other was from Charon, and it said that you were no longer my aide; that you'd left Earth."

" 'Family problems'?" I asked.

She nodded, standing there with her hands folded—clenched—in front of her.

"Did he say whose family?"

The lines in her face deepened a little more. "No one has answered my queries. What's wrong?"

I looked down, flexing my bad hand. "Charon. . . . Lazuli's gone.
He sent her away. He found out." I looked up again. Elnear's face was
white. She turned away, so that she didn't have to go on looking at me.
"Talitha too."

"Jiro—" she murmured, "I saw him, this morning. He wouldn't
speak to me, I thought it was because you—"

"It was because of me," I said. "Charon kept him here, just to hurt
her."

Elnear put a hand up to her eyes like she wanted to shut out the day.
Wondering if there wasn't something she could have done differently,
something she should have said. . . .

I couldn't answer it. My eyes kept tracing the outline of the window
frame behind her, over and over, around and around. . . . I clenched
my jaw, and stopped.

Elnear sat down heavily in a chair. "Oh, Cat . . . oh why—?" Her
hand made a fist.

I couldn't answer that one, either.

She raised her head again. I felt her registering the details of my face
—not even seeing the things that had made her eyes catch once. Seeing
past them now, maybe not to what I really was, but close enough so
that she understood why I couldn't answer her. "What are you doing
here?" she asked at last.

I wasn't sure if she meant in her office, or on the planet. Neither was
she. "Braedee won't let me go till he's got everything he wants from me.
I had to see you, just to explain—"

"There's nothing to explain." Cutting me off, so she didn't have to
discuss it further. So she didn't have to think about Lazuli's suffering,
or Jiro's or mine—or her own. Lazuli and the children were all she'd
had left to enjoy, to care about like a woman.

"Elnear," I said. "I mean, Lady . . . that other message. What
Braedee said. It's true. You are safe." I explained that much, as well as I
could. "It's all aimed at Daric's head. Braedee'll see that he doesn't get
near you. Everything'll be all right for you now." I wanted to believe
that, wanted to feel her believe it.

For just a moment, she did. I caught the giddy feel of her relief as the
burden of her secret fears fell away, as wonder and gratitude filled her.
Everything is all right— Her mind echoed it.

And then it all began to change. She was safe, and alive . . . but
what was there left to live for? She glanced away toward the pictures on
her desk, that might as well be blank frames.

"Don't even think that, damn it!"

She jerked back around. "What?"

"What you were just thinking."

She sighed and looked away again, guilty this time.

"What did Stryger want?" Changing the subject, because I had to get her mind off that.

She shook her head. "I don't know . . . he said he was just passing by."

"He never does anything without a reason."

She met my eyes, finally. "I know," she said, resigned. She wished that I'd been there, to tell her what he'd really wanted. "He did ask about you, when he saw that you weren't here." I wondered if Daric had told him something already. "Perhaps he only came to gloat." The unexpected bitterness surprised both of us. One large hand clutched the other again, twisted. Somewhere, she wasn't even sure when, she'd finally begun to believe me.

"You really think he's going to win, then?"

She shrugged slightly. "The combines that want either deregulation or Stryger aren't going to change their votes. And enough others that have no real involvement will follow along and defeat us simply because they don't care about anything beyond their own interests." She faced the false image of the world outside in the false window space on her wall. "They have no accessible nerve-endings; I can't reach them to make them react, make them *feel* that this is important—"

"That's what Jule said, once. . . ."

"What?" She turned back to me.

"That if she could only make people feel what she felt when they hurt each other . . . maybe they wouldn't hurt each other so much." I rubbed my face. My skin felt too tight. "Those Assembly reps are alive —that means they've got to have some nerve-endings. You can hardly see the sharp end of a tack, Lady, and the end of a finger's not much bigger. But you can make a big son of a bitch jump if it's sharp enough. You believe that, or you wouldn't be where you are."

She nodded, almost showing a smile. "But it's hard to find a good, sharp tack these days. That's one reason why I wanted that Council slot so badly: there can only be real equality among creatures on the same level. . . . I'm tired of wasted effort." Dreary visions of the future I'd given back to her slowly blotted out my image in her sight . . . visions of the struggle against deregulation lost, of a life controlled by the taMings, sterile and empty. . . . "I suppose that I won't be seeing you any more," she said, and the realization made her feel like she'd just lost her last friend.

"I'm still here," I said, suddenly feeling less empty because she felt more empty. "I can still be your aide. I'm staying at Argentyne's club—"

She shook her head slowly, looking away. "Charon has . . . supplied me with another aide. You have other duties now. You work for Centauri." As if I needed reminding.

"No, I—"

"Cat," she said, almost gently, wanting me to stop. "I am not your responsibility any more." She looked at me, registering the dark fatigue circles under my eyes, the tense, hollow face of a burnout. "Please . . . do what you must do for Braedee, and then leave, before Centauri ruins your life too." She put her hand on my arm. *(And before you ruin any more lives.)* She tried not to think it; didn't mean to, couldn't help herself . . . hoped I wouldn't hear it.

I looked down; looked at my own clouded image in her mind, through a long silence. Not able to tell her goodbye and leave; not like this. "Lady—" I said. My bandaged hand closed over hers where it still rested on my arm, tightened until it hurt us both. I let go again, feeling her surprise. "You haven't lost the vote, Stryger hasn't won the Council slot yet. You know you're not going to quit until it's over—and you know I can't either. There's got to be a way to get at Stryger. Whatever it takes—" My hands made the truth-swearing sign, a pledge.

She shook her head, but a little color was coming back into her face, into her thoughts. "You already know how hard it is . . . but yes, you're right, of course. It isn't over." She forced a smile, and I felt the stubbornness of her will lock it into place. "There's an old saying: 'That which has to be done usually can be done.' I'll save my despair until I'm sure I need it." The smile got warmer, until it was almost the smile I remembered.

(Whatever it takes,) I thought, looking through her eyes into her mind one last time. I left her office, still without saying goodbye. I went through the outer office without saying anything at all, without looking at the stranger who was there to take my place.

As I made my way back along the halls of the Assembly plex, the little bit of warmth her smile had left inside me faded, and I felt lousier than ever. I hadn't sworn to her that we could still get Stryger just to cheer her up . . . but I might as well have. I wondered how long it would be until she realized that. Maybe she wouldn't. But even if she did, I knew she'd keep on, now. She knew what was important to her. I wished I felt the same way. I didn't want to see Stryger lose everything because it served some higher Truth or Justice, or for the sake of the fucking Human Race. I wanted to cut him down because I knew he'd beaten the shit out of somebody that no one cared about . . . and because when he'd looked into my eyes he'd wanted to do the same thing to me.

Nobody cared. Elnear was right. If I told them what Stryger had done, what he was really like, they'd never believe me. Even if they did, even if I went to the Indy, got it on the Net, it wouldn't change anything. The vote would still come out the same. My mind tendriled out, feeling strangers pass through me, measuring their thoughts. Those might look like human beings, but they were only tools some combine or other was using to push the right button. I pushed my fists into my jacket pockets, not thinking about what I was doing until the pain in my hand made me swear.

Two people passing me in the hall swore too, and shook out their own hands; looked at me and each other, confused and half-frightened. I realized I'd projected my pain without meaning to. I kept walking, pulling my brain back together, while they went on in the other direction, muttering.

I reached the platform of the closest transit stop, stood looking back at the sloping face of the building I'd just come out of. My eyes followed its rise up into the light, past the next level of the city high over my head. And I wondered what it would take to make every smug bastard in the entire Assembly jump. Maybe if it was their own freedom, or their own pain they had to choose, they'd think about it twice before they let it happen. . . .

I looked down again, squeezed my sore hand shut. Nobody around me jumped this time; I was back under control. *"If they could only feel what I feel. . . ."* I heard Jule say it again, inside my head. And suddenly the answer was right there, so clear to me that I couldn't look away from it, no matter how hard I tried.

The transit arrived, stopped. The people around me pushed past and boarded, and it went on again, leaving me standing there like I'd been stunshot. There was a way to get at Stryger. A way to make the Assembly feel what it was like to be Stryger's victim. I could make them live it. . . . But to do that, I'd have to live through it first.

27

"YOU LOOK LIKE SHIT," Argentyne said when I got back to the club. Music and image filled the air around her, and faded again. The symb was setting up for the night's show.

"You are what you eat," I muttered. I looked up at her where she stood, and wondered if the only reason Elnear hadn't made it unanimous was because she was too polite.

Argentyne waved a hand at the rest of the players, signaling a break, and climbed down from the stage. "Was it that bad?" she asked, as she reached my side. "Your visit to the Lady?"

I shook my head, looking down. "Not exactly." It had been more the ride back, while I'd had plenty of time to think it all over. Before I could say anything else the message function on my databand began to beep. I answered it, heard Mikah's voice. I raised my wrist up close to my ear, moved away from Argentyne's sudden worried frown. "What did you get?" I murmured. "You find out who wants taMing dead?"

"Everybody wants him dead."

"Say what?"

"Almost everybody that counts." I heard him hesitate, trying to figure out how to make it clear. "What you got here is something that cuts across territories—"

"Jeezu. . . . Drugs?" I asked, because that seemed most likely; even though I couldn't imagine how Daric could be in deep enough to get himself killed.

"You said taMing's a user?"

"Yeah." I heard him grunt. Up till now I'd thought that drugs were the least of Daric's problems. Now I wasn't so sure. But one thing I was sure of—I needed Daric alive, to get at Stryger. And if the whole Market was down on him, he might not be alive much longer. "Shit. . . . Can you get me access to somebody with some control over this? Is there anybody who can say *stop* and *go?*"

There was a long silence. "You want to negotiate?"

I rubbed my face, wanting to dig my fingernails into my skin. "Yeah."

There was another long silence. I didn't have to be reading his mind to know what he was thinking: he was afraid we'd both end up dead. "You got that kind of credit with Centauri?" he asked finally.

"Yeah." Not sure if it was true, or even if I cared. "It's important. I wouldn't ask if it wasn't important."

"I'll see what I can do." The link went dead.

I let my hand drop, looked back at Argentyne. She was still standing there, with the same expression on her face. "It'll be all right," I lied, and watched her face relax into uncertainty. "I—I need to ask you some questions about your symb circuit." Daric's life wasn't the only thing I had to be sure of, before I knew whether I could set up Stryger the way I wanted to.

She looked surprised, and then just distracted. "Not now, okay— we're working it. Later I'll show you anything you want. . . . Why don't you get some sleep." She nudged my body like I was a drone. I felt her concern, and her impatience to get back to the group . . . felt my resolve start to fall apart. "You can use my bed again."

"Again?" I said.

Her mouth quirked. "You used it last night."

I realized I didn't remember anything at all about where I'd slept, anything at all about getting up again, besides the fact that it was too soon. "Were you there too?"

"How flattering." Her smile stretched a little thinner; she shook her head. "No, laddie-love. I didn't rape you while you slept."

"Decent of you." I trudged away toward the stairs. This time I didn't even remember hitting the foam. My dreams were full of strange music, full of strangers with hungry faces.

I only woke up again because somebody was shaking me hard. I jerked awake, wet with sweat, hearing my own thick gasp of relief as I opened my eyes. Mikah was standing over me in the darkness of Argentyne's room. "Cat," he was saying for the twelfth or thirteenth time.

"Yeah," I mumbled, and he let me go. I dropped back onto the bed with a grunt.

"You always sleep like that?" he asked. *Like I was in a coma.*

I rubbed my eyes. "No," I said. "Why?"

"Just wondered how you'd survived so long." He dumped my leather jacket on top of me. "Let's go."

He didn't bother to tell me where we were going, letting me figure it out for myself as I followed him downstairs. We went out a back way I hadn't seen before. I was glad I didn't have to face the wall of flesh out front, where the symb was blistering another night with lightsong.

We went on deeper into the Deep End, while he filled me in. He'd gotten what I'd asked for, some leads, access to somebody who could give me the answers I wanted. He didn't know any more than I did about what the answers would be. He didn't say much else, as he took me through dim green-lit streets toward the smell of the sea.

When we reached the Locks his soldiers were waiting for us on the quay. I stopped moving, going cold in the pit of my stomach. Mikah swung around up ahead of me, impatient. "What are they doing here?" I asked.

Surprise, and then irritation, stung through his brain as he registered my question, the look on my face.

"Sorry—" I said, before he could ask me if I really thought he'd set me up.

His body jerked in what looked like a shrug, but was too angry. He held up his hand, silently showing me the line of the healed scar on his palm.

I bent my head. "Sorry."

He nodded at his gang. "They're only here to prove to the Governor that I'm not running solo—and neither are you." His Family was backing him in this; that was how he'd gotten the meeting. "This is as far as they go, though. We're going out." He looked toward the Locks.

I thought about the billions of tons of water barely held back by the transparent wall of the domes . . . about being on the wrong side of the wall. I tried to keep my reaction off my face as I nodded, looking back at him. I remembered being down here before, seeing what looked like dim lights showing out there in the undersea night. Maybe it made a kind of security sense, to whoever we were meeting.

One of the soldiers, one who was built like the bouncers at Purgatory, held out a couple of drysuits to us as we reached the edge of the quay. "I can't swim. . . ." I said.

Mikah laughed. "Neither can I. Don't sweat it. Everything's taken care of." *One way.* But he didn't say that. I didn't ask about the return trip, figuring that if he was willing to risk it for me, the least I could do was keep my mouth shut. He wasn't armored tonight, but he stripped himself of half a dozen weapons before he took his suit. I watched him put it on, copying his moves; as I sealed the helmet, one of the smaller access locks opened in front of us like a silent invitation. Mikah made some last handtalk to his men, and we stepped inside.

Cold foaming water roared into the hollow space around us as the hatch sealed, flooding it up to my neck, then over my head, almost before I had time to hold my breath. Nothing leaked: nothing icy and wet seeped in anyplace . . . I breathed out and in again, drifting now like I was weightless. The suit's gills began processing oxygen out of the water; the feel against my skin was cool and soothing. A silver-glinting fish swam past my face.

"Okay?" Mikah gestured.

I nodded. "When you start at the bottom there's no way to sink any deeper." I knew that he could hear me, because he grinned.

A small ferry sub was waiting for us at the outer hatch. No one was in it. I had the feeling it only went to one place. As we got in its door sealed—leaving us still underwater as it started away into the darkness.

I latched myself into a seat; Mikah let himself drift, bumping restlessly against the ceiling and the walls. "The Governor—?" I said at last, remembering the name he'd mentioned back on the quay.

"The Governor's kind of like a pressure valve, you know what I mean? He settles things, when there's Market troubles. He speaks for everybody, if they need him to."

I nodded. In the distance I could make out half a dozen of the lights I thought I'd seen from back on the quay. I wondered how many more there were, and why they were out there. I glanced at Mikah. He was seeing restricted gaming holes, exclusive whorehouses, private estates. I looked back the way we'd come, saw the Deep End glowing through the murk like an emerald. *Everything looks better from the outside.* I looked ahead again. We were closing with one of the lights now. I began to see its real form, a shining sphere drifting over the sea floor, shifted slowly and constantly by the motion of the tides. I took a deep breath; still surprised when I did that I didn't drown.

"You ever met this Governor?"

Mikah shook his head. "Not yet. I made this deal through channels. You got Ichiba curious too." Ichiba headed his Family.

"Do they know about me—that I'm a psion?"

Mikah shrugged. "The Governor knows all about you. He takes the Morning Report, too."

The sub nosed in under the looming wall of the sphere, was sucked up into a narrowing funnel, into the heart of the Governor's very private estate. The heavy transparent inner hatch blinked green and swung open, but the lock hadn't drained. The quiet, normal-looking blue-green room that I could see beyond it was full of water. At the far end of the room a spiral of stairway disappeared upward.

"You sure you know what you're doing?" Mikah said.

"This's a hell of a time to ask me that," I muttered, feeling my stomach drop into my boots. I realized suddenly that I was here claiming I spoke for one of the biggest combines in the galaxy, about to face somebody who could say *stop* and *go* for the underworld of this entire planet, maybe even for the whole solar system. And there was nobody I could blame for it but myself. But then a sudden dark rush of excitement filled me, making me feel strong, eager, ready—like something was riding me that didn't know what fear meant. . . . I reached up with a shaky hand; couldn't touch the drug patch through the membranes of my suit.

We pushed off from the edge of the lock into the room, probably looking just as clumsy as we felt, and floundered toward the air fountain billowing upward at its center. Furniture was laid out in small intimate arcs on the blue and white tiles around the bubble sculpture. The furniture was made of plastic but it could have been carved from ice, cool and clear. I glanced at the readouts inside my helmet; the water here in the house was as warm as blood.

As we stopped moving and waited, I felt someone come silently down the steps at the other end of the room. I looked up, watched him come one step at a time, moving as naturally as if the room was filled with air and not water.

"Good evening," the Governor said. No bubbles came out of his smiling mouth. Somehow I actually heard him speak. It took a minute to realize he was using a bonebox and my suit was registering it. You couldn't see the wariness just beneath the surface of his skin, but it was there as he looked at me. I felt the sudden hot surge of Mikah's interest as the Governor glanced his way. The Governor wasn't young, but he looked young, and the muscles of his long body moved like an athlete's under the formfitting jumpsuit he had on. His long hair flowed around his head like seaweed; the warm brown of it matched his skin and eyes. He was barefoot; his fingers and toes were all a joint too long, with thin membranes between them.

Mikah held up his hands, palms out, and signed, *"Ichiba says hullo."*

The Governor's smile got a little friendlier. *"My regards to your Fam-*

ily," he signed back. He nodded and stepped down into the room. I wondered where he hid the ballast that let him move that normally. Maybe his suit was doing it. He wasn't breathing; he had gills behind his ears. But the rooms up above us were air-filled, and I could sense other people up there, observing, guarding, leading normal lives. He'd had himself made totally amphibian.

Mikah was still standing beside me. The Governor glanced at him again, a little curious. "You're staying?"

Mikah nodded.

"I don't think I have to tell you that you run the risk of hearing more than is good for you."

Mikah glanced at me. "Go," I said. He shook his head. "Too late," he said to the Governor. He made the sign for *Family.*

The Governor watched us, not saying anything, but watching us now with different eyes. "Sit down," he said finally. "I'm sorry for the inconvenience." He shrugged. *Security.*

I made it to the nearest group of seats, moving slowly so that I didn't look any worse than I had to. I settled on one of the benches, pretending like we were supposed to that everything was perfectly normal. Mikah settled down on another bench, his eyes still wandering back to the Governor, nervous and admiring.

The Governor's long-fingered hands touched the wide, trailing ends of the drape he wore around his neck. It came alive like a port; that was what it was. He was direct-accessing. There was a remote truthtester on the system; the water gave it a good feed. "So," he said to me, letting his hands slowly fall and clasp in front of him, "I understand that you represent the taMings." There was curiosity and a lot of incredulity inside him.

I held onto the edge of my seat. "Not exactly," I said, finally. "Centauri's Corporate Security."

He raised his eyebrows. "And why would they send you to us?" Emphasis on the *you* and the *us.*

"I'm their catspaw," I said.

He actually laughed, as the meaning registered. "That seems to be true . . ." Meaning he'd checked it. "It fits the baroque xenophobia of the corporate mentality well enough. But what legitimate business could they have that requires a meeting like this one?" His smile was full of amusement and irony.

"I think you know," I said.

He folded his arms. "Suppose you tell me, anyway, since I am not a mindreader."

And I was. He must know that it would be hard to hide things from me in a face meeting. Maybe that meant his clients were interested in negotiating. Probably it just meant that it was easier to kill me this way if the meeting turned out bad. "They want to know why you're trying to kill Daric taMing."

He looked vague for a second. At first I thought it was surprise, but then I realized his mind was listening to something—to someone, through a remote link. Everybody who had an interest in this was probably observing through his port, at a safe, anonymous distance from me, and from each other.

"Tell me why they believe that anyone at all wants to kill Gentleman Daric taMing? I understood that it was Lady Elnear you personally saved from assassination. Aren't you working as her bodyguard?"

Mikah was right; they did know all about me. Except for what I knew about them. "Yeah . . . except whoever tried to take out Daric didn't know one thing: nobody was really trying to kill Lady Elnear. It was part of a plot by Centauri to keep control over her and her holdings in ChemEnGen. So when the Market ran that hit on Daric, trying to make it look like it was meant for her, it crashed. It let Centauri know somebody else was the real target."

The Governor looked down at his feet, to hide the fact that he wasn't seeing us again while he got feedback from his listeners. I felt Mikah staring at him, at me, with *interest, excitement, fear* making neuron soup in his brain.

Finally the Governor said, "Very interesting." As close as he'd come out loud to admitting I'd just surprised the hell out of a whole lot of Marketeers. "Someone apparently took a wrong turn in the labyrinthine halls of a combine powerplay. . . . But why is Centauri so sure Daric taMing was the target?"

I took a deep breath and stepped over the edge. "I told them."

"Shit . . ." Mikah whispered, so softly that I barely heard him.

The Governor's head jerked up. He sent a sharp glance at Mikah, back at me; his attention flickered out for a second again. I felt Mikah's sudden tension like a pinched nerve. "How did you find out?" The Governor's voice turned cold.

I forced myself to smile. "I'm a telepath. Finding things out is what I'm good at." I hoped the bluff would be good enough to satisfy his truthtester, to keep him from pushing, from making me tell them who'd helped me do it. "I know you're trying to kill him, but I don't know why. The Corpses want me to find out."

The hard line of his mouth curved a little. "Why bother to come to me?"

I shrugged. "It's easier."

He laughed again; bubbles came out of his nose. The laughter stopped. "You must be smart enough to realize that you knew too much to come here safely. But you've come anyway, so I'm assuming you carry the keys to something you haven't shown me yet."

Mikah glanced at me again, hoping he was right. I hoped so too.

"Suppose we offer an exchange of data. I will tell you why we want Daric taMing . . . and then you tell me what you want."

I nodded.

The Governor wrapped his long fingers over the glowing ends of his drape, making sure of his facts. "Gentleman Daric taMing has for some years had a significant drug account with the Market. He uses heavily himself, and also deals for us to other combine vips who want to indulge their bad habits, but lack his contacts. We have granted him a degree of trust and privilege that is rather extraordinary for someone who comes to us from the Other Side. Gentleman Daric is not your typical Assembly member, obviously. . . . But these privileges were extended with the understanding that they would only last as long as he never betrayed our trust or interfered in our business in any way—that, in fact, he would keep our interests in mind when he voted on certain drug-related issues. . . ."

Now I knew one more way that Daric had found to fuck over his family. And suddenly I saw what had gone wrong. "The pentryptine deregulation vote," I said.

The Governor lifted his head slightly; his hair brushed his shoulders like a soft wing. "Yes—"

"If deregulation passes, it cuts out your profit." I leaned forward. "And he's been supporting it, supporting Stryger's push to get pentryptine deregged. He has to, because it's too important to his family, he can't go against them." Daric might be crazy, but he wasn't that crazy. "That's why you want him out. Right—?"

"Precisely," the Governor said, his voice a little strained. His hand went to his head, touched it, fell away.

"Why not just cut off his drugs? Why kill him? You want to make an example of him, or is somebody just that pissed?"

"Neither." He looked relieved that I was only asking questions again, not answering them. "Gentleman Daric is considered to be too volatile a personality to be trusted, under the circumstances. If we cut off his access to drugs, he has the influence to cause considerable trouble for us with the Fed Corpsec. But he has violated his pact with us, and we can't allow that. It's bad for . . . business."

I leaned back again, swaying with the motion of the water around me, watching the fountain weave alien landscapes out of pearls of air and light, watching them mutate and change, like data beings moving through a separate reality. Daric didn't know the Market was after his head; they'd wanted to keep it that way. You couldn't kill a Gentleman of the Board and Assembly like you squashed a flea. By finding out, and telling Centauri's Security, I'd made it a lot harder for them to finish what they'd started. They'd finish it anyway, whatever it took, unless I gave them a damn good reason why they shouldn't. And if I couldn't, I'd be dead before Daric was.

"Your turn," the Governor said, his voice nudging me gently. Right then I couldn't remember ever seeing an expression more frightening than his smile.

I wondered whether I was having trouble breathing because of my suit, or just because of the way he was looking at me. "I'm here to work a trade." Until that moment I hadn't been sure what would come out of my mouth. But as I heard the words I realized that I'd held the solution in my hands ever since I'd left Elnear's office today. Even while I'd been sleeping my brain had been fitting together pieces. And now, what I'd just heard had pushed the last of them into place. Suddenly everything I had to do stood out clear and sharp—as sharp as a knifepoint pricking my throat. I didn't have any choice. I just hoped I could make the Market believe they didn't have any choice either, without telling them too much.

The Governor was still watching me, waiting, his body shifting faintly with the slow motion of the water. "Well?" he said.

"Centauri wants Daric alive. . . ." Stalling, trying to pull my thoughts together. *So does Argentyne.* I told myself that what I thought about it didn't matter; this was business, just like Braedee had said.

"Unfortunate for them," the Governor murmured. "Because we never go back on a promise."

"But the final vote on deregulation hasn't happened yet."

He nodded. "But deregulation is certain to be approved, in spite of our efforts. Sojourner Stryger is able to keep a much higher profile than we can."

"He's a combine puppet anyway," I said. "That's where he gets his major motion. But he wants the Council slot Lady Elnear is up for, and he'll get that too if the deregulation passes. And then he'll stop being a puppet and start playing god for real."

The Governor frowned slightly, his eyes going out of focus as he listened to other voices. "Interesting. But hardly our concern."

"You're not—" My voice broke suddenly. I swallowed, and tried again. "You're not gonna like the way he plays. He wants to use deregulation and the power he gets to crush people like you and me. The Feds mostly leave you alone now. But once he's on the Council, what if he has the same kind of effect on them that he has on everybody else? Even Centauri's Security Chief thinks he's more than they bargained for."

The Governor frowned.

I pushed on, feeling his doubt stir. "I think there might still be a way to stop Stryger, and make the deregulation move fail. To make Stryger look bad enough to change some votes." I saw the sudden interest in his eyes. "But Daric has to stay alive or it can't happen."

" 'Can't' happen?" the Governor asked. "Not 'won't'—'can't'?"

I nodded.

"What makes you believe Stryger can be brought down so easily— especially if what you say is true, and he isn't even his own man?"

My hands made fists. "Because he's human."

The Governor looked down at his webbed feet. "Explain further."

I shook my head. "I can't . . . I don't know all of it exactly myself, yet. But Daric is Centauri's liaison with Stryger. He has to do his part or it can't work."

"Centauri is backing this?" he asked, looking at me again. "Why, when they stand to make a substantial profit if this deregulation goes through?"

"If Daric dies they'll lose more—they could lose an Assembly seat to some other combine. And the taMings lose a board member. Gentleman Charon wants his son alive more than he wants more profits." I wondered if he'd still feel that way if he knew what Daric really was.

The Governor was silent, staring at the fountain now but not really seeing it. His face worked, while his mind held half a dozen one-sided conversations. "No . . ." he said at last, turning back again, speaking to me. "Unless you can provide me with something more concrete— that isn't enough to lift the Silence on Daric taMing."

I hung onto the edge of the bench with all my strength, trying not to let him feel my desperation. If I told him everything, he'd probably think I was crazy. I wasn't sure he'd be wrong. But I knew—I realized I'd known all along—that there was nothing Centauri could offer the Market that would get Daric off its hook. And no way Daric could escape forever, even if they made him into a nonperson.

But if the Market let him live, they could still get what they wanted —and I could get what I wanted, too: Stryger. If I just had the guts to make it all work. . . . "Look," I said, "can't you hold off just until after the vote? Isn't it worth that much to you, at least, to hold off a few days? If he cooperates, if he does his part and deregulation fails—then he's canceled his debt to you, and maybe you don't have to kill him. . . . Killing him without anybody noticing has just gotten a lot harder for you. And if he dies before the vote, then there's no hope in hell of stopping deregulation, and it's your loss. What's a few days, against that—?"

The Governor stood, swaying gently, too many eyes watching me through his own.

"And if deregulation still passes . . . ?" he said at last.

"Then you can . . . silence him." I pushed up from the bench, controlling every movement because I couldn't afford to look stupid now.

"Oh, we will," he said. "Be sure of that. Tell him I said so." He hesitated. "In fact, we may even be forced by events to look into the continued health of Sojourner Stryger. . . ."

I felt the blood sing in my ears. But all I said was, "Then we've got a deal." Not making it a question, because I was already certain. All the voices clamoring through the circuits in his head had finally said the same thing. I moved forward, held up my gloved hand.

He slapped it; a strange slithering like the touch of wings. "Deal."

Mikah came up beside me. The Governor looked at him. *"My regards to Ichiba,"* he signed. "Tell him he's got a good man. I respect loyalty to a friend." Mikah nodded, not quite letting himself crack a smile. The Governor looked at me again. "I'm glad you came. It's been illuminating. I'm also glad that we were able to find some common ground. I hope that what has been agreed to comes to pass. It will be a considerable hardship for all concerned, if it doesn't. . . ." He looked down, up at me again. "If it does, perhaps you would consider doing some work for me, someday."

If I survived. "I'll think about it," I said.

He smiled. "Then I hope to see both of you again. Good night, gentlemen." He turned and started back up the stairs, one step at a time. When he was gone the lock finally began to cycle, across the room.

We floundered to the exit and through the hatch. Mikah sighed once —relief, or maybe regret—looking back as the sub carried us toward the city. Then he turned to look at me. "You got more guts than good sense, brother. But you made it run."

"Yeah."

"You don't look happy about it."

"I'm not." I shut my eyes.

"Because now you're on the list too, if deregulation passes?" It sounded casual; but he was thinking that if it came to that, there was nothing at all he could do to help me.

I grimaced. "Worrying about that's the least of my problems, right now," I said.

He shook his head, and looked out again at the Governor's private world fading like a memory behind us. "You catch that? He says he wants to see us again." He actually sounded a little wistful, behind the hard, ambitious grin that was pulling his mouth up.

"Yeah, I'm flattered." I opened one eye to look at him. "And I'm touched by how glad he was he didn't have to drop an electric current through the water in that room after he went upstairs."

28

I REACHED PURGATORY again just as Argentyne's doorkeeper was heading home for the day. S/he flipped me a handsign that could have meant *have a good day* or *fuck you*. Neither one seemed like much of a possibility.

I went on inside, scooping up a handful of leftovers off a table. I didn't feel hungry, and whatever it was tasted like garbage. I ate it anyway, because I couldn't remember the last time I'd eaten anything, or even felt like I wanted to. Argentyne and her symb were still shutting down, clustered together at the back of the empty stage above the empty room. Random bits of music began, fell away, segued into some-one else's melody as I crossed the dance floor.

I climbed up onto the stage, feeling self-conscious as soon as they noticed me, six heads all turning at once. The club was closed; they weren't expecting anybody to walk in on them now, while they were coming down from a performance high. A couple of them were half-naked, in the middle of peeling off costumes, but that wasn't what made them *feel* naked. It was being caught half-in and half-out of symb; not quite one being any more, not quite separate individuals either.

I stopped. "Sorry," I said. "I'll come back. . . ."

"Wait a minute," Argentyne called.

I stopped again, hearing her leave the others and cross the stage, feeling her hand catch my arm to pull me around.

Her eyes were still a little glassy, but the hard light of her need to know cut through the fog in her brain as she said, "Where did you go with that Marketeer friend of yours?"

I glanced down at her hand touching my arm. "I went to get Daric a stay of execution."

Her hand tightened, then went loose and dropped away. "Did you?" she asked softly, almost afraid to say the words.

I nodded. "For now."

"What does that mean?" She half frowned.

"It means that if Daric helps me set up Stryger for a fall, then maybe the Market will forget it wants him dead. They want him dead because he's helping Stryger push for that drug deregulation. If it costs them, it's going to cost him."

She shook her head slightly, feeling dazed again. "The Market's going after Stryger?"

"No. I am."

"You—?" She blinked at me, and made a sound that wasn't quite a laugh.

I nodded again.

"I can't deal with this right now." She waved her hand at me. "It's too surreal. . . ." She started to turn away.

"Argentyne, wait," I said. "I need your help." Finally able to make myself ask what I hadn't been able to ask her before. "Help me do it."

She turned back. "Me?" Her sense of unreality was getting stronger all the time. "How?"

"The symb. You said you could teach me how to work it."

"Just for laughs." She shook her head. "I didn't mean going political on it. Holy lights, you said to *me* you didn't want any trouble!"

"To save Daric—?"

She broke off, looked away suddenly. "If you need the symb, everybody's got to agree." She went away, spoke quietly to the players still standing inside their desultory cloud of music at the other end of the stage. I waited, trying to get my buzzing thoughts straight so I could explain everything when I had to.

She came back again after a minute. "They want to know everything first. So do I."

"That's what I figured," I said.

"Come on, then." She nodded. I followed them backstage, down a hallway to what passed for a living room. Mismatched furniture that looked like somebody had dragged it in off the street made a soft barrier along the acoustic-fiber walls. The walls were plastered with holo stick-ups of performers they admired. Old musical instruments, the kind that had never been intended to be grafted into anyone's body, lay around on the furniture like kids' toys. Everything was comfortable, loose, real—everything the club out front wasn't.

The symb spread out around me, standing, sitting, collapsing on the dusty rug . . . but still keeping physical contact. Hands touched hair, clung to ankles; bodies brushed hip against shoulder, or folded into someone else's arms. Their eyes were getting clearer as they watched me. I could feel them still shifting response centers in their brains, switching out of the instinctive, almost automatic modes of cyber-enhanced creativity. I'd never felt anything exactly like it; most humans had their logic and comm functions enhanced, not their creative side.

"How's the hand?" Aspen asked me.

I looked down at it. "Useful."

Argentyne settled onto a couch next to Kiroku, the piper, watching me with wary copper eyes. "Okay," she said, "spill your guts, kid."

I looked down at my boots, feeling all their eyes locked on me now, judging my performance. "I guess you all know how I used to work for Centauri, protecting Lady Elnear. And I guess you've all seen Sojourner Stryger. Now I'm going to tell you what I know about him." I told them what lived inside that perfect shell; how he felt about psions and what he wanted to do with the deregulated pentryptine; what he'd try to do if he got that Council slot. How the combines that were backing him were getting more than they bargained for. "I think you already know something about Lady Elnear. . . ." I glanced at Argentyne. "Lady Elnear wants that Council slot too. She deserves it. But she doesn't have the backers that Stryger does—and Stryger's done everything he can to make sure she loses. He even used me. She's going to lose, and he's going to win, and the whole Federation's going to get even worse about how it treats freaks, if he gets his way. . . . I'm a freak, and I take that personally. Okay, so maybe it doesn't matter to you, maybe it's not your problem—"

"Hey, look, nobody said that," Midnight murmured.

"But how can *you* stop Stryger, if Lady Elnear can't?" Aspen asked. "You planning to assassinate him?"

"He thinks our act's bad enough to kill him," somebody else said. There was laughter, mixed with synth sounds.

I waited until it stopped, and then I said, "There's something else about Stryger." I glanced at Argentyne again; her gaze hung on me. "He doesn't just hate freaks. He likes to hurt them. . . . You remember that girl Daric brought here—?"

"Stryger did that?" Aspen said, incredulous.

"She was a fr— a psion?" Kiroku echoed.

I nodded. "Daric is Centauri's private liaison with Stryger. He's also his pimp—he gets him victims."

"Shit, man. . . ." somebody muttered.

"—a pervert?"

"Daric. That figures. . . ."

"So what's that got to do with us?" Raya, the other piper, asked.

"I'm getting to it as fast as I can!" I rubbed my neck, trying to ease the crawling itch under the surface of my skin.

She shrugged. "Right, so he's a pervert. Why don't you just tell everybody?"

I shook my head. "That's not good enough. The Assembly's not easy to move. I've got to show them what it means . . . I've got to make the whole fucking Assembly *feel* like his victims, or it won't change anything—" I closed my fist, and opened up my mind.

The players jerked and swore in a cacophony of sudden uncontrolled sound. They shook out their hands, touched their heads; held onto each other a little tighter.

"Damn it!" Argentyne said, and then, catching her breath, "all right —so you can make everybody hurt. What's that got to do with my symb? You don't need us if you can goose the whole Assembly yourself with one thought."

"No—" I shook my head. "That's not the point. If I went in there and made them all puke, they'd fry me, and all it would prove was that Stryger was right about psions all along. He tried to use me against the Lady once already; I'm not gonna make it easy for him." I frowned. "I got to have a record, proof of what he does . . . how it really feels." I looked back at Argentyne. "You said I could actually feed feeling into the symb, right? Can I record it, and make it into a show . . . ?"

Argentyne sat forward on the couch, her own hands making fists; not listening. "Oh God . . . what do you want, you mean you want Daric to let Stryger torture him?"

"Daric—?" I said. I felt her freeze as she realized what she'd done. "Daric's not a psion." I said each word with just enough confusion; felt the surprise drain out of the minds around me. Argentyne sank back into the couch. (And if you really still give a damn about him, you'd better find some way to make yourself believe that.) She gasped, touching her head; looked back at me with gratitude and resentment blurring her sight. "Of course he's not. . . ." she murmured. "Then what do you mean—you expect us to record it while Stryger beats the crap out of another freak, is that it?"

"Yeah," I said. "That's right."

"God's teeth! You're a real vip, aren't you? Now you're going out to pick up some poor bastard off the street who's so pitiful he'd let a deeve like Stryger do that to him—"

"No." I shook my head, feeling my face flush. "I've already got my poor freak bastard."

She broke off. "Who?"

"Me."

She stared at me like she was waiting for me to laugh, like she thought it was really all just a sick joke. "Oh God. . . ." she said at last. "You really mean that."

"You really think I'd use somebody else to get what I want from Stryger? I'm not Daric," I said. I sat down on a couch, rubbed my sweating hands on the knees of my pants. The pressure of everybody's sudden silence sat on my back like an animal.

"You said . . . you said you needed Daric in this with you. Why?" Argentyne asked.

I looked up at her. "He's got to set me up. Stryger's not stupid. I can't just walk up to him and say, 'Kick the shit out of me, will you?' It's got to look good. If Daric offers to get me for him to use, he'll trust that."

"But you work for the taMings, for Centauri—you saved their lives," Argentyne protested, her mind still tumbling like a bird knocked out of the air.

"Not any more. Not that Stryger knows. Daric's probably already told him how Charon got rid of me. I'm a degenerate, I seduced Lady Lazuli. I'm a fucking freak rapist as far as the taMings are concerned." I listened to myself talk about it like I was listening to a stranger talk about someone else. "I got no friends on this world . . . no protection. . . ." The back of my hand rose up to my mouth, hard and sudden. I forced it down into my lap again; made myself stop counting the shinestones in the constellation on her tunic. "Stryger hates my guts," the stranger went on, calmly, steadily, "as much as I hate his. It's perfect."

"It's crazy." Argentyne got up from her place beside Kiroku and turned her back on me, moving away across the room. She turned around suddenly, her hands out in front of her. "What if he kills you?"

"I'm not stupid either," I said. "I'll make sure I'm protected. I'm not going to let it get serious. All I need is just enough to give those marks in the Assembly a good kick in the balls. I figure not one of them's ever felt real pain. It won't take much to scare the shit out of them. I can take that much." My lips felt numb. I pushed to my feet again, as the wild darkness inside me made me want to move. "Are you going to help me out, or not?"

Nobody said anything . . . nobody said, "No." But they didn't

know where to look, because none of them wanted to look at me, right
then.

"What do you want us to do?" Argentyne asked finally.

"Teach me how to use the symb to make a recording. Let me use
your equipment for an evening. That's all."

"You'll need a socket."

I nodded. "I know." I couldn't use Deadeye's trick-entry if I wanted
to do something that would leave a record.

"Aspen—" She gestured at him. He nodded and got up, going out of
the room to get his medical equipment. She looked back at me. "You
know, this might not even work. When I said that, about making people
live it . . . well, nobody's ever done that." She shrugged. Part of her
was afraid it wouldn't work, and part of her was afraid it would.

I didn't say anything, more afraid than she was. My fingers explored
the cracked formfoam beside me restlessly; found something hard and
pulled it out: a blunt rectangle of rusted metal, with a line of square
holes showing along its side, like teeth in a grinning mouth. I turned it
over and over, staring at it.

"Do you know anything about how a symb functions?" Argentyne
asked, a little impatient.

I looked up, shook my head.

She sat down again, resting against Kiroku like she was a chair back.
"We're all pretty heavily augmented. If I'm right, you won't need that,
because you know how to tap into our heads direct. . . . The way it
works, each of the players has their own repertoire—the songs they've
stored, new compositions happening, whatever they can get their personal system to do. Everyone's different. Everyone does their own riffs
—unique, you know, self-contained. But they feed together into a larger
pattern through the symb. Working the augmentation lets us improvise
fast enough to keep track of it, keep everyone moving and flowing,
when it's really good." Kiroku looked up at her, smiling, and kissed her
arm.

"Sometimes we work it so everyone's words and music fit the same
theme, weaving together like threads—" She lifted her hands, wove her
fingers together. "Sometimes everybody takes a different theme, and we
let it explode—" Her hands flew apart. "But it's all coming out of the
same heart, and it all has to pull back into the center, come together
again by the end. When it's right, it's like the cosmos, you know? Like
the expanding and contracting of the universe, like centripetal and
centrifugal forces, the motion of worlds and suns. . . ." Her hands

circled each other in space. She was somewhere else now, forgetting who she was talking to or even why as she groped for a way to explain something that ran so deep in her that it had no explanation. The other players were hanging on her words, all of them lost inside their own private visions of how it felt to be caught up in that epiphany.

"Like a joining," I murmured.

"A what?" Argentyne said, coming back into focus again.

"Nothing." I looked down, still turning the metal bar over and over in my hands.

"You mean sex?" Kiroku asked, and giggled.

I shook my head, still looking down. "It's something psions can do. Not very often. It's opening yourself up to somebody else, completely, until you're like one person in two bodies. . . ." I was thinking about Jule; about how our minds had caught fire with nameless colors, burning brighter and brighter . . . how for one brief moment outside of time the emptiness inside me had been filled with all the answers I'd ever need, all the comfort, the understanding, the love. . . .

"Sounds like sex to me," Argentyne said, with a strange half-smile.

I glanced up; wanting to say something . . . changing my mind. I shook my head again, not meeting her eyes. Instead I said, "Seems to me like most of the people who see your act don't catch half of what's really going on. They'd have to be cybered too, to follow it."

She shrugged, nodded. "I know. That's why I envied you, what you did at the club the other night. . . . But they get as much as they can take, and if they have a good time, that's all they care about. And we don't really do it for them, anyway, in the end."

"What about the visuals, all that holo stuff I saw that night. Where's that come from?"

"That's Argentyne," Jax said. "She's the spirit. She projects the visions. She makes it all flow."

"Shut up," she said, turning away. The sudden irritation behind it surprised me. She was afraid of being singled out, cut off, separated from the group—afraid that fate was waiting to slap her down, that in the middle of all this tech the Evil Eye was still watching. "We all input on what we're trying to make it say. I image them with what I've got up here, yeah; I mix the colors, I control the visual. But the pieces of the dreams belong to all of us." And I realized she was right: all the augmentation in the galaxy couldn't make them fuse well enough to do what they did unless their human halves, with their human egos, were willing to cooperate. I wondered if having their brains rewired like that was what made it possible, or whether collecting the right mix of per-sonalities to make this kind of art was the first, and hardest act of creation. I wondered how long it would last; how long anything that complex could hold together.

Aspen came back into the room, carrying his kit, and sat down beside me. "Lean over." My body tensed, fighting him as he tried to make me stretch my neck. "Relax," he said, sticking on a patch of painkiller. "You won't feel a thing."

That wasn't what I was afraid of; but I didn't say anything, I only bent my head. I didn't feel a thing while he wired me, until the very end: a tingling, like bells ringing inside my skull, and that was all. Getting my ear pierced had been worse.

"You feel that?" Aspen asked.

I nodded.

"Good. You're live, then." He handed me a mirror. "One of us." He grinned.

I pushed up my hair and looked, even though I didn't want to. I touched the fresh spot of synthetic flesh on the back of my neck. Nothing else even showed. I looked at my reflection, at the round, perfectly normal pupils of my eyes. *One of them.*

"Try it out on us." Aspen was still grinning. He'd already forgotten what I wanted to do with it, or the trouble it could make for me. Or maybe it had never even registered on him in the first place.

I looked around the circle, felt them waiting to *feel* something. . . . I shook my head. "I don't want to try it now." I looked down. "Just tell me how I make it do what I need it to do. Just tell me how I record what happens to me, and how do I feed it back into the heads of the Assembly?"

"We can't tell you," Argentyne said, feeling her patience slip again. "Like I said, it's not anything we've ever done. You've got to lock in so we can test it out. The symb quantifies sensory input for vision and sound, sometimes even smell, but we've never tried to code anything like whole body sensation before. I don't know if it can even handle something as unpredictable as . . . as your pain." She said the word like an obscenity, and in the back of her mind she thought an obscenity was what I'd be committing with her equipment. "We've got to take neural readings off you."

I nodded, shrugged. "What do I do?" I started to get up.

"Just stay there," she said. I sat back down again. "Wake up the jack . . . and listen through it for the music."

I called it on: it shrieked and shone and crackled inside my brain like some insane alien lifeforce. "Jeezu—!" I pressed my hand against my eyes, trying to blot out the molten highways that were linking me to the startled faces of the players. Slowly the sandpaper static faded, as my mind took its measure and tuned out everything irrelevant, bit by bit. I blinked, able to see their relief, starting to be able to feel it again past the noise. "I'm reading you . . . and you . . ." pointing to them as I was able to separate the raw data of the sounds each of their instrument systems made. Readouts flashed inside my eyes like phosphenes. "Where are you?" I looked at Argentyne, the only one I couldn't find a channel for.

"You're in my seat, playing spirit, my role," she said. "I'm just listening, reading you out this time. You'll have to play spirit to do what you want to do. You're accessing my console."

"I'm in your head?"

"Not exactly. Just on the phone. I can't feel you."

I nodded, even though I wasn't sure I understood; trusting her judgment because I didn't have any choice.

"How does it feel?" She'd never taken a reaction off a psion.

"Like having rats down your pantslegs. How the hell do you stand it?"

"I'm used to it." She shrugged. "Anyway, it never really bothered me that much. . . ." She looked away from whatever she was seeing on some built-in readout of her own, focused on my face again. Slowly she lifted her hand to touch her forehead. "You remember what I said about you feeling like silk . . . ?"

I nodded, finally understanding that much, at least. "Now what?"

"Open up the console; send data back to the others. Tell them to pick it up, ease off—something simple."

Something simple was all I could do anyway; but I did it, embarrassed and awkward, collecting my thoughts like spit and funneling them into the rigid patterns of noiselight that lay waiting, a datascan that had somehow ended up on the wrong side of my eyes. The symbsystem only recognized a narrow range of commands, a narrow band of frequencies; it was totally blind to everything else. It was like being brain-damaged . . . but remembering how I'd felt without my psi, I realized it was still better than nothing.

"Loosen up," Argentyne said. "Stop treating it like an electric shock."

"I don't know anything about making music—"

"You don't have to," she said gently. "That's their business. Just let them know what you want to hear. Nobody's judging you—try to enjoy it. That's what it's for."

I let myself settle back into the couch, into the crosscurrents of half a dozen different kinds of music playing at once. I let it fill my brain and filter down, trying to reach levels where the control would be almost instinctive. My muscles began to twitch, wanting to be what made the sounds that were filling me now. I'd always liked music. It was everywhere in Oldcity, pouring out of forbidden clubs or broken windows, trapped inside a bottle, just like I was. It was the only thing about Oldcity that ever made me feel glad I was alive. I tried to remember that, to imagine what I was hearing was like that. I let go of who and where I was, and of what I was doing here; tried to make what was happening inside me feel like the sound of an Oldcity night ricocheting off the roof of the world. By not focusing on any single player I could half-hear them all, reacting half a dozen ways at once by not trying to react. . . .

I felt it begin to change; felt the sudden surge of my own pleasure fill me until it turned into a squeal of feedback . . . until I got it under control, drifting back into the river of sound, feeling its currents divide and re-form around me.

"Good," Argentyne murmured. "You've got instincts, at least. Now try making an image."

"How?" I mumbled, hating to interrupt myself to say the word.

"The same way you're guiding the music. Concentrate on the console, give it an easy focus—a face, something in the room, to fix on, and let it start improvising, then ride it—"

I gave it the easiest thing I could think of—myself, moving to the music the way my body wanted to. I saw my own holoform image flash into being in the middle of the symb, dancing, with the walls and ceiling darkening, closing in . . . dancing the way I'd danced once years ago to someone else's music, through a sweltering Oldcity night. I stared at the image, forgetting that I was supposed to be controlling it . . . until suddenly it wavered, folded in on itself, and was gone. The music began to unravel into separate strands inside me. "Damn!"

"Don't worry," Argentyne said. "It takes practice. It's like putting your pants on while walking a fence. . . ."

I smiled with half my brain; the other half was still trying to put everything back together that I'd almost had perfect. I looked from face to face, finally understanding the kind of trust it took, the discipline, the control, to do what a player did. Creativity was only the beginning. And they did it without using psi.

"Feel something—"

"I am. . . ." I said, only half hearing her; working my mind deeper into the artificial passageways, still looking for my lost image.

"Something physical."

"Yeah. . . ." I looked down at my bandaged hand; made it into a fist.

Something happened in the artificial grid inside my head—pain went out and came back again sixfold, making me gasp. It went out and came back again, worse, caught in a circular feedback that I didn't know how to stop—

Suddenly the link went dead; Argentyne had cut me loose. I sank back into the couch, gulping in the sweet, empty void that followed like cool water.

There was silence around me in the room, too. Not even echoes. Finally Midnight said, "Shit . . . don't *ever* do that again, man." Raya put an arm around him, pulling him close.

"I won't," I said. "Not to you, anyway." There was silence again. Slowly the players began to get up, by ones and twos, putting their arms around each other and mumbling excuses as they left the room. Only Argentyne was still there when I finally looked up.

"I guess it works," she said faintly.

I nodded.

"It won't feed back like that on an open-ended link. It was just trapped."

I laughed once. "So I won't burn the brains out of the Federation Assembly. Then all I've got to worry about is putting my pants on while walking a fence with Stryger on my back."

She shook her head; tried not to grimace. "That's no problem either, if all you want from the equipment is to code a feelie . . . a straight record of your experience. You come through very clearly; some people never learn to do that. You focus like a pro."

I half smiled. "I am a pro."

"I know. . . ." she said, glancing away, and back at me. "You should really try working this more. Experiment, play with us. It wouldn't take you long to pick it up, I can tell. I want to know what you'd symb like, feeling something real good. . . ." Her gaze broke, as self-consciousness smashed the image crystallizing in her mind.

I kept my face expressionless, looking down. I picked up the small metal-plated bar that was still lying in my lap. "What's this thing?" I asked, to get my own mind off what she'd been thinking.

She looked relieved at the change of subject. "Oh, that . . . something Raya picked up in a junk shop. It's real old, like most of the stuff here—" She gestured at the other instruments lying around the room, started to smile a little. "She can't resist any old piece of crap that's supposed to make music. We like to play them . . . play with them. She said it's called a harp."

"I thought harps had long strings. Like pianos."

"She said it's a mouth harp. You blow through its teeth, and it makes noise. Try it."

I tried it. It made a whole chord of notes as I blew, a different chord when I breathed in again. The sound was smoky and lost; it put a hand around my heart and squeezed. It reminded me of something, but I couldn't remember what. I dropped it on the couch and stood up.

"Take it, if you want," Argentyne said.

I shook my head, and started for the door.

"Where are you going?" she called, mostly because she wasn't sure that I knew either.

"Back to the real world," I said.

29

"YOU'RE HOTWIRED," Braedee said, as I came into his office. He leaned forward across the desk/terminal like a snooper sniffing out drugs. The desk was a black cube, like the one on his cruiser. "Do you know what the penalty is for psions wearing bioware?"

"Fuck off, Braedee." I frowned, collapsing into a chair. "I know it better than you do." The way I felt right now, there was nothing they could do to me that wasn't already happening.

"Where did you pick up an illegal jack?"

"It doesn't matter. You're not going to turn me in." Daring him to deny it, feeling lousy enough to enjoy pissing him off. "I need it right now. I'll get rid of it as soon as I can. Wearing this shit is enough punishment—I don't know how you deadheads stand it."

He stared at me, unblinking, rigid. Finally his body eased, with a shrug that said he'd given up trying to make sense of a sociopath. "See that you do." If I didn't see to it, he would. "What have you found out concerning Daric taMing?"

I leaned back in my seat, trying to ignore the dryness in my mouth, and the way my eyes kept wanting to trace the black knife-edge outline of his desk. I glanced at the wide stretch of window behind him, at the view of Centauri's operations plex spreading out in the cold, clear morning across Longeye, as big as the city that had been there before it. I realized the whole layout of this office, and even the colors in it, were the same as the ones on his ship. He liked his world under control. No wonder he didn't like what was happening now. I looked back at him. "I think I found out how you can save Daric's life."

His face barely registered a change; but his mind was an exclamation point. "How?" he said.

"You're not going to like it. Did you tell Charon—Gentleman Charon—" as he frowned, "what happened?"

He nodded. "He knows Daric is in trouble. And he knows that you're still working for me here on Earth."

"How's he taking it?"

"With extreme prejudice." Braedee's mouth thinned. "Well—?"

There wasn't an easy way to say it. "If he wants Daric to stay alive, the pentryptine deregulation has to lose in the Assembly."

Braedee shook his head slightly, as if he thought his hearing had gone out on him.

I went over it again: Daric's drugs, Daric's Lack Market dealings, how Daric had stepped over some invisible line, and the only way back across it was the hard way. What was going on in Braedee's brain got darker with every word I spoke, as he realized what Daric had done to himself.

"It's impossible. . . ." he said finally; but he didn't mean that he didn't believe it. Only that he didn't see any way to stop it. He turned his chair until his back was to me, and stared out at the fields, the symbol of Centauri's empire. Even if Centauri suddenly changed its mind on the deregulation, he figured they'd never get enough other combines to change their votes, just to save the life of Daric taMing. They might be able to save Daric by giving him a total identity change and sending him away somewhere, but the end result would still be the same. They'd still lose his voting seat in the Assembly, and on the board. That made him as good as dead to Centauri, even if he survived.

"Maybe not," I said.

He turned back to face me again. "Explain."

"Stryger. I think Stryger's the key. I think I have a way of making his credibility lousy. And if he goes down, I think he'll drag deregulation down with him."

"Stryger . . . ?" he murmured. His eyes glazed while he called up data and fed it over and over through his mind. At last he said, "Centauri is backing Stryger in his bid for the Council slot as well as in his push for deregulation." He thought he was telling me something I didn't know.

"I know," I said.

His sudden paranoia turned into irritation, almost before he knew what he was feeling. "They are not the only combine involved in this."

"I know."

His fingers began to tap on the black expanse of tabletop. "What makes you think Stryger is vulnerable?"

"Everybody's vulnerable." I looked down. "He hates psions."

Braedee was actually surprised, for half a second. "How is that fact likely to cause him any serious trouble?" Plenty of people in positions of power hated psions.

I looked up at him again. "Because he does things to freaks that the rest of you deadheads only daydream about," I said softly.

He straightened up in his seat, staring at me. His mouth opened. But by now he knew enough not to waste his time asking me the obvious questions. "What are you planning to do?" he murmured.

"That's my business." I frowned.

He shook his head. "I can't allow that."

"Daric will know all about it. He's going to help me. If Centauri wants to keep him alive, then you've got to trust me. Leave me alone to do what I have to do."

"What are you getting out of this?" he asked, finally.

I shrugged. "Your money."

He leaned forward again, his fingers making a pyramid on the black plain. "What else?"

"You wouldn't understand. . . . Knowing Stryger won't be working for the Humane Society." He didn't understand, but it didn't matter. "You told me you think Stryger's a fanatic, maybe crazy. That he's not going to play anybody's game but his own—"

He nodded. "But that's only my opinion. I'll still have to clear it with the board. Centauri has a great deal to lose if deregulation loses. If the board disagrees, it will still be my duty to stop you."

I didn't say anything.

The Corpses who had taken me to Braedee took me back to the city again, and let me off at the waterline. It was the middle of the day by the time I walked the last few streets to Purgatory. My feet began to stumble as the angry energy from my meeting with him finally wore off. I still had to deal with Daric; but breaking the news to him was going to be like breaking glass, and I didn't feel clear-headed enough to handle it without more sleep. My brain still thought it was plugged into the sun, but my body said my brain was a liar.

Argentyne met me in the back hallway of the club, looking concerned, but not about me. "Jiro's here."

"Jiro?" I said. "Why?"

Jiro stepped out of her dressing room into the hallway behind her. His white tunic was smeared with something that looked the way it smelled, and one side of his face was red and purple. For a second I thought it was makeup. But this time it was real.

"Somebody robbed him," Argentyne said.

"I wanted to see you," he said to me. His voice couldn't decide whether to sound like a taMing, or like he wanted to cry.

"How'd you find me?"

"Auntie told me you were here."

I glanced at Argentyne.

She nodded. "Go on upstairs."

We went up to her room. Jiro looked around it, wide-eyed with curiosity in spite of himself. He sat down almost timidly on the edge of her bed. "Why doesn't Argentyne want to see Daric any more?"

I tried a lot of answers, finally settled on, "She's angry at him."

"She's been angry at him before. But this is different. Daric's real upset. He won't even leave his house. He said she's never going to come back. Even if he tells her he'll kill himself again."

"Jeezu," I muttered. "That's all I need." I looked out the window, wondering if he'd still be so eager to commit suicide once he knew that somebody wanted to do it for him.

"He said it was your fault."

I looked back at Jiro. "Daric says a lot of things that aren't true."

He bit his lip. "I know. . . ."

"How are you doing?" I asked it, even though I already knew the answer.

"I miss my mother." He twisted the edge of his belt between his fists. "And Tally."

"Me too," I said, touching the empty hole in my ear, feeling the drug patch still in place behind it. "Why'd you come down here, Jiro?"

"Because I hate Charon! I'm never going back there—" He winced as his face hurt him. "I want to stay with you."

I stared at him. "And do what?" I asked.

"We could go to Eldorado and find my mother, and you and she—"

"No," I said softly, cutting him off. "We can't. You've got to go home."

"Why not—?" A crimson rush of *anger frustration grief fear* reddened his other cheek.

"Because that's not how life works. Because Charon will stop you, no matter what you do. Because your mother doesn't really want to give up being a taMing. Because you don't really want to throw away everything you've got and live like me. . . . Because I've only started living, and I'm not ready to lose it all to a mindwipe."

"But I—"

"No. Go home, Jiro."

He half-rose from the bed, his fist coming up to take a swing at me. I blocked the move, held his hand away. It began to tremble; he collapsed onto the bed again.

I reached out, trying to be gentle as I touched his bruised face with my fingers. He flinched. "You're lucky that's all you got. How many guys did it take to do that to you?"

He looked down, his face getting red again. "Only one."

"You're still lucky."

"I tried to use my tychee training, but it didn't work very well."

"Didn't you wear a bodyguard?"

"I forgot to turn it on."

I shook my head. "How far do you figure you're going to get on your own in the galaxy if you can't even make it to Argentyne's without getting the crap knocked out of you, and everything you own stolen?"

"I've got my own credit line—" He held his wrist up. It was bare. He stared at it like his hand was missing; I heard him suck in a gulp of disbelief. He made a noise like a stepped-on puppy, and lowered his arm. "Oh, no—" His hands went into his pockets, his tunic, searching frantically for something else. "It was in my jacket, he took my jacket, it's gone!" *A handmade tapestry pouch Elnear had given him, with a holo of him and his parents inside it.* He could see it so clearly in his mind that I could see it too. He sagged forward, his shoulders hunching, his fists pressed into the space between his knees. His nose began to run as he fought back tears. "Shit. Shit. Shit!"

I sat down beside him on the bed and put my arm around him. "Jiro —" I broke off, waiting until he was ready to listen. "Jiro," I said again, at last; I barely touched the bruise on his face. "This's what it means to be on your own, and just a kid. I've been on my own as long as I can remember. When I was a kid it never got much better."

"It couldn't get any worse," he said sullenly.

"Sometimes it got a whole lot worse." He raised his head; I looked away from the questions in his eyes.

"But I hate Charon! You don't know what he's like—"

I looked down at my bandaged hand. "Yeah, I do." I sighed. "Nobody said you're not hurting, or that you don't have any reason to. Nobody said you don't feel lonelier than you thought anybody knew how to. Charon's a bastard, and he's done things to both of us that we're not going to forget." I saw his mother's face in both our memories. "But you're still a taMing, Jiro. And you're still young. That means you'll probably get everything you want, sooner or later. Your mother's not dead, and neither is your sister. Charon will get over what happened; you'll all be together again, someday. And someday you'll be an adult, a member of the board yourself; maybe even an Assembly member. Charon won't run your life any more. And then you can make him pay for this, if that's still what you need."

"But that'll take years and years—" He pulled away from my shoulder, stiffening upright, full of desperation. "How am I going to stand it, for years and years?"

"Just like I did," I said. "One day at a time."

"You're not me! That's stupid! That's not a good enough answer—" His face and his mind got blind-stubborn again.

"Neither is running away!" I rubbed my itching face, my arms. *What do you want from me? If I had all the answers, do you think I'd be sitting here like this—?* But I only said, "Look . . . your mother said you're away at school most of the time, anyhow, right?" He nodded slowly. "So you're not going to spend that much time around Charon. You can live with it. You'll have friends at school, people there that you can respect and learn from. Use that—" He stared at me, but he didn't say anything. "Everybody's got to take over their own life sooner or later, or they might as well be dead. You'll just have to do it sooner. You have to figure out for yourself what's important to you, because you won't have a family you can trust to guide you. Except your aunt . . . you can trust your Aunt Elnear." He nodded again, solemn and listening now. Suddenly I thought of something else. "What about the baby?"

"The baby?" he asked, looking confused.

"Your mother said there was going to be a baby soon. Hers and Charon's. Your brother. . . ."

He blinked, remembering.

"He's going to need you," I said. "To help him understand."

He glanced away, staring at the windows; I felt his mind begin to open up again, at last.

I stood up. "Come on. You'd better be getting home before Charon figures out you're gone." I gestured toward the door.

"Cat . . . ?"

"What?"

His mouth struggled to make the words. "Did you ever get scared

. . . when you were just a kid . . . and you didn't have anybody to take care of you?"

I looked down at the faded colors of the rug. "Yeah. I was scared all the time. Sometimes I still am."

He got up; glanced at his wrist, as if he still couldn't believe it was naked. *Shock humiliation fury grief* glanced through his brain again, with the realization that there was nothing left to take home with him out of all the things he'd brought.

"You worried what Charon's going to do when he learns you lost the deebee?"

"The what?" he said.

"Your databand."

He nodded. "He'll—" He made a face. "I don't care. Let him. It's only money, we've got plenty. . . ." The defiance fell away. "But I lost my picture . . . my picture, it's the only one I had. . . ." His hands rose, helplessly, dropped to his sides. He sniveled.

The holo in the tapestry bag that was gone with his jacket. "Where'd you get robbed?"

"Right outside the trans station."

"Let's go for a walk," I said.

"But—"

"Don't worry. You're safe now. You've got nothing left to steal."

He didn't like it, but he led me to the place where he'd been robbed. I looked up and down the street, seeing overflowing bins of garbage, only some of it plastic-sealed, waiting for a pickup. "Which way did he run after he knocked you down?" Jiro pointed straight ahead. "Come on," I said. "Let's check the dumpsters."

"Dumpsters?"

"Garbage bins," I said. "Not everybody has a home recycler. A slip'll dump anything he can't use, usually real close by."

He stared down the street. "You look for it. I don't want to touch garbage."

Rich kids— "Fuckin' ass, you will." I gave him a shove. "You're the one who knows what you lost. If you want it back so bad, you'll help me look for it."

He glared at me. I stared him down, waiting while his anger fell apart. He shrugged his shoulders, embarrassed, and nodded. As we began to walk I felt his self-consciousness and fear begin to fade; he looked into every heap and bin, more carefully as he went along.

"There—!" he shouted suddenly, running forward. Something bright stood out from the garbage colors in the shadow of a stairwell. He picked up an expensive-looking orange jacket—his jacket—shook it out, felt in the pockets. They were empty, which figured. He waded back into the trash pile, picking up a carryall and a couple of other things he seemed to recognize; dropping them again. "Here it is!" His voice shot up an octave. He laughed, waving the holo, triumphant. "I found it! We found it—!" He stumbled back to my side, tripping over cans, his eyes wide. "We really did. I don't believe it—" He laughed again. "Wow. Thanks. Thanks. . . ." He pushed the holo down inside his tunic, close to his heart. "How'd you know that, Cat? How'd you know it would be there? Because you're a psion?"

I half-smiled, turning around. "Because when I was a slip, that's what I always used to do." I started back toward the transit station, letting him catch up when he could.

He came up beside me again, panting, dragging his jacket. He looked at it while he walked, and frowned, wrinkling his nose. He tossed it at another trash heap as we passed.

I reached out, caught it before it landed. Further down the street I handed it to a drab-looking girl in a Fedworks uniform, who wasn't much bigger, or older, than he was. She gaped, grinned, and ran on down the street, clutching it in her fists; afraid we'd change our minds.

"It was dirty—" Jiro said, watching her go.

"So are you." I hit the stain on the front of his tunic with my hand, a little harder than I needed to. He winced and didn't say anything more as we headed into the station.

When the transit came, he started looking for words to tell me goodbye. I only shook my head, and got on board with him. "I'm coming back to the estates with you."

He frowned, worry and sudden fear filling his mind again. "But Charon said—"

"I've got to see Daric. Charon'll have to live with it." I slumped down in the seat, suddenly remembering how tired I still was, and hoping this wasn't a mistake. . . . I realized I was tracing the molded cube design on the plastic seat in front of me, and tried to stop.

"Cat?" Jiro said, as the trans started to pick up speed.

"What?"

"I'm sorry." *About the garbage. About the coat.*

I sighed.

30

NEITHER OF US was wearing a valid clearance any more, but Jiro managed to convince the estate security systems that we were cleared to land. He had plenty of beginner's bioware netted into his brain.

Charon himself was waiting for us on the terrace when the mod landed, standing with his hands clenched behind his back.

"Where the hell have you been? What the hell are you doing here?" he said, one question for each of us. "What happened to your clearance?" Another one for Jiro.

"I got robbed," Jiro mumbled, looking at the ground.

"What? Speak up, for God's sake—"

"I got robbed!" Jiro lifted his chin. Now Charon could see the bruise on his face, his stained clothes, the stubborn set of his jaw.

Charon's face changed: *worry, fear, anger.* He looked back at me like I'd done it.

"He's all right," I said, ignoring the look. "He came down to see me at Purgatory. He lost his databand to a slip, that's all."

Charon's relief was so strong I almost choked on it. He stood looking at Jiro, his hands tightening at his sides, fighting something inside himself. I realized it wasn't anger or wanting to hurt the boy . . . it was the urge to get down on his knees and hold him, and thank God that he was all right. Jiro stood frozen, reading it as rage, watching those hands with barely-controlled panic.

But Charon didn't move. His hands loosened. "Don't ever do anything that stupid again," he said. "You could have been killed."

"I won't," Jiro said dully.

I felt Charon do something with the hardware in his head—sending out a signal to kill Jiro's lost databand. I hoped it was too late, that some freedrop had already cleaned out his account. "Go inside," he ordered, gesturing toward the Crystal Palace waiting behind him.

Jiro hesitated, looking at me. He smiled, uncertainly. "Thank you." He patted his shirt, the holo hidden inside it.

I nodded.

"See you—?"

"Maybe," I said, not wanting to make him a promise I couldn't keep. I watched him go on, small and alone, into the shining house.

Charon stood watching Jiro, watching me as I watched. I felt his awareness of me, an ache like a knife-wound. He couldn't believe I was still here: the thing he hated most, still infesting his life, perverting his family. I was like some kind of curse on him, a living, breathing, punishment. . . . *A psion . . . Lazuli and Jiro . . . Daric . . . Jule . . . Did you sleep with my daughter too?* Wondering what he would never dare to ask me. "Get out of here," he said suddenly, thickly, jerking his head. He turned away, starting toward the house. And he was *trying not to think about it—about the thing he'd done. . . . Jule . . . Daric . . . psions. . . .*

"I have to see Daric," I said, too loudly, but he didn't notice. *What thing?* My body stood motionless, left running on autopilot while a part of my mind went after him, trying not to lose that sudden, secret thought. I followed it back through the hot-and-cold maze of his mind. *How many secrets like the one about Elnear did he have hidden inside him?*

He turned back suddenly, glaring at me. "Daric?" he said. "Why?" *He hated psions. But both his children were psions. And nobody really knew why.*

"About the trouble he's in," I said. "About how to get himself out of it." Distracting him as I probed deeper, getting closer, until I could almost feel it—*He didn't know Daric's secret. But I was sure now that somewhere inside him lived the reason for it. . . .*

"Not until you tell me everything." The same mangled rush of emotions that had hit him when he saw Jiro come home hit him again, twice as hard, *worry, fear, anger*—even something he might have called *love,* but I wouldn't have . . . for Daric, *who was perfectly normal, in spite of everything, and yet gave him nothing but grief. . . .*

"No, sir." I shook my head. "I can't do that. Ask your Security Chief. He'll explain it to you." In spite of everything, I could almost feel sorry for him. . . . *In spite of everything . . . everything that had been done to make them something more. . . .*

He opened his mouth to tell me to go to hell—broke off, seeing something in my eyes that made him afraid.

"If you want to keep Daric alive, you'll let me see him now. No conditions," I said, hitting him in the face with the words, blinding his thoughts.

He stared at me a second longer, his mind leaping and dropping between levels, and fears. "All right," he murmured. "See him, then. And then get out." He turned his back on me and went into the house.

And then I saw the answer; I knew what he'd done.

I got back into the mod again like a sleepwalker, and it took me to Daric.

"Daric!" I called, at the sealed entrance of his house. He was inside, I could feel him in there. I knew he had to be watching, listening through his house system. But there was no answer. "Come on, talk to me!" This was one thing I hadn't counted on—that he would refuse to see me. "You want to save your life—?" Still no answer. I looked around. The house was like no building I'd seen before, here on the estates, or anywhere. It was made of untreated wood, the lines of it stark and clean. There were no windows looking out anywhere, no other entrance but this one. My mind had him pinpointed behind that barrier; I slipped in through his useless defenses, and thought, (Do you want to know why you're a freak like me—like your sister?)

This time the door opened.

I went inside, down a long empty hallway of polished golden wood. At its end was a rectangular courtyard, open to the sky, dazzled with light. The center of the courtyard was a sort of garden; small, precise green-needled shrubs were set in a sea of sand and smooth black stones. The sand had been raked into lines like the ripples on a sea; every black stone had been set exactly where it was to create a calculated effect. It reminded me of standing on the Monument. . . . For just a minute standing here seemed as unreal as the memory of standing there suddenly did.

"That was very clever." Daric's voice came ahead of him out of the shadows. He pushed aside a door/wall and came into the courtyard, wearing a long, patterned black robe that seemed to suit a place like this, and an expression that didn't. The mocking arrogance was a false face, but it was all he could find to cover the naked *fear, curiosity, anger, resentment* inside him as he saw me. He looked pale and sick. "That was a lie, wasn't it? What you put into my head, about knowing why I'm a psion? You just said that to make me let you in, didn't you?"

"No," I said, "it was true." I didn't say anything more.

"Well? Are you going to tell me?"

"That depends on how good a listener you are."

He bent his head, the twisted smile spreading wider across his face. "Ah. So you've finally decided what you want from me. I knew you would." *Blackmail, for keeping his secret.*

"Yeah." I nodded. "You might say that."

"Sit down." He pointed toward the low wooden benches waiting at the center of the courtyard. The mindless gesture made me think of some vip inviting the opposition to open a round of negotiations. I realized that was what he was doing, whether he knew it or not. He sat down first, waiting.

I stepped out into the sunlight, blinking for a second until my eyes adjusted. I sat down, wary, but no warier than he was, this time.

"How much do you want?" he asked.

"It's not that easy," I said. "Have you talked to Braedee lately?"

His frown was all the answer I needed; and all I got. He knew why I was still on Earth. He knew that the human bomb had been meant for him. He wasn't sure whether he cared. . . . I probed deeper into his mind, until I found the solid, stubborn core of him that wanted to survive at any cost; that had kept him alive, living with his secret all these years.

"I found out who wants to kill you," I said.

He sat watching me, not saying anything, with his hands clenched quietly at his sides, tightening and tightening. I felt the pain growing like a flower inside him as his nails dug into his palms. I'd never noticed how long his nails were, how sharp.

"It's the Lack Market," I said.

"The Lack Market?" he murmured finally, with more disbelief than anything.

"They think you're two-timing them."

He still looked blank. He kept the two sides of his life so separate in his mind that he couldn't even imagine why.

"It's about drugs." I felt him start. "They say you made some promises to them, about doing them some favors in return for getting all you can use. They feel you haven't been keeping the promises."

"Who says so?" he asked, stalling.

"The Governor."

"You spoke to him?" His incredulity got a lot louder. "How?"

"Friends in the wrong places."

He sat a minute longer trying to decide if I was telling the truth. "They really want to kill me," he said at last. "Why?"

"Deregulation. They don't like it that you're working so hard for it. They don't like you playing on Stryger's side."

He frowned. "I explained that to them; that I couldn't go against my family's interests, or the combine's. It's too important, the potential profit gain—"

"Is their loss," I said. "They're real concerned about that."

"Oh, for God's sake—" He looked away, searching for something calm to rest his eyes on, focusing on waves of sand, black stones. "This is absurd. Some consortium of social deviants actually expects me to put them ahead of Centauri—and if I don't they threaten to kill me?" His body jerked with exasperation.

"They will kill you. They've already tried." I made him look at me. "The human bomb was just the first one. Who the hell do you think you've been playing with, Daric?" He stared at me, as the reality of what was happening to him finally began to sink in. "You think this was all some game to them, like it's been to you? They've even threatened to hit Stryger."

He flinched as my voice got loud; that wasn't supposed to happen here. None of this was supposed to be happening, here, in his life. . . . He said sullenly, "Why don't you just let them do it, then? It would get you everything you really want, wouldn't it?"

I opened my mouth, shut it again. Because there wasn't any point in asking him if he thought I wanted two more dead men on my conscience right now; in telling him that what Elnear wanted mattered to me, was important to me. I only said, "If deregulation passes, they'll kill me too."

He heard it, but it didn't seem to mean anything to him. "Tell Braedee," he said distractedly. "He'll protect me until the vote is over. . . ."

"I already told him. He's already trying. But they won't stop, not until you're dead. It's a matter of—business with them. You understand about business . . . ?" I felt my mouth try to twist into a smile. "Even Braedee knows that much about the other side. He knows that if you want to keep breathing it'll take a total identity wipe—there won't be a Gentleman Daric taMing any more. No board member, no Assembly member. You're a null set, dead or alive . . . if deregulation passes."

He was as gray as a cadaver now. "Only if it passes—?" he said weakly. I nodded. "But it's going to pass. . . ." He looked out at the still, rippling sea of black-and-whiteness around him, clutching his knees with his hands. "I can't stop it."

"You're going to try," I said. He looked back at me. "You're going to help me do it, if you want to stay alive."

"How?" There was no sullenness, no sneer on his face now. No questions about what it would mean to Centauri or his father. The survivor was in control, looking out at me through clear eyes.

"I want to show Stryger for a freakhater in front of the Assembly. I want you to tell him you can get me for him to do . . . you know what I mean." I looked away; forced myself to look at him again. "I want to make a full-sensory tape of what he does to psions, with Argentyne's equipment, then feed it through the system in the Assembly Hall before the vote, so that everybody in that room knows what he is. Is he going to be there?"

Daric nodded, picturing Stryger's final address to the members. His own mind was still caught in the middle of taking it all in.

"Good." I wiped my mouth with the back of my hand, feeling sweat on my upper lip; feeling trapped in this silent rectangle of sunlight, inside the shadowed symmetry of its perfect walls.

"Let me make certain I understand this. . . ." Daric muttered, his hands twitching in his lap like poisoned mice. "We humiliate Stryger in public, and that will weaken his support?"

"More or less," I said.

"The vote will be close; that might be enough.   . And the Council slot—" He broke off, as the full weight of the betrayal and the likely repercussions began to come down on him. "If this works, he'll lose it; Elnear will take it." He looked up at me again, wavering, as the two sides of him fought over his survival.

I had to be sure I had him. "You want to know the truth about what you are?" I asked.

His hands tightened. For once his mouth didn't get the best of him; he only said, "Tell me." And then, before I could, "It was Triple Gee, wasn't it? The marriage, somehow they managed to use that woman—" he meant his mother—"to hide defective genes. . . ." It was what his father had always hinted at, wanted everyone to believe.

I shook my head. "Your mother had nothing to do with it. Every gene in your body and Jule's was laid out like a streetmap before you were born; you really think nobody would have noticed? Your father did it."

He stared at me, his mind floundering.

"It was Charon," I said again, before he had the chance to call me a liar. "He planned it, he had the extra genes planted on purpose. Nobody else knew."

"That's insane," he whispered. "Why would he want to ruin the family line—?"

"He didn't think he was ruining it. He thought he was improving it. He wanted to give the taMings an edge—he wanted mindreaders nobody would suspect, or detect. To help you keep one up on the competition, outside Centauri and inside it."

He looked down at his hands, his body, as if he was seeing them for the first time. "But it didn't work . . . ?"

"Not the way he expected. He didn't really understand: it's like trying to make somebody a holo artist—and maybe you wind up with a musician instead, or a dancer." Jule had almost been what he'd wanted. She was an empath, she felt emotions, and projected her own—but she couldn't read a formed thought, and without any training she couldn't control what emotions she read, or when she projected. She could teleport too; that was easier to control, but it was only an extra embarrassment to her family. She'd been a setback to Charon, but still he'd tried again, one more time—

Daric's eyes moved, sliding away as I tried to make him look at me again. "Then why did they kill her—?" *Centauri. His mother.* He quivered.

"Maybe it really was an accident. Daric—she didn't die till you were old enough to remember it, and they all thought you were normal." He looked at me again, finally, a little sanity coming back into his eyes. "How did you keep them from finding out—" I asked, "all the while you were growing up?" I wondered again how he'd ever managed to keep a secret like that, when Jule couldn't.

"Jule . . . Jule hid it." He chewed his lip.

"But she was only a little girl," I said.

He nodded. "But she already knew that there was something wrong with her, that it made people hate her. She protected me, covered for me, taught me to hide what I could do. . . ." She'd tried to save him from the pain she felt, the pain that she couldn't stand to feel happening inside him too. "That's why I hated her so much." The pressure, the constant fear, the suffering that Jule felt and didn't know how to hide; he'd blamed her for all that. "I didn't know what else to do. . . . She was the only one I could trust, the only one who would forgive me. So I always hurt her. But no matter how much I hurt her, or she wanted to hurt me, she never gave away my secret. . . ." In the end, he'd even hated her for that. He shook his head, blinking too much.

He looked up at me again with bleak eyes, both of us realizing that it was too late to change anything at all; and that he'd never forgive me for letting him know the truth. But now his betrayal of his father and Centauri only seemed like justice. His mind went back over everything I'd said about the setup again, step by step. "Does Argentyne know about this . . . this perversion of her equipment?"

I nodded.

"She's agreed?"

"Yeah."

"Elnear said you were staying at Purgatory. . . ." He gave me a look that carried feeling as thick and dark as blood.

"That's right." I met it, lifting my chin a little.

"And you want me to tell Stryger he can have you?" he said. The pupils of his eyes opened wide.

My jaw tightened until it hurt. "Make it convincing. It's got to happen before the Assembly meets to vote."

"And that's all I have to do?" His eyes flickered away, following his thoughts.

"Probably."

"That won't be any problem," he murmured. I watched the knife-twisting smile come out of hiding. "In fact," he looked back at me, "it sounds like fun."

31

I SAW ELNEAR'S HOUSE falling away below me, across the open fields, as the mod rose and I left Daric behind. I had to fight the urge to turn back—to stand in the stone-walled courtyard again, to walk through those halls that smelled like another age . . . to touch a table covered with stars that shone in the firelight. To talk to Elnear, tell her what I had to do—

I told myself she wouldn't be there . . . I told myself the truth: that if she knew, she'd try to stop me. Because she wouldn't understand; because she wouldn't want to see me get hurt. The less she knew about it, the better. And the less I thought about the things, and the people, I'd shared that house with, the better off I'd be now.

When I got back to Purgatory, I found Argentyne in her dressing room, putting on her night face. She turned around in her seat, one side of her face silver, and one side reflecting light like a mirror. I squinted.

"Is Jiro okay?" she asked. "What did Charon do?"

"He's okay." I nodded. "Too much and not enough. . . . I saw Daric. It's set. He'll do what I need him to."

She didn't say anything, seeing Daric in her mind with a kind of helpless hunger.

"He says it sounds like fun."

A wave of sickness went through her. Her mouth pinched, guilt shutting her up when resentment made her want to call me a bastard. Instead she pulled her hair forward too hard, braiding it between her fingers, and said, "We've been talking this over—" meaning the symb, "about how you want to make something the Assembly's really going to live." She shook her head, glittering, the look in her eyes now telling me she was enjoying making my life harder too. "Nobody's sure that's going to work at the other end . . . if the systems are even compatible. . . ."

"The Net's the Net," I said, feeling my sudden frustration start to back up inside me. "All the systems in it work the same way."

"But they don't all use the same kind of specialty programming." She hit me with the obvious. "What the Assembly uses is basically a comm net, not a sensory net; it may not even be able to read the kind of message you want to send through it. Maybe you can make them watch a threedy of Stryger, but you probably can't make them live it. . . . What if it won't work?"

I swore. "It's got to work. . . . How can I find out? Can you test it?"

She made a noise that wasn't really a laugh. "You think we have access to the Assembly floor—?"

"Daric does," I said. "Daric can help me find out for sure."

"And what if it really doesn't work?"

"Then Daric will help me fix it." I went out of her dressing room, leaving her there to wonder, and climbed the stairs to the upper level. It seemed to take forever. I lay down across her bed, smelling the faint smell of spices and herbs that was her perfume as I shut my eyes; thinking that if I could just grab a few hours of sleep while she was downstairs in the club, then maybe I wouldn't feel like this any more, like somebody was stretching my sanity on the rack. . . .

When I woke up again, the light hardly seemed to have changed. I checked my databand, looking for the time—looked at it again and again, trying not to believe that I'd actually slept nearly a whole day. I felt worse than before. But I forced myself to get up off the bed, and stuck a fresh drug patch behind my ear. There were only half a dozen left.

I stumbled downstairs. Argentyne, Aspen, and Raya were sitting at a table out front, watching the air dancers drift through a freeform routine inside their sphere. Aspen and Raya were making an eerie, chiming music for the show, rubbing wet fingers around the rims of their drink glasses.

"Why didn't you wake me up?" I said, sounding more like I felt than I wanted to.

Argentyne looked up at me, startled. She took the camph out of her mouth. "I tried," she said. "You wouldn't."

She actually meant it. I glanced away, rubbing my neck. "Sorry," I muttered.

She shrugged. "No problem. . . . Daric called. So did Braedee."

I looked up. "What did they want?"

Trying to sound indifferent, she said, "Daric's at the Assembly. He says Stryger wants to do it."

I swallowed the sudden hard lump in my throat, and nodded. "When?"

"The night before the Assembly votes."

Two days. The buzzing in my head was so loud all of a sudden that I could hardly hear.

"I told Daric that you need him to help check out the systems compatability. He's probably still there now, if you want to go up—"

"I can't." I touched the jack on the back of my head. "It's too risky. He'd better come here."

She stiffened, but she didn't say anything.

"What about Braedee? What did he want?"

"He didn't say."

I frowned, and went to use the phone.

Daric was still in his office. He smiled when he saw me on his screen. "Did Argentyne tell you? It's all set. Two days. I told Stryger you planned to leave Earth right after the vote." He looked like he could hardly wait.

"It's not quite set," I said. "Not unless I'm sure the Assembly's really going to eat it all. I need you down here tonight to check things for me."

"At the club—?" His shoulders tightened. "Of course . . . I'll leave immediately." The screen went blank.

I stood there a minute, not sure whether to be surprised or worried. Then I called Braedee. I got a recording. That didn't make me feel any better. I called Mikah instead. He came onscreen, alive and half smiling. "Who's trying to kill you this time?" he said. I couldn't tell for sure whether that was a joke.

"Sojourner Stryger."

Now he couldn't tell. I explained everything to him, now that I was as sure as I could be that it would really happen. His smile disappeared while he listened. "You're out of your fucking mind," he said finally. "Cat, it's the drug talking. You're not indestructible. He will kill you."

"Not if you're there to back me up—"

"Uh-huh," he murmured. He hesitated, looking down, considering the possibilities. "That's different. I'll clear my calendar." He looked up at me again. "Call me when you got the details."

I nodded, fingering the patch behind my ear. "Mikah—"

"Yeah?"

"Don't get me any more topalase. No matter what I say."

"Right." He made the truth-swearing sign, his hand clenching around his closed fist, before he cut contact.

I left the phone, starting back along the hallway into the club.

Two Centauri Corpses stepped into the hall in front of me, blocking my path.

My first instinct was to turn and run; but they were ready for that. I wouldn't get two meters before they stunned me. I stopped where I was, instead. "Braedee—?" I called.

"Braedee wants you," one of the Corpses said.

There was only one reason why he'd want me picked up now: the Centauri board wouldn't cooperate. They wanted Stryger and deregulation more than they wanted Daric alive. "I'm not talking to you," I said to the Corpse. "Braedee—I'll bet tens you're monitoring this pickup. Call them off—or Charon hears everything."

The phone I'd just left began to beep. I went back to it and thumbed on the privacy screen. Braedee's face filled in on the monitor in front of me. "Leave me alone," I said, "or Charon hears about the human bomb." He'd lost his check on me, but I still had mine on him.

He stared at my image on his screen for a long minute. "All right."

I frowned. "That's too easy."

He smiled faintly. "I can leave you alone. But that doesn't mean someone else won't be watching over Stryger. Centauri is not the only combine interested in his continued well-being. I have no control over that."

"Damn it, Braedee—" I broke off, my hands spasming on the edges of the monitor. "You know what he is! You really think letting him win is going to be in Centauri's best interests?"

"I'm in no position to judge that," he said. "I simply follow orders."

"Sure you do." I looked away from his face, because I couldn't think when I looked into those eyes. "Listen. . . ." I said finally. "And you better listen good, damn you. I set it up with the Market to leave Daric alone until after the vote, because I need him. If deregulation fails, he lives; if it passes, he doesn't. But to get them to deal I had to make them believe Stryger's a threat to them. They threatened to kill him too, if deregulation passes."

He stared at me; kept staring, for a long time. But he didn't say anything.

I cancelled the connection and shut off the security screen. When I turned around, the hall was empty.

I went back into the club. Argentyne was sitting at the table alone now. Even the air dancers had gone away. "What did those Corpses want?" she asked.

"Nothing." I looked toward the door, still frowning. "Daric will be here soon."

I watched her sit there, motionless, while half a dozen different impulses burned themselves out inside her. "Oh, what the hell. . . ." she murmured. She sank back into the cushions, pushing at her hair.

I felt like my stomach was full of worms. "Argentyne. . . ."

"It's all right." She looked up at me, resigned. "It is my own fault."

I shrugged, and sat down across from her. "I'm sorry I took up your bed all day, anyway."

She laughed. "Don't lose sleep over it. I've got half a dozen others."

It took a minute before the meaning behind the words sank in. "The symb—?" I realized that I almost never saw any of them alone. They were always in twos and threes, always with each other, talking, touching.

"Yeah." She smiled now, half fond, half amused. "We all sleep together. When you get that tangled up in each others' heads, it just seems natural to get as close as you can. It's kind of like family." Her smile twitched. " 'Vice is nice, but incest is best.' "

"Where did that leave Daric?" I asked. "Or was he only in it for the pain?"

She stopped smiling; but it wasn't anger this time. "Everybody takes their serious lovers on the outside. It would get too intense otherwise. This way it stays more casual . . . maybe it'll hold together longer. . . ." She glanced down at her hands, like she was holding a bubble in her palms; she looked up again at me. "Daric is—was like nobody else I ever had. The way he touched me . . . he could touch me in impossible places. . . ." Her eyes changed; I felt her realizing for the first time why—how—he was able to do that to her. "He was so good. . . ." She pushed up from the table, looking toward the door. "I'll be in back with the others. We'll be ready with the equipment when he gets here."

I sat and waited alone for Daric, rubbing my wet fingertip around and around the lip of a half-empty glass until I could make it sing.

He came into the club at last, walking straight across the room toward me. He stopped in front of the table; his frustration showed on his face as he saw that Argentyne wasn't there.

"The Centauri board's against what we want to do to Stryger," I said, trying to get his mind off her. He frowned. He didn't know that; they'd met without him. I wondered which way Charon had voted, or if it really mattered. "I've got Braedee on hold, but he says Stryger's other backers will be watching him closer. I don't know if Braedee can control that, or not. Is that going to be a problem—?"

He shook his head, his mouth thinning. I felt the sullen betrayal smoldering in his brain. "No," he said softly. "Stryger has his own ways, and so do I . . . I assume the Governor will allow me to use them in his interest. Stryger will keep his appointment with you." I looked away. "What are you waiting for?" he asked. "Let's check the system. We want to make sure it's all perfect—" When I looked back at him, he was smiling.

I led the way into the back of the club, feeling the strangeness he felt as he followed me through this place he knew so well. All the players were there, waiting for us. Argentyne stood in the middle of them like someone wearing a human shield; she was blinking too much. Daric stopped dead as he saw her. He hadn't really believed she'd be here, meeting him face to face. I felt the air come alive between them with the static of their tension. All they felt was the silence—both of them wanting and hating this, the closeness without contact, the contact without closeness.

Argentyne looked down first, away from the sight of him. He'd never looked better to her—taller, handsomer. . . . "Hullo, Daric," she said.

"Argentyne," he muttered; broke off, when he couldn't think of what to say next.

"Here's the box." She held something out to him in the palm of her hand.

He crossed the room, took it from her; I felt the electricity as they touched. He settled the finger-sized box in the palm of his left hand, closed his own fingers over it like he was going to crush it. But his hand was more than a hand—augmented, like Elnear's, like his father's. "Activate it," he said.

She called on the symb. Daric's face got vague as something else took over inside his brain, checking, matching, reading out. After a few seconds his expression started to come back . . . he frowned. He swore with disbelief. "You were right." He glanced at Argentyne, his face going pale. He'd checked the symb with his own bioware, and it didn't match.

"Can the Assembly system be altered so it works?" I asked.

He laughed, still frowning. "Of course it could. It's simple enough. You'd only have to open up the spectrum-width the Assembly floor accepts. But you'd have to break into the Federation's security first. I guarantee you that you will grow old and die before you make that happen."

Argentyne took the box back from him, stood looking at it, holding it in her cupped hands. "He could still make a threedy. It would still show up Stryger. You could give it to the Indy, they'd run it—"

"Stryger could say it was altered, faked. A smear." I shook my head. "Nobody would believe it."

"He's right." Daric pulled at the high collar of his coat, sweating. "Stryger isn't where he is because his aura's been easy to tarnish." He started to pace. "Oh God . . . what am I going to do? They're going to kill me, Argentyne!"

Argentyne's face filled with helplessness as she watched him. She raised her hands, raising the symb box to plug it into its hidden socket again, somewhere in the back of her head.

"Wait." I held out my hand. She gave me the box, looking uncertain. "Just for a little while," I said, "that's all we need." I jerked my head at Daric. "There's still something we can try. But we have to do it without any interruptions."

She nodded, and didn't ask the questions in her mind. The other players followed her out of the room, glancing back at us as they left. Daric watched her go, watched me stay, like he was paralyzed.

(Daric,) I thought, loud, to get his attention. He spasmed, focused on me. "Can you access the Federation system from here? Or do you need some kind of special port?"

He touched his head, irritated and confused. "I can access directly through my bandphone, from anywhere on the planet. Why?"

"We're going to take a trip together into their system. And you're going to change it."

He looked at me like I'd gone insane. "I told you, there isn't any way—"

(There is for us.)

He jerked again, shuddered, as it reminded him what we had in common. "But that's impossible . . . isn't it?"

I shook my head. "I know how to get in. If you open the window, it'll be easy enough. But I have to take you with me, because I can't change anything once I get inside. You show me what I need to find, and when I find it, you'll make it change."

He shook his head, trying to imagine what I was actually telling him. "You mean . . . any psion could do that. . . . I could?"

"Not without me to find the way. I'm the eyes . . . you're the tool. We need each other." My mouth twisted into a grin that felt like one of his.

He glared at me, with his lips pressed together. "Their security—"

"—won't see us, hear us, or feel us if we're careful enough. We're outside the spectrum."

"This is incredible. . . ." he murmured. "You're really serious. How do you know all this?"

"That doesn't matter. And once we've done it, you'd better forget you ever knew it, if you want to go on passing for human."

His frown came back. He sat on a couch, twitching. "How do we do it?"

I handed him the box and sat down across from him, hoping I knew as much as I thought I did; thinking about Deadeye. "I'm going to link with you—make telepathic contact. You're going to open your access to the Assembly system. I'm going to follow it in, and take you with me."

He licked his lips. "How long does it take?"

"Not long, if it works." I shut my eyes, shutting out the sight of his face as I moved in on his mind. I kept the contact as gentle as I could, but still the fear inside him exploded, fragmenting his concentration. (Daric!) I thought. (Do this or you're dead.) I felt everything pull back together, as the survivor reintegrated and focused on his own need. Images of his father, shot through with memories, filled him/me like gall. "All right," he said bitterly. "I can stand it if you can."

(Don't talk. Just think. I'll hear you.)

(Oh, God,) he thought.

(Open the access.)

He called on his access to the Assembly floor. A rush of particle code lit up a section of his bioware with party lights; data began reforming itself into something his conscious mind could read.

(Think about how the system needs to be altered, and where.)

He did what I asked, checking and comparing the symb's system with his own, spelling it out for me until I knew what I had to look for. (Now relax and hold on; you're going for a ride.)

The open window lay right there inside his mind, waiting. Compared to what I'd gone through with Deadeye, getting in this way was easy. I dragged Daric after me into the channel of white light. His ghost clung to me, riding my back, too terrified and dazzled to even think about letting go. The access conduit swept us at lightspeed into the hidden heart of the Federation, the invisible world that made the visible one possible. Entering its data core was like being sucked into the heart of a star, drawn in through denser and denser shells of pulsing energies. My head sang with the feedback of our passage: the layers of *light/noise/ vibration* seemed endless, filling my senses with the smell of burnt cinnamon. It was hard to remember that this blazing infinity was no more than a subatomic dance to prerecorded music, locked inside a telhassium crystal the size of my thumb. It was even harder to remember that I knew where I was going inside it, and what I wanted to do when I got there.

Before I'd finished the thought we were there, inside the nexus that fed the Assembly Hall; the end of the line. (We're there,) I said to Daric, and felt him open his eyes, or something like it.

(It's hot—) he thought, because that came closer to describing the indescribable than anything he could think of, sensing something all around him, but blind to it with every sense he had any understanding of. I began to search for the nerve center he'd described, that contained the code sequence we were hunting for. As I narrowed my focus things got clearer; I began to pick out forms within the form, the kinds of things Deadeye had taught me to recognize and forced me to learn the meaning of. Every other layer here was some kind of security program, penetrating the flesh of the data core like blood vessels. Uneasy subsystems nuzzled my brain, rippling through us like fish through water. My mind wanted to hold its breath every time one did, and I was glad that Daric couldn't see what I saw as I riffled the Assembly's files.

(Here it is,) I said at last. The sequence we had to open up lay waiting, sandwiched in between security traps, but clean and simple. I deepened my penetration into Daric's mind until I was contacting the brain centers he'd be using. I opened up to him, let him see for a second through my mind's eye. (Make it change—) I felt him respond with a kind of terrified eagerness; felt an energy I'd never been able to call up surge through the circuits of his/my mind and out of him/me, turning *black to white, yes to no, open to closed.*

A different sequence was pulsing under my eyes now . . . the right one, the one that would give us both what we wanted. (Look,) I thought, trying to let him see it himself.

(Get me out of here!) he screamed. I felt him start to panic as he got too much input; struggling to get free—In another minute he was going to trigger something in the system around us, and we'd be dead. I got us out of there as fast as I could.

I got myself out of his mind even faster. In less than a heartbeat we were staring at each other, slack-faced and glassy-eyed, across the empty distance of the room again.

"We did it?" he asked finally, having trouble with his mouth. "It's going to work?"

"Yeah." I nodded. "I think we did."

He got up, rubber-kneed. "Incredible," he mumbled again, his mind still strobing with awe and energy. He held his head . . . suddenly feeling afraid that maybe he'd even enjoyed what he'd just done. "I need a drink. Or something." He turned to look back at me; his relief and revulsion were sweet-sour clogging my senses. And because he was afraid he'd liked it, he said, "God, I'd hate to be you. Why do you bother living?"

Argentyne came into the room; she'd been waiting for sounds of life. I could hear other sounds coming alive out front, the club beginning to fill up for the night. "Did you fix it—?" she asked, not sure which of us to look at. "What happened?" Not sure anything even had. She was doing everything she could think of to keep from looking at Daric too much.

"Don't ask." Daric put his hands up to his head again. But then he said, "Yes. I fixed it."

I frowned, but I didn't say anything. I watched her face soften with relief and self-doubt. "That's good," she said, meaning it. She hesitated, aching deep inside. "Are you staying . . . for the show?"

"Do you want me to?" he asked, moving closer. The urge went through him to do something to her with his mind, one of those things that had always made her want him to do more. . . . I touched his mind, just enough to let him know I was there; just enough to stop him.

She looked away, glancing at me. "I need the symb box." He gave it to her, and she went out again, her mind and body clenched.

Daric stood where he was for another minute, watching me. "I'm going out front for a drink," he said. His voice sounded strained. *(And staying for the show.)* Knowing that I could read the decision in his mind; and knowing that I would. "Are you coming?" Daring me to do anything about it.

"No," I said.

He let himself think about what he'd done to me a few nights ago . . . about what Stryger was going to do to me, two nights from now—

I watched his face flush. "See you in hell," he said. He went out of the room.

I sat where I was, trying not to follow his mind as he went away. But I couldn't stop myself, because he was still thinking about me—me on top of his stepmother; wondering how she'd liked it. Hoping his father was wondering too. Thinking about Argentyne naked. . . .

I cut contact, hating him, hating myself. But the images of naked flesh stayed in my mind. *Argentyne . . . Lazuli . . .* I wondered where Lazuli was right now, too far away to reach; remembering the soft sweetness of her body until it made my own body ache. I wondered whether she was thinking about me; whether she was hating me, and how much.

"Damn," I said, to nobody.

32

DARIC WAS THE LAST one to leave the club as Purgatory shut down for the night. I watched him go, making sure he didn't turn back or change his mind—the one thing that I could still do to hurt him.

Argentyne watched him go too, with the heavy ache still deep inside her. She looked at me once, from across the room, feeling my eyes on her. Her performance had looked good tonight, but inside it had been empty. Her mind had been somewhere else the whole time; her body felt like lead to her. She went backstage with the other players, her arms around two of them, burying her need in the security of the symb. After a while I heard them making music again in the back room, aimless and loose, unwinding.

I followed them down the hall, not knowing why, until I saw them. The players looked up at me as I came into the room, accepting the sight of me now, somehow more used to my being here than I was. Argentyne was the only one who felt any resentment.

"I thought maybe I should . . . practice." I touched the socket on my neck before she could say anything. "Like you said." My mind didn't want to face anything that took any effort, any emotion, but even working the symb was better than the emptiness I felt inside me right now.

Some of the players mumbled agreement, their curiosity reaching out to me. They were tired from the night but still riding their performance high, and nobody had interfaced with them even casually in a long while. Argentyne nodded, shrugged; I felt her own anticipation stir, almost against her will.

I crossed the room, calling my link on; the two-dimensional imagery of their artificial psi unfolded across my mind. For a while it was enough just to listen and watch, leaning against the wall, as Argentyne wove their separate colors of sound into lightsong, funneling her unhappiness into a search for something she'd never seen before. But the more

I felt the changing flow of images around them, the more it got into my blood, making me hungry to be a part of the pattern again, and not just a dead-end street.

"Come on," Argentyne said to me finally, impatiently, "feel something."

I eased into the dance, trying not to stumble and break its heart; concentrating on the way it made me feel—the *pleasure, envy, longing*—trying to focus the physical sensations the emotions caused in me. The sea of stimuli inside and outside of my head seemed to shimmer as the players reacted to a kind of input they'd never experienced before. Their disorientation faded fast; they liked it. Argentyne liked it.

I took what they gave back to me and sent it out again, filtering it this time so that the feedback stayed under control. I wanted to give them something, an extra dimension to move in, a part of myself, in return for what they were giving me. And hovering around the pattern of their energy I found something that only happened inside Argentyne: something that was a part of the vision filling her as she controlled the symb, something more real to her than reality—and yet always missing, when they played, because it was too intangible to express through the crude sensory net of the symb. I felt the ache of her frustration, always there too, because her act of creation could never be complete. . . .

I took the fragile phantom that hovered in her mind and used my psi to give it form. Then I fed it into the circuits, setting it free . . . feeling her rush of pleasure warm me like the sun's heat as her vision suddenly became perfect. She looked toward me, the wonder alive on her face. And suddenly I felt whole, a part of something more, for the first time in longer than I wanted to remember.

It was nothing like a joining . . . because a joining was like nothing else. It was a different kind of give and take, a different kind of sharing than I'd ever known; one that belonged totally to the human side of me. Holding together my concentration in the middle of such dense input was hard to do; but staying with the flow made it worth the effort. It got easier the longer we played, until I felt like I'd never felt this good and been in my right mind. . . .

And then some lousy left-out part of my brain remembered why I was wearing an illegal jack, and what I was really here for. And the pleasure went out of everything, like blight rotting a flower. I shut down my access, feeling the lines of contact wither and die.

Argentyne and the players followed me, dropping out of symbiosis, shutting down one by one until I was alone in the middle of their silent curiosity again.

"Why did you stop?" Argentyne asked.

"I've had enough," I said.

"It was really good, really something new—" There was frustration in her voice that had nothing to do with me. "It'll get better . . . work with us some more. Open up, you didn't get far enough—"

I shook my head.

"Come on, Cat," somebody else said. "Lose yourself."

"Come cloud-walking—"

"Yeah, come on, lose yourself."

"It feels better than anything—"

"I'm not doing this because it feels good! Just leave me the fuck alone." I went out of the room, away from their questions and their sudden embarrassment.

I went out the back way into the alley behind the club. I stopped when I got outside, sagged against the building wall; letting it hold me up because suddenly my legs didn't want to any more. *Tomorrow. Tomorrow night it would be me and Stryger.* . . . Something howled inside my brain, hungry for it to happen; something that wasn't me. My hands started to tremble; but this time it didn't stop there. It crawled up my arms, spreading, until my whole body was shaking like I had a fever. I wrapped my arms across my chest, holding on until it passed.

The door opened and Argentyne came out, alone. She stood looking at me, her costume sparking like a live wire in the dim light. Finally she reached into her pocket and handed me a camph. I stuck it into my mouth; she put one into her own. It didn't help much, but it kept us from having to say anything for that much longer. I looked at my distorted reflection in the mirror she'd made of half her face, looked down again.

"I'm sorry," she said at last, staring at the ground.

I nodded without meaning it, my hands still knotted over the heavy folds of my jacket. My head hurt.

She leaned against the wall beside me, studying my face. "I know we get kind of caught up in the symb, inside our own world, sometimes. . . ."

I looked away, sucking on the camph. The small cone of light we stood inside of was artificial, fragile, unreal. The night was all around us, closing in, and I was the only one who could feel it. . . .

". . . I mean," she said, "when you discover a new dimension like that . . . you want to hold onto that, get deeper into it. You don't want to let go. You kind of forget everything else, you know?"

I didn't say anything, barely listening, waiting for her to go away. She didn't go away. "All my life," she said, "I've had this thing that happened inside me—" I looked back at her finally, feeling her need force me to. "When I hear somebody's name I feel a color. Sometimes hearing music makes me see a place I've never been . . . or remember things I haven't thought about since forever, and makes it seem like they happened yesterday. . . . And always, everything has a *mood*— colors do, the sea does, or a song. Not one that has anything to do with what the thing *is*, or what I'm doing with it . . . but a separate thing that's like its soul, speaking to me. I can always feel it, inside me. But no matter what I try to do, even with the symb, I can never make anybody else feel it. All my life, I've been trying to make other people feel it." She looked away at the night, and back. "And then you came here . . . and you can. You did. You made it real for me—" She caught hold of my jacket with her jewel-gloved fist. "You can't just *stop* like that. I know it's not what you were trying to do. I know it's not what you wanted, or what's important to you. But it made you feel good, I know it did. Maybe it's what you really need, too—" She had hold of me with both hands, now.

I took a step forward; pushed her up against the cold brick wall with my body. I held her there with my mouth covering hers, my hands against the sides of her face as I kissed her, lost in her silver hair.

She struggled for about half a second, mostly from surprise. And then her body went boneless against me, the way it had done once before. Her hands slid down my back, pulling me close until it hurt. Her mouth was wet and open over mine, and the truth about what we both really needed, right now, hit us head-on like a freighter.

And the next thing I remembered we were in her room, across her bed, not bothering to take off more than would let us reach each other, and she was ready and I was inside almost before I knew what was happening to me. And then I began to move inside her, and I knew, and she knew, rising to meet me until there was nothing else but sensation. She came, and I came with her, with a desperate urgency that had almost nothing to do with sharing each other's bodies.

I rolled off of her, lying motionless across the bed; feeling like I'd never move again. She lay silently beside me for a few minutes more, staring at the ceiling, not seeing it in the rainbowed half-light filtering in from the street outside. But then she pushed up on her elbow until she was looking down into my eyes, and she smiled. She held up her finger, kissed it, ran it along my cheek. And then, slowly, piece by piece, she began to take off my clothes. I let her, too tired to protest. When I lay there completely naked she slowly took off her own, until finally I could see the body I'd wanted to see, without ever quite realizing it, ever since that first night in Purgatory. I wasn't disappointed.

She leaned over me, covering my mouth with hers again.

"Argentyne . . . I can't," I murmured.

"Don't worry. . . ." She kissed me again, used her tongue. "It's all right." The kisses moved over my face, closing my eyes, circling down into my ear. Then on down along my throat, my chest. She rolled me onto my stomach and kneeled between my sprawled legs, while her fingers slid over every inch of my back, probing the hollows along my spine, soothing and urging. "You will—" she said softly, as they moved down and in between my thighs. She did things that no woman I'd been with before had ever done to me, and each one felt better than the last. I felt myself sliding into the warm, heavy rhythm of her own patient longing, felt myself begin to come alive again, felt her feeding me strength with every touch. "How did you get that tattoo?" she asked, her voice gently laughing as she massaged my buttock.

"I don't remember," I mumbled, and she laughed again and kissed it.

I rolled onto my back, letting her hands follow, letting them work, until finally I opened my eyes and looked down, hardly believing what I saw rising like a defiant finger. She smiled, pushing up on her knees, lowering herself onto me with a sigh. She leaned forward, her breasts warm against my chest as she found my mouth again. "I want to know how it feels to a man," she whispered, starting to move, slowly, on top of me. "Let me feel what you feel. . . ." And inside her there was no fear. She wasn't Lazuli, and her mind was as open to me as her body, reaching for me, for one more experience she'd never believed she'd live long enough to have.

I entered her mind, going deep as I felt her wanting more and more. I went deeper into her body too, let my fingers move over her silver skin, her breasts, her belly; letting her surround me with her warm secrets. And I let her feel everything, my hardness, her softness, every nerve-ending in my body coming on line, and all the while as I opened my mind to show her how I felt, she was feeling what a woman felt, feeding back into my brain, feeding my own pleasure with hers, doubling it and redoubling it. I felt her excitement climbing, centering, circling that place where our bodies were fused together and making my own need

hotter. For once every touch, every motion either of us made seemed
like exactly the right one. I wanted to make it go on and on, always
almost reaching the end but never ending . . . but she couldn't wait.
She came—I felt it trigger inside her, spreading through the nerve net of
her body like a shower of stars.

And back through the link into my own, until the lightning struck
me and I couldn't stop myself. I cried out, falling like a meteor, dizzy
and spinning, into the warm sea of our release.

But even as I felt myself fading, softening, growing dim and dead, I
felt the heat still pulsing somewhere inside me. She was still on top of
me, her head back, her eyes clouded and bright as she began to move
again, her body caressing what was left of me, her hands touching my
sweating skin and her own, like she was expecting the impossible to
happen one more time. I felt her arousal growing inside me, knew at
last how it felt to be able to be ready and willing all over again, and
again; to have a capacity for pleasure as deep and endless as a sea. . . .

I let her fill the utter emptiness inside me with the sensations she was
creating, playing our bodies like she played the symb; demanding, de-
pending on me to let her go on using my mind and body along with her
own to explore this thing she'd only dreamed about. I felt her pleasure
beginning to climb again, and her need and her wonder at being two
people in one, one mind with two bodies—so different and yet so much
the same that if they could only be this way forever. . . .

And I felt myself respond, incredibly, growing hard again with a need
so hot and sudden that it was more like pain. She felt my disbelief; I felt
her own, and laughed as we began again. This time we circled the center
of each other's pleasure without any urgency at all, letting every kind of
sensation pass in slow motion through the lines of contact between us as
we rose and rose, and fell again. . . .

This time she was satisfied and more than satisfied; and I was more
than grateful. She slid off of me, moving slowly and tenderly; kept
contact, body against body, as she lay next to me, with her arm still
across my chest. "God, it feels so good. . . ." she murmured. "Stay
inside me. . . ." But she was only asking for my mind inside her now—
to go on being two in one, as she drifted away into sleep, too heavy with
pleasure and release to say anything more.

I lay where I was, stupefied with sensation, wondering as it ebbed
away where I was even going to find the strength to keep breathing. I
thought about Lazuli, felt the hollow ache start inside me again as I
remembered how she'd wanted this too. She'd been too afraid of me to

take it this far, as close to a real joining as any human without psi could ever come. I wondered, if we'd had enough time, if I could have shown her. . . . But all the while I knew, in the parts of my mind that Argentyne couldn't reach and never would, that even if Lazuli and I had been two people in one body, we'd never have been two in one mind.

33

WHEN I WOKE UP again Argentyne was still sleeping, her arm still lying across me, as if neither of us had even moved during the rest of the night. It was halfway into the next afternoon, but I felt like I'd barely slept. Sleep was trying to pull me back down, and I wanted to let it. But it was the next day. When I remembered what day that was, I felt like I'd been jabbed with a prod, and I knew I wasn't going to sleep any more.

I slid out from under Argentyne's warm arm, kissed her face gently until she smiled, her eyelids flickering. She sighed and stretched. "Again . . ." she murmured. Her eyes closed again.

I pulled on my clothes and put on another drug patch and went downstairs. A couple of the players were in the kitchen; they watched me stumble in, glanced at the ceiling and made knowing faces. Midnight pushed a plate of food at me, and shoved a cup into my hand. "Eat," he said. "Better keep up your strength." He raised his eyebrows. I gave him a sick grin, trying to look grateful. I ate a couple of bites, almost gagging, and left the rest of it.

I went to the phone and called Daric, to make sure everything was set. And then I called Mikah, to make double sure.

When I'd finished talking I went back into the empty club and sat alone, not wanting anything more than that . . . except maybe to turn today into tomorrow. After a while Argentyne came into the room, wrapped in her bathrobe, and sat down beside me. I felt the sudden hot rush of feeling inside her as she looked at me, her memory flashing back to the night, struggling to remember *now,* going *back*— But when I met her eyes something else happened, and it made her look away suddenly. Face to face in the light of day, the memory of what we'd done last night became too real for her even to think about. She tried to say something; couldn't. Because she was afraid, after all . . . so afraid that she wouldn't admit even to herself what she was really afraid of.

I sat looking at her look away, not answering what she didn't say; afraid of the same thing, deep inside.

After a while she reached up behind her head, took out the symb box and handed it to me. "I guess you'll be needing this," she said. "Try not to carry it on you; it's kind of fragile. We're not performing tonight, so there's . . . I mean, you can use it all night . . ." She broke off, sickened.

I took it, with fingers that suddenly couldn't feel anything.

"When are you meeting Daric?" She watched herself fold her hands on the tabletop, trying to sound matter-of-fact.

I grimaced. "Not soon enough."

"Is there anything else you need, that we can do?" Still looking at her hands.

"Give me a place to come back to?"

She smiled a little. "Any time." She got up again when I didn't say anything more; kissed my forehead and walked away.

I stayed where I was, glad to be alone again, and hating every second of it. I didn't know why it was so hard to wait; so hard to think about tonight. I'd set it all up, covered my ass, made sure I had backup. I didn't even have to depend on a mechanical link if I needed help. I had my psi, in perfect working order. I was going to get roughed up a little; that was all. Nothing I couldn't handle. It was my game, I was calling the throws. But still my guts turned to water every time I thought about what was going to happen to me tonight. Maybe because I'd thought I'd never have to do this kind of thing to myself again.

The message beeper on my databand suddenly came alive, making me jump. I sat listening to it, trying to decide if I should answer it here or go to the public phone; half afraid of what I might hear from anybody who'd call me now. Finally I went to the phone in the hall.

The face I found waiting for me when I answered was so unexpected that for a second I couldn't even put a name to it. "Natan Isplanasky," the face said, as if he could tell that I didn't recognize him.

I didn't say anything, because I couldn't think of anything at all to say.

"Elnear told me about your . . . falling out with the taMings. She's concerned about you," he said, sounding concerned too.

I felt myself frown as I wondered if she'd told him all the details. I wondered what was really going on in his mind. "She told you to call?" I asked, not sure whether resentment or disbelief was stronger inside me.

"No," he said. "I called because I wanted you to know I haven't forgotten about what you said."

"About what?"

He looked surprised, or at least confused. "About Contract Labor."

"Oh." I looked down, laughed once. "That."

"Elnear told me you have your reasons. I still want to hear them."

I lifted my head again. "What's the point?" Suddenly I wanted to smash the screen. I clenched my fists until the feeling passed.

He didn't answer the question. "Will you come up and see me?"

I shook my head. "I can't."

"Can't?" he repeated, as if he thought I meant something else.

"I can't."

He hesitated, nodded. "What if I come there? Or meet you somewhere else? Whenever you say."

I stared at him. "You mean that?"

He nodded again.

"I can't." I looked away from his eyes. "There's something else I've got to do. And I don't know where I'll be after that."

"Something more important to you than this."

"Yeah," I said. I was starting to tremble again. I almost said the words to cut the connection; stopped. "Look, I'll call back if—when I can. As soon as I can."

He nodded. "Good. I'll be waiting."

"Tell Elnear . . . tell her I think it'll all work out." I cut him off. Then I leaned back against the wall, waiting for the shakes to leave me alone. When I felt in control enough to move again, I left Purgatory, not telling anybody I was going, and went uptown toward Daric's.

Daric's city place was sleek and faceless on the outside, a vip's sacred ground, the kind of place that probably had almost as much to hide as its owner did. I stood in the twilight in the mall garden for a long time, looking at it, getting the feel of it; trying to force myself to go up to its door. Mikah had promised he'd track me; but there was no trace of him. I had to believe he'd keep his word, just like I had to believe nothing would go wrong that I couldn't handle. I didn't believe either thing as I crossed the vanilla-scented lawns to Daric's door.

The door opened when I stepped up onto the polished terrace, answering the security clearance Daric had given me. Daric was waiting inside. He gestured me in with a nervous hand.

"What were you doing out there for so long, for God's sake?" he hissed, as the door solidified again behind us. "Everyone in the stack could have seen you by now."

"Nobody else was watching," I said. *Nobody else at all.* Even the security scanners didn't see me, as long as the codes told them not to. It was all very discreet. I looked around me in the dim light, my hands twisting inside my jacket pockets. The asceticism of his house on the taMing estates had turned so impersonal here that it was like standing in a clinic. "Stryger's not here."

"Of course not," Daric said, still irritable. "It's early. Come inside." He wanted to play host about as much as I wanted to play guest, but I followed him down the long ramp into the ceramic hollow of his living room. There was a round enameled table in the center of it, ringed with low seats inside a cylinder of sourceless light. He sat down; I sat down on the far side of the table, staring at him.

"How is Argentyne?" he asked, almost civilly.

"Satisfied," I answered, mostly to annoy him.

He frowned. He poured himself a drink from the liquor carafe on the table in front of him, and gulped it down.

"Why don't you drop the bleeding-inside crap?" I said. "She doesn't mean anything to you. Nobody does."

His head snapped up. The *pain anger jealousy* gnawing at his gut was real enough. *"You,"* he said, his finger quivering as it pointed me out, "are a nameless bastard. You are not fit to judge me. You will not sit there and tell me what I think or feel or want in my own house!"

I flinched as his fury scraped my raw nerves. I kept my eyes on the carafe and cups on the tray in front of him. The tray was moving, slowly, around the table. There was a kind of continental drift at work in the table's heart; my hands could feel it, a faint vibration under what looked like a solid surface, carrying everything invisibly toward me. I watched them come, hypnotized. "Plate tectonics," Daric murmured, and I laughed out loud before I could stop myself. My hands rattled on the tabletop. They reminded me of his hands, as if somehow his hands had gotten attached to my body.

Daric looked at me, under control again, his expression caught somewhere between curiosity and disgust.

"Fuck you, Gentleman Daric," I said.

"Have a drink," he offered, as the carafe reached me, and stopped.

I filled a cup and looked at it. Daric's tension level jumped as I picked it up. I glanced at him, watched him take another swallow from his own cup; felt him react to the kick of high-proof alcohol. There was nothing in the liquor that didn't belong there. He relaxed again, even though I hadn't drunk anything; he didn't care if I drank his liquor or not.

I took a sip, felt it numb the inside of my mouth, burn a track down my throat, deaden my aching stomach. It felt good. Right then drinking acid would have felt good. I drank some more.

And then I started to get dizzy. The room began to run and flow as I sat staring in disbelief. "It was safe . . . How . . . ?" I forced the words out; it seemed like the longest speech I'd ever made.

"The cup wasn't." Daric shrugged. He smiled. His face was melting. "It has to look good, you know, for Stryger. Trust me."

I didn't trust him. I fell face down onto the table.

When I came to again, I was somewhere else. There was a dirty fibroid floor pressing hard against the side of my face. I lifted my head, blinking. I had a headache. The light here was white and shadowless, not like the dim half-light of the room where Daric and I had been hiding from each other's hatred. It was a square box with one hard, ugly chair and a hard metal bedframe set on a storage base. One door, shut. No windows. I could hear a ventilator running somewhere: a wheezing scream that went on and on, that sounded like the machine was being killed by this place. For a minute I thought I was in Oldcity. And then I thought I was having a nightmare.

I wasn't alone in it. Daric was leaning against the door. And Stryger was standing beside him, hidden inside so much drab, ungodly clothing that I had to touch his mind to be sure I was really seeing him. "You see," Daric said, to one or the other of us, or both. "Here he is."

I tried to push myself up, fell back on my face again, because I couldn't make my hands work. My hands were locked in binders behind my back. I rolled onto my side, got up finally, using just my legs. As I staggered to my feet one foot jerked out from under me, and I almost fell again. One of my ankles was tied to the bedframe by a piece of rope. "You son of a bitch," I said to Daric, and the choking panic in my voice was real.

He smiled. The tiny shrug of his shoulders told me, *It has to look good.*

"Hello, Cat," Stryger murmured, his voice soft and almost warm, as if we were having a perfectly normal conversation, as if I wasn't standing here like this—like some kind of human sacrifice. He began to take off the shapeless, hooded coat that made him look twice his size. My own jacket was gone; so were my boots. All I had on was a tunic and jeans, and they weren't going to give me much protection. And then I remembered the symb box. I'd put it into my jacket; and my jacket wasn't in the room. I froze, trying to make my mind hold together while I called on the link, not letting myself think about what would happen if there was no answer. But the familiar grid of energy filled my inner sight like a streetmap. I followed it, found the symb box ready for me, locked in . . . Daric was wearing it. I forced myself to take a deep breath, and another. Then I sent what was left of my concentration out through the white noise of the ventilator and my own fear in one last sweep, searching for Mikah.

He was there. Somewhere outside, nearby, close enough. He'd tracked me here, wherever here was; as good as his word. I felt him jump as I goosed him with my relief. I fed him a flood of images about where I was and what was about to happen.

And then I broke contact, because I realized Stryger had gone on talking to me, and now he was waiting for me to answer.

He'd asked me to tell him why I thought God had allowed me to be born.

"What?" I said, because even knowing what he'd asked me, that was all the answer I could think of.

He repeated the question. "I'm very interested in your religious views," he said softly. "I've had to wait such a long time for this opportunity to talk to you about them." He was leaning on his staff, shining in the white light; as if he really had made half a lifetime's journey to reach this stinking rathole room, all to talk religion with me.

"Then why this—?" I asked, feeling the binders cut into my wrists, tightening more as I jerked my hands. I tried not to look at him like he was crazy.

He sighed. "Because it's necessary. Now, the question is, why are humans and Hydrans so similar that interspecies miscegenation can even occur? Why has God permitted our pure stock to become polluted with abnormal genes? Why were you born—a halfbreed, the degenerate spawn of an unnatural act? As a warning? As an example?" I felt him goading me; goading his own hatred.

"There isn't any God," I said. "If there was, you wouldn't exist." I glanced at Daric; he was backed into the corner by the door now, with fear-sweat shining on his face. Smiling. "None of us would."

Stryger moved his hands; the bottom end of his staff shot out, tangled in my legs. I fell down, hard, with no way to stop it. I lay there for a long minute, with the pain in my bruised legs throbbing up through my body, before I rolled over and pushed onto my knees again.

He was still standing quietly, leaning on his staff again as if it had been God's hand and not his own that had struck me down. He actually believed it had been God's hand.

I managed to get up, and backed away toward the bed. I sat down on it, sending a silent finger of thought into his brain while I did. I hadn't counted on the binders: I was going to need everything I had to keep from getting maimed.

"I realize you cannot be expected to behave like a civilized person," he said. The velvet on his voice was wearing away now; the naked fist was showing through. "But I think you can give me a better answer than that."

I made a face. "I don't know why I'm alive. I don't know why I'm a halfbreed. Maybe my mother was gang-raped by deadheads."

The staff flashed out at my head. I felt him move and ducked; but it came back at me before I could get my balance again and hit me from behind, knocking me off the bed. I landed on my face. I sat up again on the floor; got to my knees, and then my feet. It took longer this time, because it was harder to do. Blood was leaking out of my nose; my mouth felt like raw meat. I stared at the grid still shining and alive inside my eyes, made sure it was getting every detail of how much it hurt. (Why—?) I thought, because I couldn't catch my breath to ask him *why;* because I wondered what he'd do. (Why do you want to do this to me?)

"Filth!" he shrieked. The staff end hit the floor with a crack, and then it hit me across the chest, staggering me. I fell down again. "Never touch me with your filthy—" He broke off, swallowing the word, shuddering. And then, with what almost sounded like grief in his voice, he said, "I don't want to do this. . . ." And the worst part was that some part of him really didn't. I watched him come forward, a step at a time. He held out his hand to me, as if he really wanted to help me up. "But God has shown me that it is necessary. You have shown me yourself that you deserve punishment. Your very existence is a blasphemy. . . . The Hydran civilization was corrupt. They set themselves up to be in God's place; that was why their civilization fell. It fell from grace. Only full-blooded humans are God's children, recognizing their role as it was meant to be. Only Earth is pure."

I looked up at him, at his outstretched hand, at the white, pitiless light ringing him with aura . . . trying not to look at the staff. "That's a lot of shit."

The staff leaped up and clipped me under the chin, knocking me back into the metal base of the bed, sending me down with a headful of stars. I pushed my way up the side of the bedframe, fell onto the stinking mattress foam again, dazed and gasping. I hoped he hadn't broken my jaw. The welts rising on me felt as thick as my arm. I wondered how I could have missed his move on me that time so completely.

"We're not . . ." I mumbled, and spat, grateful that my mouth still worked, ". . . not the different ones. Hydrans were all over. . . . It's you. You're the mutants . . . misfits . . . defectives, failures . . . !" Blood dribbled down my chin.

"Damn you—" he whispered, as something tore like rotten cloth inside his brain. And then I saw, too late, what his most terrible fear was: The fear that I was right. In the vision he'd had so long ago, when that accident had left him clinically dead—the vision he'd believed had been sent to him by God—he'd dreamed that his mind had left his body. It had hovered over him, and then crossed the impossible threshold into the minds of the people working to save him. He'd heard them speak—known their thoughts, almost known their every secret, like God. And then they'd saved him, and pulled him back into his body where he belonged. And when he'd come to, he'd known that he'd never have that feeling of pure, godlike power again . . . because he wasn't a psion. And I felt the hunger for the Gift he could never have eating him alive, and his insane hatred of the ones who had it by birthright. *Oh God,* I thought, and wished I'd thought of something else.

"I think . . ." he murmured, staring down at me with mindless sorrow, "you will profit from this." The end of his staff caught me in the stomach, doubling me over, and then came down hard across the side of my face, smashing my ear.

I lay where I'd fallen face-down on the putrid foam, listening to myself moan; hoping that if I lay still he'd let me rest for a minute. More blood was running down my neck and into my eye. I couldn't wipe it off. I wished head wounds didn't bleed so damn much. I couldn't hear out of the ear he'd hit; it was full of blood. I wondered why I was having so much trouble reading him. That wasn't right. Maybe the symb box was taking up too much of my concentration. But it had to come first, or else the rest of this had no point at all. . . . It was getting harder all the time to remember what the point of anything was.

I sat up, my ears still ringing; let him hit me in the ribs and knock me off the bed again. He didn't even give me a chance to roll over this time before the staff whacked me in the balls. I folded up, retching, and he hit me across the kidneys. (Daric—!) I tried to form the thought, to reach his mind with it, couldn't. Too little control left, too much pain— the pain leaked out of me like blood and into their minds, until I heard Stryger screaming at me again, hitting me over and over to make me stop hurting out loud. "Daric!" I was sobbing now but I didn't care. "Daric—"

"Sojourner . . ." Daric said, his voice sounding hollow and far away. "Sojourner!" Louder, almost frightened, this time. He came toward us, inching into my line of sight; clamped his hand on Stryger's arm, pulling him around. "I—I want him for a moment . . ."

Stryger froze, stared at him; moved away from me like he was in a trance, letting Daric crouch down beside me. "Enough?" Daric whispered. I nodded, shutting my eyes.

"No . . ." he said hoarsely, "I don't think so." I opened my eyes. He rubbed a finger across my torn lips; it came away red. He put it into his mouth and sucked it, smiling. He straightened up again. "By the way— " His finger swam down toward my eyes again, and there was something else on its tip. "I think this belongs to you—?" I squinted. It was a drug patch. The one from behind my ear. He'd taken it off me after I'd passed out. My psi had been slowly going dead on me all this time.

He flicked the patch away. I swore, floundering, trying to get my legs under me, trying to see where it had gone. He kicked me in the stomach, collapsing me again, and left me there. (Mikah—!) I threw everything I had into the call, praying that now, now when I really needed it, my Gift would come back to me on its own. But it didn't. "Mikah—!" I screamed it, raw-voiced. And then Stryger brought his staff down on me again, and I just screamed.

I tried to kick him, tried to crawl away, but it was all useless. He used his staff on me like an artist, now that I was down and helpless . . . used it to cause the most pain in the most ways, the most places, hurting me everywhere but never doing enough damage at once to let me lose consciousness. Somewhere in the middle of it, the lines of the grid inside my head went out. And I realized my backup was gone, I was alone in this nameless place with the two people who hated me most; two people who wanted me dead more than anything else in the universe right now. And this thing had already gone too far, way beyond the plan. Stryger was going to kill me—and Daric would lick my bloody corpse, and nobody would ever know. . . .

There was nothing left to hold onto as the pain drove me under, drowning me in fear, drowning me in memory. . . . I was back on the streets again, seven or eight years old with an empty hole in my brain where my past should have been, hungry and cold. And a man who sometimes gave me handouts said, *Come on in.* I thought I knew the streets, knew the rules, knew what I was doing. I'd never heard bad talk about him. But up in his room he'd dropped his pants and told me what he wanted me to do to him. I said I didn't want to, and his face went from smiling and soft to ugly with rage faster than I could think. He pulled a knife, and with it pressed against my throat, he said, *Do it or I'll kill you.* And I did it, whimpering and sick, but thinking if I did it I could go. I'd never heard he'd killed anybody, if I did it he'd let me go. . . .

But he wouldn't let me go. I begged him, I tried to fight, but he cut me and ripped off my clothes. He pinned me down on the bed and started doing things to me. I told myself it was only some babyfucker getting his fix, it didn't mean anything as long as I was still alive when it was over. And the things got worse and worse, hurting me until I cried out; and when I did he started to beat me, shouting it was all my fault, like I'd made him do this—until I was hurt and bleeding everywhere, but still it was only pain and it couldn't go on forever. And then he rolled me onto my stomach and climbed on top of me. Naked and helpless under his weight, I screamed as a kind of pain I'd never known existed tore something apart in my insides. "Oh God, stop—!" I screamed and screamed for somebody to save me but there was nobody at all who heard my screams and cared.

And it wasn't stopping. My screams turned hoarse, my sobs became heaves of vomit; it went on and on, until all that was left was the truth . . . blind with pain, with the black pit opening up to swallow me, I knew at last that the river of wetness that rushed through me was all my blood, that I was never going to get out of this room, that oh God I was dying right here, it was over, over, right now going down, down, into the blackness. . . .

Noise exploded the room around me, exploded my living nightmare. And then there was silence, even though inside my head I was still screaming. The blows stopped coming; even though it didn't stop the pain. I opened the one eye that would still open, blinking in the naked whiteness, watching as reality unrolled like a threedy show in front of me: Stryger standing still, gaping at something, someone standing where the door had been, but wasn't any more. Daric sidling away along the wall like a spider, as Mikah stepped into the room.

Mikah stopped dead as he saw me. His eyes squinted, and his head moved slowly from side to side; but whatever happened on his face was hidden behind the faceshield of his armor. He raised his head again, looking at Stryger. "So," he muttered, the words thick with anger as he glanced at Daric and back at Stryger. "Two-timing me again, you lousy freak. . . ." With some part of my brain that was still half working, I realized that he was covering my ass, making it look good.

Stryger was still gaping, his eyes getting wider and wider with a disbelief that was so total he couldn't breathe. He looked like he was seeing the devil in human form, and maybe he thought he was. Maybe he was right. I started to laugh, or maybe cry.

Mikah moved forward, coming toward me.

Stryger shut his mouth as Mikah shoved him aside, making him stagger . . . as he realized Mikah was only human, and a witness to what he'd done here. He lifted his staff—

Mikah stunshot him without even turning back to look; Stryger collapsed like a broken leg. Mikah crouched down, his mailed fist opening, reaching out toward me.

"No . . . don' . . ." The words bubbled out of my mouth in a bloody froth; my body cringed away from his touch, my mind still full of shattered glass.

He pulled his hand back, raised his faceguard so I could see his face. "Cat," he said, "it's Mikah."

"Mikah . . . I didn' lie t' you. . . ."

"About what?" He looked confused.

"Gettin' free. . . ."

"Yeah. I know."

"Don' let 'em beat me no more."

"I won't," he said, and then, softly, "we're not on Cinder. Not for a long time, brother. . . ."

"I know. . . ." I mumbled, trying to raise my head. "Where—?"

"—are we? Off the Deep End." His deathshead grin came back for a second.

"Figures."

He half smiled, waiting while I caught up with reality. Then he pulled the red scarf out of the neck of his armor. Lifting my head, he wiped blood and drool off my face with the end of it.

"You hear' . . . ?" I squeezed the words out, not even sure he'd be able to understand them. "You hear' me . . . ?" Right then hope hurt me almost as much as my body did.

"Heard?" He shook his head. "I didn't hear a damn thing after you hit me with your psi that once. That's why I came. It was taking too long. I figured something went wrong—"

I began to cough; choking on disappointment. The pain in my chest and ribs hurt so bad when I coughed that it made me gag. He lifted me up so I could sit, held me there. I whimpered, every crawling millimeter of my body hating the agony of being upright; but not as much as it hated lying on my raw, bleeding face. His hand touched the binders on my wrists, and he grunted with disgust.

"Daric's—" I mumbled, trying to turn my head. "Get him to . . ."

But I felt the shock as something sparked out behind me, as Mikah cancelled the lock himself. The binders fell off my hands; my arms flopped forward. Mikah propped me up like a doll against the side of the bed, and cut the rope around my ankle. He turned to look at Daric. Daric stood pressed against the pitted wall, staring at Stryger's body, at us, back at Stryger. "What happened?" Mikah asked, asking me, but still looking at Daric. "What went wrong?"

"Him. Double-crossing bastard—" I said, still looking at Daric too, not able to stop. "Took my drugs. I couldn't . . ." My voice broke. "Scumsucker, you would've let him—"

"You want me to kill 'em both?" Mikah asked, getting slowly to his feet.

"No," Daric whined, going rubber-mouthed as he tried to make it sound reasonable. "I would have stopped him, Cat. Just a little longer . . ." He wiped his face on his sleeve. "Just a little—it had to look good . . . You saw how I could control him. He's not dead, is he dead—?" He looked at Stryger.

"Not yet," Mikah said. "But I'll take care of that right now." He turned, raising his hand.

"No—!" I gasped. "Jeezu, don'." Blood splattered as I shook my head.

He looked back at me. "Why the hell not?"

"Because . . . you'll make him . . . goddamn . . . martyr." I dragged myself up the side of the bed and collapsed on it. The pain of moving that far gave me the dry heaves. Mikah stood waiting until I could speak again. "You kill him now . . . he'll win in spite of . . . everything. Besides, I wan' him to live . . . Because it wouldn't hurt enough, this way."

His face twisted. He lowered his hand. "Just wanted to be sure."

"Of what?"

He gave me a strange look. "That it wasn't because you knew how he felt." He smiled for a second, showing me his teeth. "What about the Gentleman?" He jerked his head at Daric.

"I still need him . . . until tomorrow." I looked at Daric. "You know what you have to do. If you don't do it . . . I'll kill you myself." He nodded silently, licking his lips.

"Get it out of here," Mikah said to Daric, pointing at Stryger's body.

"How?" Daric asked. He looked like he was the one who'd been stunshot.

"Drag him."

"But . . . I have to tell him something, when he wakes up . . . ?" Daric looked at me again, his face as hollow as his voice. "He'll know that something—"

"Jus' tell him . . . he made my lover . . . real jealous." I laughed, and then swore, because even that hurt more than I could stand.

Daric stared at me, his face twisting. But he nodded, and stumbled across the room. He picked up the body by the armpits. I watched him go out through the ruined doorway like an undertaker, dragging Stryger behind him, cursing under his breath.

"That's something I never did before," Mikah said, when we couldn't hear them any more.

"Wha'?"

"Let somebody live when I should have killed him."

I grunted. "I did somethin' . . . I never done, too."

"What?"

"Peed in my pants."

He looked at me and almost laughed; didn't. I didn't, either. There was red in the wet stain on my jeans. "Come on," he said, "I better get you out of here." He started back to me.

"Wait . . . Mikah. Drug patch . . ." I put up a hand, touching the pulped mess that Stryger had made of my ear. "I need it." I tried to get up, couldn't. "It's here someplace." I looked up at him. "Help me. Can't think—"

"You can't think because that scumbag busted your goddamn skull,"

Mikah said, frowning. But he turned away, searching the floor until he found it. He stuck it behind my other ear.

"Be awright now," I said. I wiped my chin with a shaky hand. I got up off the bed, and fell on my face.

He let me fall, and then he picked me up again, holding me there, almost gently. "Junkie."

I nodded, pain-tears squeezing out of my eyes. I couldn't stand up by myself. Stryger's staff was still lying on the floor in front of me, covered with my blood. "Mikah . . ."

"Yeah?"

"Is it really over?"

He looked down at the staff. He kicked it across the room. "It's over. I'll take you home."

34

MIKAH TOOK ME to a clinic before he took me anywhere else; one where they didn't ask a lot of questions. It took them the rest of the night to put me back together. They wanted to make me stay; but it was morning, and I had things to do. They took one look at Mikah, and didn't argue. We went back to Purgatory.

Argentyne stopped dead in the middle of the hallway as she saw us come in. Her hands clutched the sleeves of her smock and she hugged herself silently, waiting while we came toward her. As we reached her, she called, "Aspen—!"

"S'all right." I shook my head, moving in slow motion because of all the tranks and painkillers. Her eyes didn't believe me, looking at my face.

"Took care of it already." Mikah nodded, as Aspen materialized behind her.

"Daric has the box," I said.

"Fuck the box." Her voice wasn't steady. "Did it work for you—?"

I nodded.

"Daric did everything he promised to do—?"

"Everything . . . and more," I said sourly. "You heard from him?"

She shook her head, still looking at me uncertainly, glancing at Mikah.

"I got to go up to the Assembly." I had to know that he was there, that Stryger would be there; that everything was set.

"You can't." Argentyne looked at me like I must still be in shock.

"The jack's gone." I touched my head. They'd taken it out at the clinic. Stryger had already scrambled it, along with my brains. "I wanna be there, to watch it happen."

"You and a few billion other people," she said. "They won't let anybody near the place who doesn't have a right to be there."

I swore. "I have a right—"

"Cat," Mikah said. "You thought about this: What's going to hit after Daric feeds that program through their system? You're messing with the Federation. You better keep your head down, boy. Catch it on the Indy."

I stood glaring at him, at her; until the combined weight of their common sense finally crushed me. "Yeah . . ." Suddenly I wasn't so sure that I really wanted to be there when the entire Assembly relived what had happened to me last night. "I guess I will."

"Rest a while," Argentyne said, putting her hand on my arm. "Nothing's even starting for hours."

"Yeah. I guess I will . . ."

"You get lamped for those head wounds?" Aspen asked me, running a professional's eye over my glued-up face. I shrugged, not sure if I didn't know, or just couldn't remember.

"He got the full course," Mikah said. "They know what they're doing at Soule's. They get a lot of trauma cases."

Aspen nodded. "You'll feel like you have a new body in a few days," he said to me, looking as pleased as if he'd fixed it up himself.

"But I'll still remember being in this one." I turned my back on him, feeling the bile rise up in my throat as I stumbled away down the hall.

The stairs to the upper level looked like they led to the moon. With one eye covered, I couldn't even tell where they started. Mikah helped me make it up them and settled me in Argentyne's room. I lay on her bed with my eyes shut, not moving . . . but underneath the haze of painkiller and sedatives, my body was still trembling, still waiting for the next blow to fall. Because the last three years of my life I'd been living a lie. Pretending I was a free citizen of the Human Federation, with a mind and a name and the right to feel some kind of pride. . . . But Stryger had torn away my illusions, the way some nameless pervert had torn away my clothes so long ago, and taught me that I was nothing but a victim in a room without exits.

I rolled onto my stomach, burying my face in the smothering darkness of the bedding as I heard Mikah start to leave, leaving me there alone. But as he reached the door he hesitated. I felt him look at me. And then he turned back, very quietly, and sat down in a chair instead. I raised my head and opened my good eye halfway to look at him sitting there, staring out the window. I reached out and touched his mind with my own; not so he knew it, but only so I did. And then, finally, I felt safe, and I slept.

He was still there when I woke up a few hours later. Argentyne was there too, calling my name, telling me that coverage was starting on the Net. I felt better than I had before I went to sleep, but on a scale of one to ten my body was still about minus-five.

I got up somehow and we went downstairs into the club. The other players were there, and a few people who worked for Purgatory, already waiting. I felt their morbid curiosity glance off me as I came into the room. Nobody wanted to look at my face for long. "Anybody need a headset?" The doorkeeper waved one at me as I passed. Wearing one would bring the visuals up closer, make it that much more real. . . . I shook my head.

A threedy image of the Federation Assembly Hall was already taking up the stage as I eased myself down onto the cushions beside a table. Shander Mandragora was drifting in and out of reality up front, keeping the audience hooked with flashbacks, replaying all the controversies, real and imaginary, that had led up to this; trying to hold audience interest in a vote that he thought they knew the outcome of already. He explained it all, to the billions of present and future viewers who would never really understand what it meant any more than he would. I watched the shifting scenes and faces flow by, feeling dizzy as the background circled behind him and I searched for someone I knew. The cams showed Elnear, waiting on the speaker's platform. She'd asked for permission as a Member to address the Assembly before the vote, and she'd gotten it. . . . And then Stryger had demanded the same right. He was there too, alive and clean and perfect. The two of them sat in their places like game pieces. But there was one more face I still needed to see.

"Daric," Argentyne said, lifting her hand as a slow scan of the Assembly's faces finally passed over him. He was there and gone again almost before I saw him. But he was there. I nodded and sank back into the bed of cushions again, letting my one eye unfocus. Argentyne pressed a mugful of something hot and harmless into my bandaged hands. I drank it down.

Finally the endless shuffling and shrugging and switching accesses stopped, as the Assembly's Chosen Speaker called the delegates into the closed system for the session. I pushed myself up again as he announced the guest speakers, explaining their requests one more time, as if they actually had some meaning. He called Elnear forward first to the floating podium. Her speech was mainly what she'd said in the open debate —because there was nothing else to say; because that should have been enough. I could hear the intensity in her voice that I couldn't feel inside her, as she drove against the impossible inertia of too many preset minds. . . . And then she was finished speaking, and Stryger was walking forward to take her place.

I watched him move toward me through the gleaming white-and-blue respectability of the Federation Assembly, wearing its approval like an aura. He wasn't carrying his staff with him. But if what he'd done to me, or even what had happened to him last night, had had any effect on him, I couldn't see it in the way he moved, the way he shone. Maybe it had only made him more sure that God was on his side, that his crusade was just . . . that he was finally about to get everything he wanted. I watched him come, feeling like somehow he could actually see me; feeling like I was drowning. . . .

Mikah leaned over and nudged me. "Breathe," he said.

I sucked in air. Stryger had reached the podium now. He began to speak, while Shander Mandragora reminded us again that for Stryger speaking out loud wasn't just something he did for effect, but the only way he could communicate with his audience . . . like it was a pledge, a symbol of his purity, of his dedication to the common people.

"Because he'll never have the Gift," I muttered. "Because if he can't have it, he won't ever take second best."

Argentyne glanced at me. "I thought he hated psions—" Her eyes flickered down and away as she saw the proof of it again on my face.

"He does," I said. "Can you think of a better reason?" I watched as Stryger blessed the Assembly members, and called them upholders of peace and order . . . told them he'd come before them one last time to speak for those countless human beings who were the Federation's real reason for existence, whose strength and numbers made its existence possible . . . who trusted in the Assembly to do the right thing. . . . *Come on, Daric,* I thought. *Come on—* I shouldn't have let them talk me out of it; I should have been there. Stryger was almost finished; in another minute it would be too late, the voting would begin—

"I know you will agree with me," he said, smiling for the last time at the waiting faces below him, "because, after all, we all want the same thing . . . we are all so much alike, in our hearts." He stepped away from the podium, turning, starting back toward his seat.

"No," I said. "*No!* You bastard, you doublecrossing—" Mikah caught at my arm as I pushed to my feet.

But something was happening in the silent crowd on the Assembly floor. They began to make a sound, a restless murmuring like the sea, as larger-than-life figures suddenly materialized in the air: Stryger's image, and then mine. Daric had used himself to get a second viewpoint on the symb box. It was happening . . . it was really happening. I collapsed into my seat again, staring as cams that had been focused close-up on Stryger's face pulled back to take in the show, making Stryger seem to shrink where he stood on the stage. I watched his bloated image in the air open its mouth; I repeated the words that came out of it before they even registered on anyone else watching.

The real Stryger stopped moving, confusion showing on his face. The news recorders were hooked into the Assembly system through the Net, picking up sound to match the picture. Without any augmentation at all, he couldn't know what everyone else was seeing in the air above him, what they were hearing. . . .

He turned around, turning back toward the podium, searching for the Speaker. He stared as he saw the billowing images above him. He was standing inside them, and like a man standing inside a cloud, he couldn't make out their real form. Behind him Elnear and the Speaker stared in disbelief. I saw Elnear's hand go over her mouth as she recognized me. And then it was his own image Stryger was standing inside of, a victim's-eye view now, as the staff swung in for a blow.

I wanted to shut my eyes as the staff came at me. But I couldn't—I watched it come, saw the image change as it hit me. I heard the wood crack against my flesh, and saw what it did to me. I bit down on my fist.

Cries were registering on the audio. I heard my voice rising through them, telling Stryger why he hated psions, and I saw him answer me. . . . The image we were watching on the stage split open, half of it still focused on the beating, the other half sweeping the Hall as panic-stricken Assembly members fell over themselves and each other, screaming, vomiting, trying to get up or get away from what they were being force-fed over the inviolable link of the Assembly's system. The Speaker was up at the podium now, shoving Stryger aside as he used its access to try and force the system and its users back under control. As Stryger stumbled away he finally saw what everyone else was seeing— saw himself, larger than life, beating me to a pulp in front of billions of witnesses.

And then, as suddenly as it had come, the image disappeared from the air. It must have disappeared from the Assembly's system at the same time, because the screaming mob scene on the Assembly floor began to die down. Members fell back into their seats, the curses and cries turning into furious demands and questions. Inside of a minute there was total silence in the Hall. I couldn't tell what they were doing now, because even the info cams couldn't pick it up. I leaned forward across the table, my fists clenched, ignoring what it did to my body . . . because I had to know if it was working; and I couldn't tell anything, sitting here—

Stryger started back toward the podium with hellfire in his eyes. But before he could take control of it Elnear was there, barring his way, claiming the cameras and the Assembly's attention. The Speaker stepped aside, giving her room, giving way to one of his own.

"Sojourner Stryger," she said, flinching as he got near her, as if she was half afraid he'd attack her too. "What in God's name was your purpose in forcing this hideous thing on me . . . on everyone in this Hall?" Her voice trembled. Her face was white; her hands were clenched over the edges of the podium, holding her there. "What have you done to my aide—?"

"I—?" Stryger said, thumping his chest with his hands, still bug-eyed with disbelief. "This was not *my* doing!" I watched him struggle to control himself; struggle and win. "I was not to blame for this! This is some absurd blasphemy created in an attempt to humiliate me—"

The Speaker stepped between them. "Sojourner Stryger," he murmured, putting out his hand. "I'm sure there is some explanation for all this. But considering your current and future interests in the Federation, I think that perhaps the explanations had better come from you. Lady Elnear." He stepped back again, giving the floor to Elnear; giving her the right to ask the questions.

Stryger bristled; backed off, as he realized he didn't have any choice except to go ahead and face her down. "Surely no one—even you—" looking from the Speaker to Elnear, "takes seriously something as easily counterfeited as a threedy tape: two actors play roles, their images are altered to look like myself and a psion. . . ." Listening to him, watching him, I could almost believe he meant every word. I wondered what I'd see if I could get into his mind right now.

Elnear stiffened as he used the word *psion,* but she only said, "Tapes can certainly be counterfeited. But I have never in my life experienced pain while watching a threedy tape. Have you—?"

"Lady Elnear," he said, with patronizing calm, "I'm sure it was upsetting for you to see someone you thought you knew suffer—"

"I'm not talking about that." She cut him off, her own voice sharp and cold now. "I mean that I felt physical pain in every nerve-ending of my body—as if I was the victim every time you struck a blow."

608 ALIEN BLOOD

"That's absurd," he said, looking at her like she must be crazy.

"It should be." She nodded; her face was still white and drawn. "But everyone in this Hall felt it."

"I felt nothing of the kind," he snapped, looking out at the slack, stunned faces of the Assembly as if he thought they were all lying, or insane.

"Evidently you did not," she said bitterly. "Sojourner Stryger, why exactly did you choose a psion as your victim?"

He was still looking out into the Assembly Hall. "I did not 'choose a psion'!" he said to them, almost shouting it.

"That was how you identified him. Not as my aide—someone you knew—but as 'a psion.'"

"Someone else chose the act, and the victim, to discredit me!"

There was color back in Elnear's face now; her blue eyes were alive and intent. "Then why did they—whoever they were—choose to show you attacking a psion? Psions are not the objects of much compassion in our society. Why not a child, or an old woman?"

"I don't know," he murmured, as if he really didn't. "Perhaps they were stupid, as well as evil." He looked at her, away from her; up into the air like he was searching for guidance, wondering why God was letting this happen to him.

Her own eyes never left his face. "My aide tried to tell me, on several occasions, that you had a pathological hatred of psions," she said quietly. "I never really believed him, until now."

I sat up straight again, my teeth clenched in a grin.

"Your aide lied about me. He tried to discredit me to the entire Net!" He looked back at her, his face burning. "He tried to make them believe that I had lied—"

"You did lie. About him," she insisted. "Or have you forgotten?"

His mouth snapped shut. "That isn't true. As God is my witness . . . I may have been misinformed, but I never lie. God guides everything I do—"

"Even when he takes a piss?" Argentyne murmured beside me, and laughter drowned out the rest of his words.

"Has God told you that psions are evil?" Elnear asked. All the cams were on the two of them again.

"Yes . . ." he murmured. "That is, the evidence of society itself has shown that they are deviants of the most degraded sort, the kind of underclass I hope to eliminate through the wider use of pentryptine."

"The most degraded . . ." Elnear said softly. "Do you truly believe that, Sojourner? That all our drug dealers are psions? Our child molesters? Our contract killers? Are psions worse than someone who would set out to destroy an entire people, as some of our own ancestors have done to each other . . . all in the name of God?"

He was staring at her now. I kept waiting for the smooth denial to pour out of him. But this time it didn't come. "God . . ." he murmured finally. "God has shown me what they are. I have done nothing but follow God's Word as I understand it. . . ." His eyes narrowed. "But that does *not* mean that I persecute them! I only want to improve their lot."

Elnear folded her hands together in front of her, looked down at them, nodding as if she conceded the point. "Why is it that you have never had any augmentation done, Sojourner?" Her voice was calm now. The question sounded like a complete change of subject, but I didn't believe it.

Stryger gave her a strange look, but he answered her. "Because I see it as a violation of humanity's basic nature, the pure state which I believe God meant to be our chosen form of existence." He raised his head, back on firmer ground.

"Then God regards augmentation as wrong?" She sounded honestly surprised.

He laughed, his hands fluttering. "I'm not saying it's wrong for everyone. Our society could not function without its technological aids. God intended for us to have these tools, or we would still all be living on one planet. But to go so far as to challenge God's omniscience and power, to try to put oneself in the place that is naturally God's—that is always wrong."

"And do psions do that? I believe you said that was why the Hydran civilization fell, because they tried to put themselves in God's rightful place."

"Yes." He nodded. "Yes, I believe that . . . I—I've said that many times." A shadow touched his face as he realized the slip he'd almost made, almost acknowledging that he'd said it to me.

"How is it that you share my interest in the Security Council slot, then?" Elnear asked. "It is certainly the ultimate in augmentation available to any human being alive today. Surely the near-omniscience and power available to a Council member goes beyond the limits you believe God had in mind?"

My splinted fingers were tapping nervous code on the tabletop, like I could reach her somehow that way, when my mind couldn't reach her through the wilderness of minds between us. Even I hadn't seen the whole truth, seen the connection, until now. . . . *Make it*—I thought. *Make it, Elnear*—

I saw Stryger tense. "It really isn't the same thing. In order to continue to do God's work here in the Federation—"

"What do you plan to do, then—if not, in effect, to play God yourself?" Her voice sharpened. "Like the people you evidently hate so much?"

He frowned, like a dog trying to decide which flea to bite at first. "How dare you—"

"Sojourner, where is your staff today?" she asked, cutting him off again. "The one that you always carry, that you have said was 'the symbol of your journey toward the truth'?"

"I left it behind," he said. "It's only a piece of wood. It gets in the way."

"You seemed to use it without any difficulty when you used it to torture my aide."

His face reddened. "I am not on trial here! This is a fraud, a vicious lie, to ruin me! He was your aide—maybe you even planned it together, to hurt me, to claim the Council slot for yourself!" His voice was getting louder, as the idea took hold inside him. "That's it, isn't it? It was you, you made that tape—sent him to me, because you knew I—I—mean that it was a forgery, a lie, it never happened . . ."

His voice died, and there was silence in the Hall, and all around me in the club.

"We'll know that soon enough," Elnear said softly. She hesitated, listening to something he couldn't hear, and nodded. "The Speaker has analyzed the Assembly record of the tape. The databand keycodes of the two subjects appear to belong to my aide, and to you. There has been tampering with the Assembly system as well." She looked up at him again. "Eventually we will get to the bottom of this, and then we will know exactly how it happened. But I think that everyone already knows the truth, Sojourner Stryger." She looked back at him, with more sadness than anger showing on her face. "Even you."

"No," he said, and his mouth began to tremble. "No, it isn't true! I mean them no harm. I only want to do good—I have come to do God's work. I want to save them. Let me do good! Give me the power to bring about change! I need the power, I need it—" He was screaming now at the silent Assembly, at us where we sat watching; his face swelling, getting bigger and bigger, as the Net closed in on him pitilessly. I shut my eyes this time, but I couldn't stop hearing him, his voice, screaming, "You can't stop me! God has chosen me, and only God can stop me—" Suddenly his voice went dim. I opened my eyes. Somebody had dropped a security shield around him. Half a dozen Corpses were surrounding him on the stage now, forcing him to leave it; dragging him, when he tried to resist.

Elnear stood staring after him, her face flushed and her eyes shining; but she didn't look happy. The Speaker came up to her, subvocalizing something that the cams couldn't pick up. And then he said, "It has been suggested that the vote be postponed, because of this unfortunate—"

She turned toward him, and suddenly the outrage that I'd needed to see was on her face. She turned back to the podium, and said, "I move that we vote immediately, as planned. And I ask you all to remember that Sojourner Stryger is the man who wants you to deregulate pentryptine—who believes that you will vote his way, 'because you are all so much like him in your hearts.'" And then she left the podium, walking down and away toward her own seat on the Assembly floor.

Daric taMing seconded the motion.

The motion passed. And in less time than it took to formally announce the vote, deregulation failed to get its majority. By three votes. One of them was Daric taMing's.

35

I HARDLY REMEMBER what happened next on the Assembly floor, because suddenly the club was all whooping and music and celebration. I wouldn't have believed a dozen people could make that much crazy noise. But up in front of me I saw Elnear's face as it registered on her that she'd actually won. I saw that smile of hers come out like the sun. And then finally I could smile too, and laugh and yell and swallow the wine Mikah was pouring down my throat, and start to live again. Because it hadn't all been for nothing.

The private party lasted until the club opened, and then it became a public party, as Argentyne let everybody join in. The stage was their lightshow, full of constant threedy feed, infotainment for the masses. Somewhere in the middle of it I remember her shaking me out of a warm, nodding daze, yelling, "Look! Listen!" in my ear. And it was Daric's face up there, Daric being interviewed by Shander Mandragora as he took "exclusive responsibility" for the illegal 'cast that had burned itself into the collective brain of the Assembly, and turned Sojourner Stryger from the Chosen One of the combine gods into a dose of scratch.

"Gentleman Daric," Shander Mandragora was saying, pushing in for an uncomfortable closeup. "You took extraordinary measures to reveal Sojourner Stryger as a bigot and a dangerous fanatic. What was it that made you decide to commit such a controversial—even illegal—act, something that could ruin your position and damage your distinguished career for years to come?"

Something touched Daric's face for maybe a second, something that nobody else even saw. And for the space of that second, I almost believed he'd done it for the right reason. That he might even find the honesty somewhere to tell everybody what he really was. . . . But then he only looked uncomfortable and annoyed again. "A sense of higher duty," he said, and the answer was the empty, professional lie of a politician. He stared directly into Mandragora's third eye, facing down the watching universe with a calculated intensity that said he knew just how to work the Net. Argentyne couldn't look away from it. "I worked very closely with Sojourner Stryger, as Centauri's private liaison in matters concerning deregulation. It became clear to me that he was dangerously unstable. But because of his immense public popularity, I knew that he was almost certain to be chosen for the opening on the Security Council. When I realized that might happen, I felt someone had to stop it. And because of his popularity, I knew it would take unorthodox means to effectively prevent such a travesty. So I chose to do this."

"And what about the victim?" Mandragora said. "I interviewed him myself, when he saved several people from an assassination attempt on Lady Elnear Lyron/taMing. He was her aide—was she aware of what you were doing?"

"Absolutely not." Daric barely kept the grimace off his face. "I got to know him because he saved my life too that night. He agreed to play the victim for Stryger because of his own feelings about Stryger's bigotry. It was a courageous act on his part, and the poor fellow suffered terribly for his beliefs. He's in seclusion now, and doesn't want to be disturbed."

I swore, searching for the poisoned smile I knew was there behind the words.

"He was in no way involved in the actual carrying out of the plan, of course; beyond offering his body as bait, so to speak. . . ."

"You lousy motherfucker," I mumbled.

Argentyne turned toward me, frowning. "He's covering for you, he's taking the blame on himself. Can't you see that? He's protecting you from a criminal action. Do you know what kind of deep shit you'd be in if he didn't?"

"He's giving Charon the finger, and taking the credit for himself," I said wearily. I touched my swollen face, wincing. "Fuck him, he can have it. . . . I got what I wanted."

"He didn't have to do this. It's going to hurt him. Can't you ever give him credit for a decent act?"

"Not until he does one." I shook my head, and it made me dizzy. She looked away again.

"It has been pointed out," Shander Mandragora was saying, "that Centauri Transport had more to gain financially than almost any combine supporting deregulation. You are a member of their board, and yet you not only discredited Sojourner Stryger, but you actually voted against deregulation yourself. What made you vote against your own corporate interests?"

"Blackmail," I whispered, so softly that even Argentyne couldn't hear me.

Daric stood a little straighter, pulling at his cuffs. "There are some things," he said, with more dignity than I thought he had in him, "more important than money."

"Like his own skin," Mikah grunted. He raised his glass to me. "This one's to you, freak," he said, and swallowed down the rest of the brew in it. Then he got up, stretched, and shook himself out, blocking my view of whatever Daric did next. Every movement he made was perfectly under control, even though he'd been drinking nonstop all evening. Either he had a shunt or he held his liquor better than anybody I'd ever seen. "Looks like he's met his end of the deal. Guess that means the Market will have to do the same." He shrugged, looking down at me. "Looks like everybody wins tonight. . . . But maybe the Governor ought to send somebody out to kick his ass around a little anyway; just to let him know how lucky he is." He smiled, thinking maybe he'd suggest it himself. Argentyne frowned, but she didn't say anything. Mikah put out his hand to me; we clenched thumbs. "So long, kid. It's been real."

I half smiled and nodded. And suddenly the thing I'd sworn I wouldn't ask him for again was all I could think about. But the look in his eyes, and what lay behind it, stopped the words in my throat. I looked down; telling myself I still had three of those little red dots left on the sheet. . . . I looked up again. "Thanks."

He raised his hand, palm out, showing me the scar. "Any time, brother."

I lifted my own hand, and watched him go out of the club. I turned back to Argentyne; but she was gone. Some stranger with striped skin and a long striped tongue was lapping syrup out of a bowl beside me. I ate a few meat-filled buns, and stuck on more painkillers where the damage was starting to leak through. The striped stranger asked me to dance, but I shook my head, not up to it. I lay back in the cushions, watching the endless replays and interviews and flashbacks flowing across the empty stage until I was numb.

As I listened to Daric's confession for the third time, the real Daric entered the club. I felt him walk in, his mind like nobody else's; followed him as he made his way through the crowd to Argentyne, who'd stopped moving to watch his image again. He watched her watching it, standing motionless with her eyes fixed on his holo face as he crossed the room behind her. He wanted to take hold of her as he reached her, and prove to both of them that he was alive; prove to both of them how she still felt about him. . . . But he didn't. Holding himself under control, he only touched her once, to make her turn around. He handed her the symb box, murmuring something noncommittal.

She took it and stuck it back where it belonged. She asked him how he was, told him how glad she was that everything had gone all right; feeling every word ring hollow. She told him how he'd come across on the Net, and then, like she couldn't help herself, how it had made her feel. . . . Her hand stretched toward him, tentative until it reached his chest. And then it slid down and around him. And there was no going back for her, as he touched her with his hands . . . as his mind touched that hidden place inside her where she'd ached to feel him all these endless days.

I broke off watching, broke off *feeling* it; not sure who I was more disgusted with . . . or why I wasn't more surprised. I stared at the images on the stage, waiting for Daric to come to me, knowing that he would.

He was alone again when he finally reached my table, and the grin of satisfaction on his face faded as I looked up at him. He flinched as he saw my own face. "Get out of here," he said to the people sitting around me. They got up and left as he sat down. Dead serious, he asked, "Are you satisfied now?"

"You kept your part of it." I had to force myself to say the words.

"What about the Market? Did they see everything? Are they satisfied too? Do I get my life back?"

I shrugged, and it hurt every muscle in my shoulders, back, and chest.

"Well—?" he said, when I didn't answer.

"Yeah. This time."

He nodded, but the tight lines around his eyes didn't disappear. "And you'll keep your mouth shut—?"

I frowned, touching the scabs on my lips.

"I'm protecting you! I'm taking the blame for everything that happened, so that you don't have to! That ought to make up for a few extra bruises, for God's sake." He jerked his hands. "All right—I was angry, I wanted to see you suffer like you'd made me suffer. I admit it. But I didn't mean for it to go that far. I thought I could control him, I didn't think he'd . . . He always stopped, before. . . ." Finally admitting, to me and to himself, that at the end he'd been as powerless to stop Stryger as I had. He looked down, remembering his own fear as he'd watched Stryger go out of control.

I wished he was lying to me; but he wasn't. I looked away as he tried to meet my eyes, tried to guess what was on my mind. He'd never know what he'd really done to me . . . and telling him the truth would only make it harder for me to bear. "All right," I whispered. "You want to go on living your lie—go ahead. Maybe I don't even blame you." Realizing that if the choice was mine to make right now, I'd make the same one he would. I looked up at him again, through a single round-pupiled eye. "You know, for a minute I almost thought you felt something real while you were serving all that shit to the Net. That maybe you finally understood, why it was important to get Stryger, now. That it mattered to you that you'd stopped him." I touched my head, grimacing. "It must've been the concussion."

He glanced away. "No," he said finally. "You were right." He'd enjoyed playing his private games with Stryger, being in control, cheating him like he'd cheated the rest of the universe. Last night he'd enjoyed watching Stryger torture me; thinking that he hated me as much as Stryger did. But his own hatred had let the pain get too personal, sucked him in too close to its heart, ruptured the membrane of lies that let him feel safe—just like it had ruptured mine. He'd seen the truth about Stryger, and about himself. About his worst nightmares . . .

"In the middle of the night," he said, "while I was trying to drag that self-righteous, perverted slug to somewhere discreet and safe, all because he was no better than anybody else . . . I had something of an epiphany, I suppose. And then I actually wanted to see the son of a bitch broken on the rack of public opinion today—and not just for my own sake." His hand tightened on the tabletop. He stared at it, forced it to relax again. "Auntie was brilliant, wasn't she?" He grinned, like he'd never considered the possibility before. "You know, for a moment while I was being interviewed, I actually thought, what if I did tell them I was a psion—?" He looked back at me. "But it passed, mercifully. I'm so glad you'll be leaving soon. A little truth is a dangerous thing."

I started to smile in spite of myself, as wide as my mouth would let me; realizing I never would have heard those words out of his mouth if it hadn't been for what had happened to me last night. "What kind of trouble is the Assembly tampering going to make for you?"

He raised his eyebrows. "Everyone will sling legal and political rubbish at me. It will be unpleasant. But little of it will stick. It may even improve Centauri's relations with the Feds, in the end—I mean, I was obviously so right about Stryger. . . . And besides, I'm a taMing. You know what they say." The mocking smile came back, and he shrugged. " 'Cats and Gentlemen always land on their feet.' "

I grunted. "What about your father?"

The smile froze over. He looked away, and didn't answer. I wondered which of them would end up hating me more. "Even Argentyne has begun to forgive me, after all. . . ." He smirked as he looked up at me again. *Even though I'd done all I could to ruin it between them. . . . Even though she knew his secret.* Terror and exhilaration filled him at the thought of it. "A relationship based on trust—who knows where that will lead? I suppose I'll have to be nicer to her. . . ." He laughed, nervously, and got to his feet. "Maybe I should even thank you. But I truly hope we never meet again, Cat. Don't think I intend to forget you, though. . . ." He stopped, just out of reach, and looked back. "I have a copy of that tape of you with Stryger. I intend to use it for my own personal recreational pleasure." He laughed again, at the look on my face, and started away.

"Daric!"

He stopped, looking back, still smiling.

I got my voice under control, and said, "There's something else you ought to know. I'll keep my word about you. But before I knew you were the teek, I told Braedee there was another psion at the estates." I smiled this time, as his grin faded. "It's something to keep in mind."

He looked at me for a long time, with his throat working. And then his smile started to grow back. "Well, good for you. . . ." he murmured. "You're just as human as the rest of us." He turned away again, and went looking for Argentyne.

I lay back in the pillows with my eyes shut. "Eat shit and die," I muttered.

The threedy images were fading up on the stage, turning to fog, mutating as I opened my eyes and began to watch again: becoming Argentyne and the symb beginning a performance. She'd said they weren't going to perform tonight; I wondered which of the things that had happened today had changed her mind.

I held my psi back as the rippling wall of light and sound opened up, not wanting to find out as I let my other senses pull me into the symb's hallucinogenic vision. Maybe Argentyne had been better than this, but I hadn't been there when it happened . . . and watching, listening, letting the lightsong surround me and draw me out of myself, I realized

618 ALIEN BLOOD

that this might be the last time I'd ever see her perform. I didn't need
her any more; and she didn't need me. Whatever happened now, my
time here in Purgatory was over.

The jack was gone from the back of my head already. I wasn't real to
her or the players any more on that other plane where their minds were
now, and soon I'd hardly even be a memory to them. But I didn't really
need a socket to reach them. And now, while I still had my Gift, I
wanted to use it. I pushed out through the haze of painkillers until I
found Argentyne's mind. I let myself in, and set free the things I saw
there, feeding her mood poems into all the players' minds at once,
letting their reactions flow back to her—doing freehand what I'd done
before by tracing the lifelines of the symb . . . until I knew they knew
I was in symb with them one last time, giving them the best gift I knew
how to give. . . .

36

THE NEXT DAY'S news was full of Lady Elnear Lyron/taMing being named to fill the empty slot on the Security Council. I missed it, because when I went to bed I slept for three days straight. When I finally came to again the pain had eased up enough that I could stand it without drugs. Most of the swelling had gone down, and my reflection in the mirror looked like it belonged to somebody I knew again. I peeled the pad away from my bandaged eye. It looked like Deadeye's. But at least I could see out of it again. I thought about being blind for life; thought about Oldcity. They'd told me at Soule's that there shouldn't be any scars this time. None that showed, anyway. Two green eyes with round pupils that were beginning to seem too familiar searched my face, and looked away.

I went downstairs, one step at a time. As I limped into the kitchen, Shander Mandragora's face up on the wall was telling the Federation that Sojourner Stryger had committed suicide.

My stomach pushed up into my throat; I drank a cup of stale coffee that was sitting on the kitchen table, forcing it back down where it belonged.

"He left a message," Aspen said, putting his arm around Midnight's shoulders as he looked at me. "Something about going where he was wanted. . . ." For a second I thought he was joking; but he wasn't.

"Do you think there's a heaven?" Midnight asked.

"I don't believe in heaven," I said. "But I hope there's a hell."

They looked at me, and they didn't say anything else.

"Where's Argentyne?" I asked, to fill up the silence.

Aspen looked down; I felt the stab of his embarrassment. "Out at Daric's."

I made a noise.

"Sorry, man," Midnight said. "Don't take it too hard."

"Like they say," I muttered. "Cats and Gentlemen always land on their feet."

"Lady Elnear's been trying to reach you," Aspen said. "She left a lot of messages while you were out."

Out. I half smiled. *Out of my head.* "What did she say?"

They told me the old news then, about her appointment. I nodded, not surprised, but relieved. "She just said she wanted to talk to you as soon as possible. That it was important."

I got up. "Thanks." I went to the phone and tried to call her, but I couldn't even get through. Everyone else in the galaxy was probably trying to do the same thing, and that wouldn't end soon. I stood in the hall for a minute, letting my frustration ease off, trying to think. And then I called Natan Isplanasky. He actually came onscreen himself when I gave my ID. He stared at me, at my face, like everybody else had; but he listened to what I had to say without interrupting. He half frowned when I finished, rubbing his beard. "I don't know if it's even possible," he said. "She was installed today. The period of adjustment for a new Council member is difficult. . . ."

"I have to see her," I said. "And I've only got a couple of days left."

He looked surprised. "What happens after that?"

I shrugged. "I'm not sure."

"Are you in trouble over the Stryger affair?"

"No." I shook my head.

"Are you all right?"

"No." I looked away, knowing he could see that for himself.

"God damn it," he said. "I don't know if it's the things you do say or the things you don't say that grate on me more." He broke off as I laughed; a grudging smile pulled at his mouth. "I'll see what I can arrange."

He called me back later in the day. "Come up to the office," he said. "I'll meet you there." That he'd kept his promise surprised me nearly as much as anything that had happened the past few weeks. But I only nodded, and did what he told me.

He met me at his office door, tried not to flinch as he got a fresh look at me, and took me inside. "Elnear will join us as soon as she's able." He handed me one of his thousand-year-old beers. "You earned it," he said. "What you did took a lot of guts. The people of the Federation owe you more than a beer." *For destabilizing Stryger's orbit.*

I looked down, studying the bottle so that I didn't have to meet his eyes. "I didn't do it for them."

"Well," he said, "very few things seem to get done for the reasons they should get done." He moved restlessly. "As far as that goes, I owe you more than a beer myself."

I raised my head again. "What for?"

"For proving that I am not all-seeing. . . . Elnear finally told me about what happened to you at the Mines."

I swallowed a mouthful of beer, and didn't say anything.

He looked down, this time. "I've been exploring options to streamline the system, so that I have more direct access to all its parts." He didn't look away from the look on my face. "And to put more of its resources into protecting its clients. I don't know if that will be enough to satisfy someone who has been abused by it. . . . I hope it will be enough to make some difference." What he didn't say was what we both already knew, each of us in our own way—that even he was just another mouse in the machine, in the end. There was only so much he'd ever be able to do. The system was more than its parts.

And yet changing it still mattered to him. What had happened once to a nobody like me mattered to him, here in this private office at the top of the world, at the top of the FTA's power structure. I thought about the last time I'd stood in this office, and what I'd been feeling then. Standing here now, feeling the *anger, frustration, hope* behind his eyes, I realized suddenly that knowing he actually felt that way made a hell of a difference to me. And I realized the difference that having Elnear for a friend had made in him.

"Hello, Cat."

I turned as I heard Elnear's voice, startled because I hadn't sensed her coming in. She was standing there behind me, smiling. I started toward her; stopped again, blinking. "You're not here." It was an image, a holo. It looked real, it reacted in realtime, but there was no one inside it. I stood still, sending out my mind through wider and wider circles, searching for her. "Where are you? I can't find you—"

"I know." Her smile changed, until it wasn't really a smile any more, and I couldn't tell what lay behind it. "I'm afraid this is the best I can do. I'm on the Council now."

"I know, but . . ." I shook my head. "Where are you, then?"

She turned toward Isplanasky. "Natan, didn't you explain?"

He shrugged. "I thought he knew."

"*What—?*" I said, ready to yank it out of his mind.

"Could we have some time alone?" she asked him.

"Of course," he said. "I need to get back into the system, anyway."

He looked at me. "Goodbye, Cat. Good luck to you. Just let yourself out when you're finished."

I watched him cross the room to the wired lounge where I'd first seen him. He lay back in it, linking into the Net, taking all the energy of his mind and body with him. He was still in the room, but inside of a minute we had complete privacy. . . . I looked away from him, hunching my shoulders. Seeing Elnear but not seeing her didn't make me feel any better.

"Well, we won," she said softly, smoothing her long blue-gray robe with her hands. Her face filled with pride and something deeper as she looked at me again. "You found a pin sharp enough to make the Assembly jump, after all. What happened was your doing, wasn't it—not Daric's?"

I nodded. "But if it hadn't been for you, Stryger might still have gotten what he wanted. What I did might not have stopped anything, if it hadn't been for you—" My throat closed up; it took an effort to keep the real expression off my face.

Her smile disappeared. "But in the end, he was his own nemesis. . . ." She knew what he'd done to himself. I couldn't tell if she really believed what she said, though—that he was to blame for that, and not us. I couldn't tell if I did, either. "I am so grateful to you, once again," she said, and her voice was suddenly too full; her eyes touched my face, glanced down my body, darkened as they registered the damage that showed. "Knowing what I now know, about Stryger and about the real nature of the Security Council . . . If he had won this slot, the chaos his instability would have caused could have been unimaginable." Her hands tightened. "But if I had known what you intended to do—do to yourself—I would never have let you do it."

"That's why I didn't tell you." I shook my head, not wanting her to say any more; not wanting to hear it. "Lady . . . Why aren't you here? Is it security—"

"I'm on the Council now, Cat," she said again, and hesitated, as if finding the right words was terribly important to her, or terribly hard somehow. "I'm joined with the system, like Natan . . . but permanently."

I stared at her, feeling stupid and dazed, not able to read the context of thought that would make the words mean what they were supposed to. "Permanently?"

She nodded.

I looked back at Isplanasky. "You mean you can't ever walk away from it?"

"Yes. That's right."

"Why?" I said weakly.

"Because the Council demands total commitment. Keeping control of any network that spans interstellar distances is a nearly impossible task, and the FTA is the largest coherent network of all. There are systems within systems inside the Authority. Natan is at one level; I was on another one, far lower, before. At each level of complexity, as you ascend, more augmentation is required to make up for the structural limitations of the human mind; to give it the capacity it needs to process the increased dataflow and make meaningful judgments about it. Most combines never really function on the highest levels; they have to segment their operations, because of the limits of realtime communication. . . . Only the FTA makes policy on this level, because it has to respond to so many different factors. And at this level the interface is so complex that it has to be permanent."

"What happens, then . . . to you?" Muscles twitched in my jaw.

"My body is being maintained. They'll take excellent care of it . . . it will probably last for another fifty or seventy-five years."

I tried not to grimace. "And then what?"

"They'll have to choose someone else to fill a Council slot. The Charter does not permit Council members to . . . stay on after death."

I looked away from the thing that was standing across the room pretending to be someone I knew. "What about Elnear? I mean . . . Shit, I don't know what I mean!" My hand hit my leg in frustration; I winced. "I can't feel you. Are you alive or are you just data? Do you feel human? Do you feel anything at all any more?"

"Oh, yes . . ." she murmured. "I wish you could know what I feel, Cat. You might understand it better than most people, because of what you are."

I nodded, because I knew what she meant, better than she realized . . . maybe even better than she did. But I couldn't tell her that. "Maybe it's a nice place to visit. But I wouldn't want to live there."

She smiled a little. "I'm only just beginning to grasp what it really is. My sense of individual identity may be no more than an artificial construct, for all I know . . . and yet I still feel quite human, somehow. Perhaps I'll always feel that way, because I interact as a coherent personality, all the time, with human beings at all levels of the system—just the way I'm speaking to you."

ALIEN BLOOD

"How do I look to you?" I asked.

"Very far away . . ." she said, and there was sadness in it again. "Perhaps my sense of humanness will fade, with time . . . perhaps it's wise that our service is limited by our lifespan. But I am not alone here inside, either, which I think will help me to remember why I exist and perhaps even who I am. I am a part of the Council in a very literal sense, and we are . . . of one mind."

I thought about the shining beings I'd met inside the Council core when I'd been lost in inner space with Deadeye . . . and for just a second I went cold inside, as I imagined what it really would have meant if Stryger had become one of them. But then I thought about how it felt to make a joining. The Hydrans had been able to share a single mindspace with as many others as there was need for. But to share just one other person's mind totally was something that no normal human could ever do; it was almost impossible even for a human who was a psion . . . even for me. Something that might have been envy, but wasn't, stirred inside me. "Did you know it would be like this, all along?" It was almost more than I could believe, or wanted to. "That if you won you'd never be able to see anyone face to face again, or smell coffee or paint a picture or walk in the woods—?" The memories of all the things I'd watched her do that gave her pleasure filled my mind.

"Yes." She nodded. "I knew that much. I didn't know it would be like this—I couldn't really know. It's impossible to describe in human terms. But I knew there would be no coming back from it."

"You still wanted it." I couldn't make it a question, because the answer was obvious. "Weren't you afraid—of disappearing?"

"Weren't you afraid," she asked, "of what would happen when you let Stryger get his hands on you?"

"Yeah," I said. "I sure as hell was."

She laughed. "I sure as hell was, too. But Cat, someone described the process of augmenting the human mind as pouring indigo dye into a bucket, and then pouring the bucket into a vat, and the vat into the sea. . . . The dye is still there, no matter how diffused. It's rather like seeing God in all things. And I think that it's fitting, perhaps even the key to our survival as a species, that we stay a part of the systems we create, however we can: as cells, as organs . . . and, I hope, as souls. Because we have already set in motion our transformation, like it or not. Progress is always the process of leaving something behind. Every choice we make means that we are forced to give something up, as well; to sacrifice the thing not chosen."

I shook my head. "No regrets, then?"

"Oh . . ." The smile didn't quite work, this time. "A few. Phantom pains for my lost body. I'm told they will get worse, and then fade with time, as the past fades. But I am only my memories now, and so even my regrets are precious to me."

I looked away from her, disappointment rising up so suddenly in me that I couldn't speak. I'd come here to see Elnear, the living, breathing, human woman I'd gone through so much with, and for . . . to see her once more before the drugs wore off and I lost the ability to really see her: her mind, her soul. But because of those damned drugs I'd slept away three days of my life; I'd missed her, and now I'd never have the chance again.

"And what about you?" she asked, to my turned back.

"Lousy," I said, my hands tightening. "Really lousy."

"Are you angry?"

I shook my head.

"Disappointed, then—?"

I shrugged.

"Afraid of me?"

I turned back. "No . . ." I shook my head again. "I don't know." My voice sounded hoarse and thick. "I don't know how to feel, because I don't know what you are any more."

"Then you probably feel something like I felt when I first met you," she said gently.

I looked down again. Finally I said, "I just wish you'd told me. So I could have been . . . ready."

"We've both had painful secrets to keep, it seems." Chiding me, still gently. "What I knew about the real nature of the Security Council was not something that I was permitted to share freely. Those who do know feel—and I think justifiably—that the people of the Federation, the people the FTA is meant to serve, would rather believe that it is still run by identifiable human beings. And so they . . . we try to preserve that illusion. Now you know the secret too. You know it because I know I can trust you to keep it."

I looked at her image, my eyes unfocused, not saying anything.

"There is something I still need to discuss with you." Her voice got stronger, pulling me back. "Being on the Council leaves me in an awkward position, Cat. I am legally neither dead nor alive. I wanted to see you, not only to say goodbye, but also to discuss with you the disposition of my estate."

"With me?" I said.

"My personal holdings, including my controlling interest in ChemEnGen, will have to be overseen by a trusteeship in my . . . absence. I would like to name you to the board."

"Me?" I said again, sounding stupider than before. "I don't know sh— anything, about overseeing—"

She held up her hands. "That isn't necessary. Philipa will head the board. She will see that the actual duties are taken care of. I simply need individuals I know I can trust, to fill the other seats—I suppose that's why they call them 'trustees.' It would give you the freedom to live your life as you want to. You'd never again have to let someone like Braedee blackmail you into a job you hated."

I felt a smile start. "It wasn't such a bad job . . . But yeah." I nodded. "Maybe I'd like that." *Freedom.* But more than freedom . . . *security.* She smiled too as I looked back at her again. "You have all the seats filled?"

"Do you have candidates?"

"Jule."

She hesitated, nodded.

"Jiro."

This time her surprise showed. But then she smiled, and nodded again. "Thank you."

I shrugged, staring at her image. "I just want to know one thing. Are you really happy, Elnear?"

"Yes," she said, and there was no hesitation in it. "Yes, I am."

"Then I guess it'll be all right." I took a deep breath.

"What are your plans," she asked, "now that this ordeal has finally ended, for both of us?"

I shook my head. "I don't know. I guess I'll go back to the University, until I figure out what to do with the rest of my life." My mouth twitched, not really a smile. I reached up, feeling for the patch behind my ear; feeling my teeth clench. "But first I've got to find a place where I can be alone and scream for a while." I tried to make it sound like a joke, but it didn't.

Sympathy and pain that I couldn't feel showed in her eyes. But then her face changed. She murmured, "I know just the place. It's spring there, now. No one will bother you. It's a place that can make you remember the good. . . . Will you let me arrange it?"

Surprised, I almost said *no.* But instead I thought about it, and nodded. And as I did, I felt my body loosen with relief, letting go of a fear that I hadn't realized I'd been holding all this time. I rubbed my eyes with my hand.

"Goodbye, Cat," she said.

"Goodbye, Elnear." And then, because it was better than admitting the truth, I smiled at her, and said, "Think about me sometimes. Maybe I'll hear you."

She smiled too, and held out her hand. I even tried to touch it, before she disappeared.

After she was gone I let myself out of Isplanasky's office. I walked through the halls of the Federation plex for the last time, alone. When I reached the display area, I stopped inside the crowd of tourists who were staring at the mosaic of the People of Earth. I studied the faces on the wall, the faces around me, for a long time. Human faces. *I hadn't done it for them.* That was what I'd told Isplanasky. But somehow those faces weren't so hard to look at, this time. Somehow they'd changed; or maybe I had. "You're welcome," I said at last. No one turned to look at me as I went on my way.

EPILOGUE

I STAYED IN the cottage halfway up the mountainside for as long as it took—to learn to live with myself, and only myself, again. About once a week I had to walk down into the nearest village to pick up supplies. It was an independent crafters' commune, not a Federal outlet or a combine clave, and they didn't seem to care if I looked like hell or sometimes I couldn't make myself speak to them. I didn't want to speak to them, or even hear them speak to me. They might as well have been the hallucinations of my own sick mind, because I couldn't feel them inside my thoughts any more.

At first sometimes facing even fifteen minutes' mindless contact was more than I could stand, and I'd just go hungry. Sitting inside the one room, sometimes I wouldn't move all day. I stared at the silent, whitewashed walls, wishing they were black. All I could feel was pain. Some of the pain was physical, but that was almost a relief compared to the pain that wasn't. Sometimes I did scream. Once I called Mikah, ready to beg him to get me what I needed. Nobody answered the call.

But all the while I was healing. My battered body mended fast. The broken bones of my defenses mended a lot more slowly. In time the blackness inside me began to break up into shades of gray, telling me my inner eyes were finally adjusting to life in a darkened room. After enough time, I could even begin to see how far I'd come, in spite of everything, from the place I'd been when I first came to Earth. I started being able to look at the scars on my face and body for long enough to recognize that they were really fading . . . to look at the memories that strobed behind them directly enough that I could even begin to believe what had happened to me with Stryger wasn't the same thing that had happened to me back in Oldcity; to believe that this time it hadn't been random, meaningless suffering. This time I'd made a hard choice, for a good reason, and made a difference by doing it. And this time my survival hadn't been as random as my pain . . . this time I really hadn't been all alone in hell.

And slowly, painfully, I was able to see that even if Oldcity had been reality for me for seventeen years, it didn't make the life I had now a lie. Not the good parts of it; not the bad. I wasn't a victim any more. I wasn't a telepath any more, either. The drugs I'd used to blind me to the truth were the lie, just like they'd always been. Unless I wanted to live without my Gift forever, I had to face living without it now, for however long it took. But the truth was the bitterest drug I'd ever had to swallow; it burned my mouth every time I had to speak a word.

As my need died, day by day, I began to rediscover the world waiting for me outside. I heard birds calling, smelled damp earth and new grass, finally knew the color of the flowers and the sky. I tried to learn how to make music on the mouth harp Argentyne had given me along with one last kiss as we said our goodbyes. I watched spring turn into summer all across the valley below me, until finally I knew I was glad to be alive again . . . knew this world for a part of my heritage, a place that I had a right to love; a place I wanted to come back to again, on my own terms. And then at last I understood the real gift that Elnear had given me.

After the worst of the pain had died, I realized that what was left didn't hurt me the way it had before. That it let me reach out a little further before I ran into the wall. That maybe Jule had been right about what I'd done; that by helping someone else I'd helped myself, and the past had really gotten just a little further away for me.

One day I went into town when I didn't have to, because I wanted to hear a human voice that wasn't my own. And then I knew I felt human again, if not Hydran . . . and that I was ready to live like a human again, on their terms.

I contacted Braedee and made him take me back where he'd found me. On the way there, I made him fix my eyes. Neither of us said *thanks* as I got ready to leave the ship; but he said I ought to study chess. I told him I thought I'd stick to Square/Cubes.

The University was still in port where I'd left it, finishing up its session on the Monument. There was a tape waiting there for me, from Jule. I sat in my cabin and watched her smiling face a dozen times before I was ready to go out and start living the life of a student again.

My absence had been listed as being for "family problems." I had a hard time keeping a decent expression on my face as Kissindre Perrymeade told me I looked tired, and she hoped that everything was all right at home. She asked if I wanted to talk about it. I said *no*. She said she was sorry about what had happened between us just before I left. I couldn't remember what she meant, but I didn't say so. She offered to share credit with me on the session thesis she was finishing, because I hadn't had time to do anything for the course.

I shook my head, still having trouble even relating to what she was saying. I felt like I'd been missing for years, instead of months; the holomuraled walls of the museum hall seemed more real than she did. "No. It's all right. . . ."

"It would only be fair," she insisted, not understanding that I really didn't care. "You gave me the concept yourself. What you said before you left, about the Monument as a 'monument to Death'—"

"I said that?" I asked, and then nodded; remembering it, finally. I thought about the sunset at Goldengate, and the music of the wind, and what it had said to me. "I guess I did. . . . I'll see you later." I started to turn away.

"Where are you going?" she asked, with more gentleness than I would have expected.

"Gonna take a jump down to the surface. I want to . . . get the feel of the thing again before it's gone."

"Want some company?"

I looked back at her. "What about—" I broke off. *Ezra.* That had been his name. Her boyfriend. "Ezra?"

She made a face, and shook her head. "We're not speaking this week."

I looked away again. "I don't feel much like talking, myself."

"That's all right," she said.

I shrugged, and nodded.

We took the shuttle down together to Goldengate, and stood on the open plateau. It was barely dawn this time, and we were alone in the soft half-light. A handful of stars were still showing, and the arch of the Gate was a black silhouette that even my eyes could barely make out against the sky. The wind was still making mournful flutesong through the riddled stone, just the way I remembered it. I touched the mouth harp riding in the pocket of my jeans, finally remembering after all this time what something in its sound had always reminded me of.

I started away from the shuttle, the sandy dirt whispering under my feet. It was almost cold, and I was glad I was wearing Deadeye's sweater. Kissindre sat down cross-legged where she was, watching silently, but letting me have my space.

I sat on the rocks at the edge of the plateau, listening, feeling the wind, waiting as day broke and the light touched the arch and began to turn it gold. And I thought about the way this world had been made, put together out of ruined bits and pieces, forged into a work of art by a technology so far beyond ours that it still seemed like magic. *A monument to bad ends and broken dreams* . . . and yet that didn't seem right, when it seemed to be waiting through millennia just for something living to come here and touch it. Even the air I was breathing was a miracle; all the studies I'd ever seen said you needed a living ecosystem to produce an atmosphere a human could live in. But a human could breathe here, walk here, feel perfectly at home here . . . do everything except stay. So could a Hydran. I wondered if the Hydrans had known about this world, visited it, studied it. And I realized suddenly that it could just as well have been left here for them to find, as for the humans. Whether it had been meant for the Hydrans instead was probably a question no one had ever asked up at the museum. . . .

I tried not to let the bitterness take hold of me again as I thought it. I was still a halfbreed, even if my telepathy was gone—still made out of bits and pieces like this world was, but nobody's idea of a work of art. The two halves of me were so much alike . . . except for that one, fragile thing that made all the difference. In the way two peoples looked at life, and each other. I wondered how something like that could even have happened; what kind of cosmic joke I'd been made the butt of. I remembered Stryger asking me the same thing.

And because I couldn't face too much of that, I took the mouth harp out of my pocket and began to play, trying to make the sounds it made act like a song. The song that the wind made answered me, making me remember the symb; remember the good. There was more of it to remember than I'd expected.

I thought about Elnear then; about where and what she was now . . . about all she'd given up, and all she'd become. If I'd been given that chance, I didn't know if I could have taken it. . . . The part of me that wanted to be whole again, the Hydran part, had envied her; but the human part had known it wouldn't be the same, and it had only been afraid. It was hard enough just living with what I knew already, just being one of a hundred billion random cells in the Federation's evolving supermind.

And yet knowing she'd had the courage to make that choice, and take that final step, still made a difference . . . as much difference, in its way, as what she'd done to help me survive in my own random life.

She'd finally proved something to me about humans, and about the human side in me, that I hadn't thought anyone could make me believe again: that maybe they deserved some respect, after all.

And so did the ones who'd left this world here. I wondered what they'd been like, before they'd disappeared from our plane of existence hundreds of thousands of years ago. I'd told Stryger I didn't believe in a God; and I didn't—not any kind that he'd recognize. Probably not any kind that I would, either. But a race that could create this world, and then pull themselves into a hat and disappear . . . they could have played God a little before they left, done a little genetic tampering, planted some seeds and left them there to see what would happen. The Haves and the Have Nots. An experiment, a cosmic joke . . . the next generation.

The Hydrans had reached the stars first, but they'd depended on their Gift too much, and spread it too thin. When the humans got there after them, it had been easy enough to sweep their psi Net away like cobwebs. The Hydrans hadn't reached their transformation, and now they never would. Maybe they'd had it too easy. Maybe they'd never seen how much they'd been given . . . how much they had to lose.

Now the humans had built their own Net, and it was technogenetic, cruder but stronger. And now they were using it to climb inexorably up the same ever-steepening evolutionary curve. . . . I thought about Elnear again: about the chosen few already on the brink of something unknowable . . . and all the systems within systems below them, the individual humans who had become the core—the soul, Elnear had said —of an evolving meta-being they called a combine, creating their future almost without realizing it.

Maybe they'd never take the final step, either; maybe for humans it would always be too hard. Maybe the fear of Otherness that was always there, inside a mind that could never really put itself in somebody else's place, would always hold them back. Or maybe they'd make it just because they'd had to fight so hard simply to survive; because they'd never given up trying to bridge the impossible gulf between one human mind and another. . . .

I looked down at the fight scars on my knuckles, and out at the dawn again. Whatever happened to the human race, the Monument would be waiting here: a road sign, pointing toward an unimaginable future. Not a cemetery headstone, but a memorial to the death of Death.

I heard the soft scuff of someone's footsteps behind me; looked up as Kissindre stopped beside me.

"A credit for your thoughts," she said, almost whispering, with an embarrassed twitch in her smile.

I shook my head, smiling a little too. "Don't waste your money." She held her arms pressed tightly against her chest. She was wearing a thin, short-sleeved shirt, and I realized how much she was feeling the cold. "Sit down," I said, suddenly feeling selfish, and sorry for it.

She sat on the warming rocks beside me, and there was no tension in her body, no yearning, no anticipation in her mind. . . .

And I knew that. It wasn't much, but it was something.

I put my arm around her shoulders, but it was only to help her stay warm; something a friend would do. We sat together a while longer, like two friends, watching the day come in.

ABOUT THE AUTHOR

JOAN D. VINGE'S fiction has won many awards, including the 1981 Hugo for the best science fiction novel of the year, THE SNOW QUEEN. Her other books include WORLD'S END, PHOENIX IN THE ASHES, and the bestselling RETURN OF THE JEDI STORY-BOOK. Her stories have appeared in numerous magazines and anthologies of science fiction.

A trained anthropologist, Ms. Vinge is a former salvage archeologist. Of ALIEN BLOOD, she says, "Cat is a character I began to write about when I was seventeen. I plan to write a series of novels about him and what happens to him through his life."

Joan D. Vinge lives in Chappequa, New York, with her husband and two children.